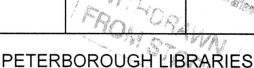

Melmoth the Wanderer

CHARLES MATURIN

. . .

PENGUIN ENGLISH
LIBRARY

PENGUIN BOOKS

Published by the Penguin Group
Penguin Books Ltd, 80 Strand, London WC2R ORL, England
Penguin Group (USA) Inc., 375 Hudson Street, New York, New York 10014, USA
Penguin Group (Canada), 90 Eglinton Avenue East, Suite 700, Toronto, Ontario, Canada M4P 2Y3
(a division of Pearson Penguin Canada Inc.)
Penguin Ireland, 25 St Stephen's Green, Dublin 2, Ireland
(a division of Penguin Books Ltd)
Penguin Group (Australia), 250 Camberwell Road,
Camberwell, Victoria 3124, Australia (a division of Pearson Australia Group Pty Ltd)
Penguin Books India Pvt Ltd, 11 Community Centre,
Panchsheel Park, New Delhi – 110 017, India
Penguin Group (NZ), 67 Apollo Drive, Rosedale, Auckland 0632, New Zealand
(a division of Pearson New Zealand Ltd)
Penguin Books (South Africa) (Pty) Ltd, Block D, Rosebank Office Park,
181 Jan Smuts Avenue, Parktown North, Gauteng 2193, South Africa

Penguin Books Ltd, Registered Offices: 80 Strand, London WC2R ORL, England

www.penguin.com

First published 1820
Published in Penguin Classics edited by Victor Sage 2000
This edition first published in the Penguin English Library 2012
001

Front cover illustration: Ben Anslow

ISBN: 978-0-141-19929-0

www.greenpenguin.co.uk

ALWAYS LEARNING   **PEARSON**

Contents

MELMOTH

THE

WANDERER:

A

TALE.

BY THE AUTHOR OF " BERTRAM," &c.

IN FOUR VOLUMES.

VOL. I.

EDINBURGH:

PRINTED FOR ARCHIBALD CONSTABLE AND COMPANY.

AND HURST, ROBINSON, AND CO. CHEAPSIDE,

LONDON.

1820.

Preface

The hint of this Romance (or Tale) was taken from a passage in one of my Sermons, which (as it is to be presumed very few have read) I shall here take the liberty to quote. The passage is this.

> At this moment is there one of us present, however we may have departed from the Lord, disobeyed his will, and disregarded his word – is there one of us who would, at this moment, accept all that man could bestow, or earth afford, to resign the hope of his salvation? – No, there is not one – not such a fool on earth, were the enemy of mankind to traverse it with the offer!

This passage suggested the idea of 'Melmoth the Wanderer'. The Reader will find that idea developed in the following pages, with what power or success *he* is to decide.

The 'Spaniard's Tale' has been censured by a friend to whom I read it, as containing too much attempt at the revivification of the horrors of Radcliffe-Romance, of the persecutions of convents, and the terrors of the Inquisition.

I defended myself, by trying to point out to my friend, that I had made the misery of conventual life depend less on the startling adventures one meets with in romances, than on that irritating series of petty torments which constitutes the misery of life in general, and which, amid the tideless stagnation of monastic existence, solitude gives its inmates leisure to invent, and power combined with malignity, the full disposition to practise. I trust this defence will operate more on the conviction of the Reader, than it did on that of my friend.

For the rest of the Romance, there are some parts of it which I have borrowed from real life.

The story of John Sandal and Elinor Mortimer is founded in fact.

The original from which the Wife of Walberg is imperfectly sketched is a living woman, and *long may she live*.

I cannot again appear before the public in so unseemly a character as that of a writer of romances, without regretting the necessity that compels me to it. Did my profession furnish me with the means of subsistence, I should hold myself culpable indeed in having recourse to any other, but – am I allowed the choice?

Dublin,
31 August 1820

Chapter One

Alive again? Then show me where he is;
I'll give a thousand pounds to look upon him.

Shakespeare

In the autumn of 1816, John Melmoth, a student in Trinity College, Dublin, quitted it to attend a dying uncle on whom his hopes for independence chiefly rested. John was the orphan son of a younger brother, whose small property scarce could pay John's college expences; but the uncle was rich, unmarried, and old; and John, from his infancy, had been brought up to look on him with that mingled sensation of awe, and of the wish, without the means to conciliate, (that sensation at once attractive and repulsive), with which we regard a being who (as nurse, domestic, and parent have tutored us to believe) holds the very threads of our existence in his hands, and may prolong or snap them when he pleases.

On receiving this summons, John set immediately out to attend his uncle.

The beauty of the country through which he travelled (it was the county Wicklow) could not prevent his mind from dwelling on many painful thoughts, some borrowed from the past, and more from the future. His uncle's caprice and moroseness, – the strange reports concerning the cause of the secluded life he had led for many years, – his own dependent state, – fell like blows fast and heavy on his mind. He roused himself to repel them, – sat up in the mail, in which he was a solitary passenger, – looked out on the prospect, – consulted his watch; – then he thought they receded for a moment, – but there was nothing to fill their place, and he was forced to invite them back for company. When the mind is thus active in calling over invaders, no wonder the conquest is soon completed. As the carriage drew near the Lodge, (the name of old Melmoth's seat), John's heart grew heavier every moment.

The recollection of this awful uncle from infancy, – when he was never permitted to approach him without innumerable lectures, – *not to be troublesome*, – not to go too near his uncle, – not to ask him any questions, – on no account to disturb the inviolable arrangement of his snuff-box, hand-bell, and spectacles, nor to suffer the glittering of the gold-headed cane to tempt him to the mortal sin of handling it, – and, finally, to pilot himself aright through his perilous course in and out of the apartment without striking against the piles of books, globes, old newspapers, wig-blocks, tobacco-pipes, and snuff-cannisters, not to mention certain hidden rocks of rat-traps and mouldy books beneath the chairs, – together with the final reverential bow at the door, which was to be closed with cautious gentleness, and the stairs to be descended as if he were 'shod with felt'. – This recollection was carried on to his school-boy years, when at Christmas and Easter, the ragged poney, the jest of the school, was dispatched to bring the reluctant visitor to the Lodge, – where his pastime was to sit vis-a-vis to his uncle, without speaking or moving, till the pair resembled Don Raymond and the ghost of Beatrice in the Monk, – then watching him as he picked the bones of lean mutton out of his mess of weak broth, the latter of which he handed to his nephew with a needless caution not to 'take more than he liked,' – then hurried to bed by daylight, even in winter, to save the expence of an inch of candle, where he lay awake and restless from hunger, till his uncle's retiring at eight o'clock gave signal to the governante of the meagre household to steal up to him with some fragments of her own scanty meal, administering between every mouthful a whispered caution not to tell his uncle. Then his college life, passed in an attic in the second square, uncheered by an invitation to the country; the gloomy summer wasted in walking up and down the deserted streets, as his uncle would not defray the expences of his journey; – the only intimation of his existence, received in quarterly epistles, containing, with the scanty but punctual remittance, complaints of the expences of his education, cautions against extravagance, and lamentations for the failure of tenants and the fall of the value of lands. All these recollections came over him, and along with them the remembrance of that last scene, where his dependence on his uncle was impressed on him by the dying lips of his father.

'John, I must leave you, my poor boy; it has pleased God to take your father from you before he could do for you what would have made this hour less painful to him. You must look up, John, to your uncle for every thing. He has oddities and infirmities, but you must learn to bear with them, and with many other things too, as you will learn too soon. And now, my poor boy, may He who is the father of the fatherless look on your desolate state, and give you favour in the eyes of your uncle.' As this scene rose to John's memory, his eyes filled fast with tears, which he hastened to wipe away as the carriage stopt to let him out at his uncle's gate.

He alighted, and with a change of linen in a handkerchief, (his only travelling equipment), he approached his uncle's gate. The lodge was in ruins, and a barefooted boy from an adjacent cabin ran to lift on its single hinge what had once been a gate, but was now a few planks so villainously put together, that they clattered like a sign in a high wind. The stubborn post of the gate, yielding at last to the united strength of John and his barefooted assistant, grated heavily through the mud and gravel stones, in which it left a deep and sloughy furrow, and the entrance lay open. John, after searching his pocket in vain for a trifle to reward his assistant, pursued his way, while the lad, on his return, cleared the road at a hop step and jump, plunging through the mud with all the dabbling and amphibious delight of a duck, and scarce less proud of his agility than of his 'sarving a gentleman'. As John slowly trod the miry road which had once been the approach, he could discover, by the dim light of an autumnal evening, signs of increasing desolation since he had last visited the spot, – signs that penury had been aggravated and sharpened into downright misery. There was not a fence or a hedge round the domain: an uncemented wall of loose stones, whose numerous gaps were filled with furze or thorns, supplied their place. There was not a tree or shrub on the lawn; the lawn itself was turned into pasture-ground, and a few sheep were picking their scanty food amid the pebblestones, thistles, and hard mould, through which a few blades of grass made their rare and squalid appearance.

The house itself stood strongly defined even amid the darkness of the evening sky; for there were neither wings, or offices, or shrubbery, or tree, to shade or support it, and soften its strong harsh outline. John, after a melancholy gaze at the grass-grown steps and boarded windows, 'addressed himself' to knock at the door; but knocker there was none: loose stones, however, there were in plenty; and John was making vigorous application to the door with one of them, till the furious barking of a mastiff, who threatened at every bound to break his chain, and whose yell and growl, accompanied by 'eyes that glow and fangs that grin', savoured as much of hunger as of rage, made the assailant raise the siege on the door, and betake himself to a well-known passage that led to the kitchen. A light glimmered in the window as he approached: he raised the latch with a doubtful hand; but, when he saw the party within, he advanced with the step of a man no longer doubtful of his welcome.

Round a turf-fire, whose well-replenished fuel gave testimony to the 'master's' indisposition, who would probably as soon have been placed on the fire himself as seen the whole *kish* emptied on it once, were seated the old housekeeper, two or three *followers*, (*i.e.* people who ate, drank, and lounged about in any kitchen

4

that was open in the neighbourhood, on an occasion of grief or joy, all for his honor's sake, and for the great rispict they bore the family), and an old woman, whom John immediately recognized as the doctress of the neighbourhood, – a withered Sybil, who prolonged her squalid existence by practising on the fears, the ignorance, and the sufferings of beings as miserable as herself. Among the better sort, to whom she sometimes had access by the influence of servants, she tried the effects of some simples, her skill in which was sometimes productive of success. Among the lower orders she talked much of the effects of the 'evil eye', against which she boasted a counter-spell, of unfailing efficacy; and while she spoke, she shook her grizzled locks with such witch-like eagerness, that she never failed to communicate to her half-terrified, half-believing audience, some portion of that enthusiasm which, amid all her consciousness of imposture, she herself probably felt a large share of; still, when the case at last became desperate, when credulity itself lost all patience, and hope and life were departing together, she urged the miserable patient to confess *'there was something about his heart'*; and when this confession was extorted from the weariness of pain and the ignorance of poverty, she nodded and muttered so mysteriously, as to convey to the bystanders, that she had had difficulties to contend with which were invincible by human power. When there was no pretext, from indisposition, for her visiting either 'his honor's' kitchen, or the cottar's hut, – when the stubborn and persevering convalescence of the whole country threatened her with starvation, – she still had a resource: – if there were no lives to be shortened, there were fortunes to be told; – she worked 'by spells, and by such daubry as is beyond our element'. No one twined so well as she the mystic yarn to be dropt into the lime-kiln pit, on the edge of which stood the shivering inquirer into futurity, doubtful whether the answer to her question of 'who holds?' was to be uttered by the voice of demon or lover.

No one knew so well as she to find where the four streams

met, in which, on the same portentous season, the chemise was to be immersed, and then displayed before the fire, (in the name of one whom we dare not mention to 'ears polite'), to be turned by the figure of the destined husband before morning. No one but herself (she said) knew the hand in which the comb was to be held, while the other was employed in conveying the apple to the mouth, – while, during the joint operation, the shadow of the phantom-spouse was to pass across the mirror before which it was performed. No one was more skilful or active in removing every iron implement from the kitchen where these ceremonies were usually performed by the credulous and terrified dupes of her wizardry, lest, instead of the form of a comely youth exhibiting a ring on his white finger, an headless figure should stalk to the rack, (*Anglicè*, dresser), take down a long spit, or, in default of that, snatch a poker from the fire-side, and mercilessly take measure with its iron length of the sleeper for a coffin. No one, in short, knew better how to torment or terrify her victims into a belief of that power which may and has reduced the strongest minds to the level of the weakest; and under the influence of which the cultivated sceptic, Lord Lyttleton, yelled and gnashed and writhed in his last hours, like the poor girl who, in the belief of the horrible visitation of the vampire, shrieked aloud, that her grandfather was sucking her vital blood while she slept, and expired under the influence of imaginary horror. Such was the being to whom old Melmoth had committed his life, half from credulity, and (*Hibernicè* speaking) *more than half* from avarice. Among this groupe John advanced, – recognizing some, – disliking more, – distrusting all. The old housekeeper received him with cordiality; – he was always her 'white-headed boy', she said, – (*imprimis*, his hair was as black as jet), and she tried to lift her withered hand to his head with an action between a benediction and a caress, till the difficulty of the attempt forced on her the conviction that that head was fourteen inches higher than her reach since she had last patted it. The men, with the national deference of the Irish to a person of superior rank, all rose at his approach, (their stools chattering on the broken flags), and wished his honor 'a thousand years, and long life to the back of that; and would not his honor take something to keep the grief out of his heart;' and so saying, five or six red and bony hands tendered him glasses of whiskey all at once. All this time the Sybil sat silent in the ample chimney-corner, sending redoubled whiffs out of her pipe. John gently declined the offer of spirits, received the attentions of the old housekeeper cordially, looked askance at the withered crone who occupied the chimney corner, and then glanced at the table, which displayed other cheer than he had been accustomed to see in his 'honor's time'. There was a wooden dish of potatoes, which old Melmoth would have considered enough for a week's subsistence. There was the salted salmon, (a luxury unknown even in London. *Vide* Miss Edgeworth's Tales, 'The Absentee').

There was the *slink-veal*, flanked with tripe; and, finally, there were lobsters and *fried* turbot enough to justify what the author of the tale asserts, 'suo periculo', that when his great grandfather, the Dean of Killala, hired servants at the deanery, they stipulated that they should not be required to eat turbot or lobster more than twice a-week. There were also bottles of Wicklow ale, long and surreptitiously borrowed from his 'honor's' cellar, and which now made their first appearance on the kitchen hearth, and manifested their impatience of further constraint, by hissing, spitting, and bouncing in the face of the fire that provoked its animosity. But the whiskey (genuine illegitimate potsheen, smelling strongly of weed and smoke, and breathing defiance to excisemen) appeared, the 'veritable Amphitryon' of the feast; every one praised, and drank as deeply as he praised.

John, as he looked round the circle, and thought of his dying uncle, was forcibly reminded of the scene at Don Quixote's departure, where, in spite of the grief caused by the dissolution of the worthy knight, we are informed that 'nevertheless the niece eat her victuals, the housekeeper drank to the repose of his soul, and even Sancho cherished his little carcase.' After returning, 'as he might', the courtesies of the party, John asked how his uncle was. 'As bad as he can be;' – 'Much better, and many thanks to your honor,' was uttered in such rapid and discordant unison by the party, that John turned from one to the other, not knowing which or what to believe. 'They say his honor has had a fright,' said a fellow, upwards of six feet high, approaching by way of whispering, and then bellowing the sound six inches above John's head. 'But then his honor has had *a cool* since,' said a man who was quietly swallowing the spirits that John had refused. At these words the Sybil who sat in the chimney corner slowly drew her pipe from her mouth, and turned towards the party: The oracular movements of a Pythoness on her tripod never excited more awe, or impressed for the moment a deeper silence. 'It's not *here*,' said she, pressing her withered finger on her wrinkled forehead, 'nor *here*, – nor *here*;' and she extended her hand to the foreheads of those who were near her, who all bowed as if they were receiving a benediction, but had immediate recourse to the spirits afterwards, as if to ensure its effects. – 'It's all *here* – it's all *about the heart*;' and as she spoke she spread and pressed her fingers on her hollow bosom with a force of action that thrilled her hearers. – 'It's all *here*,' she added, repeating the action, (probably excited by the effect she had produced), and then sunk on her seat, resumed her pipe, and spoke no more. At this moment of involuntary awe on the part of John, and of terrified silence on that of the rest, an unusual sound was heard in the house, and the whole company started as if a musket had been discharged among them: – it was the unwonted sound of old Melmoth's bell. His domestics were so few, and so constantly near him, that the sound of his bell startled them as much as if he had been ringing the knell for his own interment. 'He used always to *rap down* for me,' said the old housekeeper, hurrying out of the kitchen; 'he said pulling the bells wore out the ropes.'

The sound of the bell produced its full effect. The housekeeper rushed into the room, followed by a number of women, (the Irish præficae), all ready to prescribe for the dying or weep for the dead, – all clapping their hard hands, or wiping their dry eyes. These hags all surrounded the bed; and to witness their loud, wild, and desperate grief, their cries of 'Oh! he's going, his honor's going, his honor's going,' one would have imagined their lives were bound up in his, like those of the wives in the story of Sinbad the Sailor, who were to be interred alive with their deceased husbands.

Four of them wrung their hands and howled round the bed, while one, with all the adroitness of a Mrs Quickly, felt his honor's feet, and 'upward and upward,' and 'all was cold as any stone.'

Old Melmoth withdrew his feet from the grasp of the hag, – counted with his keen eye (keen amid the approaching dimness of death) the number assembled round his bed, – raised himself on his sharp elbow, and pushing away the housekeeper, (who attempted to settle his night-cap, that had been shoved on one side in the struggle, and gave his haggard, dying face, a kind of grotesque fierceness), bellowed out in tones that made the company start, – 'What the devil brought ye all here?' The question scattered the whole party for a moment; but rallying instantly, they communed among themselves in whispers, and frequently using the sign of the cross, muttered 'The devil, – Christ save us, the devil in his mouth the first word he spoke.' 'Aye,' roared the invalid, 'and the devil in my eye the first sight I see.' 'Where, – where?' cried the terrified housekeeper, clinging close to the invalid in her terror, and half-hiding herself in the blanket, which she snatched without mercy from his struggling and exposed limbs. 'There, there,' he repeated, (during the battle of the blanket), pointing to the huddled and terrified women, who stood aghast at hearing themselves arointed as the very demons they came to banish. 'Oh! Lord keep your honor's head,' said the housekeeper in a more soothing tone, when her fright was over; 'and sure your honor knows them all, is'n't *her* name, – and *her* name, – and *her* name,' – and she pointed respectively to each of them, adding their names, which we shall spare the English reader the torture of reciting, (as a proof of our lenity, adding the last only, Cotchleen O'Mulligan), 'Ye lie, ye b——h,' growled old Melmoth; 'their name is Legion, for they are many, – turn them all out of the room, – turn them all out of doors, – if they howl at my death, they shall howl in earnest, – not for my death, for they would see me dead and damned too with dry eyes, but for want of the whiskey that they would have stolen if they could have got at it,' (and here old Melmoth grasped a key which lay under his pillow, and shook it in vain triumph at the old housekeeper, who had long possessed the means of getting at the spirits unknown to his 'honor'), 'and for want of the victuals you have pampered them with.' '*Pampered*, oh Ch——st!' ejaculated the housekeeper. 'Aye, and what are there so many candles for, all *fours*, and the same below I warrant. Ah! you – you – worthless, wasteful old devil.' 'Indeed, your honor, they are all *sixes*.' 'Sixes, – and what the devil are you burning sixes for, d'ye think it's *the wake* already? Ha?' 'Oh! not yet, your honor, not yet,' chorussed the beldams; 'but in God's good time, your honor knows,' in a tone that spoke ill suppressed impatience for the event. 'Oh! that your honor would think of making your soul.' 'That's the first sensible word you have said,' said the dying man, 'fetch me the prayer-book, – you'll find it there under that old boot-jack, – blow off the cobwebs; – it has not been opened this many a year.' It was handed to him by the old gouvernante, on whom he turned a reproaching eye. 'What made you burn sixes in the kitchen, you extravagant jade? How many years have you lived in this house?' 'I don't know, your honor.' 'Did you ever see any extravagance or waste in it?' 'Oh never, never, your honor.' 'Was any thing but a farthing candle ever burned in the kitchen?' 'Never, never, your honor.' 'Were not you kept as tight as hand and head and heart could keep you, were you not? answer me that.' 'Oh yes, sure, your honor; every *sowl* about us knows that, – every one does your honor justice, that you kept the closest house and closest hand in the country, – your honor was always a good warrant for it.' 'And how dare you unlock my hold before death has unlocked it,' said the dying miser, shaking his meagre hand at her. 'I smelt meat in the house, – I heard voices in the house, – I heard the key turn in the door over and over. Oh that I was up,' he added, rolling in impatient agony in his bed, 'Oh that I was up, to see the waste and ruin that is going on. But it would kill me,' he continued, sinking back on the bolster, for he never allowed himself a pillow; 'it would kill me, – the very thought of it is killing me now.' The women, discomfited and defeated, after sundry winks and whispers, were huddling out of the room, till recalled by the sharp eager tones of old Melmoth. – 'Where are ye trooping to now? back to the kitchen to gormandize and guzzle? Won't one of ye stay and listen while there's a prayer read for me? Ye may want it one day for yourselves, ye hags.' Awed by this expostulation and menace, the train silently returned, and placed themselves round the bed, while the housekeeper, though a Catholic, asked if his honor would not have a clergyman to give him *the rights*, (rites) of his church. The eyes of the dying man sparkled with vexation at the proposal. 'What for, – just to have him expect a scarf and hatband at the funeral. Read the prayers yourself, you old –; that will save something.' The housekeeper made the attempt, but soon declined it, alleging, as her reason, that her eyes had been watery ever since his honor took ill. 'That's because you had always a drop in them,' said the invalid, with a spiteful sneer, which the contraction of approaching death stiffened into a hideous grin. – 'Here, – is not there one of you that's gnashing and howling there, that can get up a prayer to keep me from it?' So adjured, one of the women offered her services; and of her it might truly be said, as of the 'most desartless man of the watch' in Dogberry's time, that 'her reading and writing came by nature'; for she never had been at school, and had never before seen or opened a Protestant prayer book in her life; nevertheless, on she went, and with more emphasis than good discretion, read nearly through the service for the 'churching of women'; which in our prayer-books following that of the burial of the dead, she perhaps imagined was someway connected with the state of the invalid.

She read with great solemnity, – it was a pity that two interruptions occurred during the performance, one from old Melmoth, who, shortly after the commencement of the prayers, turned towards the old housekeeper, and said in a tone scandalously audible, 'Go down and draw the niggers of the kitchen fire closer, and lock the door, and let me *hear it locked*. I can't mind any thing till that's done.' The other was from John Melmoth gliding into the room, hearing the inappropriate words uttered by the ignorant woman, taking quietly as he knelt beside her the prayer-book from her hands, and reading in a suppressed voice part of that solemn service which, by the forms of the Church of England, is intended for the consolation of the departing.

'That is John's voice,' said the dying man; and the little kindness he had ever shewed this unfortunate lad rushed on his hard heart at this moment, and touched it. He saw himself, too, surrounded by heartless and rapacious menials; and slight as must have been his dependence on a relative whom he had always treated as a stranger, he felt at this hour he was no stranger, and grasped at his support like a straw amid his wreck. 'John, my good boy, you are there. – I kept you far from me when living, and now you are nearest me when dying. – John, *read on*.' John, affected deeply by the situation in which he beheld this *poor man*, amid all his wealth, as well as by the solemn request to impart consolation to his dying moments, read on; – but in a short time his voice became indistinct, from the horror with which he listened to the increasing hiccup of the patient, which, however, he struggled with from time to time, to ask the housekeeper if *the niggers were closed*. John, who was a lad of feeling, rose from his knees in some degree of agitation. 'What, are you leaving me like the rest?' said old Melmoth, trying to raise himself in the bed. 'No, Sir,' said John; 'but,' observing the altered looks of the dying man, 'I think you want some refreshment, some support, Sir.' 'Aye, I do, I do, but whom can I trust to get it for me. *They*, (and his haggard eye wandered round the groupe), *they* would poison me.' 'Trust me, Sir,' said John; 'I will go to the apothecary's, or whoever you may employ.' The old man grasped his hand, drew him close to his bed, cast a threatening yet fearful eye round the party, and then whispered in a voice of agonized constraint, 'I want a glass of wine, it would keep me alive for some hours, but there is not one I can trust to get it for me, – *they'd steal a bottle, and ruin me*.' John was greatly shocked. 'Sir, for God's sake, let *me* get a glass of wine for you.' 'Do you know where?' said the old man, with an expression in his face John could not understand. 'No, Sir; you know I have been rather a stranger here, Sir.' 'Take this key,' said old Melmoth, after a violent spasm; 'take this key, there is wine in that closet, – *Madeira*. I always told them there was nothing there, but they did not believe me, or I should not have been robbed as I have been. At one time I said it was whiskey, and then I fared worse than ever, for they drank twice as much of it.'

John took the key from his uncle's hand; the dying man pressed it as he did so, and John, interpreting this as a mark of kindness, returned the pressure. He was undeceived by the whisper that followed, – 'John, my lad, don't drink any of that wine while you are there.' 'Good God!' said John, indignantly throwing the key on the bed; then, recollecting that the miserable being before him was no object of resentment, he gave the promise required, and entered the closet, which no foot but that of old Melmoth had entered for nearly sixty years. He had some difficulty in finding out the wine, and indeed staid long enough to justify his uncle's suspicions, – but his mind was agitated, and his hand unsteady.

He could not but remark his uncle's extraordinary look, that had the ghastliness of fear superadded to that of death, as he gave him permission to enter his closet. He could not but see the looks of horror which the women exchanged as he approached it. And, finally, when he was in it, his memory was malicious enough to suggest some faint traces of a story, too horrible for imagination, connected with it. He remembered in one moment most distinctly, that no one but his uncle had ever been known to enter it for many years.

Before he quitted it, he held up the dim light, and looked around him with a mixture of terror and curiosity. There was a great deal of decayed and useless lumber, such as might be supposed to be heaped up to rot in a miser's closet; but John's eyes were in a moment, and as if by magic, rivetted on a portrait that hung on the wall, and appeared, even to his untaught eye, far superior to the tribe of family pictures that are left to moulder on the walls of a family mansion. It represented a man of middle age. There was nothing remarkable in the costume, or in the countenance, but *the eyes*, John felt, were such as one feels they wish they had never seen, and feels they can never forget. Had he been acquainted with the poetry of Southey, he might have often exclaimed in his after-life,

> Only the eyes had life,
> They gleamed with demon light. – THALABA

From an impulse equally resistless and painful, he approached the portrait, held the candle towards it, and could distinguish the words on the border of the painting, – Jno. Melmoth, anno 1646. John was neither timid by nature, or nervous by constitution, or superstitious from habit, yet he continued to gaze in stupid horror on this singular picture till, aroused by his uncle's cough, he hurried into his room. The old man swallowed the wine. He appeared a little revived; it was long since he had tasted such a cordial, – his heart appeared to expand to a momentary confidence. 'John, what did you see in that room?' 'Nothing, Sir.' 'That's a lie; every one wants to cheat or to rob me.' 'Sir, I don't want to do either.' 'Well, what did you see that you – you took notice of?' 'Only a picture, Sir.' 'A picture, Sir! – the original is still alive.' John, though under the impression of his recent feelings, could not but look incredulous. 'John,' whispered his uncle; – 'John, they say I am dying of this and that; and one says it is for want of nourishment, and one says it is for want of medicine, – but, John,' and his face looked hideously ghastly, 'I am dying of a fright. That man,' and he extended his meagre arm towards the closet, as if he was pointing to a living being; 'that man, I have good reason to know, is alive still.' 'How is that possible, Sir?' said John involuntarily, 'the date on the picture is 1646.' 'You have seen it, – you have noticed it,' said his uncle. 'Well,' – he rocked and nodded on his bolster for a moment, then, grasping John's hand with an unutterable look, he exclaimed, 'You will see him again, he is alive.' Then, sinking back on his bolster, he fell into a kind of sleep or stupor, his eyes still open, and fixed on John.

The house was now perfectly silent, and John had time and space for reflection. More thoughts came crowding on him than he wished to welcome, but they would not be repulsed. He thought of his uncle's habit and character, turned the matter over and over again in his mind, and he said to himself, 'The last man on earth to be superstitious. He never thought of any thing but the price of stocks, and the rate of exchange, and my college expences, that hung heavier at his heart than all; and such a man to die of a fright, – a ridiculous fright, that a man living 150 years ago is alive still, and yet – he is dying.' John paused, for facts will confute the most stubborn logician. 'With all his hardness of mind, and of heart, he is dying of a fright. I heard it in the kitchen, I have heard it from himself, – he could not be deceived. If I had ever heard he was nervous, or fanciful, or superstitious, but a character so contrary to all these impressions; – a man that, as poor Butler says, in his Remains, of the Antiquarian, would have 'sold Christ over again for the numerical piece of silver which Judas got for him,' such a man to die of fear! Yet he *is* dying,' said John, glancing his fearful eye on the contracted nostril, the glazed eye, the dropping jaw, the whole horrible apparatus of the *facies Hippocratica* displayed, and soon to cease its display.

Old Melmoth at this moment seemed to be in a deep stupor; his eyes lost that little expression they had before, and his hands, that had convulsively been catching at the blankets, let go their short and quivering grasp, and lay extended on the bed like the claws of some bird that had died of hunger, – so meagre, so yellow, so spread. John, unaccustomed to the sight of death, believed this to be only a sign that he was going to sleep; and, urged by an impulse for which he did not attempt to account to himself, caught up the miserable light, and once more ventured into the forbidden room, – the *blue chamber* of the dwelling. The motion roused the dying man; – he sat bolt upright in his bed. This John could not see, for he was now in the closet; but he heard the groan, or rather the choaked and guggling rattle of the throat, that announces the horrible conflict between muscular and mental convulsion. He started, turned away; but, as he turned away, he thought he saw the eyes of the portrait, on which his own was fixed, *move*, and hurried back to his uncle's bedside.

Old Melmoth died in the course of that night, and died as he had lived, in a kind of avaricious delirium. John could not have imagined a scene so horrible as his last hours presented. He cursed and blasphemed about three half-pence, missing, as he said, some weeks before, in an account of change with his groom, about hay to a starving horse that he kept. Then he grasped John's hand, and asked him to give him the sacrament. 'If I send to the clergyman, he will charge me something for it, which I cannot pay, – I cannot. They say I am rich, – look at this blanket; – but I would not mind that, if I could save my soul.' And, raving, he added, 'Indeed, Doctor, I am a very poor man. I never troubled a clergyman before, and all I want is, that you will grant me two trifling requests, very little matters in your way, – save my soul, and (whispering) make interest to get me a parish coffin, – I have not enough left to bury me. I always told every one I was poor, but the more I told them so, the less they believed me.'

John, greatly shocked, retired from the bed-side, and sat down in a distant corner of the room. The women were again in the room, which was very dark. Melmoth was silent from exhaustion, and there was a death-like pause for some time. At this moment John saw the door open, and a figure appear at it, who looked round the room, and then quietly and deliberately retired, but not before John had discovered in his face the living original of the portrait. His first impulse was to utter an exclamation of terror, but his breath felt stopped. He was then rising to pursue the figure, but a moment's reflection checked him. What could be more absurd, than to be alarmed or amazed at a resemblance between a living man and the portrait of a dead one! The likeness was doubtless strong enough to strike him even in that darkened room, but it was doubtless only a likeness; and though it might be imposing enough to terrify an old man of gloomy and retired habits, and with a broken constitution, John resolved it should not produce the same effect on him.

But while he was applauding himself for this resolution, the door opened, and the figure appeared at it, beckoning and nodding to him, with a familiarity somewhat terrifying. John now started up, determined to pursue it; but the pursuit was stopped by the weak but shrill cries of his uncle, who was struggling at once with the agonies of death and his housekeeper. The poor woman, anxious for her master's reputation and her own, was trying to put on him a clean shirt and nightcap, and Melmoth, who had just sensation enough to perceive they were taking something from him, continued exclaiming feebly, 'They are robbing me, – robbing me in my last moments, – robbing a dying man. John, won't you assist me, – I shall die a beggar; they are taking my last shirt, – I shall die a beggar.' – And the miser died.

Chapter Two

You that wander, scream, and groan,
Round the mansions once your own.

Rowe

A few days after the funeral, the will was opened before proper witnesses, and John was found to be left sole heir to his uncle's property, which, though originally moderate, had, by his grasping habits, and parsimonious life, become very considerable.

As the attorney who read the will concluded, he added, 'There are some words here, at the corner of the parchment, which do not appear to be part of the will, as they are neither in the form of a codicil, nor is the signature of the testator affixed to them; but, to the best of my belief, they are in the hand-writing of the deceased.' As he spoke he shewed the lines to Melmoth, who immediately recognized his uncle's hand, (that perpendicular and penurious hand, that seems determined to make the most of the very paper, thriftily abridging every word, and leaving scarce an atom of margin), and read, not without some emotion, the following words: 'I enjoin my nephew and heir, John Melmoth, to remove, destroy, or cause to be destroyed, the portrait inscribed J. Melmoth, 1646, hanging in my closet. I also enjoin him to search for a manuscript, which I think he will find in the third and lowest left-hand drawer of the mahogany chest standing under that portrait, – it is among some papers of no value, such as manuscript sermons, and pamphlets on the improvement of Ireland, and such stuff; he will distinguish it by its being tied round with a black tape, and the paper being very mouldy and discoloured. He may read it if he will; – I think he had better not. At all events, I adjure him, if there be any power in the adjuration of a dying man, to burn it.'

After reading this singular memorandum, the business of the meeting was again resumed; and as old Melmoth's will was very clear and legally worded, all was soon settled, the party dispersed, and John Melmoth was left alone.

We should have mentioned, that his guardians appointed by the will (for he was not yet of age) advised him to return to College, and complete his education as soon as proper; but John urged the expediency of paying the respect due to his uncle's memory, by remaining a decent time in the house after his decease. This was not his real motive. Curiosity, or something that perhaps deserves a better name, the wild and awful pursuit of an indefinite object, had taken strong hold of his mind. His guardians (who were men of respectability and property in the neighbourhood, and in whose eyes John's consequence had risen rapidly since the reading of the will), pressed him to accept of a temporary residence in their respective houses, till his return to Dublin. This was declined gratefully, but steadily. They called for their horses, shook hands with the heir, and rode off – Melmoth was left alone.

The remainder of the day was passed in gloomy and anxious deliberation, – in traversing his late uncle's room, – approaching the door of the closet, and then retreating from it, – in watching the clouds, and listening to the wind, as if the gloom of the one, or the murmurs of the other, relieved instead of increasing the weight that pressed on his mind. Finally, towards evening, he summoned the old woman, from whom he expected something like an explanation of the extraordinary circumstances he had witnessed since his arrival at his uncle's. The old woman, proud of the summons, readily attended, but she had very little to tell, – her communication was nearly in the following words: (We spare the reader her endless circumlocutions, her Irishcisms, and the frequent interruptions arising from her applications to her snuff-box, and to the glass of whiskey punch with which Melmoth took care to have her supplied). The old woman deposed, 'That his honor (as she always called the deceased) was always intent upon the little room inside his bed-chamber, and reading there, within the last two years; – that people, knowing his honor had money, and thinking it must be there, had broke into that room, (in other words, there was a robbery attempted there), but finding nothing but some papers, they had retired; – that he was so frightened, he had bricked up the window; but *she thought there was more in it than that*, for when his honor missed but a half-penny, he would make the house ring about it, but that, when the closet was bricked up, he never said a word; – that afterwards his honor used to lock himself up in his own room, and though he was never fond of reading, was always found, when his dinner was brought him, hanging over a paper, which he hid the moment any one came into the room, and once there was a great bustle about a picture that he tried to conceal; – that knowing there was an *odd story in the family*, she did her best to come at it, and even went to Biddy Brannigan's, (the medical Sybil before mentioned), to find out the rights of it; but Biddy only shook her head, filled her pipe, uttered some words she did not understand, and smoked on; – that it was but two evenings before his honor *was struck*, (*i.e.* took ill), she was standing at the door of the court, (which had once been surrounded by stables, pigeon-house, and all the usual etceteras of a gentleman's residence, but now presented only a ruinous range of dismantled out-offices, thatched with thistles, and tenanted by pigs), when his honor called to her to lock the door, (his honor was always *keen* about locking the doors early); she was hastening to do so, when he snatched the key from her, swearing at her, (for he was always very keen about locking the doors, though the locks were so bad, and the keys so rusty, that it was always like *the cry of the dead* in the house when the keys were turned); – that she stood aside for a minute, seeing he was angry, and gave him the key, when she heard him utter a scream, and saw him fall across the door-way; – that she hurried to raise him, *hoping* it was a fit; – that she found him stiff and stretched out, and called for help to lift him up; – that then people came from the kitchen to assist; – that she was so bewildered and terrified, she hardly knew what was done or said; but with all her terror remembered, that as they raised him up, the first sign of life he gave was lifting up his arm, and pointing it towards the court, and at that moment she saw the figure of a tall man cross the court, and go out of the court, she knew not where or how, for the outer gate was locked, and had not been opened for years, and they were all gathered round his honor at the other door; – she saw the figure, – she saw the shadow on the wall, – she saw him walk slowly through the court, and in her terror cried, 'Stop him,' but nobody minded her, all being busy about her master; and when he was brought to his room, nobody thought but of getting him to himself again. And further she could not tell. His honor (young Melmoth) knew as much as she, – he had witnessed his last illness, had heard his last words, he saw him die, – how could she know more than his honor.'

'True,' said Melmoth, 'I certainly saw him die; but – you say *there was an odd story in the family*, do you know any thing about it?' 'Not a word, it was long before my time, as old as I am.' 'Certainly it must have been so; but, was my uncle ever superstitious, fanciful?' – and Melmoth was compelled to use many synonymous expressions, before he could make himself understood. When he did, the answer was plain and decisive, 'No, never, never. When his honor sat in the kitchen in winter, to save a fire in his own room, he could never bear the talk of the old women that came in to light their pipes *betimes*, (from time to time). He used to shew such impatience of their superstitious nonsense, that they were fain to smoke them in silence, without the consolatory accompaniment of one whisper about a child that the evil eye had looked on, or another, that though apparently a mewling, peevish, crippled brat all day, went regularly out at night to dance with the *good people* on the top of a neighbouring mountain, summoned thereto by the sound of a bag-pipe, which was unfailingly heard at the cabin door every night.' Melmoth's thoughts began to take somewhat of a darker hue at this account. If his uncle was not superstitious, might he not have been guilty, and might not his strange and sudden death, and even the terrible visitation that preceded it, have been owing to some wrong that his rapacity had done the widow and the fatherless. He questioned the old woman indirectly and cautiously on the subject, – her answer completely justified the deceased. 'He was a man,' she said, 'of a hard hand, and a hard heart, but he was as jealous of another's right as of his own. He would have starved all the world, but he would not have wronged it of a farthing.'

Melmoth's last resource was to send for Biddy Brannigan, who was still in the house, and from whom he at least hoped to hear the odd story that the old woman confessed was in the family. She came, and, on her introduction to Melmoth, it was curious to observe the mingled look of servility and command, the result of the habits of her life, which was alternately one of abject mendicity, and of arrogant but clever imposture. When she first appeared, she stood at the door, awed and curtseying in the presence, and muttering sounds which, possibly intended for blessings, had, from the harsh tone and witch-like look of the speaker, every appearance of malediction; but when interrogated on the subject of the story, she rose at once into consequence, – her figure seemed frightfully dilated, like that of Virgil's Alecto, who exchanges in a moment the appearance of a feeble old woman for that of a menacing fury. She walked deliberately across the room, seated, or rather squatted herself on the hearth-stone like a hare in her form, spread her bony and withered hands towards the blaze, and rocked for a considerable time in silence before she commenced her tale. When she had finished it, Melmoth remained in astonishment at the state of mind to which the late singular circumstances had reduced him, – at finding himself listening with varying and increasing emotions of interest, curiosity, and terror, to a tale so wild, so improbable, nay, so actually incredible, that he at least blushed for the folly he could not conquer. The result of these impressions was, a resolution to visit the closet, and examine the manuscript that very night.

This resolution he found it impossible to execute immediately, for, on inquiring for lights, the gouvernante confessed the very last had been burnt at *his honor's* wake; and a barefooted boy was charged to run for life and death to the neighbouring village for candles; and if you could *borry* a couple of candlesticks, added the housekeeper. 'Are there no candlesticks in the house?' said Melmoth. 'There are, honey, plinty, but it's no time to be opening the old chest, for the plated ones, in regard of their being at the bottom of it, and the brass ones that's *in it* (in the house), one of them has no socket, and the other has no bottom.' 'And how did you make shift yourself,' said Melmoth. 'I stuck it in a potatoe,' quoth the housekeeper. So the *gossoon* ran for life and death, and Melmoth, towards the close of the evening, was left alone to meditate.

It was an evening apt for meditation, and Melmoth had his fill of it before the messenger returned. The weather was cold and gloomy; heavy clouds betokened a long and dreary continuance of autumnal rains; cloud after cloud came sweeping on like the dark banners of an approaching host, whose march is for desolation. As Melmoth leaned against the window, whose dismantled frame, and pierced and shattered panes, shook with every gust of wind, his eye encountered nothing but that most cheerless of all prospects, a miser's garden, – walls broken down, grass-grown walks whose grass was not even green, dwarfish, doddered, leafless trees, and a luxuriant crop of nettles and weeds rearing their unlovely heads where there had once been flowers, all waving and bending in capricious and unsightly forms, as the wind sighed over them. It was the verdure of the churchyard, the garden of death. He turned for relief to the room, but no relief was there, – the wainscotting dark with dirt, and in many places cracked and starting from the walls, – the rusty grate, so long unconscious of a fire, that nothing but a sullen smoke could be coaxed to issue from between its dingy bars, – the crazy chairs, their torn bottoms of rush drooping inwards, and the great leathern seat displaying the stuffing round the worn edges, while the nails, though they kept their places, had failed to keep the covering they once fastened, – the chimney-piece, which, tarnished more by time than by smoke, displayed for its garniture half a pair of snuffers, a tattered almanack of 1750, a time-keeper dumb for want of repair, and a rusty fowling-piece without a lock. – No wonder the spectacle of desolation drove Melmoth back to his own thoughts, restless and uncomfortable as they were. He recapitulated the Sybil's story word by word, with the air of a man who is cross-examining an evidence, and trying to make him contradict himself.

The first of the Melmoths, she says, who settled in Ireland, was an officer in Cromwell's army, who obtained a grant of lands, the confiscated property of an Irish family attached to the royal cause. The elder brother of this man was one who had travelled abroad, and resided so long on the Continent, that his family had lost all recollection of him. Their memory was not stimulated by their affection, for there were strange reports concerning the traveller. He was said to be (like the 'damned magician, great Glendower,') 'a gentleman profited in strange concealments.'

It must be remembered, that at this period, and even to a later, the belief in astrology and witchcraft was very general. Even so late as the reign of Charles II. Dryden calculated the nativity of his son Charles, the ridiculous books of Glanville were in general circulation, and Delrio and Wierus were so popular, that even a dramatic writer (Shadwell) quoted copiously from them, in the notes subjoined to his curious comedy of the Lancashire witches. It was said, that during the life-time of Melmoth, the traveller paid him a visit; and though he must have then been considerably advanced in life, to the astonishment of his family, he did not betray the slightest trace of being a year older than when they last beheld him. His visit was short, he said nothing of the past or the future, nor did his family question him. It was said that they did not feel themselves perfectly at ease in his presence. On his departure he left them his picture, (the same which Melmoth saw in the closet, bearing date 1646), and they saw him no more. Some years after, a person arrived from England, directed to Melmoth's house, in pursuit of the traveller, and exhibiting the most marvellous and unappeasable solicitude to obtain some intelligence of him. The family could give him none, and after some days of restless inquiry and agitation, he departed, leaving behind him, either through negligence or intention, a manuscript, containing an extraordinary account of the circumstances under which he had met John Melmoth the Traveller (as he was called).

The manuscript and portrait were both preserved, and of the original a report spread that he was still alive, and had been frequently seen in Ireland even to the present century, – but that he was never known to appear but on the approaching death of one of the family, nor even then, unless when the evil passions or habits of the individual had cast a shade of gloomy and fearful interest over their dying hour.

It was therefore judged no favourable augury for the spiritual destination of the last Melmoth, that this extraordinary person had visited, or been imagined to visit, the house previous to his decease.

Such was the account given by Biddy Brannigan, to which she added her own solemnly-attested belief, that John Melmoth the Traveller was still without a hair on his head changed, or a muscle in his frame contracted; – that she had seen those that had seen him, and would confirm their evidence by oath if necessary; – that he was never heard to speak, seen to partake of food, or known to enter any dwelling but that of his family; – and, finally, that she herself believed that his late appearance boded no good either to the living or the dead.

John was still musing on these things when the lights were procured, and, disregarding the pallid countenances and monitory whispers of the attendants, he resolutely entered the closet, shut the door, and proceeded to search for the manuscript. It was soon found, for the directions of old Melmoth were forcibly written, and strongly remembered. The manuscript, old, tattered, and discoloured, was taken from the very drawer in which it was mentioned to be laid. Melmoth's hands felt as cold as those of his dead uncle, when he drew the blotted pages from their nook. He sat down to read, – there was a dead silence through the house. Melmoth looked wistfully at the candles, snuffed them, and still thought they looked dim, (perchance he thought they burned blue, but such thought he kept to himself.) Certain it is, he often changed his posture, and would have changed his chair, had there been more than one in the apartment.

He sunk for a few moments into a fit of gloomy abstraction, till the sound of the clock striking twelve made him start, – it was the only sound he had heard for some hours, and the sounds produced by inanimate things, while all living beings around are as dead, have at such an hour an effect indescribably awful. John looked at his manuscript with some reluctance, opened it, paused over the first lines, and as the wind sighed round the desolate apartment, and the rain pattered with a mournful sound against the dismantled window, wished – what did he wish for? – he wished the sound of the wind less dismal, and the dash of the rain less monotonous. – He may be forgiven, it was past midnight, and there was not a human being awake but himself within ten miles when he began to read.

Chapter Three

Apparebat eidolon *senex*.[1]

Pliny

The manuscript was discoloured, obliterated and mutilated beyond any that had ever before exercised the patience of a reader. Michaelis himself, scrutinizing into the pretended autograph of St Mark at Venice, never had a harder time of it. – Melmoth could make out only a sentence here and there. The writer, it appeared, was an Englishman of the name of Stanton, who had travelled abroad shortly after the Restoration. Travelling was not then attended with the facilities which modern improvement has introduced, and scholars and literati, the intelligent, the idle, and the curious, wandered over the Continent for years, like *Tom Coryat*, though they had the modesty, on their return, to entitle the result of their multiplied observations and labours only 'crudities'.

Stanton, about the year 1676, was in Spain; he was, like most of the travellers of that age, a man of literature, intelligence and curiosity, but ignorant of the language of the country, and fighting his way at times from convent to convent, in quest of what was called 'Hospitality', that is, obtaining board and lodging on the condition of holding a debate in Latin, on some point theological or metaphysical, with any monk who would become the champion of the strife. Now, as the theology was Catholic, and the metaphysics, Aristotelian, Stanton sometimes wished himself at the miserable Posada from whose filth and famine he had been fighting his escape; but though his reverend antagonists always denounced his creed, and comforted themselves, even in defeat, with the assurance that he must be damned, on the double score of his being a heretic and an Englishman, they were obliged to confess that his Latin was good, and his logic unanswerable; and he was allowed, in most cases, to sup and sleep in peace. This was not doomed to be his fate on the night of the 17th August 1677, when he found himself in the plains of Valencia, deserted by a cowardly guide, who had been terrified by the sight of a cross erected as a memorial of a murder, had slipped off his mule unperceived, crossing himself every step he took on his retreat from the heretic, and left Stanton amid the terrors of an approaching storm, and the dangers of an unknown country. The sublime and yet softened beauty of the scenery around, had filled the soul of Stanton with delight, and he enjoyed that delight as Englishmen generally do, silently.

The magnificent remains of two dynasties that had passed away, the ruins of Roman palaces, and of Moorish fortresses, were around and above him; – the dark and heavy thunderclouds that advanced slowly, seemed like the shrouds of these spectres of departed greatness; they approached, but did not yet overwhelm or conceal them, as if nature herself was for once awed by the power of man; and far below, the lovely valley of Valencia blushed and burned in all the glory of sunset, like a bride receiving the last glowing kiss of the bridegroom before the approach of night. Stanton gazed around. The difference between the architecture of the Roman and Moorish ruins struck him. Among the former are the remains of a theatre, and something like a public place; the latter present only the remains of fortresses, embattled, castellated, and fortified from top to bottom, – not a loop-hole for pleasure to get in by, – the loop-holes were only for arrows; all denoted military power and despotic subjugation *a l'outrance*.[2] The contrast might have pleased a philosopher, and he might have indulged in the reflection, that though the ancient Greeks and Romans were savages, (as Dr Johnson says all people

who want a press must be, and he says truly), yet they were wonderful savages for their time, for they alone have left *traces of their
taste for pleasure* in the countries they conquered, in their superb
theatres, temples (which were also dedicated to pleasure one way
or another), and baths, while other conquering bands of savages
never left any thing behind them but traces of their rage for
power. So thought Stanton, as he still saw strongly defined,
though darkened by the darkening clouds, the huge skeleton of a
Roman amphitheatre, its arched and gigantic colonnades now
admitting a gleam of light, and now commingling with the purple thunder-cloud; and now the solid and heavy mass of a
Moorish fortress, no light playing between its impermeable
walls, – the image of power, dark, isolated, impenetrable. Stanton forgot his cowardly guide, his loneliness, his danger amid an
approaching storm and an inhospitable country, where his name
and country would shut every door against him, and every peal
of thunder would be supposed justified by the daring intrusion
of a heretic in the dwelling of an *old Christian*, as the Spanish
Catholics absurdly term themselves, to make the distinction
between them and the baptised Moors. – All this was forgot in
contemplating the glorious and awful scenery before him, – light
struggling with darkness, – and darkness menacing a light still
more terrible, and announcing its menace in the blue and livid
mass of cloud that hovered like a destroying angel in the air, its
arrows aimed, but their direction awfully indefinite. But he
ceased to forget these local and petty dangers, as the sublimity of
romance would term them, when he saw the first flash of the
lightning, broad and red as the banners of an insulting army
whose motto is *Vae victis*,[3] shatter to atoms the remains of a
Roman tower; – the rifted stones rolled down the hill and fell at
the feet of Stanton. He stood appalled, and, awaiting his summons from the Power in whose eye pyramids, palaces and the
worms whose toil has formed them, and the worms who toil out
their existence under their shadow or their pressure, are perhaps

all alike contemptible, he stood collected, and for a moment felt that defiance of danger which danger itself excites, and we love to encounter it as a physical enemy, to bid it 'do its worst', and feel that its worst will perhaps be ultimately its best for us. He stood and saw another flash dart its bright, brief and malignant glance over the ruins of ancient power, and the luxuriance of recent fertility. Singular contrast! The relics of art for ever decaying, – the productions of nature for ever renewed. – (Alas! for what purpose are they renewed, better than to mock at the perishable monuments which men try in vain to rival them by). The pyramids themselves must perish, but the grass that grows between their disjointed stones will be renewed from year to year. Stanton was thinking thus, when all power of thought was suspended, by seeing two persons bearing between them the body of a young, and apparently very lovely girl, who had been struck dead by the lightning. Stanton approached, and heard the voices of the bearers repeating, 'There is none who will mourn for her!' 'There is none who will mourn for her!' said other voices, as two more bore in their arms the blasted and blackened figure of what had once been a man, comely and graceful; – 'there is not *one* to mourn for her now!' They were lovers, and he had been consumed by the flash that had destroyed her, while in the act of endeavouring to defend her. As they were about to remove the bodies, a person approached with a calmness of step and demeanour, as if he were alone unconscious of danger, and incapable of fear; and after looking on them for some time, burst into a laugh so loud, wild and protracted, that the peasants, starting with as much horror at the sound as at that of the storm, hurried away, bearing the corse with them. Even Stanton's fears were subdued by his astonishment, and, turning to the stranger, who remained standing on the same spot, he asked the reason of such an outrage on humanity. The stranger, slowly turning round, and disclosing a countenance which – (Here the manuscript was illegible for a few lines), said in English – (A long hiatus followed here, and the next passage that was legible, though it proved to be a continuation of the narrative, was but a fragment).

*

The terrors of the night rendered Stanton a sturdy and unappeasable applicant; and the shrill voice of the old woman, repeating, 'no heretic – no English – Mother of God protect us – avaunt Satan!' – combined with the clatter of the wooden casement (peculiar to the houses in Valentia) which she opened to discharge her volley of anathematization, and shut again as the lightning glanced through the aperture, were unable to repel his importunate request for admittance, in a night whose terrors ought to soften all the miserable petty local passions into one awful feeling of fear for the Power who caused it, and compassion for those who were exposed to it. – But Stanton felt there was something more than national bigotry in the exclamations of the old woman; there was a peculiar and personal horror of the English. – and he was right; but this did not diminish the eagerness of his

*

The house was handsome and spacious, but the melancholy appearance of desertion

*

– The benches were by the wall, but there were none to sit there; the tables were spread in what had been the hall, but it seemed as if none had gathered round them for many years; – the clock struck audibly, there was no voice of mirth or of occupation to drown its sound; time told his awful lesson to silence alone; – the hearths were black with fuel long since consumed; – the family portraits looked as if they were the only tenants of the mansion; they seemed to say, from their mouldering frames, 'there are none to gaze on us;' and the echo of the steps of Stanton and his feeble guide, was the only sound audible between the peals of thunder that rolled still awfully, but more distantly, – every peal like the exhausted murmurs of a spent heart. As they passed on, a shriek was heard. Stanton paused, and fearful images of the dangers to which travellers on the Continent are exposed in deserted and remote habitations, came into his mind. 'Don't heed it,' said the old woman, lighting him on with a miserable lamp; – 'it is only he

*

The old woman having now satisfied herself, by ocular demonstration, that her English guest, even if he was the devil, had neither horn, hoof, or tail, that he could bear the sign of the cross without changing his form, and that, when he spoke, not a puff of sulphur came out of his mouth, began to take courage, and at length commenced her story, which, weary and comfortless as Stanton was,

*

Every obstacle was now removed; parents and relations at last gave up all opposition, and the young pair were united. Never was there a lovelier, – they seemed like angels who had only anticipated by a few years their celestial and eternal union. The marriage was solemnized with much pomp, and a few days after there was a feast in that very wainscotted chamber which you paused to remark was so gloomy. It was that night hung with rich tapestry, representing the exploits of the Cid, particularly that of his burning a few Moors who refused to renounce their accursed religion. They were represented beautifully tortured, writhing and howling, and 'Mahomet! Mahomet!' issuing out of their mouths, as they called on him in their burning agonies; – you could almost hear them scream. At the upper end of the room, under a splendid estrade, over which was an image of the blessed Virgin, sat Donna Isabella de Cardoza, mother to the bride, and near her Donna Ines, the bride, on rich almohadas, the bride-groom sat opposite her; and though they never spoke to each other, their eyes, slowly raised, but suddenly withdrawn, (those eyes that blushed), told to each other the delicious secret of their happiness. Don Pedro de Cardoza had assembled a large party in honour of his daughter's nuptials; among them was an English-man of the name of *Melmoth*, a traveller; no one knew who had brought him there. He sat silent like the rest, while the iced waters and the sugared wafers were presented to the company. The night was intensely hot, and the moon glowed like a sun over the ruins of Saguntum; the embroidered blinds flapped heavily, as if the wind made an effort to raise them in vain, and then desisted.

(Another defect in the manuscript occurred here, but it was soon supplied).

*

The company were dispersed through various alleys of the gar-den; the bridegroom and bride wandered through one where the delicious perfume of the orange trees mingled itself with that of the myrtles in blow. On their return to the hall, both of them asked, Had the company heard the exquisite sounds that floated through the garden just before they quitted it? No one had heard them. They expressed their surprise. The Englishman had never quitted the hall; it was said he smiled with a most particular and extraordinary expression as the remark was made. His silence had been noticed before, but it was ascribed to his ignorance of the Spanish language, an ignorance that Spaniards are not anx-ious either to expose or remove by speaking to a stranger. The subject of the music was not again reverted to till the guests were seated at supper, when Donna Ines and her young husband, exchanging a smile of delighted surprise, exclaimed they heard the same delicious sounds floating round them. The guests lis-tened, but no one else could hear it; – every one felt there was something extraordinary in this. Hush! was uttered by every voice almost at the same moment. A dead silence followed, – you would think, from their intent looks, that they listened with their very eyes. This deep silence, contrasted with the splendour of the feast, and the light effused from torches held by the domestics, produced a singular effect, – it seemed for some moments like an assembly of the dead. The silence was interrupted, though the cause of wonder had not ceased, by the entrance of Father Olavida, the Confessor of Donna Isabella, who had been called away previous to the feast, to administer extreme unction to a dying man in the neighbourhood. He was a priest of uncommon sanctity, beloved in the family, and respected in the neighbourhood, where he had displayed uncommon taste and talents for exorcism; – in fact, this was the good Father's *forte*, and he piqued himself on it accordingly. The devil never fell into worse hands than Father Olavida's, for when he was so contumacious as to resist Latin, and even the first verses of the Gospel of St John in Greek, which the good Father never had recourse to but in cases of extreme stubbornness and difficulty, – (here Stanton recollected the English story of the *Boy of Bilsdon*, and blushed even in Spain for his countrymen), – then he always applied to the Inquisition; and if the devils were ever so obstinate before, they were always seen to fly out of the possessed, just as, in the midst of their cries, (no doubt of blasphemy), they were tied to the stake. Some held out even till the flames surrounded them; but even the most stubborn must have been dislodged when the operation was over, for the devil himself could no longer tenant a crisp and glutinous lump of cinders. Thus Father Olavida's fame spread far and wide, and the Cardoza family had made uncommon interest to procure him for a Confessor, and happily succeeded. The ceremony he had just been performing, had cast a shade over the good Father's countenance, but it dispersed as he mingled among the guests, and was introduced to them. Room was soon made for him, and he happened accidentally to be seated opposite the

Englishman. As the wine was presented to him, Father Olavida, (who, as I observed, was a man of singular sanctity), prepared to utter a short internal prayer. He hesitated, – trembled, – desisted; and, putting down the wine, wiped the drops from his forehead with the sleeve of his habit. Donna Isabella gave a sign to a domestic, and other wine of a higher quality was offered to him. His lips moved, as if in the effort to pronounce a benediction on it and the company, but the effort again failed; and the change in his countenance was so extraordinary, that it was perceived by all the guests. He felt the sensation that his extraordinary appearance excited, and attempted to remove it by again endeavouring to lift the cup to his lips. So strong was the anxiety with which the company watched him, that the only sound heard in that spacious and crowded hall, was the rustling of his habit, as he attempted to lift the cup to his lips once more – in vain. The guests sat in astonished silence. Father Olavida alone remained standing; but at that moment the Englishman rose, and appeared determined to fix Olavida's regards by a gaze like that of fascination. Olavida rocked, reeled, grasped the arm of a page, and at last, closing his eyes for a moment, as if to escape the horrible fascination of that unearthly glare, (the Englishman's eyes were observed by all the guests, from the moment of his entrance, to effuse a most fearful and preternatural lustre), exclaimed, 'Who is among us? – Who? – I cannot utter a blessing while he is here. I cannot feel one. Where he treads, the earth is parched! – Where he breathes, the air is fire! – Where he feeds, the food is poison! – Where he turns, his glance is lightning! – *Who is among us? – Who?'* repeated the priest in the agony of adjuration, while his cowl fallen back, his few thin hairs around the scalp instinct and alive with terrible emotion, his outspread arms protruded from the sleeves of his habit, and extended towards the awful stranger, suggested the idea of an inspired being in the dreadful rapture of prophetic denunciation. He stood – still stood, and the Englishman stood calmly opposite to him. There was an agitated irregularity in the attitudes of those around them, which contrasted strongly the fixed and stern postures of those two, who remained gazing silently at each other. 'Who knows him?' exclaimed Olavida, starting apparently from a trance; 'who knows him? who brought him here?'

The guests severally disclaimed all knowledge of the Englishman, and each asked the other in whispers, 'who *had* brought him there?' Father Olavida then pointed his arm to each of the company, and asked each individually, 'Do you know him?' 'No! no! no!' was uttered with vehement emphasis by every individual. 'But I know him,' said Olavida, 'by these cold drops!' and he wiped them off; – 'by these convulsed joints!' and he attempted to sign the cross, but could not. He raised his voice, and evidently speaking with increased difficulty, – 'By this bread and wine, which the faithful receive as the body and blood of Christ, but which *his* presence converts into matter as viperous as the suicide foam of the dying Judas, – by all these – I know him, and command him to be gone! – He is – he is –' and he bent forwards as he spoke, and gazed on the Englishman with an expression which the mixture of rage, hatred, and fear, rendered terrible. All the guests rose at these words, – the whole company now presented two singular groupes, that of the amazed guests all collected together, and repeating, 'Who, what is he?' and that of the Englishman, who stood unmoved, and Olavida, who dropped dead in the attitude of pointing to him.

*

The body was removed into another room, and the departure of the Englishman was not noticed till the company returned to the hall. They sat late together, conversing on this extraordinary circumstance, and finally agreed to remain in the house, lest the evil spirit (for they believed the Englishman no better) should take certain liberties with the corse by no means agreeable to a Catholic, particularly as he had manifestly died without the benefit of the last sacraments. Just as this laudable resolution was formed, they were roused by cries of horror and agony from the bridal-chamber, where the young pair had retired.

They hurried to the door, but the father was first. They burst it open, and found the bride a corse in the arms of her husband.

*

He never recovered his reason; the family deserted the mansion rendered terrible by so many misfortunes. One apartment is still tenanted by the unhappy maniac; his were the cries you heard as you traversed the deserted rooms. He is for the most part silent during the day, but at midnight he always exclaims, in a voice frightfully piercing, and hardly human, 'They are coming! they are coming!' and relapses into profound silence.

The funeral of Father Olavida was attended by an extraordinary circumstance. He was interred in a neighbouring convent; and the reputation of his sanctity, joined to the interest caused by his extraordinary death, collected vast numbers at the ceremony. His funeral sermon was preached by a monk of distinguished eloquence, appointed for the purpose. To render the effect of his discourse more powerful, the corse, extended on a bier, with its face uncovered, was placed in the aisle. The monk took his text from one of the prophets, – 'Death is gone up into our palaces.' He expatiated on mortality, whose approach, whether abrupt or lingering, is alike awful to man. – He spoke of the vicissitudes of empires with much eloquence and learning, but his audience were not observed to be much affected. – He cited various passages from the lives of the saints, descriptive of the glories of martyrdom, and the heroism of those who had bled and blazed for Christ and his blessed mother, but they appeared still waiting for something to touch them more deeply. When he inveighed against the tyrants under whose bloody persecutions those holy men suffered, his hearers were roused for a moment, for it is always easier to excite a passion than a moral feeling. But when he spoke of the dead, and pointed with emphatic gesture to the corse, as it lay before them cold and motionless, every eye was fixed, and every ear became attentive. Even the lovers, who, under pretence of dipping their fingers into the holy water, were contriving to exchange amorous billets, forbore for one moment this interesting intercourse, to listen to the preacher. He dwelt with much energy on the virtues of the deceased, whom he declared to be a particular favourite of the Virgin; and enumerating the various losses that would be caused by his departure to the community to which he belonged, to society, and to religion at large; he at last worked up himself to a vehement expostulation with the Deity on the occasion. 'Why hast thou,' he exclaimed, 'why hast thou, Oh God! thus dealt with us? Why hast thou snatched from our sight this glorious saint, whose merits, if properly applied, doubtless would have been sufficient to atone for the apostacy of St Peter, the opposition of St Paul, (previous to his conversion), and even the treachery of Judas himself? Why hast thou, Oh God! snatched him from us?' – and a deep and hollow voice from among the congregation answered, – 'Because he deserved his fate.' The murmurs of approbation with which the congregation honoured this apostrophe, half-drowned this extraordinary interruption; and though there was some little commotion in the immediate vicinity of the speaker, the rest of the audience continued to listen intently. 'What,' proceeded the preacher, pointing to the corse, 'what hath laid thee there, servant of God?' – 'Pride, ignorance and fear,' answered the same voice, in accents still more thrilling. The disturbance now became universal. The preacher paused, and a circle opening, disclosed the figure of a monk belonging to the convent, who stood among them.

*

After all the usual modes of admonition, exhortation, and discipline had been employed, and the bishop of the diocese, who, under the report of these extraordinary circumstances, had visited

the convent in person to obtain some explanation from the contumacious monk in vain, it was agreed, in a chapter extraordinary,
to surrender him to the power of the Inquisition. He testified
great horror when this determination was made known to him, –
and offered to tell over and over again all that *could* relate of the
cause of Father Olavida's death. His humiliation, and repeated
offers of confession, came too late. He was conveyed to the Inquisition. The proceedings of that tribunal are rarely disclosed, but
there is a secret report (I cannot answer for its truth) of what
he said and suffered there. On his first examination, he said he
would relate all he *could*. He was told that was not enough, he
must relate all he knew.

★

'Why did you testify such horror at the funeral of Father Olavida?' – 'Every one testified horror and grief at the death of that
venerable ecclesiastic, who died in the odour of sanctity. Had I
done otherwise, it might have been reckoned a proof of my
guilt.' 'Why did you interrupt the preacher with such extraordinary exclamations?' – To this no answer. 'Why do you refuse to
explain the meaning of those exclamations?' – No answer. 'Why
do you persist in this obstinate and dangerous silence? Look, I
beseech you, brother, at the cross that is suspended against this
wall,' and the Inquisitor pointed to the large black crucifix at the
back of the chair where he sat; 'one drop of the blood shed there
can purify you from all the sin you have ever committed; but all
that blood, combined with the intercession of the Queen of
Heaven, and the merits of all its martyrs, nay, even the absolution
of the Pope, cannot deliver you from the curse of dying in unre-
pented sin.' – 'What sin, then, have I committed?' 'The greatest
of all possible sins; you refuse answering the questions put to
you at the tribunal of the most holy and merciful Inquisition; –
you will not tell us what you know concerning the death of
Father Olavida.' – 'I have told you that I believe he perished in

consequence of his ignorance and presumption.' 'What proof can you produce of that?' – 'He sought the knowledge of a secret withheld from man.' 'What was that?' – 'The secret of discovering the presence or agency of the evil power.' 'Do you possess that secret?' – After much agitation on the part of the prisoner, he said distinctly, but very faintly, 'My master forbids me to disclose it.' 'If your master were Jesus Christ, he would not forbid you to obey the commands, or answer the questions of the Inquisition.' – 'I am not sure of that.' There was a general outcry of horror at these words. The examination then went on. 'If you believed Olavida to be guilty of any pursuits or studies condemned by our mother the church, why did you not denounce him to the Inquisition?' – 'Because I believed him not likely to be injured by such pursuits; his mind was too weak, – he died in the struggle,' said the prisoner with great emphasis. 'You believe, then, it requires strength of mind to keep those abominable secrets, when examined as to their nature and tendency?' – 'No, I rather imagine strength of body.' 'We shall try that presently,' said an Inquisitor, giving a signal for the torture.

*

The prisoner underwent the first and second applications with unshrinking courage, but on the infliction of the water-torture, which is indeed insupportable to humanity, either to suffer or relate, he exclaimed in the gasping interval, he would disclose every thing. He was released, refreshed, restored and the following day uttered the following remarkable confession

*

The old Spanish woman further confessed to Stanton, that

*

and that the Englishman certainly had been seen in the neighbourhood since; – seen, as she had heard that very night. 'Great

G—d!' exclaimed Stanton, as he recollected the stranger whose demoniac laugh had so appalled him, while gazing on the lifeless bodies of the lovers, whom the lightning had struck and blasted.

As the manuscript, after a few blotted and illegible pages, became more distinct, Melmoth read on, perplexed and unsatisfied, not knowing what connexion this Spanish story could have with his ancestor, whom, however, he recognized under the title of *the Englishman*; and wondering how Stanton could have thought it worth his while to follow him to Ireland, write a long manuscript about an event that occurred in Spain, and leave it in the hands of his family, to 'verify untrue things,' in the language of Dogberry, – his wonder was diminished, though his curiosity was still more inflamed, by the perusal of the next lines, which he made out with some difficulty. It seems Stanton was now in England.

*

About the year 1677, Stanton was in London, his mind still full of his mysterious countryman. This constant subject of his contemplations had produced a visible change in his exterior, – his walk was what Sallust tells us of Catiline's, – his were, too, the *fœdi oculi*.[4] He said to himself every moment, 'If I could but trace that being, I will not call him man,' – and the next moment he said, 'and what if I could?' In this state of mind, it is singular enough that he mixed constantly in public amusements, but it is true. When one fierce passion is devouring the soul, we feel more than ever the necessity of external excitement; and our dependence on the world for temporary relief increases in direct proportion to our contempt of the world and all its works. He went frequently to the theatres, *then* fashionable, when

> The fair sat panting at a courtier's play,
> And not a mask went unimproved away

The London theatres then presented a spectacle which ought for ever to put to silence the foolish outcry against progressive deterioration of morals, – foolish even from the pen of Juvenal, and still more so from the lips of a modern Puritan. Vice is always nearly on an average: The only difference in life worth tracing, is that of manners, and there we have manifestly the advantage of our ancestors. Hypocrisy is said to be the homage that vice pays to virtue, – decorum is the outward expression of that homage; and if this be so, we must acknowledge that vice has latterly grown very humble indeed. There was, however, something splendid, ostentatious, and obtrusive, in the vices of Charles the Second's reign. – A view of the theatres alone proved it, when Stanton was in the habit of visiting them. At the doors stood on one side the footmen of a fashionable nobleman, (with arms concealed under their liveries), surrounding the sedan of a popular actress,* whom they were to carry off *vi et armis*,[5] as she entered it at the end of the play. At the other side waited the *glass coach* of a woman of fashion, who waited to take Kynaston (the Adonis of the day), in his female dress, to the park after the play was over, and exhibit him in all the luxurious splendour of effeminate beauty, (heightened by the theatrical dress), for which he was so distinguished.

Plays being then performed at four o'clock, allowed ample time for the evening drive, and the midnight assignation, when the parties met by torch-light, masked, in St James's park, and verified the title of Wycherly's play, 'Love in a Wood.' The boxes, as Stanton looked round him, were filled with females, whose naked shoulders and bosoms, well testified in the paintings of Lely, and the pages of Grammont, might save modern puritanism many a vituperative groan and affected reminiscence. They

* Mrs Marshall, the original Roxana in Lee's Alexander, and the only virtuous woman then on the stage. She was carried off in the manner described, by Lord Orrery, who, finding all his solicitations repelled, had recourse to a sham marriage performed by a servant in the habit of a clergyman.

had all taken the precaution to send some male relative, on the first night of a new play, to report whether it was fit for persons of 'honour and reputation' to appear at; but in spite of this precaution, at certain passages (which occurred about every second sentence) they were compelled to spread out their fans, or play with the still cherished love-lock, which Prynne himself had not been able to write down.

The men in the boxes were composed of two distinct classes, the 'men of wit and pleasure about town,' distinguished by their Flanders lace cravats, soiled with snuff, their diamond rings, the pretended gift of a royal mistress, (*n'importe* whether the Duchess of Portsmouth or Nell Gwynne;) their uncombed wigs, whose curls descended to their waists, and the loud and careless tone in which they abused Dryden, Lee, and Otway, and quoted Sedley and Rochester; – the other class were the lovers, the gentle 'squires of dames,' equally conspicuous for their white fringed gloves, their obsequious bows, and their commencing every sentence addressed to a lady, with the profane exclamation of* 'Oh Jesu!', or the softer, but equally unmeaning one of 'I beseech you, Madam,' or, 'Madam, I burn.†' One circumstance sufficiently extraordinary marked the manners of the day; females had not then found their proper level in life; they were alternately adored as goddesses, and assailed as prostitutes; and the man who, this moment, addressed his mistress in language borrowed from Orondates worshipping Cassandra, in the next accosted her with ribaldry that might put to the blush the piazzas of Covent Garden.‡

---

* Vide Pope, (copying from Donne).

> 'Peace, fools, or Gonson will for Papists seize you,
> If once he catch you at your Jesu, Jesu.'

† Vide the Old Bachelor, whose Araminta, wearied by the repetition of these phrases, forbids her lover to address her in any sentence commencing with them.
‡ Vide any old play you may have the patience to peruse; or, *instar omnium*, read the courtly loves of Rhodophil and Melantha, Palamede and Doralice, in Dryden's Marriage à la Mode.

The pit presented a more various spectacle. There were the critics armed cap-a-pee from Aristotle and Bossu; these men dined at twelve, dictated at a coffee-house till four, then called to the boy to brush their shoes, and strode to the theatre, where, till the curtain rose, they sat hushed in grim repose, and expecting their evening prey. There were the templars, spruce, pert, and loquacious; and here and there a sober citizen, doffing his steeple-crowned hat, and hiding his little band under the folds of his huge puritanic cloke, while his eyes, declined with an expression half leering, half ejaculatory, towards a masked female, muffled in a hood and scarf, testified what had seduced him into these 'tents of Kedar'. There were females, too, but all in vizard masks, which, though worn as well as aunt Dinah's in Tristram Shandy, served to conceal them from the 'young bubbles' they were in quest of, and from all but the orange-women, who hailed them loudly as they passed the doors.* In the galleries were the happy souls who waited for the fulfilment of Dryden's promise in one of his prologues;† no matter to them whether it were the ghost of Almanor's mother in her dripping shroud, or that of Laius, who, according to the stage directions, rises in his chariot, armed with the ghosts of his three murdered attendants behind him, – a joke that did not escape l'Abbe le Blanc,‡ in his recipe for writing an English tragedy. Some, indeed, from time to time called out for the 'burning of the Pope'; but though

> 'Space was obedient to the boundless piece,
> Which oped in Mexico and closed in Greece,'

it was not always possible to indulge them in this laudable amuse-

---

* Vide Southern's Oroonoko, – I mean the comic part.
† 'A charm, a song, a murder, and a ghost.' *Prologue to Œdipus.*
‡ Vide Le Blanc's Letters.

ment, as the scene of the popular plays was generally laid in Africa or Spain; Sir Robert Howard, Elkanah Settle, and John Dryden, all agreeing in their choice of Spanish and Moorish subjects for their principal plays. Among this joyous groupe were seated several women of fashion masked, enjoying in secrecy the licentiousness which they dared not openly patronize, and verifying Gay's characteristic description, though it was written many years later,

> 'Mobbed in the gallery Laura sits secure,
> And laughs at jests that turn the box demure.'

Stanton gazed on all this with the look of one who 'could not be moved to smile at any thing.' He turned to the stage, the play was Alexander, then acted as written by Lee, and the principal character was performed by Hart, whose god-like ardour in making love, is said almost to have compelled the audience to believe that they beheld the 'son of Ammon'.

There were absurdities enough to offend a classical, or even a rational spectator. There were Grecian heroes with roses in their shoes, feathers in their hats, and wigs down to their waists; and Persian princesses in stiff stays and powdered hair. But the illusion of the scene was well sustained, for the heroines were rivals in real as well as theatrical life. It was that memorable night, when, according to the history of the veteran Betterton,* Mrs Barry, who personated Roxana, had a greenroom squabble with Mrs Bowtell, the representative of Statira, about a veil, which the partiality of the property-man adjudged to the latter. Roxana suppressed her rage till the fifth act, when, stabbing Statira, she aimed the blow with such force as to pierce through her stays, and inflict a severe though not dangerous wound. Mrs Bowtell

---

* Vide Betterton's History of the Stage.

fainted, the performance was suspended, and, in the commotion which this incident caused in the house, many of the audience rose, and Stanton among them. It was at this moment that, in a seat opposite to him, he discovered the object of his search for four years, – the Englishman whom he had met in the plains of Valentia, and whom he believed the same with the subject of the extraordinary narrative he had heard there.

He was standing up. There was nothing particular or remarkable in his appearance, but the expression of his eyes could never be mistaken or forgotten. The heart of Stanton palpitated with violence, – a mist overspread his eyes, – a nameless and deadly sickness, accompanied with a creeping sensation in every pore, from which cold drops were gushing, announced the

*

Before he had well recovered, a strain of music, soft, solemn and delicious, breathed round him, audibly ascending from the ground, and increasing in sweetness and power till it seemed to fill the whole building. Under the sudden impulse of amazement and pleasure, he inquired of some around him from whence those exquisite sounds arose. But, by the manner in which he was answered, it was plain that those he addressed considered him insane; and, indeed, the remarkable change in his expression might well justify the suspicion. He then remembered that night in Spain, when the same sweet and mysterious sounds were heard only by the young bridegroom and bride, of whom the latter perished on that very night. 'And am I then to be the next victim?' thought Stanton; 'and are those celestial sounds, that seem to prepare us for heaven, only intended to announce the presence of an incarnate fiend, who mocks the devoted with 'airs from heaven', while he prepares to surround them with 'blasts from hell'?' It is very singular that at this moment, when his imagination had reached its highest pitch of elevation, – when the object he had pursued so long and fruitlessly, had in one moment become as it were tangible to the grasp both of mind and body, – when this spirit, with whom he had wrestled in darkness, was at last about to declare its name, that Stanton began to feel a kind of disappointment at the futility of his pursuits, like Bruce at discovering the course of the Nile, or Gibbon on concluding his History. The feeling which he had dwelt on so long, that he had actually converted it into a duty, was after all mere curiosity; but what passion is more insatiable, or more capable of giving a kind of romantic grandeur to all its wanderings and eccentricities? Curiosity is in one respect like love, it always compromises between the object and the feeling; and provided the latter possesses sufficient energy, no matter how contemptible the former may be. A child might have smiled at the agitation of Stanton, caused as it was by the accidental appearance of a stranger; but no man, in the full energy of his passions, was there, but must have trembled at the horrible agony of emotion with which he felt approaching, with sudden and irresistible velocity, the crisis of his destiny.

When the play was over, he stood for some moments in the deserted streets. It was a beautiful moonlight night, and he saw near him a figure, whose shadow, projected half across the street, (there were no flagged ways then, chains and posts were the only defence of the foot-passenger), appeared to him of gigantic magnitude. He had been so long accustomed to contend with these phantoms of the imagination, that he took a kind of stubborn delight in subduing them. He walked up to the object, and observing the shadow only was magnified, and the figure was the ordinary height of man, he approached it, and discovered the very object of his search, – the man whom he had seen for a moment in Valentia, and, after a search of four years, recognized at the theatre.

*

'You were in quest of me?' – 'I was.' 'Have you any thing to inquire of me?' – 'Much.' 'Speak, then.' – 'This is no place.' 'No place! poor wretch, I am independent of time and place. Speak, if you have any thing to ask or to learn.' – 'I have many things to ask, but nothing to learn, I hope, from you.' 'You deceive yourself, but you will be undeceived when next we meet.' – 'And when shall that be?' said Stanton, grasping his arm; 'name your hour and your place.' 'The hour shall be mid-day,' answered the stranger, with a horrid and unintelligible smile; 'and the place shall be the bare walls of a mad-house, where you shall rise rattling in your chains, and rustling from your straw, to greet me, – yet still you shall have *the curse of sanity*, and of memory. My voice shall ring in your ears till then, and the glance of these eyes shall be reflected from every object, animate or inanimate, till you behold them again.' – 'Is it under circumstances so horrible we are to meet again?' said Stanton, shrinking under the full-lighted blaze of those demon eyes. 'I never,' said the stranger, in an emphatic tone, – 'I *never desert my friends in misfortune*. When they are plunged in the lowest abyss of human calamity, *they are sure to be visited by me*.'

*

The narrative, when Melmoth was again able to trace its continuation, described Stanton, some years after, plunged in a state the most deplorable.

He had been always reckoned of a singular turn of mind, and the belief of this, aggravated by his constant talk of Melmoth, his wild pursuit of him, his strange behaviour at the theatre, and his dwelling on the various particulars of their extraordinary meetings, with all the intensity of the deepest conviction, (while he never could impress them on any one's conviction but his own), suggested to some prudent people the idea that he was deranged. Their malignity probably took part with their prudence. The selfish Frenchman* says, we feel a pleasure even in the misfortunes

* Rochefoucault.

of our friends, – *a plus forte* in those of our enemies; and as every one is an enemy to a man of genius of course, the report of Stanton's malady was propagated with infernal and successful industry. Stanton's next relative, a needy unprincipled man, watched the report in its circulation, and saw the snares closing round his victim. He waited on him one morning, accompanied by a person of a grave, though somewhat repulsive appearance. Stanton was as usual abstracted and restless, and, after a few moment's conversation, he proposed a drive a few miles out of London, which he said would revive and refresh him. Stanton objected, on account of the difficulty of getting a hackney coach, (for it is singular that at this period the number of private equipages, though infinitely fewer than they are now, exceeded the number of hired ones), and proposed going by water. This, however, did not suit the kinsman's views; and, after pretending to send for a carriage, (which was in waiting at the end of the street), Stanton and his companions entered it, and drove about two miles out of London.

The carriage then stopped. 'Come, Cousin,' said the younger Stanton, – 'come and view a purchase I have made.' Stanton absently alighted, and followed him across a small paved court; the other person followed. 'In troth, Cousin,' said Stanton, 'your choice appears not to have been discreetly made; your house has something of a gloomy aspect.' – 'Hold you content, Cousin,' replied the other; 'I shall take order that you like it better, when you have been some time a dweller therein.' Some attendants of a mean appearance, and with most suspicious visages, awaited them on their entrance, and they ascended a narrow staircase, which led to a room meanly furnished. 'Wait here,' said the kinsman, to the man who accompanied them, 'till I go for company to divertise my cousin in his loneliness.' They were left alone. Stanton took no notice of his companion, but as usual seized the first book near him, and began to read. It was a volume in manuscript, – they were then much more common than now.

The first lines struck him as indicating insanity in the writer. It was a wild proposal (written apparently after the great fire of London) to rebuild it with stone, and attempting to prove, on a calculation wild, false, and yet sometimes plausible, that this could be done out of the colossal fragments of Stonehenge, which the writer proposed to remove for that purpose. Subjoined were several grotesque drawings of engines designed to remove those massive blocks, and in a corner of the page was a note, – 'I would have drawn these more accurately, but was not allowed *a knife* to mend my pen.'

The next was entitled, 'A modest proposal for the spreading of Christianity in foreign parts, whereby it is hoped its entertainment will become general all over the world.' – This modest proposal was, to convert the Turkish ambassadors, (who had been in London a few years before), by offering them their choice of being strangled on the spot, or becoming Christians. Of course the writer reckoned on their embracing the easier alternative, but even this was to be clogged with a heavy condition, – namely, that they must be bound before a magistrate to convert twenty mussulmans a day, on their return to Turkey. The rest of the pamphlet was reasoned very much in the conclusive style of Captain Bobadil – these twenty will convert twenty more a piece, and these four hundred converts, converting their due number in the same time, all Turkey would be converted before the Grand Signior knew where he was. Then comes the *coup declat*, – one fine morning, every minaret in Constantinople was to ring out with bells, instead of the cry of the Muezzins; and the Imaum, coming out to see what was the matter, was to be encountered by the Archbishop of Canterbury, *in pontificalibus*,[6] performing Cathedral service in the church of St Sophia, which was to finish the business. Here an objection appeared to arise, which the ingenuity of the writer had anticipated. – 'It may be redargued,' saith he, 'by those who have more spleen than brain, that forasmuch as the Archbishop preacheth in English, he will not thereby much edify the Turkish folk, who do altogether hold in a vain gabble of their own.' But this (to use his own language) he 'evites,' by judiciously observing, that where service was performed in an unknown tongue, the devotion of the people was always observed to be much increased thereby; as, for instance, in the church of Rome, – that St Augustine, with his monks, advanced to meet King Ethelbert singing litanies, (in a language his majesty could not possibly have understood), and converted him and his whole court on the spot; – that the sybilline books

*

Cum multis aliis.

Between the pages were cut most exquisitely in paper the likenesses of some of these Turkish ambassadors; the hair of the beards, in particular, was feathered with a delicacy of touch that seemed the work of fairy fingers, – but the pages ended with a complaint of the operator, that his *scissars had been taken from him*. However, he consoled himself and the reader with the assurance, that he would that night catch a moon-beam as it entered through the grating, and, when he had whetted it on the iron knobs of his door, would do wonders with it. In the next page was found a melancholy proof of powerful but prostrated intellect. It contained some insane lines, ascribed to Lee the dramatic poet, commencing,

'O that my lungs could bleat like buttered pease,' &c

There is no proof whatever that these miserable lines were really written by Lee, except that the measure is the fashionable quatrain of the period. It is singular that Stanton read on without suspicion of his own danger, quite absorbed in *the album of a madhouse*, without ever reflecting on the place where he was, and which such compositions too manifestly designated.

It was after a long interval that he looked round, and perceived that his companion was gone. Bells were unusual then. He proceeded to the door, – it was fastened. He called aloud, – his voice was echoed in a moment by many others, but in tones so wild and discordant, that he desisted in involuntary terror. As the day advanced, and no one approached, he tried the window, and then perceived for the first time it was grated. It looked out on the narrow flagged yard, in which no human being was; and if there had, from such a being no human feeling could have been extracted.

Sickening with unspeakable horror, he sunk rather than sat down beside the miserable window, and 'wished for day'.

*

At midnight he started from a doze, half a swoon, half a sleep, which probably the hardness of his seat, and of the deal table on which he leaned, had not contributed to prolong.

He was in complete darkness; the horror of his situation struck him at once, and for a moment he was indeed almost qualified for an inmate of that dreadful mansion. He felt his way to the door, shook it with desperate strength, and uttered the most frightful cries, mixed with expostulations and commands. His cries were in a moment echoed by a hundred voices. In maniacs there is a peculiar malignity, accompanied by an extraordinary acuteness of some of the senses, particularly in distinguishing the voice of a stranger. The cries that he heard on every side seemed like a wild and infernal yell of joy, that their mansion of misery had obtained another tenant.

He paused, exhausted, – a quick and thundering step was heard in the passage. The door was opened, and a man of savage appearance stood at the entrance, – two more were seen indistinctly in the passage. – 'Release me, villain!' 'Stop, my fine fellow, what's all this noise for?' 'Where am I?' 'Where you ought to be.' 'Will you dare to detain me?' 'Yes, and a little more than that,' answered the ruffian, applying a loaded horse-whip to his back and shoulders, till the patient soon fell to the ground convulsed with rage and pain. 'Now you see you are where you ought to be,' repeated the ruffian, brandishing the horse-whip over him, 'and now take the advice of a friend, and make no more noise. The lads are ready for you with the darbies, and they'll clink them on in the crack of this whip, unless you prefer another touch of it first.' They then were advancing into the room as he spoke, with fetters in their hands, (strait waistcoats being then little known or used), and shewed, by their frightful countenances and gestures, no unwillingness to apply them. Their harsh rattle on the stone pavement made Stanton's blood run cold; the effect, however, was useful. He had the presence of mind to acknowledge his (supposed) miserable condition, to supplicate the forbearance of the ruthless keeper, and promise complete submission to his orders. This pacified the ruffian, and he retired.

Stanton collected all his resolution to encounter the horrible night; he saw all that was before him, and summoned himself to meet it. After much agitated deliberation, he conceived it best to continue the same appearance of submission and tranquillity, hoping that thus he might in time either propitiate the wretches in whose hands he was, or, by his apparent inoffensiveness, procure such opportunities of indulgence, as might perhaps ultimately facilitate his escape. He therefore determined to conduct himself with the utmost tranquillity, and never to let his voice be heard in the house; and he laid down several other resolutions with a degree of prudence which he already shuddered to think might be the cunning of incipient madness, or the beginning result of the horrid habits of the place.

These resolutions were put to desperate trial that very night. Just next to Stanton's apartment were lodged two most uncongenial neighbours. One of them was a puritanical weaver, who had been driven mad by a single sermon from the celebrated Hugh Peters; and was sent to the mad-house as full of election and reprobation as he could hold, – and fuller. He regularly repeated over the *five points* while day-light lasted, and imagined himself preaching in a conventicle with distinguished success; towards twilight his visions were more gloomy, and at midnight his blasphemies became horrible. In the opposite cell was lodged a loyalist tailor, who had been ruined by giving credit to the cavaliers and their ladies, – (for at this time, and much later, down to the reign of Anne, tailors were employed by females even *to make* and *fit on their stays*), – who had run mad with drink and loyalty on the burning of the Rump, and ever since had made the cells of the mad-house echo with fragments of the ill-fated Colonel Lovelace's songs, scraps from Cowley's 'Cutter of Coleman street,' and some curious specimens from Mrs Aphra Behn's plays, where the cavaliers are denominated the *heroicks*, and Lady Lambert and Lady Desborough represented as going to meeting, their large Bibles carried before them by their pages, and falling in love with two banished cavaliers by the way. – 'Tabitha, Tabitha,' cried a voice half in exultation and half in derision; 'thou shalt go with thy hair curled, and thy breasts naked;' – and then added in an affected voice, – 'I could dance the Canaries once, spouse.' This never failed to rouse the feelings, or rather operate on the instincts of the puritanic weaver, who immediately answered, 'Colonel Harrison shall come out of the west, riding on a sky-coloured mule, which signifies instruction*.' 'Ye lie, ye round-head son of a b—h,' roared the cavalier tailor, 'Colonel Harrison will be damned before he ever mounts a sky-coloured mule;' and he concluded this pithy sentence with fragments of anti-Oliverian songs.

> 'And may I live to see
> Old Noll upon a tree,
> And many such as he;
> Confound him, confound him,
> Diseases all around him'

* Vide Cutter of Coleman street.

'Ye are honest gentlemen, I can play many tunes,' squeaked a poor mad loyalist fiddler, who had been accustomed to play in the taverns to the cavalier party, and just remembered the words of a similar minstrel playing for Colonel Blunt in the committee. 'Then play me the air to "Rebellion is breaking up house", exclaimed the tailor, dancing wildly about his cell (as far as his chains allowed him) to an imaginary measure. The weaver could contain no longer. 'How long, Lord, how long,' he exclaimed, 'shall thine enemies insult thy sanctuary, in which I have been placed an anointed teacher? even here, where I am placed to preach to the souls in prison? – Open the flood-gates of thy power, and though thy waves and storms go over me, let me testify in the midst of them, even as he who spreadeth forth his hands to swim may raise one of them to warn his companion that he is about to sink. – Sister Ruth, why dost thou uncover thy bosom to discover my frailty? – Lord, let thine arm of power be with us as it was when thou brakest the shield, the sword, and the battle. – When thy foot was dipped in the blood of thine enemies, and the tongue of thy dogs was red through the same. – Dip all thy garments in blood, and let me weave thee fresh when thou art stained. – When shall thy saints tread the winepress of thy wrath? Blood! blood! the saints call for it, earth gapes to swallow it, hell thirsts for it! Sister Ruth, I pray thee, conceal thy bosom, and be not as the vain women of this generation. – Oh for a day like that, a day of the Lord of hosts, when the towers fell! – Spare me in the battle, for I am not a mighty man of war; leave me in the rear of the host, to curse, with the curse of Meroz, those who come not to the help of the Lord against the mighty, – even to curse this malignant tailor, – yea, curse him bitterly. – Lord, I am in the tents of Kedar, my feet stumble on the dark mountains, – I fall, – I fall!' – And the poor wretch, exhausted by his delirious agonies, fell, and grovelled for some time in his straw. 'Oh! I have had a grievous fall, – Sister Ruth, – Oh Sister Ruth! – Rejoice not against me, Oh mine enemy! though I fall, I shall rise again.'

Whatever satisfaction Sister Ruth might have derived from this assurance, if she could have heard it, was enjoyed tenfold by the weaver, whose amorous reminiscences were in a moment exchanged for war-like ones, borrowed from a wretched and disarranged mass of intellectual rubbish. 'The Lord is a man of war,' he shouted. – 'Look to Marston Moor! – Look to the city, the proud city, full of pride and sin! – Look to the waves of the Severn, as red with blood as the waves of the Red Sea! – There were the hoofs broken by means of the prancings, the prancings of the mighty ones. – Then, Lord, was thy triumph, and the triumph of thy saints, to bind their kings in chains, and their nobles in links of iron.' The malignant tailor burst out in his turn: 'Thank the false Scots, and their solemn league and covenant, and Carisbrook Castle, for that, ye crop-eared Puritan,' he yelled. 'If it had not been for them, I would have taken measure of the king for a velvet cloak as high as the Tower of London, and one flirt of its folds would have knocked the 'copper nose' into the Thames, and sent it a-drift to Hell.' 'Ye lie, in your teeth,' echoed the weaver; 'and I will prove it unarmed, with my shuttle against your needle, and smite you to the earth thereafter, as David smote Goliath. It was *the man's* (such was the indecent language in which Charles the First was spoken of by the Puritans) – it was the man's carnal, self-seeking, world-loving, prelatical hierarchy, that drove the godly to seek the sweet word in season from their own pastors, who righteously abominated the Popish garniture of lawn-sleeves, lewd organs, and steeple houses. Sister Ruth, tempt me not with that calf's head, it is all streaming with blood; drop it, I beseech thee, sister, it is unmeet in a woman's hand, though the brethren drink of it. – Woe be unto thee, gainsayer, dost thou not see how flames envelope the accursed city under his Arminian and Popish son? – London is on fire! – on fire!' he yelled; 'and the brands are lit by the half-papist, whole-arminian, all-damned people thereof. – Fire! – fire!' The voice in which he shrieked out the last words was powerfully horrible, but it was like the moan of an infant, compared to the voice which took up and re-echoed the cry, in a tone that made the building shake. It was the voice of a maniac, who had lost her husband, children, subsistence, and finally her reason, in the dreadful fire of London. The cry of fire never failed to operate with terrible punctuality on her associations. She had been in a disturbed sleep, and now started from it as suddenly as on that dreadful night. It was Saturday night, too, and she was always observed to be particularly violent on that night, – it was the terrible weekly festival of insanity with her. She was awake, and busy in a moment escaping from the flames; and she dramatized the whole scene with such hideous fidelity, that Stanton's resolution was far more in danger from her than from the battle between his neighbours *Testimony* and *Hothead*. She began exclaiming she was suffocated by the smoke; then she sprung from her bed, calling for a light, and appeared to be struck by the sudden glare that burst through her casement. – 'The last day,' she shrieked, 'The last day! The very heavens are on fire!' – 'That will not come till the Man of Sin be first destroyed,' cried the weaver; 'thou ravest of light and fire, and yet thou art in utter darkness. – I pity thee, poor mad soul, I pity thee!' The maniac never heeded him; she appeared to be scrambling up a staircase to her children's room. She exclaimed she was scorched, singed, suffocated; her courage appeared to fail, and she retreated. 'But my children are there!' she cried in a voice of unspeakable agony, as she seemed to make another effort; 'here I am – here I am come to save you. – Oh God! They are all blazing! – Take this arm – no, not that, it is scorched and disabled – well, any arm – take hold of my clothes – no, they are blazing too! Well, take me all on fire as I am! – And their hair, how it hisses! – Water, one drop of water for my youngest – he is but an infant – for my youngest, and let me burn!' She paused in horrid silence, to watch the fall of a blazing rafter that was about to shatter the staircase on which she stood. – 'The roof has fallen on my head!' she exclaimed. 'The earth is weak, and all the inhabitants thereof,' chaunted the weaver; 'I bear up the pillars of it.'

The maniac marked the destruction of the spot where she thought she stood by one desperate bound, accompanied by a wild shriek, and then calmly gazed on her infants as they rolled over the scorching fragments, and sunk into the abyss of fire below. 'There they go, – one – two – three – all!' and her voice sunk into low mutterings, and her convulsions into faint, cold shudderings, like the sobbings of a spent storm, as she imagined herself to 'stand in safety and despair', amid the thousand houseless wretches assembled in the suburbs of London on the dreadful nights after the fire, without food, roof, or raiment, all gazing on the burning ruins of their dwellings and their property. She seemed to listen to their complaints, and even repeated some of them very affectingly, but invariably answered them with the same words, 'But I have lost all my children – *all*!' It was remarkable, that when this sufferer began to rave, all the others became silent. The cry of nature hushed every other cry, – she was the only patient in the house who was not mad from politics, religion, ebriety, or some perverted passion; and terrifying as the outbreak of her frenzy always was, Stanton used to await it as a kind of relief from the dissonant, melancholy, and ludicrous ravings of the others.

But the utmost efforts of his resolution began to sink under the continued horrors of the place. The impression on his senses began to defy the power of reason to resist them. He could not shut out these frightful cries nightly repeated, nor the frightful sound of the whip employed to still them. Hope began to fail him, as he observed, that the submissive tranquillity (which he had imagined, by obtaining increased indulgence, might contribute to his escape, or perhaps convince the keeper of his sanity) was interpreted by the callous ruffian, who was acquainted only with the varieties of *madness*, as a more refined species of that cunning which he was well accustomed to watch and baffle.

On his first discovery of his situation, he had determined to take the utmost care of his health and intellect that the place allowed, as the sole basis of his hope of deliverance. But as that hope declined, he neglected the means of realizing it. He had at first risen early, walked incessantly about his cell, and availed himself of every opportunity of being in the open air. He took the strictest care of his person in point of cleanliness, and with or without appetite, regularly forced down his miserable meals; and all these efforts were even pleasant, as long as hope prompted them. But now he began to relax them all. He passed half the day in his wretched bed, in which he frequently took his meals, declined shaving or changing his linen, and, when the sun shone into his cell, turned from it on his straw with a sigh of heart-broken despondency. Formerly, when the air breathed through his grating, he used to say, 'Blessed air of heaven, I shall breathe you once more in freedom! – Reserve all your freshness for that delicious evening when I shall inhale you, and be as free as you myself.' Now when he felt it, he sighed and said nothing. The twitter of the sparrows, the pattering of rain, or the moan of wind, sounds that he used to sit up in his bed to catch with delight, as reminding him of nature, were now unheeded.

He began at times to listen with sullen and horrible pleasure to the cries of his miserable companions. He became squalid, list-less, torpid, and disgusting in his appearance.

*

It was one of those dismal nights, that, as he tossed on his loath-some bed, – more loathsome from the impossibility to quit it without feeling more 'unrest', – he perceived the miserable light that burned in the hearth was obscured by the intervention of some dark object. He turned feebly towards the light, without curiosity, without excitement, but with a wish to diversify the monotony of his misery, by observing the slightest change made even accidentally in the dusky atmosphere of his cell. Between him and the light stood the figure of Melmoth, just as he had seen him from the first; the figure was the same; the expression of the face was the same, – cold, stony, and rigid; the eyes, with their infernal and dazzling lustre, were still the same.

Stanton's ruling passion rushed on his soul; he felt this apparition like a summons to a high and fearful encounter. He heard his heart beat audibly, and could have exclaimed with Lee's unfortunate heroine, – 'It pants as cowards do before a battle; Oh the great march has sounded!'

Melmoth approached him with that frightful calmness that mocks the terror it excites. 'My prophecy has been fulfilled; – you rise to meet me rattling from your chains, and rustling from your straw – am I not a true prophet?' Stanton was silent. 'Is not your situation very miserable?' – Still Stanton was silent; for he was beginning to believe this an illusion of madness. He thought to himself, 'How could he have gained entrance here?' – 'Would you not wish to be delivered from it?' Stanton tossed on his straw, and its rustling seemed to answer the question. 'I have the power to deliver you from it.' Melmoth spoke very slowly and very softly, and the melodious smoothness of his voice made a frightful contrast to the stony rigour of his features, and the fiend-like brilliancy of his eyes. 'Who are you, and whence come you?' said Stanton, in a tone that was meant to be interrogatory and imperative, but which, from his habits of squalid debility, was at once feeble and querulous. His intellects had become affected by the gloom of his miserable habitation, as the wretched inmate of a similar mansion, when produced before a medical examiner, was reported to be a complete Albino. – 'His skin was bleached, his eyes turned white; he could not bear the light; and, when exposed to it, he turned away with a mixture of weakness and restlessness, more like the writhings of a sick infant than the struggles of a man.'

Such was Stanton's situation; he was enfeebled now, and the

power of the enemy seemed without a possibility of opposition from either his intellectual or corporeal powers.

*

Of all their horrible dialogue, only these words were legible in the manuscript, 'You know me now.' – 'I always knew you.' – 'that is false; you imagined you did, and that has been the cause of all the wild

*

of the

*

of your finally being lodged in this mansion of misery, where only I would seek, where only I can succour you.' 'You, demon!' – 'Demon! – Harsh words! – Was it a demon or a human being placed you here? – Listen to me, Stanton; nay, wrap not yourself in that miserable blanket, – that cannot shut out my words. Believe me, were you folded in thunderclouds, you must hear *me*! Stanton, think of your misery. These bare walls – what do they present to the intellect or the senses? – White-wash, diversified with the scrawls of charcoal or red chalk, that your happy predecessors have left for you to trace over. You have a taste for drawing, – I trust it will improve. And here's a grating, through which the sun squints on you like a step-dame, and the breeze blows, as if it meant to tantalize you with a sigh from that sweet mouth, whose kiss you must never enjoy. And where's your library, – intellectual man, – travelled man?' he repeated in a tone of bitter derision; 'where be your companions, your peaked men of countries, as your favourite Shakespeare has it? You must be content with the spider and the rat, to crawl and scratch round your flock-bed! I have known prisoners in the Bastille to feed them for companions, – why don't you begin your task? I have known a spider to descend at the tap of a finger, and a rat to come forth when the daily meal was brought, to share it with his fellow-prisoner! – How delightful to have vermin for your guests! Aye, and when the feast fails them, they make a meal of their entertainer! – You shudder – Are you, then, the first prisoner who has been devoured alive by the vermin that infested his cell? – Delightful banquet, not 'where you eat, but where you are eaten!' Your guests, however, will give you one token of repentance while they feed; there will be *gnashing of teeth*, and you shall hear it, and feel it too perchance! – And then for meals – Oh you are daintily off! – The soup that the cat has lapped; and (as her progeny has probably contributed to the hell-broth) why not? – Then your hours of solitude, deliciously diversified by the yell of famine, the howl of madness, the crash of whips, and the broken-hearted sob of those who, like you, are supposed, or *driven* mad by the crimes of others! – Stanton, do you imagine your reason can possibly hold out amid such scenes? – Supposing your reason was unimpaired, your health not destroyed, – suppose all this, which is, after all, more than fair supposition can grant, guess the effect of the continuance of these scenes on your senses alone. A time will come, and soon, when, from mere habit, you will echo the scream of every delirious wretch that harbours near you; then you will pause, clasp your hands on your throbbing head, and listen with horrible anxiety whether the scream proceeded from *you* or *them*. The time will come, when, from the want of occupation, the listless and horrible vacancy of your hours, you will feel as anxious to hear those shrieks, as you were at first terrified to hear them, – when you will watch for the ravings of your next neighbour, as you would for a scene on the stage. All humanity will be extinguished in you. The ravings of these wretches will become at once your sport and your torture. You will watch for the sounds, to mock them with the grimaces and bellowings of a fiend. The mind has a power of accommodating itself to its situation, that you will experience in its most frightful and deplorable efficacy. Then comes the dreadful doubt of one's own sanity, the terrible announcer that *that* doubt will soon become fear, and *that* fear certainty. Perhaps still more (dreadful) the *fear* will at last become a *hope*, – shut out from society, watched by a brutal keeper, writhing with all the impotent agony of an incarcerated mind without communication and without sympathy, unable to exchange ideas but with those whose ideas are only the hideous spectres of departed intellect, or even to hear the welcome sound of the human voice, except to mistake it for the howl of a fiend, and stop the ear desecrated by its intrusion, – then at last your fear will become a more fearful hope; you will wish to become one of them, to escape the agony of consciousness. As those who have long leaned over a precipice, have at last felt a desire to plunge below, to relieve the intolerable temptation of their giddiness,* you will hear them laugh amid their wildest paroxysms; you will say, "Doubtless those wretches have some consolation, but I have none; my sanity is my greatest curse in this abode of horrors. They greedily devour their miserable meals, while I loathe mine. They sleep sometimes soundly, while my sleep is – worse than their waking. They are revived every morning by some delicious illusion of cunning madness, soothing them with the hope of escaping, baffling, or tormenting their keeper; my sanity pre-cludes all such hope. *I know I never can escape*, and the preservation of my faculties is only an aggravation of my sufferings. I have all their miseries, – I have none of their consolations. They laugh, – I hear them; would I could laugh like them." You will try, and the very effort will be an invocation to the demon of insanity to come and take full possession of you from that moment for ever.'

(There were other details, both of the menaces and tempta-tions employed by Melmoth, which are too horrible for insertion. One of them may serve for an instance).

* A fact, related to me by a person who was near committing suicide in a similar situation, to escape what he called 'the excruciating torture of giddiness'.

'You think that the intellectual power is something distinct from the vitality of the soul, or, in other words, that if even your reason should be destroyed, (which it nearly is), your soul might yet enjoy beatitude in the full exercise of its enlarged and exalted faculties, and all the clouds which obscured them be dispelled by the Sun of Righteousness, in whose beams you hope to bask for ever and ever. Now, without going into any metaphysical subtleties about the distinction between mind and soul, experience must teach you, that there can be no crime into which madmen would not, and do not precipitate themselves; mischief is their occupation, malice their habit, murder their sport, and blasphemy their delight. Whether a soul in this state can be in a hopeful one, it is for you to judge; but it seems to me, that with the loss of reason, (and reason cannot long be retained in this place), you lose also the hope of immortality. – Listen,' said the tempter, pausing, 'listen to the wretch who is raving near you, and whose blasphemies might make a demon start. – He was once an eminent puritanical preacher. Half the day he imagines himself in a pulpit, denouncing damnation against Papists, Arminians, and even Sub-lapsarians, (he being a Supra-lapsarian himself). He foams, he writhes, he gnashes his teeth; you would imagine him in the hell he was painting, and that the fire and brimstone he is so lavish of, were actually exhaling from his jaws. At night his *creed retaliates on him*; he believes himself one of the reprobates he has been all day denouncing, and curses God for the very decree he has all day been glorifying Him for.

'He, whom he has for twelve hours been vociferating "is the loveliest among ten thousand," becomes the object of demoniac hostility and execration. He grapples with the iron posts of his bed, and says he is rooting out the cross from the very foundations of Calvary; and it is remarkable, that in proportion as his morning exercises are intense, vivid, and eloquent, his nightly blasphemies are outrageous and horrible. – Hark! Now he believes himself a demon; listen to his diabolical eloquence of horror!'

Stanton listened, and shuddered

*

'Escape – escape for your life,' cried the tempter; 'break forth into life, liberty, and sanity. Your social happiness, your intellectual powers, your immortal interests, perhaps, depend on the choice of this moment. – There is the door, and the key is in my hand. Choose – choose!' – 'And how comes the key in your hand? and what is the condition of my liberation?' said Stanton.

*

The explanation occupied several pages, which, to the torture of young Melmoth, were wholly illegible. It seemed, however, to have been rejected by Stanton with the utmost rage and horror, for Melmoth at last made out, – 'Begone, monster, demon! – begone to your native place. Even this mansion of horror trembles to contain you; its walls sweat, and its floors quiver, while you tread them.'

*

The conclusion of this extraordinary manuscript was in such a state, that, in fifteen mouldy and crumbling pages, Melmoth could hardly make out that number of lines. No antiquarian, unfolding with trembling hand the calcined leaves of an Hercula-neum manuscript, and hoping to discover some lost lines of the Æneis in Virgil's own autograph, or at least some unutterable abomination of Petronius or Martial, happily elucidatory of the mysteries of the Spintriæ, or the orgies of the Phallic wor-shippers, ever pored with more luckless diligence, or shook a head of more hopeless despondency over his task. He could but just make out what tended rather to excite than assuage that feverish thirst of curiosity which was consuming his inmost soul. The manuscript told no more of Melmoth, but mentioned that Stanton was finally liberated from his confinement, – that his pursuit of Melmoth was incessant and indefatigable, – that he himself allowed it to be a species of insanity, – that while he acknowledged it to be the master-passion, he also felt it the master-torment of his life. He again visited the Continent, returned to England, – pursued, inquired, traced, bribed, but in vain. The being whom he had met thrice, under circumstances so extraordinary, he was fated never to encounter again *in his lifetime*. At length, discovering that he had been born in Ireland, he resolved to go there, – went, and found his pursuit again fruitless, and his inquiries unanswered. The family knew nothing of him, or at least what they knew or imagined, they prudently refused to disclose to a stranger, and Stanton departed unsatisfied. It is remarkable, that he too, as appeared from many half-obliterated pages of the manuscript, never disclosed to mortal the particulars of their conversation in the mad-house; and the slightest allusion to it threw him into fits of rage and gloom equally singular and alarming. He left the manuscript, however, in the hands of the family, possibly deeming, from their incuriosity, their apparent indifference to their relative, or their obvious inacquaintance with reading of any kind, manuscript or books, his deposit would be safe. He seems, in fact, to have acted like men, who, in distress at sea, intrust their letters and dispatches to a bottle sealed, and commit it to the waves. The last lines of the manuscript that were legible, were sufficiently extraordinary.

*

'I have sought him every where. – The desire of meeting him once more, is become as a burning fire within me, – it is the necessary condition of my existence. I have vainly sought him at last in Ireland, of which I find he is a native. – Perhaps our final meeting will be in

*

Such was the conclusion of the manuscript which Melmoth

found in his uncle's closet. When he had finished it, he sunk down on the table near which he had been reading it, his face hid in his folded arms, his senses reeling, his mind in a mingled state of stupor and excitement. After a few moments, he raised himself with an involuntary start, and saw the picture gazing at him from its canvas. He was within ten inches of it as he sat, and the proximity appeared increased by the strong light that was accidentally thrown on it, and its being the only representation of a human figure in the room. Melmoth felt for a moment as if he were about to receive an explanation from its lips.

He gazed on it in return, – all was silent in the house, – they were alone together. The illusion subsided at length; and as the mind rapidly passes to opposite extremes, he remembered the injunction of his uncle to destroy the portrait. He seized it; – his hand shook at first, but the mouldering canvas appeared to assist him in the effort. He tore it from the frame with a cry half terrific, half triumphant; – it fell at his feet, and he shuddered as it fell. He expected to hear some fearful sounds, some unimaginable breathings of prophetic horror, follow this act of sacrilege, for such he felt it, to tear the portrait of his ancestor from his native walls. He paused and listened: – 'There was no voice, nor any that answered;' but as the wrinkled and torn canvas fell to the floor, its undulations gave the portrait the appearance of smiling. Melmoth felt horror indescribable at this transient and imaginary resuscitation of the figure. He caught it up, rushed into the next room, tore, cut and hacked it in every direction, and eagerly watched the fragments that burned like tinder in the turf-fire which had been lit in his room. As Melmoth saw the last blaze, he threw himself into bed, in hope of a deep and intense sleep. He had done what was required of him, and felt exhausted both in mind and body; but his slumber was not so sound as he had hoped for. The sullen light of the turf-fire, burning but never blazing, disturbed him every moment. He turned and turned, but still there was the same red light glaring on, but not illuminating, the dusky furniture of the apartment. The wind was high that night, and as the creaking door swung on its hinges, every noise seemed like the sound of a hand struggling with the lock, or of a foot pausing on the threshold. But (for Melmoth never could decide) was it in a dream or not, that he saw the figure of his ancestor appear at the door? – hesitatingly as he saw him at first on the night of his uncle's death, – saw him enter the room, approach his bed, and heard him whisper, 'You have burned me, then; but those are flames I can survive. – I am alive, – I am beside you.' Melmoth started, sprung from his bed, – it was broad day-light. He looked round, – there was no human being in the room but himself. He felt a slight pain in the wrist of his right arm. He looked at it, it was black and blue, as from the recent gripe of a strong hand.

Chapter Four

Haste with your weapons, cut the shrouds and stay,
And hew at once the mizen-mast away.

Falconer

The following evening Melmoth retired early. The restlessness of
the preceding night inclined him to repose, and the gloom of the
day left him nothing to wish for but its speedy conclusion. It was
now the latter end of Autumn; heavy clouds had all day been
passing laggingly and gloomily along the atmosphere, as the
hours of such a day pass over the human mind and life. Not a
drop of rain fell; the clouds went portentously off, like ships of
war after reconnoitering a strong fort, to return with added
strength and fury. The threat was soon fulfilled; the evening came
on, prematurely darkened by clouds that seemed surcharged
with a deluge. Loud and sudden squalls of wind shook the house
from time to time, and then as suddenly ceased. Towards night
the storm came on in all its strength; Melmoth's bed was shaken
so as to render it impossible to sleep. He 'liked the rocking of the
battlements', but by no means liked the expected fall of the chim-
neys, the crashing in of the roof, and the splinters of the broken
windows that were already scattered about his room. He rose
and went down to the kitchen, where he knew a fire was burning,
and there the terrified servants were all assembled, all agreeing,
as the blast came roaring down the chimney, they never had witnessed such a storm, and between the gusts, breathing shuddering
prayers for those who were 'out at sea that night'. The vicinity of

Melmoth's house to what seamen called an ironbound coast, gave a dreadful sincerity to their prayers and their fears.

In a short time, however, Melmoth perceived that their minds were occupied with terrors beside those of the storm. The recent death of his uncle, and the supposed visit of that extraordinary being in whose existence they all firmly believed, were connected in their minds inseparably with the causes or consequences of this tempest, and they whispered their fearful suggestions to each other, till the sound reached Melmoth's ears at every step that he measured across the broken floor of the kitchen. Terror is very fond of associations; we love to connect the agitation of the elements with the agitated life of man; and never did a blast roar, or a gleam of lightning flash, that was not concerned in the imagination of some one, with a calamity that was to be dreaded, deprecated, or endured, – with the fate of the living, or the destination of the dead. The tremendous storm that shook all England on the night of Cromwell's death, gave the hint to his puritanic chaplains to declare, that the Lord had caught him up in the whirlwind and chariot of fire, even thereafter, as he caught the prophet Elijah; while all the cavalier party, putting their own construction on the matter, proclaimed their confidence, that the Prince of the power of the air was vindicating his right, and carrying off the body of his victim (whose soul had long been his purchase) in a tempest, whose wild howl and triumphant ravage might have been variously, and with equal justice, interpreted by each party as giving testimony to their mutual denunciations. Just such a party (*mutatis mutandis*) were collected round the bickering fire and rocking chimney in Melmoth's kitchen. 'He is going in that blast,' said one of the hags, taking the pipe from her mouth, and trying vainly to rekindle it among the embers that the storm scattered about like dust; 'he is going in that blast.' – 'He'll come again,' cried another Sybil, 'he'll come again, – he's not at rest! – He roams and wails about till something is told that he never could tell in his life-time. – G-d save us!' she added, howling up the chimney, as if addressing the troubled spirit; 'tell us what you want, and *stop the blast*, will ye?' – The wind came like thunder down the chimney; the hag shuddered and retreated. 'If it's this you want – and this – and this,' cried a young female whom Melmoth had not noticed before, 'take them;' and she eagerly tore the papers out of her hair, and flung them into the fire. Then Melmoth recollected a ridiculous story told him the day before of this girl, who had had the 'bad luck', as she called it, to curl her hair with some of the old and useless law-papers of the family, and who now imagined that they 'who kept this dreadful pudder o'er her head', were particularly provoked by her still retaining about her whatever belonged to the deceased; and as she flung the fragments of paper into the fire, she cried aloud, 'There stop for the holy J—s' sake, and let us have no more about it! – You have what you wanted, and will you have done?' The laugh that Melmoth could hardly resist, was checked by a sound which he heard distinctly amid the storm. 'Hush – silence! that was a signal gun! – there is a vessel in distress.' They all paused and listened. We have already mentioned the closeness of Melmoth's abode to the sea-shore. This had well-accustomed its inmates to all the terrors of shipwrecked vessels and drowning passengers. To their honour be it spoken, they never heard those sounds but as a claim, a piteous, irresistible claim on their humanity. They knew nothing of the barbarous practice on the English coast, of fastening a lanthorn to the limbs of a spanselled horse, whose plungings were to misdirect the wrecked and sinking wretches, in the vain hope that the light they saw was a beacon, and thus to double the horrors of death by the baffled expectation of relief.

The party in the kitchen all watched Melmoth's countenance intently, as if its expression could have told them 'the secrets of the hoary deep'. The storm ceased for a moment, and there was a deep and dreary silence of fearful expectation. The sound was heard again, – it could not be mistaken. 'It is a gun,' cried

Melmoth; 'there is a vessel in distress!' and he hurried out of the kitchen, calling on the men to follow him.

The men partook eagerly of the excitement of enterprise and danger. A storm without doors is, after all, better than a storm within; without we have something to struggle with, within we have only to suffer; and the severest storm, by exciting the energy of its victim, gives at once a stimulus to action, and a solace to pride, which those must want who sit shuddering between rocking walls, and almost driven to wish they had only to suffer, not to fear.

While the men were in search of a hundred coats, boots, and hats of their old master, to be sought for in every part of the house, – while one was dragging a great coat from the window, before which it had long hung as a blind, in total default of glass or shutters, – another was snatching a wig from the jack, where it had been suspended for a duster, – and a third was battling with a cat and her brood of kittens for a pair of old boots which she had been pleased to make the seat of her accouchement, – Melmoth had gone up to the highest room in the house. The window was driven in; – had there been light, this window commanded a view of the sea and the coast. He leaned far out of it, and listened with fearful and breathless anxiety. The night was dark, but far off, his sight, sharpened by intense solicitude, descried a light at sea. The gust drove him from the window for a moment; at returning the next, he saw a faint flash, and then the report of a gun followed.

There needed no more; and in a few moments after, Melmoth was on the shore. Their way was short, and they walked with their utmost speed; but the violence of the storm made their progress very slow, and their anxiety made it seem still slower. From time to time they said to each other, in choaked and breathless accents, 'Call up the people in those cabins – there is a light in that house – they are all up – no wonder – who could sleep in such a night – hold the lanthorn low – it is impossible to keep footing on the strand.' 'Another gun!' they exclaimed, as the flash faintly broke through the darkness, and the heavy sound rolled round the shore, as if fired over the grave of the sufferers. 'Here's the rock, hold fast, and cling together.' They scaled it. 'Great God!' cried Melmoth, who was among the first, 'what a night! and what a spectacle! – Hold up your lanthorns – do you hear cries? – shout to them – tell them there is help and hope near them. – Stay,' he added, 'let me scramble up that crag – they will hear my voice from that.' He dashed desperately through the water, while the foam of the breakers from a distant rock almost choaked him, gained the point, and, elated by his success, shouted aloud with his utmost strength. But his voice, baffled and drowned by the tempest, was lost even to his own hearing. Its sound was faint and querulous, more like the wail of grief, than the encouraging cry of hope. At this moment, the racking clouds flying rapidly across the sky, like the scattered fugitives of a routed army, the moon burst forth with the sudden and appalling effulgence of lightning. Melmoth caught a full view of the vessel, and of her danger. She lay beating against a rock, over which the breakers dashed their foam to the height of thirty feet. She was half in the water, a mere hulk, her rigging torn to shreds, her main mast cut away, and every sea she shipped, Melmoth could hear distinctly the dying cries of those who were swept away, or perhaps of those whose mind and body, alike exhausted, relaxed their benumbed hold of hope and life together, – knew that the next shriek that was uttered must be their own and their last. There is something so very horrible in the sight of human beings perishing so near us, that we feel one firm step rightly planted, one arm steadily held out, might save at least one, – yet feel we know not where to fix that step, and cannot stretch that arm, that Melmoth's senses reeled under the shock, and for a moment he echoed the storm with yells of actual insanity. By this time the country, having been alarmed by the news of a vessel going to pieces on the shore, had poured down in multitudes; and those who, from experience or confidence, or even ignorance, repeated incessantly, 'it is impossible to save her, – every soul on board must perish,' involuntarily quickened their steps as they uttered the words, as if they were anxious to behold the fulfilment of their own prediction, while they appeared hurrying to avert it.

Of one man, in particular, it was observed, that during their hurried rush to the shore, he was, with what breath his haste allowed him, assuring the rest every moment, 'she would be down before they could get there,' and heard the ejaculations of 'Christ save us! don't say that,' 'No, please God, we'll do some good,' with a laugh almost of triumph. When they arrived, this man scaled a rock at the risk of his life, caught a view of the vessel, pointed out her desperate situation to those below, and shouted, 'Didn't I tell you so? wasn't I right?' And as the storm increased, his voice was still heard, 'wasn't I right?' And when the cries of the perishing crew were distinctly wafted to their ears, he was still heard in the interval repeating, 'But wasn't I right?' Singular sentiment of pride, that can erect its trophies amid the grave. 'Tis in this spirit we give advice to those who suffer from life, as well as from the elements; and when the heart of the victim breaks, console ourselves by exclaiming, '*Didn't I foretell it all?* did I not tell you how it would be?' It is remarkable that this man lost his life that very night in the most desperate and fruitless attempt to save the life of one of the crew who was swimming within six yards of him. The whole shore was now crowded with helpless gazers, every crag and cliff was manned; it seemed like a battle fought at once by sea and land, between hope and despair. No effectual assistance could be rendered, – not a boat could live in that gale, – yet still, and to the last, cheers were heard from rock to rock, – terrible cheers, that announced safety was near and – impossible; – lanthorns held aloft in all directions, that displayed to the sufferers the shore all peopled with life, and the roaring and impassable waves between; – ropes flung out, with loud cries of help and encouragement, and caught at by some chilled, nerveless, and despairing hand, that only grasped the wave, – relaxed its hold, – was tossed once over the sinking head, –

and then seen no more. It was at this moment that Melmoth, starting from his trance of terror, and looking round him, saw all, to the number of hundreds, anxious, restless, and occupied; and, though obviously in vain, the sight cheered his heart. 'How much good there is in man,' he cried, 'when it is called forth by the sufferings of his fellows!' He had no leisure or inclination, then, to analyse the compound he called good, and resolve it into its component parts of curiosity, strong excitement, the pride of physical strength, or the comparative consciousness of safety. He had, indeed, no leisure, for just then he descried, standing a few yards above him on the rock, a figure that shewed neither sympathy or terror, – uttered no sound, – offered no help. Melmoth could hardly keep his footing on the slippery and rocking crag on which he stood; the figure, who stood still higher, appeared alike unmoved by the storm, as by the spectacle. Melmoth's surtout, in spite of his efforts to wrap it round him, was fluttering in rags, – not a thread of the stranger's garments seemed ruffled by the blast. But this did not strike him so much as his obvious insensibility to the distress and terror around him, and he exclaimed aloud, 'Good God! is it possible that any thing bearing the human form should stand there without making an effort, without expressing a feeling, for those perishing wretches!' A pause ensued, or the blast carried away the sound; but a few moments after, Melmoth distinctly heard the words, 'Let them perish.' He looked up, the figure still stood unmoved, the arms folded across the breast, the foot advanced, and fixed as in defiance of the white and climbing spray of the wave, and the stern profile caught in the glimpses of the stormy and doubtful moon-light, seeming to watch the scene with an expression formidable, revolting, and unnatural. At this moment, a tremendous wave breaking over the deck of the hulk, extorted a cry of horror from the spectators; they felt as if they were echoing that of the victims whose corses were in a few moments to be dashed against their feet, mangled and lifeless.

When the cry had ceased, Melmoth heard a laugh that chilled

his blood. It was from the figure that stood above him. Like lightning then glanced on his memory the recollection of that night in Spain, when Stanton first encountered that extraordinary being, whose charmed life, 'defying space and time', held such fatal influence over his, and when he first recognized his supposed demoniac character by the laugh with which he hailed the spectacle of the blasted lovers. The echo of that laugh rung in Melmoth's ears; he believed it was indeed that mysterious being who was standing so near him. His mind, by its late intense and bewildering pursuits, at once heated and darkened, like the atmosphere under an incumbent thunder-cloud, had now no power of inquiry, of conjecture, or of calculation. He instantly began to climb the rock, – the figure was but a few feet above him, – the object of his daily and nightly dreams was at last within the reach of his mind and his arm, – was almost tangible. *Fang and Snare** themselves, in all the enthusiasm of professional zeal, never uttered, 'if I but once get him within my vice', with more eagerness than did Melmoth, as he scrambled up his steep and perilous path, to the ledge of the rock where the figure stood so calm and dark. Panting from the fury of the storm, the vehemence of his own exertions, and the difficulty of the task, he was now almost foot to foot, and face to face, with the object of his pursuit, when, grasping at the loosened fragment of a stone whose fall could not have hurt a child, though on its tottering insecurity hung the life-grasp of a man, his hold failed – he fell backwards, – the roaring deep was beneath, seeming to toss its ten thousand arms to receive and devour him. He did not feel the instantaneous giddiness of his fall, but as he sunk he felt the splash, he heard the roar. He was engulphed, then for a moment thrown to the surface. He struggled with nothing to grasp at. He sunk with a vague thought, that if he could reach the bottom, if he could arrive at any thing solid, he was safe. Ten thousand

* See Henry IV. Second Part.

trumpets then seemed to ring in his ears; lights flashed from his eyes. 'He seemed to go through fire and water,' and remembered no more till several days afterwards, when he found himself in bed, the old gouvernante beside him, and uttered faintly, 'What a horrid dream!' then sinking back as he felt his exhaustion, 'and how weak it has left me!'

Chapter Five

'I have heard,' said the Squire, 'that from hell there is no *retention*.'

Cervantes

For some hours after this exclamation, Melmoth lay silent, his memory returning, – his senses gradually defecated, – the intellectual lord slowly returning to his abdicated throne. –

'I remember all now,' he cried, starting up in his bed with a sudden vehemence, that terrified his old nurse with the apprehension of returning insanity; but when she approached the bed, candle in hand, cautiously veiling her eyes with the other, while she threw the full glare of the light on the face of the patient, she saw in a moment the light of sanity in his eyes, and the strength of health in his movements. To his eager inquiries of how he had been saved, how the storm had terminated, and whether any but himself had survived the wreck, she could not deny herself the gratification of answering, though conscious of his weakness, and solemnly charged neither to let him speak or hear, as she valued the recovery of his reason. She had faithfully observed the charge for several days, – a dreadful trial! – and now she felt like Fatima in Cymon, who, when threatened by the magician with the loss of speech, exclaims, 'Barbarian, will not my death then satisfy you?'

She began her narrative, the effect of which was, to lull Melmoth into a profound repose before half of it was concluded; he felt the full benefit of the invalids mentioned in Spenser, who used to hire Irish story-tellers, and found those indefatigable persons still pursuing the tale when they awoke. At first Melmoth listened with eager attention; soon he was in the situation of him described by Miss Baillie,

> 'Who, half asleep, but faintly hears,
> The gossip's tale hum in his ears.'

Soon after his lengthened respiration gave token that she was only 'vexing the dull ear of a drowsy man'; while, as she closed the curtain, and shaded the light, the images of her story were faintly painted on his dream, that still seemed half a waking one.

In the morning Melmoth sat up, gazed round, remembered every thing in a moment, though nothing distinctly, but felt the most intense anxiety to see the stranger saved from the shipwreck, who, he remembered the gouvernante had told him, (while her words seemed to falter on the threshold of his closing senses), was still alive, and an inmate in his house, but weak and ill from the bruises he had received, and the exhaustion and terror he had undergone. The opinions of the household on the subject of this stranger were various. The knowledge of his being a Catholic had conciliated their hearts, for the first act of his recovered reason was to request that a Catholic priest might be sent for, and the first use of his speech was to express his satisfaction that he was in a country where he might enjoy the benefits of the rites of his own church. So far all was well; but there was a mysterious haughtiness and reserve about him, that somewhat repelled the officious curiosity of his attendants. He spoke often to himself in a language they did not understand; they hoped relief from the priest on this point, but the priest, after listening long at the invalid's door, pronounced the language in which he was soliloquizing *not to be Latin*, and, after a conversation of some hours with him, refused to tell what language the stranger spoke to himself in, and forbid all inquiry on the subject. This was bad enough; but, still worse, the stranger spoke English with ease and fluency, and therefore could have no right, as all the household argued, to torment them with those unknown sounds, that, sonorous and powerful as they were, seemed to their ears like an evocation of some invisible being.

'He asks for what he wants in English,' said the harassed housekeeper, 'and he can call for candle in English, and he can say he'll go to bed in English; and why the devil can't he do every thing in English? – He can say his prayers too in English to that picture he's always pulling out of his breast and talking to, though it's no saint, I am sure, he prays to, (from the glimpse I got of it), but more like the devil, – Christ save us!' All these strange rumours, and ten thousand more, were poured into Melmoth's ears, fast and faster than he could receive them. 'Is Father Fay in the house,' said he at last, understanding that the priest visited the stranger every day; 'if he be, let me see him.' Father Fay attended him as soon as he quitted the stranger's apartment.

He was a grave and decent priest, well 'spoken of by those that were without' the pale of his own communion; and as he entered the room, Melmoth smiled at the idle tattle of his domestics. 'I thank you for your attention to this unfortunate gentleman, who, I understand, is in my house.' – 'It was my duty.' – 'I am told he sometimes speaks in a foreign tongue.' The priest assented. 'Do you know what countryman he is?' 'He is a Spaniard,' said the priest. This plain, direct answer, had the proper effect on Melmoth, of convincing him of its veracity, and of there being no mystery in the business, but what the folly of his servants had made.

The priest proceeded to tell him the particulars of the loss of the vessel. She was an English trader bound for Wexford or Waterford, with many passengers on board; she had been driven up the Wicklow coast by stress of weather, had struck on the night of the 19th October, during the intense darkness that accompanied the storm, on a hidden reef of rocks, and gone to pieces. Crew, passengers, all had perished, except this Spaniard. It was singular, too, that this man had saved the life of Melmoth.

While swimming for his own, he had seen him fall from the rock he was climbing, and, though his strength was almost exhausted, had collected its last remains to preserve the life of a being who, as he conceived, had been betrayed into danger by his humanity. His efforts were successful, though Melmoth was unconscious of them; and in the morning they were found on the strand, locked in each other's hold, but stiff and senseless. They shewed some signs of life when an attempt was made to remove them, and the stranger was conveyed to Melmoth's house. 'You owe your life to him,' said the priest, when he had ended. 'I shall go and thank him for it this moment,' said Melmoth; but as he was assisted to rise, the old woman whispered to him with visible terror, 'Jasus' sake, dear, don't tell him ye're a Melmoth, for the dear life! he has been as mad as any thing out of Bedlam, since some jist mintioned the name before him the ither night.' A sickening recollection of some parts of the manuscript came over Melmoth at these words, but he struggled with himself, and proceeded to the apartment of the stranger.

The Spaniard was a man about thirty, of a noble form and pre-possessing manners. To the gravity of his nation was super-added a deeper tint of peculiar melancholy. He spoke English fluently; and when questioned on it by Melmoth, he remarked with a sigh, that he had learnt it in a painful school. Melmoth then changed the subject, to thank him with earnest gratitude for the preservation of his life. 'Senhor,' said the Spaniard, 'spare me; if your life was no dearer to you than mine, it would not be worth thanks.' 'Yet you made the most strenuous exertions to save it,' said Melmoth. 'That was instinct,' said the Spaniard. 'But you also struggled to save mine,' said Melmoth. 'That was instinct too at the moment,' said the Spaniard; then resuming his stately polite-ness, 'or I should say, the influence of my better genius. I am wholly a stranger in this country, and must have fared miserably but for the shelter of your roof.'

Melmoth observed that he spoke with evident pain, and he

confessed a few moments afterwards, that though he had escaped without any serious injury, he had been so bruised and lacerated, that he still breathed with difficulty, and hardly possessed the use of his limbs. As he concluded the account of his sufferings during the storm, the wreck, and the subsequent struggle for life, he exclaimed in Spanish, 'God! why did the Jonah survive, and the mariners perish?' Melmoth, imagining he was engaged in some devotional ejaculation, was going to retire, when the Spaniard detained him. 'Senhor, I understand your name is –' He paused, shuddered, and with an effort that seemed like convulsion, disgorged the name of Melmoth. 'My name is Melmoth.' 'Had you an ancestor, a very remote one, who was – at a period perhaps beyond family-tradition – It is useless to inquire,' said the Spaniard, covering his face with both his hands, and groaning aloud. Melmoth listened in mingled excitement and terror. 'Perhaps, if you would proceed, I could answer you – go on, Senhor.' 'Had you,' said the Spaniard, forcing himself to speak, abruptly and rapidly, 'had you, then, a relative who was, about one hundred and forty years ago, said to be in Spain.' 'I believe – yes, I fear – I had.' 'It is enough, Senhor – leave me – to-morrow perhaps – leave me now.' 'It is impossible to leave you now,' said Melmoth, catching him in his arms before he sunk on the floor. He was not senseless, for his eyes were rolling with terrible expression, and he attempted to articulate. They were alone. Melmoth, unable to quit him, called aloud for water; and while attempting to open his vest, and give him air, his hand encountered a miniature portrait close to the heart of the stranger. As he touched it, his touch operated on the patient with all the force of the most powerful restorative. He grasped it with his own cold hand with a force like that of death, and muttered in a hollow but thrilling voice, 'What have you done?' He felt eagerly the ribbon by which it was suspended, and, satisfied that his terrible treasure was safe, turned his eyes with a fearful calmness of expression on Melmoth, 'You know all, then?' – 'I know nothing,' said Melmoth faultering. The

Spaniard rose from the ground, to which he had almost fallen, disengaged himself from the arms that supported him, and eagerly, but staggeringly, hurrying towards the candles, (it was night), held up the portrait full before Melmoth's eye. It was a miniature likeness of that extraordinary being. It was painted in a coarse and unartist-like style, but so faithfully, that the pencil appeared rather held by the mind than by the fingers.

'Was he – was the original of this – your ancestor? – Are you his descendant? – Are you the depository of that terrible secret which –' He again fell to the ground convulsed, and Melmoth, for whose debilitated state this scene was too much, was removed to his own apartment.

It was several days before he again saw his visitor; his manner was then calm and collected, till he appeared to recollect the necessity of making an apology for his agitation at their last meeting. He began – hesitated – stopped; tried in vain to arrange his ideas, or rather his language; but the effort so obviously renewed his agitation, that Melmoth felt an exertion on his part necessary to avert its consequences, and began most inauspiciously to inquire into the motive of his voyage to Ireland. After a long pause, the Spaniard said, 'That motive, Senhor, a few days past I believed it was not in mortal power to compel me to disclose. I deemed it incommunicable as it was incredible. I conceived myself to be alone on the earth, without sympathy and beyond relief. It is singular that accident should have placed me within the reach of the only being from whom I could expect either, and perhaps a development of those circumstances which have placed me in a situation so extraordinary.' This exordium, delivered with a composed but thrilling gravity, had an effect on Melmoth. He sat down and prepared to listen, and the Spaniard began to speak; but after some hesitation, he snatched the picture from his neck, and trampling on it with true continental action, exclaimed, 'Devil! devil! thou choakest me!' and crushing the portrait, glass and all, under his feet, exclaimed, 'Now I am easier.'

The room in which they sat was a low, mean, wretchedly furnished apartment; the evening was tempestuous, and as the windows and doors rattled in the blast, Melmoth felt as if he listened to some herald of 'fate and fear.' A deep and sickening agitation shook his frame; and in the long pause that preceded the narrative of the Spaniard, the beating of his heart was audible to him. He rose, and attempted to arrest the narration by a motion of his hand; but the Spaniard mistook this for the anxiety of his impatience, and commenced his narrative, which, in mercy to the reader, we shall give without the endless interruptions, and queries, and anticipations of curiosity, and starts of terror, with which it was broken by Melmoth.

Tale of the Spaniard

'I am, Senhor, as you know, a native of Spain, but you are yet to learn I am a descendant of one of its noblest houses, – a house of which she might have been proud in her proudest day, – the house of Monçada. Of this I was not myself conscious during the first years of my life; but during those years, I remember experiencing the singular contrast of being treated with the utmost tenderness, and kept in the most sordid privacy. I lived in a wretched house in the suburbs of Madrid with an old woman, whose affection for me appeared prompted as much by interest as inclination. I was visited every week by a young cavalier and a beautiful female; they caressed me, called me their beloved child, and I, attached by the grace with which my young father's *capa* was folded, and my mother's veil adjusted, and by a certain air of indescribable superiority over those by whom I was surrounded, eagerly returned their caresses, and petitioned them to take me *home* with them; at these words they always wept, gave a valuable present to the woman I lived with, whose attention was always redoubled by this expected stimulant, and departed.

'I observed their visits were always short, and paid late in the evening; thus a shadow of mystery enveloped my infant days, and perhaps gave its lasting and ineffaceable tinge to the pursuits, the character, and the feelings of my present existence. A sudden change took place; – one day I was visited, splendidly dressed, and carried in a superb vehicle, whose motion made me giddy with novelty and surprise, to a palace whose front appeared to me to reach the heavens. I was hurried through several apartments, whose splendour made my eyes ache, amid an army of bowing domestics, to a cabinet where sat an old nobleman, whom, from the tranquil majesty of his posture, and the silent magnificence that surrounded him, I felt disposed to fall down and worship as we do those saints, whom, after traversing the aisles of an immense church, we find niched in some remote and solitary shrine. My father and mother were there, and both seemed awed by the presence of that aged vision, pale and august; their awe increased mine, and as they led me to his feet, I felt as if about to be sacrificed. He embraced me, however, with some reluctance and more austerity; and when this ceremony was performed, during which I trembled, I was removed by a domestic, and conducted to an apartment where I was treated like the son of a grandee; in the evening I was visited by my father and mother; they shed tears over me as they embraced me, but I thought I could perceive they mingled the tears of grief with those of fondness. Every thing around appeared so strange, that perhaps I felt something appropriate in this change. I was so much altered myself, that I expected an alteration in others, and the reverse would have struck me as a phenomenon.

'Change followed change with such rapidity, that it produced on me an effect like that of intoxication. I was now twelve years old, and the contracted habits of my early life had had their usual effect, of exalting my imagination, while they impaired every other faculty. I expected an adventure whenever the door opened, and that was but seldom, to announce the hours of devotion, food, and exercise. On the third day after I was received into the palace of Monçada, the door was opened at an unusual hour, (a circumstance that made me tremble with anticipation), and my father and mother, attended by a number of domestics, entered, accompanied by a youth whose superior height and already distinguished figure, made him appear my senior, though he was in fact a year younger.

'"Alonzo,"' said my father to me, "embrace your brother." I advanced with all the eagerness of youthful affection, that feels delight from new claims on its store, and half wishes those new claims were endless; but the slow step of my brother, the measured air with which he extended his arms, and declined his head on my left shoulder for a moment, and then raising it, viewed me with eyes in whose piercing and haughty lustre there was not one beam of fraternity, repelled and disconcerted me. We had obeyed our father, however, and embraced. "Let me see you hand in hand together," said my father, as if he would have enjoyed the sight. I held out my hand to my brother, and we stood thus linked for a few moments, my father and mother remaining at some distance to gaze on us; during these *few* moments, I had leisure to glance from my parents to my brother, and judge of the comparative effect our appearance thus contrasted might produce on them. The contrast was by no means favourable to me. I was tall, but my brother was much taller; he had an air of confidence, of conquest I might say; the brilliancy of his complexion could be equalled only by that of his dark eyes, which turned from me to our parents, and seemed to say, "Chuse between us, and reject me if you dare."

'My father and mother advanced and embraced us both. I clung round their necks; my brother submitted to their caresses with a kind of proud impatience, that seemed to demand a more marked recognition.

'I saw no more of them, – that evening the whole household, which perhaps contained two hundred domestics, were in despair.

The Duke de Monçada, that awful vision of anticipated mortality whom I had seen but once, was dead. The tapestry was torn from the walls; every room was filled with ecclesiastics; I was neglected by my attendants, and wandered through the spacious rooms, till I by chance lifted up a curtain of black velvet, and saw a sight which, young as I was, paralyzed me. My father and mother, dressed in black, sat beside a figure which I believed to be my grandfather asleep, but his sleep was very profound; my brother was there too, in a mourning dress, but its strange and grotesque disfigurement could not conceal the impatience with which he wore it, and the flashing eagerness of his expression, and the haughty brilliancy of his eye, shewed a kind of impatience of the part he was compelled to act. – I rushed forward; – I was withheld by the domestics; – I asked, "Why am I not permitted to be here, where my younger brother is?" An ecclesiastic drew me from the apartment. I struggled with him, and demanded, with an arrogance which suited my pretensions better than my prospects, "Who I was?" "The grandson of the late Duke of Monçada," was the answer. "And why am I thus treated?" To this no answer. I was conveyed to my apartment, and closely watched during the interment of the Duke of Monçada. I was not permitted to attend his funeral. I saw the splendid and melancholy cavalcade depart from the palace. I ran from window to window to witness the funeral pomp, but was not allowed to accompany it. Two days after I was told a carriage waited for me at the gate. I entered it, and was conveyed to a convent of ex-Jesuits, (as they were well known to be, though no one in Madrid dared to say so), where an agreement had been made for my board and education, and where I became an inmate that very day. I applied myself to my studies, my teachers were pleased, my parents visited me frequently, and gave the usual marks of affection, and all was well; till one day as they were retiring, I heard an old domestic in their suite remark, how singular it was, that the eldest son of the (now) Duke de Monçada should be educated in a convent, and brought up to a monastic life, while the younger, living in a superb palace, was surrounded by teachers suited to his rank. The word 'monastic life' thrilled in my ears; it furnished me with an interpretation not only of the indulgence I had experienced in the convent, (an indulgence quite inconsistent with the usual severity of their discipline), but of the peculiar language in which I had been always addressed by the Superior, the brethren, and the boarders. The former, whom I saw once a week, bestowed the most flattering praises on the progress I had made in my studies, (praises that covered me with blushes, for I well knew it was very moderate compared with that of the other boarders), and then gave me his benediction, but never without adding, "My God! thou wilt not suffer this lamb to wander from thy fold."

'The brethren always assumed before me an air of tranquillity, that eulogized their situation more powerfully than the most exaggerated eloquence. The petty squabbles and intrigues of the convent, the bitter and incessant conflicts of habits, tempers, and interests, the efforts of incarcerated minds for objects of excitement, the struggles to diversify endless monotony, and elevate hopeless mediocrity; – all that makes monastic life like the wrong side of tapestry, where we see only uncouth threads, and the harsh outlines, without the glow of the colours, the richness of the tissue, or the splendour of the embroidery, that renders the external surface so rich and dazzling; all this was carefully concealed. I heard something of it, however, and, young as I was, could not help wondering how men who carried the worst passions of life into their retreat, could imagine *that* retreat was a refuge from the erosions of their evil tempers, the monitions of conscience, and the accusations of God. The same dissimulation was practised by the boarders; the whole house was in masquerade from the moment I entered it. If I joined the latter at the time of recreation, they went through the few amusements allowed them with a kind of languid impatience, as if it was an interruption of better pursuits to which they were devoted. One of them, coming up to me, would say, "What a pity that these exercises are necessary for the support of our frail nature! what a pity we cannot devote its whole powers to the service of God!" Another would say, "I never am so happy as in the choir! What a delightful eulogy was that pronounced by the Superior on the departed Fre Jose! How thrilling was that requiem! I imagined the heavens opened, and angels descending to receive his soul, as I listened to it!"

'All this, and much more, I had been accustomed to hear every day. I now began to understand it. I suppose they thought they had a very weak person to deal with; but the bare-faced coarseness of their manœuvres only quickened my penetration, which began to be fearfully awake. I said to them, "Are you, then, intended for the monastic life?" "We hope so." "Yet I have heard you, Oliva, *once* (it was when you did not think I overheard you) I heard you complain of the length and tediousness of the homilies delivered on the eves of the saints." – "I was then under the influence of the evil spirit doubtless," said Oliva, who was a boy not older than myself; "Satan is sometimes permitted to buffet those whose vocation is but commencing, and whom he is therefore more afraid to lose." "And I have heard you, Balcastro, say you had not taste for music; and to me, I confess, that of the choir appears least likely to inspire a taste for it." "God has touched my heart since," replied the young hypocrite, crossing himself; "and you know, friend of my soul, there is a promise, that the ears of the deaf shall be opened." "Where are those words?" "In the Bible." "The Bible? – But we are not permitted to read it." "True, dear Monçada, but we have the word of our Superior and the brethren for it, and that is enough." "Certainly; our spiritual guides must take on themselves the whole responsibility of that state, whose enjoyments and punishments they reserve in their own hands; but, Balcastro, are you willing to take this life on their word, as well as the next, and resign it before you have tried it?" "My dear friend, you only speak to tempt me." "*I do not speak to tempt*," said I, and was turning indignantly away, when the bell ringing, produced its usual effect on us all. My companions assumed a more sanctified air, and I struggled for a more composed one.

'As we went to the church, they conversed in whispers, but those whispers were intended to reach my ear. I could hear them say, "It is in vain that he struggles with grace; there never was a more decided vocation; God never obtained a more glorious victory. Already he has the look of a child of heaven; – the monastic gait, – the downcast look; – the motion of his arms naturally imitates the sign of the cross, and the very folds of his mantle arrange themselves, by a divine instinct, into those of a Monk's habit." And all this while my gait was disturbed, my countenance flushed, and often lifted to heaven, and my arms employed in hastily adjusting my cloak, that had fallen off my shoulder from my agitation, and whose disordered folds resembled any thing but those of a Monk's habit. From that evening I began to perceive my danger, and to meditate how to avert it. I had no inclination for the monastic life; but after vespers, and the evening exercise in my own cell, I began to doubt if this very repugnance was not itself a sin. Silence and night deepened the impression, and I lay awake for many hours, supplicating God to enlighten me, to enable me not to oppose his will, but clearly to reveal that will to me; and if he was not pleased to call me to a monastic life, to support my resolution in undergoing every thing that might be inflicted on me, sooner than profane that state by extorted vows and an alienated mind. That my prayers might be more effectual, I offered them up first in the name of the Virgin, then in that of the Patron-saint of the family, and then of the Saint on whose eve I was born. I lay in great agitation till morning, and went to matins without having closed my eyes. I had, however, I felt, acquired *resolution*, – at least I thought so. Alas! I knew not what I had to encounter. I was like a man going to sea with a day's provision, and imagining he is victualled for a voyage to the poles. I went through my exercises (as they were called) with uncommon assiduity that day; already I felt the necessity of imposition, – fatal lesson of monastic institutions. We dined at noon; and soon after my father's carriage arrived, and I was permitted to go for an hour on the banks of the Manzanares. To my surprise my father was in the carriage, and though he welcomed me with a kind of embarrassment, I was delighted to meet him. He was a layman at least, – *he might have a heart*.

'I was disappointed at the measured phrase he addressed me in, and this froze me at once into a rigid determination, to be as much *on my guard with him*, as I must be within the walls of the convent. The conversation began, "You like your convent, my son?" "Very much," (there was not a word of truth in my answer, but the fear of circumvention always teaches falsehood, and we have only to thank our instructors). "The Superior is very fond of you." "He seems so." "The brethren are attentive to your studies, and capable of directing them, and appreciating your progress." "They seem so." "And the boarders – they are sons of the first families in Spain, they appear all satisfied with their situation, and eager to embrace its advantages." "They seem so." "My dear son, why have you thrice answered me in the same monotonous, unmeaning phrase?" "Because I thought it all *seeming*." "How, then, would you say that the devotion of those holy men, and the profound attention of their pupils, whose studies are alike beneficial to man, and redounding to the glory of the church to which they are dedicated –" "My dearest father, – I say nothing of them, – but I *dare* to speak of myself, – I can never be a monk, – if that is your object – spurn me, – order your lacqueys to drag me from this carriage, – leave me a beggar in the streets to cry *'fire and water'*,* – but do not make me a monk." My father appeared stunned by this apostrophe. He did not utter a word. He had not expected such a premature development of the secret which he imagined *he* had to disclose, not to hear disclosed. At this moment

* 'Fire for the cigars, and iced-water for drink,' – A cry often heard in Madrid.

the carriage turned into the *Prado*; a thousand magnificent equipages, with plumed horses, superb caparisons, and beautiful
women bowing to the cavaliers, who stood for a moment on the
foot-board, and then bowed their adieus to the 'ladies of their
love', passed before our eyes. I saw my father, at this moment,
arrange his superb mantle, and the silk net in which his long black
hair was bound, and give the signal to his lacqueys to stop, that he
might mingle among the crowd. I caught this moment, – I grasped
his mantle. – "Father, you find this world delightful then, – would
you ask me to resign it, – me, – who am your child." – "But you
are too young for it, my son." "Oh, then, my father, I am surely
much *too young for another world*, to which you would force me."
"Force you, my child, my first-born!" And these words he uttered
with such tenderness, that I involuntarily kissed his hands, while
his lips eagerly pressed my forehead. It was at this moment that I
studied, with all the eagerness of hope, my father's physiognomy,
or what artists would call his *physique*.

'He had been my parent before he was sixteen; his features
were beautiful, his figure the most graceful and lover-like I ever
beheld, and his early marriage had preserved him from all the
evils of youthful excess, and spared the glow of feature, and elasticity of muscle, and grace of juvenility, so often withered by
vice, almost before they have bloomed. He was now but twenty-
eight, and looked ten years younger. He was evidently conscious
of this, and as much alive to the enjoyments of youth, as if he
were still in its spring. He was at the same moment rushing into
all the luxuries of youthful enjoyment and voluptuous splendour, and dooming one, who was at least young enough to be his
son, to the frozen and hopeless monotony of a cloister. I laid hold
of this with the grasp of a drowning man. But a drowning man
never grasped a straw so weak as he who depends on the worldly
feeling of another for the support of his own.

'Pleasure is very selfish; and when selfishness pleads to selfishness for relief, it is like a bankrupt asking his fellow-prisoner to go

bail for him. This was my conviction at the moment, yet still I reflected, (for suffering supplies the place of experience in youth, and they are most expert casuists who have graduated only in the school of misfortune), I reflected, that a taste for pleasure, while it renders a man selfish in one sense, renders him generous in another. The real voluptuary, though he would not part with his slightest indulgence to save the world from destruction, would yet wish all the world to be enjoying itself, (provided it was not at his expence), because his own would be increased by it. To this I clung, and intreated my father to indulge me with another view of the brilliant scene before us. He complied, and his feelings, softened by this compliance, and exhilarated by the spectacle, (which interested *him* more than me, who observed it only for its effect on him), became more favourable than ever. I availed myself of this, and, while returning to the convent, threw the whole power of my nature and intellect into one (almost) shrieking appeal to his heart. I compared myself to the unhappy Esau, deprived of his birthright by a younger brother, and I exclaimed in his language, "Hast thou no blessing for me! Bless me, even me also, Oh my Father!" My father was affected; he promised my intreaty every consideration; but he hinted some difficulty to be encountered on my mother's part, much on that of her Director, who (I afterwards found) governed the whole family, and still more remotely hinted at something insurmountable and inexplicable. He suffered me, however, to kiss his hands at parting, and vainly struggled with his emotions when he felt it damp with my tears.

'It was not till two days after, that I was summoned to attend my mother's Director, who was waiting for me in the parlour. I deemed this delay the result of a long family debate, or (as it seemed to me) conspiracy; and I tried to prepare myself for the multifarious warfare in which I had now to engage with parents, directors, superiors, and monks, and boarders, all sworn to win the day, and not caring whether they carried their point by storm, sap, mine, or blockade. I began to measure the power of the assailants, and to try to furnish myself with weapons suited to their various modes of attack. My father was gentle, flexible, and vacillating. I had *softened* him in my favour, and I felt that was all that could be done with him. But the Director was to be encountered with different arms. As I went down to the parlour, I composed my looks, my gait, I modulated my voice, I adjusted my dress. I was on my guard, body, mind, mien, clothes, every thing. He was a grave, but mild-looking ecclesiastic; one must have had the treachery of Judas to suspect him of treachery. I felt disarmed, I even experienced some compunction. "Perhaps," said I, "I have all this while armed myself against a message of reconciliation." The Director began with some trifling inquiries about my health, and my progress in study, but he asked them in a tone of interest. I said to myself, it would not be decorous for him to enter on the subject of his visit too soon; – I answered him calmly, but my heart palpitated with violence. A silence ensued, and then suddenly turning towards me, he said, "My dear child, I understand your objections to a monastic life are insurmountable. I do not wonder at it; its habits must appear very unconciliating to youth, and, in fact, I know not to what period of life abstinence, privation, and solitude, are particularly agreeable; it was the wish of your parents doubtless; but" – This address, so full of candour, almost overpowered me; caution and every thing else forsook me as I exclaimed, "But what then, my father?" "But, I was going to observe, how rarely our own views coincide with those which others entertain for us, and how difficult it is to decide which are the least erroneous." "Was that all?" said I, shrinking with disappointment. "That was all; for instance, some people, (of whom I once happened to be one), might be fanciful enough to imagine, that the superior experience and proved affection of parents should qualify them to decide on this point better than their children; nay, I have heard some carry their absurdity so far, as to talk of the rights of nature, the obligations of duty, and the useful coercion of restraint; but since I had the pleasure of becoming acquainted with your resolution, I am beginning to be of opinion, that a youth, not thirteen years of age, may be an incomparable judge in the last resort, particularly when the question bears a trifling relation to his eternal as well as temporal interest; in such a case, he has doubtless the double advantage of dictating both to his spiritual and natural parents." "My father, I beg you to speak without irony or ridicule; you may be very clever, but I merely wish you to be intelligible and serious." "Do you wish me, then, to speak seriously?" and he appeared to *collect* himself as he asked this question. "Certainly." "Seriously, then, my dear child, do you not believe that your parents love you? Have you not received from your infancy every mark of affection from them? Have you not been pressed to their bosoms from your very cradle?" At these words I struggled vainly with my feelings, and wept, while I answered, "Yes." "I am sorry, my dear child, to see you thus overpowered; my object was to appeal to your reason, (for you have no common share of reasoning power), – and to your reason I appeal; – can you suppose that parents, who have treated you with such tenderness, who love you as they do their own souls, could act (as your conduct charges them) with causeless and capricious cruelty towards you? Must you not be aware there is a reason, and that it must be a profound one? Would it not be more worthy of your duty, as well as your superior sense, to inquire into, than contend with it?" "Is it founded upon any thing in my conduct, then? – I am willing to do every thing, – to sacrifice every thing." – "I understand, – you are willing to do every thing but what is required of you, – and to sacrifice every thing but your own inclination." "But you have hinted at a reason." The Director was silent. "You urged me to inquire into it." The Director was silent still. "My father, I adjure you, by the habit you wear, unmuffle this terrible phantom to me; there is nothing I cannot encounter" – "Except the commands of your parents. But am I at liberty to discover this secret to you?" said the Director, in a tone of internal debate. "Can I imagine that you, who have in the very outset outraged parental authority, will revere parental feelings?" "My father, I do not understand you." "My dear child, I am compelled to act with a caution and reserve unsuited to my character, which is naturally as open as yours. I dread the disclosure of a secret; it is repugnant to my habits of profound confidence; and I dread disclosing any thing to a character impetuous like yours. I feel myself reduced to a most painful situation." "My father, act and speak with candour, my situation requires it, and your own profession demands it from you. My father, remember the inscription over the confessional which thrilled my very blood to read, 'God hears thee.' Remember God hears you always, and will you not deal sincerely with one whom God has placed at your mercy?" I spoke with much agitation, and the Director appeared affected for a moment; that is, he passed his hand over his eyes, which were as dry as – his heart. He paused for several minutes, and then said, "My dear child, dare I trust you? I confess I came prepared to treat you like a boy, but I feel I am disposed to consider you as a man. You have the intelligence, the penetration, the decision of a man. Have you the feelings of one?" "Try me, my father." I did not perceive that his irony, his *secret*, and his parade of feeling, were all alike theatrical, and substitutionary for real interest and sincerity. "If I should be inclined to trust you, my dear child," – "I shall be grateful." "And secret." "And secret, my father." "Then imagine yourself" – "Oh! my father, let me not have to *imagine* any thing – tell me the truth." "Foolish boy, – am I then so bad a painter, that I must write the name under the figure." "I understand you, my father, and shall not interrupt you again." "Then imagine to yourself the honour of one of the first houses in Spain; the peace of a whole family, – the feelings of a father, – the honour of a mother, – the interests of religion, – the eternal salvation of an individual, all suspended in one scale. What do you think could outweigh them?" "Nothing," I replied ardently. "Yet, in the opposite scale you throw *nothing*, – the caprice of a boy not

thirteen years old; – this is all you have to oppose to the claims of
nature, of society, and of God." "My father, I am penetrated with
horror at what you have said, – does all this depend on me?" "It
does, – it does all depend on you." "But how, then, – I am bewildered, – I am willing to make a sacrifice, – tell me what I am to
do." "Embrace, my dear child, the monastic life; this will accomplish the views of all who love you, ensure your own salvation,
and fulfil the will of God, who is calling you at this moment by
the voices of your affectionate parents, and the supplications of
the minister of heaven, who is now kneeling before you." And he
sunk on his knees before me.

'This prostration, so unexpected, so revolting, and so like the
monastic habit of artificial humiliation, completely annihilated
the effect of his language. I retreated from his arms, which were
extended towards me. "My father, *I cannot*, – I will never become
a monk." "Wretch! and you refuse, then, to listen to the call of
your conscience, the adjuration of your parents, and the voice of
God?" The fury with which he uttered these words, – the change
from a ministering angel to an infuriated and menacing demon,
had an effect just contrary to what he expected. I said calmly, "My
conscience does not reproach me, – I have never disobeyed its
calls. My parents have adjured me only through your mouth; and
I hope, for their sakes, the organ has not been inspired by them.
And the voice of God, echoed from my own heart, bids me not
to obey you, by adulterating his service with prostituted vows."
As I spoke thus, the Director changed the whole character of his
figure, his attitude, and his language; – from the extreme of supplication or of terror, he passed in a moment, with the facility of
an actor, to a rigid and breathless sternness. His figure rose from
the ground before me like that of the Prophet Samuel before the
astonished eyes of Saul. He dropt the dramatist, and was the
monk in a moment. "And you will not take the vows?" "I will not,
my father." "And you will brave the resentment of your parents,
and the denunciations of the church." "I have done nothing to

deserve either." "But you will encounter both, to cherish your horrid resolution of being the enemy of God." "I am not the enemy of God for speaking the truth." "Liar and hypocrite, you blaspheme!" "Stop, my father, these are words unbecoming to your profession, and unsuited to this place." "I acknowledge the justice of the rebuke, and submit to it, though uttered by the mouth of a child." – And he dropped his hypocritical eyes, folded his hands on his breast, and murmured, "Fiat voluntas tua.[7] My dear child, my zeal for the service of God, and the honour of your family, to which I am attached equally by principle and affection, have carried me too far, – I confess it; but have I to ask pardon of you also, my child, for a redundance of that affection and zeal for your house, which its descendant has proved himself destitute of?" The mingled humiliation and irony of this address had no effect on me. He saw it had not; for after slowly raising his eyes to watch that effect, he saw me standing in silence, not trusting my voice with a word, lest I should utter something rash and disrespectful, – not daring to lift up my eyes, lest their expression should speak without making language necessary.

'I believe the Director felt his situation rather critical; his interest in the family depended on it, and he attempted to cover his retreat with all the expertness and fertility of manœuvre which belong to an ecclesiastical tactician. "My dear child, we have been both wrong, I from zeal, and you from – no matter what; our business is to exchange forgiveness with each other, and to implore it of God, whom we have both offended. My dear child, let us prostrate ourselves before him, and even while our hearts are glowing with human passion, God may seize that moment to impress the seal of his grace on both, and fix it there for ever. Often the earthquake and the whirlwind are succeeded by the still, small voice, and God is there. – Let us pray." I fell on my knees, resolved to pray in my heart; but in a short time, the fervour of his language, the eloquence and energy of his prayers, dragged me along with him, and I felt myself compelled to pray

against every dictate of my own heart. He had reserved this display for the last, and he had judged well. I never heard any thing
so like inspiration; as I listened, and involuntarily, to effusions
that seemed to issue from no mortal lips, I began to doubt my
own motives, and search my heart. I had disdained his taunts,
I had defied and conquered his passion, but as he prayed, I wept.
This going over the same ground with the heart, is one of the
most painful and humiliating of all exercises; the virtue of yesterday becomes the vice of to-day; we ask with the desponding and
restless scepticism of Pilate, 'What is truth?' but the oracle that
was so eloquent one moment, is dumb the next, or if it answers,
it is with that ambiguity that makes us dread we have to consult
again – again – and for ever – in vain.

'I was now in a state quite fit for the Director's purpose; but he
was fatigued with the part he had played with so little success,
and took his leave, imploring me to continue my importunities to
Heaven to direct and enlighten me, while he himself would supplicate all the saints in Heaven to touch the hearts of my parents,
and reveal to them some means of saving me from the crime and
perjury of a forced vocation, without *involving themselves in a
crime, if possible, of blacker dye and greater magnitude*. Saying so he
left me, to urge my parents, with all his influence, to pursue the
most rigorous measures to enforce my adoption of the conventual life. His motives for doing so were sufficiently strong when
he visited me, but their strength was increased tenfold before his
departure. He had reckoned confidently on the power of his
remonstrances; he had been repulsed; the disgrace of such a
defeat rankled in the core of his heart. He had been only a *partizan* in the cause, but he was now a *party*. What was a matter of
conscience before, was now a matter of honour with him; and
I rather believe that the Director laid a greater stress on the latter,
or made a great havock of confusion between both in his mind.
Be that as it may, I passed a few days after his visit in a state of
indescribable excitement. I had something to hope, and that is

often better than something to enjoy. The cup of hope always excites thirst, that of fruition disappoints or quenches it. I took long walks in the garden alone. I framed imaginary conversations to myself. The boarders observed me, and said to each other, according to their instructions, "He is meditating on his vocation, he is supplicating for illuminating grace, let us not disturb him." I did not undeceive them; but I reflected with increasing horror on a system that *forced* hypocrisy to a precocity unparalleled, and made the last vice of life the earliest of conventual youth. But I soon forgot reflection, to plunge into reverie. I imagined myself at the palace of my father; I saw him, my mother, and the Director, engaged in debate. I spoke for each, and felt for all. I supplied the passionate eloquence of the Director, his strong representations of my aversion to the habit, his declaration that further importunity on their part would be as impious as it was fruitless. I saw all the impression I once flattered myself I had made on my father revived. I saw my mother yield. I heard the murmur of doubtful acquiescence, – the decision, the congratulations. I saw the carriage approaching, – I heard the convent doors fly open. Liberty, – liberty, – I was in their arms; no, I was at their feet. Let those who smile at me, ask themselves whether they have been indebted most to imagination or reality for all they have enjoyed in life, if indeed they have ever enjoyed any thing. In these internal dramas, however, I always felt that the persons did not speak with the interest I wished; and the speeches I put into their mouths would have been spoken with ten thousand times more animation by myself. Still I felt the most exquisite enjoyment in these reveries, and perhaps it was not diminished by the thought of how I was deceiving my companions the whole time. But dissimulation always teaches dissimulation; and the only question is, whether we shall be the masters of the art or its victims? a question soon decided by our self-love.

'It was on the sixth day that I heard, with a beating heart, a carriage stop. I could have sworn to the sound of its wheels. I was in the hall before I was summoned. I felt I could not be in the wrong, nor was I. I drove to my father's palace in a delirium, – a vision of repulse and of reconciliation, of gratitude and of despair. I was ushered into a room, where were assembled my father, my mother, and the Director, all seated, and silent as statues. I approached, I kissed their hands, and then stood at a small distance breathless. My father was the first to break silence, but he spoke very much with the air of a man who was repeating a part dictated to him; and the tone of his voice contradicted every word he *prepared* to utter. "My son, I have sent for you, no longer to contend with your weak and wicked obstinacy, but to announce to you my own resolution. The will of Heaven and of your parents has devoted you to its service, and your resistance can only make us miserable, without in the least frustrating that resolution." At these words, gasping for breath, my lips involuntarily unclosed; my father imagined this was an attempt to reply, though in fact I was not capable of uttering a syllable, and hastened to prevent it. "My son, all opposition is unavailing, all discussion fruitless. Your destiny is decided, and though your struggles may render it wretched, they cannot reverse it. Be reconciled, my child, to the will of Heaven and your parents, which you may insult, but cannot violate. This reverend person can better explain to you the necessity of your obedience than I can." And my father, evidently weary of a task which he had reluctantly undertaken, was rising to go away, when the Director detained him. "Stay, Senhor, and assure your son before you depart, that, since I last saw him, I have fulfilled my promise, and urged every topic on your mind, and that of the duchess, that I thought might operate for his *best interests*." I was aware of the hypocritical ambiguity of this expression; and, collecting my breath, I said, "Reverend father, as a son I seek not to employ an intercessor with my own parents. I stand before them, and if I have not an intercessor in their hearts, your mediation must be ineffectual altogether. I implored you merely to state to them my

invincible reluctance." They all interrupted me with exclamations, as they repeated my last words, – "Reluctance! invincible! Is
it for this you have been admitted to our presence? Is it for this we
have borne so long with your contumacy, only to hear it repeated
with aggravations?" "Yes, my father, – yes, for this or nothing. If
I am not permitted to speak, why am I suffered in your presence?"
"Because we hoped to witness your submission." "Allow me to
give the proofs of it on my knees;" – and I fell on my knees, hoping that my posture might soften the effect of the words I could
not help uttering. I kissed my father's hand, – he did not withdraw it, and I felt it tremble. I kissed the skirt of my mother's
robe, – she attempted to withdraw it with one hand, but with the
other she hid her face, and I thought I saw tears bursting through
her fingers. I knelt to the Director too, and besought his benediction, and struggled, though with revolting lips, to kiss his hand;
but he snatched his habit from my hand, elevated his eyes, spread
out his fingers, and assumed the attitude of a man who recoils in
horror from a being who merits the extreme of malediction and
reprobation. Then I felt my only chance was with my parents.
I turned to them, but they shrunk from me, and appeared willing
to devolve the remainder of the task on the Director. He
approached me. "My child, you have pronounced your reluctance
to *the life of God* invincible, but may there not be things more
invincible even to your resolution? The curses of that God, confirmed by those of your parents, and deepened by all the
fulminations of the church, whose embraces you have rejected,
and whose holiness you have desecrated by that rejection."
"Father, these are terrible words, but I have no time now but for
meanings." "Besotted wretch, I do not understand you, – you do
not understand yourself." "Oh! I do, – I do!" I exclaimed. And
turning to my father, still on my knees, I cried, "My dear father, is
life, – human life, all shut up from me?" "It is," said the Director,
answering for my father. "Have I no resource?" "None." "No profession?" "*Profession!* degenerate wretch!" "Let me embrace the

meanest, but do not make me a monk." "Profligate as weak."
"Oh! my father," still calling on my father, "let not this man answer
for you. Give me a sword, – send me into the armies of Spain to
seek death, – death is all I ask, in preference to that life you doom
me to." "It is impossible," said my father, gloomily returning from
the window against which he had been leaning; "the honour of an
illustrious family, – the dignity of a Spanish grandee –" "Oh! my
father, of how little value will that be, when I am consuming in
my early grave, and you die broken-hearted on it, over the flower
your own voice has doomed to wither there." My father trembled.
"Senhor," I entreated, – "I command you to retire; this scene will
unfit you for the devotional duties you must perform this evening." "And you leave me then?" I cried as they departed.
"Yes, – yes," – repeated the Director; "leave you burdened with the
curse of your father." "Oh no!" exclaimed my father; but the Director had hold of his hand, and pressed it strongly. "Of your
mother," he repeated. I heard my mother weep aloud, and felt it
like a repeal of that curse; but she dared not speak, and I could not.
The Director had now two victims in his hands, and the third at
his feet. He could not avoid showing his triumph. He paused, collected the full power of his sonorous voice, and thundered forth,
"And of God!" And as he rushed from the room, accompanied by
my father and mother, whose hands he grasped, I felt as if struck
by a thunderbolt. The rushing of their robes, as he dragged them
out, seemed like the whirlwind that attends the presence of the
destroying angel. I cried out, in my hopeless agony of destitution,
"Oh! That my brother were here to intercede for me," – and, as I
uttered these words, I fell. My head struck against a marble table,
and I sunk on the floor covered with blood.

'The domestics (of whom, according to the custom of the
Spanish nobility, there were about two hundred in the palace)
found me in this situation. They uttered outcries, – assistance
was procured, – it was believed that I had attempted to kill myself;
but the surgeon who attended me happened to be a man both of

science and humanity, and having cut away the long hair clotted with blood, and surveyed the wound, he pronounced it trifling. My mother was of his opinion, for within three days I was summoned to her apartment. I obeyed the summons. A black bandage, severe head-ache, and an unnatural paleness, were the only testimonies of my accident, as it was called; and the Director had suggested to her that this was the time to FIX THE IMPRESSION. How well religious persons understand the secret of making every event of the present world operate on the future, while they pretend to make the future predominate over the present. Were I to outlive the age of man, I should never forget my interview with my mother. She was alone when I entered, and seated with her back to me. I knelt and kissed her hand. My paleness and my submission seemed to affect her, – but she struggled with her emotions, overcame them, and said in a cold *dictated* tone, "To what purpose are those marks of exterior reverence, when your heart disowns them?" "Madam, I am not conscious of that." "Not conscious! How then are you here? How is it that you have not, long before this, spared your father the shame of supplicating his own child, – the shame, still more humiliating, of supplicating him in vain; spared the Father Director the scandal of seeing the authority of the church violated in the person of its minister, and the remonstrances of duty as ineffectual as the calls of nature? And me, – oh! why have you not spared me this hour of agony and shame?" and she burst into a flood of tears, that drowned my soul as she shed them. "Madam, what have I done that deserves the reproach of your tears? My disinclination to a monastic life is no crime?" "In you it is a crime." "But how then, dear mother, were a similar choice offered to my brother, would his rejection of it be deemed a crime?" I said this almost involuntarily, and merely by way of comparison. I had no ulterior meaning, nor the least idea that one could be developed by my mother, except a reference to an unjustifiable partiality. I was undeceived, when she added, in a voice that chilled my blood,

"There is a great difference between you." "Yes, Madam, he is your favourite." "No, I take Heaven to witness, – no;" and she, who had appeared so severe, so decisive, and so impenetrable before, uttered these words with a sincerity that penetrated to the bottom of my heart; – she appeared to be appealing to Heaven against the prejudices of her child. I was affected – I said, "But, Madam, this difference of circumstances is inexplicable." "And would you have it explained *by me*?" "By any one, Madam." "*By me!*" she repeated, not hearing me; then kissing a crucifix that hung on her bosom, "My God! the chastisement is just, and I submit to it, though inflicted by my own child. You are illegitimate," she added, turning suddenly towards me; "you are illegitimate, – your brother is not: and your intrusion into your father's house is not only its disgrace, but a perpetual monitor of that crime which it aggravates without absolving." I stood speechless. "Oh! my child," she continued, "have mercy on your mother. Has not this confession, extorted from her by her own son, been sufficient to expiate her offence?" "Go on, Madam, I can bear any thing now." "You must bear it, for you have forced me to this disclosure. I am of rank far inferior to your father, – you were our first child. He loved me, and forgiving my weakness as a proof of my devotion to him, we were married, and your brother is our lawful child. Your father, anxious for my reputation, since I was united to him, agreed with me, as our marriage was private, and its date uncertain, that you should be announced as our legitimate offspring. For years your grandfather, incensed at our marriage, refused to see us, and we lived in retirement, – would that I had died there. A few days before his death he relented, and sent for us; it was no time to acknowledge the imposition practised on him, and you were introduced as the child of his son, and the heir of his honours. But from that hour I have never known a moment's peace. The lie I had dared to utter before God and the world, and to a dying parent, – the injustice done to your brother, – the violation of natural duties and of legal claims, – the convulsions of my conscience, that heavily upbraided me, not only with vice and perjury, but with sacrilege." "Sacrilege!" "Yes; every hour you delay the assumption of the habit is a robbery of God. Before you were born, I devoted you to him, as the only expiation of my crime. While I yet bore you in my bosom without life, I dared to implore his forgiveness only on the condition of your future intercession for me as a minister of religion. *I relied on your prayers before you could speak.* I proposed to intrust my penitence to one, who, in becoming the child of God, had atoned for *my* offence in making him the child of sin. In imagination I knelt already at your confessional, – heard you, by the authority of the church, and the commission of Heaven, pronounce me forgiven. I saw you stand beside my dying bed, – I felt you press the cross to my cold lips, and point to that heaven where I hoped my vow had already secured a seat for you. Before your birth I had laboured to lift you to heaven, and my recompence is, that your obstinacy threatens to drag us both into the gulph of perdition. Oh! my child, if our prayers and intercessions are available to the delivery of the souls of our departed relatives from punishment, hear the adjuration of a living parent, who implores you not to seal her everlasting condemnation!" I was unable to answer, my mother saw it, and redoubled her efforts. "My son, if I thought that my kneeling at your feet would soften your obduracy, I would prostrate myself before them this moment." "Oh! Madam, the sight of such unnatural humiliation ought to kill me." "And yet you will not yield – the agony of this confession, the interests of my salvation and your own, nay, the preservation of my life, are of no weight with you." She perceived that these words made me tremble, and repeated, "Yes, my life; beyond the day that your inflexibility exposes me to infamy, I will not live. If you have resolution, I have resolution too; nor do I dread the result, for God will charge on your soul, not on mine, the crime an unnatural child has forced me to – and yet you will not yield. – Well, then, the prostration of my body is nothing to that prostration of soul you have already driven me to. I kneel to my own child for life and for salvation," and she knelt to me. I attempted to raise her; she repelled me, and exclaimed, in a voice hoarse with despair, "And you will not yield?" "I do not say so." "And what, then, do you say? – raise me not, approach me not, till you answer me." "That I will think." "Think! you must decide." "I do, then, I do." "But how?" "To be whatever you would have me." As I uttered these words, my mother fell in a swoon at my feet. As I attempted to lift her up, scarce knowing if it was not a corse I held in my arms, I felt I never could have forgiven myself if she had been reduced to that situation by my refusing to comply with her last request.

*

'I was overpowered with congratulations, blessings, and embraces. I received them with trembling hands, cold lips, a rocking brain and a heart that felt turned to stone. Everything passed before me as in a dream. I saw the pageant move on, without a thought of who was to be the victim. I returned to the convent – I felt my destiny was fixed – I had no wish to avert or arrest it – I was like one who sees an enormous engine (whose operation is to crush him to atoms) put in motion, and, stupefied with horror, gazes on it with a calmness that might be mistaken for that of one who was coolly analysing the complication of its machinery, and calculating the resistless crush of its blow. I have read of a wretched Jew, who, by the command of a Moorish emperor, was exposed in an arena to the rage of a lion who had been purposely kept fasting for eight and forty hours. The horrible roar of the famished and infuriated animal made even the executioners tremble as they fastened the rope round the body of the screaming victim. Amid hopeless struggles, supplications for mercy, and shrieks of despair, he was bound, raised and lowered into the arena. At the moment he touched the ground, he fell prostrate, stupefied, annihilated. He uttered no cry – he did not draw a breath – he did not make an effort – he fell contracting his whole body into a ball, and lay as senseless as a lump of earth. – So it fared with me; my cries and struggles were over, – I had been flung into the arena, and I lay there. I repeated to myself, "I am to be a monk," and there the debate ended. If they commended me for the performance of my exercises, or reproved me for my deficiency, I showed neither joy nor sorrow, – I said only, "I am to be a monk." If they urged me to take exercise in the garden of the convent, or reproved me for my excess in walking beyond the allotted hours, I still answered, "I am to be a monk." I was showed much indulgence in these wanderings. A son – the eldest son of the Duke de Monçada, taking the vows, was a glorious triumph for the ex-Jesuits, and they did not fail to make the most of it. They asked what books I would like to read, – I answered, "What they pleased." They saw I was fond of flowers, and vases of porcelain, filled with the most exquisite produce of their garden, (renewed every day), embellished my apartment. I was fond of music, – that they perceived from my involuntary joining in the choir. My voice was good, and my profound melancholy gave an expression to my tones, which these men, always on the watch to grasp at any thing that may aggrandize them, or delude their victims, assured me were like the tones of inspiration.

'Amid these displays of indulgence, I exhibited an ingratitude totally foreign from my character. I never read the books they furnished me with, – I neglected the flowers with which they filled my room, – and the superb organ they introduced into my apartment, I never touched, except to elicit some deep and melancholy chords from its keys. To those who urged me to employ my talents for painting and music, I still answered with the same apathetic monotony, "I am to be a monk." "But, my brother, the love of flowers, of music, of all that can be consecrated to God, is also worthy of the attention of man – you abuse the indulgence of the Superior." "Perhaps so." "You must, in gratitude to God, thank him for these lovely works of his creation;" – the room was at this time filled with carnations and roses; – "you must also be grateful to him for the powers with which he has distinguished you in hymning his praises – your voice is the richest and most powerful in the church." "I don't doubt it." "My brother, you answer at random." "Just as I feel – but don't heed that." "Will you take a turn in the garden?" "If you please." "Or will you seek a moment's consolation from the Superior?" "If you please." "But why do you speak with such apathy? are the odour of the flowers, and the consolations of your Superior, to be appreciated in the same breath?" "I believe so." "Why?" "Because I am to be a monk." "Nay, brother, will you never utter any thing but that phrase, which carried no meaning with it but that of stupefaction or delirium?" "Imagine me, then, stupefied, delirious – what you please – you know I must be a monk." At these words, which I suppose I uttered in a tone unlike that of the usual *chaunt* of monastic conversation, another interposed, and asked what I was uttering in so loud a key? "I am only saying," I replied, "that I must be a monk." "Thank God it is no worse," replied the querist, "your contumacy must long ago have wearied the Superior and the brethren – thank God it's no worse." At these words I felt my passions resuscitated, – I exclaimed, "*Worse!* what have I to dread? – am I not to be a monk?" From that evening, (I forget when it occurred), my liberty was abridged; I was no longer suffered to walk, to converse with the boarders or novices, – a separate table was spread for me in the refectory, – the seats near mine were left vacant at service, – yet still my cell was embellished with flowers and engravings, and exquisitely-wrought toys were left on my table. I did not perceive they were treating me as a lunatic, yet certainly my foolishly reiterated expressions might have justified them in doing so, – they had their own plans in concert with the Director, – my silence went for proof. The Director came often to visit me, and the hypocritical wretches *would* accompany him to my cell. I was generally (for want of other occupation) attending to my flowers, or gazing at the engravings, – and they would say, "You see he is as happy as he wishes to be – he wants for nothing – he is quite occupied in watching those roses." "No, I am not occupied," I returned, "it is occupation I want." Then they shrugged their shoulders, exchanged mysterious looks with the Director, and I was glad when they were gone, without reflecting on the mischief their absence threatened me with. At this moment, consultation after consultation was held at the palace de Monçada, whether I could be induced to shew sufficient intellect to enable me to pronounce the vows. It seems the reverend fathers were as anxious as their old enemies the Moors, to convert an idiot into a saint. There was now a party combined against me, that it would have required more than the might of man to resist. All was uproar from the palace de Monçada to the convent, and back again. I was mad, *contumacious*, heretical, idiotical, – any thing – every thing – that could appease the jealous agony of my parents, the cupidity of the monks, or the ambition of the ex-Jesuits, who laughed at the terror of all the rest, and watched intently over their own interests. Whether I was mad or not, they cared very little; to enroll a son of the first house of Spain among their converts, or to imprison him as a madman, or to exorcise him as a demoniac, was all the same to them. There was a *coup de theatre* to be exhibited, and provided they played first parts, they cared little about the catastrophe. Luckily, during all this uproar of imposture, fear, falsehood and misrepresentation, the Superior remained steady. He let the tumult go on, to aggrandize his importance; but he was resolved all the time that I should have sanity enough to enable me to take the vows. I knew nothing of all this, but was astonished at being summoned to the parlour on the last eve of my noviciate. I had performed my religious exercises with regularity, had received no rebukes from the master of the novices, and was totally unprepared for the scene that awaited me. In the parlour were assembled my father, mother, the Director, and some other persons whom I did not recognize. I advanced with a calm look, and equal step. I believe I was as much in possession of my reason as any one present. The Superior, taking my arm, led me round the room, saying, "You see –" I interrupted him – "Sir, what is this intended for?" He answered only by putting his finger on his lips, and then desired me to exhibit my drawings. I brought them, and offered them on one knee, first to my mother, and then to my father. They were sketches of monasteries and prisons. My mother averted her eyes – and my father said, pushing them away, "I have no taste in those things." "But you are fond of music doubtless," said the Superior; "you must hear his performance." There was a small organ in the room adjacent to the parlour; my mother was not admitted there, but my father followed to listen. Involuntarily I selected an air from the "Sacrifice of Jephtha". My father was affected, and bid me cease. The Superior imagined this was not only a tribute to my talent, but an acknowledgement of the power of his party, and he applauded without measure or judgement. Till that moment, I had never conceived I could be the object of a party in the convent. The Superior was determined to make me a Jesuit, and therefore was pledged for my *sanity*. The monks wished for an exorcism, an *auto da fe*,[8] or some such bagatelle, to diversify the dreariness of monasticism, and therefore were anxious I should be, or appear, deranged or possessed. Their pious wishes, however, failed. I had appeared when summoned, *behaved* with scrupulous correctness, and the next day was appointed for my taking the vows.

'That next day – Oh! that I could describe it! – but it is impossible – the profound stupefaction in which I was plunged prevented my noticing things which would have inspired the most uninterested spectator. I was so absorbed, that though I remember facts, I cannot paint the slightest trace of the feelings which they excited. During the night I slept profoundly, till I was awoke by a knock at my door. – "My dear child, how are you employed?" I knew the voice of the Superior, and I replied, "My father, I was sleeping." "And I was macerating myself at the foot

of the altar for you, my child, – the scourge is red with my blood."
I returned no answer, for I felt the maceration was better merited
by the betrayer than the betrayed. Yet I was mistaken; for in fact,
the Superior felt some compunction, and had undergone this
penance on account of my repugnance and alienation of mind,
more than for his own offences. But Oh! *how false is a treaty made
with God, which we ratify with our own blood*, when he has declared
there is but one sacrifice he will accept, even that of the Lamb
slain from the foundation of the world! Twice in the night, I was
thus disturbed, and twice answered in the same language. The
Superior, I make no doubt, was sincere. He thought he was doing
all for God, and his bleeding shoulders testified his zeal. But I was
in such a state of mental ossification, that I neither felt, heard, or
understood; and when he knocked a second and third time at the
door of my cell to announce the severity of his macerations, and
the efficacy of his intercessions with God, I answered, "Are not
criminals allowed to sleep the night before their execution?" At
hearing these words, which must have made him shudder, the
Superior fell prostrate before the door of my cell, and I turned to
sleep again. But I could hear the voices of the monks as they
raised the Superior, and bore him to his cell. They said, "He is
incorrigible – you humiliate yourself in vain – when he is *ours*,
you shall see him a different being – he shall then prostrate himself before you." I heard this, and slept on. The morning came – I
knew what it would bring – I dramatized the whole scene in my
own mind. I imagined I witnessed the tears of my parents, the
sympathy of the congregation. I thought I saw the hands of the
priests tremble as they tossed the incense, and even the acolytes
shiver as they held their robes. Suddenly my mind changed: I
felt – what was it I felt? – a union of malignity, despair and power,
the most formidable. Lightning seemed flashing from my eyes as
I reflected, – I might make the sacrificers and the sacrificed change
places in one moment, – I might blast my mother as she stood, by
a word, – I might break my father's heart, by a single sentence, – I

might scatter more desolation around me, than it was apparently possible for human vice, human power, or human malignity, more potent than both, to cause to its most abject victim. – Yes! – on that morning I felt within myself the struggles of nature, feeling, compunction, pride, malevolence and despair. – The former I had brought with me, the latter had been all acquired in the convent. I said to those who attended me that morning, "You are arraying me for a victim, but I can turn the executioners into the victims if I please" – and I laughed. The laugh terrified those who were about me – they retreated – they represented my state to the Superior. He came to my apartment. The whole convent was by this time alarmed – their credit was at stake – the preparations had all been made – the whole world was determined I was to be a monk, mad or not.

'The Superior was terrified, I saw, as he entered my apartment. "My son, what means all this?" "Nothing, my father – nothing but a sudden thought that has struck me." "We will discuss it another time, my son; at present –" "*At present,*" I repeated with a laugh that must have lacerated the Superior's ears – "At present I have but one alternative to propose – let my father or my brother take my place – that is all. I will never be a monk." The Superior, at these words, ran in despair round the cell. I followed him, exclaiming, in a voice that must have filled him with horror, "I exclaim against the vows – let those who forced me to it, take the guilt on themselves – let my father, in his own person, expiate his guilt in bringing me into the world – let my brother sacrifice his pride – why must I be the only victim of the crime of the one, and the passions of the other?" "My son, all this was arranged before." "Yes, I know that – I know that by a decree of the Almighty I was doomed to be cursed even in my mother's womb, but I will never subscribe that decree with my own hand." "My son, what can I say to you – you have passed your noviciate." "Yes, in a state of stupefaction." "All Madrid is assembled to hear you take your vows." "Then all Madrid shall hear me renounce them, and disavow them." "This is the very day fixed on. The ministers of God are prepared to yield you to his arms. Heaven and earth, – all that is valuable in time, or precious in eternity, are summoned, are waiting for the irrevocable words that seal your salvation, and ensure that of those you love. What demon has taken possession of you, my child, and seized the moment you were coming to Christ, to cast you down, and tear you? How shall I – how shall the fraternity, and all the souls who are to escape from punishment by the merit of your prayers, answer to God for your horrible apostacy?" "Let them answer for themselves – let every one of us answer for ourselves – that is the dictate of reason." "Of reason, my deluded child, – when had reason any thing to do with religion?" I had sat down, folded my arms on my breast, and forbore to answer a word. The Superior stood with his arms crossed, his head declined, his whole figure in an air of profound and mortified contemplation. Any one else would have imagined him seeking God in the abysses of meditation, but I felt he was only seeking him where he is never to be found, – in the abyss of that heart which is 'deceitful and desperately wicked'. He approached – I exclaimed, "Come not near me! – you will renew again the story of my submission – I tell you it was artificial; – of my regularity in devotional exercises – it was all mechanism or imposture; – of my conformity to discipline – it was all practised with the hope of escaping from it ultimately. Now, I feel my conscience discharged and my heart lightened. Do you hear, do you understand me? These are the first words of truth I ever uttered since I entered these walls – the only ones that will, perhaps, ever be uttered within them – aye, treasure them up, knit your brows, and cross yourself, and elevate your eyes as you will. Go on with your religious drama. What is there you see before you so horrible, that you recoil, that you cross yourself, that you lift your eyes and hands to heaven? – a creature whom despair has driven to utter desperate truth! Truth may be horrible to the inmates of a convent, whose whole life is artificial and perverted, – whose very hearts are sophisticated beyond the hand even of Heaven (which they alienate by their hypocrisy) to touch. But I feel I am at this moment an object of less horror in the sight of the Deity, than if I were standing at his altar, to (as you would urge me) insult him with vows, which my heart was bursting from my bosom to contradict, at the moment I uttered them."

'At these words, which I must have uttered with the most indecent and insulting violence, I almost expected the Superior would have struck me to the earth, – would have summoned the lay-brothers to bear me to confinement, – would have shut me up in the dungeon of the convent, for I knew there was such a place. Perhaps I wished for all this. Driven to extremity myself, I felt a kind of pride in driving others to it in return. Any thing of violent excitement, of rapid and giddy vicissitude, or even of intense suffering, I was prepared for, and equal to, at that moment. But these paroxysms soon exhaust themselves and us by their violence.

'Astonished by the Superior's silence, I raised my eyes to him. I said, in a tone of moderation that seemed unnatural to my own ears, "Well, let me hear my sentence." He was silent still. He had *watched the crisis*, and now skilfully seized the turn of the mental disease, to exhibit his applications. He was standing before me meek and motionless, his arms crossed, his eyes depressed, not the slightest indication of resentment to be traced in his whole figure. The folds of his habit, refusing to announce his internal agitation, seemed as they were cut out of stone. His silence imperceptibly softened me, – I blamed myself for my violence. Thus men of the world command us by their passions, and men of the other world by the apparent suppression of them. At last he said, "My son, you have revolted from God, resisted his Holy Spirit, profaned his sanctuary, and insulted his minister, – in his name and my own I forgive you all. Judge of the various characters of our systems, by their different results on us two. You revile, defame and accuse, – I bless and forgive; which of us is then under the influence of the gospel of Christ, and within the pale of the church's benediction? But leaving this question, which you are not at present in a frame to decide, I shall urge but one topic more; if that fails, I shall no longer oppose your wishes, or urge you to prostitute a sacrifice which man would despise, and God must disdain. I add, I will even do my utmost to facilitate your wishes, which are now in fact my own." At these words, so full of truth and benignity, I was rushing to prostrate myself at his feet, but fear and experience checked me, and I only bowed. "Promise me merely that you will wait with patience till this last topic is urged; whether it succeeds or not I have now little interest, and less care." I promised, – he went out. A few moments after he returned. His air was a little more disturbed, but still struggling for a calmness of expression. There was agitation about him, but I knew not whether it was felt on his own account or mine. He held the door half open, and his first sentence astonished me. – "My son, you are well acquainted with the classical histories." "But what is that to the purpose, my father?" "You remember a remarkable story of the Roman general, who spurned from the steps of his tribune, people, senators and *priests*, – trampled on all law, – outraged all religion, – but was at last moved by nature, for, when his mother prostrated herself before him, and exclaimed, "My son, before you tread the streets of Rome, you must first tread on the body of her who bore you!" he relented. "I remember all, but to what does this tend?" "*To this*," and he threw open the door; "now, prove yourself, if you can, more obdurate than a heathen." As the door opened, across the threshold lay my mother, prostrate on her face. She said in a stifled voice, "Advance, – break your vows, – but you must rush to perjury over the body of your mother." I attempted to raise her, but she clung to the ground, repeating the same words; and her magnificent dress, that overspread the floor of stone with gems and velvet, frightfully contrasted her posture of humiliation, and the despair that burned in her eyes, as she raised them to me for a moment. Convulsed with agony and horror, I reeled into the arms of the Superior, who seized that moment to bear me to the church. My mother followed, – the ceremony proceeded. I vowed chastity, poverty, and obedience, and in a few moments my destiny was decided.

*

'Day followed day for many a month, of which I have no recollections, nor wish to have any. I must have experienced many emotions, but they all subsided like the waves of the sea under the darkness of a midnight sky, – their fluctuation continues, but there is no light to mark their motion, or trace when they rise and fall. A deep stupor pervaded my senses and soul; and perhaps, in this state, I was best fitted for the monotonous existence to which I was doomed. It is certain that I performed all the conventual functions with a regularity that left nothing to be blamed, and an apathy that left nothing for praise. My life was a sea without a tide. The bell did not toll for service with more mechanical punctuality than I obeyed the summons. No automaton, constructed on the most exquisite principles of mechanism, and obeying those principles with a punctuality almost miraculous, could leave the artist less room for complaint or disappointment, than I did the Superior and community. I was always first in my place in the choir. I received no visits in the parlour, – when I was permitted to go, I declined the permission. If penance was enjoined, I submitted; if relaxation was permitted, I never partook of it. I never asked a dispensation from morning prayers, or from vigils. I was silent in the refectory, – in the garden I walked alone. I neither thought, nor felt, nor lived, – if life depends on consciousness, and the motions of the will. I slept through my existence like the Simorgh in the Eastern fable, but this sleep was not to last long. My abstraction and calmness would not do for the Jesuits. My stupor, my noiseless tread, my fixed eyes, my ghastly silence, might indeed have impressed a superstitious community with the idea that it was no human creature who stalked through their cloisters, and haunted their choir. But they had quite different ideas. They considered all this as a tacit reproach to the struggles, the squabbles, the intrigues, and the circumventions, in which they were immersed, body and soul, from morn till night. Perhaps they thought I was lying in reserve, only to watch them. Perhaps there might have been a dearth of some matter of curiosity or complaint in the convent just then, – a very little serves for either. However it was, they began to revive the old story of my being deranged, and resolved to make the most of it. They whispered in the refectory, consulted in the garden, – shook their heads, pointed at me in the cloister, and finally, I faithfully believe, worked themselves into the conviction that what they wished or imagined was actually true. Then they all felt their consciences interested in the investigation; and a select party, headed by an old monk of influence and reputation, waited on the Superior. They stated to him my abstraction, my mechanical movements, my automaton figure, my meaningless words, my stupefied devotion, my total alienation from the spirit of the monastic life, while my scrupulous, *wooden*, *jointless* exactness in its forms was only a mockery. The Superior heard them with great indifference. He had held secret intelligence with my family, had communicated with the Director, and pledged himself that I should be a monk. He had succeeded by dint of exertions, (the result of which has been seen), and now cared very little whether I was mad or not. With a grave air he forbid their further interference in the matter, and reserved its future cognizance to himself. They retired defeated, but not disappointed, and they all pledged themselves to each other to *watch me*; that is, to harass, persecute, and torment me into being the very character with which their malice, their curiosity, or their mere industry of idleness and wantonness of unoccupied invention, had invested me already. From that hour the whole convent was in a tumult of conspiracy and combination. Doors were clapped to wherever I was heard to approach; and three or four would stand whispering near where I walked, and clear their throats, and exchange signs, and pass *audibly* to the most trifling topics in my hearing, as if to intimate, while they affected to conceal it, that their last topic had been *me*. I laughed at this internally. I said to myself, "Poor perverted beings, with what affectation of dramatic bustle and contrivance you labour to diversify the misery of your hopeless vacancy; – you struggle, – I submit." Soon the toils they were preparing began to tighten round me. They would throw themselves in my way with an assiduity I could not avoid, and an appearance of kindness I did not willingly repel. They would say, in the blandest tones, "My dear brother, you are melancholy, – you are devoured with chagrin, – would to God our fraternal efforts could banish your regrets. But from what arises that melancholy that appears to consume you?" At these words I could not help fixing on them eyes full of reproaches, and I believe of tears, – but I did not utter a word. The state in which they saw me, was a sufficient cause for the melancholy with which I was reproached.

*

'This attack having failed, another method was tried. They attempted to make me a party in the parties of the convent. They told me a thousand things of unjust partialities, – of unjust punishments, daily to be witnessed in the convent. They talked of a sickly brother being compelled to attend matins, while the physician pronounced his attendance on them must be his death, – *and he died,* – while a young favourite, in the bloom of health, had a dispensation from matins whenever he pleased to lie till nine in the morning; – of complaints that the confessional was not attended to as it ought, – and this might have made some impression on me, till another complainant added, and the *turning-box is not attended as it ought to be.* This union of dissonant sounds, – this startling transition from a complaint of neglecting the mysteries of the soul in its profoundest communion with God, to the lowest details of the abuses of conventual discipline, revolted me at once. I had with difficulty concealed my disgust till then, and it was now so obvious, that the *party* gave up their attempt for the moment, and beckoned to an *experienced* monk to join me in my solitary walk, as I broke from them. He approached, "My brother, you are alone." "I wish to be so." "But why?" "I am not obliged to announce my reasons." "True, but you may confide them to me." "I have nothing to confide." "I know that, – I would not for the world intrude on your confidence; reserve that for friends more honoured." It struck me as rather odd, that he should, in the same breath, ask for my confidence, – declare that he was conscious I had nothing to intrust to him, – and, lastly, request a reserve of my confidence for some more favoured friend. I was silent, however, till he said, "But, my brother, you are devoured with ennui." I was silent still. "Would to God I could find the means to dissipate it." I said, looking on him calmly. "Are those means to be found within the walls of a convent?" "Yes, my dear brother, – yes, certainly, – the debate in which the convent is now engaged about the proper hour for matins, which the Superior wants to have restored to the original hour." "What is the difference?" "*Full five minutes*." "I confess the importance of the question." "Oh! if you once begin to feel it, there will be no end of your happiness in a convent. There is something every moment to inquire, to be anxious about, and to contend for. Interest yourself, my dear brother, in these questions, and you will not have a moment's ennui to complain of." At these words I fixed my eyes on him. I said calmly, but I believe emphatically, "I have, then, only to excite in my own mind, spleen, malignity, curiosity, every passion that your retreat should have afforded me protection against, to render that retreat supportable. Pardon me, if I cannot, like you, beg of God permission to take his enemy into compact against the corruption which I promote, while I presume to pray against it." He was silent, lifted up his hands, and crossed himself; and I said to myself, "God forgive your hypocrisy," as he went into another walk, and repeated to his companions, "He is mad, irrecoverably mad." "But how, then?" said several voices. There was a stifled whisper. I saw several heads bent together. I did not know what they were meditating, nor did I care. I was walking alone, – it was a delicious moon-light evening. I saw the moon-beams through the trees, but the trees all looked to me like walls. Their trunks were as adamant, and the interlaced branches seemed to twine themselves into folds that said, "Beyond us there is no passing." I sat down by the side of a fountain, – there was a tall poplar over it, – I remember their situation well. An elderly priest (who, I did not see, was detached by the party) sat down beside me. He began some common-place observations on the transiency of human existence. I shook my head, and he understood, by a kind of tact not uncommon among Jesuits, that *it would not do*. He shifted the subject, remarked on the beauty of the foliage, and the limpid purity of the fountain. I assented. He added, "Oh that life were pure as that stream!" I sighed, "Oh that life were verdant and fertile to me as that tree!" "But, my son, may not fountains be dried up, and trees be withered?" "Yes, my father, – yes, – the fountain of my life has been dried up, and the green branch of my life has been blasted for ever." As I uttered these words, I could not suppress some tears. The father seized on what he called the moment when God was breathing on my soul. Our conversation was very long, and I listened to him with a kind of reluctant and stubborn attention, because I had involuntarily been compelled to observe, that he was the only person in the whole community who had never harassed me by the slightest importunity either before my profession or after; and when the worst things were said of me, never seemed to attend; and when the worst things were predicted of me, shook his head and said nothing. His character was unimpeached, and his religious performances as exemplary and punctual as my own. With all this I felt no confidence in him, or in any human being; but I listened to him with patience, and my patience must have had no trivial trial, for, at the end of an hour,

(I did not perceive that our conference was permitted quite beyond the usual hour of retirement), he continued repeating, "My dear son, you will become reconciled to the conventual life." "My father, never, never, – unless this fountain is dried up, and this tree withered, by to-morrow." "My son, God has often performed greater miracles for the salvation of a soul."

'We parted, and I retired to my cell. I know not how he and the others were employed, but, before matins, there was such a tumult in the convent, that one would have thought Madrid was on fire. Boarders, novices and monks, ran about from cell to cell, up and down the staircase, through all the corridors, unrestrained and unquestioned, – all order was at an end. No bell was rung, no commands for restoring tranquillity issued; the voice of authority seemed to have made peace for ever with the shouts of uproar. From my window I saw them running through the garden in every direction, embracing each other, ejaculating, praying, and counting their beads with hands tremulous, and eyes uplifted in extacy. The hilarity of a convent has something in it uncouth, unnatural and even alarming. I suspected some mischief immediately, but I said to myself, "The worst is over, they cannot make me more than a monk." – I was not long left in doubt. Many steps approached my cell, numerous voices were repeating, "Hasten, dear brother, hasten to the garden." I was left no choice; they surrounded and almost bore me to the garden.

'The whole community were assembled there, the Superior among them not attempting to suppress the confusion, but rather encouraging it. There was a suffusion of joy in every countenance, and a kind of artificial light in every eye, but the whole performance struck me as hollow and hypocritical. I was led, or rather hurried to the spot where I had sat and conversed so long the preceding evening. *The fountain was dried up, and the tree was withered*. I stood speechless with astonishment, while every voice around me repeated, "A miracle! a miracle! – God himself has sealed your vocation with his own hand" The Superior made a signal to them to stop. He said to me in a calm voice, "My son, you are required only to believe the evidence of your own eyes. Will you make infidels of your very senses, sooner than believe God? Prostrate yourself, I adjure you, before him this moment, and, by a public and solemn act of faith, recognize that mercy that has not scrupled a miracle to invite you to salvation." I was amazed more than touched by what I saw and heard, but I threw myself on my knees before them all, as I was directed. I clasped my hands and said aloud, "My God, if you have indeed vouch-safed this miracle on my account, you will also doubtless enrich and illuminate me with grace to apprehend and appreciate it. My mind is dark, but you can illuminate it. My heart is hard, but it is not beyond the power of omnipotence to touch and subdue it. An impression made on it this moment, a whisper sent to its recesses, is not less worthy of your mercy than an impression on inanimate matter, which only confounds my senses." The Supe-rior interrupted me. He said, "Hold, those are not the words you should use. Your very faith is incredulous, and your prayer an ironical insult on the mercy it pretends to supplicate." "My father, put what words you please in my mouth, and I will repeat them, – if I am not convinced, I am at least subdued." "You must ask pardon of the community for the offence your *tacit* repugnance to the life of God has caused them." I did so. "You must express your gratitude to the community for the joy they have testified at this miraculous evidence of the truth of your vocation." I did so. "You must also express your gratitude to God, for a visible inter-position of supernatural power, not more to the vindication of his grace, than to the eternal honour of this house, which he has been pleased to irradiate and dignify by *a miracle*." I hesitated a little. I said, "My father, may I be permitted to utter this prayer internally?" The Superior hesitated too; he thought it might not be well to push matters too far, and he said at length, "As you please." I was still kneeling on the ground, close to the tree and the fountain. I now prostrated myself with my face to the earth, and prayed internally and intensely, while they all stood around me; but the language of my prayer was very different from what they flattered themselves I was uttering. On rising from my knees, I was embraced by half the community. Some of them actually shed tears, the source of whose fountain was surely not in their hearts. Hypocritical joy insults only its dupe, but hypocritical grief degrades the professor. That whole day was passed in a kind of revelry. Exercises were abridged, – the refections embellished with confectionery, – every one had permission to go from cell to cell, without an order from the Superior. Presents of chocolate, snuff, iced water, liqueurs and (what was more acceptable and necessary than any of them) napkins and towels of the finest and whitest damask, circulated among all the members. The Superior was shut up half the day with two *discreet* brethren, as they are called, (that is, men who are elected to take part with the Superior, on supposition of their utter, superannuated incapacity, as Pope Sixtus was elected for his (supposed) imbecility), preparing an authenticated account of the miracle, to be dispatched to the principal convents in Spain. There was no need to distribute the intelligence through Madrid, – they were in possession of it an hour after it happened, – the malicious say *an hour before*.

'I must confess the agitating exhilaration of this day, so unlike what I had ever witnessed before in a convent, produced an effect on me I cannot describe. I was caressed, – made the hero of the *fete*, – (a conventual *fete* has always something odd and unnatural in it), – almost deified. I gave myself up to the intoxication of the day, – I did verily believe myself the favourite of the Deity for some hours. I said to myself a thousand flattering things. If this deception was criminal, I expiated my crime very soon. The next day every thing was restored to its usual order, and I found that the community could pass from the extreme of disorder in a moment to the rigidity of their usual habits.

'My conviction of this was certainly not diminished within the few following days. The oscillations of a convent vibrate within a

very short interval. One day all is relaxation, another all is inexorable discipline. Some following days I received a striking proof
of that foundation on which, in despite of a miracle, my repugnance to a monastic life rested. Some one, it was said, had
committed a slight breach of monastic duty. The *slight breach* was
fortunately committed by a distant relation of the Archbishop of
Toledo, and consisted *merely in his entering the church intoxicated*,
(a rare vice in Spaniards), attempting to drag the matin preacher
from the pulpit, and failing in that, getting astride as well as he
could on the altar, dashing down the tapers, overturning the
vases and the pyx, and trying to scratch out, as with the talons of
a demon, the painting that hung over the table, uttering all the
while the most horrible blasphemies, and even *soliciting the portrait of the Virgin* in language not to be repeated. A consultation
was held. The community, as may be guessed, was in an uproar
while it lasted. Every one but myself was anxious and agitated.
There was much talk of the Inquisition, – the scandal was so
atrocious, – the outrage so unpardonable, – and atonement is
impracticable. Three days afterwards the archbishop's mandate
came to stop all proceedings; and the following day the youth
who had committed this sacrilegious outrage appeared in the
hall of the Jesuits, where the Superior and a few monks were
assembled, read a short exercise which one of them had written
for him on the pithy word 'Ebrietas', and departed to take possession of a large benefice in the diocese of the archbishop his
relative. The very next day after this scandalous scene of com-
promise, imposture, and profanation, a monk was detected in the
act of going, after the permitted hour, to an adjacent cell to
return a book he had borrowed. As a punishment for this offence,
he was compelled to sit for three days at refection, while we were
dining, barefooted and his tunic reversed, on the stone floor of
the hall. He was compelled to accuse himself aloud of every
crime, and of many not at all fit to be mentioned to our ears, and
exclaim at every interval, "My God, my punishment is just."

On the second day, it was found that a mat had been placed under him by some merciful hand. There was an immediate commotion in the hall. The poor wretch was labouring under a complaint that made it worse than death to him to be compelled to sit or rather lie on a stone floor; some merciful being had surreptitiously conveyed to him this mat. An investigation was immediately commenced. A youth whom I had not noticed before, started from the table, and kneeling to the Superior, confessed *his guilt*. The Superior assumed a stern look, retired with some old monks to consult on this new crime of humanity, and in a few moments the bell was rung, to give every one notice to retire to their cells. We all retired trembling, and while we prostrated ourselves respectively before the crucifix in our cells, wondered who would be the next victim, or what might be his punishment. I saw that youth but once again. He was the son of a wealthy and powerful family, but even his wealth was no balance against his contumacy, in the opinion of the convent, that is, of four monks of rigid principles, whom the Superior consulted that very evening. The Jesuits are fond of courting power, but they are still fonder of keeping it, if they can, to themselves. The result of their debate was, that the offender should undergo a severe humiliation and penance in their presence. His sentence was announced to him, and he submitted to it. He repeated every word of contrition they dictated to him. He then bared his shoulders, and applied the scourge till the blood flowed, repeating between every stroke, "My God, I ask pardon of thee for having given the slightest comfort or relief to Fra Paolo, during his merited penance." He performed all this, cherishing in the bottom of his soul an intention still to comfort and relieve Fra Paolo, whenever he could find opportunity. He then thought all was over. He was desired to retire to his cell. He did so, but the monks were not satisfied with this examination. They had long suspected Fra Paolo of irregularity, and imagined they might extort the confession of it from this youth, whose humanity increased their suspicion. The virtues of nature are always deemed vices in a convent. Accordingly, he had hardly been in bed when they surrounded him. They told him they came by command of the Superior to enjoin him a further penance, unless he disclosed the secret of the interest he felt for Fra Paolo. It was in vain he exclaimed, "I have no interest but that of humanity and compassion." Those were words they did not understand. It was in vain he urged, "I will inflict whatever penance the Superior is pleased to order, but my shoulders are bleeding still," – and he shewed them. The executioners were pitiless. They compelled him to quit his bed, and applied the scourge with such outrageous severity, that at last, mad with shame, rage and pain, he burst from them, and ran through the corridor calling for assistance or for mercy. The monks were in their cells, none dared to stir, – they shuddered, and turned on their straw pallets. It was the vigil of Saint John the Lesser, and I had been commanded what is called in convents an hour of recollection, which was to be passed in the church. I had obeyed the order, and remained with my face and body prostrate on the marble steps of the altar, till I was almost unconscious, when I heard the clock strike twelve. I reflected the hour had elapsed without a single recollection on my part. "And thus it is to be always," I exclaimed, rising from my knees; "they deprive of the power of thinking, and then they bid me recollect." As I returned through the corridor, I heard frightful cries – I shuddered. Suddenly a phantom approached me – I dropt on my knees – I cried, "*Satana vade retro – apage Satana.*"[9] A naked human being, covered with blood, and uttering screams of rage and torture, flashed by me; four monks pursued him – they had lights. I had shut the door at the end of the gallery – I felt they must return and pass me – I was still on my knees, and trembling from head to foot. The victim reached the door, found it shut, and rallied. I turned, and saw a groupe worthy of Murillo. A more perfect human form never existed than that of this unfortunate youth. He stood in an attitude of despair – he was streaming with blood. The monks, with their lights, their scourges, and their dark habits, seemed like a groupe of demons who had made prey of a wandering angel, – the groupe resembled the infernal furies pursuing a mad Orestes. And, indeed, no ancient sculptor ever designed a figure more exquisite and perfect than that they had so barbarously mangled. Debilitated as my mind was by the long slumber of all its powers, this spectacle of horror and cruelty woke them in a moment. I rushed forward in his defence – I struggled with the monks – I uttered some expressions which, though I hardly was conscious of, they remembered and exaggerated with all the accuracy of malice.

'I have no recollection of what followed; but the issue of the business was, that I was confined to my cell for the following week, for my daring interference in the discipline of the convent. And the additional penance of the unfortunate novice, for resisting that discipline, was inflicted with such severity, that he became delirious with shame and agony. He refused food, he got no rest, and died the eighth night after the scene I had witnessed. He was of a temper unusually mild and amiable – he had a taste for literature, and even the disguise of a convent could not conceal the distinguished graces of his person and manners. Had he lived in the world, how these qualities would have embellished it! Perhaps the world would have abused and perverted them – true; but would the abuses of the world ever have brought them to so frightful and disastrous a conclusion? – would he have been first lashed into madness, and then lashed out of existence? He was interred in the church of the convent, and the Superior himself pronounced his eulogium – the Superior! by whose order, or else permission, or at least connivance, he had been driven mad, in order to obtain a trivial and imaginary secret.

'During this exhibition, my disgust arose to a degree incalculable. I had loathed the conventual life – I now despised it; and every judge of human nature knows, that it is harder to eradicate the latter sentiment than the former. I was not long without an occasion for the renewed exercise of both feelings. The weather was intensely hot that year – an epidemic complaint broke out in the convent – every day two or three were ordered to the infirmary, and those who had merited slight penances were allowed, by way of commutation, to attend the sick. I was most anxious to be of the number – I was even resolved, by some slight deviation, to tempt this punishment, which would have been to me the highest gratification. Dare I confess my motive to you, Sir? I was anxious to see those men, if possible, divested of the conventual disguise, and forced to sincerity by the pangs of disease, and the approach of death. I triumphed already in the idea of their dying confession, of hearing them acknowledge the seductions employed to ensnare me, deplore the miseries in which they had involved me, and implore, with convulsed lips, my pardon in – *no* – *not in vain*.

'This wish, though vindictive, was not without its palliations; but I was soon saved the trouble of realizing it at my own expence. That very evening the Superior sent for me, and desired me to attend in the infirmary, allowing me, at the same time, remission from vespers. The first bed I approached, I found Fra Paolo extended on. He had never recovered the effects of the complaint he laboured under at the time of his penance; and the death of the young novice (so fruitlessly incurred) had been mortal to him.

'I offered him medicines – I attempted to adjust him in his bed. He had been greatly neglected. He repelled both offers, and, feebly waving his hand, said, "Let me, at least, die in peace." A few moments after, he unclosed his eyes, and recognized me. A gleam of pleasure trembled over his countenance, for he remembered the interest I had shewn for his unfortunate friend. He said, in a voice hardly intelligible, "It is you, then?" "Yes, my brother, it is I – can I do any thing for you?" After a long pause, he added, "Yes, you can." "Tell me then." He lowered his voice, which was before almost inaudible, and whispered, "Let none of them come near me in my dying moments – it will not give you much trouble – those moments are approaching." I pressed his hand in token of acquiescence. But I felt there was something at once terrifying and improper in this request from a dying man. I said to him, "My dear brother, you are then dying? – would you not wish an interest in the prayers of the community? – would you not wish the benefit of the last sacraments?" He shook his head, and I fear that I understood him too well. I ceased any further importunity; and a few moments he uttered, in tones I could hardly distinguish, *"Let them, let me die.* – They have left me no power to form another wish." His eyes closed, – I sat beside his bed, holding his hand in mine. At first, I could feel he attempted to press it – the attempt failed, his hold relaxed. Fra Paolo was no more.

'I continued to sit holding the dead hand in mine, till a groan from an adjacent bed roused me. It was occupied by the old monk with whom I had held a long conversation the night before the miracle, in which I still believed most firmly.

'I have observed, that this man was of a temper and manners remarkably mild and attractive. Perhaps this is always connected with great weakness of intellect, and coldness of character *in men.* (It may be different in women – but my own experience has never failed in the discovery, that where there was a kind of feminine softness and pliability in the male character, there was also treachery, dissimulation and heartlessness.) At least, if there be such a union, a conventual life is sure to give it every advantage in its range of internal debility, and external seductiveness. – That pretence of a wish to assist, without the power, or even the wish, that is so flattering both to the weak minds that exercise it, and the weaker on whom it is exercised. This man had been always judged very weak, and yet very fascinating. He had been always employed to ensnare the young novices. He was now dying – overcome by his situation, I forgot every thing but its tremendous claims, and offered him every assistance in my power. "I want nothing but to die," was his answer. His countenance was perfectly calm, but its calmness was rather that of apathy than of resignation. "You are, then, perfectly sure of your approach to blessedness?" "I know nothing about it." "How, my brother, are those words for a dying man to utter?" "Yes, if he speaks the truth." "But a monk? – a Catholic?" "Those are but names – I feel *that truth*, at least, now." "You amaze me!" "I care not – I am on the verge of a precipice – I must plunge from it – and whether the by-standers utter outcries or not, is a matter of little consequence to me." "And yet, you expressed a willingness to die?" "Willingness! Oh impatience! – I am a clock that has struck the same minutes and hours for sixty years. Is it not time for the machine to long for its winding up? The monotony of my existence would make a transition, even to pain, desirable. I am weary, and would change – that is all." "But to me, and to all the community, you seemed to be resigned to the monastic life." "I seemed a lie – I lived a lie – I was a lie – I ask pardon of my last moments for speaking the truth – I presume they neither can refuse me, or discredit my words – I hated the monastic life. Inflict pain on man, and his energies are roused – condemn him to insanity, and he slumbers like animals that have been found inclosed in wood and stone, torpid and content; but condemn him at once to pain and inanity, as they do in convents, and you unite the sufferings of hell and of annihilation. For sixty years I have cursed my existence. I never woke to hope, for I had nothing to do or to expect. I never lay down with consolation, for I had, at the close of every day, only to number so many deliberate mockeries of God, as exercises of devotion. The moment life is put beyond the reach of your will, and placed under the influence of mechanical operations, it becomes, to thinking beings, a torment insupportable.

"'I never ate with appetite, because I knew, that with or without it, I must go to the refectory when the bell rung. I never lay down to rest in peace, because I knew the bell was to summon me in defiance of nature, whether it was disposed to prolong or shorten my repose. I never prayed, for my prayers were dictated to me.

I never hoped, for my hopes were founded not on the truth of God, but on the promises and threatenings of man. My salvation hovered on the breath of a being as weak as myself, whose weakness I was nevertheless obliged to flatter, and struggle to obtain a gleam of the grace of God, through the dark distorted medium of the vices of man. *It never reached me* – I die without light, hope, faith, or consolation." – He uttered these words with a calmness that was more terrific than the wildest convulsions of despair. I gasped for breath – "But, my brother, you were always punctual in your religious exercises." "That was mechanism – will you not believe a dying man?" "But you urged me, in a long conversation, to embrace the monastic life; and your importunity must have been sincere, for it was after my profession." "It is natural for the miserable to wish for companions in their misery. This is very selfish, very misanthropic, you will say, but it is also very natural. You have yourself seen the cages suspended in the cells – are not the tame birds always employed to allure the wild ones? We were caged birds, can you blame us for the deception?" In these words I could not help recognizing that *simplicity of profound corruption*,* – that frightful paralysis of the soul, which leaves it incapable of receiving any impression or making one, – that says to the accuser, Approach, remonstrate, upbraid – I defy you. My conscience is dead, and can neither hear, utter, or echo a reproach. I was amazed – I struggled against my own conviction. I said, "But your regularity in religious exercises –" *"Did you never hear a bell toll?"* "But your voice was always the loudest and most distinct in the choir." *"Did you never hear an organ played?"*

*

'I shuddered, yet I still went on with my queries – I thought I could not know too much. I said, "But, my brother, the religious exercises in which you were constantly engaged, must have

* Vide Madame Genlis's 'Julien Delmour.'

imperceptibly instilled something of their spirit into you? – is it not so? You must have passed from the forms of religion into its spirit ultimately? – is it not so, my brother? Speak on the faith of a dying man. May I have such a hope! I would undergo any thing – any thing, to obtain it." "There is no such hope," said the dying man, "deceive not yourself with it. The repetition of religious duties, without the feeling or spirit of religion, produces an incurable callosity of heart. There are not more irreligious people to be found on earth than those who are occupied always in its *externals*. I verily believe half our lay-brothers to be Atheists. I have heard and read something of those whom we call heretics. They have people to open their pews, (shocking profanation you will call it, to sell seats in the house of God, and you are right), they have people to ring bells when their dead are to be interred; and these wretches have no other indication of religion to give, but watching during the whole time of service, (in which their duties forbid them to partake), for the fees which they extort, and dropping upon their knees, ejaculating the names of Christ and God, amid the rattling of the pew-doors, which always operates on their associations, and makes them bound from their knees to gape for a hundredth part of the silver for which Judas sold his Saviour and himself. Then their bell-ringers – one would imagine *death might humanize them*. Oh! no such thing – they *extort money in proportion to the depth of the grave*. And the bell-ringer, the sexton and the survivors, fight sometimes a manual battle over the senseless remains, whose torpidity is the most potent and silent reproach to this unnatural conflict." I knew nothing of this, but I grasped at his former words, "You die, then, without hope or confidence?" He was silent. "Yet you urged me by eloquence almost divine, by a miracle verified before my own eyes." He laughed. There is something very horrible in the laugh of a dying man: hovering on the verge of both worlds, he seems to give the lie to both, and proclaim the enjoyments of one, and the hopes of another, alike an imposture. "I performed that miracle myself," he said with all the calmness, and, alas! something of the triumph of a deliberate impostor. "I knew the reservoir by which the fountain was supplied – by consent of the Superior it was drawn off in the course of the night. We worked hard at it, and laughed at your credulity every pump we drew." "But the tree –" "I was in possession of some chemical secrets – I have not time to disclose them now – I scattered a certain fluid over the leaves of the poplar that night, and they *appeared* withered by the morning – go look at them a fortnight hence, and you will see them as green as ever." "And these are your dying words?" "They are." "And why did you deceive me thus?" He struggled a short time at this question, and then rising almost upright in his bed, exclaimed, "Because I was a monk, and wished for victims of my imposture to gratify my pride! and companions of my misery, to soothe its malignity!" He was convulsed as he spoke, the natural mildness and calmness of his physiognomy were changed for something that I cannot describe – something at once derisive, triumphant and diabolical. I forgave him every thing in that horrible moment. I snatched a crucifix that lay by his bed – I offered it to his lips. He pushed it away. "If I wanted to have this farce acted, I should choose another actor. You know I might have the Superior and half the convent at my bed-side this moment if I pleased, with their tapers, their holy water, and their preparations for extreme unction, and all the masquerade of death, by which they try to dupe even the dying, and insult God even on the threshold of his own eternal mansion. I suffered you to sit beside me, because I thought, from your repugnance to the monastic life, you might be a willing hearer of its deceptions, and its despair."

'Deplorable as had been the image of that life to me before, this representation exceeded my imagination. I had viewed it as excluding all the enjoyments of life, and thought the prospect blasting; but now the other world was weighed in the balance, and found wanting. The genius of monasticism seemed to wield a two-edged sword, and to lift it between and against time and eternity. The blade bore a two-fold inscription – on the side next the world was written the word "suffer", – on that opposed to eternity, "despair". In the utter hopelessness of my soul, I still continued to question *him* for hope – him! while he was bereaving me of its very shadow, by every word he uttered. "But, must all be plunged in this abyss of darkness? Is there no light, no hope, no refuge, for the sufferer? May not some of us become reconciled to our situation – first patient of it, then attached to it? Finally, may we not (if our repugnance be invincible) make a merit of it with God, and offer to him the sacrifice of our earthly hopes and wishes, in the confidence of an ample and glorious equivalent? Even if we are unable to offer this sacrifice with the unction which would ensure its acceptance, still may we not hope it will not be wholly neglected? – that we may become tranquil, if not happy – resigned, if not content. Speak, tell me if this may be?" "And you wish to extort deception from the lips of death – but you will fail. Hear your doom – Those who are possessed of what may be called the religious character, that is, those who are visionary, weak, morose and ascetic, may elevate themselves to a species of intoxication in the moments of devotion. They may, while clasping the images, work themselves into the delusion, that the dead stone thrills to their touch; that the figures move, assent to their petitions, and turn their lifeless eyes on them with an expression of benignity. They may, while kissing the crucifix, believe that they hear celestial voices pronouncing their pardon; that the Saviour of the world extends his arms to them, to invite them to beatitude; that all heaven is expanded to their view, and the harmonies of paradise are enriched to glorify their apotheosis. But this is a mere inebriation that the most ignorant physician could produce in his patients by certain medicines. The secret of this ecstatic swoon might be traced to an apothecary's shop, or purchased at a cheaper rate. The inhabitants of the north of Europe procure this state of exaltation by the use of liquid fire – the Turks by opium – the Dervises by dancing – and Christian monks by spiritual pride operating on the exhaustion of a macerated frame. It is all intoxication, with this difference only, that the intoxication of men of this world produces always *self*-complacency – that of men of the other world, a complacency whose supposed source is derived from God. The intoxication is, therefore, more profound, more delusive, and more dangerous. But nature, violated by these excesses, exacts a most usurious interest for this illicit indulgence. She makes them pay for moments of rapture with hours of despair. Their precipitation from extasy to horror is almost instantaneous. In the course of a few moments, they pass from being the favourites of Heaven to becoming its outcasts. They doubt the truth of their raptures, – the truth of their vocation. They doubt every thing – the sincerity of their prayers, even the efficacy of the Saviour's atonement, and the intercession of the blessed Virgin. They plunge from paradise to hell. They howl, they scream, they blaspheme. From the bottom of the infernal gulph in which they imagine themselves plunged, they bellow imprecations against their Creator – they denounce themselves as damned from all eternity for their sins, while their only sin is their inability to support preternatural excitement. The paroxysm ceases [and] they become the elect of God again in their own imaginations. And to those who interrogate them with regard to their late despair, they answer, That Satan was permitted to buffet them – that they were under the hidings of God's face, &c. All saints, from Mahomet down to Francis Xavier, were only a compound of insanity, pride and self-imposition; – the latter would have been of less consequence, but that men always revenge their impositions on themselves, by imposing to the utmost on others."

'There is no more horrible state of mind than that in which we are *forced by conviction to listen on, wishing every word to be false, and knowing every word to be true*. Such was mine, but I tried to palliate it by saying, "It was never my ambition to be a saint; but is the lot of all, then, so deplorable?" The monk, who appeared to rejoice in this opportunity to discharge the concentrated malignity of sixty years of suffering and hypocrisy, collected his dying voice to answer. He seemed as if he never could inflict enough, for what had been inflicted on himself. "Those who possess strong sensibility, without the religious character, are of all others the most unhappy, but their miseries are soonest terminated. They are harassed by trivial constraints, stupefied by monotonous devotion, exasperated by full insolence and bloated superiority. They struggle, they resist. Penance and punishment are applied. Their own violence justifies increased violence of treatment; and, at all events, it would be applied without this justification, for there is nothing that delights the pride of power, more than a victorious strife with the pride of intellect. The remainder is easily to be conceived by you, who have witnessed it. You saw the unfortunate youth who interfered about Paolo. He was lashed to madness. Tortured first to phrenzy, then to stupefaction, – he died! I was the secret, unsuspected adviser of the whole proceeding." "Monster!" I exclaimed, for truth had made us equal *now*, and even precluded the language that humanity would dictate when uttered to a dying man. – "But why?" – said he, with that calmness which had once attracted, and now revolted me, but which had at all times undisputed possession of his physiognomy; – "his sufferings were shorter, do you blame me for diminishing their duration?" – There was something cold, ironical and jeering, even in the suavity of this man, that gave a certain force to his simplest observations. It seemed as if he had reserved the truth all his life, to utter it at his dying hour. "Such is the fate of those who possess strong sensibility; those who have less languish away in an imperceptible decline. They spend their time in watching a few flowers, in tending birds. They are punctual in their religious exercises, they receive neither blame or praise, – they melt away in torpor and ennui. They wish for death, as the preparation it might put the convent to might produce a short excitement, but they are disappointed, for their state forbids excitement, and they die as they have lived, – unexcited, unawakened. The tapers are lit, they do not see them, – the unction is applied, they do not feel it, – prayers are uttered, they cannot partake in them; – in fact, the whole drama is acted, but the principal performer is absent, – is gone. Others indulge themselves in perpetual reverie. They walk alone in the cloister, – in the garden. They feed themselves with the poison of delicious, innutritive illusion. They dream that an earthquake will shake the walls to atoms, that a volcano will burst forth in the centre of the garden. They imagine a revolution of government, – an attack of banditti, – any thing, however improbable. Then they take refuge in the possibility of a fire, (if a fire bursts out in a convent, the doors are thrown open, and 'Sauve qui peut,' is the word). At this thought they conceived the most ardent hope, – they could rush out, – they could precipitate themselves into the streets, into the country, – in fact, they would fly any where to escape. Then these hopes fail, – they begin to get nervous, morbid, restless. If they have interest, they are indulged with remission from their duties, and they remain in their cells, relaxed, – torpid, – idiotical; if they have not interest, they are forced to the punctual performance of their duties, and then idiotism comes on much sooner, as diseased horses, employed in a mill, become blind sooner than those who are suffered to wear out existence in ordinary labour. Some of them take refuge in religion, as they call it. They call for relief on the Superior, but what can the Superior do? He is but human too, and perhaps feels the despair that is devouring the wretches who supplicate him to deliver them from it. Then they prostrate themselves before the images of the saints, – they invoke, they sometimes revile them. They call for their intercession, deplore its inefficacy, and fly to some other, whose merits they imagine are higher in the sight of God. They supplicate for an interest in the intercession of Christ and the Virgin, as their last resort. That resort fails them too, – the Virgin herself is inexorable, though they wear out her pedestal with their knees, and her feet with their kisses. Then they go about the galleries all night, they rouse the sleepers. They knock at every door, – they cry, 'Brother Saint Jerome, pray for me, – Brother Saint Augustine, pray for me.' Then the placard is seen fastened to the rails of the altar, 'Dear brothers, pray for the wandering soul of a monk.' The next day the placard bears this inscription, 'The prayers of the community are implored for a monk who is in despair.' Then they find human intercession as unavailing as divine, to procure them a remission of the sufferings which, while *their profession* continues to inflict on them, no power can reverse or mitigate. They crawl to their cells, – in a few days the toll of the bell is heard, and the brethren exclaim, 'He died in the odour of sanctity,' and hasten to spread their snares for another victim." "And is this, then, monastic life?" "It is, – there are but two exceptions, that of those who can every day renew, by the aid of imagination, the hope of escape, and who cherish that hope even on their dying bed; and those who, like me, diminish their misery by dividing it, and, like the spider, feel relieved of the poison that swells, and would burst them, by instilling a drop of it into every insect that toils, agonizes and perishes in their net, – *like you.*" At these last words, a glare of malignity flashed on the features of the dying wretch, that appalled me. I retreated from his bed for a moment. I returned, I looked at him, – his eyes were closed, – his hands extended. I touched him, – raised him, – he was dead, – those were his last words. The expression of his features was the physiognomy of his soul, – they were calm and pale, but still a cold expression of derision lingered about the curve of his lips.

'I rushed from the infirmary. I was at that time indulged, like all the other visitants of the sick, to go to the garden beyond the allotted hours perhaps to diminish the chance of infection. I was but too ready to avail myself of this permission. The garden, with its calm moon-light beauty, its innocence of heaven, its theology of the stars, was at once a reproach and a consolation to me. I tried to reflect, to feel, – both efforts failed; and perhaps it is in this silence of the soul, this suspension of all the clamorous voices of the passions, that we are most ready to hear the voice of God. My imagination suddenly represented to me the august and ample vault above me as a church, – the images of the saints grew dim in my eyes as I gazed on the stars, and even the altar, over which the crucifixion of the Saviour of the world was represented, turned pale to the eye of the soul, as I gazed on the moon "walking in her brightness". I fell on my knees. I knew not to whom I was about to pray, but I never felt so disposed to pray. I felt my habit touched at this moment. I at first trembled, from the idea of being detected in a forbidden act. I started up. A dark figure stood beside me, who said in indistinct and faultering tones, "Read this," and he thrust a paper into my hand; "I have worn it sewed into my habit for four days. I have watched you night and day. I had no opportunity but this, – you were in your cell, in the choir, or in the infirmary. Tear it in pieces, throw the fragments into the fountain, or *swallow them*, the moment you have read it. – Adieu. I have risked every thing for you," and he glided away. I recognized his figure as he departed; it was the porter of the convent. I well understood the risk he must have run in delivering this paper, for it was the regulation of the convent, that all letters, whether addressed to or written by boarders, novices, or monks, were first to be read by the Superior, and I never knew an instance of its infringement. The moon gave me sufficient light. I began to read, while a vague hope, that had neither object or basis, trembled at the bottom of my heart. The paper contained these words:

"'My dearest brother, (My God; how I started!) I see you revolt at the first lines which I address to you, – I implore you, for both our sakes, to read them with calmness and attention. We have been both the victims of parental and priestly imposition; the former we must forgive, for our parents are the victims of it too. The Director has their consciences in his hand, and their destiny and ours at his feet. Oh, my brother, what a tale have I to disclose to you! I was brought up, by the Director's orders, whose influence over the domestics is as unbounded as it is over their unhappy master, in complete hostility against you, as one who was depriving me of my natural rights, and degrading the family by your illegitimate intrusion. May not this palliate, in some degree, my unnatural repulsiveness when we first met? I was taught from my cradle to hate and fear you, – to hate you as an enemy, and fear you as an impostor. This was the Director's plan. He thought the hold he had over my father and mother too slight to gratify his ambition of domestic power, or realize his hopes of professional distinction. The basis of all ecclesiastical power rests upon fear. A crime must be discovered or invented. The vague reports circulated in the family, my mother's constant dejection, my father's occasional agitation, offered him a clue, which he followed with incessant industry through all its windings of doubt, mystery, and disappointment, till, in a moment of penitence, my mother, terrified by his constant denunciations if she concealed any secret of her heart or life from him, disclosed the truth.

'"We were both infants then. He adopted immediately the plan he has since realized at the expence of all but himself. I am convinced he had not, from the first hour of his machinations, the least malignity against you. The aggrandizement of his interest, which ecclesiastics always individualize with that of the church, was his only object. To dictate, to tyrannize, to manage a whole family, and that of rank, by his knowledge of the frailty of one of its members, was all he looked to. Those who by their vows are excluded from the interest which natural affections give us in life, must seek for it in the artificial ones of pride and domination, and the Director found it there. All thenceforth was conducted and inspired by him. It was he who caused us to be kept asunder from our infancy, fearful that nature might frustrate his plans, – it was he who reared me in sentiments of implacable animosity against you. When my mother fluctuated he reminded her of her vow, with which she had rashly intrusted him. When my father murmured, the shame of my mother's frailty, the bitter feuds of domestic discussion, the tremendous sounds of imposture, perjury, sacrilege, and the resentment of the church, were thundered in his ears. You may conceive there is nothing this man would shrink at, when, almost in my childhood, he disclosed to me my mother's frailty, to insure my early and zealous participation in his views. Heaven blast the wretch who could thus contaminate the ears, and wither the heart of a child, with the tale of a parent's shame, to secure a partizan for the church! This was not all. From the first hour I was able to hear and comprehend him, he poisoned my heart by every channel he could approach. He exaggerated my mother's partiality for you, which he assured me often contended vainly with her conscience. He represented my father as weak and dissipated, but affectionate; and, with the natural pride of a boy-father, immoveably attached to his eldest offspring. He said, 'My son, prepare yourself to struggle with a host of prejudices, – the interests of God, as well as of society, demand it. *Assume a high tone with your parents,* – you are in possession of the secret that corrodes their consciences, make your own use of it.' Judge the effect of these words on a temper naturally violent, – words, too, uttered by one whom I was taught to regard as the agent of the Divinity.

"'All this time, as I have since been informed, he was debating in his own mind whether he would not adopt your part instead of mine, or at least vacillate between both, so as to augment his influence over our parents, by the additional feature of suspicion. Whatever influenced his determination, the effect of his lessons on me may be easily calculated. I became restless, jealous, and vindictive; – insolent to my parents, and suspicious of all around me. Before I was eleven years of age I reviled my father for his partiality to you, – I insulted my mother with her crime, – I tyrannized over the domestics, – I was the dread and the torment of the whole household; and the wretch who had made me thus a premature demon, had outraged nature, and compelled me to trample on every tie he should have taught me to hallow and cherish, consoled himself with the thought that he was obeying the calls of his function, and strengthening the hands of the church.

'Scire volunt secreta domus et inde timeri.'

'"On the day preceding our first meeting, (which had not been intended before), the Director went to my father; he said, 'Senhor, I think it best the brothers should meet. Perhaps God may touch their hearts, and by his merciful influence over them, enable you to reverse the decree that threatens one of them with seclusion, and both with a cruel and final separation.' My father assented with tears of delight. Those tears did not melt the heart of the Director; he hastened to my apartment, and said, 'My child, summon all your resolution, your artful, cruel, partial parents, are *preparing a scene* for you, – they are determined on introducing you to your spurious brother.' 'I will spurn him before their faces, if they dare to do so,' said I, with the pride of premature tyranny. 'No, my child, that will not do, you must appear to comply with their wishes, but you must not be their victim, – promise me that, my dear child, – promise me resolution and dissimulation.' 'I promise you resolution, keep the dissimulation for yourself.' 'Well, I will do so, since your interests require it.' He hurried back to my father. 'Senhor, I have employed all the eloquence of heaven and nature with your younger son. He is softened, – he melts already, – he longs to precipitate himself into the fraternal embrace, and hear your benediction poured over the united hearts and bodies of your two children, – they are both your children. You must banish all prejudices, and –' 'I have no prejudices!' said my poor father; 'let me but see my children embrace, and if Heaven summoned me at that moment, I should obey it by dying of joy.' – The Director reproved him for the expressions which gushed from his heart, and, wholly unmoved by them, hurried back to me, full of his commission. 'My child, I have warned you of the conspiracy formed against you by your own family. You will receive a proof of it to-morrow, – your brother is to be introduced, – you will be required to embrace him, – your consent is reckoned on, but at the moment you do so, your father is resolved to interpret this as the signal, on your part, of the resignation of all your natural rights. Comply with your hypocritical parents, embrace this brother, but give an air of repugnance to the action that will justify your conscience, while it deceives those who would deceive you. Watch the signal-word, my dear child; embrace him as you would a serpent, – his art is not less, and his poison as deadly. Remember that your resolution will decide the event of this meeting. Assume the appearance of affection, but remember you hold your deadliest enemy in your arms.' At these words, unnatural as I was, I shuddered. I said, 'My brother!' 'Never mind,' said the Director, 'he is the enemy of God, – an illegitimate impostor. Now, my child, are you prepared?' and I answered, 'I am prepared.' That night, however, I was very restless. I required the Director to be summoned. I said in my pride, 'But how is this poor wretch (meaning you) to be disposed of?' 'Let him embrace the monastic life,' said the Director. At these words I felt an interest on your account I had never recognized before. I said decidedly, for he had taught me to assume a tone of decision, 'He shall never be a monk.' The Director appeared staggered, yet he trembled before the spirit he had himself raised. 'Let him go into the army,' I said; 'let him inlist as a common soldier, I can supply him with the means of promotion; – let him engage in the meanest profession, I shall not blush to acknowledge him, but, father, he shall never be a monk.' 'But, my dear child, on what foundation does this extraordinary objection rest? It is the only means to restore peace to the family, and procure it for the unfortunate being for whom you are so much interested.' 'My father, have done with this language. Promise me, as the condition of my obedience to your wishes to-morrow, that my brother shall never be compelled to be a monk.' 'Compelled, my dear child! there can be no compulsion in a holy vocation.' 'I am not certain of that; but I demand from you the promise I have mentioned.' The Director hesitated, at last he said, 'I promise.' And he hastened to tell my father there was no longer any opposition to our meeting, and that I was delighted with the determination which had been announced to me of my brother eagerly embracing the monastic life. Thus was our first meeting arranged. When, at the command of my father, our arms were entwined, I swear to you, my brother, I felt them thrill with affection. But the instinct of nature was soon superseded by the force of habit, and I recoiled, collected all the forces of nature and passion in the terrible expression that I dared to direct towards our parents, while the Director stood behind them smiling, and encouraging me by gestures. I thought I had acted my part with applause, at least I gave myself enough, and retired from the scene with as proud a step as if I had trampled on a prostrate world, – I had only trampled on nature and my own heart. A few days after I was sent to a convent. The Director was alarmed at the dogmatizing tone he himself had taught me to assume, and he urged the necessity of my education being attended to. My parents complied with every thing he required. I, for a wonder, consented; but, as the carriage conveyed me to the convent, I repeated to the Director, 'Remember, my brother is not to be a monk.'"

'(After these lines several were unintelligible to me, apparently from the agitation under which they were written; – the precipitancy and fiery ardor of my brother's character communicated itself to his writings. After many a defaced page I could trace the following words.)

*

"'It was singular enough that you, who were the object of my inveterate hatred before my residence in the convent, became the object of my interest from that moment. I had adopted your cause from pride, I now upheld it from experience. Compassion, instinct, whatever it was, began to assume the character of a duty. When I saw the indignity with which the lower classes were treated, I said to myself, 'No, he shall never suffer that, – he is my brother.' When I succeeded in my exercises, and was applauded, I said, 'This is applause in which he never can share.' When I was punished, and that was much more frequently, I said, 'He shall never feel this mortification.' My imagination expanded. I believed myself your future patron, I conceived myself redeeming the injustice of nature, aiding and aggrandizing you, forcing you to confess that you owed more to me than to your parents, and throwing myself, with a disarmed and naked heart, on your gratitude alone for affection. I heard you call me brother, – I bid you stop, and call me benefactor. My nature, proud, generous, and fiery, had not yet quite emancipated itself from the influence of the Director, but every effort it made pointed, by an indescribable impulse, towards you. Perhaps the secret of this is to be found in the elements of my character, which always struggled against dictation, and loved to teach itself all it wished to know, and inspire itself with the object of its own attachments. It is certain that I wished for your friendship, at the moment I was instructed to hate you. Your mild eyes and affectionate looks haunted me perpetually in the convent. To the professions of friendship repeatedly made me by the boarders, I answered, 'I want a brother.' My conduct was eccentric and violent, – no wonder, for my conscience had begun to operate against my habits. Sometimes I would apply with an eagerness that made them tremble for my health; at others, no punishment, however severe, could make me submit to the ordinary discipline of the house. The community grew weary of my obstinacy, violence, and irregularities. They wrote to the Director to have me removed, but before this could be accomplished I was seized with a fever. They paid me unremitting attention, but there was something on my mind no cares of theirs could remove. When they brought me medicine with the most scrupulous punctuality, I said, 'Let my

brother fetch it, and if it be poison I will drink it from his hand;
I have injured him much.' When the bell tolled for matins and
vespers, I said, 'Are they going to make my brother a monk? The
Director promised me differently, but you are all deceivers.' At
length they muffled the bell. I heard its stifled sound, and I
exclaimed, 'You are tolling for his funeral, but I, – I am his murderer!' The community became terrified at these exclamations so
often repeated, and with the meaning of which they could not
accuse themselves. I was removed in a state of delirium to my
father's palace in Madrid. A figure like yours sat beside me in the
carriage, alighted when we stopped, accompanied me where I
remained, assisted me when I was placed again in the carriage. So
vivid was the impression, that I was accustomed to say to the
attendants, 'Stop, my brother is assisting me.' When they asked
me in the morning how I had rested? I answered, 'Very well, –
Alonzo has been all night at my bed-side.' I invited this visionary
companion to continue his attentions; and when the pillows were
arranged to my satisfaction, I would say, 'How kind my brother
is, – how useful, – but *why will he not speak?*' At one stage I absolutely refused nourishment, because the phantom appeared to
decline it. I said, 'Do not urge me, my brother, you see, will not
accept of it. Oh, I entreat his pardon, it is a day of abstinence, –
that is his reason, you see how he points to his habit, – that is
enough.' It is very singular that the food at this house happened
to be poisoned, and that two of my attendants died of partaking
of it before they could reach Madrid. I mention these circumstances, merely to prove the rivetted hold you had taken both on
my imagination and my affections. On the recovery of my intellect, my first inquiry was for you. This had been foreseen, and my
father and mother, shunning the discussion, and even trembling
for the event, as they knew the violence of my temper, intrusted
the whole business to the Director. He undertook it, – how he
executed it is yet to be seen. On our first meeting he approached
me with congratulations on my convalescence, with regrets for

the constraints I must have suffered in the convent, with assurances that my parents would make my home a paradise. When he had gone on for some time, I said, 'What have you done with my brother?' 'He is in the bosom of God,' said the Director, crossing himself. I understood him in a moment, – I rushed past him before he had finished. 'Where are you going, my son?' 'To my parents.' 'Your parents, – it is impossible that you can see them now.' 'But it is certain that I will see them. Dictate to me no longer, – degrade yourself not by this prostituted humiliation,' for he was putting himself in a posture of intreaty, – 'I *will* see my parents. Procure for me an introduction to them this moment, or tremble for the continuance of your influence in the family.' At these words he trembled. He did not indeed dread my influence, but he dreaded my passions. His own lessons were bitterly retaliated on him that moment. He had made me fierce and impetuous, because that suited his purpose, but he had neither calculated on, or prepared himself for, this extraordinary direction which my feelings had taken, so opposite to that which he had laboured to give them. He thought, in exciting my passions, he could ascertain their direction. Woe be to those, who, in teaching the elephant to direct his trunk against their foes, forget that by a sudden convolution of that trunk, he may rend the driver from his back, and trample him under his feet into the mire. Such was the Director's situation and mine. I insisted on going instantly to my father's presence. He interposed, he supplicated; at last, as a hopeless resource, he reminded me of his continual indulgence, his flattery of my passions. My answer was brief, but Oh that it might sink into the souls of such tutors and such priests! 'And that has made me what I am. Lead the way to my father's apartment, or I will spurn you before me to the door of it.' At this threat, which he saw I was able to execute, (for you know my frame is athletic, and my stature twice that of his), he trembled; and I confess this indication of both physical and mental debility completed my contempt for him. He crawled before me to the apartment where my father and mother were seated, in a balcony that overlooked the garden. They had imagined all was settled, and were astonished to see me rush in, followed by the Director, with an aspect that left them no reason to hope of an auspicious result of our conference. The Director gave them a sign which I did not observe, and which they had not time to profit by, – and as I stood before them livid from my fever, on fire with passion, and trembling with inarticulate expressions, they shuddered. Some looks of reproach were levelled by them at the Director, which he returned, as usual, by signs. I did not understand *them*, but I made them understand me in a moment. I said to my father, 'Senhor, is it true you have made my brother a monk?' My father hesitated; at last he said, 'I thought the Director had been commissioned to speak to you on that subject.' 'Father, what has a Director to do in the concerns of a parent and child? That man never can be a parent, – never can have a child, how then can he be a judge in a case like this?' 'You forget yourself, – you forget the respect due to a minister of the church.' 'My father, I am but just raised from a death-bed, my mother and you trembled for my life, – that life still depends on your words. I promised submission to this wretch, on a condition which he has violated, which –' 'Command yourself, Sir,' said my father, in a tone of authority which ill suited the trembling lips it issued from, 'or quit the apartment.' 'Senhor,' interposed the Director, in a softened tone, 'let not me be the cause of dissension in a family whose happiness and honour have been always my object, next to the interests of the church. Let him go on, the remembrance of my crucified Master will sustain me under his insults,' and he crossed himself. 'Wretch!' I cried, grasping his habit, 'you are a hypocrite, a deceiver!' and I know not of what violence I might have been guilty, but my father interposed. My mother shrieked with terror, and a scene of a confusion followed, in which I recollect nothing but the hypocritical exclamations of the Director, appearing to struggle between my father and me, while he mediated with God for both. He repeated incessantly, 'Senhor, do not interpose, every indignity I suffer I make a sacrifice to Heaven; it will qualify me to be an intercessor for my traducer with God;' and, crossing himself, he called on the most sacred names, and exclaimed, 'Let insults, calumnies, and blows, be added to that preponderance of merit which is already weighed in the scales of heaven against my offences,' and he dared to mix the claims of the intercession of the saints, the purity of the immaculate Virgin, and even the blood and agony of Jesus Christ, with the vile submissions of his own hypocrisy. The room was by this time filled with attendants. My mother was conveyed away, still shrieking with terror. My father, who loved her, was driven by this spectacle, and by my outrageous conduct, to a pitch of fury, – he drew his sword. I burst into a laugh, that froze his blood as he approached me. I expanded my arms, and presented my breast, exclaiming, 'Strike! – this is the consummation of monastic power, – it begun by violating nature, and ends in filicide. Strike! give a glorious triumph to the influence of the church, and add to the merits of the holy Director. You have sacrificed your Esau, your first-born, already, let Jacob be your next victim.' My father retreated from me, and, revolted by the disfigurement which the violence of my agitation had caused, almost to convulsion, he exclaimed, 'Demon!' and stood at a distance viewing, and shuddering at me. 'And who has made me so? *He* who fostered my evil passions for his own purposes; and, because one generous impulse breaks out on the side of nature, would represent or drive me mad, to effectuate his purposes. My father, I see the whole power and system of nature reversed, by the arts of a corrupt ecclesiastic. By his means my brother has been imprisoned for life; – by his means our birth has been made a curse to my mother and to you. What have we had in the family since his influence was fatally established in it, but dissension and misery? Your sword was pointed against my heart this moment; was it nature or a monk that armed a parent against his child, whose crime was – interceding for his brother? Dismiss this man, whose presence eclipses our hearts, and let us confer together for a moment as father and son, and if I do not humiliate myself before you, spurn me for ever. My father, for God's sake examine the difference between this man and me, as we stand before you. We are together at the bar of your heart, judge between us. A dry and featureless image of selfish power, consecrated by the name of the church, occupies his whole soul, – I plead to you by the interests of nature, that must be sincere, because they are contrary to my own. He only wishes to wither your soul, – I seek to touch it. Is his heart in what he says? does he shed a tear? does he employ one impassioned expression? he calls on God, – while I call only on you. The very violence which you justly condemn, is not only my vindication but my eulogy. They who prefer their cause to themselves, need no proof of their advocacy being sincere.' 'You aggravate your crime, by laying it on another; you have always been violent, obstinate, and rebellious.' 'But who has made me so? Ask himself, – ask this shameful scene, in which his duplicity has driven me to act such a part.' 'If you wish to show submission, give me the first proof of it, by promising never to torture me by renewing the mention of this subject. Your brother's fate is decided, – promise not to utter his name again, and –' 'Never, – never,' I exclaimed, 'never will I violate my conscience by such a vow; and his who could propose it must be seared beyond the power of Heaven to touch it.' Yet, in uttering these words, I knelt to my father, but he turned from me. I turned in despair to the Director. I said, 'If you are the minister of Heaven, prove the truth of your commission, – make peace in a distracted family, reconcile my father to both his children. You can effect this by a word, you know you can, yet you will not utter it. My unfortunate brother was not so inflexible to your appeals, and yet were they inspired by a feeling as justifiable as mine.' I had offended the Director beyond all forgiveness. I knew this, and spoke indeed rather to expose than to persuade him.

I did not expect an answer from him, and I was not disappointed, – he did not utter a word. I knelt in the middle of the floor between them. I cried, 'Deserted by my father and by you, I yet appeal to Heaven. I call on it to witness my vow never to abandon my persecuted brother, whom I have been made a tool to betray. I know you have power, – I defy it. I know every art of circumvention, of imposture, of malignant industry, – every resource of earth and hell, will be set at work against me. I take Heaven to witness against you, and demand only its aid to insure my victory.' My father had lost all patience; he desired the attendants to raise and remove me by force. This mention of force, so repugnant to my habits of imperious indulgence, operated fatally on intellects scarcely recovering from delirium, and too strongly tried in the late struggle. I relapsed into partial insanity. I said wildly, 'My father, you know not how mild, generous, and forgiving is the being you thus persecute, – I owe my life to him. *Ask your domestics if he did not attend me, step by step, during my journey?* If he did not administer my food, my medicines, and smoothe the pillows on which I was supported?' 'You rave,' cried my father, as he heard this wild speech, but he cast a look of fearful inquiry on the attendants. The trembling servants swore, one and all, as well they might, that not a human being but themselves had been suffered to approach me since I quitted the convent, till my arrival at Madrid. The small remains of reason forsook me completely at this declaration, which was however true every word of it. I gave the lie to the last speaker with the utmost fury, – I struck those who were next me. My father, astonished at my violence, suddenly exclaimed, 'He is mad.' The Director, who had till then been silent, instantly caught the word, and repeated, 'He is mad.' The servants, half in terror, half in conviction, re-echoed the cry.

'"I was seized, dragged away; and this violence, which always excited corresponding violence in me, realized all my father feared, and the Director wished for. I behaved just as a boy, scarce out of a fever, and still totally delirious, might be supposed to behave. In my apartment I tore down the hangings, and there was not a porcelain vase in the room that I did not dash at their heads. When they seized me, I bit their hands; when at length they were compelled to bind me, I gnawed the strings, and finally snapt them by a violent effort. In fact, I completely realized all the hopes of the Director. I was confined to my apartment for several days. During this time, I recovered the only powers that usually revive in a state of isolation, – those of inflexible resolution and profound dissimulation. I had soon exercise enough for both of them. On the twelfth day of my confinement, a servant appeared at the door of my apartment, and, bowing profoundly, announced, that if my health was recovered, my father wished to see me. I bowed in complete imitation of his mechanical movements, and followed him with the steps of a statue. I found my father, armed with the Director at his side. He advanced, and addressed me with an abruptness which proved that he forced himself to speak. He hurried over a few expressions of pleasure at my recovery, and then said, 'Have you reflected on the subject of our last conversation?' 'I have *reflected on it. – I had time to do so.*' – 'And you have employed that time well?' – 'I hope so.' – 'Then the result will be favourable to the hopes of your family, and the interests of the church.' The last words chilled me a little, but I answered as I ought. In a few moments after the Director joined me, he spoke amicably and turned the conversation on neutral topics. I answered him, – what an effort did it cost me! – yet I answered him in all the bitterness of extorted politeness. All went on well, however. The family appeared gratified by my renovation. My father, harassed out, was content to procure peace on any terms. My mother, still weaker, from the struggles between her conscience and the suggestions of the Director, wept, and said she was happy. A month has now elapsed in profound but treacherous peace on all sides. They think me subdued, but

*

"'In fact, the efforts of the Director's power in the family would alone be sufficient to precipitate my determinations. He has placed you in a convent, but that is not enough for the persevering proselytism of the church. The palace of the Duke de Monçada is, under his influence, turned into a convent itself. My mother is almost a nun, her whole life is exhausted in imploring forgiveness for a crime for which the Director, to secure his own influence, orders her a new penance every hour. My father rushes from libertinism to austerity, – he vacillates between this world and the next; – in the bitterness of exasperated feeling, sometimes reproaches my mother, and then joins her in the severest penance. Must there not be something very wrong in the religion which thus substitutes external severities for internal amendment? I feel I am of an inquiring spirit, and if I could obtain a book they call the Bible, (which, though they say it contains the words of Jesus Christ, they never permit us to see) I think — but no matter. The very domestics have assumed the *in ordine ad spiritualia*[11] character already. They converse in whispers – they cross themselves when the clock strikes – they dare to talk, even in my hearing, of the glory which will redound to God and the church, by the sacrifice my father may yet be induced to make of his family to its interests.

*

"'My fever has abated – I have not lost a moment in consulting your interests – I have heard that there is a possibility of your reclaiming your vows – that is, as I have been told, of declaring they were extorted under impressions of fraud and terror. Observe me, Alonzo, I would rather see you rot in a convent, than behold you stand forth as a living witness of our mother's shame. But I am instructed that this reclamation of your vows may be carried on in a civil court: If this be practicable, you may yet be free, and I shall be happy. Do not hesitate for resources, I am able to supply them. If you do not fail in resolution, I have no doubt of our ultimate success. – *Ours* I term it, for I shall not know a moment's peace till you are emancipated. With the half of my yearly allowance I have bribed one of the domestics, who is brother to the porter of the convent, to convey these lines to you. Answer me by the same channel, it is secret and secure. You must, I understand, furnish a memorial, to be put into the hands of an advocate. It must be strongly worded, – but remember, not a word of our unfortunate mother; – I blush to say this to her son. Procure paper by some means. If you find any difficulty, I will furnish you; but, to avoid suspicion, and too frequent recurrences to the porter, try to do it yourself. You conventual duties will furnish you with a pretext of writing out your confession, – I will undertake for its safe delivery. I commend you to the holy keeping of God, – not the God of monks and directors, but the God of nature and mercy. – I am your affectionate brother,

Juan De Monçada."

'Such were the contents of the papers which I received in fragments, and from time to time, by the hands of the porter. I swallowed the first the moment I had read it, and the rest I found means to destroy unperceived as I received them, – my attendance on the infirmary entitling me to great indulgences.'

At this part of the narrative, the Spaniard became so much agitated, though apparently more from emotion than fatigue, that Melmoth intreated him to suspend it for some days, and the exhausted narrator willingly complied.

Chapter Six

Τηλε μὲιργονοι ψυχαι, ειδοωλα καμουτων.[12]

Homer

When, after some days interval, the Spaniard attempted to describe his feelings on the receipt of his brother's letter, the sudden resuscitation of heart, and hope, and existence, that followed its perusal, he trembled, – uttered some inarticulate sounds, – wept; – and his agitation appeared to Melmoth, with *his uncontinental feelings*, so violent, that he entreated him to spare the description of his feelings, and proceed with his narrative.

'You are right,' said the Spaniard, drying his tears, 'joy is a convulsion, but grief is a habit, and to describe what we never can communicate, is as absurd as to talk of colours to the blind. I will hasten on, not to tell of my feelings, but of the results which they produced. A new world of hope was opened to me. I thought I saw liberty on the face of heaven when I walked in the garden. I laughed at the jar of the doors as they opened, and said to myself, "You shall soon expand to me for ever". I behaved with uncommon complacency to the community. But I did not, amid all this, neglect the most scrupulous precautions suggested by my brother. Am I confessing the strength or the weakness of my heart? In the midst of all the systematic dissimulation that I was prepared and eager to carry on, the only circumstance that gave me real compunction, was my being obliged to destroy the letters of that dear and generous youth who had risked every thing for my emancipation. In the mean time, I pursued my preparations with industry inconceivable to you, who have never been in a convent.

'Lent was now begun, – all the community were preparing themselves for the great confession. They shut themselves up, – they prostrated themselves before the shrines of the saints, – they occupied themselves whole hours in taking minutes of their consciences, and magnifying the trivial defects of conventual discipline into offences in the eye of God, in order to give consequence to their penitence in the hearing of the confessor, – in fact, they would have been glad to accuse themselves of a crime, to escape from the monotony of a monastic conscience. There was a kind of silent bustle in the house, that very much favoured my purposes. Hour after hour I demanded paper for my confession. I obtained it, but my frequent demands excited suspicion, – they little knew what I was writing. Some said, for every thing excites inquiry in a convent, "He is writing the history of his family; he will discharge it into the ears of the confessor, along with the secrets of his own soul." Others said, "He has been in a state of *alienation* for some time, he is giving an account to God for it, – we shall never hear a word about it." Others, who were more judicious, said, "He is weary of the monastic life, he is writing an account of his monotony and ennui, doubtless that must be very long;" and the speakers yawned as they uttered these words, which gave a very strong attestation to what they said. The Superior watched me in silence. He was alarmed, and with reason. He consulted with some of the *discreet* brethren, whom I mentioned before, and the result was a restless vigilance on their part, to which I supplied an incessant fuel, by my absurd and perpetual demand for paper. Here, I acknowledge, I committed a great oversight. It was impossible for the most exaggerated conscience to charge itself, even in a convent, with crimes enough to fill all the paper I required. I was filling them all the time with *their* crimes, not my own. Another great mistake I made, was being wholly unprepared for the great confession when it came on. I received intimations of this as we walked in the garden, – I have before mentioned that I had assumed an amicability of habit toward them. They would say to me, "You have made ample preparations for the great confession." "I have prepared myself." "But we expect great edification from its results." "I trust you will receive it." – I said no more, but I was very much disturbed at these hints. Others would say, "My brother, amid the multitudinous offences that burden your conscience, and which you have found necessary to employ quires of paper to record, would it not be a relief to you to open your mind to the Superior, and ask for a few previous moments of consolation and direction from *him*." To this I answered, "I thank you, and will consider of it." – I was thinking all the time of something else.

'It was a few nights before the time of the great confession, that I had to entrust the last packet of my memorial to the porter. Our meetings had been hitherto unsuspected. I had received and answered my brother's communications, and our correspondence had been conducted with a secrecy unexampled in convents. But this last night, as I put my packet into the porter's hand, I saw a change in his appearance that terrified me. He had been a comely, robust man, but now, even by the moon-light, I could perceive he was wasted to a shadow, – his hands trembled as he took the papers from me, – his voice faultered as he promised his usual secrecy. The change, which had been observed by the whole convent, had escaped me till that night; my mind had been too much occupied by my own situation. I noticed it then, however, and I said, "But what is the matter?" "Can you then ask? I am withered to a spectre by the terrors of the office I have been bribed to. Do you know what I risk? – incarceration for life, or rather for death, – perhaps a denunciation to the Inquisition. Every line I deliver from you, or to you, seems a charge against my own soul, – I tremble when I meet you. I know that you have the sources of life and death, temporal and eternal, in your hands. The secret in which I am an agent should never be intrusted but to *one*, and *you are another*. As I sit in my place, I think every step in the cloister is advancing to summon me to the presence of the

Superior. When I attend in the choir, amid the sounds of devotion your voice swells to accuse me. When I lie down at night, the evil spirit is beside my bed, reproaching me with perjury, and reclaiming his prey; – his emissaries surround me wherever I move, – I am beset by the tortures of hell. The saints from their shrines frown on me, – I see the painting of the traitor Judas on every side I turn to. When I sleep for a moment, I am awakened by my own cries. I exclaim, 'Do not betray me, he has not yet violated his vows, I was but an agent, – I was bribed, – do not kindle those fires for me.' I shudder, – I start up in a cold sweat. My rest, my appetite, are gone. Would to God you were out of this convent; – and O! would that I had never been instrumental to your release, then both of us might have escaped damnation to all eternity." I tried to pacify him, to assure him of his safety, but nothing could satisfy him but my solemn and sincere assurance that this was the last packet I would ever ask him to deliver. He departed tranquillized by this assurance; and I felt the dangers of my attempt multiplying around me every hour.

'This man was faithful, but he was timid; and what confidence can we have in a being whose right hand is held out to you, while his left trembles to be employed in transferring your secret to your enemy. This man died a few weeks after. I believe I owed his dying fidelity to the delirium that seized on his last moments. But what I suffered during those moments! – his death under such circumstances, and the unchristian joy I felt at it, were only in my mind stronger evidences against the unnatural state of life that could render such an event, and such feelings, almost necessary. It was on the evening after this, that I was surprised to see the Superior, with four of the monks, enter my cell. I felt this visit boded me no good. I trembled all over, while I received them with deference. The Superior seated himself opposite to me, arranging his seat so as that I was opposite the light. I did not understand what this precaution meant, but I conceive now, that he wished to watch every change in my countenance, while his was concealed from me. The four monks stood at the back of his chair; their arms were folded, their lips closed, their eyes half shut, their heads declined – they looked like men assembled reluctantly to witness the execution of a criminal. The Superior began, in a mild voice, "My son, you have been intently employed on your confession for some time – that was laudable. But have you, then, accused yourself of every crime your conscience charges you with?" "I have, my father." "Of all, you are sure?" "My father, I have accused myself of all I was conscious of. Who but God can penetrate the abysses of the heart? I have searched mine as far as I could." "And you have recorded all the accusations you found there?" "I have." "And you did not discover among them the crime of obtaining the means of writing out your confession, to abuse them to a very different purpose?" – This was coming to the point. I felt it necessary to summon my resolution – and I said, with a venial equivocation, "That is a crime of which my conscience *does not accuse me*." "My son, do not dissemble with your conscience, or with me. I should be even above it in your estimation; for if it errs and deceives you, it is to me you should apply to enlighten and direct it. But I see it is in vain to attempt to touch your heart. I make my last appeal to it in these plain words. A few moments only of indulgence await you – use them or abuse them, as you will. I have to ask you a few plain questions, which, if you refuse to answer, or do not answer truly, your blood be on your own head." I trembled, but I said, "My father, have I then refused to answer your questions?" "Your answers are all either interrogations or evasions. They must be direct and simple to the questions I am about to propose in the presence of these brethren. More depends on your answer than you are aware of. The warning voice breaks forth in spite of me." – Terrified at these words, and humbled to the wish to propitiate them, I rose from my chair – then gasping, I leant on it for support. I said, "My God! what is all this terrible preparation for? Of what am I guilty? Why am I summoned by this warning voice so often, whose warnings are only so many mysterious threatenings? Why am I not told of my offence?"

'The four monks, who had never spoken or lifted up their heads till that moment, now directed their livid eyes at me, and repeated, all together, in a voice that seemed to issue from the bottom of a sepulchre, "Your crime is –" The Superior gave them a signal to be silent, and this interruption increased my consternation. It is certain, that when we are conscious of guilt, we always suspect that a greater degree of it will be ascribed to us by others. Their consciences avenge the palliations of our own, by the most horrible exaggerations. I did not know of what crime they might be disposed to accuse me; and already I felt the accusation of my clandestine correspondence as dust in the balance of their resentment. I had heard the crimes of convents were sometimes unutterably atrocious; and I felt as anxious now for a distinct charge to be preferred against me, as I had a few moments before to evade it. These indefinite fears were soon exchanged for real ones, as the Superior proposed his questions. "You have procured a large quantity of paper – how did you employ it?" I recovered myself, and said, "As I ought to do." "How, in unburdening your conscience?" "Yes, in unburdening my conscience." "That is false; the greatest sinner on earth could not have blotted so many pages with the record of his crimes." "I have often been told in the convent, I *was* the greatest sinner on earth." "You equivocate again, and convert your ambiguities into reproaches – this will not do – you must answer plainly: For what purpose did you procure so much paper, and how have you employed it?" "I have told you already." "It was, then, employed in your confession?" – I was silent, but bowed assentingly. – "You can, then, shew us the proofs of your application to your duties. Where is the manuscript that contains your confession?" I blushed and hesitated, as I showed about half-a-dozen blotted and scrawled pages as my confession. It was ridiculous. It did not occupy more than a tenth part of the paper which I had received. "And this is your confession?" "It is."

"And you dare to say that you have employed all the paper entrusted to you for that purpose." – I was silent. "Wretch!" said the Superior, losing all patience, "disclose instantly for what purpose you have employed the paper granted you. Acknowledge instantly that it was for some purpose contrary to the interests of this house." – At these words I was roused. I saw again the cloven foot of interest peeping from beneath the monastic garb. I answered, "Why am I suspected if *you* are not guilty? What could I accuse you of? What could I complain of if there were no cause? Your own consciences must answer this question for me." At these words, the monks were again about to interpose, when the Superior, silencing them by a signal, went on with his matter-of-fact questions, that paralyzed all the energy of passion. "You will not tell me what you have done with the paper committed to you?" – I was silent. – "I enjoin you, by your holy obedience, to disclose it this moment." – His voice rose in passion as he spoke, and this operated as a signal on mine. I said, "You have no right, my father, to demand such a declaration." "Right is not the question now. I command you to tell me. I require your oath on the altar of Jesus Christ, and by the image of his blessed Mother." "You have no right to demand such an oath. I know the rules of the house – I am responsible to the confessor." "Do you, then, make a question between right and power? You shall soon feel, within these walls, they are the same." "I make no question – perhaps they are the same." "And you will not tell what you have done with those papers, blotted, doubtless, with the most infernal calumnies?" "I will not." "And you will take the consequences of your obstinacy on your own head?" "I will." And the four monks chorussed again, all in the same unnatural tone, "The consequences be on his own head." But while they spoke thus, two of them whispered in my ears, "Deliver up your papers, and all is well. The whole convent knows you have been writing." I answered, "I have nothing to give up – nothing on the faith of a monk. I have not a single page in my possession, but what you

162

have seized on." The monks, who had whispered in a conciliatory tone to me before, quitted me. They conversed in whispers with the Superior, who, darting on me a terrible look, exclaimed, "And you will not give up your papers?" "I have nothing to give up: Search my person – search my cell – every thing is open to you." "Every thing shall be soon," said the Superior in fury. In a moment the examination commenced. There was not an article of furniture in my cell that was not the object of their investigation. My chair and table were overturned, shaken, and finally broken, in the attempt to discover whether any papers had been secreted in them. The prints were snatched from the walls, – held up between them and the light. – Then the very frames were broken, to try if any thing was concealed in them. Then they examined my bed; – they threw all the furniture about the floor, they unripped the mattress, and tore out the straw; one of them, during this operation, actually applied his teeth to facilitate it, – and this malice of activity formed a singular contrast to the motionless and rigid torpor with which they had clothed themselves but a few moments before. All this time, I stood in the centre of the floor, as I was ordered, without turning to right or left. Nothing was found to justify their suspicions. They then surrounded me; and the examination of my person was equally rapid, minute, and indecorous. Every thing I wore was on the floor in a moment: The very seams of my habit were ript open; and, during the examination, I covered myself with one of the blankets they had taken from my bed. When it was over, I said, "Have you discovered any thing?" The Superior answered, in a voice of rage, struggling proudly, but vainly, with disappointment, "I have other means of discovery – prepare for them, and tremble when they are resorted to." At these words he rushed from my cell, giving a sign to the four monks to follow him. I was left alone. I had no longer any doubt of my danger. I saw myself exposed to the fury of men who would risk nothing to appease it. I watched, waited, trembled, at every step I heard in the gallery – at the sound of every door that opened or shut near me. Hours went on in this agony of suspense, and terminated at last without an event. No one came near me that night – the next was to be that of the great confession. In the course of the day, I took my place in the choir, trembling, and watching every eye. I felt as if every countenance was turned on me, and every tongue said in silence, "Thou art the man". Often I wished that the storm I felt was gathering around me, would burst at once. It is better to hear the thunder than to watch the cloud. It did not burst, however, then. And when the duties of the day were over, I retired to my cell, and remained there, pensive, anxious, and irresolute.

'The confession had begun; and as I heard the penitents, one by one, return from the church, and close the doors of their cells, I began to dread that I was to be excluded from approaching the holy chair, and that this exclusion from a sacred and indispensible right, was to be the commencement of some mysterious course of rigour. I waited, however, and was at last summoned. This restored my courage, and I went through my duties more tranquilly. After I had made my confession, only a few simple questions were proposed to me, as, Whether I could accuse myself of any *inward* breach of conventual duty? of any thing I had *reserved*? any thing in my conscience? &c. – and on my answering them in the negative, was suffered to depart. It was on that very night the porter died. My last packet had gone some days before, – all was safe and well. Neither voice or line could bear witness against me now, and hope began to revisit me, as I reflected that my brother's zealous industry would discover some other means for our future communication.

'All was profound calm for a few days, but the storm was to come soon enough. On the fourth evening after the confession, I was sitting alone in my cell, when I heard an unusual bustle in the convent. The bell was rung, – the new porter seemed in great agitation, – the Superior hurried to the parlour first, then to his cell, – then some of the elder monks were summoned. The younger whispered in the galleries, – shut their doors violently, – all seemed in agitation. In a domestic building, occupied by the smallest family, such circumstances would hardly be noticed, but, in a convent, the miserable monotony of what may be called their internal existence, gives an importance, – an interest, to the most trivial external circumstance in common life. I felt all this. I said to myself, "Something is going on." – I added, "Something is going on against me." I was right in both my conjectures. Late in the evening I was ordered to attend the Superior in his own apartment, – I said I was ready to go. Two minutes after the order was reversed, and I was desired to remain in my cell, and await the approach of the Superior, – I answered I was willing to obey. But this sudden change of orders filled me with an *indefinite* fear; and in all the changes of my life, and vicissitude of my feelings, I have never felt any fear so horrible. I walked up and down, I repeated incessantly, "My God protect me! my God strengthen me!" Then I dreaded to ask the protection of God, doubting whether the cause in which I was engaged merited his protection. My ideas, however, were all scattered by the sudden entrance of the Superior and the four monks who had attended him on the visit previous to the confession. At their entrance I rose, – no one desired me to sit down. The Superior advanced with a look of fury, and, dashing some papers on my table, said, "Is that your writing?" I threw a hurried and terrified eye over the papers, – *they were a copy of my memorial.* I had presence of mind enough to say, "That is not my writing." "Wretch! you equivocate, it is a copy of your writing." – I was silent. – "Here is a proof of it," he added, throwing down another paper. It was a copy of the memoir of the advocate, addressed to me, and which, by the influence of a superior court, they had not the power of withholding from me. I was expiring with anxiety to examine it, but I did not dare to glance at it. The Superior unfolded page after page. He said, "Read, wretch! read, – look into it, examine it line by line." I approached trembling, – glanced at it, – in the very first lines

I read *hope*. My courage revived. – I said, "My father, I acknowledge this to be the copy of my memorial. I demand your permission to read the answer of the advocate, you cannot refuse me this right." "Read it," said the Superior, and he flung it towards me.

'You may readily believe, Sir, that, under such circumstances, I could not read with very steady eyes; and my penetration was not at all quickened by the four monks disappearing from the cell, at a signal I did not see. The Superior and I were now alone. He walked up and down my cell, while I appeared to hang over the advocate's memoir. Suddenly he stopped; – he struck his hand with violence on the table, – the pages I was trembling over quivered from the violence of the blow, – I started from my chair. "Wretch," said the Superior, "when have such papers as those profaned the convent before? When, till your unhallowed entrance, were we insulted with the memoirs of legal advocates? How comes it that you have dared to –" "Do what, my father?" "Reclaim your vows, and expose *us* to all the scandal of a civil court and its proceedings." "I weighed it all against my own misery." "Misery! is it thus you speak of a conventual life, the only life that can promise tranquillity here, or ensure salvation hereafter." These words, uttered by a man convulsed by the most frantic passion, were their own refutation. My courage rose in proportion to his fury; and besides, I was driven to a point, and forced to act on my defence. The sight of the papers added to my confidence. I said, "My father, it is in vain to endeavour to diminish my repugnance to the monastic life; the proof that that repugnance is invincible lies before you. If I have been guilty of a step that violates the decorum of a convent, I am sorry, – but I am not reprehensible. Those who forced me into a convent, are guilty of the violence which is falsely ascribed to me. I am determined, if it be possible, to change my situation. You see the efforts I have already made, be assured they will never cease. Disappointment will only redouble their energy; and if it be in the power of heaven or earth to procure the annulment of my vows, there is no power in either I will not have recourse to." I expected he would not have heard me out, but he did. He even listened with calmness, and I prepared myself to encounter and repel that alternation of reproach and remonstrance, of solicitation and menace, which they so well know how to employ in a convent. "Your repugnance to a conventual life is then invincible?" "It is." "But to what do you object? – not to your duties, for you perform them with the most edifying punctuality, – not to the treatment you receive, for it has been the most indulgent that our discipline admits of, – not to the community itself, who are all disposed to cherish and love you; – of what do you complain?" "Of the life itself, – that comprehends every thing. I am not fit to be a monk." "Remember, I implore you, that though the forms of earthly courts must be obeyed, from the necessity that makes us dependent on human institutions, in all matters between man and man, they never can be available in matters between God and man. Be assured, my deluded child, that if all the courts on earth pronounced you absolved from your vows this moment, your own conscience never can absolve you. All your ignominious life, it will continue to reproach you with the violation of a vow, whose breach man has connived at, but God has not. And, at your last hour, how horrible will those reproaches be!" "Not so horrible as at the hour I took that vow, or rather at the hour when it was extorted." "Extorted!" "Yes, my father, yes, – I take Heaven to witness against you. On that disastrous morning, your anger, your remonstrances, your pleadings, were as ineffectual as they are now, till you flung the body of my mother before my feet." "And do you reproach me with my zeal in the cause of your salvation?" "I do not wish to reproach you. You know the step I have taken, you must be aware I will pursue it with all the powers of nature, – that I will never rest till my vows are annulled, while a hope of it remains, – and that a soul, determined as mine, can convert despair itself into hope. Surrounded, suspected, watched as I have been, I yet found the means of conveying my papers to the hands of the advocate. Calculate the strength of that resolution which could effectuate such a measure in the very heart of a convent. Judge of the futility of all future opposition, when you failed in defeating, or even detecting, the first steps of my design." At these words the Superior was silent. I believed I had made an impression on him. I added, "If you wish to spare the community the disgrace of my prosecuting my appeal within its walls, the alternative is easy. Let the door be left unguarded some day, connive at my escape, and my presence shall never molest or dishonour you another hour." "How! would you make me not only a witness, but an accomplice in your crime? Apostate from God, and plunged in perdition as you are, do you repay the hand stretched out to save you, by seizing it, that you may drag me into the infernal gulph along with you?" and he walked up and down the cell in the most violent agitation. This unlucky proposal operated on his master-passion, (for he was exemplarily rigid in discipline), and produced only convulsions of hostility. I stood waiting till this fresh burst had subsided, while he continued to exclaim incessantly, "My God, for what offence am I thus humiliated? – for what inconceivable crime is this disgrace precipitated on the whole convent? What will become of our character? What will all Madrid say?" "My father, whether an obscure monk lives, dies, or recalls his vows, is an object of little importance beyond the walls of his convent. They will forget me soon, and you will be consoled by the restored harmony of the discipline, in which I should always be a jarring note. Besides, all Madrid, with all the interest you ascribe to it, could never be made responsible for my salvation." He continued to walk up and down, repeating, "What will the world say? What will become of us?" till he had worked himself into a state of fury; and, suddenly turning on me, he exclaimed, "Wretch! renounce your horrible resolution, – renounce it this moment! I give you but five minutes for consideration." "Five thousand would make no change." "Tremble, then, lest you should not have life spared to see the fulfilment of your impious purposes."

'As he uttered these words he rushed from my cell. The

moments I passed during his absence were, I think, the most horrible of my life. Their terror was aggravated by darkness, for it
was now night, and he had carried away the light along with him.
My agitation did not at first permit me to observe this. I felt I was
in the dark, but knew not how or why. A thousand images of
indescribable horror rushed in a host on me. I had heard much of
the terrors of convents, – of their punishments, often carried to
the infliction of death, or of reducing their victim to a state in
which death would have been a blessing. Dungeons, chains and
scourges, swam before my eyes in a fiery mist. The threatening
words of the Superior appeared emblazoned on the darkened
walls of my cell in characters of flame. I shuddered, – I cried
aloud, though conscious that my voice would be echoed by no
friendly answering tones in a community of sixty persons, – such
is the sterility of humanity in a convent. At last my very fears
recovered me by their excess. I said to myself, "They dare not murder me, – they dare not incarcerate me; – they are answerable to
the court to which I have appealed for my forthcoming, – they
dare not be guilty of any violence." Just as I had come to this
comfortable conclusion, which indeed was the triumph of the
sophistry of hope, the door of my cell was thrown open, and the
Superior, attended by his four satellites, re-entered. My eyes were
dim from the darkness in which I had been left, but I could distinguish that they carried with them a rope and a piece of sackcloth.
I drew the most frightful presages from this apparatus. I altered
my reasoning in a moment, and instead of saying they dare not do
so and so, I instantly argued, "What dare they not do? I am in their
power, – they know it. I have provoked them to the utmost, – what
is it monks will not do in the impotence of their malignity? – what
is to become of me?" They advanced, and I imagined the rope was
to strangle me, and the sackcloth to inclose my murdered body.
A thousand images of blood swam before me, – a gush of fire
choaked up my respiration. The groans of a thousand victims
seemed to rise from the vaults of the convent, to which they had

been hurried by a fate like mine. I know not what is death, but I am convinced I suffered the agonies of many deaths in that moment. My first impulse was to throw myself on my knees. I said, "I am in your power, – I am guilty in your eyes, – accomplish your purpose, but do not keep me long in pain." The Superior, without heeding, or perhaps hearing me, said, "Now you are in the posture that becomes you." At hearing these words, which sounded less dreadful than I had feared, I prostrated myself to the ground. A few moments before I would have thought this a degradation, but fear is very debasing. I had a dread of violent means, – I was very young, and life was not the less attractive from its being arrayed only in the brilliant drapery of imagination. The monks observed my posture, – they feared its effect on the Superior. They said, in that choral monotony, – that *discordant unison* that had frozen my blood when I knelt in the same posture but a few nights before, "Reverend father, do not suffer yourself to be imposed on by this prostituted humiliation, – the time for mercy is past. You gave him his moments of deliberation, – he refused to avail himself of them. You come now not to listen to pleadings, but to inflict justice." At these words, that announced every thing horrible, I went on my knees from one to the other, as they all stood in a grim and executioner-like row. I said to each with tears, "Brother Clement, – Brother Justin, – why do you try to irritate the Superior against me? Why do you precipitate a sentence which, whether just or not, must be severe, since you are to be the executioners? What have I done to offend you? I interceded for you when you were guilty of any slight deviation – Is this my return?" "This is wasting time," said the monks. "Hold," said the Superior; "give him leave to speak. Will you avail yourself of the last moment of indulgence I can ever afford you, to renounce your horrible resolution of recalling your vows?" Those words renewed all my energies. I stood upright before them all. I said, in a loud distinct voice, "Never – I stand at the bar of God." "Wretch! you have renounced God." "Well, then, my father, I have only to hope that God will not renounce me. I have appealed to a bar also, over which you have no power." "But we have power here, and that you shall feel." He made a signal, and the four monks approached. I uttered one short cry of fear, but submitted the next moment. I felt convinced it was to be my last. I was astonished, when, instead of fastening the cords round my neck, they bound my arms with them. They then took off my habit, and covered me with the sackcloth. I made no resistance; but shall I confess to you, Sir, I felt some disappointment. I was prepared for death, but something worse than death appeared threatened in these preparations. When we are driven to the precipice of mortality, we spring forward with resolution, and often defeat the triumph of our murderers, by merging it in our own. But when we are led to it step by step, held often over it, and then withdrawn, we lose our resolution along with our patience; and feel, that the last blow would be mercy, compared with its long-suspended, slowly descending, wavering, mutilating, hesitating stroke. I was prepared for every thing but what followed. Bound with this rope as fast as a felon, or a galley-slave, and covered only with the sackcloth, they dragged me along the gallery. I uttered no cry, made no resistance. They descended the stairs that led to the church. I followed, or rather was dragged after them. They crossed the aisle; there was a dark passage near it which I had never observed before. We entered it. A low door at the end presented a frightful perspective. At sight of it I cried aloud, "You will not immure me? You will not plunge me in that horrible dungeon, to be withered by damps, and devoured by reptiles? No, you will not, – remember you are answerable for my life." At these words, they surrounded me; then, for the first time, I struggled, – I called for help; – this was the moment they waited for; they wanted some repugnance on my part. The signal was instantly given to a lay-brother, who waited in the passage, – the bell was rung, – that terrible bell, that requires every member of a convent to plunge into his cell, as something extraordinary is going on in the house. At the first toll I lost all hope. I felt as if not a living being was in existence but those who surrounded me, and who appeared, in the livid light of one taper burning faintly in that dismal passage, like spectres hurrying a condemned soul to his doom. They hurried me down the steps to this door, which was considerably below the level of the passage. It was a long time before they could open it; many keys were tried; perhaps they might have felt some agitation at the thoughts of the violence they were going to commit. But this delay increased my terrors beyond expression; I imagined this terrible vault had never been unclosed before; that I was to be the first victim inhumed within it; and that their determination was, I should never quit it alive. As these thoughts occurred, in unutterable agony I cried aloud, though I felt I was beyond all human hearing; but my cries were drowned in the jarring of the heavy door, as it yielded to the efforts of the monks, who, uniting their strength, pushed it with extended arms, grating all the way against the floor of the stone. The monks hurried me in, while the Superior stood at the entrance with the light, appearing to shudder at the view it disclosed. I had time to view all the furniture of what I thought my last abode. It was of stone: the roof formed an arch; a block of stone supported a crucifix, and a death's head, with a loaf and a pitcher of water. There was a mat on the floor, to lie on; another rolled up at the end of it formed a pillow. They flung me on it, and prepared to depart. I no longer struggled, for I knew escape was in vain, but I supplicated them at least to leave me a light; and I petitioned for this with as much earnestness as I could have done for my liberty. Thus it is that misery always breaks down the mind into petty details. We have not strength to comprehend the whole of our calamity. We feel not the mountain which is heaped on us, but the nearest grains press on and grind us. I said, "In Christian mercy leave me a light, if it be but to defend myself against the reptiles that must swarm here." And already I saw this was true, for some of extraordinary size, disturbed by the phænomenon of the light, came crawling down the walls. All this time the monks were straining their strength to close the heavy door; they did not utter a word. "I adjure you to leave me light, *if it is but to gaze on that skull*; fear not the exercise of sight can be any indulgence in this place; but still let me have a light; think that when I wish to pray, I must *feel my way* to that crucifix." As I spoke, the door was with difficulty closed and locked, and I heard their departing steps. You will hardly believe, Sir, that I slept profoundly; yet I did; but I would rather never sleep again, than awake so horribly. I awoke in *the darkness of day*. I was to behold the light no more; nor to watch those divisions of time, which by measuring our portions of suffering, appear to diminish them. When the clock strikes, we know an hour of wretchedness is past, never to return. My only time-keeper was the approach of the monk, who every day renewed my allowance of bread and water; and had he been the object I loved most on earth, the sound of his steps could not have made more delicious music. These æras by which we compute the hours of darkness and inanity are inconceivable to any but those who are situated as I was. You have heard, Sir, no doubt, that the eye which, on its being first immersed into darkness, appears deprived of the power of vision for ever, acquires, imperceptibly, a power of accommodating itself to its darkened sphere, and even of distinguishing objects by a kind of conventional light. The mind certainly possesses the same power, otherwise, how could I have had the power to reflect, to summon some resolution, and even to indulge some hope, in this frightful abode? Thus it is, when all the world seems sworn to hostility against us, we turn friends to ourselves with all the obstinacy of despair; – and *while all the world is flattering and deifying us, we are the perpetual victims of lassitude and self-reproach*.

'The prisoner whose hours are visited by a dream of emancipation, is less a prey to ennui than the sovereign on a throne, begirt with adulation, voluptuousness and satiety. I reflected that all my papers were safe, – that my cause was prosecuting with vigour, – that, owing to my brother's zeal, I had the ablest advocate in Madrid, – that they dared not murder me, and were answerable with the whole credit of the house for my re-appearance whenever the courts demanded it, – that the very rank of my family was a powerful protection, though none of them but my generous fiery Juan was probably favourable to me; – that if I was permitted to receive and read the advocate's first memoir, even through the hands of the Superior, it was absurd to imagine that I could be denied intercourse with him in a more advanced and important stage of the business. These were the suggestions of my hope, and they were plausible enough. What were the suggestions of my despair, I shudder even at this moment to reflect on. The most terrible of all was, that I might be murdered *conventually* before it was possible that my liberation could be accomplished.

'Such, Sir, were my reflections; you may ask, what were my occupations? My situation supplied me with those, and, revolting as they were, they were still occupations. I had my devotions to perform; religion was my only resource in solitude and darkness, and while I prayed only for liberty and peace, I felt I was not at least insulting God by the prayers of hypocrisy, which I would have been compelled to utter in the choir. There I was obliged to join in a sacrifice that was odious to me, and offensive to him; – in my dungeon I offered up the sacrifice of my heart, and felt it was not unacceptable. During the glimpse of light afforded me by the approach of the monk who brought me bread and water, I arranged the crucifix so as that I could feel it when I awoke. This was very often, and not knowing whether it was day or night, I uttered my prayers at random. I knew not whether it was matins or vespers; there was neither morning or evening for me, but it was like a talisman to me to touch the crucifix, and I said as I felt for it, "My God is with me in the darkness of my dungeon; he is a God who has suffered, and can pity me. My extremest point of wretchedness can be nothing to what this symbol of divine humiliation for the sins of man, has undergone for mine!" – and I kissed the sacred image (with lips wandering from the darkness) with more emotion than I had ever felt when I saw it illuminated by the blaze of tapers, amid the elevation of the Host, the tossing of the perfumed censers, the gorgeous habits of the priests, and the breathless prostration of the faithful. I had other occupations less dignified, but quite as necessary. The reptiles, who filled the hole into which I had been thrust, gave me opportunity for a kind of constant, miserable, ridiculous hostility. My mat had been placed in the very seat of warfare; – I shifted it, – still they pursued me; – I placed it against the wall, – the cold crawling of their bloated limbs often awoke me from my sleep, and still oftener made me shudder when awake. I struck at them; – I tried to terrify them by my voice, to arm myself against them by the help of my mat; but above all, my anxiety was ceaseless to defend my bread from their loathsome incursions, and my pitcher of water from their dropping into it. I adopted a thousand precautions, trivial as they were inefficacious, but still there was occupation. I do assure you, Sir, I *had more to do in my dungeon than in my cell*. To be fighting with reptiles in the dark appears the most horrible struggle that can be assigned to man; but what is it compared to his combat with those reptiles which his own heart hourly engenders in a cell, and of which, if his heart be the mother, solitude is the father. I had another employment, – I cannot call it occupation. I had calculated with myself, that sixty minutes made an hour, and sixty seconds a minute. I began to think I could keep time as accurately as any clock in a convent, and measure the hours of my confinement or – my release. So I sat and counted sixty; a doubt always occurred to me, that I *was counting them faster than the clock*. Then I wished to be the clock, that I might have no feeling, no *motive for hurrying on the approach of time*. Then I reckoned slower. Sleep sometimes overtook me in this exercise, (perhaps I adopted it from that hope); but when I awoke,

I applied to it again instantly. Thus I oscillated, reckoned, and measured time on my mat, while time withheld its delicious diary of rising and setting suns, – of the dews of dawn and of twilight, – of the glow of morning and the shades of the evening. When my reckoning was broken by my sleep, (and I knew not whether I slept by day or by night), I tried to eke it out by my incessant repetition of minutes and seconds, and I succeeded; for I always consoled myself, that whatever hour it was, sixty minutes must go to an hour. Had I led this life much longer, I might have been converted into the idiot, who as I have read, from the habit of watching a clock, imitated its mechanism so well, that when it was down, he sounded the hour as faithfully as ear could desire. Such was my life. On the fourth day, (as I reckoned by the visits of the monk), he placed my bread and water on the block of stone as usual, but hesitated for some time before he departed. In fact, he felt a repugnance at delivering an intimation of hope; it was not consonant either to his profession, or the office which, in the wantonness of monastic malignity, he had accepted as penance. You shudder at this, Sir, but it is nevertheless true; this man thought he was doing service to God, by witnessing the misery of a being incarcerated amid famine, darkness, and reptiles. He recoiled when his penance terminated. Alas! how false is that religion which makes our aggravating the sufferings of others our mediator with that God who willeth all men to be saved. But this is a question to be solved in convents. This man hesitated long, struggled with the ferocity of his nature, and at last departed and bolted the door, that he might indulge it a few moments longer. Perhaps in those moments he prayed to God, and ejaculated a petition, that this protraction of *my* sufferings might be accepted as a melioration of his own. I dare say he was very sincere; but if men were taught to look to the *one great Sacrifice*, would they be so ready to believe that their own, or those of others, could ever be accepted as a commutation for it? You are surprised, Sir, at these sentiments from a Catholic; but another part of my story will disclose the cause of my uttering them. At length this man could delay his commission no longer. He was obliged to tell me that the Superior was moved by my sufferings, that God had touched his heart in my behalf, and that he permitted me to quit my dungeon. The words were scarce out of his mouth, before I rose, and rushed out with a shout that electrified him. Emotion is very unusual in convents, and the expression of joy a phænomenon. I had gained the passage before he recovered his surprise; and the convent walls, which I had considered as those of a prison, now appeared the area of emancipation. Had its doors been thrown open to me that moment, I don't think I could have felt a more exquisite sensibility of liberty. I fell on my knees in the passage to thank God. I thanked him for the light, for the air, for the restored power of respiration. As I was uttering these effusions, (certainly not the least sincere that were ever poured forth within those walls), suddenly I became sick, – my head swam round, – I had feasted on the light to excess. I fell to the ground, and remember nothing for many hours afterwards. When I recovered my senses, I was in my cell, which appeared just as I had left it; it was day-light, however; and I am persuaded that circumstance contributed more to my restoration, than the food and cordials with which I was now liberally supplied. All that day I heard nothing, and had time to meditate on the motives of the indulgence with which I had been treated. I conceived that an order might have been issued to the Superior to produce me, or, at all events, that he could not prevent those interviews between the advocate and me, which the former might insist on as necessary while my cause was carrying on. Towards evening some monks entered my cell; they talked of indifferent matters, – affected to consider my absence as the result of indisposition, and I did not undeceive them. They mentioned, as if incidentally, that my father and mother, overwhelmed with grief at the scandal I had brought on religion by appealing against my vows, had quitted Madrid. At this intelligence I felt much more emotion than I

showed. I asked them how long I had been *ill*? They answered,
Four days. This confirmed my suspicions with regard to the cause
of my liberation, for the advocate's letter had mentioned, that
on the fifth day he would require an interview with me on the
subject of my appeal. They then departed; but I was soon to
receive another visitor. After vespers, (from which I was excused),
the Superior entered my cell alone. He approached my bed. I
attempted to rise, but he desired me to compose myself, and sat
down near me with a calm but penetrating look. He said, "You
have now found we have it in our power to punish." – "I never
doubted it." – "Before you tempt that power to an extremity,
which, I warn you, you will not be able to endure, I come to
demand of you to resign this desperate appeal against your vows,
which can terminate only in dishonouring God, and disappoint-
ing yourself." – "My father, without entering into details, which
the steps taken on both sides have rendered wholly unneces-
sary, I can only reply, that I will support my appeal with every
power Providence puts within my reach, and that my punishment has only confirmed my resolution." – "And this is your final
determination?" – "It is, and I implore you to spare me all further
importunity, – it will be useless." He was silent for a long time; at
length he said, "And you will insist on your right to an interview
with the advocate to-morrow?" – "I shall claim it." – "It will not
be necessary, however, to mention to him your late punishment."
These words struck me. I comprehended the meaning which he
wished to conceal in them, and I answered, "It may not be necessary, but it will probably be expedient." – "How? – would you
violate the secrets of the house, while you are yet within its
walls?" – "Pardon me, my father, for saying, that you must be
conscious of having exceeded your duty, to be so anxious for its
concealment. It is not, then, the secrets of your discipline, but the
violation of it, I shall have to disclose." – He was silent, and I
added, "If you have abused your power, though I have been the
sufferer, it is you who are guilty." – The Superior rose, and quit-

ted my cell in silence. The next morning I attended matins. Service went on as usual, but at its conclusion, when the community were about to rise from their knees, the Superior, striking the desk violently with his hand, commanded them all to remain in the same posture. He added, in a thundering voice, "The intercession of this whole community with God is supplicated for a monk who, abandoned by the Spirit of God, is about to commit an act dishonourable to Him, disgraceful to the church, and infallibly destructive of his own salvation." At these terrible sounds the monks, all shuddering, sunk on their knees again. I was kneeling among them, when the Superior, calling me by my name, said aloud, "Rise, wretch! rise, and pollute not our incense with your unhallowed breath!" I rose trembling and confounded, and shrunk to my cell, where I remained till I was summoned by a monk to the parlour, to meet the advocate, who waited for me there. This interview was rendered quite ineffective by the presence of the monk, who was desired by the Superior to witness our conference, and whom the advocate could not order away. When we entered into details, he interrupted us with declarations, that his duty would not permit such a violation of the rules of the parlour. When I asserted a fact, he contradicted it, gave me the lie repeatedly, and finally disturbed the purpose of our conference so completely, that in mere self-defence, I spoke of the subject of my punishment, which he could not deny, and to which my livid looks bore a testimony invincible. The moment I spoke on this subject the monk became silent, (he was treasuring every word for the Superior), and the advocate redoubled his attention. He took minutes of every thing I said, and appeared to lay more stress on the matter than I had imagined, or indeed wished for. When the conference was over, I retired again to my cell. The advocate's visits were repeated for some days, till he had obtained the information requisite for carrying on my suit; and during this time, my treatment in the convent was such as to give me no cause of complaint; and this doubtless was the motive of

their forbearance. But the moment those visits ceased, the warfare of persecution commenced. They considered me as one
with whom no measures were to be kept, and they treated me
accordingly. I am convinced it was their intention that I should
not survive the events of my appeal; at least it is certain they left
nothing unaccomplished that could verify that intention. This
began, as I mentioned, on the day of the advocate's last visit. The
bell rung for refection; – I was going to take my place as usual,
when the Superior said, "Hold, – place a mat for him in the midst
of the hall." This was done, and I was required to sit down on it,
and supplied with bread and water. I eat a little, which I moist-
ened with my tears. I foresaw what I had to undergo, and did not
attempt to expostulate. When grace was about to be said, I was
desired to stand without the door, lest my presence should frustrate the benediction they implored.

'I retired, and when the bell rung for vespers, I presented myself
among the rest at the door of the church. I was surprised to find it
shut, and they all assembled. When the bell ceased, the Superior
appeared, the door was opened, and the monks hurried in. I was
following, when the Superior repelled me, exclaiming, "*You wretch,
you!* Remain where you are." I obeyed; and the whole community
entered the church, while I remained at the door. This species of
excommunication produced its full effect of terror on me. As the
monks slowly came out, and cast on me looks of silent horror,
I thought myself the most abject being on earth; I could have hid
myself under the pavement till the event of my appeal was over.

'The next morning, when I went to matins, the same scene
was renewed, with the horrible addition of audible reproaches,
and almost imprecations, denounced against me, as they entered
and returned. I knelt at the door. I did not answer a word.
I returned not "railing for railing", and lifted up my heart with a
trembling hope, that this offering might be as acceptable to God
as the sonorous chaunt of the choir, which I still felt it was miserable to be excluded from joining.

'In the course of the day, every sluice of monastic malignity and vengeance was thrown open. I appeared at the door of the refectory. I did not dare to enter. Alas! Sir, how are monks employed in the hour of refection? It is an hour, when, while they swallow their meal, they banquet on the little scandal of the convent. They ask, 'Who was late at prayers? Who is to undergo penance?' This serves them for conversation; and the details of their miserable life supply no other subject for that mixture of exhaustless malignity and curiosity, which are the inseparable twins of monastic birth. As I stood at the door of the refectory, a lay-brother, to whom the Superior nodded, bid me retire. I went to my cell, waited for several hours, and just when the bell for vespers had rung, was supplied with food, which famine itself would have shrunk from. I tried to swallow it, but could not, and hurried away, as the bell tolled, to attend vespers; for I wished to have no cause of complaint against my neglect of duties. I hastened down. The door was again shut; service began; and again I was compelled to retire without partaking of it. The next day I was excluded from matins; the same degrading scene was acted over when I appeared at the door of the refectory. Food was sent to my cell, that a dog would have rejected; and the door was shut when I attempted to enter the church. A thousand circumstances of persecution, too contemptible, too minute, either for recollection or repetition, but infinitely harassing to the sufferer, were heaped on me every day. Imagine, Sir, a community of upwards of sixty persons, all sworn to each other to make the life of one individual insupportable; joined in a common resolution to insult, harass, torment, and persecute him; and then imagine how that individual can support such a life. I began to dread the preservation of my reason – of my existence, which, miserable as it was, still fed on the hope of my appeal. I will sketch one day of my life for you. *Ex uno disce omnes.*[12] I went down to matins, and knelt at the door; I did not dare to enter. When I retired to my cell, I found the crucifix taken away. I was about to go to the

Superior's apartment to complain of this outrage; in the passage I happened to meet a monk and two boarders. They all shrunk close to the walls; they drew in their garments, as if trembling to encounter the pollution of my touch. I said mildly, "There is no danger; the passage is wide enough." The monk replied, "Apage Satana.[13] My children," addressing the boarders, "repeat with me, apage Satana; avoid the approach of that demon, who insults the habit he desecrates." They did so; and to render the exorcism complete, they spit in my face as they passed. I wiped it off, and thought how little of the spirit of Jesus was to be found in the house of his nominal brethren. I proceeded to the apartment of the Superior, and knocked timidly at the door. I heard the words, "Enter in peace;" and I prayed that it might be in peace. As I opened the door, I saw several monks assembled with the Superior. The latter uttered an exclamation of horror when he saw me, and threw his robe over his eyes; the monks understood the signal; the door was closed, and I was excluded. That day I waited several hours in my cell before any food was brought me. There is no state of feeling that exempts us from the wants of nature. I had no food for many days requisite for the claims of adolescence, which were then rapidly manifesting themselves in my tall, but attenuated frame. I descended to the kitchen to ask for my share of food. The cook crossed himself as I appeared at the door; for even at the door of the kitchen I faultered at the threshold. He had been taught to consider me as a demon incarnate, and shuddered, while he asked, "What do you want?" – "Food," I replied; "food; – that is all." – "Well, you shall have it – but come no further – there is food." And he flung me the offal of the kitchen on the earth; and I was so hungry, that I devoured it eagerly. The next day I was not so lucky; the cook had learned the secret of the convent, (that of tormenting those whom they no longer have hopes of commanding), and mixed the fragments he threw to me, with ashes, hair and dust. I could hardly pick out a morsel that, famished as I was, was eatable. They allowed me no water in my cell; I was not permitted to partake of it at refection; and, in the agonies of thirst, aggravated by my constant solicitude of mind, I was compelled to kneel at the brink of the well, (as I had no vessel to drink out of), and take up the water in my hand, or lap it like a dog. If I descended to the garden for a moment, they took the advantage of my absence to enter my cell, and remove or destroy every article of furniture. I have told you that they took away my crucifix. I had still continued to kneel and repeat my prayers before the table on which it stood. That was taken away, – table, chair, missal, rosary, every thing, disappeared gradually; and my cell presented nothing but four bare walls, with a bed, on which they had rendered it impossible for me to taste repose. Perhaps they dreaded I might, however, and they hit on an expedient, which, if it had succeeded, might have deprived me of reason as well as repose.

'I awoke one night, and saw my cell in flames; I started up in horror, but shrunk back on perceiving myself surrounded by demons, who, clothed in fire, were breathing forth clouds of it around me. Desperate with horror, I rushed against the wall, and found what I touched was cold. My recollection returned, and I comprehended, that these were hideous figures scrawled in phosphorus, to terrify me. I then returned to my bed, and as the day-light approached, observed these figures gradually decline. In the morning, I took a desperate resolution of forcing my way to the Superior, and speaking to him. I felt my reason might be destroyed amid the horrors they were surrounding me with.

'It was noon before I could work myself up to execute this resolution. I knocked at his cell, and when the door was opened, he exhibited the same horror as at my former intrusion, but I was not to be repelled. "My father, I require you to hear me, nor will I quit this spot till you do so." – "Speak." – "They famish me, – I am not allowed food to support nature." – "Do you deserve it?" – "Whether I do or not, neither the laws of God or man have yet condemned me to die of hunger; and if *you* do, you commit murder." – "Have you any thing else to complain of?" – "Every thing; I am not allowed to enter the church, – I am forbid to pray, – they have stripped my cell of crucifix, rosary and the vessel for holy water. It is impossible for me to perform my devotions even alone." – "*Your* devotions!" – "My father, though I am not a monk, may I not still be a Christian?" – "In renouncing your vows, you have abjured your claim to either character." – "But I am still a human being, and as such – But I appeal not to your humanity, I call on your authority for protection. Last night, my cell was covered with representations of fiends. I awoke in the midst of flames and spectres." – "So you will at the last day!" – "My punishment will then be enough, it need not commence already." – "These are the phantoms of your conscience." – "My father, if you will deign to examine my cell, you will find the traces of phosphorus on the walls." – "*I* examine your cell? *I* enter it?" – "Am I then to expect no redress? Interpose your authority for the sake of the house over which you preside. Remember that, when my appeal becomes public, all these circumstances will become so too, and you are to judge what degree of credit they will attach to the community." "Retire!" I did so, and found my application attended to, at least with regard to food, but my cell remained in the same dismantled state, and I continued under the same desolating interdiction from all communion, religious or social. I assure you, with truth, that so horrible was this amputation from life to me, that I have walked hours in the cloister and the passages, to place myself in the way of the monks, who, I knew, as they passed, would bestow on me some malediction or reproachful epithet. Even this was better than the withering silence which surrounded me. I began almost to receive it as a customary salutation, and always returned it with a benediction. In a fortnight my appeal was to be decided on; this was a circumstance I was kept in ignorance of, but the Superior had received a notification of it, and this precipitated his resolution to deprive me of the benefit of its eventual success, by one of the most horrible schemes that ever entered the human (I retract the expression) the monastic heart. I received an indistinct intimation of it the very night after my application to the Superior; but had I been apprised, from the first, of the whole extent and bearings of their purpose, what resources could I have employed against it?

'That evening I had gone into the garden; my heart felt unusually oppressed. Its thick troubled beatings, seemed like the vibrations of a time-piece, as it measures our approach to some hour of sorrow.

'It was twilight; the garden was empty; and kneeling on the ground, in the open air, (the only oratory they had left me), I attempted to pray. The attempt was in vain; – I ceased to articulate sounds that had no meaning; – and, overcome by a heaviness of mind and body inexpressible, I fell on the ground, and remained extended on my face, torpid, but not senseless. Two figures passed, without perceiving me; they were in earnest conversation. One of them said, "More vigorous measures must be adopted. You are to blame to delay them so long. You will be answerable for the disgrace of the whole community, if you persist in this foolish lenity." – "But his resolution remains unbroken," said the Superior, (for it was he). – "It will not be proof against the measure I have proposed." – "He is in your hands then; but remember I will not be accountable for –" They were by this time out of hearing. I was less terrified than you will believe, by what I had heard. Those who have suffered much, are always ready to exclaim, with the unfortunate Agag, "Surely the bitterness of death is past." They know not, that that is the very moment when the sword is unsheathed to hew them in pieces. That night, I had not been long asleep, when I was awoke by a singular noise in my cell: I started up, and listened. I thought I heard some one hurry away barefooted. I knew I had no lock to my door, and could not prevent the intrusion of any one into my cell who pleased to visit it; but still I believed the discipline of the convent too strict to allow of this. I composed myself again, but was hardly asleep, when I was again awoke by something that touched me. I started up again; a soft voice near me said in whispers, "Compose yourself; I am your friend." – "My friend? Have I one? – but why visit me at this hour?" – "It is the only hour at which I am permitted to visit you." – "But who are you, then?" – "One whom these walls can never exclude. One to whom, if you devote yourself, you may expect services beyond the power of man." – There was something frightful in these words. I cried out, "Is it the enemy of souls that is tempting me?" As I uttered these words, a monk rushed in from the passage, (where he had been evidently waiting, for his dress was on). He exclaimed, "What is the matter? You have alarmed me by your cries, – you pronounced the name of the infernal spirit, – what have you seen? what is it you fear?" I recovered myself, and said, "I have seen or heard nothing extraordinary. I have had frightful dreams, that is all. Ah! Brother St Joseph, no wonder, after passing such days, my nights should be disturbed."

'The monk retired, and the next day passed as usual; but at night the same whispering sounds awoke me again. The preceding night these sounds had only startled me; they now alarmed me. In the darkness of night, and the solitude of my cell, this repeated visitation overcame my spirits. I began almost to admit the idea that I was exposed to the assaults of the enemy of man. I repeated a prayer, but the whisper, which seemed close to my ear, still continued. It said, "Listen, – listen to me, and be happy. Renounce your vows, place yourself under my protection, and you shall have no cause to complain of the exchange. Rise from your bed, trample on the crucifix which you will find at the foot of it, spit on the picture of the Virgin that lies beside it, and –" At these words I could not suppress a cry of horror. The voice ceased in a moment, and the same monk, who occupied the cell next to mine, rushed in with the same exclamations as on the preceding night; and, as he entered my cell, the light in his hand shewed a crucifix, and a picture of the blessed Virgin, *placed* at the foot of my bed. I had sprung up when the monk entered my cell; I saw them, and recognized them to be the very crucifix and picture of the Virgin which had been taken from my cell. All the hypocritical outcries of the monk, at the disturbance I had again caused him, could not efface the impression which this slight circumstance made on me. I believed, and not without reason, they had been left there by the hands of some human tempter. I started, awake to this horrible imposition, and required the monk to leave my cell. He demanded, with a frightful paleness in his looks, why I had again disturbed him? said it was impossible to obtain repose while such noises were occurring in my cell; and, finally, stumbling over the crucifix and picture, demanded how they came there. I answered, "You know best." – "How, then, do you accuse me of a compact with the infernal demon? By what means could these have been brought to your cell?" – "By the very hands that removed them," I answered; and these words appeared to produce an effect on him for a moment; but he retired, declaring, that if the nightly disturbance in my cell continued, he must represent it to the Superior. I answered, the disturbance did not proceed from me, – but I trembled for the following night.

'I had reason to tremble. That night, before I lay down, I repeated prayer after prayer, the terrors of my excommunication pressing heavy on my soul. I also repeated the prayers against possession or temptation by the evil spirit. These I was compelled to utter from memory, for I have told you that they had not left a book in my cell. In repeating these prayers, which were very long, and somewhat verbose, I at last fell asleep. That sleep was not to continue long. I was again addressed by the voice that whispered close to my bed. The moment I heard it, I rose without fear. I crept around my cell with my hands extended, and my feet bare. I could feel nothing but the empty walls, – not a single object, tangible or visible, could I encounter. I lay down again, and had hardly begun the prayer with which I tried to fortify myself, when the same sounds were repeated close to my ear, without the possibility either of my discovering from whence they proceeded, or preventing their reaching me. Thus I was completely deprived of sleep; and if I dozed for a moment, the same terrible sounds were re-echoed in my dreams. I became feverish from want of rest. The night was passed in watching for these sounds, or listening to them, and the day in wild conjectures or fearful anticipations. I felt a mixture of terror and impatience inconceivable at the approach of night. I had a consciousness of imposture the whole time, but this gave me no consolation, for there is a point to which human malice and mischief may be carried, that would baffle those of a demon. Every night the persecution was renewed, and every night it became more terrible. At times the voice would suggest to me the most unutterable impurities, – at another, blasphemies that would make a demon shudder. Then it would applaud me in a tone of derision, and assure me of the final success of my appeal, then change to the most appalling menaces. The wretched sleep I obtained, during the intervals of this visitation, was any thing but refreshing. I would awake in a cold perspiration, catching at the bed-furniture, and repeating in an inarticulate voice, the last sounds that had rung in my closing ears. I would start up and see the bed surrounded by monks, who assured me they had been disturbed by my cries, – that they had hurried in terror to my cell. Then they would cast looks of fear and consternation on each other and on me; say, "something extraordinary is the matter, – something presses on your mind that you will not disburden it of." They implored me, in the most awful names, and for the interests of my salvation, to disclose the cause of these extraordinary visitations. At these words, however agitated before, I always became calm. I said, "Nothing is the matter, – why do you intrude into my cell?" They shook their heads, and affected to retire slowly and reluctantly, as if from pity of my dreadful situation, while I repeated, "Ah, Brother Justin, ah Brother Clement, I see you, I understand you, – remember there is a God in heaven."

'One night I lay for a considerable time without hearing any sound. I fell asleep, but was soon awoke by an extraordinary light. I sat up in my bed, and beheld displayed before me the mother of God, in all the glorious and irradiated incarnation of beatitude. She hovered, rather than stood, in an atmosphere of light at the foot of my bed, and held a crucifix in her hand, while she appeared to invite me, with a benign action, to kiss the five mysterious wounds.* For a moment I almost believed in the actual presence of this glorious visitor, but just then *the voice* was heard louder than ever, "Spurn them, – spit on them, – you are mine, and I claim this homage from my vassal." At these words the figure disappeared instantly, and the voice was renewing its whispers, but they were repeated to an insensible ear, for I fell into a swoon. I could easily distinguish between this state and sleep, by the deadly sickness, the cold sweats, and the horrid sense of *eva-nition*, that preceded it, and by the gasping, sobbing, choking efforts that attended my recovery. In the mean time the whole community carried on and even aggravated the terrible delusion, which, while it was my torment to detect, it was my greater to be the victim of. When art assumes the omnipotence of reality, when we feel we suffer as much from an illusion as from truth, our sufferings lose all dignity and all consolation. We turn demons against ourselves, and laugh at what we are writhing under. All day long I was exposed to the stare of horror, the shudder of sus-picion, and, worst of all, the hastily-averted glance of hypocritical commiseration, that dropt its pitying ray on me for a moment, and was then instantly raised to heaven, as if to implore forgive-ness for the involuntary crime of compassionating one whom God had renounced. When I encountered any of them in the gar-den, they would strike into another walk, and cross themselves in

---

* Vide Mosheim's *Ecclesiastical History* for the truth of this part of the narra-tive. I have suppressed circumstances in the original too horrible for modern ears.

my sight. If I met them in the passages of the convent, they drew their garments close, turned their faces to the wall, and told their beads as I went by. If I ventured to dip my hands in the holy water that stood at the door of the church, it was thrown out before my face. Certain extraordinary precautions were adopted by the whole community against the power of the evil one. Forms of exorcism were distributed, and additional prayers were used in the service of matins and vespers. A report was industriously diffused, that Satan was permitted to visit a favoured and devoted servant of his in the convent, and that all the brethren might expect the redoubled malice of his assaults. The effect of this on the young boarders was indescribable. They flew with the speed of lightning from me, whenever they saw me. If accident forced us to be near each other for a moment, they were armed with holy water, which they flung at me in pailfuls; and when that failed, what cries, – what convulsions of terror! They knelt, – they screamed, – they shut their eyes, – they cried, "Satan have mercy on me, – do not fix your infernal talons on me, – take your victim," and they mentioned my name. The terror that I inspired I at last began to feel. I began to believe myself – I know not what, whatever they thought me. This is a dreadful state of mind, but one impossible to avoid. In some circumstances, where the whole world is against us, we begin to take its part against ourselves, to avoid the withering sensation of being alone on our own side. Such was my appearance, too, my flushed and haggard look, my torn dress, my unequal gait, my constant internal muttering, and my complete isolation from the habits of the house, that it was no wonder I should justify, by my exterior, all of horrible and awful that might be supposed passing in my mind. Such an impression I must have made on the minds of the younger members. They had been taught to hate me, but their hatred was now combined with fear, and such a union is the most terrible amid all the complications of human passion. Desolate as my cell was, I retired to it early, as I was excluded from the exercises of the community. The bell for vespers would ring, I would hear the steps of those who were hastening to join in the service of God, and tedious as that service had once appeared to me, I would now have given worlds to be permitted to join in it, as a defence against that *horrible midnight mass of Satan**, that I was awaiting to be summoned to. I knelt however in my cell, and repeated what prayers I could recollect, while every toll of the bell struck on my heart, and the chaunt of the choir from below sounded like a repulsive echo to an answer which my fears already anticipated from heaven.

'One evening that I still continued to pray, and audibly, as the monks passed my cell they said, "Do *you* presume to pray? Die, desperate wretch, – die and be damned. Precipitate yourself into the infernal gulph at once, no longer desecrate these walls by your presence." At these words I only redoubled my prayers; but this gave greater offence, for churchmen cannot bear to hear prayers uttered in a form different from their own. The cry of a solitary individual to God, sounds like profanation in their ears. They ask, Why do they not employ our form? How dare they hope to be heard? Alas! is it forms then that God regards? or is it not rather the prayer of the heart which alone reaches him, and prospers in its petition? As they called out, passing my cell, "Perish, impious wretch, perish, – God will not hear you," I answered them on my knees with blessings – which of us had the spirit of prayer? That night was one of trial I could no longer support. My frame was exhausted, my mind excited, and, owing to our frail nature, this battle of the senses and soul is never long carried on without the worst side remaining conqueror. I was no sooner laid down than the voice began to whisper. I began to pray, but my head swam round, my eyes flashed fire, – fire almost tangible, my

* This expression is not exaggerated. In the dreams of sorcery, or of imposture, the evil spirit was supposed to perform a mass in derision; and in Beaumont and Fletcher there is mention of *'howling a black Santis'*, i.e. Satan's mass.

cell appeared in flames. Recollect my frame worn out with famine, my mind worn out with persecution. I struggled with what I was conscious was delirium, – but this consciousness aggravated its horror. It is better to be mad at once, than to believe that all the world is sworn to think and *make* you be so, in spite of your own consciousness of your sanity. The whispers this night were so horrible, so full of ineffable abominations, of – I cannot think of them, – that they *maddened my very ear*. My senses seemed deranged along with my intellect. I will give you an instance, it is but a slight one, of the horrors which –' Here the Spaniard whispered Melmoth.* The hearer shuddered, and the Spaniard went on in an agitated tone.

'I could bear it no longer. I sprung from my bed, I ran through the gallery like a maniac, knocking at the doors of the cells, and exclaiming, "Brother such a one, pray for me, – pray for me, I beseech you." I roused the whole convent. Then I flew down to the church; it was open, and I rushed in. I ran up the aisle, I precipitated myself before the altar, I embraced the images, I clung to the crucifix with loud and reiterated supplications. The monks, awakened by my outcries, or perhaps on the watch for them, descended in a body to the church, but, perceiving I was there, they would not enter, – they remained at the doors, with lights in their hands, gazing on me. It was a singular contrast between me, hurrying round the church almost in the dark, (for there were but a few lamps burning dimly), and the groupe at the door, whose expression of horror was strongly marked by the light, which appeared to have deserted me to concentrate itself among them. The most impartial person on earth might have supposed me deranged, or possessed, or both, from the state in which they saw

---

* We do not venture to guess at the horrors of this whisper, but every one conversant with ecclesiastical history knows, that *Tetzel* offered indulgences in Germany, even on the condition that the sinner had been guilty of the *impossible* crime of violating the mother of God.

me. Heaven knows, too, what construction might have been put on my wild actions, which the surrounding darkness exaggerated and distorted, or on the prayers which I uttered, as I included in them the horrors of the temptation against which I implored protection. Exhausted at length, I fell to the ground, and remained there, without the power of moving, but able to hear and observe every thing that passed. I heard them debate whether they should leave me there or not, till the Superior commanded them to remove that abomination from the sanctuary; and such was the terror of me into which they had *acted* themselves, that he had to repeat his orders before he could procure obedience to them. They approached me at last, with the same caution that they would an infected corse, and dragged me out by the habit, leaving me on the paved floor before the door of the church. They then retired, and in this state I actually fell asleep, and continued so till I was awoke by the bell for matins. I recollected myself, and attempted to rise; but my having slept on a damp floor, when in a fever from terror and excitement, had so cramped my limbs, that I could not accomplish this without the most exquisite pain. As the community passed in to matins, I could not suppress a few cries of pain. They must have seen what was the matter, but not one of them offered me assistance, nor did I dare to implore it. By slow and painful efforts, I at last reached my cell; but, shuddering at the sight of the bed, I threw myself on the floor for repose.

'I was aware that some notice must be taken of a circumstance so extraordinary – that such a subversion of the order and tranquillity of a convent, would force an inquiry, even if the object was less remarkable. But I had a sad foreboding, (for suffering makes us full of presages), that this inquiry, however conducted, would terminate unfavourably to me. I was the Jonah of the vessel – let the storm blow from what point it would, I felt the lot was to fall on me. About noon, I was summoned to the apartment of the Superior. I went, but not as at former times, with a mixture of supplication and remonstrance on my lips, – with hope and fear in my heart, – in a fever of excitement or of terror, – I went sullen, squalid, listless, reckless; my physical strength, borne down by fatigue and want of sleep; my mental, by persecution, incessant and insupportable. I went no longer shrinking from, and deprecating *their worst*, but defying, almost desiring it, in the terrible and indefinite curiosity of despair. The apartment was full of monks; the Superior stood among them, while they formed a semicircle at a respectful distance from him. I must have presented a miserable contrast to these men arrayed against me in their pride of power, – their long and not ungraceful habits, giving their figures an air of solemnity, perhaps more imposing than splendour – while I stood opposed to them, ragged, meagre, livid and obdurate, the very personification of an evil spirit summoned before the angels of judgement. The Superior addressed me in a long discourse, in which he but slightly touched on the scandal given by the attempt to repeal my vows. He also suppressed any allusion to the circumstance which was known to every one in the convent but myself, that my appeal would be decided on in a few days. But he adverted in terms that (in spite of my consciousness that they were hollow) made me shudder, to the horror and consternation diffused through the convent by my late tremendous visitation, as he called it. "Satan hath desired to have you," he said, "because you have put yourself within his power, by your impious reclamation of your vows. You are the Judas among the brethren; a branded Cain amid a primitive family; a scapegoat that struggles to burst from the hands of the congregation into the wilderness. The horrors that your presence is hourly heaping on us here, are not only intolerable to the discipline of a religious house, but to the peace of civilized society. There is not a monk who can sleep within three cells of you. You disturb them by the most horrible cries – you exclaim that the infernal spirit is perpetually beside your bed – that he is whispering in your ears. You fly from cell to cell, supplicating the prayers of the brethren. Your shrieks disturb the holy sleep of the community – that sleep which they snatch only in the intervals of devotion. All order is broken, all discipline subverted, while you remain among us. The imaginations of the younger members are at once polluted and inflamed, by the idea of the infernal and impure orgies which the demon celebrates in your cell; and of which we know not whether your cries, (which all can hear), announce triumph in, or remorse for. You rush at midnight into the church, deface the images, revile the crucifix, spurn at the altar; and when the whole community is forced, by this unparalleled atrocity of blasphemy, to drag you from the spot you are desecrating, you disturb, by your cries, those who are passing to the service of God. In a word, your howls, your distortions, your demoniac language, habits and gestures, have but too well justified the suspicion entertained when you first entered the convent. You were abominable from your very birth, – you were the offspring of sin – you are conscious of it. Amid the livid paleness, that horrible unnatural white that discolours your very lips, I see a tingle like crimson burning on your cheek at the mention of it. The demon who was presiding at your natal hour – the demon of impurity and antimonasticism – pursues you in the very walls of a convent. The Almighty, in my voice, bids you begone; – depart, and trouble us no more. – Stop," he added, as he saw I was obeying his directions literally, "hold, the interests of religion, and of the community, have required that I should take particular notice of the extraordinary circumstances that have haunted your unhallowed presence within these walls. In a short time you may expect a visit from the Bishop – prepare yourself for it as you may." I considered these as the final words addressed to me, and was about to retire, when I was recalled. I was desired to utter some words, which every one was eager to put into my mouth, of expostulation, of remonstrance, of supplication. I resisted them all as steadily as if I had known (which I did not) that the Bishop had himself instituted the examination into the deranged state of the convent; and that instead of the Superior inviting the

Bishop to examine into the cause of the disturbance in his convent, (the very last step he would have taken), the Bishop, (a man whose character will shortly be developed), had been apprized of the *scandal* of the convent, and had determined to take the matter into his own hands. Sunk in solitude and persecution, I knew not that all Madrid was on fire, – that the Bishop had determined to be no longer a passive hearer of the extraordinary scenes reported to pass in the convent, – that, in a word, my *exorcism* and my appeal were quivering in alternate scales, and that the Superior himself doubted which way the scale might incline. All this I was ignorant of, for no one dared to tell it to me. I therefore was about to retire without uttering a word in answer to the many whispered speeches to humble myself to the Superior, to implore his intercession with the Bishop to suspend this disgraceful examination that threatened *us* all. I broke from them as they surrounded me; and standing calm and sullen at the door, I threw a retorting look at them, and said, "God forgive you all, and grant you such an acquittal at his judgement-seat, as I hesitate not to claim at that of the Bishop-visitant." These words, though uttered by a ragged demoniac, (as they thought me), made them tremble. Truth is rarely heard in convents and therefore its language is equally emphatical and portentous.

'The monks crossed themselves, and, as I left the apartment, repeated, "But how then, – what if we *prevented* this mischief?" – "By what means?" – "By any that the interests of religion may suggest, – the character of the convent is at stake. The Bishop is a man of a strict and scrutinizing character, – he will keep his eyes open to the truth, – he will inquire into facts, – what will become of us? Were it not better that –" "What?" – "You comprehend us." – "And if I dared to comprehend you, *the time is too short.*" – "We have heard of the death of maniacs being very sudden, of –" "What do you dare to hint at?" – "Nothing, we only spoke of what every one knows, that a profound sleep is often a restorative to lunatics. *He* is a lunatic, as all the convent are ready to swear, – a wretch possessed by the infernal spirit, whom he invocates every night in his cell, – he disturbs the whole convent by his outcries."

'The Superior all this time walked impatiently up and down his apartment. He entangled his fingers in his rosary, – he threw on the monks angry looks from time to time; at last he said, "I am myself disturbed by his cries, – his wanderings, – his undoubted commerce with the enemy of souls. I need rest, – I require a profound sleep to repair my exhausted spirits, – *what would you prescribe*?" Several pressed forward, not understanding the hint, and eagerly recommended the common opiates – Mithridate, &c. &c. An old monk whispered in his ear, "Laudanum, – it will procure a deep and sound sleep. Try it, my father, if you want rest; but to make the experiment sure, were it not best to try it first on another?" The Superior nodded, and the party were about to disperse, when the Superior caught the old monk by his habit, and whispered, "But no murder!" – "Oh no! only profound sleep. – What matter when he wakes? It must be to suffering in this life or the next. *We* are not guilty in the business. What signifies a few moments sooner or later?" The Superior was of a timid and passionate character. He still kept hold of the monk's habit; – he whispered, "But it must not be known." – "But who can know it?" At this moment the clock struck, and an old ascetic monk, who occupied a cell adjacent to the Superior's, and who had accustomed himself to the exclamation, "God knoweth all things", whenever the clock struck, repeated it aloud. The Superior quitted his hold of the monk's habit, – the monk crawled to his cell *God-struck*, if I may use the expression, – the laudanum was not administered that night, – the voice did not return, – I slept the entire night, and the whole convent was delivered from the harassings of the infernal spirit. Alas! none haunted it, but that spirit which the natural *malignity of solitude* raises within the circle of every heart, and forces us, from the terrible economy of misery, to feed on the vitals of others, that we may spare our own.

'This conversation was repeated to me afterwards by a monk

who was on his dying bed. He had witnessed it, and I have no reason to doubt his sincerity. In fact, I always considered it as rather a palliation than an aggravation of their cruelty to me. They had made me suffer worse than many deaths, – the single suffering would have been instantaneous, – the single act would have been mercy. The next day the visit of the Bishop was expected. There was an indescribable kind of terrified preparation among the community. This house was the first in Madrid, and the singular circumstance of the son of one of the highest families in Spain having entered it in early youth, – having protested against his vows in a few months, – having been accused of being in a compact with the infernal spirit a few weeks after, – the hope of a scene of exorcism, – the doubt of the success of my appeal, – the probable interference of the Inquisition, – the *possible* festival of an *auto da fe*, – had set the imagination of all Madrid on fire; and never did an audience long more for the drawing up of the curtain at a popular opera, than the religious and irreligious of Madrid did for the development of the scene which was acting at the convent of the ex-Jesuits.

'In Catholic countries, Sir, religion is the national drama; the priests are the principal performers, the populace the audience; and whether the piece concludes with a 'Don Giovanni' plunging in flames, or the beatification of a saint, the applause and the enjoyment is the same.

'I feared my destiny was to be the former. I knew nothing of the Bishop, and hoped nothing from his visit; but my hopes began to rise in proportion to the visible fears of the society. I argued, with the natural malignity of wretchedness, "If they tremble, I may exult." When suffering is thus weighed against suffering, the hand is never steady; we are always disposed to make the balance incline a little on our own side. The Bishop came early, and passed some hours with the Superior in his own apartment. During this interval, there was a stillness in the house that was strongly contrasted with its previous agitation. I stood alone in my cell, – *stood*, for I had no seat left me. I said to myself, "This event bodes neither good or evil to me. I am not guilty of what they accuse me of. They never can prove it, – an accomplice with Satan! – the victim of diabolical delusion! – Alas! my only crime is my involuntary subjection to the delusions they have practised on me. This man, this Bishop, cannot give me freedom, but he may at least do me justice." All this time the community were in a fever – the character of the house was at stake – my situation was notorious. They had laboured to represent me as a possessed being beyond their walls, and to *make* me appear as one within them. The hour of trial approached. For the honour of human nature, – from the dread of violating decency, – from the dread of apparently violating truth, I will not attempt to relate the means they had recourse to the morning of the Bishop's visitation, to qualify me to perform the part of a possessed, insane, and blasphemous wretch. The four monks I have before mentioned, were the principal executioners, (I must call them so). – Under pretence that there was no part of my person which was not under the influence of the demon,

*

'This was not enough. I was deluged almost to suffocation with aspersions of holy water. Then followed, &c.

*

'The result was, that I remained half-naked, half-drowned, gasping, choking and delirious with rage, shame and fear, when I was summoned to attend the Bishop, who, surrounded by the Superior and the community, awaited me in the church. This was the moment they had fixed on – I yielded myself to them. I said, stretching out my arms, "Yes, drag me naked, mad – religion and nature alike violated in my abused figure – before your Bishop. If he speaks truth, – if he feels conscience, – woe be to you, hypocritical, tyrannical wretches. You have half-driven me mad! – half-murdered me, by the unnatural cruelties you have exercised on me! and in this state you drag me before the Bishop! Be it so, I must follow you." As I uttered these words, they bound my arms and legs with ropes, carried me down, and placed me at the door of the church, standing close to me. The Bishop was at the altar, the Superior near him; the community filled the choir. They flung me down like a heap of carrion, and retreated as if they fled from the pollution of my touch. This sight struck the Bishop: He said, in a loud voice, "Rise, *unhappy*, and come forward." I answered, in a voice whose tones appeared to thrill him, "Bid them unbind me, and I will obey you." The Bishop turned a cold and yet indignant look on the Superior, who immediately approached and whispered him. This whispering consultation was carried on for some time; but, though lying on the ground, I could perceive the Bishop shook his head at every whisper of the Superior; and the end of the business was an order to unbind me. I did not fare much the better for this order, for the four monks were still close to me. They held my arms as they led me up the steps to the altar. I was then, for the first time, placed opposite to the Bishop. He was a man, the effect of whose physiognomy was as indelible as that of his character. – The one left its impress on the senses, as strongly as the other did on the soul. He was tall, majestic and hoary; not a feeling agitated his frame – not a passion had left its trace on his features. He was a marble statue of Episcopacy, chiselled out by the hand of Catholicism, – a figure magnificent and motionless. His cold black eyes did not seem to see you, when they were turned on you. His voice, when it reached you, did not address *you*, but your *soul*. Such was his exterior: – for the rest, his character was unimpeachable, his discipline exemplary, his life that of an Anchorite hewed out in stone. But he was partially suspected of what is called *liberality* in opinions, (that is, of an inclination to Protestantism), and the sanctity of his character went bail in vain for this imputed heterodoxy, which the Bishop could hardly redeem by his rigid cognizance of every conventual abuse in his district, among which my convent happened to be. Such was the man before whom I stood. At the command to unloose me, the Superior shewed much agitation; but the command was positive, and I was released. I was then between the four monks, who held me, and I felt that my appearance must have justified the impression he had received. I was ragged, famished, livid and on fire, with the horrible treatment I had just received. I hoped, however, that my submission to whatever was to be performed, might, in some degree, redeem the opinion of the Bishop. He went with evident reluctance through the forms of exorcism, which were delivered in Latin, while all the time, the monks crossed themselves, and the *Acolytes* were not sparing of holy water and of incense. Whenever the terms "diabole te adjuro"[14] occurred, the monks who held me twisted my arms, so that I appeared to make contortions, and uttered cries of pain. This, at first, seemed to disturb the Bishop; but when the form of exorcism was over, he commanded me to approach the altar alone. I attempted to do so; but the four monks surrounding me, made it appear an act of great difficulty. He said, "Stand apart – let him alone." They were compelled to obey. I advanced alone, trembling. I knelt. The Bishop, placing his stole on my head, demanded, "Did I believe in God, and the holy Catholic church?" Instead of answering, I shrieked, flung off the stole, and trampled in agony on the steps of the altar. The Bishop retreated, while the Superior and the rest advanced. I collected courage as I saw them approach; and, without uttering a word, pointed to the pieces of broken glass which had been thrown on the steps where I stood, and which had pierced me through my torn sandals. The Bishop instantly ordered a monk to sweep them away with the sleeve of his tunic. The order was obeyed in a moment, and the next I stood before him without fear or pain. He continued to ask, "Why do you not pray in the church?" – "Because its doors are shut against me." – "How? what is this? A memorial is in my hands urging many complaints against you, and this among the first, that you do not pray in the church." – "I have told you the doors of the church are shut against me. – Alas! I could no more open them, than I could open the hearts of the community – everything is shut against me here." He turned to the Superior, who answered, "The doors of the church are always shut to the enemies of God." The Bishop said, with his usual stern calmness, "I am asking a plain question – evasive and circuitous answers will not do. Have the doors of the church been shut against this wretched being? – have you denied him the privilege of addressing God?" – "I did so, because I thought and believed –" "I ask not what you thought or believed; I ask a plain answer to a matter-of-fact question. Did you, or did you not, deny him access to the house of God?" – "I had reason to believe that –" "I warn you, these answers may compel me to make you exchange situations in one moment with the object you accuse. Did you, or did you not, shut the doors of the church against him? – answer yes or no." The Superior, trembling with fear and rage, said, "I did; and I was justified in doing so." – "That is for another tribunal to judge. But it seems you plead guilty to the fact of which you accuse him." The Superior was dumb. The Bishop then examining his paper, addressed me again, "How is it that the monks cannot sleep in their cells from the disturbance you cause?" – "I know not – you must ask them." – "Does not the evil spirit visit you nightly? Are not your blasphemies, your execrable impurities, disgorged even in the ears of those who have the misfortune to be placed near you? Are you not the terror and the torment of the whole community?" I answered, "I am what they have made me. I do not deny there are extraordinary noises in my cell, but they can best account for them. I am assailed by whispers close to my bed-side: It seems these whispers reach the ears of the brethren, for they burst into my cell, and take advantage of the terror with which I am overwhelmed, to put the most incredible constructions on it." – "Are there no cries, then, heard in your cell at night?" – "Yes, cries of terror – cries uttered not by one who is celebrating infernal orgies, but dreading them." – "But the blasphemies, the imprecations, the impurities, which proceed from your lips?" – "Sometimes, in irrepressible terror, I have repeated the sounds that were suggested to my ears; but it was always with an exclamation of horror and aversion, that proved these sounds were not *uttered* but *echoed* by me, – as a man may take up a reptile in his hand, and gaze on its hideousness a moment, before he flings it from him. I take the whole community to witness the truth of this. The cries I uttered, the expressions I used, were evidently those of hostility to the infernal suggestions which had been breathed into my ears. Ask the whole community – they must testify, that when they broke into my cell, they found me alone, trembling, convulsed. That I was the victim of those disturbances, they affected to complain of; and though I never was able to guess the means by which this persecution was effected, I am not rash in ascribing it to the hands that covered the walls of my cell with representations of demons, the traces of which still remain." – "You are also accused of having burst into the church at midnight, defaced the images, trampled on the crucifix, and performed all the acts of a demon violating the sanctuary." At this accusation, so unjust and cruel, I was agitated beyond control. I exclaimed, "I flew to the church for protection in a paroxysm of terror, which their machinations had filled me with! I flew there at night, because it was shut against me during the day, as you have discovered! I prostrated myself before the cross, instead of trampling on it! I embraced the images of the blessed saints, instead of violating them! And I doubt whether prayers more sincere were ever offered within these walls, than those I uttered that night amid helplessness, terror, and persecutions!" – "Did you not obstruct and deter the community next morning by your cries, as they attempted to enter the church?" – "I was paralyzed from the effects of lying all night on the stone pavement, where they had flung me. I attempted to rise and crawl away at their approach, and a few cries of pain were extorted from me by my efforts to do so – efforts rendered more painful by their refusing to offer me the slightest assistance. In a word, the whole is a fabrication. I flew to the church to implore for mercy, and they represent it as the outrages of an apostate spirit. Might not the same arbitrary and absurd construction be put on the daily visits of multitudes of afflicted souls, who weep and groan audibly as I did? If I attempted to overturn the crucifix, to deface the images, would not the marks of this violence remain? Would they not have been preserved with care, to substantiate the accusation against me? Is there a trace of them? – there is not, there cannot be, because they never existed." The Bishop paused. An appeal to his feelings would have been vain, but this appeal to facts had its full effect. After some time, he said, "You can have no objection, then, to render before the whole community the same homage to the representations of the Redeemer and the holy saints, that you say it was your purpose to render them that night?" – "None." A crucifix was brought me, which I kissed with reverence and unction, and prayed, while the tears streamed from my eyes, an interest in the infinite merits of the sacrifice it represented. The Bishop then said, "Make a deed of faith, of love, of hope." I did so; and though they were extempore, my expressions, I could perceive, made the dignified ecclesiastics who attended on the Bishop, cast on each other looks in which were mingled compassion, interest and admiration. The Bishop said, "Where did you learn those prayers?" – "My heart is my only teacher – I have no other – I am allowed no book." – "How! – recollect what you say." – "I repeat I have none. They have taken away my breviary, my crucifix; – they have stript my cell of all its furniture. I kneel on the floor – I pray from the heart. If you deign to visit my cell, you will find I have told you the truth." At these words, the Bishop cast a terrible look on the Superior. He recovered himself, however, immediately, for he was a man unaccustomed to any emotion, and felt it at once a suspension of his habits, and an infringement of his rank. In a cold voice he bid me retire; then, as I was obeying him, he recalled me, – my appearance for the first time seemed to strike him. He was a man so absorbed in the contemplation of that waveless and frozen tide of duty in which his mind was anchored, without fluctuation, progress, or improvement, that physical objects must be presented before him a long time before they made the least impression on him, – his senses were almost ossified. Thus he had come to examine a supposed demoniac; but he had made up his mind that there must be injustice and imposture in the case, and he acted in the matter with a spirit, decision and integrity, that did him honour.

'But, all the time, the horror and misery of my appearance, which would have made the first impression on a man whose feelings were at all *external*, made the last. They struck him as I slowly and painfully crawled from the steps of the altar, and the impression was forcible in proportion to its slowness. He called me back and inquired, as if he saw me for the first time, "How is it your habit is so scandalously ragged?" At these words I thought I could disclose a scene that would have added to the Superior's humiliation, but I only said, "It is the consequence of the ill treatment I have experienced." Several other questions of the same kind, relating to my appearance, which was deplorable enough, followed, and at last I was forced to make a full discovery. The Bishop was incensed at the detail more than was credible. Rigid minds, when they yield themselves to emotion, do it with a vehemence inconceivable, for to them every thing is a duty, and passion (when it occurs) among the rest. Perhaps the novelty of emotion, too, may be a delightful surprise to them.

'More than all this was the case now with the good Bishop, who was as pure as he was rigid, and shrunk with horror, disgust and indignation, at the detail I was compelled to give, which the Superior trembled at my uttering, and which the community dared not to contradict. He resumed his cold manner; for to him feeling was an effort, and rigour a habit, and he ordered me again

to retire. I obeyed, and went to my cell. The walls were as bare as
I had described them, but, even contrasted with all the splendour
and array of the scene in the church, they seemed emblazoned
with my triumph. A dazzling vision passed before me for a
moment, then all subsided; and, in the solitude of my cell, I knelt
and implored the Almighty to touch the Bishop's heart, and
impress on him the moderation and simplicity with which I had
spoken. As I was thus employed, I heard steps in the passage.
They ceased for a moment, and I was silent. It appeared the persons overheard me, and paused; and these few words, uttered in
solitude, made, I found, a deep impression on them. A few
moments after the Bishop, with some dignified attendants, followed by the Superior, entered my cell. The former all stopped,
horror-struck at its appearance.

'I have told you, Sir, that my cell now consisted of four bare
walls and a bed; – it was a scandalous, degrading sight. I was
kneeling in the middle of the floor, God knows, without the least
idea of producing an effect. The Bishop gazed around him for
some time, while the ecclesiastics who attended him testified
their horror by looks and attitudes that needed no interpretation.
The Bishop, after a pause, turned to the Superior, "Well, what do
you say to this?" The Superior hesitated, and at last said, "I was
ignorant of this." – "That is false," said the Bishop; "and even if it
was true, it would be your crimination, not your apology. Your
duty binds you to visit the cells every day; how could you be
ignorant of the shameful state of this cell, without neglecting
your own duties?" He took several turns about the cell, followed
by the ecclesiastics, shrugging their shoulders, and throwing on
each other looks of disgust. The Superior stood dismayed. They
went out, and I could hear the Bishop say, in the passage, "All this
disorder must be rectified before I quit the house." And to the
Superior, "You are unworthy of the situation you hold, – you
ought to be deposed." And he added in severer tones, "Catholics,
monks, Christians, this is shocking, – horrible! tremble for the

consequences of my next visit, if the same disorders exist, – I promise you it shall be repeated soon." He then returned, and standing at the door of my cell, said to the Superior, "Take care that all the abuses committed in this cell are rectified before to-morrow morning." The Superior signified his submission to this order in silence.

'That evening I went to sleep on a bare mattress, between four dry walls. I slept profoundly, from exhaustion and fatigue. I awoke in the morning far beyond the time for matins, and found myself surrounded by all the comforts that can be bestowed on a cell. As if magic had been employed during my sleep, crucifix, breviary, desk, table, every thing was replaced. I sprung from bed, and actually gazed in extasy around my cell. As the day advanced, and the hour for refection approached, my extasy abated, and my terrors increased; – it is not easy to pass from extreme humilia-tion and utter abhorrence, to your former state in the society of which you are a member. When the bell rung I went down. I stood at the door for a moment, – then, with an impulse like despair, I entered, and took my usual place. No opposition was made, – not a word was said. The community separated after din-ner. I watched for the toll of the bell for vespers, – I imagined that would be decisive. The bell tolled at last, – the monks assembled. I joined them without opposition, – I took my place in the choir, – my triumph was complete, and I trembled at it. Alas! in what moment of success do we not feel a sensation of terror! Our des-tiny always acts the part of the ancient slave to us, who was required every morning to remind the monarch that he was a man; and it seldom neglects to fulfil its own predictions before the evening. Two days passed away, – the storm that had so long agitated us, seemed to have sunk into a sudden calm. I resumed my former place, – I performed the customary duties, – no one congratulated or reviled me. They all seemed to consider me as one beginning monastic life *de novo*. I passed two days of perfect tranquillity, and I take God to witness, I enjoyed this triumph with moderation. I never reverted to my former situation, – I never reproached those who had been agents in it, – I never uttered a syllable on the subject of the visitation, which had made me and the whole convent change places in the space of a few hours, and the oppressed take the part (if he pleased) of the oppressor. I bore my success with temperance, for I was supported by the hope of liberation. The Superior's triumph was soon to come.

'On the third morning I was summoned to the parlour, where a messenger put into my hands a packet, containing (as I well understood) the result of my appeal. This, according to the rules of the convent, I was compelled to put first into the hands of the Superior to read, before I was permitted to read it myself. I took the packet, and slowly walked to the Superior's apartment. As I held it in my hand, I considered it, felt every corner, weighed it over and over again in my hand, tried to catch an omen from its very shape. Then a withering thought crossed me, that, if its intelligence was auspicious, the messenger would have put it into my hands with an air of triumph, that, in spite of convent etiquette, I might break open the seals which inclosed the sentence of my liberation. We are very apt to take our presages from our destination, and mine being that of a monk, no wonder its auguries were black, – and were verified.

'I approached the Superior's cell with the packet. I knocked, was desired to enter, and, my eyes cast down, could only distinguish the hems of many habits, whose wearers were all assembled in the Superior's apartment. I offered the packet with reverence. The Superior cast a careless eye over it, and then flung it on the floor. One of the monks approached to take it up. The Superior exclaimed, "Hold, let *him* take it up." I did so, and retired to my cell, making first a profound reverence to the Superior. I then went to my cell, where I sat down with the fatal packet in my hands. I was about to open it, when a voice from within me seemed to say, – It is useless, you must know the contents already.

208

It was some hours before I perused it, – it contained the account of the failure of my appeal. It seemed, from the detail, that the advocate had exerted his abilities, zeal and eloquence to the utmost; and that, at one time, the court had been near deciding in favour of my claims, but the precedent was reckoned too dangerous. The advocate on the other side had remarked, "If this succeeds, we shall have all the monks in Spain appealing against their vows." Could a stronger argument have been used in favour of my cause? An impulse so universal must surely originate in nature, justice, and truth.'

*

On reverting to the disastrous issue of his appeal, the unfortunate Spaniard was so much overcome, that it was some days before he could resume his narrative.

Chapter Seven

Pandere res alta terra et caligine mersas.[15]

I'll shew your Grace the strangest sight, –
Body o'me, what is it, Butts? –

Henry the Eighth

'Of the desolation of mind into which the rejection of my appeal plunged me, I can give no account, for I return no distinguishing image. All colours disappear in the night, and despair has no diary, – monotony is her essence and her curse. Hours have I walked in the garden, without retaining a single impression but that of the sounds of my footsteps; – thought, feeling, passion, and all that employs them, – life and futurity, extinct and swallowed up. I was already like an inhabitant of the land where "all things are forgotten". I hovered on the regions of mental twilight, where the "light is as darkness". The clouds were gathering that portended the approach of utter night, – they were scattered by a sudden and extraordinary light.

'The garden was my constant resort, – a kind of instinct supplying the place of that choice I had no longer energy enough to make, directed me there to avoid the presence of the monks. One evening I saw a change in its appearance. The fountain was out of repair. The spring that supplied it was beyond the walls of the convent, and the workmen, in prosecuting the repairs, had found it necessary to excavate a passage under the garden-wall, that communicated with an open space in the city. This passage, however, was closely watched during the day while the workmen were employed, and well secured at night by a door erected for the purpose, which was chained, barred, and bolted, the moment the workmen quitted the passage. It was, however, left open during the day; and this tantalizing image of escape and freedom, amid the withering certainty of eternal imprisonment, gave a kind of awakened sting to the pains that were becoming obtuse. I entered the passage, and drew as close as possible to the door that shut me out from life. My seat was one of the stones that were scattered about, my head rested on my hand, and my eyes were sadly fixed on the *tree and the well*, the scene of that false miracle. I knew not how long I sat thus. I was aroused by a slight noise near me, and perceived a paper, which some one was thrusting under the door, where a slight inequality in the ground rendered the attempt just practicable. I stooped and attempted to seize it. It was withdrawn: but a moment after a voice, whose tones my agitation did not permit me to distinguish, whispered, "Alonzo." – "Yes, – yes," I answered eagerly. The paper was instantly thrust into my hands, and I heard a sound of steps retreating rapidly. I lost not a moment in reading the few words it contained. "Be here to-morrow evening at the same hour. I have suffered much on your account, – destroy this." It was the hand of my brother Juan, that hand so well remembered from our late eventful correspondence, – that hand whose traces I never beheld without feeling corresponding characters of hope and confidence retraced in my soul, as lines before invisible appear on exposure to the heat that seems to vivify them. I am surprised that between this and the following evening my agitation did not betray me to the community. But perhaps it is only agitation arising from frivolous causes, that vents itself in external indications, – I was absorbed in mine. It is certain, at least, that my mind was all that day vacillating like a clock that struck every minute the alternate sounds, *"There is hope, – there is no hope."* The day, – the eternal day, was at last over. Evening came on; how I watched the advancing shades! At vespers, with what delight did

I trace the gradual mellowing of the gold and purple tinges that gleamed through the great eastern window, and calculated that their western decline, though slower, must come at last! – It came. Never was a more propitious evening. It was calm and dark – the garden deserted, not a form to be seen, not a step to be heard in the walks. – I hurried on. Suddenly I thought I heard the sound of something pursuing me. I paused, – it was but the beating of my own heart, audible in the deep stillness of that eventful moment. I pressed my hand on my breast, as a mother would on an infant whom she tried to pacify; – it did not cease to throb, however. I entered the passage. I approached the door, of which hope and despair seemed to stand the alternate portresses. The words still rung in my ears. "Be here to-morrow evening at the same hour." I stooped, and saw, with eyes that devoured the sight, a piece of paper appear under the door. I seized and buried it in my habit. I trembled with such ecstasy, that I thought I never should be able to carry it undiscovered to my cell. I succeeded, however; and the contents, when I read them, justified my emotion. To my unspeakable uneasiness, great part of it was illegible, from being crushed amid the stones and damp clay contiguous to the door, and from the first page I could hardly extract that he had been kept in the country almost a prisoner, through the influence of the Director; that one day, while shooting with only one attendant, the hope of liberation suddenly filled him with the idea of terrifying this man into submission. Presenting his loaded fowling piece at the terrified wretch, he threatened him with instant death, if he made the least opposition. The man suffered himself to be bound to a tree; and the next page, though much defaced, gave me to understand he had reached Madrid in safety, and heard for the first time the event of my ill-fated appeal. The effect of this intelligence on the impetuous, sanguine, and affectionate Juan, could be easily traced in the broken and irregular lines in which he vainly attempted to describe it. The letter then proceeded. "I am now in Madrid, pledged body and soul never to quit it till you are liberated. If you possess resolution, this is not impossible, – the doors even of convents are not inaccessible to a silver key. My first object, that of obtaining a communication with you, appeared as impracticable as your escape, yet it has been accomplished. I understood that repairs were going on in the garden, and stationed myself at the door evening after evening, whispering your name, but it was not till the sixth that you were there."

'In another part he detailed his plans more fully. "Money and secrecy are the primary objects, – the latter I can insure by the disguises I wear, but the former I scarce know how to obtain. My escape was so sudden, that I was wholly unprovided, and have been obliged to dispose of my watch and rings since I reached Madrid, to purchase disguises and procure subsistence. I could command what sums I pleased by disclosing my name, but this would be fatal. The report of my being in Madrid would immediately reach my father's ears. My resource must be a Jew; and when I have obtained money, I have little doubt of effecting your liberation. I have already heard of a person in the convent under very extraordinary circumstances, who would probably not be disinclined to"

*

'Here a long interval occurred in the letter, which appeared to be written at different times. The next lines that I could trace, expressed all the light-heartedness of this most fiery, volatile, and generous of created beings.

*

' "Be not under the least uneasiness about me, it is impossible that I should be discovered. At school I was remarkable for a dramatic talent, a power of personation almost incredible, and which I now find of infinite service. Sometimes I strut as a *Majo*,*

* Something between a bully and a rake.

with enormous whiskers. Sometimes I assume the accent of a Biscayan, and, like the husband of Donna Rodriguez, 'am as good a gentleman as the king, because I came from the mountains.' But my favourite disguise is that of a mendicant or a fortune-teller, – the former procures me access to the convent, the other money and intelligence. Thus I am paid, while I appear to be the buyer. When the wanderings and stratagems of the day are over, you would smile to see the loft and pallet to which the heir of Monçada retires. This masquerade amuses *me* more than the spectators. A consciousness of our superiority is often more delightful when confined to our own breasts, than when expressed by others. Besides, I feel as if the squalid bed, the tottering seat, the cobwebbed rafters, the rancid oil, and all the other *agremens* of my new abode, were a kind of atonement for the wrongs I have done you, Alonzo. My spirits sometimes sink under privations so new to me, but still a kind of playful and wild energy, peculiar to my character, supports me. I shudder at my situation when I retire at night, and place, for the first time *with my own hands*, the lamp on the miserable hearth; but I laugh when, in the morning, I attire myself in fantastic rags, discolour my face, and modulate my accent, so that the people in the house, (where I tenant a garret), when they meet me on the stairs, do not know the being they saw the preceding evening. I change my abode and costume every day. Feel no fears for me, but come every evening to the door in the passage, for every evening I shall have fresh intelligence for you. My industry is indefatigable, my zeal unquenchable, my heart and soul are on fire in the cause. Again I pledge myself, soul and body, never to quit this spot till you are free, – *depend on me, Alonzo.*"

'I will spare you, Sir, the detail of the feelings, – feelings! Oh my God, pardon me the prostration of heart with which I kissed those lines, with which I could have consecrated the hand that traced them, and which are worthy only to be devoted to the image of the great Sacrifice. Yet a being so young, so generous, so devoted, with a heart at once so wild and warm, sacrificing all that rank, and youth, and pleasure could offer, – submitting to the vilest disguises, undergoing the most deplorable privations, struggling with what must have been most intolerable to a proud voluptuous boy, (and I knew he was all this), hiding his revoltings under a gaiety that was assumed, and a magnanimity that was real – and all this for me! – Oh what I felt!

*

'The next evening I was at the door; no paper appeared, though I sat watching for it till the declining light made it impossible for me to discover it, had it been there. The next I was more fortunate; it appeared. The same disguised voice whispered "Alonzo," in tones that were the sweetest music that ever reached my ears. This billet contained but a very few lines, (so I found no difficulty in *swallowing it* immediately after perusal). It said, "I have found a Jew, at last, who will advance me a large sum. He pretends not to know me, though I am satisfied he does. – But his usurious interest and illegal practices are my full security. I shall be master of the means of liberating you in a few days; and I have been fortunate enough to discover how those means may be applied. There is a wretch –"

'Here the billet ended; and for four following evenings the state of the repairs excited so much curiosity in the convent, (where it is so easy to excite curiosity), that I dared not to remain in the passage, without the fear of exciting suspicion. All this time I suffered not only the agony of suspended hope, but the dread of this accidental communication being finally closed; for I knew the workmen could not have more than a few days to employ on their task. This I conveyed the intelligence of to my brother in the same way in which I received his billets. Then I reproached myself for hurrying him. I reflected on the difficulties of his concealment – of his dealing with Jews – of his bribing the servants of the convent. I thought of all he had undertaken, and all he had undergone. Then I dreaded that all might be in vain. I would not live over those four days again to be sovereign of the earth. I will give you one slight proof of what I must have felt, when I heard the workmen say, "It will be finished soon." I used to rise at an hour before matins, displace the stones, trample on the mortar, which I mingled with the clay, so as to render it totally useless; and finally, *re-act Penelope's web* with such success, that the workmen believed the devil himself was obstructing their operations, and latterly never came to their task unless armed with a vessel of holy water, which they dashed about with infinite sanctimony and profusion. On the fifth evening I caught the following lines beneath the door. "All is settled – I have fixed the Jew on *Jewish terms*. He affects to be ignorant of my real rank, and certain (*future*) wealth, but he knows it all, and dare not, for his own sake, betray me. The Inquisition, to which I could expose him in a moment, is my best security – I must add, my *only*. There is a wretch in your convent, who took sanctuary from *parricide*, and consented to become a monk, to escape the vengeance of heaven in this life at least. I have heard, that this monster cut his own father's throat, as he sat at supper, to obtain a small sum which he had lost at gambling. His partner, who was a loser also, had, it seems, made a vow to an image of the Virgin, that was in the neighbourhood of the wretched house where they gamed, to present two wax tapers before it in the event of his success. He lost; and, in the fury of a gamester, as he repassed the image, he struck and spit at it. This was very shocking – but what was it to the crime of him who is now an inmate of your convent? The one defaced an image, the other murdered his father: Yet the former expired under tortures the most horrible, and the other, after some vain efforts to elude justice, *took sanctuary*, and is now a lay-brother in your convent. On the crimes of this wretch I build all my hopes. His soul must be saturated with avarice, sensuality, and desperation. There is nothing he will hesitate at if he be bribed; – for money he will undertake your liberation – for money he will undertake to strangle you in your cell. He envies Judas the thirty pieces of silver for which the Redeemer of mankind was sold. *His* soul might be purchased at half-price. Such is the instrument with which I must work. – It is horrible, but necessary. I have read, that from the most venomous reptiles and plants, have been extracted the most sanative medicines. I will squeeze the juice, and trample on the weed.

'"Alonzo, tremble not at these words. Let not your habits prevail over your character. Entrust your liberation to me, and the instruments I am compelled to work with; and doubt not, that the hand which traces these lines, will soon be clasping that of a brother in freedom."

'I read these lines over and over again in the solitude of my cell, when the excitement of watching for, secreting, and perusing it *for the first time*, were over, and many doubts and fears began to gather round me like twilight clouds. In proportion as Juan's confidence increased, mine appeared to diminish. There was a terrifying contrast between the fearlessness, independence, and enterprise of *his* situation, and the loneliness, timidity, and danger of mine. While the hope of escape, through his courage and address, still burnt like an inextinguishable light in the depth of my heart, I still dreaded entrusting my destiny to a youth so impetuous, though so affectionate; one who had fled from his parents' mansion, was living by subterfuge and imposture in Madrid, and had engaged, as his coadjutor, a wretch whom nature must revolt from. Upon whom and what did my hopes of liberation rest? On the affectionate energies of a wild, enterprising, and unaided being, and the co-operation of a demon, who might snatch at a bribe, and then shake it in triumph in his ears, as the seal of our mutual and eternal despair, while he flung the key of liberation into an abyss where no light could penetrate, and from which no arm could redeem it.

'Under these impressions, I deliberated, I prayed, I wept in the agony of doubt. At last I wrote a few lines to Juan, in which

I honestly stated my doubts and apprehensions. I stated first my doubts of the possibility of my escape. I said, "Can it be imagined that a being whom all Madrid, whom all Spain, is on the watch for, can elude their detection? Reflect, dear Juan, that I am staked against a community, a priesthood, a nation. The escape of a monk is almost impossible, – but his concealment afterwards is down-right impossible. Every bell in every convent in Spain would ring out *untouched* in pursuit of the fugitive. The military, civil, and ecclesiastical powers, would all be on the 'qui vive'. Hunted, panting, and despairing, I might fly from place to place – no place affording me shelter. The incensed powers of the church – the fierce and vigorous gripe of the law – the execration and hatred of society – the suspicions of the lowest order among whom I must lurk, to shun and curse their penetration; think of encountering all this, while the fiery cross of the Inquisition blazes in the van, followed by the whole pack, shouting, cheering, hallooing on to the prey. Oh Juan! if you knew the terrors under which I live – under which I would rather die than encounter them again, even on the condition of liberation! Liberation! Great God! what chance of liberation for a monk in Spain? There is not a cottage where I could rest one night in security – there is not a cavern whose echoes would not resound to the cry of my apostacy. If I was hid in the bowels of the earth, they would discover me, and tear me from its entrails. My beloved Juan, when I consider the omnipotence of the ecclesiastical power in Spain, may I not address it in the language applied to Omnipotence itself: 'If I climb up to heaven, thou art *there*; – if I go down to hell, thou art *there* also; – if I take the wings of the morning, and flee unto the *uttermost parts of the sea, even there –*' And suppose my liberation was accomplished – suppose the convent plunged in a profound torpor, and the unsleeping eye of the Inquisition winked at my apostacy – where am I to reside? how am I to procure subsistence? The luxurious indolence of my early years unfit me for active employment. The horrible conflict of apathy the deepest, with hostility the most deadly, in monastic life, disqualifies me for society. Throw the doors of every convent in Spain open, and for what will their inmates be fit? For nothing that will either embellish or improve it. What could I do to serve myself? – what could I do that would not betray me? I should be a persecuted, breathless fugitive, – a branded *Cain*. Alas! – perhaps expiring in flames, I might see *Abel* not *my* victim, but that of the Inquisition."

'When I had written these lines, with an impulse for which all can account but the writer, I tore them to atoms, burnt them deliberately by the assistance of the lamp in my cell, and went to watch again at the door in the passage – the door of hope. In passing through the gallery, I encountered, for a moment, a person of a most forbidding aspect. I drew on one side – for I had made it a point not to mix, in the slightest degree, with the community, beyond what the discipline of the house compelled me to. As he passed, however, he touched my habit, and gave a most significant look. I immediately comprehended this was the person Juan alluded to in his letter. And in a few moments after, on descending to the garden, I found a note that confirmed my conjectures. It contained these words: "I have procured the money – I have secured our agent. He is an incarnate devil, but his resolution and intrepidity are unquestionable. Walk in the cloister to-morrow evening – some one will touch your habit – grasp his left wrist, that will be the signal. If he hesitates, whisper to him – 'Juan,' he will answer – 'Alonzo.' That is your man, consult with him. Every step that I have taken will be communicated to you by him."

'After reading these lines, I appeared to myself like a piece of mechanism wound up to perform certain functions, in which its co-operation was irresistible. The precipitate vigour of Juan's movements seemed to impel mine without my own concurrence; and as the shortness of the time left me no opportunity for deliberation, it left me also none for choice. I was like a clock whose hands are pushed forward, and I struck the hours I was impelled to strike. When a powerful agency is thus exercised on us, – when another undertakes to think, feel, and act for us, we are delighted to transfer to him, not only our physical, but our moral responsibility. We say, with selfish cowardice, and self-flattering passiveness, "Be it so – you have decided for me," – without reflecting that at the bar of God there is no bail. So I walked the next evening in the cloister. I composed my habit, – my looks; any one would have imagined me plunged in profound meditation, – and so I was, but not on the subjects with which they conceived I was occupied. As I walked, some one touched my habit. I started, and, to my consternation, one of the monks asked my pardon for the sleeve of his tunic having touched mine. Two minutes after another touched my habit. I felt the difference, – there was an intelligential and communicative force in his grasp. He seized it as one who did not fear to be known, and who had no need to apologize. How is it that crime thus seizes us in life with a fearless grasp, while the touch of conscience trembles on the verge of our garment. One would almost parody the words of the well known Italian proverb, and say that guilt is masculine, and innocence feminine. *I grasped his wrist* with a trembling hand, and whispered – "Juan," in the same breath. He answered – "Alonzo," and passed me onward in a moment. I had then a few moments leisure to reflect on a destiny thus singularly entrusted to a being whose affections honoured humanity, and a being whose crimes disgraced it. I was suspended like Mahomet's tomb between heaven and earth. I felt an antipathy indescribable to hold any communication with a monster who had tried to hide the stains of parricide, by casting over their bloody and ineffaceable traces the shroud of monasticism. I felt also an inexpressible terror of Juan's passions and precipitancy; and I felt ultimately that I was in the power of all I dreaded most, and must submit to the operation of that power for my liberation.

'I was in the cloisters the following evening. I cannot say

I walked with a step so equal, but I am sure I did with a step much more artificially regular. For the second time the same person touched my habit, and whispered the name of Juan. After this I could no longer hesitate. I said, in passing, "I am in your power." A hoarse repulsive voice answered, "No, I am in yours." I murmured, "Well, then, I understand you, we belong to each other." – "Yes. We must not speak here, but a fortunate opportunity presents itself for our communication. To-morrow will be the eve of the feast of Pentecost; the vigil is kept by the whole community, who go two and two every hour to the altar, pass their hour in prayer, and then are succeeded by two more, and this continues all night. Such is the aversion with which you have inspired the community, that they have one and all refused to accompany you during your hour, which is to be from two till three. You will therefore be alone, and during your hour I will come and visit you, – we shall be undisturbed and unsuspected." At these words he quitted me. The next night was the eve of Pentecost, the monks went two and two all night to the altar, – at two o'clock my turn arrived. They rapped at my cell, and I descended to the church alone.'

Chapter Eight

Ye monks and nuns throughout the land,
　　Who go to church at night in pairs,
Never take bell-ropes in your hands,
　　To raise you up again from prayers.

Colman

'I am not superstitious, but, as I entered the church, I felt a chill of body and soul inexpressible. I approached the altar, and attempted to kneel, – an invisible hand repelled me. A voice seemed to address me from the recesses of the altar, and demand what brought me there? I reflected that those who had just quitted that spot had been absorbed in prayer, that those who were to succeed me would be engaged in the same profound homage, while I sought the church with a purpose of imposture and deception, and abused the hour allotted to the divine worship in contriving the means to escape from it. I felt I was a deceiver, shrouding my fraud in the very veils of the temple. I trembled at my purpose and at myself. I knelt, however, though I did not dare to pray. The steps of the altar felt unusually cold, – I shuddered at the silence I was compelled to observe. Alas! how can we expect that object to succeed, which we dare not entrust to God. Prayer, Sir, when we are deeply engaged in it, not only makes us eloquent, but communicates a kind of answering eloquence to the objects around us. At former times, while I poured out my heart before God, I felt as if the lamps burnt brighter, and the images smiled, – the silent midnight air was filled with forms and voices, and every breeze that sighed by the casement bore to my ear the harpings of a thousand angels. Now all was stilled, – the lamps, the images, the altar, the roof, seemed to behold me in silence. They surrounded me like witnesses, whose presence alone is enough to condemn you, without their uttering a word. I dared not look up, – I dared not speak, – I dared not pray, lest it would unfold a thought I could not supplicate a blessing on; and this kind of keeping a secret, which God must know, is at once so vain and impious.

'I had not remained long in this state of agitation, when I heard a step approach, – it was that of him I expected. "Rise," said he, for I was on my knees; "rise, – we have no time to lose. You have but an hour to remain in the church, and I have much to tell you in that hour." I rose. "To-morrow night is fixed for your escape." – "To-morrow night, – merciful God!" – "Yes; in desperate steps there is always more danger from delay than from precipitation. A thousand eyes and ears are on the watch already, – a single sinister or ambiguous movement would render it impossible to escape their vigilance. There may be some danger in hastening matters thus, but it is unavoidable. To-morrow night, after midnight, descend to the church, it is probable no one will then be here. If any one should, (engaged in recollection or in penance), retire to avoid suspicion. Return as soon as the church is empty, – I will be here. Do you observe that door?" and he pointed to a low door which I had often observed before, but never remembered to have seen opened; "I have obtained the key of that door, – no matter by what means. It formerly led to the vaults of the convent, but, for some extraordinary reasons, which I have not time to relate, another passage has been opened, and the former has not been employed or frequented for many years. From thence branches another passage, which, I have heard, opens by a trapdoor into the garden." – "Heard," I repeated; "Good God! is it on report, then, you depend in a matter so momentous? If you are not certain that such a passage exists, and that you will be able to trace its windings, may we not be wandering amid them all night?

Or perhaps –" "Interrupt me no more with those faint objections; I have no time to listen to fears which I can neither sympathize with or obviate. When we get through the trap-door into the garden, (if ever we do), another danger awaits us." He paused, I thought, like a man who is watching the effect of the terrors he excites, not from malignity but vanity, merely to magnify his own courage in encountering them. I was silent; and, as he heard neither flattery nor fear, he went on. "Two fierce dogs are let loose in the garden every night, – but they must be taken care of. The wall is sixteen feet high, – but your brother has provided a ladder of ropes, which he will fling over, and by which you may descend on the other side in safety." – "Safety! but then Juan will be in danger." – "Interrupt me no more, – the danger within the walls is the least you have to dread, beyond them, where can you seek for refuge or secrecy? Your brother's money will enable you possibly to escape from Madrid. He will bribe high, and every inch of your way must be paved with his gold. But, after that, so many dangers present themselves, that the enterprise and the danger seem but just begun. How will you cross the Pyrenees? How –" and he passed his hand over his forehead, with the air of a man engaged in an effort beyond his powers, and sorely perplexed about the means to effect it. This expression, so full of sincerity, struck me forcibly. It operated as a balance against all my former prepossessions. But still the more confidence I felt in him, the more I was impressed by his fears. I repeated after him, "How is it possible for me to escape ultimately? I may, by your assistance, traverse those intricate passages, whose cold dews I feel already distilling on me. I may emerge into light, ascend and descend the wall, but, after that, how am I to escape? – how am I even to live? All Spain is but one great monastery, – I must be a prisoner every step that I take." – "Your brother must look to that," said he abruptly; "I have done what I have undertaken." I then pressed him with several questions relating to the details of my escape. His answer was monotonous, unsatisfactory, and evasive, to a degree that again filled me first with suspicion, and then with terror. I asked, "But how have you obtained possession of the keys?" – "It is not your business to inquire." It was singular that he returned the same answer to every question I put to him, relative to his becoming possessed of the means to facilitate my escape, so that I was compelled to desist unsatisfied, and revert to what he had told me. – "But, then, that terrible passage near the vaults, – the chance, the fear that we may never emerge to light! Think of wandering amid sepulchral ruins, of stumbling over the bones of the dead, of encountering what I cannot describe, – the horror of being among those who are neither the living or the dead; – those dark and shadowless things that sport themselves with the reliques of the dead, and feast and love amid corruption, – ghastly, mocking, and terrific. *Must* we pass near the vaults?" – "What matter? perhaps I have more reason to dread them than you. Do *you* expect the spirit of your father to start from the earth to blast you?" At these words, which he uttered in a tone intended to inspire me with confidence, I shuddered with horror. They were uttered by a parricide, boasting of his crime in a church at midnight, amid saints, whose images were silent, but seemed to tremble. For relief I reverted to the unscaleable wall, and the difficulty of managing the ladder of ropes without detection. The same answer was on his lips, – "Leave that to me, – all that is settled." While he answered thus, he always turned his face away, and broke his words into monosyllables. At last I felt that the case was desperate, – that I must trust every thing to him. *To him*! Oh, my God! what I felt when I said this to myself! The conviction thrilled on my soul, – I am in his power. And yet, even under the impression, I could not help recurring to the impracticable difficulties that appeared to obstruct my escape. He then lost patience, – reproached me with timidity and ingratitude; and, while resuming his naturally ferocious and menacing tone, I actually felt more confidence in him than when he had attempted to disguise it. Half-remonstrance, half-invective as it was, what he said displayed so much ability, intrepidity, and art, that I began to feel a kind of doubtful security. I conceived, at least, that if any being on earth could effect my liberation, this was the man. He had no conception of fear, – no idea of conscience. When he hinted at his having murdered his father, it was done to impress me with an idea of his hardihood. I saw this from his expression, for I had involuntarily looked up at him. His eye had neither the hollowness of remorse, or the wandering of fear, – it glared on me bold, challenging, and prominent. He had but one idea annexed to the word danger, – that of strong excitement. He undertook a perilous attempt as a gamester would sit down to encounter an antagonist worthy of him; and, if life and death were the stake, he only felt as if he were playing at a higher rate, and the increased demands on his courage and talent actually supplied him with the means of meeting them. Our conference was now nearly at an end, when it occurred to me that this man was exposing himself to a degree of danger which it was almost incredible he should brave on my account; and this mystery, at least, I was resolved to penetrate. I said, "But how will you provide for your own safety? What will become of you when my escape is discovered? Would not the most dreadful punishments attend even the suspicion of your having been an agent in it, and what must be the result when that suspicion is exchanged for the most undeniable certainty?" It is impossible for me to describe the change his expression underwent while I uttered these words. He looked at me for some time without speaking, with an indefinable mixture of sarcasm, contempt, doubt, and curiosity in his countenance, and then attempted to laugh, but the muscles of his face were too stubborn and harsh to admit of this modulation. To features like his, frowns were a habit, and smiles a convulsion. He could produce nothing but a *rictus Sardonicus*,[16] the terrors of which there is no describing. It is very frightful to behold crime in its merriment, – its smile must be purchased by many groans. My blood ran cold as I looked at him. I waited for the sound of his voice as a kind of relief. At length he said, "Do you imagine me such an ideot as to promote your escape at the risk of imprisonment for life, – perhaps of immurement, – perhaps of the Inquisition?" and again he laughed. "No, we must escape together. Could you suppose I would have so much anxiety about an event, in which I had no part but that of an assistant? It was of my own danger I was thinking, – it was of my own safety I was doubtful. Our situation has happened to unite very opposite characters in the same adventure, but it is an union inevitable and *inseparable*. Your destiny is now bound to mine by a tie which no human force can break, – we part no more for ever. The secret that each is in possession of, must be watched by the other. Our lives are in each other's hands, and a moment of absence might be that of treachery. We must pass life in each watching every breath the other draws, every glance the other gives, – in dreading sleep as an involuntary betrayer, and watching the broken murmurs of each other's restless dreams. We may hate each other, torment each other, – worst of all, we may be weary of each other, (for hatred itself would be a relief, compared to the tedium of our inseparability), but separate we must never." At this picture of the liberty for which I had risked so much, my very soul recoiled. I gazed on the formidable being with whom my existence was thus incorporated. He was now retiring, when he paused at some distance to repeat his last words, or perhaps to observe their effect. I was sitting on the altar, – it was late, – the lamps in the church burned very dimly, and, as he stood in the aisle, he was placed in such a position, with regard to that which hung from the roof, that the light fell only on his face and one hand, which he extended towards me. The rest of his figure, enveloped in darkness, gave to this bodyless and spectre head an effect truly appalling. The ferocity of his features, too, was softened into a heavy and death-like gloom, as he repeated, "We part never, – I must be near you for ever," and the deep tones of his voice rolled like subterranean thunder round the church. A long pause followed. He continued to stand in the same posture, nor had I power to change mine. The clock struck three, its sound reminded me that my hour had expired. We separated, each taking different directions; and the two monks who succeeded me luckily came a few minutes late, (both of them yawning most fearfully), so our departure was unobserved.

'The day that followed I have no more power of describing, than of analysing a dream to its component parts of sanity, delirium, defeated memory, and triumphant imagination. The sultan in the eastern tale who plunged his head in a bason of water, and, before he raised it again, passed through adventures the most vicissitudinous and incredible – was a monarch, a slave, a husband, a widower, a father, childless, – in five minutes, never underwent the changes of *mind* that I did during that memorable day. I was a prisoner, – free, – a happy being, surrounded by smiling infants, – a victim of the Inquisition, writhing amid flames and execrations. I was a maniac, oscillating between hope and despair. I seemed to myself all that day to be pulling the rope of a bell, whose alternate knell was *heaven – hell*, and this rung in my ears with all the dreary and ceaseless monotony of the bell of the convent. Night came at last. I might almost say *day came*, for that day had been my night. Every thing was propitious to me, – the convent was all hushed. I put my head several times out of my cell, to be assured of this, – *all was hushed*. There was not a step in the corridor, – not a voice, not a whisper to be heard under a roof containing so many souls. I stole from my cell, I descended to the church. This was not unusual for those whose consciences or nerves were disturbed, during the sleepless gloom of a conventual night. As I advanced to the door of the church, where the lamps were always kept burning, I heard a human voice. I retreated in terror; – then I ventured to give a glance. An old monk was at prayers before one of the images of the saints, and the object of his prayers was to be relieved, not from the anguish of conscience, or the annihilation of monasticism, but from the

pains of a toothache, for which he had been desired to apply his
gums to the image of a saint quite notorious for her efficacy in
such cases.* The poor, old, tortured wretch, prayed with all the
fervency of agony, and then rubbed his gums over and over again
on the cold marble, which increased his complaint, his suffering,
and his devotion. I watched, listened, – there was something at
once ludicrous and frightful in my situation. I felt inclined to
laugh at my own distress, while it was rising almost to agony
every moment. I dreaded, too, the approach of another intruder,
and feeling my fear about to be realized by the approach of some
one, I turned round, and, to my inexpressible relief, saw my companion. I made him comprehend, by a sign, how I was prevented
from entering the church; he answered me in the same way, and
retreated a few steps, but not without shewing me a bunch of
huge keys under his habit. This revived my spirits, and I waited
for another half-hour in a state of mental excruciation, which,
were it inflicted on the bitterest enemy I have on earth, I think
I would have cried, "Hold, – hold, spare him." The clock struck
two, – I writhed and stamped with my feet, as loud as I dared, on
the floor of the passage. I was not at all tranquillized by the visible impatience of my companion, who started, from time to
time, from his hiding-place behind a pillar of the cloister, flung
on me a glance – no, a glare – of wild and restless inquiry, (which
I answered with one of despondency), and retired, grinding
curses between his teeth, whose horrible grating I could hear distinctly in the intervals of my long-withheld breath. At last I took
a desperate step. I walked into the church, and, going straight up
to the altar, prostrated myself on the steps. The old monk
observed me. He believed that I had come there with the same
purpose, if not with the same feelings, as himself; and he
approached me, to announce his intention of joining in my aspi-
rations, and intreating an interest in them, *as the pain had now*

* Vide Moore's View of France and Italy.

reached from the lower jaw to the upper. There is something that one can hardly describe in this union of the lowest with the highest interests of life. I was a prisoner, panting for emancipation, and staking my existence on the step I was compelled to take, – my whole interest for time, and perhaps for eternity, hung on a moment; and beside me knelt a being whose destiny was decided already, who could be nothing but a monk for the few years of his worthless existence, and who was supplicating a short remission from a temporary pain, that I would have endured my whole life for an hour's liberty. As he drew near me, and supplicated an interest in my prayers, I shrunk away. I felt a difference in the object of our addresses to God, that I dared not search my heart for the motive of. I knew not, at the moment, which of us was right, – he, whose prayer did no dishonour to the place, – or I, who was to struggle against a disorganized and unnatural state of life, whose vows I was about to violate. I knelt with him, how-ever, and prayed for the removal of his pain with a sincerity that cannot be questioned, as the success of my petitions might be the means of procuring his absence. As I knelt, I trembled at my own hypocrisy. I was profaning the altar of God, – I was mocking the sufferings of the being I supplicated for, – I was the worst of all hypocrites, a hypocrite on my knees, and at the altar. Yet, was I not compelled to be so? If I *was* a hypocrite, who had made me one? If I profaned the altar, who had dragged me there, to insult it by vows my soul belied and reversed faster than my lips could utter them? But this was no time for self-examination. I knelt, prayed, and trembled, till the poor sufferer, weary of his ineffec-tual and unanswered supplications, rose, and began to crawl away. For a few minutes I shivered in horrible anxiety, lest some other intruder might approach, but the quick decisive step that trod the aisle restored my confidence in a moment, – it was my companion. He stood beside me. He uttered a few curses, which sounded very shocking in my ears, more from the force of habit, and influence of the place, than from the meaning attached to them, and then hurried on *to the door*. A large bunch of keys was in his hand, and I followed instinctively this pledge of my liberation.

'The door was very low – we descended to it by four steps. He applied his key, muffling it in the sleeve of his habit to suppress the sound. At every application he recoiled, gnashed his teeth, stamped – then applied both hands. The lock did not give way – I clasped my hands in agony – I tossed them over my head. "Fetch a light," he said in a whisper; "take a lamp from before one of those figures." The levity with which he spoke of the holy images appalled me, and the act appeared to me nothing short of sacrilege; yet I went and took a lamp, which, with a shuddering hand, I held to him as he again tried the key. During this second attempt, we communicated in whispers those fears that left us scarce breath even for whispers. "Was not that a noise?" – "No, it was the echo of this jarring, stubborn lock. Is there no one coming?" – "Not one." – "Look out into the passage." – "Then I cannot hold the light to you." – "No matter – any thing but detection." – "Any thing for escape," I retorted with a courage that made him start, as I set down the lamp, and joined my strength to his to turn the key. It grated, resisted; the lock seemed invincible. Again we tried, with cranched teeth, indrawn breath, and fingers stripped almost to the bone, – in vain. – Again – in vain. – Whether the natural ferocity of his temper bore disappointment worse than mine, or that, like many men of undoubted courage, he was impatient of a *slight* degree of physical pain, in a struggle where he would have risked and lost life without a murmur, – or how it was, I know not, – but he sunk down on the steps leading to the door, wiped away the big drops of toil and terror from his forehead with the sleeve of his habit, and cast on me a look that was at once the pledge of sincerity and of despair. The clock struck three. The sound rung in my ears like the trumpet of the day of doom – the trumpet that *will sound*. He clasped his hands with a fierce and convulsive agony, that might have pictured the last struggles of the impenitent malefactor, – that agony without remorse, that suffering without requital or consolation, that, if I may say so, arrays crime in the dazzling robe of magnanimity, and makes us admire the fallen spirit, with whom we dare not sympathize. "We are undone," he cried; "*you* are undone. At the hour of three another monk is to enter on his hour of recollection." And he added, in a lower tone of horror inexpressible, "I hear his steps in the passage." At the moment he uttered these words, the key, that I had never ceased to struggle with, turned in the lock. The door opened, the passage lay free to us. My companion recovered himself at the sight, and in the next moment we were both in the passage. Our first care was to remove the key, and lock the door on the inside; and during this, we had the satisfaction to discover, that there was no one in the church, no one approaching it. Our fears had deceived us; we retired from the door, looked at each other with a kind of breathless, half-revived confidence, and began our progress through the vault in silence and in safety. In safety! my God! I yet tremble at the thought of that subterranean journey, amid the vaults of a convent, with a parricide for my companion. But what is there that danger will not familiarize us with? Had I been told such a story of another, I would have denounced him as the most reckless and desperate being on earth – yet *I was the man*. I had secured the lamp, (whose light appeared to reproach me with sacrilege at every gleam it shed on our progress), and followed my companion in silence. Romances have made your country, Sir, familiar with tales of subterranean passages, and supernatural horrors. All these, painted by the most eloquent pen, must fall short of the breathless horror felt by a being engaged in an enterprise beyond his powers, experience, or calculation, driven to trust his life and liberation to hands that reeked with a father's blood. It was in vain that I tried *to make up my mind*, – that I said to myself, "This is to last but for a short time," – that I struggled to force on myself the conviction that it was necessary to have such associates in desperate enterprises; – it was all in vain. I trembled at my situation, – at myself, and that is a terror we can never overcome. I stumbled over the stones, – I was chilled with horror at every step. A blue mist gathered before my eyes, – it furred the edges of the lamp with a dim and hazy light. My imagination began to operate, and when I heard the curses with which my companion reproached my involuntary delay, I began almost to fear that I was following the steps of a demon, who had lured me there for purposes beyond the reach of imagination to picture. Tales of superstition crowded on me like images of terror on those who are in the dark. I had heard of infernal beings who deluded monks with the hopes of liberation, seduced them into the vaults of the convent, and then proposed conditions which it is almost as horrible to relate as to undergo the performance of. I thought of being forced to witness the unnatural revels of a diabolical feast, – of seeing the rotting flesh distributed, – of drinking the dead corrupted blood, – of hearing the anthems of fiends howled in insult, on that awful verge where life and eternity mingle, – of hearing the hallelujahs of the choir, echoed even through the vaults, where demons were yelling the *black mass* of their infernal Sabbath. – I thought of all that the interminable passages, the livid light, and the diabolical companion, might suggest.

'Our wanderings in the passage seemed to be endless. My companion turned to right, to left, – advanced, retreated, paused, – (the pause was dreadful)! – Then advanced again, tried another direction, where the passage was so low that I was obliged to crawl on my hands and knees to follow him, and even in this posture my head struck against the ragged roof. When we had proceeded for a considerable time, (at least so it appeared to me, for minutes are hours in the *noctuary* of terror, – terror has no *diary*), this passage became so narrow and so low, that I could proceed no farther, and wondered how my companion could have advanced beyond me. I called to him, but received no answer; and, in the darkness of the passage, or rather hole, it was impossible to see ten inches before me. I had the lamp, too, to watch, which I had held with a careful trembling hand, but which began to burn dim in the condensed and narrow atmosphere. A gush of terror rose in my throat. Surrounded as I was by damps and dews, my whole body felt in a fever. I called again, but no voice answered. In situations of peril, the imagination is unhappily fertile, and I could not help recollecting and *applying* a story I had once read of some travellers who attempted to explore the vaults of the Egyptian pyramids. One of them, who was advancing, as I was, on his hands and knees, stuck in the passage, and, whether from terror, or from the natural consequences of his situation, swelled so that it was impossible for him to retreat, advance, or allow a passage for his companions. The party were on their return, and finding their passage stopped by this irremoveable obstruction, their lights trembling on the verge of extinction, and their guide terrified beyond the power of direction or advice, proposed, in the selfishness to which the feeling of vital danger reduces all, to cut off the limbs of the wretched being who obstructed their passage. He heard this proposal, and, contracting himself with agony at the sound, was reduced, by that strong muscular spasm, to his usual dimensions, dragged out, and afforded room for the party to advance. He was suffocated, however, in the effort, and left behind a corse. All this detail, that takes many words to tell, rushed on my soul in a moment; – on my soul? – no, on my body. I was all physical feeling, – all intense corporeal agony, and God only knows, and man only can feel, how that agony can absorb and annihilate all other feeling within us, – how we could, in such a moment, feed on a parent, to gnaw out our passage into life and liberty, as sufferers in a wreck have been known to gnaw their own flesh, for the support of that existence which the unnatural morsel was diminishing at every agonizing bite.

'I tried to crawl backwards, – I succeeded. I believe the story I recollected had an effect on me, I felt a contraction of muscles corresponding to what I had read of. I felt myself almost liberated by the sensation, and the next moment I was actually so; – I had got out of the passage I knew not how. I must have made one of those extraordinary exertions, whose energy is perhaps not only increased by, but dependent on, our unconsciousness of them. However it was, I was extricated, and stood breathless and exhausted, with the dying lamp in my hand, staring around me, and seeing nothing but the black and dripping walls, and the low arches of the vault, that seemed to lower over me like the frown of an eternal hostility, – a frown that forbids hope or escape. The lamp was rapidly extinguishing in my hand, – I gazed on it with a fixed eye. I knew that my life, and, what was dearer than my life, my liberation, depended on my watching its last glimpse, yet I gazed on it with the eye of an ideot, – a stupified stare. The lamp glimmered more faintly, – its dying gleams awoke me to recollection. I roused myself, – I looked around. A strong flash discovered an object near me. I shuddered, – I uttered cries, though I was unconscious of doing so, for a voice said to me, – "Hush, be silent; I left you only to reconnoitre the passages. I have made out the way to the trap-door, – be silent, and all is well." I advanced trembling, my companion appeared trembling too. He whispered, "Is the lamp so nearly extinguished?" – "You see." – "Try to keep it in for a few moments." – "I will; but, if I cannot, what then?" – "Then we must perish," he added, with an execration that I thought would have brought down the vaults over our heads. It is certain, Sir, however, that desperate sentiments are best suited to desperate emergencies, and this wretch's blasphemies gave me a kind of horrible confidence in his courage. On he went, muttering curses before me; and I followed, watching the last light of the lamp with agony increased by my fear of further provoking my horrible guide. I have before mentioned how our feelings, even in the most fearful exigencies, dwindle into petty and wretched details. With all my care, however, the lamp declined, – quivered, – flashed a pale light, like the smile of despair on me, and was extinguished. I shall never forget the look my guide threw on me by its sinking light. I had watched it like the last beatings of an expiring heart, like the shiverings of a spirit about to part for eternity. I saw it extinguished, and believed myself already among those for "whom the blackness of darkness is reserved for ever."

'It was at this moment that a faint sound reached our frozen ears; – it was the chaunt of matins, performed by candlelight at this season of the year, which was begun in the chapel now far above us. This voice of heaven thrilled us, – we seemed the pioneers of darkness, on the very frontiers of hell. This superb insult of celestial triumph, that amid the strains of hope spoke despair to us, announced a God to those who were stopping their ears against the sound of his name, had an effect indescribably awful. I fell to the ground, whether from stumbling from the darkness, or shrinking from emotion, I know not. I was roused by the rough arm, and rougher voice of my companion. Amid execrations that froze my blood, he told me this was no time for failing or for fear. I asked him, trembling, what I was to do? He answered, "Follow me, and feel your way in darkness." Dreadful sounds! – Those who tell us *the whole* of our calamity always appear malignant, for our hearts, or our imaginations, always flatter us that it is not so great as reality proves it to be. Truth is told us by any mouth sooner than our own.

'In darkness, total darkness, and on my hands and knees, for I could no longer stand, I followed him. This motion soon affected my head; I grew giddy first, then stupified. I paused. He growled a curse, and I instinctively quickened my movements, like a dog who hears the voice of a chiding master. My habit was now in rags from my struggles, my knees and hands stript of skin. I had received several severe bruises on my head, from striking against the jagged and unhewn stones which formed the irregular sides and roof of this eternal passage. And, above all, the unnatural atmosphere, combined with the intensity of my emotion, had produced a thirst, the agony of which I can compare to nothing but that of a burning coal dropt into my throat, which I seemed to suck for moisture, but which left only drops of fire on my tongue. Such was my state, when I called out to my companion that I could proceed no farther. "Stay there and rot, then," was the answer; and perhaps the most soothing words of encouragement could not have produced so strong an effect on me. This confidence of despair, this bravado against danger, that menaced the power in his very citadel, gave me a temporary courage – but what is courage amid darkness and doubt? From the faultering steps, the suffocated breath, the muttered curses, I guessed what was going on. I was right. The final – hopeless stop followed instantly, announced by the last wild sob, the cranching of despairing teeth, the clasping, or rather clap, of the locked hands, in the terrible extasy of utter agony. I was kneeling behind him at that moment, and I echoed every cry and gesture with a violence that started my guide. He silenced me with curses. Then he attempted to pray; but his prayers sounded so like curses, and his curses were so like prayers to the evil one, that, choaking with horror, I implored him to cease. He did cease, and for nearly half an hour neither of us uttered a word. We lay beside each other like two panting dogs that I have read of, who lay down to die close to the animal they pursued, whose fur they fanned with their dying breath, while unable to mouthe her.

'Such appeared emancipation to us, – so near, and yet so hopeless. We lay thus, not daring to speak to each other, for who could speak but of despair, and which of us dared to aggravate the despair of the other. This kind of fear which we know already felt by others, and which we dread to aggravate by uttering, *even to those who know it*, is perhaps the most horrible sensation ever experienced. The very thirst of my body seemed to vanish in this fiery thirst of the soul for communication, where all communication was unutterable, impossible, hopeless. Perhaps the condemned spirits will feel thus at their final sentence, when they know all that is to be suffered, and dare not disclose to each other that horrible truth which is no longer a secret, but which the profound silence of their despair would seem to make one. The secret of silence is the only secret. Words are a blasphemy against that taciturn and invisible God, whose presence enshrouds us in our last extremity. These moments that appeared to me endless, were soon to cease. My companion sprung up, – he uttered a cry of joy. I imagined him deranged, – he was not. He exclaimed, "Light, light, – the light of heaven; we are near the trap-door, I see the light through it." Amid all the horrors of our situation, he had kept his eye constantly turned upwards, for he knew that, if we were near it, the smallest glimmering of light would be visible in the intense darkness that enveloped us. He was right. I started up, – I saw it too. With locked hands, with dropt and wordless lips, with dilated and thirsting eyes, we gazed upwards. A thin line of grey light appeared above our heads. It broadened, it grew brighter, – it *was* the light of heaven, and its breezes too came fluttering to us through the chinks of the trap-door that opened into the garden.'

Chapter Nine

'Though life and liberty seemed so near, our situation was still very critical. The morning light that aided our escape, might open many an eye to mark it. There was not a moment to be lost. My companion proposed to ascend first, and I did not venture to oppose him. I was too much in his power to resist; and in early youth superiority of depravity always seems like a superiority of power. We reverence, with a prostituted idolatry, those who have passed through the degrees of vice before us. This man was criminal, and crime gave him a kind of heroic immunity in my eyes. Premature knowledge in life is always to be purchased by guilt. He knew more than I did, – he was my all in this desperate attempt. I dreaded him as a demon, yet I invoked him as a god.

'In the end I submitted to his proposal. I was very tall, but he was much stronger than I. He rose on my shoulders, I trembled under his weight, but he succeeded in raising the trap-door, – the full light of day broke on us both. In a moment he dropt his hold of the door, – he fell to the ground with a force that struck me down. He exclaimed, "The workmen are there, they have come about the repairs, we are lost if we are discovered. They are there, the garden is full of them already, they will be there the whole day. That cursed lamp, it has undone us! Had it but kept in for a few moments, we might have been in the garden, might have crossed the wall, might have been at liberty, and now –" He fell to the ground convulsed with rage and disappointment, as he spoke. To me there was nothing so terrible in this intelligence. That we were disappointed for a time was evident, but we had been relieved from the most horrible of all fears, that of wandering in famine and darkness till we perished, – we had found the way to the trap-door. I had unfailing confidence in Juan's patience and zeal. I was sure that if he was watching for us on that night, he would watch for many a successive night. Finally, I felt we had but twenty-four hours or less to wait, and what was that to the eternity of hours that must otherwise be wasted in a convent. I suggested all this to my companion as I closed the trap-door; but I found in his complaints, imprecations, and tossing restlessness of impatience and despair, the difference between man and man in the hour of trial. He possessed active, and I passive fortitude. Give him something to do, and he would do it at the risk of limb, and life, and soul, – he never murmured. Give me something to suffer, to undergo, to submit, and I became at once the *hero of submission*. While this man, with all his physical strength, and all his mental hardihood, was tossing on the earth with the imbecility of an infant, in a paroxysm of unappeasable passion, I was his consoler, adviser, and supporter. At last he suffered himself to hear reason; he agreed that we must remain twenty-four hours more in the passage, on which he bestowed a whole litany of curses. So we determined to stand in stillness and darkness till night; but such is the restlessness of the human heart, that this arrangement, which a few hours before we would have embraced as the offer of a benignant angel for our emancipation, began to display, as we were compelled to examine its aspect more closely, certain features that were repulsive almost to hideousness. We were exhausted nearly to death. Our physical exertions had been, for the last few hours, almost incredible; in fact, I am convinced that nothing but the consciousness that we were engaged in a struggle for life or death, could have enabled us to support it, and now that the struggle was over, we began to feel our weakness. Our mental sufferings had not been less, – we had been excruciated body and soul alike. Could our mental struggles have operated like our bodily ones, we would have been seen to weep drops of blood, as we felt we were doing at every step of our progress. Recollect too, Sir, the unnatural atmosphere we had breathed so long, amid darkness and danger, and which now began to show its anti-vital and pestilent effect, in producing alternately on our bodies deluges of perspiration, succeeded by a chill that seemed to freeze the very marrow. In this state of mental fever, and bodily exhaustion, we had now to wait many hours, in darkness, without food, till Heaven pleased to send us night. But how were those hours to be passed? The preceding day had been one of strict abstinence, – we began already to feel the gnawings of hunger, a hunger not to be appeased. We must fast till the moment of liberation, and we must fast amid stone walls, and damp seats on floors of stone, which diminished every moment the strength necessary to contend with their impenetrable hardness, – their withering chillness.

'The last thought that occurred to me was, – with what a companion those hours must be passed. With a being whom I abhorred from my very soul, while I felt that his presence was at once an irrepealable curse, and an invincible necessity. So we stood, shivering under the trap-door, not daring to whisper our thoughts to each other, but feeling *that despair of incommunication* which is perhaps the severest curse that can be inflicted on those who are compelled to be together, and compelled, by the same necessity that imposes their ungenial union, not even to communicate their fears to each other. We *hear* the throb of each other's hearts, and yet dare not say, "My heart beats in unison with yours."

'As we stood thus, the light became suddenly eclipsed. I knew not from what this arose, till I felt a shower, the most violent perhaps that ever was precipitated on the earth, make its way even through the trap-door, and drench me in five minutes to the skin. I retreated from the spot, but not before I had received it in every pore of my body. You, Sir, who live in happy Ireland, blessed by God with an exemption from those vicissitudes of the atmosphere, can have no idea of their violence in continental countries. This rain was followed by peals of thunder, that made me fear God was pursuing me into the abysses where I had shrunk to

escape from his vengeance, and drew from my companion blasphemies more loud than thunder, as he felt himself drenched by
the shower, that now, flooding the vault, rose almost to our
ancles. At last he proposed our retiring to a place which he said he
was acquainted with, and which would shelter us. He added, that
it was but a few steps from where we stood, and that we could
easily find our way back. I did not dare to oppose him, and followed to a dark recess, only distinguished from the rest of the
vault by the remains of what had once been a door. It was now
light, and I could distinguish objects plainly. By the deep hollows
framed for the shooting of the bolt, and the size of the iron
hinges that still remained, though covered with rust, I saw it must
have been of no common strength, and probably intended to
secure the entrance to a dungeon, – there was no longer a door,
yet I shuddered to enter it. As we did so, both of us, exhausted in
body and mind, sunk on the hard floor. We did not say a word to
each other, an inclination to sleep irresistibly overcame us; and
whether that sleep was to be my last or not, I felt a profound
indifference. Yet I was now on the verge of liberty, and though
drenched, famishing, and comfortless, was, in any rational estimate, an object much more enviable than in the heart-withering
safety of my cell. Alas! it is too true that our souls always contract
themselves on the approach of a blessing, and seem as if their
powers, exhausted in the effort to obtain it, had no longer energy
to embrace the object. Thus we are always compelled to substitute the pleasure of the pursuit for that of the attainment, – to
reverse the means for the end, or confound them, in order to
extract any enjoyment from either, and at last fruition becomes
only another name for lassitude. These reflections certainly did
not occur to me, when, worn out with toil, terror, and famine,
I fell on the stone floor in a sleep that was not sleep, – it seemed
the suspension both of my mortal and immortal nature. I ceased
from animal and intellectual life at once. There are cases, Sir,
where the thinking power appears to accompany us to the very

verge of slumber, where we sleep full of delightful thoughts, and sleep only to review them in our dreams: But there are also cases when we feel that our sleep is a "sleep for ever", – when we resign the hope of immortality for the hope of a profound repose, – when we demand from the harassings of fate, "Rest, rest," and no more, – when the soul and body faint together, and all we ask of God or man is to let us sleep.

'In such a state I fell to the ground; and, at that moment, would have bartered all my hopes of liberation for twelve hours' profound respose, as Esau sold his birth-right for a small but indispensable refreshment. I was not to enjoy even this repose long. My companion was sleeping too. Sleeping! great God! what was his sleep? – that in whose neighbourhood no one could close an eye, or, worse, an ear. He talked as loudly and incessantly as if he had been employed in all the active offices of life. I heard involuntarily the secret of his dreams. I knew he had murdered his father, but I did not know that the vision of parricide haunted him in his broken visions. My sleep was first broken by sounds as horrible as any I ever had heard at my bed-side in the convent. I heard sounds that disturbed me, but I was not yet fully awake. They increased, they redoubled, – the terrors of my habitual associations awoke me. I imagined the Superior and the whole community pursuing us with lighted torches. I felt the blaze of the lights in contact with my very eye-balls. I shrieked. I said, "Spare my sight, do not blind me, do not drive me mad, and I will confess all." A deep voice near me muttered, "Confess." I started up fully awake, – it was only the voice of my sleeping companion. I stood on my feet, viewed him as he lay. He heaved and wallowed on his bed of stone, as if it had been down. He seemed to have a frame of adamant. The jagged points of stone, the hardness of the floor, the ruts and rudenesses of his inhospitable bed, produced no effect on him. He could have slept, but his dreams were from within. I have heard, I have read, of the horrors attending the dying beds of the guilty. They often told us of such in the convent. One monk in particular, who was a priest, was fond of dwelling on a death-bed scene he had witnessed, and of describing its horrors. He related that he had urged a person, who was sitting calmly in his chair, though evidently dying, to intrust him with his confession. The dying person answered, "I will, when those leave the room." The monk, conceiving that this referred to the relatives and friends, motioned them to retire. They did so, and again the monk renewed his demands on the conscience of the penitent. The room was now empty. The monk renewed his adjuration to the dying man to disclose the secrets of his conscience. The answer was the same, – "I will, when those are gone." – "*Those!*" – "Yes, those whom you cannot see, and cannot banish, – send them away, and I will tell you the truth." – "Tell it now, then; there are none here but you and me." – "There are," answered the dying man. "There are none that I can see," said the monk, gazing round the room. "But there are those that I do see," replied the dying wretch; "and that see me; that are watching, waiting for me, the moment the breath is out of my body. I see them, I feel them, – stand on my right side." The monk changed his position. "Now they are on the left." The monk shifted again. "Now they are on my right." The monk commanded the children and relatives of the dying wretch to enter the room, and surround the bed. They obeyed the command. "Now they are every where," exclaimed the sufferer, and expired.*

'This terrible story came freshly to my recollection, accompanied by many others. I had heard much of the terrors that surrounded the dying bed of the guilty, but, from what I was compelled to hear, I almost believe them to be less than the terrors of a guilty sleep. I have said my companion began at first with low mutterings, but among them I could distinguish sounds that reminded me too soon of all I wished to forget, at least while we were together. He murmured, "An old man? – yes, – well, the

* Fact, – me ipso teste.[18]

less blood in him. Grey hairs? – no matter, my crimes have helped to turn them grey, – he ought to have rent them from the roots long ago. They are white, you say? – well, to-night they shall be dyed in blood, then they will be white no longer. Aye, – he will hold them up at the day of judgment, like a banner of condemnation against me. He will stand at the head of an army stronger than the army of martyrs, – the host of those whose murderers have been their own children. What matter whether they cut their parents' hearts or their throats. I have cut *one* through and through, to the very core, – now for the other, it will give him less pain, I feel that," – and he laughed, shuddered, and writhed on his stony bed. Trembling with horror ineffable, I tried to awake him. I shook his muscular arms, I rolled him on his back, on his face, – nothing could awake him. It seemed as if I was only rocking him on his cradle of stone. He went on, "Secure the purse, I know the drawer of the cabinet where it lies, but secure him first. Well, then, you cannot, – you shudder at his white hairs, at his calm sleep! – ha! ha! that villains should be fools. Well, then, I must be the man, it is but a short struggle with him or me, – he may be damned, and I must. Hush, – how the stairs creak, they will not tell him it is his son's foot that is ascending? – They dare not, the stones of the wall would give them the lie. Why did you not oil the hinges of the door? – now for it. He sleeps intensely, – aye, how calm he looks! – the calmer the fitter for heaven. Now, – now, my knee is on his breast, – where is the knife? – where is the knife! – if he looks at me I am lost. The knife, – I am a coward; the knife, – if he opens his eyes I am gone; the knife, ye cursed cravens, – who dare shrink when I have gripped my father's throat? There, – there, – there, – blood to the hilt, – the old man's blood; look for the money, while I wipe the blade. I cannot wipe it, the grey hairs are mingled with the blood, – those hairs brushed my lips the last time he kissed me. I was a child then. I would not have taken a world to murder him then, now, – now, what am I? Ha! ha! ha! Let Judas shake his bag of silver against mine, – he betrayed his Saviour, and I have murdered my father. Silver against silver, and soul against soul. I have got more for mine, – he was a fool to sell his for thirty. But for which of us will the last fire burn hotter? – no matter, I am going to try." At these horrible expressions, repeated over and over, I called, I shrieked to my companion to awake. He did so, with a laugh almost as wild as the chattering of his dreams. "Well, what have you heard? I murdered him, – you knew that long before. You trusted me in this cursed adventure, which will risk the life of both, and can you not bear to hear me speak to myself, though I am only telling what you knew before?" – "No, I cannot bear it," I answered, in an agony of horror; "not even to effect my escape, could I undertake to sustain another hour like the past, – the prospect of seclusion here for a whole day amid famine, damps, and darkness, listening to the ravings of a —. Look not at me with that glare of mockery, I know it all, I shudder at your sight. Nothing but the iron link of necessity could have bound me to you even for a moment. I *am* bound to you, – I must bear it while it continues, but do not make those moments insupportable. My life and liberty are in your hands, – I must add my reason, too, in the circumstances in which we are plunged, – I cannot sustain your horrible eloquence of sleep. If I am forced to listen to it again, you may bear me alive from these walls, but you will bear me away an ideot, stupified by terror which my brain is unable to support. Do not sleep, I adjure you. Let me watch beside you during this wretched day, – this day which is to be measured by darkness and suffering, instead of light and enjoyment. I am willing to famish with hunger, to shudder with cold, to couch on these hard stones, but I cannot bear your dreams, – if you sleep, I must rouse you in defence of my reason. All physical strength is failing me fast, and I am become more jealous of the preservation of my intellect. Do not cast at me those looks of defiance, I am your inferior in strength, but despair makes us equal." As I spoke, my voice sounded like thunder in my own ears, my eyes flashed visibly to myself. I felt the power that passion gives us, and I saw that my companion felt it too. I went on, in a tone that made myself start, "If you dare to sleep, I will wake you, – if you dose even, you shall not have a moment undisturbed, – you shall wake with me. For this long day we must starve and shiver together, I have wound myself up to it. I can bear every thing, – every thing but the dreams of him whose sleep reveals to him the vision of a murdered parent. Wake, – rave, – blaspheme, – but sleep you shall not!"

'The man stared at me for some time, almost incredulous of my being capable of such energy of passion and command. But when he had, by the help of his dilated eyes, and gaping mouth, appeared to satisfy himself fully of the fact, his expression suddenly changed. He appeared to feel a community of nature with me for the first time. Any thing of ferocity appeared congenial and balsamic to him; and, with oaths, that froze my blood, swore he liked me the better for my resolution. "I *will* keep awake," he added, with a yawn that distended like the jaws of an Ogre preparing for his cannibal feast. Then suddenly relaxing, "But how shall we keep awake? We have nothing to eat, nothing to drink, what shall we do to keep awake?" And incontinently he uttered a volley of curses. Then he began to sing. But what songs? – full of such ribaldry and looseness, that, bred as I was first in domestic privacy, and then in the strictness of a convent, made me believe it was an incarnate demon that was howling beside me. I implored him to cease, but this man could pass so instantaneously from the extremes of atrocity to those of levity, – from the ravings of guilt and horror ineffable, to songs that would insult a brothel, that I knew not what to make of him. This *union of antipodes*, this unnatural alliance of the extremes of guilt and light-mindedness, I had never met or imagined before. He started from the visions of a parricide, and sung songs that would have made a harlot blush. How ignorant of life I must have been, not to know that guilt and insensibility often join to tenant and deface the same mansion, and that there is not a more strong and indissoluble alliance on earth, than that between the hand that dare do any thing, and the heart that can feel nothing.

'It was in the midst of one of his most licentious songs, that my companion suddenly paused. He gazed about him for some time; and faint and dismal as the light was by which we beheld each other, I thought I could observe an extraordinary expression overshadow his countenance. I did not venture to notice it. "Do you know where we are?" he whispered. "Too well; – in the vault of a convent, beyond the help or reach of man, – without food, without light, and almost without hope." – "Aye, so its last inhabitants might well say." – "Its last inhabitants! – who were they?" – "I can tell you, if you can bear it." – "*I cannot bear it*," I cried, stopping my ears, "I will not listen to it. I feel by the narrator it must be something horrid." – "It was indeed a horrid night," said he, unconsciously adverting to some circumstance in the narrative; and his voice sunk into mutterings, and he forbore to mention the subject further. I retired as far from him as the limits of the vault admitted; and, burying my head between my knees, tried to *forbear to think*. What a state of mind must that be, in which we are driven to wish we no longer had one! – when we would willingly become "as the beasts that perish", to forget that privilege of humanity, which only seems an undisputed title to superlative misery! To sleep was impossible. Though sleep seems to be only a necessity of nature, it always requires an act of the mind to concur in it. And if I had been willing to rest, the gnawings of hunger, which now began to be exchanged for the most deadly sickness, would have rendered it impossible. Amid this complication of physical and mental suffering, it is hardly credible, Sir, but it is not the less true, that my principal one arose from the inanity, the want of occupation, inevitably attached to my dreary situation. To inflict a suspension of the action on a being conscious of possessing the powers of action, and burning for their employment, – to forbid all interchange of mutual ideas, or acquirement of new ones to an intellectual being, – to do this, is to invent a torture that might make Phalaris blush for his impotence of cruelty.

'I had felt other sufferings almost intolerable, but I felt this impossible to sustain; and, will you believe it, Sir, after wrestling with it during an hour (as I counted hours) of unimaginable misery, I rose, and supplicated my companion to relate the circumstance he had alluded to, as connected with our dreadful abode. His ferocious good nature took part with this request in a moment; and though I could see that his strong frame had suffered more than my comparatively feeble one, from the struggles of the night and the privations of the day, he prepared himself with a kind of grim alacrity for the effort. He was now in his element. He was enabled to daunt a feeble mind by the narration of horrors, and to amaze an ignorant one with a display of crimes; – and he needed no more to make him commence. "I remember," said he, "an extraordinary circumstance connected with this vault. I wondered how I felt so familiar with this door, this arch, at first. – I did not recollect immediately, so many strange thoughts have crossed my mind every day, that events which would make a life-lasting impression on others, pass like shadows before me, while thoughts appear like substances. *Emotions are my events* – you know what brought me to this cursed convent – well, don't shiver or look *paler* – you were pale before. However it was, I found myself in the convent, and I was obliged to subscribe to its discipline. A part of it was, that extraordinary criminals should undergo what they called extraordinary penance; that is, not only submit to every ignominy and rigour of conventual life, (which, fortunately for its penitents, is never wanting in such amusing resources), but act the part of executioner whenever any distinguished punishment was to be inflicted or witnessed. They did me the honour to believe me particularly qualified for this species of recreation, and perhaps they did not flatter me. I had all the humility of a saint on trial; but still I had a kind of confidence in my talents of this description, provided they were put to a proper test; and the monks had the goodness to assure me, that I never could long be without one in a convent. This was a very tempting picture of my situation, but I found these worthy people had not in the least exaggerated. An instance occurred a few days after I had the happiness to become a member of this amiable community, of whose merits you are doubtless sensible. I was desired to attach myself to a young monk of distinguished family, who had lately taken the vows, and who performed his duties with that heartless punctuality that intimated to the community that his heart was elsewhere. I was soon put in possession of the business; from their ordering me to *attach* myself to him, I instantly conceived I was bound to the most deadly hostility against him. The friendship of convents is always a treacherous league – we watch, suspect, and torment each other, for the love of God. This young monk's only crime was, that he was suspected of cherishing an earthly passion. He was, in fact, as I have stated, the son of a distinguished family, who (from the fear of his contracting what is called a degrading marriage, *i.e.* of marrying a woman of inferior rank whom he loved, and who would have made him happy, as fools, that is, half mankind, estimate happiness) forced him to take the vows. He appeared at times broken-hearted, but at times there was a light of hope in his eye, that looked somewhat ominous in the eyes of the community. It is certain, that hope not being an indigenous plant in the parterre of a convent, must excite suspicion with regard both to its origin and its growth.

'"Some time after, a young novice entered the convent. From the moment he did so, a change the most striking took place in the young monk. He and the novice became inseparable companions – there was something suspicious in that. My eyes were on the watch in a moment. Eyes are particularly sharpened in discovering misery when they can hope to aggravate it. The attachment between the young monk and the novice went on. They were for ever in the garden together – they inhaled the odours of the flowers – they cultivated the same cluster of carnations – they entwined themselves as they walked together – when they were in the choir, their voices were like mixed incense. Friendship is often carried to excess in conventual life, but this friendship was too like love. For instance, the psalms sung in the choir sometimes breathe a certain language; at these words, the young monk and the novice would direct their voices to each other in sounds that could not be misunderstood. If the least correction was inflicted, one would intreat to undergo it for the other. If a day of relaxation was allowed, whatever presents were sent to the cell of one, were sure to be found in the cell of the other. This was enough for me. I saw that secret of mysterious happiness, which is the greatest misery to those who never can share it. My vigilance was redoubled, and it was rewarded by the discovery of a secret – a secret that I had to communicate and raise my consequence by. You cannot guess the importance attached to the discovery of a secret in a convent, (particularly when the remission of our own offences depends on the discovery of those of others.)

' "One evening as the young monk and his darling novice were in the garden, the former plucked a peach, which he immediately offered to his favourite; the latter accepted it with a movement I thought rather awkward – it seemed like what I imagined would be the reverence of a female. The young monk divided the peach with a knife; in doing so, the knife grazed the finger of the novice, and the monk, in agitation inexpressible, tore his habit to bind up the wound. I saw it all – my mind was made up on the business – I went to the Superior that very night. The result may be conceived. They were watched, but cautiously at first. They were probably on their guard; for, for some time it defied even my vigilance to make the slightest discovery. It is a situation incomparably tantalizing, when suspicion is satisfied of her own suggestions, as of the truth of the gospel, but still wants the *little fact* to make them credible to others. One night that I had, by direction of the Superior, taken my station in the gallery, (where I was contented to remain hour after hour, and night after night, amid solitude, darkness, and cold, for the chance of the power of retaliating on others the misery inflicted on myself) – One night, I thought I heard a step in the gallery – I have told you that I was in the dark – a light step passed me. I could hear the broken and palpitating respiration of the person. A few moments after, I heard a door open, and knew it to be the door of the young monk. I knew it; for by long watching in the dark, and accustoming myself to number the cells, by the groan from one, the prayer from another, the faint shriek of restless dreams from a third, my ear had become so finely graduated, that I could instantly distinguish the opening of *that door*, from which (to my sorrow) no sound had ever before issued. I was provided with a small chain, by which I fastened the handle of the door to a contiguous one, in such a manner, that it was impossible to open either of them from the inside. I then hastened to the Superior, with a pride of which none but the successful tracer of a guilty secret in convents, can have any conception. I believe the Superior was himself agitated by the luxury of the same feelings, for he was awake and up in his apartment, attended by *four monks*, whom you may remember." I shuddered at the remembrance. "I communicated my intelligence with a voluble eagerness, not only unsuited to the respect I owed these persons, but which must have rendered me almost unintelligible, yet they were good enough not only to overlook this violation of decorum, which would in any other case have been severely punished, but even to supply certain pauses in my narrative, with a condescension and facility truly miraculous. I felt what it was to acquire importance in the eyes of a Superior, and gloried in all the dignified depravity of an informer. We set out without losing a moment, – we arrived at the door of the cell, and I pointed out with triumph the chain unremoved, though a slight vibration, perceptible at our approach, showed the wretches within were already apprized of their danger. I unfastened the door, – how they must have shuddered! The Superior and his satellites burst into the cell, and *I* held the light. You tremble, – why? I was guilty, and I wished to witness guilt that palliated mine, at least in the opinion of the convent. I had only violated the laws of nature, but they had outraged the decorum of a convent, and, of course, in the creed of a convent, there was no proportion between our offences. Besides, I was anxious to witness misery that might perhaps equal or exceed my own, and this is a curiosity not easily satisfied. It is actually possible to become *amateurs in suffering*. I have heard of men who have travelled into countries where horrible executions were to be daily witnessed, for the sake of that excitement which the sight of suffering never fails to give, from the spectacle of a tragedy, or an *auto da fe*, down to the writhings of the meanest reptile on whom you can inflict torture, and feel that torture is the result of your own power. It is a species of feeling of which we never can divest ourselves, – a triumph over those whose sufferings have placed them below us, and no wonder, – suffering is always an indication of weakness, – we glory in our impenetrability. *I* did, as we burst into the cell. The wretched husband and wife were locked in each other's arms. You may imagine the scene that followed. Here I must do the Superior reluctant justice. He was a man (of course from his conventual feelings) who had no more idea of the intercourse between the sexes, than between two beings of a different species. The scene that he beheld could not have revolted him more, than if he had seen the horrible loves of the baboons and the Hottentot women, at the Cape of Good Hope; or those still more loathsome unions between the serpents of South America and their human victims,* when they can catch them, and twine round them in folds of unnatural and ineffable union. He really stood as much astonished and appalled, to see two human beings of different sexes, who dared

* Vide Charlevoix's History of Paraguay.

to love each other in spite of monastic ties, as if he had witnessed the horrible conjunctions I have alluded to. Had he seen vipers engendering in that frightful knot which seems the pledge of mortal hostility, instead of love, he could not have testified more horror, – and I do him the justice to believe he felt all he testified. Whatever affectation he might employ on points of conventual austerity, there was none here. Love was a thing he always believed connected with sin, even though consecrated by the name of a sacrament, and called marriage, as it is in our church. But, love in a convent! – Oh, there is no conceiving his rage; still less is it possible to conceive the majestic and overwhelming extent of that rage, when strengthened by principle, and sancti- fied by religion. I enjoyed the scene beyond all power of description. I saw those wretches, who had triumphed over me, reduced to my level in a moment, – their passions all displayed, and the display placing me a hero triumphant above all. I had crawled to the shelter of their walls, a wretched degraded out- cast, and what was my crime? Well, – you shudder, I have done with that. I can only say want drove me to it. And here were beings whom, a few months before, I would have knelt to as to the images round the shrine, – to whom, in the moments of my desperate penitence, I would have clung as to the 'horns of the altar', all brought as low, and lower than myself. 'Sons of the morning', as I deemed them in the agonies of my humiliation, 'how were they fallen'! I feasted on the degradation of the apos- tate monk and novice, – I enjoyed, to the core of my ulcerated heart, the passion of the Superior, – I felt that they were all men like myself. Angels, as I had thought them, they had all proved themselves mortal; and, by watching their motions, and flatter- ing their passions, and promoting their interest, or setting up my own in opposition to them all, while I made them believe it was only theirs I was intent on, I might make shift to contrive as much misery to others, and to carve out as much occupation to myself, as if I were actually living in the world. Cutting my father's throat was a noble feat certainly, (I ask your pardon, I did not mean to extort that groan from you), but here were hearts to be cut, – and to the core, every day, and all day long, so I never could want employment."

'Here he wiped his hard brow, drew his breath for a moment, and then said, "I do not quite like to go through the details by which this wretched pair were deluded into the hope of effecting their escape from the convent. It is enough that I was the principal agent, – that the Superior connived at it, – that I led them through the very passages you have traversed to-night, they trembling and blessing me at every step, – that –" "Stop," I cried; "wretch! you are tracing my course this night step by step." – "What?" he retorted, with a ferocious laugh, "you think I am betraying you, then; and if it were true, what good would your suspicions do you, – you are in my power? My voice might summon half the convent to seize you this moment, – my arm might fasten you to that wall, till those dogs of death, that wait but my whistle, plunged their fangs into your very vitals. I fancy you would not find their bite less keen, from their tusks being so long sharpened by an immersion in holy water." Another laugh, that seemed to issue from the lungs of a demon, concluded this sentence. "I know I am in your power," I answered; "and were I to trust to that, or to your heart, I had better dash out my brains at once against these walls of rock, which I believe are not harder than the latter. But I know your interests to be some way or other connected with my escape, and therefore I trust you, – because I must. Though my blood, chilled as it is by famine and fatigue, seems frozen in every drop while I listen to you, yet listen I must, and trust my life and liberation to you. I speak to you with the horrid confidence our situation has taught me, – I hate, – I dread you. If we were to meet in life, I would shrink from you with loathings of unspeakable abhorrence, but here mutual misery has mixed the most repugnant substances in unnatural coalition. The force of the alchemy must cease at the moment of my escape from the convent and from you; yet, for these miserable hours, my life is as much dependent on your exertions and presence, as my power of supporting them is on the continuance of your horrible tale, – go on, then. Let us struggle through this dreadful day. *Day!* a name unknown *here*, where noon and night shake hands that never unlock. Let us struggle through it, 'hateful and hating one another', and when it has passed, let us curse and part."

'As I uttered these words, Sir, I felt that terrible *confidence of hostility* which the worst beings are driven to in the worst of circumstances, and I question whether there is a more horrible situation than that in which we cling to each other's hate, instead of each other's love, – in which, at every step of our progress, we hold a dagger to our companion's breast, and say, "If you faulter for a moment, this is in your heart. I hate, – I fear, but I must bear with you." It was singular to me, though it would not be so to those who investigate human nature, that, in proportion as my situation inspired me with a ferocity quite unsuited to our comparative situations, and which must have been the result of the madness of despair and famine, my companion's respect for me appeared to increase. After a long pause, he asked, might he continue his story? I could not speak, for, after the slightest exertion, the sickness of deadly hunger returned on me, and I could only signify, by a feeble motion of my hand, that he might go on.

'"They were conducted here," he continued; "I had suggested the plan, and the Superior consented to it. He would not be present, but his dumb nod was enough. I was the conductor of their (intended) escape; they believed they were departing with the connivance of the Superior. I led them through those very passages that you and I have trod. I had a map of this subterranean region, but my blood ran cold as I traversed it; and it was not at all inclined to resume its usual temperament, as I felt what was to be the destination of my attendants. Once I turned the lamp, on pretence of trimming it, to catch a glimpse of the devoted wretches. They were embracing each other, – the light of joy trembled in their eyes. They were whispering to each other hopes of liberation and happiness, and blending my name in the interval they could spare from their prayers for each other. That sight extinguished the last remains of compunction with which my horrible task had inspired me. They dared to be happy in the sight of one who must be for ever miserable, – could there be a greater insult? I resolved to punish it on the spot. This very apartment was near, – I knew it, and the map of their wanderings no longer trembled in my hand. I urged them to enter this recess, (the door was then entire), while I went to examine the passage. They entered it, thanking me for my precaution, – they knew not they were never to quit it alive. But what were their lives for the agony their happiness cost me? The moment they were inclosed, and clasping each other, (a sight that made me grind my teeth), I closed and locked the door. This movement gave them no immediate uneasiness, – they thought it a friendly precaution. The moment they were secured, I hastened to the Superior, who was on fire at the insult offered to the sanctity of his convent, and still more to the purity of his penetration, on which the worthy Superior piqued himself as much as if it had ever been possible for him to acquire the smallest share of it. He descended with me to the passage, – the monks followed with eyes on fire. In the agitation of their rage, it was with difficulty they could discover the door after I had repeatedly pointed it out to them. The Superior, with his own hands, drove several nails, which the monks eagerly supplied, into the door, that effectually joined it to the staple, *never to be disjoined*; and every blow he gave, doubtless he felt as if it was a reminiscence to the accusing angel, to strike out a sin from the catalogue of his accusations. The work was soon done, – the work never to be undone. At the first sound of steps in the passage, and blows on the door, the victims uttered a shriek of terror. They imagined they were detected, and that an incensed party of monks were breaking open the door. These terrors were soon exchanged for others, – and worse, – as they heard the door nailed up, and listened to our departing steps. They uttered another shriek, but O how different was the accent of its despair! – they knew their doom.

*

'"It was my penance (no, – my delight) to watch at the door, under the pretence of precluding the possibility of their escape, (of which they knew there was no possibility); but, in reality, not only to inflict on me the indignity of being the convent gaoler, but of teaching me that callosity of heart, and induration of nerve, and stubbornness of eye, and apathy of ear, that were best suited to my office. But they might have saved themselves the trouble, – I had them all before ever I entered the convent. Had I been the Superior of the community, I should have undertaken the office of watching the door. You will call this cruelty, I call it curiosity, – that curiosity that brings thousands to witness a tragedy, and makes the most delicate female feast on groans and agonies. I had an advantage over them, – the groan, the agony I feasted on, were real. I took my station at *the door* – that door which, like that of Dante's hell, might have borne the inscription, 'Here is no hope', – with a face of mock penitence, and genuine – cordial delectation. I could hear every word that transpired. For the first hours they tried to comfort each other, – they suggested to each other hopes of liberation, – and as my shadow, crossing the threshold, darkened or restored the light, they said, 'That is he;' – then, when this occurred repeatedly, without any effect, they said, 'No, – no, it is not he,' and swallowed down the sick sob of despair, to hide it from each other. Towards night a monk came to take my place, and to offer me food. I would not have quitted my place for worlds; but I talked to the monk in his own language, and told him I would make a merit with God of my sacrifices; and was resolved to remain there all night, with the permission of the Superior. The monk was glad of having a substitute on such easy terms, and I was glad of the food he left me, for I was hungry now, but I reserved the appetite of my soul for richer luxuries. I heard them talking within. While I was eating, I actually lived on the famine that was devouring them, but of which they did not dare to say a word to each other. They debated, deliberated, and, as misery grows ingenious in its own defence, they at last assured each other that it was impossible the Superior had locked them in there to perish by hunger. At these words I could not help laughing. This laugh reached their ears, and they became silent in a moment. All that night, however, I heard their groans, – those groans of physical suffering, that laugh to scorn all the sentimental sighs that are exhaled from the hearts of the most intoxicated lovers that ever breathed. I heard them all that night. I had read French romances and all their unimaginable nonsense. Madame Sevigné herself says she would have been tired of her daughter in a long tete-a-tete journey, but clamp me two lovers into a dungeon, without food, light, or hope, and I will be damned (that I am already, by the by) if they do not grow sick of each other within the first twelve hours. The second day hunger and darkness had their usual influence. They shrieked for liberation, and knocked loud and long at their dungeon door. They exclaimed they were ready to submit to any punishment; and the approach of the monks, which they would have dreaded so much the preceding night, they now solicited on their knees. What a jest, after all, are the most awful vicissitudes of human life! – they supplicated now for what they would have sacrificed their souls to avert four-and-twenty hours before. Then the agony of hunger increased, they shrunk from the door, and grovelled apart from each other. *Apart!* – how I watched that. They were rapidly becoming objects of hostility to each other, – oh what a feast to me! They could not disguise from each other the revolting circumstances of their mutual sufferings. It is one thing for lovers to sit down to a feast magnificently spread, and another for lovers to couch in darkness and famine, – to exchange that appetite which cannot be supported without dainties and flattery, for that which would barter a descended Venus for a morsel of food. The second night they raved and groaned, (as occurred); and, amid their agonies, (I must do justice to women, whom I hate as well as men), the man often accused the female as the cause of all his sufferings, but the woman never, – never reproached him. Her groans might indeed have reproached him bitterly, but she never uttered a word that could have caused him pain. There was a change which I well could mark, however, in their physical feelings. The first day they clung together, and every movement I felt was like that of one person. The next the man alone struggled, and the woman moaned in helplessness. The third night, – how shall I tell it? – but you have bid me go on. All the horrible and loathsome excruciations of famine had been undergone; the disunion of every tie of the heart, of passion, of nature, had commenced. In the agonies of their famished sickness they loathed each other, – they could have cursed each other, if they had had breath to curse. It was on the fourth night that I heard the shriek of the wretched female, – her lover, in the agony of hunger, had fastened his teeth in her shoulder; – that bosom on which he had so often luxuriated, became a meal to him now."

*

'"Monster! and you laugh?" – "Yes, I laugh at all mankind, and the imposition they dare to practise when they talk of hearts. I laugh at human passions and human cares, – vice and virtue, religion and impiety; they are all the result of petty localities, and artificial situation. One physical want, one severe and abrupt lesson from the tintless and shrivelled lip of necessity, is worth all the logic of the empty wretches who have presumed to prate it, from Zeno down to Burgersdicius. Oh! it silences in a second all the feeble sophistry of *conventional* life, and ascititious passion. Here were a pair who would not have believed all the world on their knees, even though angels had descended to join in the attestation, that it was possible for them to exist without each other. They had risked every thing, trampled on every thing human and divine, to be in each other's sight and arms. One hour of hunger undeceived them. A trivial and ordinary want, whose claims at another time they would have regarded as a vulgar interruption of their spiritualized intercourse, not only, by its natural operation, sundered it for ever, but, before it ceased, converted that intercourse into a source of torment and hostility inconceivable, except among cannibals. The bitterest enemies on earth could not have regarded each other with more abhorrence than *these lovers*. Deluded wretches! you boasted of having hearts, I boast I have none, and which of us gained most by the vaunt, let life decide. My story is nearly finished, and so I hope is the day. When I was last here I had something to excite me; – talking of those things is poor employment to one who has been a witness to them. On the *sixth* day all was still. The door was unnailed, we entered, – they were no more. They lay far from each other, farther than on that voluptuous couch into which their passion had converted the mat of a convent bed. She lay contracted in a heap, a lock of her long hair in her mouth. There was a slight scar on her shoulder, – the rabid despair of famine had produced no farther outrage. He lay extended at his length, – his hand was between his lips; it seemed as if he had not strength to execute the purpose for which he had brought it there. The bodies were brought out for interment. As we removed them into the light, the long hair of the female, falling over a face no longer disguised by the novice's dress, recalled a likeness I thought I could remember. I looked closer, she was my own sister, – my only one, – and I had heard her voice grow fainter and fainter. I had heard –" and his own voice grew fainter – it ceased.

'Trembling for a life with which my own was linked, I staggered towards him. I raised him half up in my arms, and recollecting there must be a current of air through the trap-door, I attempted to trail him along thither. I succeeded, and, as the

breeze played over him, I saw with delight unutterable the dimi-
nution of the light that streamed through it. It was *evening*, – there
was no longer any necessity, no longer any time for delay. He
recovered, for his swoon arose not from exhausted sensibility, but
from mere inanition. However it was, I found my interest in
watching his recovery; and, had I been adequate to the task of
observing extraordinary vicissitudes of the human mind, I would
have been indeed amazed at the change that he manifested on his
recovery. Without the least reference to his late story, or late feelings, he started from my arms at the discovery that the light had
diminished, and prepared for our escape through the trap-door,
with a restored energy of strength, and sanity of intellect, that
might have been deemed miraculous if it had occurred in a
convent: – Happening to occur full thirty feet below the proper
surface for a miracle, it must be put to the account of strong
excitement merely. I could not indeed dare to believe a miracle
was wrought in favour of my profane attempt, and so I was glad
to put up with second causes. With incredible dexterity he
climbed up the wall, with the help of the rugged stones and my
shoulders, – threw open the trap-door, pronounced that all was
safe, assisted me to ascend after him, – and, with gasping delight,
I once more breathed the breath of heaven. The night was perfectly dark. I could not distinguish the buildings from the trees,
except when a faint breeze gave motion to the latter. To this darkness, I am convinced, I owe the preservation of my reason under
such vicissitudes, – the glory of a resplendent night would have
driven me mad, emerging from darkness, famine, and cold.
I would have wept, and laughed, and knelt, and turned idolater. I
would have "worshipped the host of heaven, and the moon walking in her brightness." Darkness was my best security, in every
sense of the word. We traversed the garden, without feeling the
ground under our feet. As we approached the wall, I became
again deadly sick, – my senses grew giddy, I reeled. I whispered to
my companion, "Are there not lights gleaming from the convent

windows?" – "No, the lights are flashing from your own eyes, – it is only the effect of darkness, famine, and fear, – come on." – "But I hear a sound of bells." – "The bells are ringing only in your ears, – an empty stomach is your sexton, and you fancy you hear bells. Is this a time to faulter? – come on, come on. Don't hang such a dead weight on my arm, – don't fall, if you can help it. Oh God, he has swooned!"

'These were the last words I heard. I had fallen, I believe, into his arms. With that instinct that acts most auspiciously in the absence of both thought and feeling, he dragged me in his brawny arms to the wall, *and twisted my cold fingers* in the ropes of the ladder. The touch restored me in a moment; and, almost before my hand had touched the ropes, my feet began to ascend them. My companion followed extempore. We reached the summit, – I tottered from weakness and terror. I felt a sickly dread, that, though the ladder was there, Juan was not. A moment after a lanthorn flashed in my eyes, – I saw a figure below. I sprung down, careless, in that wild moment, whether I met the dagger of an assassin, or the embrace of a brother. "Alonzo, dear Alonzo," murmured a voice. "Juan, dear Juan," was all I could utter, as I felt my shivering breast held close to that of the most generous and affectionate of brothers. "How much you must have suffered, – how much I have suffered," he whispered; "during the last horrible twenty-four hours, I almost gave you up. Make haste, the carriage is not twenty paces off." And, as he spoke, the shifting of a lanthorn shewed me those imperious and beautiful features, which I had once dreaded as the pledge of eternal emulation, but which I now regarded as the smile of the proud but benignant god of my liberation. I pointed to my companion, I could not speak, – hunger was consuming my vitals. Juan supported me, consoled me, encouraged me; did all, and more, than man ever did for man, – than man ever did, perhaps, for the most shrinking and delicate of the other sex under his protection. Oh, with what agony of heart I retrace his manly tenderness! We waited for my companion, – he descended the wall. "Make haste, make haste," Juan whispered; "I am famishing too. I have not tasted food for four-and-twenty hours, watching for you." We hurried on. It was a waste place, – I could only distinguish a carriage by the light of a dim lanthorn, but that was enough for me. I sprung lightly into it. *"He is safe,"* cried Juan, following me. *"But are you?"* answered a voice of thunder. Juan staggered back from the step of the carriage, – he fell. I sprung out, I fell too – on his body. I was bathed in his blood, – he was no more.'

Chapter Ten

Men who with mankind were foes.

*

Or who, in desperate doubt of grace. –

*

Scott's Marmion

'One wild moment of yelling agony, – one flash of a fierce and fiery light, that seemed to envelope and wither me soul and body, – one sound, that swept through my ears and brain like the last trumpet, as it will thrill on the senses of those who slept in guilt, and awake in despair, – one such moment, that condenses and crowds all imaginable sufferings in one brief and intense pang, and appears exhausted itself by the blow it has struck, – one such moment I remember, and no more. Many a month of gloomy unconsciousness rolled over me, without date or notice. One thousand waves may welter over a sunk wreck, and be felt as *one*. I have a dim recollection of refusing food, of resisting change of place, &c. but they were like the faint and successless attempts we make under the burden of the night-mare; and those with whom I had to do, probably regarded any opposition I could make no more than the tossings of a restless sleeper.

'From dates that I have since been enabled to collect, I must have been four months at least in this state; and ordinary persecutors would have given me up as a hopeless subject for any further sufferings; but religious malignity is too industrious, and too ingenious, to resign the hope of a victim but with life. If the fire is extinguished, it sits and watches the embers. If the strings of the heart crack in its hearing, it listens if it be the *last* that has broken. It is a spirit that delights to ride on the *tenth wave*, and view it whelm and bury the sufferer for ever.

*

'Many changes had taken place, without any consciousness on my part of them. Perhaps the profound tranquillity of my *last* abode contributed more than any thing else to the recovery of my reason. I distinctly remember awaking at once to the full exercise of my senses and reason, and finding myself in a place which I examined with the most amazed and jealous curiosity. My memory did not molest me in the least. Why I was there? or what I had suffered before I was brought there? it never occurred to me to inquire. The return of the intellectual powers came slowly in, like the waves of an advancing tide, and happily for me memory was the last, – the occupation of my senses was at first quite enough for me. You must expect no romance-horrors, Sir, from my narrative. Perhaps a life like mine may revolt the taste that has feasted to fastidiousness; but truth sometimes gives full and dreadful compensation, in presenting us facts instead of images.

'I found myself lying on a bed, not very different from that in my cell, but the apartment was wholly unlike the latter. It was somewhat larger, and covered with matting. There was neither crucifix, painting, or vessel for holy water; – the bed, a coarse table which supported a lighted lamp, and a vessel containing water for the purpose, were all the furniture. There was no window; and some iron knobs in the door, to which the light of the lamp gave a kind of dismal distinctness and prominence, proved that it was strongly secured. I raised myself on my arm, and gazed round me with the apprehensiveness of one who fears that the slightest motion may dissolve the spell, and plunge him again in darkness. At that moment the recollection of all the past struck me like a thunder-bolt. I uttered a cry, that seemed to drain me of breath and being at once, and fell back on the bed, not senseless but exhausted. I remembered every event in a moment, with an intenseness that could only be equalled by actual and present agency in them, – my escape, – my safety, – my despair. I felt Juan's embrace, – then I felt his blood stream over me. I saw his eyes turn in despair, before they closed for ever, and I uttered another cry, such as had never before been heard within those walls. At the repetition of this sound the door opened, and a person, in a habit I had never seen before, approached, and signified to me by signs, that I must observe the most profound silence. Nothing, indeed, could be more expressive of this meaning, than his denying himself the use of his voice to convey it. I gazed on this apparition in silence, – my amazement had all the effect of an apparent submission to his injunctions. He retired, and I began to wonder where I was. Was it among the dead? or some subterranean world of the mute and voiceless, where there was no air to convey sounds, and no echo to repeat them, and the famished ear waited in vain for its sweetest banquet, – the voice of man? These wanderings were dispelled by the re-entrance of the person. He placed bread, water, and a small portion of meat on the table, motioned me to approach, (which I did mechanically), and, when I was seated, *whispered* me, That my unhappy situation having hitherto rendered me incapable of understanding the regulations of the place where I was, he had been compelled to postpone acquainting me with them; but *now* he was obliged to warn me, that my voice must never be raised beyond the key in which he addressed me, and which was sufficient for all proper purposes of communication; finally, he assured me that cries, exclamations of any kind, or even *coughing too loud*,★ (which might be interpreted as a signal), would be considered as an attempt on the inviolable habits of the place, and punished with the utmost severity. To my repeated questions of "Where am I? what is this place, with its

★ This is a fact well established.

mysterious regulations?" he replied in a whisper, that his business was to issue orders, not to answer questions; and so saying he departed. However extraordinary these injunctions appeared, the manner in which they were issued was so imposing, peremptory, and *habitual*, – it seemed so little a thing of local contrivance and temporary display, – so much like the established language of an absolute and long-fixed system, that obedience to it seemed inevitable. I threw myself on the bed, and murmured to myself, "Where am I?" till sleep overcame me.

'I have heard that the first sleep of a recovered maniac is intensely profound. Mine was not so, it was broken by many troubled dreams. One, in particular, brought me back to the convent. I thought I was a boarder in it, and studying Virgil. I was reading that passage in the second book, where the vision of Hector appears to Æneas in his dream, and his ghastly and dishonoured form suggests the mournful exclamation,

> "– Heu quantum mutatus ab illo, –
> – Quibus ab oris, Hector expectate venis?"[18]

'Then I thought Juan was Hector, – that the same pale and bloody phantom stood calling me to fly – "Heu fuge," while I vainly tried to obey him. Oh that dreary mixture of truth and delirium, of the real and visionary, of the conscious and unconscious parts of existence, that visits the dreams of the unhappy! He was Pantheus, and murmured,

> "Venit summa dies, et ineluctabile tempus."

'I appeared to weep and struggle in my dream. I addressed the figure that stood before me sometimes as Juan, and sometimes as the image of the Trojan vision. At last the figure uttered, with a kind of querulous shriek, – that *vox stridula*[19] which we hear only in dreams,

"Proximus ardet Ucalegon,"

and I started up fully awake, in all the horrors of an expected conflagration.

'It is incredible, Sir, how the senses and the mind can operate thus, during the apparent suspension of both; how sound can affect organs that seem to be shut, and objects affect the sight, while its sense appears to be closed, – can impress on its dreaming consciousness, images more horribly vivid than even reality ever presented. I awoke with the idea that flames were raging in contact with my eye-balls, and I saw only a pale light, held by a paler hand – close to my eyes indeed, but withdrawn the moment I awoke. The person who held it shrouded it for a moment, and then advanced and flashed its full lights on me, and along with it – the person of my companion. The associations of our last meeting rushed on me. I started up, and said, "Are we free, then?" – "Hush, – one of us is free; but you must not speak so loud." – "Well, I have heard that before, but I cannot comprehend the necessity of this whispering secrecy. If I am free, tell me so, and tell me whether Juan has survived that last horrible moment, – my intellect is but just respiring. Tell me how Juan fares." – "Oh, sumptuously. No prince in all the land reposes under a more gorgeous canopy, – marble pillars, waving banners, and nodding plumes. He had music too, but he did not seem to heed it. He lay stretched on velvet and gold, but he appeared insensible of all these luxuries. There was a curl on his cold white lip, too, that seemed to breathe ineffable scorn on all that was going on, – but he was proud enough even in his life-time." – "His life-time!" I shrieked; "then he *is* dead?" – "Can you doubt that, when you know who struck the blow? None of my victims ever gave me the trouble of a second." – "You, – you?" I swam for some moments in a sea of flames and blood. My frenzy returned, and I remember only uttering curses that would have exhausted divine vengeance in all its plenitude to fulfil. I might have continued to rave till my reason was totally lost, but I was silenced and stunned by his laugh bursting out amid my curses, and overwhelming them.

'That laugh made me cease, and lift up my eyes to him, as if I expected to see another being, – it was still the same. "And you dreamt," he cried, "in your temerity, you dreamt of setting the vigilance of a convent at defiance? Two boys, one the fool of fear, and the other of temerity, were fit antagonists for that stupendous system, whose roots are in the bowels of the earth, and whose head is among the stars, – *you* escape from a convent! *you* defy a power that has defied sovereigns! A power whose influence is unlimited, indefinable, and unknown, even to those who exercise it, as there are mansions so vast, that their inmates, to their last hour, have never visited all the apartments; – a power whose operation is like its motto, – one and indivisible. The soul of the Vatican breathes in the humblest convent in Spain, – and you, an insect perched on a wheel of this vast machine, imagined you were able to arrest its progress, while its rotation was hurrying on to crush you to atoms." While he was uttering these words, with a rapidity and energy inconceivable, (a rapidity that literally made one word seem to devour another), I tried, with that effort of intellect which seems like the gasping respiration of one whose breath has long been forcibly suppressed or suspended, to comprehend and follow him. The first thought that struck me was one not very improbable in my situation, that he was not the person he appeared to be, – that it was not the companion of my escape who now addressed me; and I summoned all the remains of my intellect to ascertain this. A few questions must determine this point, if I had breath to utter them. "Were you not the agent in my escape? Were you not the man who – What tempted you to this step, in the defeat of which you appear to rejoice?" – "A bribe." – "And you have betrayed me, you say, and boast of your treachery, – what tempted you to this?" – "A higher bribe. Your brother gave gold, but the convent promised me salvation, – a business I was very willing to commit to their hands, as I was

totally incompetent to manage it myself." – "Salvation, for treachery and murder?" – "Treachery and murder, – hard words. Now,
to talk sense, was not yours the vilest treachery? You reclaimed
your vows, – you declared before God and man, that the words
you uttered before both were the babble of an infant; then you
seduced your brother from his duty to his and your parents, – you
connived at his intriguing against the peace and sanctity of a
monastic institution, and dare *you* talk of treachery? And did you
not, with a callosity of conscience unexampled in one so young,
accept, nay, cling to an associate in your escape whom you knew
you were seducing from his vows, – from all that man reveres as
holy, and all that God (if there be a God) must regard as binding
on man? You knew my crime, you knew my atrocity, yet you
brandished me as your banner of defiance against the Almighty,
though its inscription was, in glaring characters, – impiety –
parricide – irreligion. Torn as the banner was, it still hung near
the altar, till you dragged it away, to wrap yourself from detection in its folds, – and *you* talk of treachery? – there is not a more
traitorous wretch on earth than yourself. Suppose that I was all
that is vile and culpable, was it for you to double-dye the hue of
my crime in the crimson of your sacrilege and apostasy? And for
murder, I know I am a parricide. I cut my father's throat, but he
never felt the blow, – nor did I, – I was intoxicated with wine, with
passion, with blood, – no matter which; but you, with cold deliberate blows, struck at the hearts of father and mother. You killed
by inches, – I murdered at a blow, – which of us is the murderer? –
And *you* prate of treachery and murder? I am as innocent as the
child that is born this hour, compared to you. Your father and
mother have separated, – she is gone into a convent, to hide her
despair and shame at your unnatural conduct, – your father is
plunging successively into the abysses of voluptuousness and
penitence, wretched in both; your brother, in his desperate
attempt to liberate you, has perished, – you have scattered desolation over a whole family, – you have stabbed the peace and

heart of each of them, with a hand that deliberated and paused
on its blow, and then struck it calmly, – and you dare to talk of
treachery and murder? You are a thousand times more culpable
than I am, guilty as you think me. I stand a blasted tree, – I am
struck to the heart, to the root, – I wither alone, – but you are the
Upas, under whose poisonous droppings all things living have
perished, – father – mother – brother, and last yourself; – the erosions of the poison, having nothing left to consume, strike
inward, and prey on your own heart. Wretch, condemned beyond
the sympathy of man, beyond the redemption of the Saviour,
what can you say to this?" – I answered only, "Is Juan dead, and
were you his murderer, – were you indeed? I believe all you say,
I must be very guilty, but is Juan dead?" As I spoke, I lifted up to
him eyes that no longer seemed to see, – a countenance that bore
no expression but that of the stupefaction of intense grief. I could
neither utter nor feel reproaches, – I had suffered beyond the
power of complaint. I awaited his answer; he was silent, but his
diabolical silence spoke. "And my mother retired to a convent?" he
nodded. "And my father?" he smiled, and I closed my eyes. I could
bear any thing but his smile. I raised my head a few moments
after, and saw him, with an habitual motion, (it could not have
been more), make the sign of the cross, as a clock in some distant
passage struck. This sight reminded me of the play so often acted
in Madrid, and which I had seen in my few days of liberation, – *El
Diablo Predicador*. You smile, Sir, at such a recollection operating
at such a moment, but it is a fact; and had you witnessed that play
under the singular circumstances I did, you would not wonder at
my being struck with the coincidence. In this performance the
infernal spirit is the hero, and in the disguise of a monk he appears
in a convent, where he torments and persecutes the community
with a mixture of malignity and mirth truly Satanic. One night
that I saw it performed, a groupe of monks were carrying the
Host to a dying person; the walls of the theatre were so slight,
that we could distinctly hear the sound of the bell which they

ring on that occasion. In an instant, actors, audience, and all, were on their knees, and the devil, who happened to be on the stage, knelt among the rest, and crossed himself with visible marks of a devotion equally singular and edifying. You will allow the coincidence to be irresistibly striking.

'When he had finished his monstrous profanation of the holy sign, I fixed my eyes on him with an expression not to be mistaken. He saw it. There is not so bitter a reproach on earth as silence, for it always seems to refer the guilty to their own hearts, whose eloquence seldom fails to fill up the pause very little to the satisfaction of the accused. My look threw him into a rage, that I am now convinced not the most bitter upbraidings could have caused. The utmost fury of imprecation would have fallen on his ear like the most lulling harmony; – it would have convinced him that his victim was suffering all he could possibly inflict. He betrayed this in the violence of his exclamations. "What, wretch!" he cried; – "Do you think it was for your masses and your mummeries, your vigils, and fasts, and mumbling over senseless unconsoling beads, and losing my rest all night watching for the matins, and then quitting my frozen mat to nail my knees to stone till they grew there, – till I thought the whole pavement would rise with me when I rose, – do you think it was for the sake of listening to sermons that the preachers did not believe, – and prayers that the lips that uttered them yawned at in the listlessness of their infidelity, – and penances that might be hired out to a lay-brother to undergo for a pound of coffee or of snuff, – and the vilest subserviencies to the caprice and passion of a Superior, – and the listening to men with God for ever in their mouths, and the world for ever in their hearts, – men who think of nothing but the aggrandizement of their temporal distinction, and screen, under the most revolting affectation of a concern in spiritualities, their ravening cupidity after earthly eminence: – Wretch! do you dream that it was for this? – that this *atheism of bigotry*, – this creed of all the priests that ever have existed in connexion with the state, and in hope of extending their interest by that connexion, – could have any influence over *me*? I had sounded every depth in the mine of depravity before them. I knew them, – I despised them. I crouched before them in body, I spurned them in my soul. With all their sanctimony, they had hearts so worldly, that it was scarce worth while to watch their hypocrisy, the secret developed itself so soon. There was no discovery to be made, no place for detection. I have seen them on their high festivals, prelates, and abbots, and priests, in all their pomp of office, appearing to the laity like descended gods, blazing in gems and gold, amid the lustre of tapers and the floating splendour of an irradiated atmosphere alive with light, and all soft and delicate harmonies and delicious odours, till, as they disappeared amid the clouds of incense so gracefully tossed from the gilded censers, the intoxicated eye dreamed it saw them ascending to Paradise. Such was the *scene*, but what was *behind the scene? – I saw it all*. Two or three of them would rush from service into the vestry together, under the pretence of changing their vestments. One would imagine that these men would have at least the decency to refrain, while in the intervals of the holy mass. No, I overheard them. While shifting their robes, they talked incessantly of promotions and appointments, – of this or that prelate, dying or dead, – of a wealthy benefice being vacant, – of one dignitary having bargained hard with the state for the promotion of a relative, – of another who had well-founded hopes of obtaining a bishoprick, for what? neither for learning or piety, or one feature of the pastoral character, but because he had valuable benefices to resign in exchange, that might be divided among numerous candidates. Such was their conversation, – such and such only were their thoughts, till the last thunders of the allelujah from the church made them start, and hurry to resume their places at the altar. Oh what a compound of meanness and pride, of imbecility and pretension, of sanctimony so transparently and awkwardly worn, that the naked frame of the natural mind was visible to every eye beneath it, – that mind which is 'earthly, sensual, devilish'. Was it to live among such wretches, who, all-villain as I was, made me hug myself with the thought that at least I was not like them, a passionless prone reptile, – a thing made of forms and dressings, half satin and shreds, half ave's and credo's, – bloated and abject, – creeping and aspiring, – winding up and up the pedestal of power at the rate of an inch a day, and tracking its advance to eminence by the flexibility of its writhings, the obliquity of its course, and the filth of its slime, – was it for this?" – he paused, half-choked with his emotions.

'This man might have been a better being under better circumstances; he had at least a disdain of all that was mean in vice, with a wild avidity for all that was atrocious. "Was it for this," he continued, "that I have sold myself to work their works of darkness, – that I have become in this life as it were an apprentice to Satan, to take anticipated lessons of torture, – that I have sealed those indentures here, which must be fulfilled below? No, I despise – I loathe it all, the agents and the system, – the men and their matters. But it is the creed of that system, (and true or false it avails not, – some kind of creed is necessary, and the falser perhaps the better, for falsehood at least flatters), that the greatest criminal may expiate his offences, by vigilantly watching, and severely punishing, those of the enemies of heaven. Every offender may purchase his immunity, by consenting to become the executioner of the offender whom he betrays and denounces. In the language of the laws of another country, they may turn 'king's evidence', and buy their own lives at the price of another's, – a bargain which every man is very ready to make. But, in religious life, this kind of transfer, this substitutional suffering, is adopted with an avidity indescribable. How we love to punish those whom the church calls the enemies of God, while conscious that, though our enmity against him is infinitely greater, we become acceptable in his sight by tormenting those who may be less guilty, but who are in our power! I hate you, not because I have any natural or social cause to do so, but because the exhaustion of my resentment on you, may diminish that of the Deity towards me. If I persecute and torment the enemies of God, must I not be the friend of God? Must not every pang I inflict on another, be recorded in the book of the All-remembering, as an expurgation of at least one of the pangs that await me hereafter? I have no religion, I believe in no God, I repeat no creed, but I have that superstition of fear and of futurity, that seeks its wild and hopeless mitigation in the sufferings of others when our own are exhausted, or when (a much more common case) we are unwilling to undergo them. I am convinced that my own crimes will be obliterated, by whatever crimes of others I can promote or punish. Had I not, then, every motive to urge you to crime? Had I not every motive to watch and aggravate your punishment? Every coal of fire that I heaped on your head, was removing one from that fire that burns for ever and ever for mine. Every drop of water that I withheld from your burning tongue, I expect will be repaid to me in slaking the fire and brimstone into which I must one day be hurled. Every tear that I draw, every groan that I extort, will, I am convinced, be repaid me in the remission of my own! – guess what a price I set on yours, or those of any other victim. The man in ancient story trembled and paused over the scattered limbs of his child, and failed in the pursuit, – the true penitent rushes over the mangled members of nature and passion, collects them with a hand in which there is no pulse, and a heart in which there is no feeling, and holds them up in the face of the Divinity as a peace-offering. Mine is the best theology, – the theology of utter hostility to all beings whose sufferings may mitigate mine. In this flattering theory, your crimes become my virtues, – I need not any of my own. Guilty as I am of the crime that outrages nature, your crimes (the crimes of those who offend against the church) are of a much more heinous order. But your guilt is my exculpation, your sufferings are my triumph. I need not repent, I need not believe; if you suffer,

I am saved, – that is enough for me. How glorious and easy it is to erect at once the trophy of our salvation, on the trampled and buried hopes of another's! How subtle and sublime that alchemy, that can convert the iron of another's contumacy and impenitence into the precious gold of your own redemption! I have literally worked out *my* salvation by *your* fear and trembling. With this hope I appeared to concur in the plan laid by your brother, every feature of which was in its progress disclosed to the Superior. With this hope I passed that wretched night and day in the dungeon with you, for, to have effected our escape by daylight, would have startled credulity as gross as even yours. But all the time I was feeling the dagger I bore in my breast, and which I had received for a purpose amply accomplished. As for you, – the Superior consented to your attempt to escape, merely that he might have you more in his power. He and the community were tired of you, they saw you would never make a monk, – your appeal had brought disgrace on them, your presence was a reproach and a burden to them. The sight of you was as thorns in their eyes, – they judged you would make a better victim than a proselyte, and they judged well. You are a much fitter inmate for your present abode than your last, and from hence there is no danger of your escaping." – "And where, then, am I?" – "*You are in the prison of the Inquisition.*"'

Chapter Eleven

Oh! torture me no more, I will confess.

Henry the Sixth

*

You have betrayed her to her own reproof.

Comedy of Errors

'And it was true, – I was a prisoner in the Inquisition. Great emergencies certainly inspire us with the feelings they demand; and many a man has braved a storm on the wide wild ocean, who would have shrunk from its voice as it pealed down his chimney. I believe so it fared with me, – the storm had risen, and I braced myself to meet it. I was in the Inquisition, but I knew that my crime, heinous as it was, was not one that came properly under the cognizance of the Inquisition. It was a conventual fault of the highest class, but liable only to be punished by the ecclesiastical power. The punishment of a monk who had dared to escape from his convent, might be dreadful enough, – immurement, or death perhaps, but still I was not legitimately a prisoner of the Inquisition. I had never, under all my trials, spoken a disrespectful word of the holy Catholic church, or a doubtful one of our most holy faith, – I had not dropped one heretical, obnoxious, or equivocal expression, relative to a single point of duty, or article of faith. The preposterous charges of sorcery and possession, brought against me in the convent, had been completely disproved at the visitation of the Bishop. My aversion to the monastic state was indeed sufficiently known and fatally proved, but that was no subject for the investigation or penalties of the Inquisition. I had nothing to fear from the Inquisition, – at least so I said to myself in my prison, and I believed myself. The seventh day after the recovery of my reason was fixed on for my examination, and of this I received due notice, though I believe it is contrary to the usual forms of the Inquisition to give this notice; and the examination took place on the day and hour appointed.

'You are aware, Sir, that the tales related in general of the interior discipline of the Inquisition, must be in nine out of ten mere fables, as the prisoners are bound by an oath never to disclose what happens within its walls; and they who could violate this oath, would certainly not scruple to violate truth in the details with which their emancipation from it indulges them. I am forbidden, by an oath which I shall never break, to disclose the circumstances of my imprisonment or examination. I am at liberty to mention some general features of both, as they are connected with my extraordinary narrative. My first examination terminated rather favourably; my contumacy and aversion to monasticism were indeed deplored and reprobated, but there was no ulterior hint, – nothing to alarm the peculiar fears of an inmate of the Inquisition. So I was as happy as solitude, darkness, straw, bread, and water, could make me, or any one, till, on the fourth night after my first examination, I was awoke by a light gleaming so strongly on my eyes, that I started up. The person then retired with his light, and I discovered a figure sitting in the farthest corner of my cell. Delighted at the sight of a human form, I yet had acquired so much of the habit of the Inquisition, that I demanded, in a cold and peremptory voice, who had ventured to intrude on the cell of a prisoner? The person answered in the blandest tones that ever soothed the human ear, that he was, like myself, a prisoner in the Inquisition; – that, by its indulgence, he had been permitted to visit me, and hoped – "And is *hope* to be named here?" I could not help exclaiming. He answered in the same soft and deprecatory tone; and, without adverting to our peculiar circumstances, suggested the consolation that might be derived from the society of two sufferers who were indulged with the power of meeting and communicating with each other.

'This man visited me for several successive nights; and I could not help noticing three extraordinary circumstances in his visits and his appearance. The first was, that he always (when he could) concealed his eyes from me; he sat sideways and backways, shifted his position, changed his seat, held up his hand before his eyes; but when at times he was compelled or *surprised* to turn their light on me, I felt that I had never beheld such eyes blazing in a mortal face, – in the darkness of my prison, I held up my hand to shield myself from their preternatural glare. The second was, that he came and retired apparently without help or hindrance, – that he came, like one who had a key to the door of my dungeon, at all hours, without leave or forbiddance, – that he traversed the prisons of the Inquisition, like one who had a master-key to its deepest recesses. Lastly, he spoke not only in a tone of voice clear and audible, totally unlike the whispered communications of the Inquisition, but spoke his abhorrence of the whole system, – his indignation against the Inquisition, Inquisitors, and all their aiders and abettors, from St Dominic down to the lowest official, – with such unqualified rage of vituperation, such caustic inveteracy of satire, such unbounded licence of ludicrous and yet withering severity, that I trembled.

'You know, Sir, or perhaps have yet to know, that there are persons *accredited* in the Inquisition, who are permitted to solace the solitude of the prisoners, on the condition of obtaining, under the pretence of friendly communication, those secrets which even torture has failed to extort. I discovered in a moment that my visitor was not one of these, – his abuse of the system was too gross, his indignation too unfeigned. Yet, in his continued visits, there was one circumstance more, which struck me with a feeling of terror that actually paralysed and annihilated all the terrors of the Inquisition.

'He constantly alluded to events and personages beyond his *possible memory*, – then he checked himself, – then he appeared to go on, with a kind of wild and derisive sneer at his own *absence*. But this perpetual reference to events long past, and men long buried, made an impression on me I cannot describe. His conversation was rich, various and intelligent, but it was interspersed with such reiterated mention of the dead, that I might be pardoned for feeling as if the speaker was one of them. He dealt much in anecdotical history, and I, who was very ignorant of it, was delighted to listen to him, for he told every thing with the fidelity of an eye-witness. He spoke of the *Restoration* in England, and repeated the well-remembered observation of the queen-mother, Henriette of France, – that, had she known as much of the English on her first arrival, as she did on her second, she never would have been driven from the throne; then he added, to my astonishment, I was beside her carriage,* *it was the only one then in London*. He afterwards spoke of the superb fetes given by Louis Quatorze, and described, with an accuracy that made me start, the magnificent chariot in which that monarch personated the god of day, while all the titled pimps and harlots of the court followed as the rabble of Olympus. Then he reverted to the death of the Duchesse d'Orleans, sister to Charles II. – to Pere Bourdaloue's awful sermon, preached at the death-bed of the royal beauty, dying of poison, (as suspected); and added, I saw the roses heaped on her toilette, to array her for a fete that very night, and near them stood the pyx, and tapers, and oil, shrouded with the lace of that very toilette. Then he passed to England; he spoke of the wretched and well-rebuked pride of the wife of James II, who "thought it scorn" to sit at the same table with an Irish officer who informed her husband (then Duke of York) that *he* had sat at

---

* I have read this somewhere, but cannot believe it. Coaches are mentioned by Beaumont and Fletcher, and even glass-coaches by [Samuel] Butler, in his 'Remains.'

table, as an officer in the Austrian service, where the Duchess's father (Duke of Modena) had stood behind a chair, as a vassal to the Emperor of Germany.

'These circumstances were trifling, and might be told by any one, but there was a minuteness and circumstantiality in his details, that perpetually forced on the mind the idea that he had himself seen what he described, and been conversant with the personages he spoke of. I listened to him with an indefinable mixture of curiosity and terror. At last, while relating a trifling but characteristic circumstance that occurred in the reign of Louis the Thirteenth, he used the following expressions:* "One night that the king was at an entertainment, where Cardinal Richelieu also was present, the Cardinal had the insolence to rush out of the apartment before his Majesty, just as the coach of the latter was announced. The King, without any indignant notice of the arrogance of the minister, said, with much *bon hommie*, 'His Eminence the Cardinal will always be first.' – 'The first to attend your Majesty,' answered the Cardinal, with admirable polite presence of mind; and, snatching a flambeau from a page who *stood near me*, he lighted the King to his carriage." I could not help catching at the extraordinary words that had escaped him; and I asked him, "Were you there?" He gave some indirect answer; and, avoiding the subject, went on to amuse me with some other curious circumstances of the private history of that age, of which he spoke with a minute fidelity somewhat *alarming*. I confess my pleasure in listening to them was greatly diminished by the singular sensation with which this man's presence and conversation inspired me. He departed, and I regretted his absence, though I could not account for the extraordinary feeling which I experienced during his visits.

'A few days after I was to encounter my second examination. The night before it one of the *officials* visited me. These are men

---

* This circumstance is related, I believe, in the *Jewish Spy*.

who are not the common officers of a prison, but accredited in some degree by the higher powers of the Inquisition, and I paid due respect to his communications, particularly as they were delivered more in detail, and with more emphasis and energy than I could have expected from an inmate of that speechless mansion. This circumstance made me expect something extraordinary, and his discourse verified all, and more than I expected. He told me in plain terms, that there had been lately a cause of disturbance and inquietude, which had never before occurred in the Inquisition. That it was reported a human figure had appeared in the cells of some of the prisoners, uttering words not only hostile to the Catholic religion, and the discipline of the most holy Inquisition, but to religion in general, to the belief of a God and a future state. He added, that the utmost vigilance of the officials, on the rack for discovery, had never been able to trace this being in his visits to the cells of the prisoners; that the guards had been doubled, and every precaution that the circumspection of the Inquisition could employ, was had recourse to, hitherto without success; and that the only intimation they had of this singular visitor, was from some of the prisoners whose cells he had entered, and whom he had addressed in language that seemed lent him by the enemy of mankind, to accomplish the perdition of these unhappy beings. He himself had hitherto eluded all discovery; but he trusted, that, with the means lately adopted, it was impossible for this agent of the evil one to insult and baffle the holy tribunal much longer. He advised me to be prepared on this point, as it would undoubtedly be touched on at my next examination, and perhaps more urgently than I might otherwise imagine; and so, commending me to the holy keeping of God, he departed.

'Not wholly unconscious of the subject alluded to in this extraordinary communication, but perfectly innocent of any ulterior signification, as far as related to myself, I awaited my next examination rather with hope than fear. After the usual questions of – Why I was there? who had accused me? for what offence?

whether I could recollect any expression that had ever intimated a disregard for the tenets of the holy church? &c. &c. &c. – after all this had been gone through, in a detail that may be spared the hearer, certain extraordinary questions were proposed to me, that appeared to relate indirectly to the appearance of my late visitor. I answered them with a sincerity that seemed to make a frightful impression on my judges. I stated plainly, in answer to their questions, that a person had appeared in my dungeon. "You must call it cell," said the Supreme. "In my cell, then. He spoke with the utmost severity of the holy office, – he uttered words that it would not be respectful for me to repeat. I could scarcely believe that such a person would be permitted to visit the dungeons (cells, I should say) of the holy Inquisition." As I uttered these words, one of the judges, trembling on his seat, (while his shadow, magnified by the imperfect light, pictured the figure of a paralytic giant on the wall opposite to me), attempted to address some question to me. As he spoke, there came a hollow sound from his throat, his eyes were rolled upwards in their sockets, – he was in an apoplectic paroxysm, and died before he could be removed to another apartment. The examination terminated suddenly, and in some confusion; but, as I was remanded back to my cell, I could perceive, to my consternation, that I had left an impression the most unfavourable on the minds of the judges. They interpreted this accidental circumstance in a manner the most extraordinary and unjust, and I felt the consequences of it at my next examination.

'That night I received a visit in my cell from one of the judges of the Inquisition, who conversed with me a considerable time, and in an earnest and dispassionate manner. He stated the atrocious and revolting character under which I appeared from the first before the Inquisition, – that of a monk who had apostatized, had been accused of the crime of sorcery in his convent, and, in his impious attempt at escape, had caused the death of his brother, whom he had seduced to join in it, and had overwhelmed one of the first families with despair and disgrace. Here I was going to reply, but he stopped me, and observed, that he came not to listen, but to speak; and went on to inform me, that though I had been acquitted of the charge of communication with the evil spirit at the visitation of the Bishop, certain suspicions attached to me had been fearfully strengthened, by the fact that the visits of the extraordinary being, of whom I had heard enough to assure me of his actuality, had never been known in the prison of the Inquisition till my entrance into it. That the fair and probable conclusion was, that I was really the victim of the enemy of mankind, whose power (through the reluctant permission of God and St Dominic, and he crossed himself as he spoke) had been suffered to range even through the walls of the holy office. He cautioned me, in severe but plain terms, against the danger of the situation in which I was placed, by the suspicions universally and (he feared) too justly attached to me; and, finally, adjured me, as I valued my salvation, to place my entire confidence in the mercy of the holy office, and, if *the figure* should visit me again, to watch what its impure lips might suggest, and faithfully report it to the holy office.

'When the Inquisitor had departed, I reflected on what he had said. I conceived it was something like the conspiracies so often occurring in the convent. I conceived that this might be an attempt to involve me in some plot against myself, something in which I might be led to be active in my own condemnation, – I felt the necessity of vigilant and breathless caution. I knew myself innocent, and this is a consciousness that defies even the Inquisition itself; but, within the walls of the Inquisition, the consciousness, and the defiance it inspires, are alike vain. I finally resolved, however, to watch every circumstance that might occur within the walls of my cell very closely, threatened as I was at once by the powers of the Inquisition, and those of the infernal demon, and I had not long to watch. It was on the second night after my examination, that I saw this person enter my cell. My first impulse was to call aloud for the officials of the Inquisition. I felt a kind of vacillation I cannot describe, between throwing myself into the power of the Inquisition, or the power of this extraordinary being, more formidable perhaps than all the Inquisitors on earth, from Madrid to Goa. I dreaded imposition on both sides. I believed that they were playing off terror against terror; I knew not what to believe or think. I felt myself surrounded by enemies on every side, and would have given my heart to those who would first throw off the mask, and announce themselves as my decided and avowed enemy. After some reflection, I judged it best to *distrust the Inquisition*, and to hear all that this extraordinary visitor had to say. In my secret soul I believed him their secret agent, – I did them great injustice. His conversation on this second visit was more than usually amusing, but it was certainly such as might justify all the suspicions of the Inquisitors. At every sentence he uttered, I was disposed to start up and call for the officials. Then I represented to myself his turning accuser, and pointing *me* out as the victim of their condemnation. I trembled at the idea of committing myself by a word, while in the power of that dreadful body that might condemn me to expire under the torture, – or, worse, to die the long and lingering death of inanity, – the mind famished, the body scarcely fed, – the annihilation of hopeless and interminable solitude, – the terrible inversion of natural feeling, that makes life the object of deprecation, and death of indulgence.

'The result was, that I sat and listened to the conversation (if it may be called so) of this extraordinary visitor, who appeared to regard the walls of the Inquisition no more than those of a domestic apartment, and who seated himself beside me as quietly as if he had been reposing on the most luxurious sofa that ever was arrayed by the fingers of voluptuousness. My senses were so bewildered, my mind so disarranged, that I can hardly remember his conversation. Part of it ran thus: "You are a prisoner of the Inquisition. The holy office, no doubt, is instituted for wise purposes, beyond the cognizance of sinful beings like us; but, as far as we can judge, its prisoners are not only insensible of, but shamefully ungrateful for, the benefits they might derive from its provident vigilance. For instance, you, who are accused of sorcery, fratricide and plunging an illustrious and affectionate family in despair, by your atrocious misconduct, and who are now fortunately restrained from farther outrages against nature, religion and society, by your salutary confinement here; – you, I venture to say, are so unconscious of these blessings, that it is your earnest desire to escape from the further enjoyment of them. In a word, I am convinced that the secret wish of your heart (unconverted by all the profusion of charity which has been heaped on you by the holy office) is not on any account to increase the burden of your obligation to them, but, on the contrary, to diminish as much as possible the grief these worthy persons must feel, as long as your residence pollutes their holy walls, by abridging its period, even long before they intend you should do so. Your wish is to escape from the prison of the holy office, if possible, – you know it is." I did not answer a word. I felt a terror at this wild and fierce irony, – I felt a terror at the mention of escape, (I had fatal reasons for this feeling), – a terror of every thing, and every one near me, indescribable. I believed myself tottering on a narrow ridge, – an Al-araf, between the alternate gulphs which the infernal spirit and the Inquisition (not less dreaded) disclosed on each side of my trembling march. I compressed my lips, – I hardly suffered my breath to escape.

'The speaker went on. "With regard to your escape, though I can promise that to you, (and that is what no *human power* can promise you), you must be aware of the difficulty which will attend it, – and, should that difficulty terrify you, will you hesitate?" Still I was silent; – my visitor perhaps took this for the silence of doubt. He went on. "Perhaps you think that your lingering here, amid the dungeons of the Inquisition, will infallibly secure your salvation. There is no error more absurd, and yet more rooted in the heart of man, than the belief that his sufferings will promote his spiritual safety." Here I thought myself safe in rejoining, that I felt, – I trusted, my sufferings here would indeed be accepted as a partial mitigation of my well-merited punishment hereafter. I acknowledged my many errors, – I professed myself as penitent for my misfortunes as if they had been crimes; and the energy of my grief combining with the innocence of my heart, I commended myself to the Almighty with an unction I really felt, – I called on the names of God, the Saviour, and the Virgin, with the earnest supplication of sincere devoutness. When I had risen from my knees, my visitor had retired.

*

'Examination followed examination before the judges, with a rapidity unexampled in the annals of the Inquisition. Alas! that they should be *annals*, – that they should be more than records of *one day* of abuse, oppression, falsehood and torture. At my next examination before the judges, I was interrogated according to the usual forms, and afterwards was led, by questions as artfully constructed, as if there was any necessity for art to lead me, to speak to the question on which I longed to disburden myself. The moment the subject was mentioned, I entered on my narrative with an eagerness of sincerity that would have undeceived any but Inquisitors. I announced that I had received another visit from this unknown being. I repeated, with breathless and trembling eagerness, every word of our late conference. I did not suppress a syllable of the insults on the holy office, the wild and fiend-like acrimony of his satire, the avowed atheism, the diabolism of his conversation, – I dwelt on every particular. I hoped to *make merit* with the Inquisition, by accusing their enemy, and that of mankind. Oh! there is no telling the agony of zeal with which we work between two mortal adversaries, hoping to make a friend of one of them! I had suffered enough already from the Inquisition, but at this moment I would have crouched at the

knees of the Inquisitors, – I would have pleaded for the place of
the meanest official in their prison, – I would have supplicated for
the loathsome office of their executioner, – I would have encountered any thing that the Inquisition could inflict, to be spared the
horror of being imagined the ally of the enemy of souls. To my
distraction, I perceived that every word I uttered, in all the agony
of truth, – in all the hopeless eloquence of a soul struggling with
the fiends who are bearing it beyond the reach of mercy, was
disregarded. The judges appeared struck, indeed, by the earnestness with which I spoke. They gave, for a moment, a kind of
instinctive credit to my words, extorted by terror; but, a moment
after, I could perceive that *I*, and not my communication, was the
object of that terror. They seemed to view me through a distort-
ing atmosphere of mystery and suspicion. They urged me, over
and over again, for further particulars, – for ulterior circumstances, – for something that was in *their* minds, but not in mine.
The more pains they took to construct their questions skilfully,
the more unintelligible they became to me. I had told all I knew,
I was anxious to tell all, but I could not tell more than I knew, and
the agony of my solicitude to meet the object of the judges, was
aggravated in proportion to my ignorance of it. On being
remanded to my cell, I was warned, in the most solemn manner,
that if I neglected to watch, remember, and report every word
uttered by the extraordinary being, whose visits they tacitly
acknowledged they could neither prevent or detect, I might
expect the utmost severity of the holy office. I promised all this, –
all that could be demanded, and, finally, as the last proof I could
give of my sincerity, I implored that some one might be allowed
to pass the night in my cell, – or, if that was contrary to the rules
of the Inquisition, that one of the guards might be stationed in
the passage communicating with my cell, to whom I could, by a
signal agreed on, intimate when this nameless being burst on me,
and his impious intrusion might be at once detected and punished. In speaking thus, I was indulged with a privilege very

unusual in the Inquisition, where the prisoner is only to answer questions, but never to speak unless when called on. My proposal, however, caused some consultation; and it was with horror I found, in its termination, that not one of the officials, even under the discipline of the Inquisition, would undertake the task of watching at the door of *my* cell.

'I went back to it in an agony inexpressible. The more I had laboured to clear myself, the more I had become involved. My only resource and consolation was in a determination to obey, to the strictest letter, the injunctions of the Inquisition. I kept myself studiously awake, – *he* came not all that night. Towards the morning I slept, – Oh what a sleep was mine! – the genii, or the demons of the place, seemed busy in the dream that haunted me. I am convinced that a real victim of an *auto da fe* (so called) never suffered more during his horrible procession to flames temporal and eternal, than I did during that dream. I dreamed that the judgement had passed, – the bell had tolled, – and we marched out from the prison of the Inquisition; – my crime was proved, and my sentence determined, as an apostate monk and a *diabolical* heretic. The procession commenced, – the Dominicans went first, then followed the penitents, arms and feet bare, each hand holding a wax taper, some with *san benitos*, some without, all pale, haggard, and breathless, the hue of their faces frightfully resembling that of their clay-coloured arms and feet. Then followed those who had on their black dresses the *fuego revolto*.* Then followed – I saw *myself*; and this horrid tracing of yourself in a dream, – this haunting of yourself by your own spectre, while you still live, is perhaps a curse almost equal to your crimes visiting you in the punishments of eternity. I saw myself in the garment of condemnation, *the flames pointing upwards*, while the demons painted on my dress were mocked by the demons who beset my feet, and hovered round my temples. The Jesuits on

---

* *Flames reversed*, intimating that the criminal is not to be burned.

each side of me, urged me to consider the difference between these painted fires, and those which were about to enwrap my writhing soul for an eternity of ages. All the bells of Madrid seemed to be ringing in my ears. There was no light but a dull twilight, such as one always sees in his sleep, (no man ever dreamed of sun-light); – there was a dim and smoky blaze of torches in my eyes, whose flames were soon to *be in my eyes*. I saw the stage before me, – I was chained to the chair, amid the ringing of bells, the preaching of the Jesuits, and the shouts of the multitude. A splendid amphitheatre stood opposite, – the king and queen of Spain, and all the nobility and hierarchy of the land, were there to see us burn. Our thoughts in dreams wander; I had heard a story of an *auto da fe*, where a young Jewess, not sixteen, doomed to be burnt alive, had prostrated herself before the queen, and exclaimed, "Save me, – save me, do not let me burn, my only crime is believing in the God of my fathers;" – the queen (I believe Elizabeth of France, wife of Philip) wept, but the procession went on. Something like this crossed my dream. I saw the supplicant rejected; the next moment the figure was that of my brother Juan, who clung to me, shrieking, "Save me, save me." The next moment I was chained to my chair again, – the fires were lit, the bells rang out, the litanies were sung; – my feet were scorched to a cinder, – my muscles cracked, my blood and marrow hissed, my flesh consumed like shrinking leather, – the bones of my legs hung two black withering and moveless sticks in the ascending blaze; – it ascended, caught my hair, – I was crowned with fire, – my head was a ball of molten metal, my eyes flashed and melted in their sockets; – I opened my mouth, it drank fire, – I closed it, the fire was within, – and still the bells rung on, and the crowd shouted, and the king and queen, and all the nobility and priesthood, looked on, and we burned, and burned! – I was a cinder body and soul in my dream.

'I awoke from it with the horrible exclamation – ever shrieked, never heard – of those wretches, when the fires are climbing fast and fell, – *Misericordia por amor di Dios* –[20] My own screams awoke me, – I was in my prison, and beside me stood the tempter. With an impulse I could not resist, – an impulse borrowed from the horrors of my dream, I flung myself at his feet, and called on him to "save me".

'I know not, Sir, nor is it a problem to be solved by human intellect, whether this inscrutable being had not the power to influence my dreams, and dictate to a tempting demon the images which had driven me to fling myself at his feet for hope and safety. However it was, he certainly took advantage of my agony, half-visionary, half-real as it was, and, while proving to me that he had the power of effecting my escape from the Inquisition, proposed to me that incommunicable condition which I am forbid to reveal, except in the act of confession.'

Here Melmoth could not forbear remembering the *incommunicable condition* proposed to Stanton in the mad-house, – he shuddered, and was silent. The Spaniard went on.

'At my next examination, the questions were more eager and earnest than ever, and I was more anxious to be heard than questioned; so, in spite of the eternal circumspection and formality of an inquisitorial examination, we soon came to understand each other. I had an object to gain, and they had nothing to lose by my gaining that object. I confessed, without hesitation, that I had received another visit from that most mysterious being, who could penetrate the recesses of the Inquisition, without either its leave or prevention, (the judges trembled on their seats, as I uttered these words); – that I was most willing to disclose all that had transpired at our last conference, but that I required to first confess to a priest, and receive absolution. This, though quite contrary to the rules of the Inquisition, was, on this extraordinary occasion, complied with. A black curtain was dropt before one of the recesses; I knelt down before a priest, and confided to him that tremendous secret, which, according to the rules of the Catholic church, can never be disclosed by the confessor but to the Pope. I do not understand how the business was managed, but I was called on to repeat the same confession before the Inquisitors. I repeated it word for word, saving only the words that my oath, and my consciousness of the holy secret of confession, forbade me to disclose. The sincerity of this confession, I thought, would have worked a miracle for me, – and so it did, but not the miracle that I expected. They required from me that incommunicable secret; I announced it was in the bosom of the priest to whom I had confessed. They whispered, and seemed to debate about the torture.

'At this time, as may be supposed, I cast an anxious and miserable look round the apartment, where the large crucifix, thirteen feet high, stood bending above the seat of the Supreme. At this moment I saw a person seated at the table covered with black cloth, intensely busy as a secretary, or person employed in taking down the depositions of the accused. As I was led near the table, this person flashed a look of recognition on me, – he was my dreaded companion, – he was an official now of the Inquisition. I gave all up the moment I saw his ferocious and lurking scowl, like that of the tiger before he springs from his jungle, or the wolf from his den. This person threw on me looks, from time to time, which I could not mistake, and I dared not interpret; and I had reason to believe that the tremendous sentence pronounced against me, issued, if not from his lips, at least from his dictation. – "You, Alonzo de Monçada, monk, professed of the order of –, accused of the crimes of heresy, apostacy, fratricide, ('Oh no, – no!' I shrieked, but no one heeded me), and conspiracy with the enemy of mankind against the peace of the community in which you professed yourself a votary of God, and against the authority of the holy office; accused, moreover, of intercourse in your cell, the prison of the holy office, with an infernal messenger of the foe of God, man, and your own apostatized soul; condemned on your own confession of the infernal spirit having had access to your cell, – are hereby delivered to –"

'I heard no more. I exclaimed, but my voice was drowned in the murmur of the officials. The crucifix suspended behind the chair of the judge, rocked and reeled before my eyes; the lamp that hung from the ceiling, seemed to send forth twenty lights. I held up my hands in abjuration – they were held down by stronger hands. I tried to speak – my mouth was stopped. I sunk on my knees – on my knees I was about to be dragged away, when an aged Inquisitor giving a sign to the officials, I was released for a few moments, and he addressed me in these words – words rendered terrible by the sincerity of the speaker. From his age, from his sudden interposition, I had expected mercy. He was a very old man – he had been blind for twenty years; and as he rose to speak my malediction, my thoughts wandered from Appius Claudius of Rome, – blessing the loss of sight, that saved him from beholding the disgrace of his country, – to that blind chief Inquisitor of Spain, who assured Philip, that in sacrificing his son, he imitated the Almighty, who had sacrificed his Son also for the salvation of mankind. – Horrid profanation! yet striking application to the bosom of a Catholic. The words of the Inquisitor were these: "Wretch, apostate and excommunicate, I bless God that these withered balls can no longer behold you. The demon has haunted you from your birth – you were born in sin – fiends rocked your cradle, and dipt their talons in the holy font, while they mocked the sponsors of your unsanctified baptism. Illegitimate and accursed, you were always the burden of the holy church; and now, the infernal spirit comes to claim his own, and you acknowledge him as your lord and master. He has sought and sealed you as his own, even amid the prison of the Inquisition. Begone, accursed, we deliver you over to the secular arm, praying that it may deal with you not too severely." At these terrible words, whose meaning I understood but too well, I uttered one shriek of agony – the only *human* sound ever heard within the walls of the Inquisition. But I was borne away; and that cry into which I had thrown the whole strength of nature, was heeded no more than a cry from the torture room. On my return to my cell, I felt convinced the whole was a scheme of inquisitorial art, to involve me in self-accusation, (their constant object when they can effect it), and punish me for a crime, while I was guilty only of an extorted confession.

'With compunction and anguish unutterable, I execrated my own beast-like and credulous stupidity. Could any but an idiot, a driveller, have been the victim of such a plot? Was it in nature to believe that the prisons of the Inquisition could be traversed at will by a stranger whom no one could discover or apprehend? That such a being could enter cells impervious to human power, and hold conversation with the prisoners at his pleasure – appear and disappear – insult, ridicule and blaspheme – propose escape, and point out the means with a precision and facility, that must be the result of calm and profound calculation – and this within the walls of the Inquisition, almost in the hearing of the judges – actually in the hearing of the guards, who night and day paced the passages with sleepless and inquisitorial vigilance? – ridiculous, monstrous, impossible! it was all a plot to betray me to self-condemnation. My visitor was an agent and accomplice of the Inquisition, and I was my own betrayer and executioner. Such was my conclusion; and, hopeless as it was, it certainly seemed probable.

'I had now nothing to await but the most dreadful of all destinations, amid the darkness and silence of my cell, where the total suspension of the stranger's visits confirmed me every hour in my conviction of their nature and purport, when an event occurred, whose consequences alike defeated fear, hope and calculation. This was the great fire that broke out within the walls of the Inquisition, about the close of the last century.

'It was on the night of the 29th November 17—, that this extraordinary circumstance took place – extraordinary from the well-known precautions adopted by the vigilance of the holy office against such an accident, and also from the very small quantity of fuel consumed within its walls. On the first intimation that the fire was spreading rapidly, and threatened danger, the prisoners were ordered to be brought from their cells, and guarded in a court of the prison. I must acknowledge we were treated with great humanity and consideration. We were conducted deliberately from our cells, placed each of us between two guards, who did us no violence, nor used harsh language, but assured us, from time to time, that if the danger became imminent, we would be permitted every fair opportunity to effect our escape. It was a subject worthy of the pencil of Salvator Rosa, or of Murillo, to sketch us as we stood. Our dismal garbs and squalid looks, contrasted with the equally dark, but imposing and authoritative looks of the guards and officials, all displayed by the light of torches, which burned, or appeared to burn, fainter and fainter, as the flames rose and roared in triumph above the towers of the Inquisition. The heavens were all on fire – and the torches, held no longer in firm hands, gave a tremulous and pallid light. It seemed to me like a wildly painted picture of the last day. God appeared descending in the light that enveloped the skies – and we stood pale and shuddering in the light below.

'Among the groupe of prisoners, there were fathers and sons, who perhaps had been inmates of adjacent cells for years, without being conscious of each other's vicinity or existence – but they did not dare to recognize each other. Was not this like the day of judgement, where similar mortal relations may meet under different classes of the sheep and goats, without presuming to acknowledge the strayed one amid the flock of a different shepherd? There were also parents and children who *did* recognize and stretch out their wasted arms to each other, though feeling they must never meet, – some of them condemned to the flames, some to imprisonment, and some to the official duties of the Inquisition, as a mitigation of their sentence, – and was not this like the day of judgement, where parent and child may be allotted different destinations, and the arms that would attest the last proof of mortal affection, are expanded in vain over the gulph of eternity. Behind and around us stood the officials and guards of the Inquisition, all watching and intent on the progress of the flames, but fearless of the result with regard to themselves. Such may be the feeling of those spirits who watch the doom of the Almighty, and know the destination of those they are appointed to watch. And is not this like the day of judgement? Far, far, above us, the flames burst out in volumes, in solid masses of fire, spiring up to the burning heavens. The towers of the Inquisition shrunk into cinders – that tremendous monument of the power, and crime, and gloom of the human mind, was wasting like a scroll in the fire. Will it not be thus also at the day of judgement? Assistance was slowly brought – Spaniards are very indolent – the engines played imperfectly – the danger increased – the fire blazed higher and higher – the persons employed to work the engines, paralyzed by terror, fell to the ground, and called on every saint they could think of, to arrest the progress of the flames. Their exclamations were so loud and earnest, that really the saints must have been deaf, or must have felt a particular predilection for a conflagration, not to attend to them. However it was, the fire went on. Every bell in Madrid rang out. – Orders were issued to every Alcaide to be had. – The king of Spain himself, (after a hard day's shooting*), attended in person. The churches were all lit up, and thousands of the devout supplicated on their knees by torch-light, or whatever light they could get, that the reprobate souls confined in the Inquisition might feel the fires that were consuming its walls, as merely a slight foretaste of the fires that glowed for them for ever and ever. The fire went on, doing its dreadful work, and heeding kings and priests no more than if they were firemen. I am convinced twenty able men, accustomed to such business, could have quenched the fire; but when our workmen should have played their engines, they were all on their knees.

* The passion of the late king of Spain for field sports was well known.

'The flames at last began to descend into the court. Then commenced a scene of horror indescribable. The wretches who had been doomed to the flames, imagined their hour was come. Idiots from long confinement, and submissive as the holy office could require, they became delirious as they saw the flames approaching, and shrieked audibly, "Spare me – spare me – put me to as little torture as you can." Others, kneeling to the approaching flames, invoked them as saints. They dreamt they saw the visions they had worshipped, – the holy angels, and even the blessed virgin, descending in flames to receive their souls as parting from the stake; and they howled out their allelujahs half in horror, half in hope. Amid this scene of distraction, the Inquisitors stood their ground. It was admirable to see their firm and solemn array. As the flames prevailed, they never faultered with foot, or gave a sign with hand, or winked with eye; – their duty, their stern and heartless duty, seemed to be the only principle and motive of their existence. They seemed a phalanx clad in iron impenetrable. When the fires roared, they crossed themselves calmly; – when the prisoners shrieked, they gave a signal for silence; – when they dared to pray, they tore them from their knees, and hinted the inutility of prayer at such a juncture, when they might be sure that the flames they were deprecating would burn hotter in a region from which there was neither escape or hope of departure. At this moment, while standing amid the groupe of prisoners, my eyes were struck by an extraordinary spectacle. Perhaps it is amid the moments of despair, that imagination has most power, and they who have suffered, can best describe and feel. In the burning light, the steeple of the Dominican church was as visible as at noon-day. It was close to the prison of the Inquisition. The night was intensely dark, but so strong was the light of the conflagration, that I could see the spire blazing, from the reflected lustre, like a meteor. The hands of the clock were as visible as if a torch was held before them; and this calm and silent progress of time, amid the tumultuous confusion of midnight horrors, – this scene of the physical and mental world in an agony of fruitless and incessant motion, might have suggested a profound and singular image, had not my whole attention been rivetted to a human figure placed on a pinnacle of the spire, and surveying the scene in perfect tranquillity. It was a figure not to be mistaken – it was the figure of him who had visited me in the cells of the Inquisition. The hopes of my justification made me forget every thing. I called aloud on the guard, and pointed out the figure, visible as it was in that strong light to every eye. No one had time, however, to give a glance towards it. At that very moment, the archway of the court opposite to us gave way, and sunk in ruins at our feet, dashing, as it fell, an ocean of flames against us. One wild shriek burst from every lip at that moment. Prisoners, guards, and Inquisitors, all shrunk together, mingled in one groupe of terror.

'The next instant, the flames being suppressed by the fall of such a mass of stone, there arose such a blinding cloud of smoke and dust, that it was impossible to distinguish the face or figure of those who were next you. The confusion was increased by the contrast of this sudden darkness, to the intolerable light that had been drying up our sight for the last hour, and by the cries of those who, being near the arch, lay maimed and writhing under its fragments. Amid shrieks, and darkness, and flames, a space lay open before me. The thought, the motion, were simultaneous – no one saw – no one pursued; – and hours before my absence could be discovered, or an inquiry be made after me, I had struggled safe and secret through the ruins, and was in the streets of Madrid.

'To those who have escaped present and extreme peril, all other peril seems trifling. The wretch who has swum from a wreck cares not on what shore he is cast; and though Madrid was in fact only a wider prison of the Inquisition to me, in knowing that I was no longer in the hands of the officials, I felt a delirious and indefinite consciousness of safety. Had I reflected for a moment, I must have known, that my peculiar dress and *bare feet* must betray me wherever I went. The conjuncture, however, was very favourable to me – the streets were totally deserted; – every inhabitant who was not in bed, or bed-rid, was in the churches, deprecating the wrath of heaven, and praying for the extinction of the flames.

'I ran on, I know not where, till I could run no longer. The pure air, which I had been so long unaccustomed to breathe, acted like the most torturing spicula on my throat and lungs as I flew along, and utterly deprived me of the power of respiration, which at first it appeared to restore. I saw a building near me, whose large doors were open. I rushed in – it was a church. I fell on the pavement panting. It was the aisle into which I had burst – it was separated from the chancel by large grated railings. Within I could see the priests at the altar, by the lamps recently and rarely lighted, and a few trembling devotees on their knees, in the body of the chancel. There was a strong contrast between the glare of the lamps within the chancel, and the faint light that trembled through the windows of the aisle, scarcely showing me the monuments, on one of which I leaned to rest my throbbing temples for a moment. I could not rest – I dared not – and rising, I cast an involuntary glance on the inscription which the monument bore. The light appeared to increase maliciously, to aid my powers of vision. I read, "Orate pro anima."[21] I at last came to the name – "Juan de Monçada". I flew from the spot as if pursued by demons – my brother's early grave had been my resting place.'

Chapter Twelve

Juravi lingua, mentem injuratam gero.—[22]
Who brought you first acquainted with the devil?

  Shirley's St Patrick for Ireland

'I ran on till I had no longer breath or strength, (without perceiving that I was in a dark passage), till I was stopt by a door. In
falling against it, I burst it open, and found myself in a low dark
room. When I raised myself, for I had fallen on my hands and
knees, I looked round, and saw something so singular, as to suspend even my personal anxiety and terror for a moment.

'The room was very small; and I could perceive by the rents,
that I had not only broken open a door, but a large curtain which
hung before it, whose ample folds still afforded me concealment
if I required it. There was no one in the room, and I had time to
study its singular furniture at leisure.

'There was a table covered with a cloth; on it were placed a
vessel of a singular construction, a book, into whose pages
I looked, but could not make out a single letter. I therefore wisely
took it for a book of magic, and closed it with a feeling of excul-
patory horror. (It happened to be a copy of the Hebrew Bible,
marked with the Samaritan points). There was a knife too; and a
cock was fastened to the leg of the table, whose loud crows
announced his impatience of further constraint.*

---

* Quilibet postea paterfamilias, cum *gallo* præ manibus, in medium primus
  prodit.

  *

'I felt that this apparatus was somewhat singular – it looked like a preparation for a sacrifice. I shuddered, and wrapt myself in the volumes of the drapery which hung before the door my fall had broken open. A dim lamp, suspended from the ceiling, discovered to me all these objects, and enabled me to observe what followed almost immediately. A man of middle age, but whose physiognomy had something peculiar in it, even to the eye of a Spaniard, from the clustering darkness of his eye-brows, his prominent nose, and a certain lustre in the balls of his eyes, entered the room, knelt before the table, kissed the book that lay on it, and read from it some sentences that were to precede, as I imagined, some horrible sacrifice; – felt the edge of the knife, knelt again, uttered some words which I did not understand, (as they were in the language of that book), and then called aloud on some one by the name of Manasseh-ben-Solomon. No one answered. He sighed, passed his hand over his eyes with the air of a man who is asking pardon of himself for a short forgetfulness, and then pronounced the name of "Antonio". A young man immediately entered, and answered, "Did you call me, Father?" – But while he spoke, he threw a hollow and wandering glance on the singular furniture of the room.

"I called you, my son, and why did you not answer me?" – "I did not hear you, father – I mean, I did not think it was on me you called. I heard only a name I was never called by before. When you said 'Antonio,' I obeyed you – I came." – "But *that* is the name by which you must in future be called and be known, to me at

---

Deinde expiationem aggreditur et capiti suo ter gallum allidit, singulosque ictus his vocibus prosequitur. Hic Gallus sit permutio pro me, &c.

*

Gallo deinde imponens manus, eum statim mactat, &c[23]

Vide Buxtorf, as quoted in Dr Magee (Bishop of Raphoe's) work on the atonement. Cumberland in his Observer, I think, mentions the discovery to have been reserved for the feast of the Passover. It is just as probable it was made on the day of expiation.

least, unless you prefer another. – You shall have your choice." –
"My father, I shall adopt whatever name you choose." – "No; the
choice of your new name must be your own – you must, for the
future, either adopt the name you have heard, or another." –
"What other, Sir?" – *"That of parricide."* The youth shuddered with
horror, less at the words than at the expression that accompanied
them; and, after looking at his father for some time in a posture
of tremulous and supplicating inquiry, he burst into tears. The
father seized the moment. He grasped the arms of his son, "My
child, I gave you life, and you may repay the gift – my life is in
your power. You think me a Catholic – I have brought you up as
one for the preservation of our mutual lives, in a country where
the confession of the true faith would infallibly cost both. I am
one of that unhappy race every where stigmatized and spoken
against, yet on whose industry and talent the ungrateful country
that anathematizes us, depends for half the sources of its national
prosperity. I am a Jew, 'an Israelite', one of those to whom, even
by the confession of a Christian apostle, 'pertain the adoption,
and the glory, and the covenants, and the giving of the law, and
the service of God, and the promises; whose are the fathers, and
of whom as concerning the flesh –" 'Here he paused, not willing
to go on with a quotation that would have contradicted his sentiments. He added, "The Messias will come, whether suffering or
triumphant.* I am a Jew. I called you at the hour of your birth by
the name of Manasseh-ben-Solomon. I called on you by that
name, which I felt had clung to the bottom of my heart from that
hour, and which, echoing from its abyss, I almost hoped you
would have recognized. It was a dream, but will you not, my
beloved child, realize that dream? Will you not? – will you not?
The God of your fathers is waiting to embrace you – and your
father is at your feet, imploring you to follow the faith of your

* The Jews believe in two Messias, a suffering and a triumphant one, to reconcile
the prophecies with their own expectations.

father Abraham, the prophet Moses, and all the holy prophets who are with God, and who look down on this moment of your soul's vacillation between the abominable idolatries of those who not only adore the Son of the carpenter, but even impiously compel you to fall down before the image of the woman his mother, and adore her by the blasphemous name of Mother of God, – and the pure voice of those who call on you to worship the God of your fathers, the God of ages, the eternal God of heaven and earth, without son or mother, without child or descendant, (as impiously presumed in their blasphemous creed), without even worshipper, save those who, like me, sacrifice their hearts to him in solitude, at the risk of those hearts being PIERCED BY THEIR OWN CHILDREN."

'At these words, the young man, overcome by all he saw and heard, and quite unprepared for this sudden transition from Catholicism to Judaism, burst into tears. The father seized the moment, "My child, you are now to profess yourself the slave of these idolaters, who are cursed in the law of Moses, and by the commandment of God, – or to enrol yourself among the faithful, whose rest shall be in the bosom of Abraham, and who, reposing there, shall see the unbelieving crawling over the burning ashes of hell, and supplicate you in vain for a drop of water, according to the legends of their own prophet. And does not such a picture excite your pride to deny them a drop?" – "I would not deny them a drop," sobbed the youth, "I would give them these tears." – "Reserve them for your father's grave," added the Jew, "for to the grave you have doomed me. – I have lived, sparing, watching, temporizing, with these accursed idolaters, for *you*. And now – and now you reject a God who is alone able to save, and a father kneeling to implore you to accept that salvation." – "No, I do not," said the bewildered youth. – "What, then, do you determine? – I am at your feet to know your resolution. Behold, the mysterious instruments of your initiation are ready. There is the uncorrupted book of Moses, the prophet of God, as these idolaters themselves confess. There are all the preparations for the year of expiation – determine whether those rites shall now dedicate you to the true God, or seize your father, (who has put his life into your hands), and drag him by the throat into the prisons of the Inquisition. You may – you can – *will you?*"

'In prostrate and tremulous agony, the father held up his locked hands to his child. I seized the moment – despair had made me reckless. I understood not a word of what was said, except the reference to the Inquisition. I seized on that last word – I grasped, in my despair, at the heart of father and child. I rushed from behind the curtain, and exclaiming, "If he does not betray you to the Inquisition. *I will.*" I fell at his feet. This mixture of defiance and prostration, my squalid figure, my inquisitorial habit, and my bursting on this secret and solemn interview, struck the Jew with a horror he vainly gasped to express, till, rising from my knees, on which I had fallen from my weakness, I added, "Yes, I will betray you to the Inquisition, unless you instantly promise to shelter me from it." The Jew glanced at my dress, perceived his danger and mine, and, with a *physical* presence of mind un-paralleled, except in a man under strong impressions of mental excitation and personal danger, bustled about to remove every trace of the expiatory sacrifice, and of my inquisitorial costume, in a moment. In the same breath he called aloud for *Rebekah*, to remove the vessels from the table; bid *Antonio* quit the apart-ment, and hastened to clothe me in some dress that he had snatched from a wardrobe collected from centuries; while he tore off my inquisitorial dress with a violence that left me actually naked, and the habit in rags.

'There was something at once fearful and ludicrous in the scene that followed. Rebekah, an old Jewish woman, came at his call; but, seeing a third person, retreated in terror, while her mas-ter, in his confusion, called her in vain by her *Christian* name of Maria. Obliged to remove the table alone, he overthrew it, and broke the leg of the unfortunate animal fastened to it, who, not to be without his share in the tumult, uttered the most shrill and intolerable screams, while the Jew, snatching up the sacrificial knife, repeated eagerly, "Statim mactat gallum",[24] and put the wretched bird out of its pain; then, trembling at this open avowal of his Judaism, he sat down amid the ruins of the over thrown table, the fragments of the broken vessels, and the remains of the martyred cock. He gazed at me with a look of stupified and ludicrous inanity, and demanded in delirious tones, what "my lords the Inquisitors had pleased to visit his humble but highly-honoured mansion for?" I was scarce less deranged than he was; and, though we both spoke the same language, and were forced by circumstances into the same strange and desperate confidence with each other, we really needed, for the first half-hour, a rational interpreter of our exclamations, starts of fear, and bursts of disclosure. At last our mutual terror acted honestly between us, and we understood each other. The end of the matter was, that, in less than an hour, I felt myself clad in a comfortable garment, seated at a table amply spread, watched over by my involuntary host, and watching him in turn with red wolfish eyes, which glanced from his board to his person, as if I could, at a moment's hint of danger from *his* treachery, have changed my meal, and feasted on his life-blood. No such danger occurred, – my host was more afraid of me than I had reason to be of him, and for many causes. He was a Jew *innate*, an impostor, – a wretch, who, drawing sustenance from the bosom of our holy mother the church, had turned her nutriment to poison, and attempted to infuse that poison into the lips of his son. I was but a fugitive from the Inquisition, – a prisoner, who had a kind of instinctive and very venial dislike to giving the Inquisitors the trouble of lighting the faggots for *me*, which would be much better employed in consuming the adherent to the law of Moses. In fact, impartiality considered, there was every thing in my favour, and the Jew just acted as if he felt so, – but all this I ascribed to his terrors of the Inquisition.

'That night I slept, – I know not how or where. I had wild

dreams before I slept, if I did sleep; and after, – such visions, – such *things*, passed in dread and stern reality before me. I have often in my memory searched for the traces of the first night I passed under the roof of the Jew, but can find nothing, – nothing except a conviction of my utter insanity. It might not have been so, – I know not how it was. I remember his lighting me up a narrow stair, and my asking him, was he lighting me *down* the steps of the dungeons of the Inquisition? – he throwing open a door, and my asking him, was it the door of the torture-room? – his attempting to undress me, and my exclaiming, "Do not bind me too tight, – I know I must suffer, but be merciful;" – his throwing me on the bed, while I shrieked, "Well, you have bound me on the rack, then? – strain it hard, that I may forget myself the sooner; but let your surgeon not be near to watch my pulse, – let it cease to throb, and let me cease to suffer." I remember no more for many days, though I have struggled to do so, and caught from time to time glimpses of thoughts better lost. Oh, Sir, there are some *criminals of the imagination*, whom if we could plunge into the *oubliettes* of its magnificent but lightly-based fabric, its lord would reign more happy.

*

'Many days elapsed, indeed, before the Jew began to feel his immunity somewhat dearly purchased, by the additional maintenance of a troublesome, and, I fear, a deranged inmate. He took the first opportunity that the recovery of my intellect offered, of hinting this to me, and inquired mildly what I purposed to do, and where I meant to go. This question for the first time opened to my view that range of hopeless and interminable desolation that lay before me, – the Inquisition had laid waste the whole track of life, as with fire and sword. I had not a spot to stand on, a meal to earn, a hand to grasp, a voice to greet, a roof to crouch under, in the whole realm of Spain.

'You are not to learn, Sir, that the power of the Inquisition, like that of death, separates you, by its single touch, from all mortal relations. From the moment its grasp has seized you, all human hands unlock their hold of yours, – you have no longer father, mother, sister, or child. The most devoted and affectionate of all those relatives, who, in the natural intercourse of human life, would have laid their hands under your feet to procure you a smoother passage over its roughnesses, would be the first to grasp the faggot that was to reduce you to ashes, if the Inquisition were to demand the sacrifice. I knew all this; and I felt, besides, that, had I never been a prisoner in the Inquisition, I was an isolated being, rejected by father and mother, – the involuntary murderer of my brother, the only being on earth who loved me, or whom I could love or profit by, – that being who seemed to flash across my brief *human* existence, to illuminate and to blast. The bolt had perished with the victim. In Spain it was impossible for me to live without detection, unless I plunged myself into an imprisonment as profound and hopeless as that of the Inquisition. And, if a miracle were wrought to convey me out of Spain, ignorant as I was of the language, the habits, and the modes of obtaining subsistence, in that or any other country, how could I support myself even for a day? Absolute famine stared me in the face, and a sense of degradation accompanying my consciousness of my own utter and desolate helplessness, was the keenest shaft in the quiver, whose contents were lodged in my heart. My consequence was actually lessened in my own eyes, by ceasing to become the victim of persecution, by which I had suffered so long. *While people think it worth their while to torment us, we are never without some dignity, though painful and imaginary.* Even in the Inquisition I belonged to somebody, – I was watched and guarded; – now, I was the outcast of the whole earth, and I wept with equal bitterness and depression at the hopeless vastness of the desert I had to traverse.

'The Jew, not at all disturbed by these feelings, went daily out for intelligence, and returned one evening in such raptures, that

I could easily discover he had ascertained his own safety at least, if not mine. He informed me that the current report in Madrid was, that I had perished in the fall of the burning ruins on the night of the fire. He added, that this report had received additional currency and strength from the fact, that the bodies of those who had perished by the fall of the arch, were, when discovered, so defaced by fire, and so crushed by the massive fragments, as to be utterly undistinguishable; – their remains had been collected, however, and mine were supposed to be among the number. A mass had been performed for them, and *their cinders, occupying but a single coffin*, were interred in the vaults of the Dominican church, while some of the first families of Spain, in the deepest mourning, and their faces veiled, testified their grief in silence for those whom they would have shuddered to acknowledge their mortal relationship to, had they been still living. Certainly a lump of cinders was no longer an object even of religious hostility. My mother, he added, was among the number of mourners, but with a veil so long and thick, and attendance so few, that it would have been impossible to have known the Duchess di Monçada, but for the whisper that her appearance there had been enjoined for penance. He added, what gave me more perfect satisfaction, that the holy office was very glad to accredit the story of my death; they wished me to be believed dead, and what the Inquisition wishes to be believed, is rarely denied belief in Madrid. This signing my certificate of death, was to me the best security for life. In the communicativeness of his joy, which had expanded his heart, if not his hospitality, the Jew, as I swallowed my bread and water, (for my stomach still loathed all animal food), informed me that there was a procession to take place that evening, the most solemn and superb ever witnessed in Madrid. The holy office was to appear in all the pomp and plenitude of its glory, accompanied by the standards of St Dominic and the cross, while all the ecclesiastical orders in Madrid were to attend with their appropriate insignia, invested by a strong military guard, (which, for some reason or other, was judged necessary or proper), and, attended by the whole populace of Madrid, was to proceed to the principal church to humiliate themselves for the recent calamity they had undergone, and implore the saints to be more personally active in the event of a future conflagration.

'The evening came on – the Jew left me; and, under an impression at once unaccountable and irresistible, I ascended to the highest apartment in his house, and, with a beating heart, listened for the toll of the bells that was to announce the commencement of the ceremony. I had not long to wait. At the close of twilight, every steeple in the city was vibrating with the tolls of their well-plied bells. I was in an upper room of the house. There was but one window; but, hiding myself behind the blind, which I withdrew from time to time, I had a full view of the spectacle. The house of the Jew looked out on an open space, through which the procession was to pass, and which was already so filled, that I wondered how the procession could ever make its way through such a wedged and impenetrable mass. At last, I could distinguish a motion like that of a distant power, giving a kind of indefinite impulse to the vast body that rolled and blackened beneath me, like the ocean under the first and far-felt agitations of the storm.

'The crowd rocked and reeled, but did not seem to give way an inch. The procession commenced. I could see it approach, marked as it was by the crucifix, banner, and taper – (for they had reserved the procession till a late hour, to give it the imposing effect of torch-light) and I saw the multitude at a vast distance give way at once. Then came on the stream of the procession, rushing, like a magnificent river, between two banks of human bodies, who kept as regular and strict distance, as if they had been ramparts of stone, – the banners, and crucifixes, and tapers, appearing like the crests of foam on advancing billows, sometimes rising, sometimes sinking. At last they came on, and the whole grandeur of the procession burst on my view, and nothing was ever more imposing, or more magnificent. The habits of the ecclesiastics, the glare of the torches struggling with the dying twilight, and seeming to say to heaven, "We have a sun though yours is set;" – the solemn and resolute look of the whole party, who trod as if their march were on the bodies of kings, and looked as if they would have said, What is the sceptre to the cross? – the black crucifix itself, trembling in the rear, attended by the banner of St Dominic, with its awful inscription. – It was a sight to convert all hearts, and I exulted I was a Catholic. Suddenly a tumult seemed to arise among the crowd – I knew not from what it could arise – all seemed so pleased and so elated.

'I drew away the blind, and saw, by torch-light, among a crowd of officials who clustered round the standard of St Dominic, the figure of my companion. His story was well known. At first a faint hiss was heard, then a wild and smothered howl. Then I heard voices among the crowd repeat, in audible sounds, "What is this for? Why do they ask why the Inquisition has been half-burned? – why the virgin has withdrawn her protection? – why the saints turn away their faces from us? – when a parricide marches among the officials of the Inquisition. Are the hands that have cut a father's throat fit to support the banner of the cross?" These were the words but of a few at first, but the whisper spread rapidly among the crowd; and fierce looks were darted, and hands were clenched and raised, and some stooped to the earth for stones. The procession went on, however, and every one knelt to the crucifixes as they advanced, held aloft by the priests. But the murmurs increased too, and the words, "parricide, profanation and victim", resounded on every side, even from those who knelt in the mire as the cross passed by. The murmur increased – it could no longer be mistaken for that of adoration. The foremost priests paused in terror ill concealed – and this seemed the signal for the terrible scene that was about to follow. An officer belonging to the guard at this time ventured to intimate to the chief Inquisitor the danger that might be apprehended, but was dismissed with the short and sullen answer, "Move on – the servants of Christ have nothing to fear." The procession attempted to proceed, but their progress was obstructed by the multitude, who now seemed bent on some deadly purpose. A few stones were thrown; but the moment the priests raised their crucifixes, the multitude were on their knees again, still, however, holding the stones in their hands. The military officers again addressed the chief Inquisitor, and intreated his permission to disperse the crowd. They received the same dull and stern answer, "The cross is sufficient for the protection of its servants – whatever fears you may feel, I feel none." Incensed at the reply, a young officer sprung on his horse, which he had quitted from respect while addressing the Suprema, and was in a moment levelled by the blow of a stone that fractured his skull. He turned his blood-swimming eyes on the Inquisitor, and died. The multitude raised a wild shout, and pressed closer. Their intentions were now too plain. They pressed close on that part of the procession among which their victim was placed. Again, and in the most urgent terms, the officers implored leave to disperse the crowd, or at least cover the retreat of the obnoxious object to some neighbouring church, or even to the walls of the Inquisition. And the wretched man himself, with loud outcries, (as he saw the danger thickening around him), joined in their petition. The Suprema, though looking pale, bated not a jot of his pride. "These are my arms!" he exclaimed, pointing to the crucifixes, "and their inscription is ἐν-τούτῳ-νίκα.[25] I forbid a sword to be drawn, or a musket to be levelled. On, in the name of God." And on they attempted to move, but the pressure now rendered it impossible. The multitude, unrepressed by the military, became ungovernable; the crosses reeled and rocked like standards in a battle; the ecclesiastics, in confusion and terror, pressed on each other. Amid that vast mass, every particle of which seemed in motion, there was but one emphatic and discriminate movement – that which bore a certain part of the crowd strait on to the spot where their victim, though inclosed and inwrapt by all that is formidable in earthly, and all that is awful in spiritual power – sheltered by the crucifix and the sword – stood trembling to the bottom of his soul. The Suprema saw his error too late, and now called loudly on the military to advance, and disperse the crowd by any means. They attempted to obey him; but by this time they were mingled among the crowd themselves. All order had ceased; and besides, there appeared a kind of indisposition to this service, from the very first, among the military. They attempted to charge, however; but, entangled as they were among the crowd, who clung round their horses' hoofs, it was impossible for them even to form, and the first shower of stones threw them into total confusion. The danger increased every moment, for one spirit now seemed to animate the whole multitude. What had been the stifled growl of a few, was now the audible yell of all – "Give him to us – we must have him;" and they tossed and roared like a thousand waves assailing a wreck. As the military retreated, a hundred priests instantly closed round the unhappy man, and with generous despair exposed themselves to the fury of the multitude. While the Suprema, hastening to the dreadful spot, stood in the front of the priests, with the cross uplifted, – his face was like that of the dead, but his eye had not lost a single flash of its fire, nor his voice a stone of its pride. It was in vain; the multitude proceeded calmly, and even respectfully, (when not resisted), to remove all that obstructed their progress; in doing so, they took every care of the persons of priests whom they were compelled to remove, repeatedly asking their pardon for the violence they were guilty of. And this tranquillity of resolved vengeance was the most direful indication of its never desisting till its purpose was accomplished. The last ring was broken – the last resister overcome. Amid yells like those of a thousand tigers, the victim was seized and dragged forth, grasping in both hands fragments of the robes of those he had clung to in vain, and holding them up in the impotence of despair.

'The cry was hushed for a moment, as they felt him in their talons, and gazed on him with thirsty eyes. Then it was renewed, and the work of blood began. They dashed him to the earth – tore him up again – flung him into the air – tossed him from hand to hand, as a bull gores the howling mastiff with horns right and left. Bloody, defaced, blackened with earth, and battered with stones, he struggled and roared among them, till a loud cry announced the hope of a termination to a scene alike horrible to humanity, and disgraceful to civilization. The military, strongly reinforced, came galloping on, and all the ecclesiastics, with torn habits, and broken crucifixes, following fast in the rear, – all eager in the cause of human nature – all on fire to prevent this base and barbarous disgrace to the name of Christianity and of human nature.

'Alas! this interference only hastened the horrible catastrophe. There was but a shorter space for the multitude to work their furious will. I saw, I felt, but I cannot describe, the last moments of this horrible scene. Dragged from the mud and stones, they dashed a mangled lump of flesh right against the door of the house where I was. With his tongue hanging from his lacerated mouth, like that of a baited bull; with one eye torn from the socket, and dangling on his bloody cheek; with a fracture in every limb, and a wound for every pore, he still howled for "life – life – life – mercy!" till a stone, aimed by some pitying hand, struck him down. He fell, trodden in one moment into sanguine and discoloured mud by a thousand feet. The cavalry came on, charging with fury. The crowd, saturated with cruelty and blood, gave way in grim silence. But they had not left a joint of his little finger – a hair of his head – a slip of his skin. Had Spain mortgaged all her reliques from Madrid to Monserrat, from the Pyrennees to Gibraltar, she could not have recovered the paring of a nail to canonize. The officer who headed the troop dashed his horse's hoofs into a bloody formless mass, and demanded, "Where was the victim?" He was answered, "Beneath your horse's feet,*" and they departed.

*

'It is a fact, Sir, that while witnessing this horrible execution, I felt all the effects vulgarly ascribed to fascination. I shuddered at the first movement – the dull and deep whisper among the crowd. I shrieked involuntarily when the first decisive movements began among them; but when at last the human shapeless carrion was dashed against the door, I echoed the wild shouts of the multitude with a kind of savage instinct. I bounded – I clasped my hands for a moment – then I echoed the screams of the thing that seemed no longer to live, but still could scream; and I screamed aloud and wildly for life – life – and mercy! One face was turned towards me as I shrieked in unconscious tones. The glance, fixed on me for a moment, was in a moment withdrawn. The flash of the well-known eyes made no impression on me then. My existence was so purely mechanical, that, without the least consciousness of my own danger, (scarce less than that of the victim, had I been detected), I remained uttering shout for shout, and scream for scream – offering worlds in imagination to be able to remove from the window, yet feeling as if every shriek I uttered was as a nail that fastened me to it – dropping my eye-lids, and feeling as if a hand held them open, or cut them away – forcing me to gaze on all that passed below, like Regulus, with his lids cut off, compelled to gaze on the sun that withered up his eye-balls – till sense, and sight, and soul, failed me, and I fell grasping by the bars of the window, and mimicking, in my horrid trance, the

* This circumstance occurred in Ireland 1797, after the murder of the unfortunate Dr Hamilton. The officer was answered, on inquiring what was that heap of mud at his horse's feet, – 'The man you came for.'

shouts of the multitude, and the yell of the devoted.* I actually for a moment believed myself the object of their cruelty. The drama of terror has the irresistible power of converting its audience into its victims.

'The Jew had kept apart from the tumult of the night. He had, I suppose, been saying within himself, in the language of your admirable poet,

"Oh, Father Abraham, what these Christians are!"

'But when he returned at a late hour, he was struck with horror at the state in which he found me. I was delirious, – raving, and all he could say or do to soothe me, was in vain. My imagination had been fearfully impressed, and the consternation of the poor Jew was, I have been told, equally ludicrous and dismal. In his terror, he forgot all the technical formality of the Christian names by which he had uniformly signalized his household, since his residence in Madrid at least. He called aloud on Manasseh-ben-Solomon his son, and Rebekah his maid, to assist in holding me. "Oh, Father Abraham, my ruin is certain, this maniac will discover all, and Manasseh-ben-Solomon, my son, will die uncircumcised."

'These words operating on my delirium, I started up, and,

---

* In the year 1803, when Emmett's insurrection broke out in Dublin – (*the fact* from which this account is drawn was related to me by an eye-witness) – Lord Kilwarden, in passing through Thomas Street, was dragged from his carriage, and murdered in the most horrid manner. Pike after pike was thrust through his body, till at last he was *nailed to a door*, and called out to his murderers to 'put him out of his pain.' At this moment, a shoemaker, who lodged in the garret of an opposite house, was drawn to the window by the horrible cries he heard. He stood at the window, gasping with horror, his wife attempting vainly to drag him away. He saw the last blow struck – he heard the last groan uttered, as the sufferer cried, 'put me out of pain,' while sixty pikes were thrusting at him. The man stood at his window as if nailed to it; and when dragged from it, became – an *idiot for life*.

grasping the Jew by the throat, arraigned him as a prisoner of the Inquisition. The terrified wretch, falling on his knees, vociferated, "My cock, – my cock, – my cock! oh! I am undone!" Then, grasping my knees, "I am no Jew, – my son, Manasseh-ben-Solomon, is a Christian; you will not betray him, you will not betray *me*, – me who have saved your life. Manasseh, – I mean Antonio, – Rebekah, – no, Maria, help me to hold him. Oh God of Abraham, my cock, and my sacrifice of expiation, and this maniac to burst on the recesses of our privacy, to tear open the veil of the tabernacle!" – "Shut the tabernacle," said Rebekah, the old domestic whom I have before mentioned; "yea, shut the tabernacle, and close up the veils thereof, for behold there be men knocking at the door, – men who are children of Belial, and they knock with staff and stone; and, verily, they are about to break in the door, and demolish the carved work thereof with axes and hammers." – "Thou liest," said the Jew, in much perturbation: "there is no carved work thereabout, nor dare they break it down with axes and hammers; peradventure it is but an assault of the children of Belial, in their rioting and drunkenness. I pray thee, Rebekah, to watch the door, and keep off the sons of Belial, even the sons of the mighty of the sinful city – the city of Madrid, while I remove this blaspheming carrion, who struggleth with me, – yea, struggleth mightily," (and struggle I did mightily). But, as I struggled, the knocks at the door became louder and stronger; and, as I was carried off, the Jew continued to repeat, "Set thy face against them, Rebekah; yea, set thy face like a flint." As he retired, Rebekah exclaimed, "Behold I have set my back against them, for my face now availeth not. My back is that which I will oppose, and verily I shall prevail." – "I pray thee, Rebekah," cried the Jew, "oppose thy FACE unto them, and verily that shall prevail. Try not the adversary with thy back, but oppose thy face unto them; and behold, if they are men, they shall flee, even though they were a thousand, at the rebuke of one. I pray thee try thy face once more, Rebekah, while I send this scape-goat into the wilderness.

Surely thy face is enough to drive away those who knocked by night at the door of that house in Gibeah, in the matter of the wife of the Benjamite." The knocking all this time increased. "Behold my back is broken," cried Rebekah, giving up her watch and ward, "for, of a verity, the weapons of the mighty do smite the lintels and door-posts; and mine arms are not steel, neither are my ribs iron, and behold I fail, – yea, I fail, and fall backwards into the hands of the uncircumcised." And so saying, she fell backwards as the door gave way, and fell not, as she feared, into the hands of the uncircumcised, but into those of two of her countrymen, who, it appeared, had some extraordinary reason for this late visit and forcible entrance.

'The Jew, apprized who they were, quitted me, after securing the door, and sat up the greater part of the night, in earnest conversation with his visitors. Whatever was their subject, it left traces of the most intense anxiety on the countenance of the Jew the next morning. He went out early, did not return till a late hour, and then hastened to the room I occupied, and expressed the utmost delight at finding me sane and composed. Candles were placed on the table, Rebekah dismissed, the door secured, and the Jew, after taking many uneasy turns about the narrow apartment, and often clearing his throat, at length sat down, and ventured to entrust me with the cause of his perturbation, in which, with the fatal consciousness of the unhappy, I already began to feel *I* must have a share. He told me, that though the report of my death, so universally credited through Madrid, had at first set his mind at ease, there was now a wild story, which, with all its falsehood and impossibility, might, in its circulation, menace us with the most fearful consequences. He asked me, was it possible I could have been so imprudent as to expose myself to view on the day of that horrible execution? and when I confessed that I had stood at a window, and had involuntarily uttered cries that I feared might have reached some ears, he wrung his hands, and a sweat of consternation burst out on his pallid features. When he recovered himself, he told me it was universally believed that my spectre had appeared on that terrible occasion, – that I had been seen hovering in the air, to witness the sufferings of the dying wretch, – and that my voice had been heard summoning him to his eternal doom. He added, that this story, possessing all the credibility of superstition, was now repeated by a thousand mouths; and whatever contempt might be attached to its absurdity, it would infallibly operate as a hint to the restless vigilance, and unrelaxing industry of the holy office, and might ultimately lead to my discovery. He therefore was about to disclose to me a secret, the knowledge of which would enable me to remain in perfect security even in the centre of Madrid, until some means might be devised of effecting my escape, and procuring me the means of subsistence in some Protestant country, beyond the reach of the Inquisition.

'As he was about to disclose this secret on which the safety of both depended, and which I bent in speechless agony to hear, a knock was heard at the door, very unlike the knocks of the preceding night. It was single, solemn, peremptory, – and followed by a demand to open the doors of the house in the name of the most holy Inquisition. At these terrible words, the wretched Jew flung himself on his knees, blew out the candles, called on the names of the twelve patriarchs, and slipped a large rosary on his arm, in less time than it is possible to conceive any human frame could go through such a variety of movements. The knock was repeated, – I stood paralyzed; but the Jew, springing on his feet, raised one of the boards of the floor in a moment, and, with a motion between convulsion and instinct, pointed to me to descend. I did so, and found myself in a moment in darkness and in safety.

'I had descended but a few steps, on the last of which I stood trembling, when the officers of the Inquisition entered the room, and stalked over the very board that concealed me. I could hear every word that passed. "Don Fernan," said an officer to the Jew, who re-entered with them, after respectfully opening the door, "why were we not admitted sooner?" – "Holy Father," said the trembling Jew, "my only domestic, Maria, is old and deaf, the youth my son is in his bed, and I was myself engaged in my devotions." – "It seems you can perform them in the dark," said another, pointing to the candles, which the Jew was re-lighting. – "When the eye of God is on me, most reverend fathers, I am never in darkness." – "The eye of God *is* on you," said the officer, sternly seating himself; "and so is another eye, to which he has deputed the sleepless vigilance and resistless penetration of his own, – the eye of the holy office. Don Fernan di Nunez," the name by which the Jew went, "you are not ignorant of the indulgence extended by the church, to those who have renounced the errors of that accursed and misbelieving race from which you are descended, but you must be also aware of its incessant vigilance being directed towards such individuals, from the suspicion necessarily attached to their doubtful conversation, and possible relapse. We know that the black blood of Grenada flowed in the tainted veins of your ancestry, and that not more than four centuries have elapsed, since your forefathers trampled on that cross before which you are now prostrate. You are an old man, Don Fernan, but not an *old Christian*; and, under these circumstances, it behoves the holy office to have a watchful scrutiny over your conduct."

'The unfortunate Jew, invoking all the saints, protested he would feel the strictest scrutiny with which the holy office might honour him, as a ground of obligation and a matter of thanksgiving, – renouncing at the same time the creed of his race in terms of such exaggeration and vehemence, as made me tremble for his probable sincerity in any creed, and his fidelity to me. The officers of the Inquisition, taking little notice of his protestations, went on to inform him of the object of their visit. They stated that a wild and incredible tale of the spectre of a deceased prisoner of the Inquisition having been seen hovering in the air near his house, had suggested to the wisdom of the holy office, that the living individual might be concealed within its walls.

'I could not see the trepidation of the Jew, but I could feel the vibration of the boards on which he stood communicated to the steps that supported me. In a choaked and tremulous voice, he implored the officers to search every apartment of his house, and to raze it to the ground, and inter him under its dust, if aught were found in it which a faithful and orthodox son of the church might not harbour. "That shall doubtless be done," said the officer, taking him at his word with the utmost *sang froid*; "but, in the mean time, suffer me to apprize you, Don Fernan, of the peril you incur, if at any future time, however remote, it shall be discovered that you harboured or aided in concealing a prisoner of the Inquisition, and an enemy of the holy church, – the very first and lightest part of that penalty will be your dwelling being razed to the ground." The Inquisitor raised his voice, and paused with emphatic deliberation between every clause of the following sentences, measuring as it were the effect of his blows on the increasing terror of his auditor. "You will be conveyed to our prison, under the suspected character of a relapsed Jew. Your son will be committed to a convent, to remove him from the pestilential influence of your presence; – and your whole property shall be confiscated, to the last stone in your walls, the last garment on your person, and the last denier in your purse."

'The poor Jew, who had marked the gradations of his fear by groans more audible and prolonged at the end of every tremendous denunciatory clause, at the mention of confiscation so total and desolating, lost all self-possession, and, ejaculating – "Oh Father Abraham, and all the holy prophets!" – fell, as I conjectured from the sound, prostrate on the floor. I gave myself up for lost. Exclusive of his pusillanimity, the words he had uttered were enough to betray him to the officers of the Inquisition; and, without a moment's hesitation between the danger of falling into their hands, and plunging into the darkness of the recess into which I had descended, I staggered down a few remaining steps, and attempted to feel my way along a passage, in which they seemed to terminate.'

Chapter Thirteen

There sat a spirit in the vault,
In shape, in hue, in lineaments, like life.

Southey's Thalaba

'I am convinced, that, had the passage been as long and intricate as any that ever an antiquarian pursued to discover the tomb of Cheops in the Pyramids, I would have rushed on in the blindness of my desperation, till famine or exhaustion had compelled me to pause. But I had no such peril to encounter, – the floor of the passage was smooth, and the walls were matted, and though I proceeded in darkness, I proceeded in safety; and provided my progress removed me far enough from the pursuit or discovery of the Inquisition, I scarcely cared how it might terminate.

'Amid this temporary magnanimity of despair, this state of mind which unites the extremes of courage and pusillanimity, I saw a faint light. Faint it was, but it was distinct, – I saw clearly it was light. Great God! what a revulsion in my blood and heart, in all my physical and mental feelings, did this sun of my world of darkness create! I venture to say, that my speed in approaching it was in the proportion of one hundred steps to one, compared to my crawling progress in the preceding darkness. As I approached, I could discover that the light gleamed through the broad crevices of a door, which, disjointed by subterranean damps, gave me as full a view of the apartment within, as if it were opened to me by the inmate. Through one of these crevices, before which I knelt in a mixture of exhaustion and curiosity, I could reconnoitre the whole of the interior.

'It was a large apartment, hung with dark-coloured baize within four feet of the floor, and this intermediate part was thickly matted, probably to intercept the subterranean damps. In the centre of the room stood a table covered with black cloth; it supported an iron lamp of an antique and singular form, by whose light I had been directed, and was now enabled to descry furniture that appeared sufficiently extraordinary. There were, amid maps and globes, several instruments, of which my ignorance did not permit me then to know the use, – some, I have since learned, were anatomical; there was an electrifying machine, and a curious *model of a rack* in ivory; there were few books, but several scrolls of parchment, inscribed with large characters in red and ochre coloured ink; and around the room were placed *four* skeletons, not in cases, but in a kind of upright coffin, that gave their bony emptiness a kind of ghastly and imperative prominence, as if they were the real and rightful tenants of that singular apartment. Interspersed between them were the stuffed figures of animals I knew not then the names of, – an alligator, – some gigantic bones, which I took for those of Samson, but which turned out to be fragments of those of the Mammoth, – and antlers, which in my terror I believed to be those of the devil, but afterwards learned to be those of an Elk. Then I saw figures smaller, but not less horrible, – human and brute abortions, in all their states of anomalous and deformed construction, not preserved in spirits, but standing in the ghastly nakedness of their white diminutive bones; these I conceived to be the attendant imps of some infernal ceremony, which the grand wizard, who now burst on my sight, was to preside over.

'At the end of the table sat an old man, wrapped in a long robe; his head was covered with a black velvet cap, with a broad border of furs, his spectacles were of such a size as almost to hide his face, and he turned over some scrolls of parchment with an anxious and trembling hand; then seizing a scull that lay on the table, and grasping it in fingers hardly less bony, and not less yellow, seemed to apostrophize it in the most earnest manner. All my personal fears were lost in the thought of my being the involuntary witness of some infernal orgie. I was still kneeling at the door, when my long suspended respiration burst forth in a groan, which reached the figure seated at the table in a moment. Habitual vigilance supplied all the defects of age on the part of the listener. It was but the sensation of a moment to feel the door thrown open, my arm seized by an arm powerful though withered by age, and myself, as I thought, in the talons of a demon.

'The door was closed and bolted. An awful figure stood over me, (for I had fallen on the floor), and thundered out, "Who art thou, and why art thou here?" I knew not what to answer, and gazed with a fixed and speechless look on the skeletons and the other furniture of this terrible vault. "Hold," said the voice, "if thou art indeed exhausted, and needest refreshment, drink of this cup, and thou shalt be refreshed as with wine; verily, it shall come into thy bowels as water, and as oil into thy bones," – and as he spoke he offered to me a cup with some liquid in it. I repelled him and his drink, which I had not a doubt was some magical drug, with horror unutterable; and losing all other fears in the overwhelming one of becoming a slave of Satan, and a victim of one of his agents, as I believed this extraordinary figure, I called on the name of the Saviour and the saints, and, crossing myself at every sentence, exclaimed, "No, tempter, keep your infernal potions for the leprous lips of your imps, or swallow them yourself. I have but this moment escaped from the hands of the Inquisition, and a million times rather would I return and yield myself their victim, than consent to become yours, – your tender mercies are the only cruelties I dread. Even in the prison of the holy office, where the faggots appeared to be lit before my eyes, and the chain already fastened round my body to bind it to the stake, I was sustained by a power that enabled me to embrace objects so terrible to nature, sooner than escape them at the price of my salvation. The choice was offered me, and I made my election, – and so would I do were it to be offered a thousand times, though the last were at the stake, and the fire already kindling."'

Here the Spaniard paused in some agitation. In the enthusiasm of his narration, he had in some degree disclosed that secret which he had declared was incommunicable, except in confessing to a priest. Melmoth, who, from the narrative of Stanton, had been prepared to suspect something of this, did not think prudent to press him for a farther disclosure, and waited in silence till his emotion had subsided, without remark or question. Monçada at length resumed his narrative.

'While I was speaking, the old man viewed me with a look of calm surprise, that made me ashamed of my fears, even before I had ceased to utter them. "What!" said he at length, fixing apparently on some expressions that struck him, "art thou escaped from the arm that dealeth its blow in darkness, even the arm of the Inquisition? Art thou that Nazarene youth who sought refuge in the house of our brother Solomon, the son of Hilkiah, who is called Fernan Nunez by the idolaters in this land of his captivity? Verily I trusted thou shouldst this night have eat of my bread, and drank of my cup, and been unto me as a scribe, for our brother Solomon testified concerning thee, saying, His pen is even as the pen of a ready writer."

'I gazed at him in astonishment. Some vague recollections of Solomon's being about to disclose some safe and secret retreat wandering over my mind; and, while trembling at the singular apartment in which we were seated, and the employment in which he seemed engaged, I yet felt a hope hover about my heart, which his knowledge of my situation appeared to justify. "Sit down," said he, observing with compassion that I was sinking alike under the exhaustion of fatigue and the distraction of terror; "sit down, and eat a morsel of bread, and drink a cup of wine, and comfort thine heart, for thou seemest to be as one who hath escaped from the snare of the fowler, and from the dart of the hunter." I obeyed him involuntarily. I needed the refreshment he offered, and was about to partake of it, when an irresistible feeling of repugnance and horror overcame me; and, as I thrust away the food he offered me, I pointed to the objects around me as the cause of my reluctance. He looked round for a moment, as doubting whether objects so familiar to him, could be repulsive to a stranger, and then shaking his head, "Thou art a fool," said he, "but thou art a Nazarene, and I pity thee; verily, those who had the teaching of thy youth, not only have shut the book of knowledge to thee, but have forgot to open it for themselves. Were not thy masters, the Jesuits, masters also of the healing art, and art thou not acquainted with the sight of its ordinary implements? Eat, I pray thee, and be satisfied that none of these will hurt thee. Yonder dead bones cannot weigh out or withhold thy food; nor can they bind thy joints, or strain them with iron, or rend them with steel, as would the living arms that were stretched forth to seize thee as their prey. And, as the Lord of hosts liveth, their prey wouldst thou have been, and a prey unto their iron and steel, were it not for the shelter of the roof of Adonijah to-night.'

'I took some of the food he offered me, crossing myself at every mouthful, and drank the wine, which the feverish thirst of terror and anxiety made me swallow like water, but not without an internal prayer that it might not be converted into some deleterious and diabolical poison. The Jew Adonijah observed me with increasing compassion and contempt. – "What," said he, "appals thee? Were I possessed of the powers the superstition of thy sect ascribes to me, might I not make thee a banquet for fiends, instead of offering thee food? Might I not bring from the caverns of the earth the voices of those that 'peep and mutter', instead of speaking unto thee with the voice of man? Thou art in my power, yet have I no power or will to hurt thee. And dost thou, who art escaped from the dungeons of the Inquisition, look as one that feareth on the things that thou seest around thee, the furniture of the cell of a secluded leach? Within this apartment I have passed the term of sixty years, and dost thou shudder to visit it for a moment? These be the skeletons of bodies, but in the den thou hast escaped from were the skeletons of perished souls. Here are relics of the wrecks or the caprices of nature, but thou art come from where the cruelty of man, permanent and persevering, unrelenting and unmitigated, hath never failed to leave the proofs of its power in abortive intellects, crippled frames, distorted creeds, and ossified hearts. Moreover, there are around thee parchments and charts scrawled as it were with the blood of man, but, were it even so, could a thousand such volumes cause such terror to the human eye, as a page of the history of thy prison, written as it is in blood, drawn, not from the frozen veins of the dead, but from the bursting hearts of the living. Eat, Nazarene, there is no poison in thy food, – drink, there is no drug in thy cup. Darest thou promise thyself that in the prison of the Inquisition, or even in the cells of the Jesuits? Eat and drink without fear in the vault, even in the vault of Adonijah the Jew. If thou daredst to have done so in the dwellings of the Nazarenes, I had never beheld thee here. Hast thou fed?" he added, and I bowed. "Hast thou drank of the cup I gave thee?" my torturing thirst returned, and I gave him back the cup. He smiled, but the smile of age, – the smile of lips over which more than an hundred years have passed, has an expression more repulsive and hideous than can be deemed; it is never the smile of pleasure, – it is a *frown of the mouth*, and I shrunk before its grim wrinkles, as the Jew Adonijah added, "If thou hast eat and drank, it is time for thee to rest. Come to thy bed, it may be harder than they have given thee in thy prison, but behold it shall be safer. Come and rest thee there, it may be that the adversary and the enemy shall not there find thee out."

'I followed him through passages so devious and intricate, that, bewildered as I was with the events of the night, they forced on my memory the well-known fact, that in Madrid the Jews have subterranean passages to each other's habitations, which have hitherto baffled all the industry of the Inquisition. I slept that night, or rather day, (for the sun had risen), on a pallet laid on the floor of a room, small, lofty, and matted half-way up the walls. One narrow and grated window admitted the light of the sun, that arose after that eventful night; and amid the sweet sound of bells, and the still sweeter of human life, awake and in motion around me, I sunk into a slumber that was unbroken even by a dream, till the day was closing; or, in the language of Adonijah, "till the shadows of the evening were upon the face of all the earth."'

Chapter Fourteen

Unde iratos deos timent, qui sic propitios merentur?[26]

Seneca

'When I awoke, he was standing by my pallet. "Arise," said he, "eat and drink, that thy strength may return unto thee." He pointed to a small table as he spoke, which was covered with food of the plainest kind, and dressed with the utmost simplicity. Yet he seemed to think an apology was necessary for the indulgence of this temperate fare. "I myself," said he, "eat not the flesh of any animal, save on the new moons and the feasts, yet the days of the years of my life have been one hundred and seven; sixty of which have been passed in the chamber where thou sawest me. Rarely do I ascend to the upper chamber of this house, save on occasions like this, or peradventure to pray, with my window open towards the east, for the turning away wrath from Jacob, and the turning again the captivity of Zion. Well saith the ethnic leach,

'Aer exclusus confert ad longevitatem.'[27]

'"Such hath been my life, as I tell thee. The light of heaven hath been hidden from mine eyes, and the voice of man is as the voice of a stranger in mine ears, save those of some of mine own nation, who weep for the affliction of Israel; yet the silver cord is not loosed, nor the golden bowl broken; and though mine eye be waxing dim, my natural force is not abated." (As he spoke, my eyes hung in reverence on the hoary majesty of his patriarchal figure, and I felt as if I beheld an embodied representation of the old law in all its stern simplicity – the unbending grandeur, and primeval antiquity.) "Hast thou eaten, and art full? Arise, then, and follow me."

'We descended to the vault, where I found the lamp was always burning. And Adonijah, pointing to the parchments that lay on the table, said, "This is the matter wherein I need thy help; the collection and transcription whereof hath been the labour of more than half a life, prolonged beyond the bounds allotted to mortality; but," pointing to his sunk and blood-shot eyes, "those that look out of the windows begin to be darkened, and I feel that I need help from the quick hand and clear eye of youth. Wherefore, it being certified unto me by our brother, that thou wert a youth who couldst handle the pen of a scribe, and, moreover, wast in need of a city of refuge, and a strong wall of defence, against the laying-in-wait of thy brethren round about thee, I was willing that thou shouldst come under my roof, and eat of such things as I set before thee, and such as thy soul desireth, excepting only the abominable things forbidden in the law of the prophet; and shouldst, moreover, receive wages as an hired servant."

'You will perhaps smile, Sir; but even in my wretched situation, I felt a slight but painful flush tinge my cheek, at the thought of a Christian, and a peer of Spain, becoming the amanuensis of a Jew for hire. Adonijah continued, "Then, when my task is completed, then will I be gathered to my fathers, trusting surely in the Hope of Israel, that mine eyes shall 'behold the King in his beauty, – they shall see the land that is very far off.' And peradventure," he added, in a voice that grief rendered solemn, mellow, and tremulous, "peradventure there shall I meet in bliss, those with whom I parted in woe – even thou, Zachariah, the son of my loins, and thou, Leah, the wife of my bosom;" apostrophizing two of the silent skeletons that stood near. "And in the presence of the God of our fathers, the redeemed of Zion shall meet – and meet as those who are to part no more for ever and ever." At these words, he closed his eyes, lifted up his hands, and appeared to be

absorbed in mental prayer. Grief had perhaps subdued my prejudices – it had certainly softened my heart – and at this moment I
half-believed that a Jew might find entrance and adoption amid
the family and fold of the blessed. This sentiment operated on
my human sympathies, and I inquired, with unfeigned anxiety,
after the fate of Solomon the Jew, whose misfortune in harbour-
ing me had exposed him to the visit of the Inquisitors. "Be at
peace," said Adonijah, waving his bony and wrinkled hand, as if
dismissing a subject below his present feelings, "our brother Solomon is in no peril of death; neither shall his goods be taken for a
spoil. If our adversaries are mighty in power, so are we mighty
also to deal with them by our wealth or our wisdom. Thy flight
they never can trace, thy existence on the face of the earth shall
also be unknown to them, so thou wilt hearken to me, and heed
my words."

'I could not speak, but my expression of mute and imploring anxiety spoke for me. "Thou didst use words," said Adonijah,
"last night, whereof, though I remember not all the purport, the
sound yet maketh mine ears to tingle; even mine, which have not
vibrated to such sounds for four times the space of thy youthful
years. Thou saidst thou wert beset by a power that tempted thee
to renounce the Most High, whom Jew and Christian alike profess to worship; and that thou didst declare, that were the fires
kindled around thee, thou wouldst spit at the tempter, and trample on the offer, though thy foot pressed the coal which the
sons of Dominick were lighting beneath its naked sole." – "I did,"
I cried, "I did – and I would – So help me God in mine extremity."

'Adonijah paused for a moment, as if considering whether this
were a burst of passion, or a proof of mental energy. He seemed
at last inclined to believe it the latter, though all men of far-
advanced age are apt to distrust any marks of emotion as a
demonstration rather of weakness than of sincerity. "Then," said
he, after a long and solemn pause, "then thou shalt know the
secret that hath been a burthen to the soul of Adonijah, even as

his hopeless solitude is a burthen to the soul of him who tra-
verseth the desert, none accompanying him with step, or cheering
him with voice. From my youth upward, even until now, have
I laboured, and behold the time of my deliverance is at hand; yea,
and shall be accomplished speedily.

'"In the days of my childhood, a rumour reached mine ears,
even mine, of a being sent abroad on earth to tempt Jew and
Nazarene, and even the disciples of Mohammed, whose name is
accursed in the mouth of our nation, with offers of deliverance
at their utmost need and extremity, so they would do that which
my lips dare not utter, even though there be no ear to receive it
but thine. Thou shudderest – well, then, thou art sincere, at least,
in thy faith of errors. I listened to the tale, and mine ears received
it, even as the soul of the thirsty drinketh in rivers of water, for
my mind was full of the vain fantasies of the Gentile fables, and
I longed, in the perverseness of my spirit, to see, yea, and to con-
sort with, yea, and to deal with, the evil one in his strength. Like
our fathers in the wilderness, I despised angel's food, and lusted
after forbidden meats, even the meats of the Egyptian sorcerers.
And my presumption was rebuked as thou seest: – childless, wife-
less, friendless, at the last period of an existence prolonged
beyond the bounds of nature, am I now left, and, save thee alone,
without one to record its events. I will not trouble thee now with
the tale of my eventful life, farther than to tell thee, that the skeletons thou tremblest to behold, were once clothed in flesh far
fairer than thine. They are those of my wife and child, whose history thou must not now hear – but those of the two others thou
must both hear and relate." And he pointed to the two other skeletons opposite, in their upright cases. "On my return to my
country, even Spain, if a Jew can be said to have a country, I set
myself down on this seat, and, lighted by this lamp, I took in my
hand the pen of a scribe, and vowed by a vow, that this lamp
should not expire, nor this seat be forsaken, nor this vault unten-
anted, until that the record is written in a book, and sealed as

with the king's signet. But, behold, I was traced by those who are keen of scent, and quick of pursuit, even the sons of Dominick. And they seized me, and laid my feet fast in the bonds; but my writings they could not read, because they were traced in a character unknown to this idolatrous people. And behold, after a space they set me free, finding no cause of offence in me; and they bade me depart, and trouble them no more. Then vowed I a vow unto the God of Israel, who had delivered me from their thraldom, that none but he who could read these characters should ever transcribe them. Moreover, I prayed, and said, O Lord God of Israel! who knowest that we are the sheep of thy fold, and our enemies as wolves round about us, and as lions who roar for their evening prey, grant, that a Nazarene escaped from their hands, and fleeing unto us, even as a bird chased from her nest, may put to shame the weapons of the mighty, and laugh them to scorn. Grant also, Lord God of Jacob, that he may be exposed to the snare of the enemy, even as those of whom I have written, and that he may spit at it with his mouth, and spurn at it with his feet, and trample on the ensnarer, even as they have trampled; and then shall my soul, even mine, have peace at the last. Thus I prayed – and my prayer was heard, for behold, *thou* art here."

'As I heard these words, a horrid foreboding, like a nightmare of the heart, hung heavily on me. I looked alternately at the withering speaker, and the hopeless task. To bear about that horrible secret inurned in my heart, was not that enough? but to be compelled to scatter its ashes abroad, and to rake into the dust of others for the same purpose of unhallowed exposure, revolted me beyond feeling and utterance. As my eye fell listlessly on the manuscripts, I saw they contained only *the Spanish language* written in *the Greek characters* – a mode of writing that, I easily conceived, must have been as unintelligible to the officers of the Inquisition, as the Hieroglyphics of the Egyptian priests. Their ignorance, sheltered by their pride, and that still more strongly fortified by the impenetrable secrecy attached to their most minute proceedings, made them hesitate to entrust to any one the circumstance of their being in possession of manuscript which they could not decypher. So they returned the papers to Adonijah, and, in his own language, "Behold, he abode in safety." But to me this was a task of horror unspeakable. I felt myself as an added link to the chain, the end of which, held by an invisible hand, was drawing me to perdition; and I was now to become the recorder of my own condemnation.

'As I turned over the leaves with a trembling hand, the towering form of Adonijah seemed dilated with preternatural emotion. "And what dost thou tremble at, child of the dust?" he exclaimed, "if thou hast been tempted, so have they – if they are at rest, so shalt thou be. There is not a pang of soul or body thou hast undergone, or canst undergo, that they have not suffered before thy birth was dreamt of. Boy, thy hand trembles over pages it is unworthy to touch, yet still I must employ thee, for I need thee. Miserable link of necessity, that binds together minds so uncongenial! I would that the ocean were my ink, and the rock my page, and mine arm, even mine, the pen that should write thereon letters that should last like those on the written mountains for ever and ever – even the mount of Sinai, and those that still bear the record, 'Israel hath passed the flood'*". As he spoke, I again turned over the manuscripts. "Does thy hand tremble still?" said Adonijah; "and dost thou still hesitate to record the story of those whose destiny a link, wondrous, invisible, and indissoluble, has bound to thine. Behold, there are those near thee, who, though they have no longer a tongue, speak to thee with that eloquence which is stronger than all the eloquence of living tongues.

* Written mountains, i.e. rocks inscribed with characters recordative of some remarkable event, are well known to every oriental traveller. I think it is in the notes of Dr Coke, on the book of Exodus, that I have met with the circumstance alluded to above. A rock near the Red Sea is said once to have borne the inscription, 'Israel hath passed the flood'.

Behold, there are those around thee, whose mute and motionless arms of bone plead to thee as no arms of flesh ever pleaded. Behold, there are those who, being speechless, yet speak – who, being dead, are yet alive – who, though in the abyss of eternity, are yet around thee, and call on thee, as with a mortal voice. Hear them! – take the pen in thine hand, and write." I took the pen in my hand, but could not write a line. Adonijah, in a transport of ecstasy, snatching a skeleton from its receptacle, placed it before me. "Tell him thy story thyself, peradventure he will believe thee, and record it." And supporting the skeleton with one hand, he pointed with the other, as bleached and bony as that of the dead, to the manuscript that lay before me.

'It was a night of storms in the world above us; and, far below the surface of the earth as we were, the murmur of the winds, sighing through the passages, came on my ear like the voices of the departed, – like the pleadings of the dead. Involuntarily I fixed my eye on the manuscript I was to copy, and never withdrew till I had finished its extraordinary contents.'

Tale of the Indians

'There is an island in the Indian sea, not many leagues from the mouth of the Hoogly, which, from the peculiarity of its situation and internal circumstances, long remained unknown to Europeans, and unvisited by the natives of the contiguous islands, except on remarkable occasions. It is surrounded by shallows that render the approach of any vessel of weight impracticable, and fortified by rocks that threatened danger to the slight canoes of the natives, but it was rendered still more formidable by the terrors with which superstition had invested it. There was a tradition that the first temple to the black goddess Seeva*, had been erected

* Vide Maurice's Indian Antiquities.

there; and her hideous idol, with its collar of human skulls, forked tongues darting from its twenty serpent mouths, and seated on a matted coil of adders, had there first received the bloody homage of the mutilated limbs and immolated infants of her worshippers.

'The temple had been overthrown, and the island half depopulated, by an earthquake, that agitated all the shores of India. It was rebuilt, however, by the zeal of the worshippers, who again began to re-visit the island, when a tufaun of fury unparalleled even in those fierce latitudes, burst over the devoted spot. The pagoda was burnt to ashes by the lightning; the inhabitants, their dwellings, and their plantations, swept away as with the besom of destruction, and not a trace of humanity, cultivation, or life, remained in the desolate isle. The devotees consulted their imagination for the cause of these calamities; and, while seated under the shade of their cocoa-trees they told their long strings of coloured beads, they ascribed it to the wrath of the goddess Seeva at the increasing popularity of the worship of Juggernaut. They asserted that her image had been seen ascending amid the blaze of lightning that consumed her shrine and blasted her worshippers as they clung to it for protection, and firmly believed she had withdrawn to some happier isle, where she might enjoy her feast of flesh, and draught of blood, unmolested by the worship of a rival deity. So the island remained desolate, and without inhabitant for years.

'The crews of European vessels, assured by natives that there was neither animal, or vegetable, or water, to be found on its surface, forbore to visit; and the Indian of other isles, as he passed it in his canoe, threw a glance of melancholy fear at its desolation, and flung something overboard to propitiate the wrath of Seeva.

'The Island, thus left to itself, became vigorously luxuriant, as some neglected children improve in health and strength, while pampered darlings die under excessive nurture. Flowers bloomed, and foliage thickened, without a hand to pluck, a step to trace, or a lip to taste them, when some fishermen, (who had been driven by a strong current toward the isle, and worked with oar and sail in vain to avoid its dreaded shore), after making a thousand prayers to propitiate Seeva, were compelled to approach within an oar's length of it; and, on their return in unexpected safety, reported they had heard sounds so exquisite, that some other goddess, milder than Seeva, must have fixed on that spot for her residence. The younger fishermen added to this account, that they had beheld a female figure of supernatural loveliness, glide and disappear amid the foliage which now luxuriantly over-shadowed the rocks; and, in the spirit of Indian devotees, they hesitated not to call this delicious vision an incarnated emanation of Vishnu, in a lovelier form than ever he had appeared before, – at least far beyond that which he assumed, when he made one of his avatars in the figure of a tiger.

'The inhabitants of the islands, as superstitious as they were imaginative, deified the vision of the isles after their manner. The old devotees, while invoking her, stuck close to the bloody rites of Seeva and Haree, and muttered many a horrid vow over their beads, which they took care to render effectual by striking sharp reeds into their arms, and tinging every bead with blood as they spoke. The young women rowed their light canoes as near as they dared to the haunted isle, making vows to Camdeo*, and sending their paper vessels, lit with wax, and filled with flowers, towards its coast, where they hoped their darling deity was about to fix his residence. The young men also, at least those who were in love and fond of music, rowed close to the island to solicit the god Krishnoo† to sanctify it by his presence; and not knowing what to offer to the deity, they sung their wild airs standing high on the prow of the canoe, and at last threw a figure of wax, with a kind of lyre in its hand, towards the shore of the desolate isle.

* The Cupid of the Indian mythology.
† The Indian Apollo.

'For many a night these canoes might be seen glancing past each other over the darkened sea, like *shooting stars of the deep*, with their lighted paper lanthorns, and their offerings of flowers and fruits, left by some trembling hand on the sands, or hung by a bolder one in baskets of cane on the rocks; and still the simple islanders felt joy and devotion united in this "voluntary humility". It was observed, however, that the worshippers departed with very different impressions of the object of their adoration. The women all clung to their oars in breathless admiration of the sweet sounds that issued from the isle; and when that ceased they departed, murmuring over in their huts those "notes angelical", to which their own language furnished no appropriate sounds. The men rested long on their oars, to catch a glimpse of the form which, by the report of the fishermen, wandered there; and, when disappointed, they rowed home sadly.

'Gradually the isle lost its bad character for terror; and in spite of some old devotees, who told their blood-discoloured beads, and talked of Seeva and Haree, and even held burning splinters of wood to their scorched hands, and stuck sharp pieces of iron, which they had purchased or stolen from the crews of European vessels, in the most fleshy and sensitive parts of their bodies, – and, moreover, talked of suspending themselves from trees with the head downwards, till they were consumed by insects, or calcined by the sun, or rendered delirious by their position, – in spite of all this, which must have been very affecting, the young people went on their own way, – the girls offering their wreaths to Camdeo, and the youths invoking Krishnoo, till the devotees, in despair, vowed to visit this accursed island, which had set every body mad, and find out how the unknown deity was to be recognized and propitiated; and whether flowers, and fruits, and love-vows, and the beatings of young hearts, were to be substituted for the orthodox and legitimate offering of nails grown into the hands till they appeared through their backs, and *setons* of ropes inserted into the sides, on which the religionist danced his dance of agony, till the ropes or his patience failed. In a word, they were determined to find out what this deity was, who demanded no suffering from her worshippers, – and they fulfilled their resolution in a manner worthy of their purpose.

'One hundred and forty beings, crippled by the austerities of their religion, unable to manage sail or oar, embarked in a canoe to reach what they called the accursed isle. The natives, intoxicated with the belief of their sanctity, stripped themselves naked, to push their boat through the surf, and then, making their *salams*, implored them to use oars at least. The devotees, all too intent on their beads, and too well satisfied of their importance in the eyes of their favourite deities, to admit a doubt of their safety, set off in triumph, – and the consequence may be easily conjectured. The boat soon filled and sunk, and the crew perished without a single sigh of lamentation, except that they had not feasted the alligators in the sacred waters of the Ganges, or perished at least under the shadow of the domes of the *holy city* of Benares, in either of which cases their salvation must have been unquestionable.

'This circumstance, apparently so untoward, operated favourably on the popularity of the new worship. The old system lost ground every day. Hands, instead of being scorched over the fire, were employed only in gathering flowers. Nails (with which it was the custom of the devotees to lard their persons) actually fell in price; and a man might sit at his ease on his hams with as safe a conscience, and as fair a character, as if fourscore of them occupied the interval between. On the other hand, fruits were every day scattered on the shores of the favourite isle; flowers, too, blushed on its rocks, in all the dazzling luxuriance of colouring with which the Flora of the East delights to array herself. There was that brilliant and superb lily, which, to this day, illustrates the comparison between it and Solomon, who, in all his glory, was not arrayed like one of them. There was the rose unfolding its "paradise of leaves", and the scarlet blossom of the bombex, which an English traveller has voluptuously described as banqueting the eye with "its mass of vegetable splendour" unparalleled. And the female votarists at last began to imitate some of "those sounds and sweet airs" that every breeze seemed to waft to their ears, with increasing strength of melody, as they floated in their canoes round this isle of enchantment.

'At length one circumstance occurred that put its sanctity of character, and that of its inmate, out of all doubt. A young Indian who had in vain offered to his beloved the mystical bouquet, in which the arrangement of the flowers is made to express love, rowed his canoe to the island, to learn his fate from its supposed inhabitant; and as he rowed, composed a song, which expressed that his mistress despised him, as if he were a Paria, but that he would love her though he were descended from the head of Brahma, – that her skin was more polished than the marble steps by which you descend to the tank of a Rajah, and her eyes brighter than any whose glances were watched by presumptuous strangers through the rents of the embroidered purdah* of a Nawaub, – that she was loftier in his eyes than the black pagoda of Juggernaut, and more brilliant than the trident of the temple of Mahadeva, when it sparkled in the dreams of the moon. And as both these objects were visible to his eyes from the shore, as he rowed on in the soft and glorious serenity of an Indian night, no wonder they found a place in his verse. Finally, he promised, that if she was propitious to his suit, he would build her a hut, raised four feet above the ground to avoid the serpents; – that her dwelling should be overshadowed by the boughs of the tamarind; and that while she slept, he would drive the mosquitoes from her with a fan, composed of the leaves of the first flowers which she accepted as a testimony of his passion.

'It so happened, that the same night, the young female, whose reserve had been the result of any thing but indifference, attended

---

* The curtain behind which women are concealed.

by two of her companions, rowed her canoe to the same spot, with the view of discovering whether the vows of her lover were sincere. They arrived about the same time; and though it was now twilight, and the superstition of these timid beings gave a darker tinge to the shadows that surrounded them, they ventured to land; and, bearing their baskets of flowers in trembling hands, advanced to hang them on the ruins of the pagoda, amid which it was presumed the new goddess had fixed her abode. They proceeded, not without difficulty, through thickets of flowers that had sprung spontaneously in the uncultivated soil – not without fear that a tiger might spring on them at every step, till they recollected that those animals chose generally the large jungles for their retreat, and seldom harboured amid flowers. Still less was the alligator to be dreaded, amid the narrow streams that they could cross without tinging their ancles with its pure water. The tamarind, the cocoa, and the palm-tree, shed their blossoms, and exhaled their odours, and waved their leaves, over the head of the trembling votarist as she approached the ruin of the pagoda. It had been a massive square building, erected amid rocks, that, by a caprice of nature not uncommon in the Indian isles, occupied its centre, and appeared the consequence of some volcanic explosion. The earthquake that had overthrown it, had mingled the rocks and ruins together in a shapeless and deformed mass, which seemed to bear alike the traces of the impotence of art and nature, when prostrated by the power that has formed and can annihilate both. There were pillars, wrought with singular characters, heaped amid stones that bore no impress but that of some fearful and violent action of nature, that seemed to say, Mortals, write your lines with the chisel, I write my hieroglyphics in fire. There were the disjointed piles of stones carved into the form of snakes, on which the hideous idol of Seeva had once been seated; and close to them the rose was bursting through the earth which occupied the fissures of the rock, as if nature preached a milder theology, and deputed her darling flower as her missionary to her children. The idol itself had fallen, and lay in fragments. The horrid mouth was still visible, into which human hearts had been formerly inserted. But now, the beautiful peacocks, with their rain-bow trains and arched necks, were feeding their young amid the branches of the tamarind that overhung the blackened fragments. The young Indians advanced with diminished fear, for there was neither sight or sound to inspire the fear that attends the approach to the presence of a spiritual being – all was calm, still, and dark. Yet their feet trod with involuntary lightness as they advanced to these ruins, which combined the devastations of nature with those of the human passions, perhaps more bloody and wild than the former. Near the ruins there had formerly been a tank, as is usual, near the pagodas, both for the purposes of refreshment and purification; but the steps were now broken, and the water was stagnated. The young Indians, however, took up a few drops, invoked the "goddess of the isle", and approached the only remaining arch. The exterior front of this building had been constructed of stones, but its interior had been hollowed out of the rock; and its recesses resembled, in some degree, those in the island of Elephanta. There were monstrous figures carved in stone, some adhering to the rock, others detached from it, all frowning in their shapeless and gigantic hideousness, and giving to the eye of superstition the terrible representation of *"gods of stone"*.

'Two of the young votarists, who were distinguished for their courage, advanced and performed a kind of wild dance before the ruins of the ancient gods, as they called them, and invoked (as they might) the new resident of the isle to be propitious to the vows of their companion, who advanced to hang her wreath of flowers round the broken remains of an idol half-defaced and half-hidden among the fragments of stone, but clustered over with that rich vegetation which seems, in oriental countries, to announce the eternal triumph of nature amid the ruins of art. Every year renews the rose, but what year shall see a pyramid rebuilt? As the young Indian hung her wreath on the shapeless stone, a voice murmured, "There is a *withered* flower there." – "Yes – yes – there is," answered the votarist, "and that withered flower is an emblem of my heart. I have cherished many roses, but suffered one to wither that was the sweetest to me of all the wreath. Wilt thou revive him for me, unknown goddess, and my wreath shall no longer be a dishonour to thy shrine?" – "Wilt *thou* revive the rose by placing it in the warmth of thy bosom," said the young lover, appearing from behind the fragments of rock and ruin that had sheltered him, and from which he had uttered his oracular reply, and listened with delight to the emblematical but intelligible language of his beloved. "Wilt thou revive the rose?" he asked, in the triumph of love, as he clasped her to his bosom. The young Indian, yielding at once to love and superstition, seemed half-melting in his embrace, when, in a moment, she uttered a wild shriek, repelled him with all her strength, and crouched in an uncouth posture of fear, while she pointed with one quivering hand to a figure that appeared, at that moment, in the perspective of that tumultuous and indefinite heap of stone. The lover, unalarmed by the shriek of his mistress, was advancing to catch her in his arms, when his eye fell on the object that had struck hers, and he sunk on his face to the earth, in mute adoration.

The form was that of a female, but such as they had never before beheld, for her skin was perfectly white, (at least in their eyes, who had never seen any but the dark-red tint of the natives of the Bengalese islands). Her drapery (as well as they could see) consisted only of flowers, whose rich colours and fantastic grouping harmonized well with the peacock's feathers twined among them, and altogether composed a feathery fan of wild drapery, which, in truth, beseemed an "island goddess". Her long hair, of a colour they had never beheld before, pale auburn, flowed to her feet, and was fantastically entwined with the flowers and the feathers that formed her dress. On her head was a coronal of shells, of hue and lustre unknown except in the Indian seas – the purple and the green vied with the amethyst, and the emerald. On her white bare shoulder a loxia was perched, and round her neck was hung a string of their pearl-like eggs, so pure and pellucid, that the first sovereign in Europe might have exchanged her richest necklace of pearls for them. Her arms and feet were perfectly bare, and her step had a goddess-like rapidity and lightness, that affected the imagination of the Indians as much as the extraordinary colour of her skin and hair. The young lovers sunk in awe before this vision as it passed before their eyes. While they prostrated themselves, a delicious sound trembled on their ears. The beautiful vision spoke to them, but it was in a language they did not understand; and this confirming their belief that it was the language of the gods, they prostrated themselves to her again. At that moment, the loxia, springing from her shoulder, came fluttering towards them. "He is going to seek for fire-flies to light his cell*," said the Indians to each other. But the bird, who, with an intelligence peculiar to his species, understood and adopted the predilection of the fair being he belonged to, for the fresh flowers in which he saw her arrayed every day, darted at the withered rose-bud in the wreath of the young Indian; and, striking his slender beak through it, laid it at her feet. The omen was interpreted auspiciously by the lovers, and, bending once more to the earth, they rowed back to their island, but no longer in separate canoes. The lover steered that of his mistress, while she sat beside him in silence; and the young couple who accompanied them chaunted verses in praise of the *white* goddess, and the island sacred to her and to lovers.'

* From the fire-flies being so often found in the nest of the loxia, the Indians imagine he illuminates his nest with them. It is more likely they are the food of his young.

Chapter Fifteen

But tell me to what saint, I pray,
    What martyr, or what angel bright,
Is dedicate this holy day,
    Which brings you here so gaily dight?

Dost thou not, simple Palmer, know,
    What every child can tell thee here? –
Nor saint nor angel claims this show,
    But the bright season of the year.

Queen-Hoo Hall, by Strutt

'The sole and beautiful inmate of the isle, though disturbed at the appearance of her worshippers, soon recovered her tranquillity. She could not be conscious of fear, for nothing of that world in which she lived had ever borne a hostile appearance to her. The sun and the shade – the flowers and foliage – the tamarinds and figs that prolonged her delightful existence – the water that she drank, wondering at the beautiful being who seemed to drink whenever she did – the peacocks, who spread out their rich and radiant plumage the moment they beheld her – and the loxia, who perched on her shoulder and hand as she walked, and answered her sweet voice with imitative chirpings – all these were her friends, and she knew none but these.

'The human forms that sometimes approached the island, caused her a slight emotion; but it was rather that of curiosity than alarm; and their gestures were so expressive of reverence and mildness, their offerings of flowers, in which she delighted, so acceptable, and their visits so silent and peaceful, that she saw them without reluctance, and only wondered, as they rowed away, how they could move on the water in safety; and how creatures so dark, and with features so unattractive, happened to *grow* amid the beautiful flowers they presented to her as the productions of their abode. The elements might be supposed to have impressed her imagination with some terrible ideas; but the periodical regularity of these phænomena, in the climate she inhabited, divested them of their terrors to one who had been accustomed to them, as to the alternation of night and day – who could not remember the fearful impression of the first, and, above all, who had never heard any terror of them expressed *by another*, – perhaps the primitive cause of fear in most minds. Pain she had never felt – of death she had no idea – how, then, could she become acquainted with fear?

'When a north-wester, as it is termed, visited the island, with all its terrific accompaniments of midnight darkness, clouds of suffocating dust, and thunders like the trumpet of doom, she stood amid the leafy colonnades of the banyan-tree, ignorant of her danger, watching the cowering wings and dropping heads of the birds, and the ludicrous terror of the monkeys, as they skipt from branch to branch with their young. When the lightning struck a tree, she gazed as a child would on a fire-work played off for its amusement; but the next day she wept, when she saw the leaves would no longer grow on the blasted trunk. When the rains descended in torrents, the ruins of the pagoda afforded her a shelter; and she sat listening to the rushing of the mighty waters, and the murmurs of the troubled deep, till her soul took its colour from the sombrous and magnificent imagery around her, and she believed herself precipitated to earth with the deluge – borne downward, like a leaf, by a cataract – engulphed in the depths of the ocean – rising again to light on the swell of the enormous billows, as if she were heaved on the back of a whale – deafened with the roar – giddy with the rush – till terror and delight embraced in that fearful exercise of imagination. So she lived like a flower amid sun and storm, blooming in the light, and bending to the shower, and drawing the elements of her sweet and wild existence from both. And both seemed to mingle their influences kindly for her, as if she was a thing that nature loved, even in her angry mood, and gave a commission to the storm to nurture her, and to the deluge to spare the ark of her innocence, as it floated over the waters. This existence of felicity, half physical, half imaginative, but neither intellectual or impassioned, had continued till the seventeenth year of this beautiful and mild being, when a circumstance occurred that changed its hue for ever.

'On the evening of the day after the Indians had departed, Immalee, for that was the name her votarists had given her, was standing on the shore, when a being approached her unlike any she had ever beheld. The colour of his face and hands resembled her own more than those she was accustomed to see, but his garments, (which were European), from their square uncouthness, their shapelessness, and their disfiguring projection about the hips, (it was the fashion of the year 1680), gave her a mixed sensation of ridicule, disgust, and wonder, which her beautiful features could express only by a smile – that smile, a *native of the face* from which not even surprise could banish it.

'The stranger approached, and the beautiful vision approached also, but not like an European female with low and graceful bendings, still less like an Indian girl with her low salams, but like a young fawn, all animation, timidity, confidence, and cowardice, expressed in almost a single action. She sprung from the sands – ran to her favourite tree; – returned again with her guard of peacocks, who expanded their superb trains with a kind of instinctive motion, as if they felt the danger that menaced their protectress, and, clapping her hands with exultation, seemed to invite them to share in the delight she felt in gazing at the *new flower that had grown in the sand*.

'The stranger advanced, and, to Immalee's utter astonishment, addressed her in the language which she had retained some words of since her infancy, and had endeavoured in vain to make her peacocks, parrots, and loxias, answer her in corresponding sounds. But her language, from want of practice, had become so limited, that she was delighted to hear its most unmeaning sounds uttered by human lips; and when he said, according to the form of the times, "How do you, fair maid?" she answered, "God made me," from the words of the Christian Catechism that had been breathed into her infant lip. "God never made a fairer creature," replied the stranger, grasping her hand, and fixing on her eyes that still burn in the sockets of that arch-deceiver. "Oh yes!" answered Immalee, "he made many things more beautiful. The rose is redder than I am – the palm-tree is taller than I am – and the wave is bluer than I am; – but they all change, and I never change. I have grown taller and stronger, though the rose fades every six moons; and the rock splits to let in the bats, when the earth shakes; and the waves fight in their anger till they turn grey, and far different from the beautiful colour they have when the moon comes dancing on them, and sending all the young, broken branches of her light to kiss my feet, as I stand on the soft sand. I have tried to gather them every night, but they all broke in my hand the moment I dipt it into water." – "And have you fared better with the stars?" said the stranger smiling. – "No," answered the innocent being, "the stars are the flowers of heaven, and the rays of the moon the boughs and branches; but though they are so bright, they only blossom in the night, – and I love better the flowers that I can gather, and twine in my hair. When I have been all night wooing a star, and it has listened and descended, springing downwards like a peacock from its nest, it has hid itself often afterwards playfully amid the mangoes and tamarinds where it fell; and though I have searched for it till the moon looked wan and weary of lighting me, I never could find it. But where do you come from? – you are not scaly and voiceless like those who grow in the waters, and show their strange shapes as I sit on the shore at sun-set; – nor are you red and diminutive like those who come over the waters to me from other worlds, in houses that can live on the deep, and walk so swiftly, with their legs plunged in the water. Where do you come from? – you are not so bright as the stars that live in the blue sea above me, nor so deformed as those that toss in the darker sea at my feet. Where did you grow, and how came you here? – there is not a canoe on the sand; and though the shells bear the fish that live in them so lightly over the waters, they never would bear me. When I placed my foot on their scolloped edge of crimson and purple, they sunk into the sand." – "Beautiful creature," said the stranger, "I come from a world where there are thousands like me." – "That is impossible," said Immalee, "for I live here alone, and other worlds must be like this." – "What I tell you is true, however," said the stranger. Immalee paused for a moment, as if making the first effort of reflection – an exertion painful enough to a being whose exist-ence was composed of felicitous tacts and unreflecting instincts – and then exclaimed, "We both must have grown in the world of voices, for I know what you say better than the chirp of the loxia, or the cry of the peacock. That must be a delightful world where they all speak – what would I give that my roses grew in the world of answers!"

'At this moment the stranger made certain signals of hunger, which Immalee understood in a moment, and told him to follow her to where the tamarind and the fig were shedding their fruit – where the stream was so clear, you could count the purple shells in its bed – and where she would scoop for him in the cocoa-shell the cool waters that flowed beneath the shade of the mango. As they went, she gave him all the information about herself that she could. She told him that she was the daughter of a palm-tree, under whose shade she had been first conscious of existence, but that her poor father had been long withered and dead – that she was very old, having seen many roses decay on their stalks; and though they were succeeded by others, she did not love them so well as the first, which were a great deal larger and brighter – that, in fact, every thing had grown smaller latterly, for she was now able to reach to the fruit which formerly she was compelled to wait for till it dropt on the ground; – but that the water was grown taller, for once she was forced to drink it on her hands and knees, and now she could scoop in a cocoa-shell. Finally, she added, she was much older than the moon, for she had seen it waste away till it was dimmer than the light of a fire-fly; and the moon that was lighting them now would decline too, and its successor be so small, that she would never again give it the name she had given to the first – Sun of the Night. "But," said her companion, "how are you able to speak a language you never learned from your loxias and peacocks?" – "I will tell you," said Immalee, with an air of solemnity, which her beauty and innocence made at once ludicrous and imposing, and in which she betrayed a slight tendency to that wish to mystify that distinguishes her delightful sex, – "there came a spirit to me from the world of voices, and it whispered to me sounds that I never have forgotten, long, long before I was born." – "Really?" said the stranger. "Oh yes! – long before I could gather a fig, or gather the water in my hand, and that must be before I was born. When I *was* born, I was not so high as the rose-bud, at which I tried to catch, now I am as near the moon as the palm-tree – sometimes I catch her beams sooner than he does, therefore I must be very old, and very high." At these words, the stranger, with an expression indescribable, leaned against a tree. He viewed that lovely and helpless being, while he refused the fruits and water she offered him, with a look, that, for the first time, intimated compassion. The stranger feeling did not dwell long in a mansion it was unused to. The expression was soon exchanged for that half-ironical, half-diabolical glance Immalee could not understand. "And you live here alone," he said, "and you have lived in this beautiful place without a companion?" – "Oh no!" said Immalee, "I have a companion more beautiful than all the flowers in the isle. There is not a rose-leaf that drops in the river so bright as its cheek. My friend lives under the water, but its colours are so bright. It kisses me too, but its lips are very cold; and when I kiss it, it seems to dance, and its beauty is all broken into a thousand faces, that come smiling at me like little stars. But, though my friend has a thousand faces, and I have but one, still there is one thing that troubles me. There is but one stream where it meets me, and that is where are no shadows from the trees – and I never can catch it but when the sun is bright. Then when I catch it in the stream, I kiss it on my knees; but my friend has grown so tall, that sometimes I wish it were smaller. Its lips spread so much wider, that I give it a thousand kisses for one that I get." "Is your friend male or female," said the stranger. – "What is that?" answered Immalee. – "I mean, of what sex is your friend?"

'But to this question he could obtain no satisfactory answer; and it was not till his return the next day, when he revisited the isle, that he discovered Immalee's friend was what he suspected. He found this innocent and lovely being bending over a stream that reflected her image, and wooing it with a thousand wild and graceful attitudes of joyful fondness. The stranger gazed at her for some time, and thoughts it would be difficult for man to penetrate into, threw their varying expression over his features for a moment. It was the first of his intended victims he had ever beheld with compunction. The joy, too, with which Immalee received him, almost brought back human feelings to a heart that had long renounced them; and, for a moment, he experienced a sensation like that of his master when he visited paradise, – pity for the flowers he resolved to wither for ever. He looked at her as she fluttered round him with outspread arms and dancing eyes; and sighed, while she welcomed him in tones of such wild sweetness, as suited a being who had hitherto conversed with nothing but the melody of birds and the murmur of waters. With all her ignorance, however, she could not help testifying her amazement

at his arriving at the isle without any visible means of convey-
ance. He evaded answering her on this point, but said, "Immalee,
I come from a world wholly unlike that you inhabit, amid inanimate flowers, and unthinking birds. I come from a world where
all, as I do, think and speak." Immalee was speechless with wonder and delight for some time; at length she exclaimed, "Oh, how
they must love each other! even I love my poor birds and flowers,
and the trees that shade, and the waters that sing to me!" The
stranger smiled. "In all that world, perhaps there is not another
being beautiful and innocent as you. It is a world of suffering,
guilt, and care." It was with much difficulty she was made to
comprehend the meaning of these words, but when she did, she
exclaimed, "Oh, that I could live in that world, for I would make
every one happy!" – "But you could not, Immalee," said the
stranger; "this world is of such extent that it would take your
whole life to traverse it, and, during your progress, you never
could be conversant with more than a small number of sufferers
at a time, and the evils they undergo are in many instances
such as you or no human power could relieve." At these words,
Immalee burst into an agony of tears. "Weak, but lovely being,"
said the stranger, "could your tears heal the corrosions of disease? – cool the burning throb of a cancered heart? – wash the
pale slime from the clinging lips of famine? – or, more than all,
quench the fire of forbidden passion?" Immalee paused aghast at
this enumeration, and could only faulter out, that wherever she
went, she would bring her flowers and sunshine among the
healthy, and they should all sit under the shade of her own tamarind. That for disease and death, she had long been accustomed
to see flowers wither and die their beautiful death of nature. "And
perhaps," she added, after a reflective pause, "as I have often
known them to retain their delicious odour even after they were
faded, perhaps *what thinks* may live too after the form has faded,
and that is a thought of joy." Of passion, she said she knew nothing, and could propose no remedy for an evil she was unconscious

of. She had seen flowers fade with the season, but could not imagine why the flower should destroy itself. "But did you never trace a worm in the flower?" said the stranger, with the sophistry of corruption. "Yes," answered Immalee, "but the worm was not the native of the flower; its own leaves never could have hurt it." This led to a discussion, which Immalee's impregnable innocence, though combined with ardent curiosity and quick apprehension, rendered perfectly harmless to her. Her playful and desultory answers, – her restless eccentricity of imagination, – her keen and piercing, though ill-poised intellectual weapons, – and, above all, her instinctive and unfailing *tact* in matters of right and wrong, formed altogether an array that discomfited and baffled the tempter more than if he had been compelled to encounter half the *wranglers* of the European academies of that day. In the logic of the schools he was well-versed, but in this logic of the heart and of nature, he was "ignorance itself". It is said, that the "awless lion" crouches before "a maid in the pride of her purity." The tempter was departing gloomily, when he saw tears start from the bright eyes of Immalee, and caught a wild and dark omen from her innocent grief. "And you weep, Immalee?" "Yes," said the beautiful being, "I always weep when I see the sun set in clouds; and will you, the sun of my heart, set in darkness too? and will you not rise again? will you not?" and, with the graceful confidence of pure innocence, she pressed her red delicious lip to his hand as she spoke. "Will you not? I shall never love my roses and peacocks if you do not return, for they cannot speak to me as you do, nor can I give them one thought, but you can give me many. Oh, I would like to have many thoughts about *the world that suffers*, from which you came; and I believe you came from it, for, till I saw you, I never felt a pain that was not pleasure; but now it is all pain when I think you will not return." – "I will return," said the stranger, "beautiful Immalee, and will shew you, at my return, a glimpse of that world from which I come, and in which you will soon be an inmate." – "But shall I see you there," said Immalee, "otherwise how shall I *talk thoughts*?" – "Oh yes, – oh certainly." – "But why do you repeat the same words twice; *your once* would have been enough." – "Well then, yes." – "Then take this rose from me, and let us inhale its odour together, as I say to my friend in the fountain, when I bend to kiss *it*; but my friend withdraws *its* rose before I have tasted it, and I leave mine on the water. Will you not take my rose," said the beautiful suppliant, bending towards him. "I will," said the stranger; and he took a flower from the cluster Immalee held out to him. It was a withered one. He snatched it, and hid it in his breast. "And will you go without a canoe across that dark sea?" said Immalee. – "We shall meet again, and meet in the *world of suffering*," said the stranger. – "Thank you, – oh, thank you," repeated Immalee, as she saw him plunge fearless amid the surf. The stranger answered only, "We shall meet again." Twice, as he parted, he threw a glance at the beautiful and isolated being; a lingering of humanity trembled round his heart, – but he tore the withered rose from his bosom, and to the waved arm and angel-smile of Immalee, he answered, "We shall meet again."'

Chapter Sixteen

Più non ho la dolce speranza.

Didone

'Seven mornings and evenings Immalee paced the sands of her lonely isle, without seeing the stranger. She had still his promise to console her, that they should meet in the world of suffering; and this she repeated to herself as if it was full of hope and consolation. In this interval she tried to educate herself for her introduction into this world, and it was beautiful to see her attempting, from vegetable and animal analogies, to form some image of the incomprehensible destiny of man. In the shade she watched the withering flower. – "The blood that ran red through its veins yesterday is purple to-day, and will be black and dry to-morrow," she said; "but it feels no pain – it dies patiently, – and the ranunculus and tulip near it are untouched by grief for their companion, or their colours would not be so resplendent. But can it be thus in the world that thinks? Could I see *him* wither and die, without withering and dying along with him. Oh no! when that flower fades, I will be the dew that falls over him!"

'She attempted to enlarge her comprehension, by observing the animal world. A young loxia had fallen dead from its pendent nest; and Immalee, looking into the aperture which that intelligent bird forms at the lower extremity of the nest to secure it from birds of prey, perceived the old ones with fire-flies in their small beaks, their young one lying dead before them. At this sight Immalee burst into tears. – "Ah! you cannot weep," she said, "what an advantage I have over you! You eat, though your young one, your own one, is dead; but could I ever drink of the milk of the cocoa, if *he* could no longer taste it? I begin to comprehend what he said – to think, then, is to suffer – and a world of thought must be a world of pain! But how delicious are these tears! Formerly I wept for pleasure – but there is a pain sweeter than pleasure, that I never felt till I beheld *him*. Oh! who would not think, to have the joy of tears?"

'But Immalee did not occupy this interval solely in reflection; a new anxiety began to agitate her; and in the intervals of her meditation and her tears, she searched with avidity for the most glowing and fantastically wreathed shells to deck her arms and hair with. She changed her drapery of flowers every day, and never thought them fresh after the first hour; then she filled her largest shells with the most limpid water, and her hollow cocoa nuts with the most delicious figs, interspersed with roses, and arranged them picturesquely on the stone bench of the ruined pagoda. The time, however, passed over without the arrival of the stranger, and Immalee, on visiting her fairy banquet the next day, wept over the withered fruit, but dried her eyes, and hastened to replace them.

'She was thus employed on the eighth morning, when she saw the stranger approach; and the wild and innocent delight with which she bounded towards him, excited in him for a moment a feeling of gloomy and reluctant compunction, which Immalee's quick susceptibility traced in his pausing step and averted eye. She stood trembling in lovely and pleading diffidence, as if intreating pardon for an unconscious offence, and asking permission to approach by the very attitude in which she forbore it, while tears stood in her eyes ready to fall at another repelling motion. This sight "whetted his almost blunted purpose." She must learn to suffer, to qualify her to become my pupil, he thought. "Immalee, you weep," he added, approaching her. "Oh yes!" said Immalee, smiling like a spring morning through her tears; "you are to teach me to suffer, and I shall soon be very fit for your world – but I had

rather weep for you, than smile on a thousand roses." – "Immalee,"
said the stranger, repelling the tenderness that melted him in
spite of himself, "Immalee, I come to shew you something of the
world of thought you are so anxious to inhabit, and of which you
must soon become an inmate. Ascend this hill where the palm-
trees are clustering, and you shall see a glimpse of part of
it." – "But I would like to see the whole, and all at once!" said
Immalee, with the natural avidity of thirsty and unfed intellect,
that believes it can swallow all things, and digest all things. "The
whole, and all at once!" said her conductor, turning to smile at
her as she bounded after him, breathless and glowing with newly
excited feeling. "I doubt the part you will see to-night will be
more than enough to satiate even your curiosity." As he spoke he
drew a tube from his vest, and bid her apply it to her sight. The
Indian obeyed him; but, after gazing a moment, uttered the
emphatic exclamation, "I am there! – or are they here?" and sunk
on the earth in a frenzy of delight. She rose again in a moment,
and eagerly seizing the telescope, applied it in a wrong direction,
which disclosed merely the sea to her view, and exclaimed sadly,
"Gone! – gone! – all that beautiful world lived and died in a
moment – all that I love die so – my dearest roses live not half so
long as those I neglect – you were absent for seven moons since I
first saw you, and the beautiful world lived only a moment."

'The stranger again directed the telescope towards the shore
of India, from which they were not far distant, and Immalee
again exclaimed in rapture, "Alive and more beautiful than ever! –
all living, thinking things! – their *very walk thinks*. No mute fishes,
and senseless trees, but wonderful rocks*, on which they look
with pride, as if they were the works of their own hands. Beautiful rocks! how I love the perfect straitness of your sides, and the
crisped and flower-like knots of your decorated tops! Oh that
flowers grew, and birds fluttered round you, and then I would

* Intellige 'buildings'.

prefer you even to the rocks under which I watch the setting sun! Oh what a world must that be where nothing is natural, and every thing beautiful! – thought must have done all that. But, how *little every thing is!* – thought should have made every thing larger – *thought should be a god.* But," she added with quick intelligence and self-accusing diffidence, "perhaps I am wrong. Sometimes I have thought I could lay my hand on the top of a palm-tree, but when, after a long, long time, I came close to it, I could not have reached its lowest leaf were I ten times higher than I am. Perhaps your beautiful world may grow higher as I approach it." – "Hold, Immalee," said the stranger, taking the telescope from her hands, "to enjoy this sight you should understand it." – "Oh yes!" said Immalee, with submissive anxiety, as the world of sense rapidly lost ground in her imagination against the new-found world of mind, – "yes – let me think." – "Immalee, have you any religion?" said the visitor, as an indescribable feeling of pain made his pale brow still paler. Immalee, quick in understanding and sympathizing with physical feeling, darted away at these words, returned in a moment with a banyan leaf, with which she wiped the drops from his livid forehead; and then seating herself at his feet, in an attitude of profound but eager attention, repeated, *"Religion!* what is that? is it a new thought?" – "It is the consciousness of a Being superior to all worlds and their inhabitants, because he is the Maker of all, and will be their judge – of a Being whom we cannot see, but in whose power and presence we must believe, though invisible – of one who is every where unseen; always acting, though never in motion; hearing all things, but never heard." Immalee interrupted with an air of distraction – "Hold! too many thoughts will kill me – let me pause. I have seen the shower that came to refresh the rose-tree beat it to the earth." After an effort of solemn recollection, she added, "The voice of dreams told me something like that before I was born, but it is so long ago, – sometimes I have had thoughts within me like that voice. I have thought I loved the things around me too much, and that I should love things *beyond* me – flowers that could not fade, and a sun that never sets. I could have sprung, like a bird into the air, after such a thought – but there was no one to shew me that path upward." And the young enthusiast lifted towards heaven eyes in which trembled the tears of ecstatic imaginings, and then turned their mute pleadings on the stranger.

'"It is right," he continued, "not only to have thoughts of this Being, but to express them by some outward acts. The inhabitants of the world you are about to see, call this, *worship*, – and they have adopted (a Satanic smile curled his lip as he spoke) very different modes; so different, that, in fact, there is but one point in which they all agree – that of making their religion a torment; – the religion of some prompting them to torture themselves, and the religion of some prompting them to torture others. Though, as I observed, they all agree in this important point, yet unhappily they differ so much about the mode, that there has been much disturbance about it in the world that thinks." – "In the world that *thinks!*" repeated Immalee, "Impossible! Surely they must know that a difference cannot be acceptable to Him who is One." – "And have you then adopted no mode of expressing your thoughts of this Being, that is, of worshipping him?" said the stranger. – "I smile when the sun rises in its beauty, and I weep when I see the evening star rise," said Immalee. – "And do you recoil at the inconsistencies of varied modes of worship, and yet you yourself employ smiles and tears in your address to the Deity?" – "I do, – for they are both the expressions of joy with me," said the poor Indian; "the sun is as happy when he smiles through the rain-clouds, as when he burns in the mid-height of heaven, in the fierceness of his beauty; and I am happy whether I smile or I weep." – "Those whom you are about to see," said the stranger, offering her the telescope, "are as remote in their forms of worship as smiles from tears; but they are not, like you, equally happy in both." Immalee applied her eye to the telescope, and exclaimed in rapture at what she saw. "What do you see?" said the stranger.

Immalee described what she saw with many imperfect expressions, which, perhaps, may be rendered more intelligible by the explanatory words of the stranger.

'"You see," said he, "the coast of India, the shores of the world near you. – There is the black pagoda of Juggernaut, that enormous building on which your eye is first fixed. Beside it stands a Turkish mosque – you may distinguish it by a figure like that of the half-moon. It is the will of him who rules that world, that its inhabitants should worship him by that sign.* At a small distance you may see a low building with a trident on its summit – that is the temple of Maha-deva, one of the ancient goddesses of the country." – "But the houses are nothing to me," said Immalee, "shew me the living things that go there. The houses are not half so beautiful as the rocks on the shore, draperied all over with seaweeds and mosses, and shaded by the distant palm-tree and cocoa." – "But those buildings," said the tempter, "are indicative of the various modes of thinking of those who frequent them. If it is into their thoughts you wish to look, you must see them expressed by their actions. In their dealings with each other, men are generally deceitful, but in their dealings with their gods, they are tolerably sincere in the expression of the character they assign them in their imaginations. If that character be formidable, they express fear; if it be one of cruelty, they indicate it by the sufferings they inflict on themselves; if it be gloomy, the image of the god is faithfully reflected in the visage of the worshipper. Look and judge."

'Immalee looked and saw a vast sandy plain, with the dark pagoda of Juggernaut in the perspective. On this plain lay the bones of a thousand skeletons, bleaching in the burning and unmoistened air. A thousand human bodies, hardly more alive,

---

* Tippoo Saib wished to substitute the Mohamedan for the Indian mythology throughout his dominions. This circumstance, though long antedated, is therefore imaginable.

and scarce less emaciated, were trailing their charred and blackened bodies over the sands, to perish under the shadow of the temple, hopeless of ever reaching that of its walls.

'Multitudes of them dropt dead as they crawled. Multitudes still living, faintly waved their hands, to scare the vultures that hovered nearer and nearer at every swoop, and scooped the poor remnants of flesh from the living bones of the screaming victim, and retreated, with an answering scream of disappointment at the scanty and tasteless morsel they had torn away.

'Many tried, in their false and fanatic zeal, to double their torments, by crawling through the sands on their hands and knees; but hands through the backs of which the nails had grown, and knees worn literally to the bone, struggled but feebly amid the sands and the skeletons, and the bodies that were soon to be skeletons, and the vultures that were to make them so.

'Immalee withheld her breath, as if she inhaled the abominable effluvia of this mass of putrefaction, which is said to desolate the shores near the temple of Juggernaut, like a pestilence.

'Close to this fearful scene, came on a pageant, whose splendour made a brilliant and terrible contrast to the loathsome and withering desolation of animal and intellectual life, amid which its pomp came towering, and sparkling, and trembling on. An enormous fabric, more resembling a moving palace than a triumphal car, supported the inshrined image of Juggernaut, and was dragged forward by the united strength of a thousand human bodies, priests, victims, brahmins, faqueers and all. In spite of this huge force, the impulse was so unequal, that the whole edifice rocked and tottered from time to time, and this singular union of instability and splendour, of trembling decadence and terrific glory, gave a faithful image of the meretricious exterior, and internal hollowness, of idolatrous religion. As the procession moved on, sparkling amid desolation, and triumphant amid death, multitudes rushed forward from time to time, to prostrate themselves under the wheels of the enormous machine, which crushed

them to atoms in a moment, and passed on; – others "cut themselves with knives and lancets after their manner," and not
believing themselves worthy to perish beneath the wheels of the
idol's chariot, sought to propitiate him by dying the tracks of
those wheels with their blood; – their relatives and friends
shouted with delight as they saw the streams of blood dye the car
and its line of progress, and hoped for an interest in these voluntary sacrifices, with as much energy, and perhaps as much reason,
as the Catholic votarist does in the penance of St Bruno, or the
ex-oculation of St Lucia, or the martyrdom of St Ursula and her
eleven thousand virgins, which, being interpreted, means the
martyrdom of a single female named *Undecimilla*, which the
Catholic legends read *Undecim Mille*.

'The procession went on, amid that mixture of rites that
characterizes idolatry in all countries, – half resplendent, half
horrible – appealing to nature while they rebel against her –
mingling flowers with blood, and casting alternately a screaming
infant, or a garland of roses, beneath the car of the idol.

'Such was the picture that presented to the strained, incredulous eyes of Immalee, those mingled features of magnificence
and horror, – of joy and suffering, – of crushed flowers and
mangled bodies, – of magnificence calling on torture for its triumph, – and the steam of blood and the incense of the rose,
inhaled at once by the triumphant nostrils of an incarnate demon,
who rode amid the wrecks of nature and the spoils of the heart!
Immalee gazed on in horrid curiosity. She saw, by the aid of the
telescope, a boy seated on the front of the moving temple, who
"perfected the praise" of the loathsome idol, with all the outrageous lubricities of the Phallic worship. From the slightest
consciousness of the meaning of this phenomenon, her
unimaginable purity protected her as with a shield. It was in vain
that the tempter plied her with questions, and hints of explanation, and offers of illustration. He found her chill, indifferent,
and even incurious. He gnashed his teeth and gnawed his lip *en*

parenthese. But when she saw mothers cast their infants under the wheels of the car, and then turn to watch the wild and wanton dance of the Almahs, and appear, by their open lips and clapped hands, to keep time to the sound of the silver bells that tinkled round their slight ankles, while their infants were writhing in their dying agony, – she dropt the telescope in horror, and exclaimed, "The world that thinks does not feel. I never saw the rose kill the bud!"

'"But look again," said the tempter, "to that square building of stone, round which a few stragglers are collected, and whose summit is surmounted by a trident, – that is the temple of Mahadeva, a goddess who possesses neither the power or the popularity of the great idol Juggernaut. Mark how her worshippers approach her." Immalee looked, and saw women offering flowers, fruits and perfumes; and some young girls brought birds in cages, whom they set free; others, after making vows for the safety of some absent, sent a small and gaudy boat of paper, illuminated with wax, down the stream of an adjacent river, with injunctions never to sink till it reached him.

'Immalee smiled with pleasure at the rites of this harmless and elegant superstition. "This is not the religion of torment," said she. – "Look again," said the stranger. She did, and beheld those very women whose hands had been employed in liberating birds from their cages, suspending, on the branches of the trees which shadowed the temple of Mahadeva, baskets containing their newborn infants, who were left there to perish with hunger, or be devoured by the birds, while their mothers danced and sung in honour of the goddess.

'Others were occupied in conveying, apparently with the most zealous and tender watchfulness, their aged parents to the banks of the river, where, after assisting them to perform their ablutions, with all the intensity of filial and divine piety, they left them half immersed in the water, to be devoured by alligators, who did not suffer their wretched prey to linger in long expectation of their horrible death; while others were deposited in the jungles near the banks of the river, where they met with a fate as certain and as horrible, from the tigers who infested it, and whose yell soon hushed the feeble wail of their unresisting victims.

'Immalee sunk on the earth at this spectacle, and clasping both hands over her eyes, remained speechless with grief and horror.

'"Look yet again," said the stranger, "the rites of all religions are not so bloody." Once more she looked, and saw a Turkish mosque, towering in all the splendour that accompanied the first introduction of the religion of Mahomet among the Hindoos. It reared its gilded domes, and carved minarets, and crescented pinnacles, rich with all the profusion which the decorative imagination of Oriental architecture, at once light and luxuriant, gorgeous and aerial, delights to lavish on its favourite works.

'A group of stately Turks were approaching the mosque, at the call of the muezzin. Around the building arose neither tree nor shrub; it borrowed neither shade nor ornament from nature; it had none of those soft and graduating shades and hues, which seem to unite the works of God and the creature for the glory of the former, and calls on the inventive magnificence of art, and the spontaneous loveliness of nature, to magnify the Author of both; it stood the independent work and emblem of vigorous hands and proud minds, such as appeared to belong to those who now approached it as worshippers. Their finely featured and thoughtful countenances, their majestic habits, and lofty figures, formed an imposing contrast to the unintellectual expression, the crouching posture, and the half naked squalidness of some poor Hindoos, who, seated on their hams, were eating their mess of rice, as the stately Turks passed on to their devotions. Immalee viewed them with a feeling of awe and pleasure, and began to think there might be some good in the religion professed by these noble-looking beings. But, before they entered the mosque, they spurned and spit at the unoffending and terrified Hindoos; they struck them in the flats of their sabres, and, terming them dogs of idolaters, they cursed them in the name of God and the prophet. Immalee, revolted and indignant at the sight, though she could not hear the words that accompanied it, demanded the reason of it. "Their religion," said the stranger, "binds them to hate all who do not worship as they do." – "Alas!" said Immalee, weeping, "is not that hatred which their religion teaches, a proof that theirs is the worst? But why," she added, her features illuminated with all the wild and sparkling intelligence of wonder, while flushed with recent fears, "why do I not see among them some of those lovelier beings, whose habits differ from theirs, and whom you call women? Why do they not worship also; or have they a milder religion of their own?" – "*That* religion," replied the stranger, "is not very favourable to those beings, of whom you are the loveliest; it teaches that men shall have different companions in the world of souls; nor does it clearly intimate that women shall ever arrive there. Hence you may see some of these excluded beings wandering amid those stones that designate the place of their dead, repeating prayers for the dead whom they dare not hope to join; and others, who are old and indigent, seated at the doors of the mosque, reading aloud passages from a book lying on their knees, (which they call the Koran), with the hope of soliciting alms, not of exciting devotion." At these desolating words, Immalee, who had in vain looked to any of these systems for that hope or solace which her pure spirit and vivid imagination alike thirsted for, felt a recoiling of the soul unutterable at religion thus painted to her, and exhibiting only a frightful picture of blood and cruelty, of the inversion of every principle of nature, and the disruption of every tie of the heart.

'She flung herself on the ground, and exclaiming, "There is no God, if there be none but theirs!" then, starting up as if to take a last view, in the desperate hope that all was an illusion, she discovered a small obscure building overshaded by palm-trees, and surmounted by a cross; and struck by the unobtrusive simplicity of its appearance, and the scanty number and peaceable demeanour of the few who were approaching it, she exclaimed, that this must be a new religion, and eagerly demanded its name and rites. The stranger evinced some uneasiness at the discovery she had made, and testified still more reluctance to answer the questions which it suggested; but they were pressed with such restless and coaxing importunity, and the beautiful being who urged them made such an artless transition from profound and meditative grief to childish, yet intelligent curiosity, that it was not in man, or more or less than man, to resist her.

'Her glowing features, as she turned them toward him, with an expression half impatient, half pleading, were indeed those "of a stilled infant smiling through its tears.*" Perhaps, too, another cause might have operated on this prophet of curses, and made him utter a blessing where he meant malediction; but into this we dare not inquire, nor will it ever be fully known till the day when all secrets must be disclosed. However it was, he felt himself compelled to tell her it was a new religion, the religion of Christ, whose rites and worshippers she beheld. "But what are the rites?" asked Immalee. "Do they murder their children, or their parents, to prove their love to God? Do they hang them on baskets to perish, or leave them on the banks of rivers to be devoured by fierce and hideous animals?" – "The religion they profess forbids that," said the stranger, with reluctant truth; "it requires them to honour their parents, and to cherish their children." – "But why do they not spurn from the entrance to their church those who do not think as they do?" – "Because their religion enjoins them to be mild, benevolent, and tolerant; and neither to reject or disdain those who have not attained its purer light." – "But why is there no splendour or magnificence in their worship; nothing grand or attractive?" – "Because they know that God cannot be acceptably worshipped but by pure hearts and crimeless hands; and though

* I trust the absurdity of this quotation here will be forgiven for its beauty. It is borrowed from Miss Baillie, the first dramatic poet of the age.

their religion gives every hope to the penitent guilty, it flatters none with false promises of external devotion supplying the homage of the heart; or artificial and picturesque religion standing in the place of that single devotion to God, before whose throne, though the proudest temples erected to his honour crumble into dust, the heart burns on the altar still, an inextinguishable and acceptable victim."

'As he spoke, (perhaps constrained by a higher power), Immalee bowed her glowing face to the earth, and then raising it with the look of a new-born angel, exclaimed, "Christ shall be my God, and I will be a Christian!" Again she bowed in the deep prostration which indicates the united submission of soul and body, and remained in this attitude of absorption so long, that, when she rose, she did not perceive the absence of her companion. – He fled murmuring, and with him fled the shades of night.'

Chapter Seventeen

'Why, I did say something about getting a licence from the Cadi.'

Blue Beard

'The visits of the stranger were interrupted for some time, and when he returned, it seemed as if their purpose was no longer the same. He no longer attempted to corrupt her principles, or sophisticate her understanding, or mystify her views of religion. On the latter subject he was quite silent, seemed to regret he had ever touched on it, and not all her restless avidity of knowledge, or caressing importunity of manner, could extract from him another syllable on the subject. He repayed her amply, however, by the rich, varied and copious stores of a mind, furnished with matter apparently beyond the power of human experience to have collected, confined, as it is, within the limits of threescore years and ten. But this never struck Immalee; she took "no note of time"; and the tale of yesterday, or the record of past centuries, were synchronized in a mind to which facts and dates were alike unknown; and which was alike unacquainted with the graduating shades of manner, and the linked progress of events.

'They often sat on the shore of the isle in the evening, where Immalee always prepared a seat of moss for her visitor, and gazed together on the blue deep in silence; for Immalee's newly-awaked intellect and heart felt that bankruptcy of language, which profound feeling will impress on the most cultivated intellect, and which, in her case, was increased alike by her innocence and her ignorance; and her visitor had perhaps reasons still stronger for his silence. This silence, however, was often broken. There was not a vessel that sailed in the distance which did not suggest an eager question from Immalee, and did not draw a slow and extorted reply from the stranger. His knowledge was immense, various and profound, (but this was rather a subject of delight than of curiosity to his beautiful pupil); and from the Indian canoe, rowed by naked natives, to the splendid, and clumsy, and ill-managed vessels of the Rajahs, that floated like huge and gilded fish tumbling in uncouth and shapeless mirth on the wave, to the gallant and well-manned vessels of Europe, that came on like the gods of ocean bringing fertility and knowledge, the discoveries of art, and the blessings of civilization, wherever their sails were unfurled and their anchors dropt, – he could tell her all, – describe the destination of every vessel, – the feelings, characters and national habits of the many-minded inmates, – and enlarge her knowledge to a degree which books never could have done; for colloquial communication is always the most vivid and impressive medium, and lips have a prescriptive right to be the first intelligencers in instruction and in love.

'Perhaps this extraordinary being, with regard to whom the laws of mortality and the feelings of nature seemed to be alike suspended, felt a kind of sad and wild repose from the destiny that immitigably pursued him, in the society of Immalee. We know not, and can never tell, what sensations her innocent and helpless beauty inspired him with, but the result was, that he ceased to regard her as his victim; and, when seated beside her listening to her questions, or answering them, seemed to enjoy the few lucid intervals of his insane and morbid existence. Absent from her, he returned to the world to torture and to tempt in the mad-house where the Englishman Stanton was tossing on his straw –'

'Hold!' said Melmoth; 'what name have you mentioned?' – 'Have patience with me, Senhor,' said Monçada, who did not like interruption; 'have patience, and you will find we are all beads strung on the same string. Why should we jar against each other?

our union is indissoluble.' He proceeded with the story of the unhappy Indian, as recorded in the parchments of Adonijah, which he had been compelled to copy, and of which he was anxious to impress every line and letter on his listener, to substantiate his own extraordinary story.

'When absent from her, his purpose was what I have described; but while present, that purpose seemed suspended; he gazed often on her with eyes whose wild and fierce lustre was quenched in a dew that he hastily wiped away, and gazed on her again. While he sat near her on the flowers she had collected for him, – while he looked on those timid and rosy lips that waited his signal to speak, like buds that did not dare to blow till the sun shone on them, – while he heard accents issue from those lips which he felt it would be as impossible to pervert as it would be to teach the nightingale blasphemy, – he sunk down beside her, passed his hand over his livid brow, and, wiping off some cold drops, thought for a moment he was not the Cain of the moral world, and that the brand was effaced, – at least for a moment. The habitual and impervious gloom of his soul soon returned. He felt again the gnawings of the worm that never dies, and the scorchings of the fire that is never to be quenched. He turned the fatal light of his dark eyes on the only being who never shrunk from their expression, for her innocence made her fearless. He looked intensely at her, while rage, despair and pity, convulsed his heart; and as he beheld the confiding and conciliating smile with which this gentle being met a look that might have withered the heart of the boldest within him, – a Semele gazing in supplicating love on the lightnings that were to blast her, – one human drop dimmed their portentous lustre, as its softened rays fell on her. Turning fiercely away, he flung his view on the ocean, as if to find, in the sight of human life, some fuel for the fire that was consuming his vitals. The ocean, that lay calm and bright before them as a sea of jasper, never reflected two more different countenances, or sent more opposite feelings to two hearts. Over

Immalee's, it breathed that deep and delicious reverie, which those forms of nature that unite tranquillity and profundity diffuse over souls whose innocence gives them a right to an unmingled and exclusive enjoyment of nature. None but crimeless and unimpassioned minds ever truly enjoyed earth, ocean and heaven. At our first transgression, nature expels us, as it did our first parents, from her paradise for ever.

'To the stranger the view was fraught with far different visions. He viewed it as a tiger views a forest abounding with prey; there might be the storm and the wreck; or, if the elements were obstinately calm, there might be the gaudy and gilded pleasure barge, in which a Rajah and the beautiful women of his haram were inhaling the sea breeze under canopies of silk and gold, overturned by the unskilfulness of their rowers, and their plunge, and struggle, and dying agony, amid the smile and beauty of the calm ocean, produce one of those contrasts in which his fierce spirit delighted. Or, were even this denied, he could watch the vessels as they floated by, and, from the skiff to the huge trader, be sure that every one bore its freight of woe and crime. There came on the European vessels full of the passions and crimes of another world, – of its sateless cupidity, remorseless cruelty, its intelligence, all awake and ministrant in the cause of its evil passions, and its very refinement operating as a stimulant to more inventive indulgence, and more systematized vice. He saw them approach to traffic for "gold, and silver, and the souls of men;" to grasp, with breathless rapacity, the gems and precious produce of those luxuriant climates, and deny the inhabitants the rice that supported their inoffensive existence; – to discharge the load of their crimes, their lust and their avarice, and after ravaging the land, and plundering the natives, depart, leaving behind them famine, despair and execration; and bearing with them back to Europe, blasted constitutions, inflamed passions, ulcerated hearts, and consciences that could not endure the extinction of a light in their sleeping apartment.

'Such were the objects for which he watched; and one evening, when solicited by Immalee's incessant questions about the worlds to which the vessels were hastening, or to which they were returning, he gave her a description of the world, after his manner, in a spirit of mingled derision, malignity, and impatient bitterness at the innocence of her curiosity. There was a mixture of fiendish acrimony, biting irony, and fearful truth, in his wild sketch, which was often interrupted by the cries of astonishment, grief and terror, from his hearer. "They come," said he, pointing to the European vessels, "from a world where the only study of the inhabitants is how to increase their own sufferings, and those of others, to the utmost possible degree; and, considering they have only had 4000 years' practice at the task, it must be allowed they are tolerable proficients." – "But is it possible?" – "You shall judge. In aid, doubtless, of this desirable object, they have been all originally gifted with imperfect constitutions and evil passions; and, not to be ungrateful, they pass their lives in contriving how to augment the infirmities of the one, and aggravate the acerbities of the other. They are not like you, Immalee, a being who breathes amid roses, and subsists only on the juices of fruits, and the lymph of the pure element. In order to render their thinking powers more gross, and their spirits more fiery, they devour animals, and torture from abused vegetables a drink, that, without quenching thirst, has the power of extinguishing reason, inflaming passion, and shortening life – the best result of all – for life under such circumstances owes its only felicity to the shortness of its duration."

'Immalee shuddered at the mention of animal food, as the most delicate European would at the mention of a cannibal feast; and while tears trembled in her beautiful eyes, she turned them wistfully on her peacocks with an expression that made the stranger smile. "Some," said he, by way of consolation, "have a taste by no means so sophisticated, – they content themselves at their need with the flesh of their fellow-creatures; and as human life is always miserable, and animal life never so, (except from elementary causes), one would imagine this the most humane and salutary way of at once gratifying the appetite, and diminishing the mass of human suffering. But as these people pique themselves on their ingenuity in aggravating the sufferings of their situation, they leave thousands of human beings yearly to perish by hunger and grief, and amuse themselves in feeding on animals, whom, by depriving of existence, they deprive of the only pleasure their condition has allotted them. When they have thus, by unnatural diet and outrageous stimulation, happily succeeded in corrupting infirmity into disease, and exasperating passion into madness, they proceed to exhibit the proofs of their success, with an expertness and consistency truly admirable. They do not, like you, Immalee, live in the lovely independence of nature – lying on the earth, and sleeping with all the eyes of heaven unveiled to watch you – treading the same grass till your light step feels a friend in every blade it presses – and conversing with flowers, till you feel yourself and them children of the united family of nature, whose mutual language of love you have almost learned to speak to each other – no, to effect their purpose, their food, which is of itself poison, must be rendered more fatal by the air they inhale; and therefore the more civilized crowd all together into a space which their own respiration, and the exhalation of their bodies, renders pestilential, and which gives a celerity inconceivable to the circulation of disease and mortality. Four thousand of them will live together in a space smaller than the last and lightest colonnade of your young banyan-tree, in order, doubtless, to increase the effects of fœtid air, artificial heat, unnatural habits and impracticable exercise. The result of these judicious precautions is just what may be guessed. The most trifling complaint becomes immediately infectious, and, during the ravages of the pestilence, which this habit generates, ten thousand lives a-day are the customary sacrifice to the habit of living in cities." – "But they die in the arms of those they love," said

Immalee, whose tears flowed fast at this recital; "and is not that better than even *life* in solitude, – as mine was before I beheld you?"

'The stranger was too intent on his description to heed her. "To these cities they resort nominally for security and protection, but really for the sole purpose to which their existence is devoted, – that of aggravating its miseries by every ingenuity of refinement. For example, those who live in uncontrasted and untantalized misery, can hardly feel it – suffering becomes their habit, and they feel no more jealousy of their situation than the bat, who clings in blind and famishing stupefaction to the cleft of a rock, feels of the situation of the butterfly, who drinks of the dew, and bathes in the bloom of every flower. But the people of the *other worlds* have invented, by means of living in cities, a new and singular mode of aggravating human wretchedness – that of contrasting it with the wild and wanton excess of superfluous and extravagant splendour."

'Here the stranger had incredible difficulty to make Immalee comprehend how there could be an unequal division of the means of existence, and when he had done his utmost to explain it to her, she continued to repeat, (her white finger on her scarlet lip, and her small foot beating the moss), in a kind of pouting inquietude, "Why should some have more than they can eat, and others nothing to eat?" – "This," continued the stranger, "is the most exquisite refinement on that art of torture which those beings are so expert in – to place misery by the side of opulence – to bid the wretch who dies for want feed on the sound of the splendid equipages which shake his hovel as they pass, but leave no relief behind – to bid the industrious, the ingenious, and the imaginative, starve, while bloated mediocrity pants from excess – to bid the dying sufferer feel that life might be prolonged by one drop of that exciting liquor, which, wasted, produces only sickness or madness in those whose lives it undermines; – to do this is their principal object, and it is fully attained. The sufferer through whose rags the wind of winter blows, like arrows lodging in every pore – whose tears freeze before they fall – whose soul is as dreary as the night under whose cope his resting-place must be – whose glued and clammy lips are unable to receive the food which famine, lying like a burning coal at his vitals, craves – and who, amid the horrors of a houseless winter, might prefer its desolation to that of the den that abuses the name of home – without food – without light – where the howlings of the storm are answered by the fiercer cries of hunger – and he must stumble to his murky and strawless nook over the bodies of his children, who have sunk on the floor, not for rest, but despair. Such a being, is he not sufficiently miserable?"

'Immalee's shudderings were her only answer, (though of many parts of his description she had a very imperfect idea). "No, he is not enough so yet," pursued the stranger, pressing the picture on her; "let his steps, that know not where they wander, conduct him to the gates of the affluent and the luxurious – let him feel that plenty and mirth are removed from him but by the interval of a wall, and yet more distant than if severed by worlds – let him feel that while *his* world is darkness and cold, the eyes of those within are aching with the blaze of light, and hands relaxed by artificial heat, are soliciting with fans the refreshment of a breeze – let him feel that every groan he utters is answered by a song or a laugh – and let him die on the steps of the mansion, while his last conscious pang is aggravated by the thought, that the price of the hundredth part of the luxuries that lie untasted before heedless beauty and sated epicurism, would have protracted his existence, while it poisons theirs – let him *die of want on the threshold of a banquet-hall*, and then admire with me the ingenuity that displays itself in this new combination of misery. The inventive activity of the people of the world, in the multiplication of calamity, is inexhaustibly fertile in resources. Not satisfied with diseases and famine, with sterility of the earth, and tempests of the air, they must have laws and marriages, and kings and tax-gatherers, and wars and fetes, and every variety of artificial misery inconceivable to you."

'Immalee, overpowered by this torrent of words, to her unintelligible words, in vain asked a connected explanation of them. The demon of his superhuman misanthropy had now fully possessed him, and not even the tones of a voice as sweet as the strings of David's harp, had power to expel the evil one. So he went on flinging about his fire-brands and arrows, and then saying, "Am I not in sport? These people,"* said he, "have made unto themselves kings, that is, beings whom they voluntarily invest with the privilege of draining, by taxation, whatever wealth their vices have left to the rich, and whatever means of subsistence their want has left to the poor, till their extortion is cursed from the castle to the cottage – and this to support a few pampered favourites, who are harnessed by silken reins to the car, which they drag over the prostrate bodies of the multitude. Sometimes exhausted by the monotony of perpetual fruition, which has no parallel even in the monotony of suffering, (for the latter has at least the excitement of hope, which is for ever denied to the former), they amuse themselves by making war, that is, collecting the greatest number of human beings that can be bribed to the task, to cut the throat of a less, equal, or greater number of beings, bribed in the same manner for the same purpose. These creatures have not the least cause of enmity to each other – they do not know, they never beheld each other. Perhaps they might, under other circumstances, wish each other well, as far as human malignity would suffer them; but from the moment they are

---

* As, by a mode of criticism equally false and unjust, the worst sentiments of my worst characters, (from the ravings of Bertram to the blasphemies of Cardonneau), have been represented as *my own*, I must here trespass so far on the patience of the reader as to assure him, that the sentiments ascribed to the stranger are diametrically opposite to mine, and that I have purposely put them into the mouth of an agent of the enemy of mankind.

hired for legalized massacre, hatred is their duty, and murder their delight. The man who would feel reluctance to destroy the reptile that crawls in his path, will equip himself with metals fabricated for the purpose of destruction, and smile to see it stained with the blood of a being, whose existence and happiness he would have sacrificed his own to promote, under other circumstances. So strong is this habit of aggravating misery under artificial circumstances, that it has been known, when in a sea-fight a vessel has blown up, (here a long explanation was owed to Immalee, which may be spared the reader), the people of that world have plunged into the water to save, at the risk of their own lives, the lives of those with whom they were grappling amid fire and blood a moment before, and whom, though they would sacrifice to their passions, their pride refused to sacrifice to the elements." – "Oh that is beautiful! – that is glorious!" said Immalee, clasping her white hands; "I could bear all you describe to see that sight!"

'Her smile of innocent delight, her spontaneous burst of high-toned feeling, had the usual effect of adding a darker shade to the frown of the stranger, and a sterner curve to the repulsive contraction of his upper lip, which was never raised but to express hostility or contempt.

' "But what do the kings do?" said Immalee, "while they are making men kill each other for nothing?" – "You are ignorant, Immalee," said the stranger, "very ignorant, or you would not have said it was for *nothing*. Some of them fight for ten inches of barren sand – some for the dominion of the salt wave – some for any thing – and some for nothing – but all for pay and poverty, and the occasional excitement, and the love of action, and the love of change, and the dread of home, and the consciousness of evil passions, and the hope of death; and the admiration of the showy dress in which they are to perish. The best of the jest is, they contrive not only to reconcile themselves to these cruel and wicked absurdities, but to dignify them with the most imposing names their perverted language supplies – the names of fame, of glory, of recording memory, and admiring posterity.

'"Thus a wretch whom want, idleness, or intemperance, drives to this reckless and heart-withering business, – who leaves his wife and children to the mercy of strangers, or to famish, (terms nearly synonimous), the moment he has assumed the blushing badge that privileges massacre, becomes, in the imagination of this intoxicated people, the defender of his country, entitled to her gratitude and to her praise. The idle stripling, who hates the cultivation of intellect, and despises the meanness of occupation, feels, perhaps, a taste for arraying his person in colours as gaudy as the parrot's or the peacock's; and this effeminate propensity is baptised by the prostituted name of the love of glory – and this complication of motives borrowed from vanity and from vice, from the fear of distress, the wantonness of idleness, and the appetite for mischief, finds one convenient and sheltering appellation in the single sound – patriotism. And those beings who never knew one generous impulse, one independent feeling, ignorant of either the principles or the justice of the cause for which they contend, and wholly uninterested in the result, except so far as it involves the concerns of their own vanity, cupidity and avarice, are, while living, hailed by the infatuated world as its benefactors, and when dead, canonized as its martyrs. He died in his country's cause, is the epitaph inscribed by the rash hand of indiscriminating eulogy on the grave of ten thousand, who had ten thousand different motives for their choice and their fate, – who might have lived to be their country's enemies if they had not *happened* to fall in her defence, – and whose love of their country, if fairly analysed, was, under its various forms of vanity, restlessness, the love of tumult, or the love of show – purely love of themselves. There let them rest – nothing but the wish to disabuse their idolaters, who prompt the sacrifice, and then applaud the victim they have made, could have tempted me to dwell thus

long on beings as mischievous in their lives, as they are insignifi-
cant in their death.

'"Another amusement of these people, so ingenious in multiplying the sufferings of their destiny, is what they call law. They
pretend to find in this a security for their persons and their
properties – with how much justice, their own felicitous experience must inform them! Of the security it gives to the latter,
judge, Immalee, when I tell you, that you might spend your life
in their courts, without being able to prove that those roses you
have gathered and twined in your hair were your own – that you
might starve for this day's meal, while proving your right to a
property which must incontestibly be yours, on the condition of
your being able to fast on a few years, and survive to enjoy it –
and that, finally, with the sentiments of all upright men, the
opinions of the judges of the land, and the fullest conviction of
your own conscience in your favour, you cannot obtain the possession of what you and all feel to be your own, while your
antagonist can start an objection, purchase a fraud, or invent a lie.
So pleadings go on, and years are wasted, and property consumed, and hearts broken, – and law triumphs. One of its most
admirable triumphs is in that ingenuity by which it contrives to
convert a difficulty into an impossibility, and punish a man for not
doing what it has rendered impracticable for him to do.

'"When he is unable to pay his debts, it deprives him of liberty
and credit, to insure that inability still further; and while destitute
alike of the means of subsistence, or the power of satisfying his
creditors, he is enabled, by this righteous arrangement, to console himself, at least, with the reflection, that he can injure his
creditor as much as he has suffered from him – that certain loss is
the reward of immitigable cruelty – and that, while he famishes
in prison, the page in which his debt is recorded rots away
faster than his body; and the angel of death, with one obliterat-
ing sweep of his wing, cancels misery and debt, and presents,

grinning in horrid triumph, the release of debtor and debt, signed by a hand that makes the judges tremble on their seats." – "But they have religion," said the poor Indian, trembling at this horrible description; "they have that religion which you shewed me – its mild and peaceful spirit – its quietness and resignation – no blood – no cruelty." – "Yes, – true," said the stranger, with some reluctance, "they have religion; for in their zeal for suffering, they feel the torments of one world not enough, unless aggravated by the terrors of another. They have such a religion, but what use have they made of it? Intent on their settled purpose of discovering misery wherever it could be traced, and inventing it where it could not, they have found, even in the pure pages of that book, which, they presume to say, contains their title to peace on earth, and happiness hereafter, a right to hate, plunder and murder each other. Here they have been compelled to exercise an extraordinary share of perverted ingenuity. The book contains nothing but what is good, and evil must be the minds, and hard the labour of those evil minds, to extort a tinge from it to colour their pretensions withal. But mark, in pursuance of their great object, (the aggravation of general misery), mark how subtilly they have wrought. They call themselves by various names, to excite passions suitable to the names they bear. Thus some forbid the perusal of that book to their disciples, and others assert, that from the exclusive study of its pages alone, can the hope of salvation be learned or substantiated. It is singular, however, that with all their ingenuity, they have never been able to extract a subject of difference from the *essential* contents of that book, to which they all appeal – so they proceed after their manner.

'"They never dare to dispute that it contains irresistible injunctions, – that those who believe in it should live in habits of peace, benevolence and harmony, – that they should love each other in prosperity, and assist each other in adversity. They dare not deny that the spirit that book inculcates and inspires, is a spirit whose fruits are love, joy, peace, long-suffering, mildness and truth. On these points they never presumed to differ. – They are too plain to be denied, so they contrive to make matter of difference out of the various habits they wear; and they cut each other's throats for the love of God, on the important subject,* whether their jackets should be red or white – or whether their priests should be arrayed in silk ribbons,† or white linen,‡ or black household garments§ – or whether they should immerse their children in water, or sprinkle them with a few drops of it – or whether they should partake of the memorials of the death of him they all profess to love, standing or on their knees – or – But I weary you with this display of human wickedness and absurdity. One point is plain, they all agree that the language of the book is, 'Love one another,' while they all translate that language, 'Hate one another.' But as they can find neither materials or excuse from that book, they search for them in their own minds, – and there they are never at a loss, for human minds are inexhaustible in malignity and hostility; and when they borrow the name of that book to sanction them, the deification of their passions becomes a duty, and their worst impulses are hallowed and practised as virtues." – "Are there no parents or children in these horrible worlds?" said Immalee, turning her tearful eyes on this traducer of humanity; "none that love each other as I loved the tree under which I was first conscious of existence, or the flowers that grew with me?" – "Parents? – children?" said the stranger; "Oh yes! There are fathers who instruct their sons –" And his voice was lost – he struggled to recover it.

After a long pause, he said, "There are some kind parents among those sophisticated people." – "And who are they?" said

---

* The Catholics and Protestants were thus distinguished in the wars of the League.
† Catholics.
‡ Protestants.
§ Dissenters.

Immalee, whose heart throbbed spontaneously at the mention of kindliness. – "Those," said the stranger, with a withering smile, "who murder their children at the hour of their birth, or, by medical art, dismiss them before they have seen the light; and, in so doing, they give the only credible evidence of parental affection."

'He ceased, and Immalee remained silent in melancholy meditation on what she had heard. The acrid and searing irony of his language had made no impression on one with whom "speech was truth," and who could have no idea why a circuitous mode of conveying meaning could be adopted, when even a direct one was often attended with difficulty to herself. But she could understand, that he had spoken much of evil and of suffering, names unknown to her before she beheld him, and she turned on him a glance that seemed at once to thank and reproach him for her painful initiation into the mysteries of a new existence. She had, indeed, tasted of the tree of knowledge, and her eyes were opened, but its fruit was bitter to her taste, and her looks conveyed a kind of mild and melancholy gratitude, that would have wrung the heart for giving its first lesson of pain to the heart of a being so beautiful, so gentle, and so innocent. The stranger marked this blended expression, and exulted.

'He had distorted life thus to her imagination, perhaps with the purpose of terrifying her from a nearer view of it; perhaps in the wild hope of keeping her for ever in this solitude, where he might sometimes see her, and catch, from the atmosphere of purity that surrounded her, the only breeze that floated over the burning desert of his own existence. This hope was strengthened by the obvious impression his discourse had made on her. The sparkling intelligence, – the breathless curiosity, – the vivid gratitude of her former expression, – were all extinguished, and her down cast and thoughtful eyes were full of tears.

'"Has my conversation wearied you, Immalee?" said he. – "It has grieved me, yet I wish to listen still," answered the Indian. "I love to hear the murmur of the stream, though the crocodile may be beneath the waves." – "Perhaps you wish to encounter the people of this world, so full of crime and misfortune." – "I do, for it is the world, you came from, and when you return to it all will be happy but me." – "And is it, then, in my power to confer happiness?" said her companion; "is it for this purpose I wander among mankind?" A mingled and indefinable expression of derision, malevolence and despair, overspread his features, as he added, "You do me too much honour, in devising for me an occupation so mild and so congenial to my spirit."

'Immalee, whose eyes were averted, did not see this expression, and she replied, "I know not, but you have taught me the joy of grief; before I saw you I only smiled, but since I saw you, I weep, and my tears are delicious. Oh! They are far different from those I shed for the setting sun, or the faded rose! And yet I know not –" And the poor Indian, oppressed by emotions she could neither understand or express, clasped her hands on her bosom, as if to hide the secret of its new palpitations, and, with the instinctive diffidence of her purity, signified the change of her feelings, by retiring a few steps from her companion, and casting on the earth eyes which could contain their tears no longer. The stranger appeared troubled, – an emotion new to himself agitated him for a moment, – then a smile of self-disdain curled his lip, as if he reproached himself for the indulgence of human feeling even for a moment. Again his features relaxed, as he turned to the bending and averted form of Immalee, and he seemed like one conscious of agony of soul himself, yet inclined to sport with the agony of another's. This union of inward despair and outward levity is not unnatural. Smiles are the legitimate offspring of happiness, but laughter is often the misbegotten child of madness, that mocks its parent to her face. With such an expression he turned towards her, and asked, "But what is your meaning, Immalee?" – A long pause followed this question, and at length the Indian answered, "I know not," with that natural and delicious art which teaches the sex to disclose their meaning in words that seem to contradict it. "I know not," means, "I know too well." Her companion understood this, and enjoyed his anticipated triumph. "And why do your tears flow, Immalee?" – "I know not," said the poor Indian, and her tears flowed faster at the question.

'At these words, or rather at these tears, the stranger forgot himself for a moment. He felt that melancholy triumph which the conqueror is unable to enjoy; that triumph which announces a victory over the weakness of others, obtained at the expence of a greater weakness in ourselves. A human feeling, in spite of him, pervaded his whole soul, as he said, in accents of involuntary softness, "What would you have me do, Immalee?" The difficulty of speaking a language that might be at once intelligible and reserved, – that might convey her wishes without betraying her heart, – and the unknown nature of her new emotions, made Immalee faulter long before she could answer, "Stay with me, – return not to that world of evil and sorrow. – Here the flowers will always bloom and the sun be as bright as on the first day I beheld you. – Why will you go back to the world to think and to be unhappy?" The wild and discordant laugh of her companion, startled and silenced her. "Poor girl," he exclaimed, with that mixture of bitterness and commiseration, that at once terrifies and humiliates; "and is this the destiny I am to fulfil? – to listen to the chirping of birds, and watch the opening of buds? Is this to be my lot?" and with another wild burst of unnatural laughter, he flung away the hand which Immalee had extended to him as she had finished her simple appeal. – "Yes, doubtless, I am well fitted for such a fate, and such a partner. Tell me," he added, with still wilder fierceness, "tell me from what line of my features, – from what accent of my voice, – from what sentiment of my discourse, have you extracted the foundation of a hope that insults me with the view of felicity?" Immalee, who might have replied, "I understand a fury in your words, but not your words," had yet sufficient aid from her maiden pride, and female penetration, to discover that she was rejected by the stranger; and a brief emotion of indignant grief struggled with the tenderness of her exposed and devoted heart. She paused a moment, and then checking her tears, said, in her firmest tones, "Go, then, to your world, – since you wish to be unhappy – go! – Alas! it is not necessary to go there to be unhappy, for I must be so here. Go, – but take with you these roses, for they will all wither when you are gone! – take with you these shells, for I shall no longer love to wear them when you no longer see them!" And as she spoke, with simple, but emphatic action, she untwined from her bosom and hair the shells and flowers with which they were adorned, and threw them at his feet; then turning to throw one glance of proud and melancholy grief at him, she was retiring. "Stay, Immalee, – stay, and hear me for a moment," said the stranger; and he would, at that moment, have perhaps discovered the ineffable and forbidden secret of his destiny, but Immalee, in silence, which her look of profound grief made eloquent, shook sadly her averted head, and departed.'

Chapter Eighteen

Miseram me omnia terrent, et maris sonitus, et scopuli, et solitudo,
et sanctitudo Apollinis.[28]

    Latin Play

'Many days elapsed before the stranger revisited the isle. How he
was occupied, or what feelings agitated him in the interval, it
would be beyond human conjecture to discover. Perhaps he sometimes exulted in the misery he had inflicted, – perhaps he
sometimes pitied it. His stormy mind was like an ocean that had
swallowed a thousand wrecks of gallant ships, and now seemed to
dally with the loss of a little slender skiff, that could hardly make
way on its surface in the profoundest calm. Impelled, however, by
malignity, or tenderness, or curiosity, or weariness of artificial life,
so vividly contrasted by the unadulterated existence of Immalee,
into whose pure elements nothing but flowers and fragrance, the
sparkling of the heavens, and the odours of earth, had transfused
their essence – or, possibly, by a motive more powerful than all, –
his own will; which, never analysed, and hardly ever confessed to
be the ruling principle of our actions, governs nine-tenths of
them. – He returned to the shore of the haunted isle, the name by
which it was distinguished by those who knew not how to classify
the new goddess who was supposed to inhabit it, and who were as
much puzzled by this new specimen in their theology, as Linnæus
himself could have been by a non-descript in botany. Alas! the varieties in moral botany far exceed the wildest anomalies of those
in the natural. However it was, the stranger returned to the isle.
But he had to traverse many paths, where human foot but his had

never been, and to rend away branches that seemed to tremble at a human touch, and to cross streams into which no foot but his had ever been dipped, before he could discover where Immalee had concealed herself.

'Concealment, however, was not in her thoughts. When he found her, she was leaning against a rock; the ocean was pouring its eternal murmur of waters at her feet; she had chosen the most desolate spot she could find; – there was neither flower or shrub near her; – the calcined rocks, the offspring of volcano – the restless roar of the sea, whose waves almost touched her small foot, that seemed by its heedless protrusion at once to court and neglect danger – these objects were all that surrounded her. The first time he had beheld her, she was embowered amid flowers and odours, amid all the glorious luxuries of vegetable and animal nature; the roses and the peacocks seemed emulous which should expand their leaves or their plumes, as a shade to that loveliness which seemed to hover between them, alternately borrowing the fragrance of the one, and the hues of the other. Now she stood as if deserted even by nature, whose child she was; the rock was her resting-place, and the ocean seemed the bed where she purposed to rest; she had no shells on her bosom, no roses in her hair – her character seemed to have changed with her feelings; she no longer loved all that is beautiful in nature; she seemed, by an anticipation of her destiny, to make alliance with all that is awful and ominous. She had begun to love the rocks and the ocean, the thunder of the wave, and the sterility of the sand, – awful objects, the incessant recurrence of whose very sound seems intended to remind us of grief and of eternity. Their restless monotony of repetition, corresponds with the beatings of a heart which asks its destiny from the phenomena of nature, and feels the answer is – "Misery".

'Those who love may seek the luxuries of the garden, and inhale added intoxication from its perfumes, which seem the offerings of nature on that altar which is already erected and burning in the heart of the worshipper; – but let those who *have* loved seek the shores of the ocean, and they shall have their answer too.

'There was a sad and troubled air about her, as she stood so lonely, that seemed at once to express the conflict of her internal emotions, and to reflect the gloom and agitation of the physical objects around her; for nature was preparing for one of those awful convulsions – one of those abortive throes of desolation, that seems to announce a more perfect wrath to come; and while it blasts the vegetation, and burns up the soil of some visited portion, seems to proclaim in the murmur of its receding thunders, that it will return in that day, when the universe shall pass away as a scroll, and the elements melt with fervent heat, and return to fulfil the dreadful promise, which its partial and initiatory devastation has left incomplete. Is there a peal of thunder that does not mutter a menace, "For *me*, the dissolution of the world is reserved, I depart, but I shall return?" Is there a flash of lightning that does not say, *visibly*, if not audibly, "Sinner, I cannot now penetrate the recesses of your soul; but how will you encounter my glare, when the hand of the judge is armed with me, and my penetrating glance displays you to the view of assembled worlds?"

'The evening was very dark; heavy clouds, rolling on like the forces of an hostile army, obscured the horizon from east to west. There was a bright but ghastly blue in the heaven above, like that in the eye of the dying, where the last forces of life are collected, while its powers are rapidly forsaking the frame, and feeling their extinguishment must shortly be. There was not a breath of air to heave the ocean, – the trees drooped without a whisper to woo their branches or their buds, – the birds had retired, with that instinct which teaches them to avoid the fearful encounter of the elements, and nestled with cowering wings and drooping heads among their favourite trees. There was not a human sound in the isle; the very rivulet seemed to tremble at its own tinklings, and its small waves flowed as if a subterranean hand arrested and

impeded their motion. Nature, in these grand and terrific operations, seems in some degree to assimilate herself to a parent,
whose most fearful denunciations are preceded by an awful
silence, or rather to a judge, whose final sentence is *felt* with less
horror than the pause that intervenes before it is pronounced.

'Immalee gazed on the awful scene by which she was surrounded, without any emotion derived from physical causes. To
her, light and darkness had hitherto been the same; she loved the
sun for its lustre, and the lightning for its transitory brilliancy, and
the ocean for its sonorous music, and the tempest for the agitation which it gave to the trees, under whose bending and
welcoming shadow she danced, in time kept by the murmur of
their leaves, that hung low, as if to crown their votarist. And she
loved the night, when all was still, but what she was accustomed
to call the music of a thousand streams, that made the stars rise
from their beds, to sparkle and nod to that wild melody.

'Such she had been. Now, her eye was intently fixed on the
declining light, and the approaching darkness, – that preternatural gloom, that seems to say to the brightest and most
beautiful of the works of God, "Give place to me, thou shalt
shine no more."

'The darkness increased, and the clouds collected like an army
that had mustered its utmost force, and stood in obdured and collected strength against the struggling light of heaven. A broad,
red and dusky line of gloomy light, gathered round the horizon,
like an usurper watching the throne of an abdicated sovereign,
and expanding its portentous circle, sent forth alternately flashes
of lightning, pale and red; – the murmur of the sea increased, and
the arcades of the banyan-tree, that had struck its patriarchal root
not five hundred paces from where Immalee stood, resounded
the deep and almost unearthly murmur of the approaching
storm through all its colonnades; the primeval trunk rocked
and groaned, and the everlasting fibres seemed to withdraw
their grasp from the earth, and quiver in air at the sound. Nature,

with every voice she could inspire from earth, or air, or water, announced danger to her children.

'That was the moment the stranger chose to approach Immalee; of danger he was insensible, of fear he was unconscious; his miserable destiny had exempted him from both, but what had it left him? No hope – but that of plunging others into his own condemnation. No fear – but that his victim might escape him. Yet with all his diabolical heartlessness, he *did* feel some relentings of his human nature, as he beheld the young Indian; her cheek was pale, but her eye was fixed, and her figure, turned from him, (as if she preferred to encounter the tremendous rage of the storm), seemed to him to say, "Let me fall into the hands of God, and not into those of man."

'This attitude, so unintentionally assumed by Immalee, and so little expressive of her real feelings, restored all the malignant energies of the stranger's feelings; the former evil-purposes of his heart, and the habitual character of his dark and fiendish pursuit, rushed back on him. Amid this contrasted scene of the convulsive rage of nature, and the passive helplessness of her unsheltered loveliness, he felt a glow of excitement, like that which pervaded him, when the fearful powers of his "charmed life" enabled him to penetrate the cells of a madhouse, or the dungeons of an Inquisition.

'He saw this pure being surrounded by the terrors of nature, and felt a wild and terrible conviction, that though the lightning might blast her in a moment, yet there was a bolt more burning and more fatal, which was wielded by his own hand, and which, if he could aim it aright, must transfix her very soul.

'Armed with all his malignity and all his power, he approached Immalee, armed only with her purity, and standing like the reflected beam of the last ray of light on whose extinction she was gazing. There was a contrast in her form and her situation, that might have touched any feelings but those of the wanderer.

'The light of her figure shining out amid the darkness that

enveloped her, – its undulating softness rendered still softer to the eye by the rock against which it reclined, – its softness, brightness and flexibility, presenting a kind of playful hostility to the tremendous aspect of nature overcharged with wrath and ruin.

'The stranger approached her unobserved; his steps were unheard amid the rush of the ocean, and the deep, portentous murmur of the elements; but, as he advanced, he heard sounds that perhaps operated on his feelings as the whispers of Eve to her flowers on the organs of the serpent. Both knew their power, and felt their time. Amid the fast approaching terrors of a storm, more terrible than any she had ever witnessed, the poor Indian, unconscious, or perhaps insensible of its dangers, was singing her wild song of desperation and love to the echoes of the advancing storm. Some words of this strain of despair and passion reached the ear of the stranger. They were thus:

'"The night is growing dark – but what is that to the darkness that his absence has cast on my soul? The lightnings are glancing round me – but what are they to the gleam of his eye when he parted from me in anger?

'"I lived but in the light of his presence – why should I not die when that light is withdrawn? Anger of the clouds, what have I to fear from you? You may scorch me to dust, as I have seen you scorch the branches of the eternal trees – but the trunk still remained, and my heart will be his for ever.

'"Roar on, terrible ocean! thy waves, which I cannot count, can never wash his image from my soul, – thou dashest a thousand waves against a rock, but the rock is unmoved – and so would be my heart amid the calamities of the world with which he threatens me, – whose dangers I never would have known but for him, and whose dangers for him I will encounter."

'She paused in her wild song, and then renewed it, regardless alike of the terrors of the elements, and the possible presence of one whose subtle and poisonous potency was more fatal than all the elements in their united wrath.

'"When we first met, my bosom was covered with roses – now it is shaded with the dark leaves of the ocynum. When he saw me first, the living things all loved me – now I care not whether they love me or not – I have forgot to love them. When he came to the isle every night, I hoped the moon would be bright – now I care not whether she rises or sets, whether she is clouded or bright. Before he came, every thing loved me, and I had more things to love than I could reckon by the hairs of my head – now I feel I can love but one, and that one has deserted me. Since I have seen him all things have changed. The flowers have not the colours they once had – there is no music in the flow of the waters – the stars do not smile on me from heaven as they did, – and I myself begin to love the storm better than the calm."

'As she ended her melancholy strain, she turned from the spot where the increasing fury of the storm made it no longer possible for her to stand, and turning, met the gaze of the stranger fixed on her. A suffusion, the most rich and vivid, mantled over her from brow to bosom; she did not utter her usual exclamation of joy at his sight, but, with averted eyes and faultering step, followed him as he pointed her to seek shelter amid the ruins of the pagoda. They approached it in silence; and, amid the convulsions and fury of nature, it was singular to see two beings walk on together without exchanging a word of apprehension, or feeling a thought of danger, – the one armed by despair, the other by innocence. Immalee would rather have sought the shelter of her favourite banyan-tree, but the stranger tried to make her comprehend, that her danger would be much greater there than in the spot he pointed out to her. "Danger!" said the Indian, while a bright and wild smile irradiated her features; "can there be danger when you are near me?" – "Is there, then, no danger in my presence? – few have met me without dreading, and without feeling it too!" and his countenance, as he spoke, grew darker than the heaven at which he scowled. "Immalee," he added, in a voice still deeper and more thrilling, from the unwonted operation of human emotion in its tones; "Immalee, you cannot be weak enough to believe that I have power of controuling the elements? If I had," he continued, "by the heaven that is frowning at me, the first exertion of my power should be to collect the most swift and deadly of the lightnings that are hissing around us, and transfix you where you stand!" – "Me?" repeated the trembling Indian, her cheek growing paler at his words, and the voice in which they were uttered, than at the redoubling fury of the storm, amid whose pauses she scarce heard them. – "Yes – you – you – lovely as you are, and innocent, and pure, before a fire more deadly consumes your existence, and drinks your heart-blood – before you are longer exposed to a danger a thousand times more fatal than those with which the elements menace you – the danger of my accursed and miserable presence!"

'Immalee, unconscious of his meaning, but trembling with impassioned grief at the agitation with which he spoke, approached him to soothe the emotion of which she knew neither the name or the cause. Through the fractures of the ruin the red and ragged lightnings disclosed, from time to time, a glimpse of her figure, – her dishevelled hair, – her pallid and appealing look, – her locked hands, and the imploring bend of her slight form, as if she was asking pardon for a crime of which she was unconscious, – and soliciting an interest in griefs not her own. All around her wild, unearthly and terrible, – the floor strewed with fragments of stone, and mounds of sand, – the vast masses of ruined architecture, whose formation seemed the work of no human hand, and whose destruction appeared the sport of demons, – the yawning fissures of the arched and ponderous roof, through which heaven darkened and blazed alternately with a gloom that wrapt every thing, or a light more fearful than that gloom. – All around her gave to her form, when it was momently visible, a relief so strong and so touching, that it might have immortalized the hand who had sketched her as the embodied presence of an angel who had descended to the regions of

woe and wrath, – of darkness and of fire, on a message of reconciliation, – and descended in vain.

'The stranger threw on her, as she bent before him, one of
those looks that, but her own, no mortal eye had yet encountered
unappalled. Its expression seemed only to inspire a higher feeling
of devotedness in the victim. Perhaps an involuntary sentiment of
terror mingled itself with that expression, as this beautiful being
sunk on her knees before her writhing and distracted enemy; and,
by the silent supplication of her attitude, seemed to implore him
to have mercy on himself. As the lightnings flashed around her, –
as the earth trembled beneath her white and slender feet, – as
the elements seemed all sworn to the destruction of every living
thing, and marched on from heaven to the accomplishment
of their purpose, with *Væ victis* written and legible to every eye, in
the broad unfolded banners of that resplendent and sulphurous
light that seemed to display the *day of hell* – the feelings of the
devoted Indian seemed concentrated on the ill-chosen object of
their idolatry alone. Her graduating attitudes beautifully, but
painfully, expressed the submission of a female heart devoted to
its object, to his frailties, his passions, and his very crimes. When
subdued by the image of power, which the mind of man exercises
over that of woman, that impulse becomes irresistibly humiliating. Immalee had at first bowed to conciliate her beloved, and her
spirit had taught her frame that first inclination. In her next stage
of suffering, she had sunk on her knees, and, remaining at a distance from him, she had trusted to this state of prostration to
produce that effect on his heart which those who love always hope
compassion may produce, – that illegitimate child of love, often
more cherished than its parent. In her last efforts she clung to his
hand – she pressed her pale lips to it, and was about to utter a few
words – her voice failed her, but her fast dropping tears *spoke* to
the hand which she held, – and its grasp, which for a moment
convulsively returned hers, and then flung it away, answered her.

'The Indian remained prostrate and aghast. "Immalee," said

the stranger, in a struggling voice, "Do you wish me to tell you
the feelings with which my presence should inspire you?" – "No –
no – no!" said the Indian, applying her white and delicate hands
to her ears, and then clasping them on her bosom; "I feel them
too much." – "Hate me – curse me!" said the stranger, not heeding her, and stamping till the reverberation of his steps on the
hollow and loosened stones almost contended with the thunder;
"hate me, for I hate you – I hate all things that live – all things that
are dead – I am myself hated and hateful!" – "Not by me," said
the poor Indian, feeling, through the blindness of her tears, for
his averted hand. "Yes, by you, if you knew whose I am, and
whom I serve." Immalee aroused her newly-excited energies of
heart and intellect to answer this appeal. "Who you are, I know
not – but I am yours. – Whom you serve, I know not – but him
will *I* serve – I will be yours for ever. Forsake me if you will, but
when I am dead, come back to this isle, and say to yourself, The
roses have bloomed and faded – the streams have flowed and
been dried up – the rocks have been removed from their places –
and the lights of heaven have altered in their courses, – but there
was one who never changed, and she is not here!"

'As she spoke the enthusiasm of passion struggling with grief,
she added, "You have told me you possess the happy art of writing thought. – Do not write one thought on my grave, for one
word traced by your hand would revive me. Do not weep, for one
tear would make me live again, perhaps to draw a tear from
you." – "Immalee!" said the stranger. The Indian looked up, and,
with a mingled feeling of grief, amazement, and compunction,
beheld him shed tears. The next moment he dashed them away
with the hand of despair; and grinding his teeth, burst into that
wild shriek of bitter and convulsive laughter that announces the
object of its derision is ourselves.

'Immalee, whose feelings were almost exhausted, trembled in
silence at his feet. "Hear me, wretched girl!" he cried in tones that
seemed alternately tremulous with malignity and compassion,

with habitual hostility and involuntary softness; "hear me! I know the secret sentiment you struggle with better than the innocent heart of which it is the inmate knows it. Suppress, banish, destroy it. Crush it as you would a young reptile before its growth had made it loathsome to the eye, and poisonous to existence!" – "I never crushed even a reptile in my life," answered Immalee, unconscious that this matter-of-fact answer was equally applicable in another sense. "You love, then," said the stranger; "but," after a long and ominous pause, "do you know whom it is you love?" – "You!" said the Indian, with that purity of truth that consecrates the impulse it yields to, and would blush more for the sophistications of art than the confidence of nature; "you! You have taught me to think, to feel and to weep." – "And you love me for this?" said her companion, with an expression half irony, half commiseration. "Think, Immalee, for a moment, how unsuitable, how unworthy, is the object of the feelings you lavish on him. A being unattractive in his form, repulsive in his habits, separated from life and humanity by a gulph impassable; a disinherited child of nature, who goes about to curse or to tempt his more prosperous brethren; one who – what withholds me from disclosing all?"

'At this moment a flash of such vivid and terrific brightness as no human sight could sustain, gleamed through the ruins, pouring through every fissure instant and intolerable light. Immalee, overcome by terror and emotion, remained on her knees, her hands closely clasped over her aching eyes.

'For a few moments that she remained thus, she thought she heard other sounds near her, and that the stranger was answering a voice that spoke to him. She heard him say, as the thunder rolled to a distance, "This hour is mine, not thine – begone, and trouble me not." When she looked up again, all trace of human emotion was gone from his expression. The dry and burning eye of despair that he fixed on her, seemed never to have owned a tear; the hand with which he grasped her, seemed never to have felt the flow of blood, or the throb of a pulse; amid the intense and increasing heat of an atmosphere that appeared on fire, its touch was as cold as that of the dead.

' "Mercy!" cried the trembling Indian, as she in vain endeavoured to read a human feeling in those eyes of stone, to which her own tearful and appealing ones were uplifted – "mercy!" And while she uttered the word, she knew not what she deprecated or dreaded.

'The stranger answered not a word, relaxed not a muscle; it seemed as if he felt not with the hands that grasped her, – as if he saw her not with the eyes that glared fixedly and coldly on her. He bore, or rather dragged, her to the vast arch that had once been the entrance to the pagoda, but which, now shattered and ruinous, resembled more the gulphing yawn of a cavern that harbours the inmates of the desert, than a work wrought by the hands of man, and devoted to the worship of a deity. "You have called for mercy," said her companion, in a voice that froze her blood even under the burning atmosphere, whose air she could scarce respire. "You have cried for mercy, and mercy you shall have. Mercy has not been dealt to me, but I have courted my horrible destiny, and my reward is just and sure. Look forth, trembler – look forth, – I command thee!" And he stamped with an air of authority and impatience that completed the terror of the delicate and impassioned being who shuddered in his grasp, and felt half-dead at his frown.

'In obedience to his command, she removed the long tresses of her auburn hair, which had vainly swept, in luxuriant and fruitless redundance, the rock on which the steps of him she adored had been fixed. With that mixture of the docility of the child, and the mild submission of woman, she attempted to comply with his demand, but her eyes, filled with tears, could not encounter the withering horrors of the scene before her. She wiped those brilliant eyes with hairs that were every day bathed in the pure and crystal lymph, and seemed, as she tried to gaze on the desolation, like some bright and shivering spirit, who, for its further purification, or perhaps for the enlargement of the knowledge necessary for its destination, is compelled to witness some evidence of the Almighty's wrath, unintelligible in its first operations, but doubtless salutary in its final results.

'Thus looking and thus feeling, Immalee shudderingly approached the entrance of that building, which, blending the ruins of nature with those of art, seemed to announce the power of desolation over both, and to intimate that the primeval rock, untouched and unmodulated by human hands, and thrown upwards perhaps by some volcanic eruption, perhaps deposited there by some meteoric discharge, and the gigantic columns of stone, whose erection had been the work of two centuries, – were alike dust beneath the feet of that tremendous conqueror, whose victories alone are without noise and without resistance, and the progress of whose triumph is marked by tears instead of blood.

'Immalee, as she gazed around her, felt, for the first time, terror at the aspect of nature. Formerly, she had considered all its phenomena as equally splendid or terrific. And her childish, though active imagination, seemed to consecrate alike the sunlight and the storm, to the devotion of a heart, on whose pure altar the flowers and the fires of nature flung their undivided offering.

'But since she had seen the stranger, new emotions had pervaded her young heart. She learned to weep and to fear; and perhaps she saw, in the fearful aspect of the heavens, the development of that mysterious terror, which always trembles at the bottom of the hearts of those who dare to love.

'How often does nature thus become an involuntary interpreter between us and our feelings! Is the murmur of the ocean without a meaning? – Is the roll of the thunder without a voice? – Is the blasted spot on which the rage of both has been exhausted without its lesson? – Do not they all tell us some mysterious secret, which we have in vain searched our hearts for? – Do we not find in them, an answer to those questions with which we are for ever importuning the mute oracle of our destiny? – Alas! how deceitful and inadequate we feel the language of man, after love and grief have made us acquainted with that of nature! – the only one, perhaps, capable of a corresponding sign for those emotions, under which all human expression faints. What a difference between *words without meaning,* and that *meaning without words,* which the sublime phenomena of nature, the rocks and the ocean, the moon and the twilight, convey to those who have "ears to hear."

'How eloquent of truth is nature in her very silence! How fertile of reflections amid her profoundest desolations! But the desolation now presented to the eyes of Immalee, was that which is calculated to cause terror, not reflection. Earth and heaven, the sea and the dry land, seemed mingling together, and about to replunge into chaos. The ocean, deserting its eternal bed, dashed its waves, whose white surf gleamed through the darkness, far into the shores of the isle. They came on like the crests of a thousand warriors, plumed and tossing in their pride, and, like them, perishing in the moment of victory. There was a fearful inversion of the natural appearance of earth and sea, as if all the barriers of nature were broken, and all her laws reversed.

'The waves deserting their station, left, from time to time, the sands as dry as those of the desert; and the trees and shrubs tossed and heaved in ceaseless agitation, like the waves of a midnight storm. There was no light, but a livid grey that sickened the eye to behold, except when the bright red lightning burst out like the eye of a fiend, glancing over the work of ruin, and closing as it beheld it completed.

'Amid this scene stood two beings, one whose appealing loveliness seemed to have found favour with the elements even in their wrath, and one whose fearless and obdurate eye appeared to defy them. "Immalee," he cried, "is this a place or an hour to talk of love! – all nature is appalled – heaven is dark – the animals have hid themselves – and the very shrubs, as they wave and shrink, seem alive with terror." – "It is an hour to implore protection," said the Indian, clinging to him timidly. "Look up," said the stranger, while his own fixed and fearless eye seemed to return flash for flash to the baffled and insulted elements; "Look up, and if you cannot resist the impulses of your heart, let me at least point out a fitter object for them. Love," he cried, extending his arm towards the dim and troubled sky, "love the storm in its might of destruction – seek alliance with those swift and perilous travellers of the groaning air, – the meteor that rends, and the thunder that shakes it! Court, for sheltering tenderness, those masses of dense and rolling cloud, – the baseless mountains of heaven! Woo the kisses of the fiery lightnings, to quench themselves on your smouldering bosom! Seek all that is terrible in nature for your companions and your lover! – woo them to burn and blast you – perish in their fierce embrace, and you will be happier, far happier, than if you lived in mine! *Lived*! – Oh who can be mine and live! Hear me, Immalee!" he cried, while he held her hands locked in his – while his eyes, rivetted on her, sent forth a light of intolerable lustre – while a new feeling of indefinite enthusiasm seemed for a moment to thrill his whole frame, and new-modulate the tone of his nature; "Hear me! If you will be mine, it must be amid a scene like this for ever – amid fire and darkness – amid hatred and despair – amid –" and his voice swelling to a demoniac shriek of rage and horror, and his arms extended, as if to grapple with the fearful objects of some imaginary struggle, he was rushing from the arch under which they stood, lost in the picture which his guilt and despair had drawn, and whose images he was for ever doomed to behold.

'The slender form that had clung to him was, by this sudden movement, prostrated at his feet; and, with a voice choked with terror, yet with that perfect devotedness which never issued but from the heart and lip of woman, she answered his frightful questions with the simple demand, *"Will you be there?"* – "Yes! – THERE I must be, and for ever! And *will* you, and *dare* you, be with me?" And a kind of wild and terrible energy nerved his frame, and strengthened his voice, as he spoke and cowered over pale and prostrate loveliness, that seemed in profound and reckless humiliation to court its own destruction, as if a dove exposed its breast, without flight or struggle, to the beak of a vulture. "Well, then," said the stranger, while a brief convulsion crossed his pale visage, "amid thunder I wed thee – bride of perdition! mine shalt thou be for ever! Come, and let us attest our nuptials before the reeling altar of nature, with the lightnings of heaven for our bed-lights, and the curse of nature for our marriage-benediction!" The Indian shrieked in terror, not at his words, which she did not understand, but at the expression which accompanied them. "Come," he repeated, "while the darkness yet is witness to our ineffable and eternal union." Immalee, pale, terrified, but reso-lute, retreated from him.

'At this moment the storm, which had obscured the heavens and ravaged the earth, passed away with the rapidity common in those climates, where the visitation of an hour does its work of destruction unimpeded, and is instantly succeeded by the smiling lights and brilliant skies of which mortal curiosity in vain asks the question, Whether they gleam in triumph or in consolation over the mischief they witness?

'As the stranger spoke, the clouds passed away, carrying their diminished burden of wrath and terror where sufferings were to be inflicted, and terrors to be undergone, by the natives of other climes – and the bright moon burst forth with a glory unknown in European climes. The heavens were as blue as the waves of the ocean, which they seemed to reflect; and the stars burst forth with a kind of indignant and aggravated brilliancy, as if they resented the usurpation of the storm, and asserted the eternal predominance of nature over the casual influences of the storms that obscured her. Such, perhaps, will be the development of the moral world. We shall be told why we suffered, and for what; but a bright and blessed lustre shall follow the storm, and all shall yet be light.

'The young Indian caught from this object an omen alike aus-picious to her imagination and her heart. She burst from him – she rushed into the light of nature, whose glory seemed like the promise of redemption, gleaming amid the darkness of the fall. She pointed to the moon, that sun of the eastern nights, whose broad and brilliant light fell like a mantle of glory over rock and ruin, over tree and flower.

'"Wed me by this light," cried Immalee, "and I will be yours for ever!" And her beautiful countenance reflected the full light of the glorious planet that rode bright through the cloudless heaven – and her white and naked arms, extended towards it, seemed like two pure attesting pledges of the union. "Wed me by this light," she repeated, sinking on her knees, "and I will be yours for ever!"'

'As she spoke, the stranger approached, moved with what feelings no mortal thought can discover. At that moment a trifling phenomenon interfered to alter his destiny. A darkened cloud at that moment covered the moon – it seemed as if the departed storm collected in wrathful haste the last dark fold of its tremendous drapery, and was about to pass away for ever.

'The eyes of the stranger flashed on Immalee the brightest rays of mingled fondness and ferocity. He pointed to the darkness, – "WED ME BY THIS LIGHT!" he exclaimed, *"and you shall be mine for ever and ever!"* Immalee, shuddering at the grasp in which he held her, and trying in vain to watch the expression of his countenance, yet felt enough of her danger to tear herself from him. "Farewell for ever!" exclaimed the stranger, as he rushed from her.

'Immalee, exhausted by emotion and terror, had fallen senseless on the sands that filled the path to the ruined pagoda. He returned – he raised her in his arms – her long dark hair streamed over them like the drooping banners of a defeated army – her arms sunk down as if declining the support they seemed to implore – her cold and colourless cheek rested on his shoulder.

'"Is she dead?" he murmured. "Well, be it so – let her perish – let her be any thing *but mine!*" He flung his senseless burden on the sands, and departed – nor did he ever revisit the island.'

Chapter Nineteen

Que donne le monde aux siens plus souvent,
    Echo *Vent*.
Que dois-je vaincre ici, sans jamais relacher,
    Echo *la chair*.
Qui fit le cause des maux, qui me sont survenus,
    Echo *Venus*.
Que faut dire après d'une telle infidelle,
    Echo *Fi d'elle*.

Magdalèniade, *by Father Pierre de St Louis.*

'Three years had elapsed since the parting of Immalee and the stranger, when one evening the attention of some Spanish gentlemen, who were walking in a public place in Madrid, was arrested by a figure that passed them, habited in the dress of the country, (only without a sword), and walking very slowly. They stopt by a kind of simultaneous movement, and seemed to ask each other, with silent looks, what had been the cause of the impression this person's appearance had made on them. There was nothing remarkable in his figure, – his demeanour was quiet; it was the singular expression of his countenance which had struck them with a sensation they could neither define or account for.

'As they paused, the person returned alone, and walking slowly – and they again encountered that singular expression of the features, (the eyes particularly), which no human glance could meet unappalled. Accustomed to look on and converse with all things revolting to nature and to man, – for ever exploring the mad-house, the jail, or the Inquisition, – the den of famine, the dungeon of crime, or the death-bed of despair, – his eyes had acquired a light and a language of their own – a light that none could gaze on, and a language that few dare understand.

'As he passed slowly by them, they observed two others whose attention was apparently fixed on the same singular object, for they stood pointing after him, and speaking to each other with gestures of strong and obvious emotion. The curiosity of the groupe for once overcame the restraint of Spanish reserve, and approaching the two cavaliers, they inquired if the singular personage who had passed was not the subject of their conversation, and the cause of the emotion which appeared to accompany it. The others replied in the affirmative, and hinted at their knowledge of circumstances in the character and history of that extraordinary being that might justify even stronger marks of emotion at his presence. This hint operated still more strongly on their curiosity – the circle of listeners began to deepen. Some of them, it appeared, had, or pretended to have, some information relative to this extraordinary subject. And that kind of desultory conversation commenced, whose principal ingredients are a plentiful proportion of ignorance, curiosity and fear, mingled with some small allowance of information and truth; – that conversation, vague, unsatisfactory, but not uninteresting, to which every speaker is welcome to contribute his share of baseless report, – wild conjecture, – anecdote the more incredible the better credited, – and conclusion the more falsely drawn the more likely to carry home conviction.

'The conversation passed very much in language incoherent as this. – "But why, if he be what he is described, what he is known to be, – why is he not seized by order of government? – why is he not immured in the Inquisition?" – "He has been often in the prison of the holy office – oftener, perhaps, than the holy fathers wished," said another. "But it is a well-known fact, that whatever transpired on his examination, he was liberated almost immediately." Another added, "that the stranger had been in almost every prison in Europe, but had always contrived either to defeat or defy the power in whose grasp he appeared to be inclosed, – and to be active in his purposes of mischief in the remotest parts of Europe at the moment he was supposed to be expiating them in others." Another demanded, "if it was known to what country he belonged?" and was answered, "He is said to be a native of Ireland – (a country that no one knows, and which the natives are particularly reluctant to dwell in from various causes) – and his name is Melmoth." The Spaniard had great difficulty in expressing that *theta*, unpronounceable by continental lips. Another, who had an appearance of more intelligence than the rest, added the extraordinary fact of the stranger's being seen in various and distant parts of the earth within a time in which no power merely human could be supposed to traverse them – that his marked and fearful habit was every where to seek out the most wretched, or the most profligate, of the community among which he flung himself – what was his object in seeking them was unknown. – "It is well known," said a deep-toned voice, falling on the ears of the startled listeners like the toll of a strong but muffled bell, – "it is well known both to him and them."

'It was now twilight, but the eyes of all could distinguish the figure of the stranger as he passed; and some even averred they could see the ominous lustre of those eyes which never rose on human destiny but as planets of woe. The groupe paused for some time to watch the retreat of the figure that had produced on them the effect of the torpedo. It departed slowly, – no one offered it molestation.

'"I have heard," said one of the company, 'that a delicious music precedes the approach of this person when his destined victim, – the being whom he is permitted to tempt or to torture, – is about to appear or to approach him. I have heard a strange tale of such music being heard; and – Holy Mary be our guide! did you ever hear such sounds?" – "Where – what?" – and the astonished listeners took off their hats, unclasped their mantles, opened their lips, and drew in their breath, in delicious ecstasy at the sounds that floated round them. "No wonder," said a young gallant of the party, "no wonder that such sounds harbinger the approach of a being so heavenly. She deals with the good spirits; and the blessed saints alone could send such music from above to welcome her." As he spoke, all eyes were turned to a figure, which, though moving among a groupe of brilliant and attractive females, appeared the only one among them on whom the eye could rest with pure and undivided light and love. She did not catch observation – observation caught her, and was proud of its prize.

'At the approach of a large party of females, there was all that anxious and flattering preparation among the cavaliers, – all that eager arrangement of capas, and hats, and plumes, – that characterized the manners of a nation still half-feudal, and always gallant and chivalrous. These preliminary movements were answered by corresponding ones on the part of the fair and fatal host approaching. The creaking of their large fans – the tremulous and purposely-delayed adjustment of their floating veils, whose partial concealment flattered the imagination beyond the most full and ostentatious disclosure of the charms they seemed jealous of – the folds of the mantilla, of whose graceful falls, and complicated manœuvres, and coquettish undulations, the Spanish women know how to avail themselves so well – all these announced an attack, which the cavaliers, according to the modes of gallantry in that day (1683), were well prepared to meet and parry.

'But, amid the bright host that advanced against them, there was one whose arms were not artificial, and the effect of whose singular and simple attractions made a strong contrast to the studied arrangements of her associates. If her fan moved, it was only to collect air – if she arranged her veil, it was only to hide her face – if she adjusted her mantilla, it was but to hide that

406

form, whose exquisite symmetry defied the voluminous drapery of even that day to conceal it. Men of the loosest gallantry fell back as she approached, with involuntary awe – the libertine who looked on her was half-converted – the susceptible beheld her as one who realized that vision of imagination that must never be embodied here – and the unfortunate as one whose sight alone was consolation – the old, as they gazed on her, dreamt of their youth – and the young for the first time dreamt of love – the only love which deserves the name – that which purity alone can inspire, and perfect purity alone can reward.

'As she mingled among the gay groupes that filled the place, one might observe a certain air that distinguished her from every female there, – not by pretension to superiority, (of that her unequalled loveliness must have acquitted her, even to the vainest of the groupe), but by an untainted, unsophisticated character, diffusing itself over look and motion, and even thought – turning wildness into grace – giving an emphasis to a single exclamation, that made polished sentences sound trifling – for ever trespassing against etiquette with vivid and fearless enthusiasm, and apologizing the next moment with such timid and graceful repentance, that one doubted whether the offence or the apology were most delightful.

'She presented altogether a singular contrast to the measured tones, the mincing gait, and the organized uniformity of dress, and manner, and look, and feeling, of the females about her. The harness of art was upon every limb and feature from their birth, and its trappings concealed or crippled every movement which nature had designed for graceful. But in the movement of this young female, there was a bounding elasticity, a springiness, a luxuriant and conscious vitality, that made every action the expression of thought; and then, as she shrunk from the disclosure, made it the more exquisite interpreter of feeling. There was around her a mingled light of innocence and majesty, never united but in *her* sex. Men may long retain, and even confirm, the character of power which nature has stamped on their frames, but they very soon forfeit their claim to the expression of innocence.

'Amid the vivid and eccentric graces of a form that seemed like a comet in the world of beauty, bound by no laws, or by laws that she alone understood and obeyed, there was a shade of melancholy, that, to a superficial observer, seemed transitory and assumed, perhaps as a studied relief to the glowing colours of a picture so brilliant, but which, to other eyes, announced, that with all the energies of intellect occupied, – with all the instincts of sense excited, – the heart had as yet no inmate, and wanted one.

'The groupe who had been conversing about the stranger, felt their attention irresistibly attracted by this object; and the low murmur of their fearful whispers was converted into broken exclamations of delight and wonder, as the fair vision passed them. She had not long done so, when the stranger was seen slowly returning, seeming, as before, known to all, but knowing none. As the female party turned, they encountered him. His emphatic glance selected and centred in one alone. She saw him too, recognized him, and, uttering a wild shriek, fell on the earth senseless.

'The tumult occasioned by this accident, which so many witnessed, and none knew the cause of, for some moments drew off the attention of all from the stranger – all were occupied either in assisting or inquiring after the lady who had fainted. She was borne to her carriage by more assistants than she needed or wished for – and just as she was lifted into it, the voice of some one near her uttered the word "Immalee!" She recognized the voice, and turned, with a look of anguish and a feeble cry, towards the direction from which it proceeded. Those around her had heard the sound, – but as they did not understand its meaning, or know to whom it was addressed, they ascribed the lady's emotion to indisposition, and hastened to place her in her carriage. It drove away, but the stranger pursued its course with his eyes – the company dispersed, he remained alone – twilight faded into darkness – he appeared not to notice the change – a few still continued lingering at the extremity of the walk to mark him – they were wholly unmarked by him.

'One who remained the longest said, that he saw him use the action of one who wipes away a tear hastily. To his eyes the tear of penitence was denied for ever. Could this have been the tear of passion? If so, how much woe did it announce to its object!'

Chapter Twenty

Oh what was love made for, if 'tis not the same
Through joy and through torment, through glory and shame!
I know not, I ask not, what guilt's in thine heart,
I but know I must love thee, whatever thou art.

Moore

'The next day, the young female who had excited so much interest the preceding evening, was to quit Madrid, to pass a few weeks at a villa belonging to her family, at a short distance from the city. That family, including all the company, consisted of her mother Donna Clara di Aliaga, the wife of a wealthy merchant, who was monthly expected to return from the Indies; her brother Don Fernan di Aliaga, and several servants; for these wealthy citizens, conscious of their opulence and formerly high descent, piqued themselves upon travelling with no less ceremony and pompous tardiness than accompanied the progress of a grandee. So the old square-built, lumbering carriage, moved on like a hearse; the coachman sat fast asleep on the box; and the six black horses crawled at a pace like the progress of time when he visits affliction. Beside the carriage rode Fernan di Aliaga and his servants, with umbrellas and huge spectacles; and within it were placed Donna Clara and her daughter. The interior of this arrangement was the counterpart of its external appearance, – all announced dullness, formality and withering monotony.

'Donna Clara was a woman of a cold and grave temper, with all the solemnity of a Spaniard, and all the austerity of a bigot. Don Fernan presented that union of fiery passion and saturnic

410

manners not unusual among Spaniards. His dull and selfish pride was wounded by the recollection of his family having been in trade; and, looking on the unrivalled beauty of his sister as a possible means of his obtaining an alliance with a family of rank, he viewed her with that kind of selfish partiality as little honourable to him who feels it, as to her who was its object.

'And it was amid such beings that the vivid and susceptible Immalee, the daughter of nature, "the gay creature of the elements", was doomed to wither away the richly-coloured and exquisitely-scented flower of an existence so ungenially transplanted. Her singular destiny seemed to have removed her from a physical wilderness, to place her in a moral one. And, perhaps, her last state was worse than her first.

'It is certain that the gloomiest prospect presents nothing so chilling as the aspect of human faces, in which we try in vain to trace one corresponding expression; and the sterility of nature itself is luxury compared to the sterility of human hearts, which communicate all the desolation they feel.

'They had been some time on their way, when Donna Clara, who never spoke till after a long preface of silence, perhaps to give what she said a weight it might otherwise have wanted, said, with oracular deliberation, "Daughter, I hear you fainted in the public walks last night – did you meet with any thing that surprised or terrified you?" – "No, Madam," – "What, then, could be the cause of the emotion you betrayed at the sight, as I am told – I know nothing – of a personage of extraordinary demeanour?" – "Oh, I cannot, dare not tell!" said Isidora, dropping her veil over her burning cheek. Then the irrepressible ingenuousness of her former nature, rushing over her heart and frame like a flood, she sunk from the cushion on which she sat at Donna Clara's feet, exclaiming, "Oh, mother, I will tell you all!" – "No!" said Donna Clara, repelling her with a cold feeling of offended pride; "no! – there is no occasion. I seek no confidence withheld and bestowed in the same breath; nor do I like these violent emotions – they are unmaidenly. Your duties as a child are easily understood – they are merely perfect obedience, profound submission, and unbroken silence, except when you are addressed by me, your brother, or Father Jose. Surely no duties were ever more easily performed – rise, then, and cease to weep. If your conscience disturbs you, accuse yourself to Father Jose, who will, no doubt, inflict a penance proportioned to the enormity of your offence. I trust only he will not err on the side of indulgence." And so saying, Donna Clara, who had never uttered so long a speech before, reclined back on her cushion, and began to tell her beads with much devotion, till the arrival of the carriage at its destination awoke her from a profound and peaceful sleep.

'It was near noon, and dinner in a cool low apartment near the garden awaited only the approach of Father Jose, the confessor. He arrived at length. He was a man of an imposing figure, mounted on a stately mule. His features, at first view, bore strong traces of thought; but, on closer examination, those traces seemed rather the result of physical conformation, than of any intellectual exercise. The channel was open, but the stream had not been directed there. However, though defective in education, and somewhat narrow in mind, Father Jose was a good man, and meant well. He loved power, and he was devoted to the interests of the Catholic church; but he had frequently doubts, (which he kept to himself), of the absolute necessity of celibacy, and he felt (strange effect!) a chill all over him when he heard of the fires of an *auto da fe*. Dinner was concluded; the fruit and wine, the latter untasted by the females, were on the table, – the choicest of them placed before Father Jose, – when Isidora, after a profound reverence to her mother and the priest, retired, as usual, to her apartment. Donna Clara turned to the confessor with a look that demanded to be answered. "It is her hour for siesta," said the priest, helping himself to a bunch of grapes. "No, Father, no!" said Donna Clara sadly; "her maid informs me she does not retire to sleep. She was, alas! too well accustomed to that burning climate where she was lost in her infancy, to feel the heat as a Christian should. No, she retires neither to pray or sleep, after the devout custom of Spanish women, but, I fear, to" – "To do what?" said the priest, with horror in his voice – "To think, I fear," said Donna Clara; "for often I observe, on her return, the traces of tears on her face. I tremble, Father, lest those tears be shed for that heathen land, that region of Satan, where her youth was past." – "I'll give her a penance," said Father Jose, "that will save her the trouble of shedding tears on the score of memory at least – these grapes are delicious." – "But, Father," pursued Donna Clara, with all the weak but restless anxiety of a superstitious mind, "though you have made me easy on that subject, I still am wretched. Oh, Father, how she will talk sometimes! – like a creature self-taught, that needed neither director or confessor but her own heart." – "How!" exclaimed Father Jose, "need neither confessor or director! – she must be beside herself." – "Oh, Father," continued Donna Clara, "she will say things in her mild and unanswerable manner, that, armed with all my authority, I" – "How – how is that?" said the priest, in a tone of severity – "does she deny any of the tenets of the Holy Catholic church?" – "No! no! no!" said the terrified Donna Clara crossing herself. "How then?" – "Why, she speaks in a manner in which I never heard you, reverend Father, or any of the reverend brethren, whom my devotion to the holy church has led me to hear, speak before. It is in vain I tell her that true religion consists in hearing mass – in going to confession – in performing penance – in observing the fasts and vigils – in undergoing mortification and abstinence – in believing all that the holy church teaches – and hating, detesting, abhorring and execrating –" "Enough, daughter – enough," said Father Jose; "there can be no doubt of the orthodoxy of your creed?" – "I trust not, holy Father," said the anxious Donna Clara. "I were an infidel to doubt it," interposed the priest; "I might as well deny this fruit to be exquisite, or this glass of Malaga to be worthy the table of his Holiness the Pope, if he feasted all the Cardinals. But how, daughter, as touching the supposed or apprehended defalcations in Donna Isidora's creed?" – "Holy Father, I have already explained my own religious sentiments." – "Yes – yes – we have had enough of them; now for your daughter's." – "She will sometimes say," said Donna Clara, bursting into tears – "she will say, but never till greatly urged, that religion ought to be a system whose spirit was universal love. Do you understand any thing of that, Father?" – "Humph – humph!" – "That it must be something that bound all who professed it to habits of benevolence, gentleness and humility, under every difference of creed and of form." – "Humph – humph!" – "Father," said Donna Clara, a little piqued at the apparent indifference with which Father Jose listened to her communications, and resolved to rouse him by some terrific evidence of the truth of her suspicions, "Father, I have heard her dare to express a hope that the heretics in the train of the English ambassador might not be everlastingly" – "Hush! – I must not hear such sounds, or it might be my duty to take severer notice of these lapses. However, daughter," continued Father Jose, "thus far I will venture for your consolation. As sure as this fine peach is in my hand – another, if you please – and as sure as I shall finish this other glass of Malaga" – here a long pause attested the fulfilment of the pledge – "so sure" – and Father Jose turned the inverted glass on the table – "Madonna Isidora has – has the elements of a Christian in her, however improbable it may seem to you – I swear it to you by the habit I wear; – for the rest, a little penance – a – I shall consider of it. And now, daughter, when your son Don Fernan has finished his siesta, – as there is no reason to suspect him of retiring to *think*, – please to inform him I am ready to continue the game of chess which we commenced four months ago. I have pushed my pawn to the last square but one, and the next step gives me a queen." – "Has the game continued so long?" said Donna Clara. "Long!" repeated the priest, "Aye, and may continue much longer – we have never played more than three hours a-day on an average."

'He then retired to sleep, and the evening was passed by the priest and Don Fernan, in profound silence at their chess – by Donna Clara, in silence equally profound, at her tapestry – and by Isidora at the casement, which the intolerable heat had compelled them to leave open, in gazing at the lustre of the moon, and inhaling the odour of the tube-rose, and watching the expanding leaves of the night-blowing cereus. The physical luxuries of her former existence seemed renewed by these objects. The intense blue of the heavens, and the burning planet that stood in sole glory in their centre, might have vied with all that lavish and refulgent opulence of light in which nature arrays an Indian night. Below, too, there were flowers and fragrance; colours, like veiled beauty, mellowed, not hid; and dews that hung on every leaf, trembling and sparkling like the tears of spirits, that wept to take leave of the flowers.

'The breeze, indeed, though redolent of the breath of the orange blossom, the jasmine, and the rose, had not the rich and balmy odour that scents the Indian air by night.

Ενθα νησον μακαρων Αυραι περιπνεουσιν.[29]

'Except this, what was not there that might not renew the delicious dream of her former existence, and make her believe herself again the queen of that fairy isle? – One image was wanting – an image whose absence made that paradise of islands, and all the odorous and flowery luxury of a moonlight garden in Spain, alike deserts to her. In her heart alone could she hope to meet that image, – to herself alone did she dare to repeat his name, and those wild and sweet songs of his country* which he had taught her in his happier moods. And so strange was the contrast between her former and present existence, – so subdued was she by constraint and coldness, – so often had she been told that every thing she did, said, or thought, was wrong, – that she began to yield up

* Ireland.

the evidences of her senses, to avoid the perpetual persecutions of teazing and imperious mediocrity, and considered the appearance of the stranger as one of those visions that formed the trouble and joy of her dreamy and illusive existence.

' "I am surprised, sister," said Fernan, whom Father Jose's gaining his queen had put in unusually bad humour – "I am surprised that you never busy yourself, as young maidens use, at your needle, or in some quaint niceties of your sex." – "Or in reading some devout book," said Donna Clara, raising her eyes one moment from her tapestry, and then dropping them again; "there is the legend of that Polish saint*, born, like *her,* in a land of darkness, yet chosen to be a vessel – I have forgot his name, reverend Father." – "Check to the king," said Father Jose in reply. 'You regard nothing but watching a few flowers, or hanging over your lute, or gazing at the moon," continued Fernan, vexed alike at the success of his antagonist and the silence of Isidora. "She is eminent in alms-deeds and works of charity," said the good-natured priest. "I was summoned to a miserable hovel near your villa, Madonna Clara, to a dying sinner, a beggar rotting on rotten straw!" – "Jesu!" cried Donna Clara with involuntary horror, "I washed the feet of thirteen beggars, on my knees in my father's hall, the week before my marriage with her honoured father, and I never could abide the sight of a beggar since." – "Associations are sometimes indelibly strong," said the priest drily; – then he added, "I went as was my duty, but your daughter was there before me. She had gone uncalled, and was uttering the sweetest words of consolation from a homily, which a certain poor priest, who shall be nameless, had lent her from his humble store."

'Isidora blushed at this anonymous vanity, while she mildly

---

* I have read the legend of this Polish saint, which is circulated in Dublin, and find recorded among the indisputable proofs of his vocation, that he infallibly swooned if an indecent expression was uttered in his presence – *when in his nurse's arms!*

smiled or wept at the harassings of Don Fernan, and the heartless austerity of her mother. "I heard her as I entered the hovel; and, by the habit I wear, I paused on the threshold with delight. Her first words were – Check-mate!" he exclaimed, forgetting his homily in his triumph, and pointing, with appealing eye, and emphatic finger, to the desperate state of his adversary's king. "That was a very extraordinary exclamation!" said the literal Donna Clara, who had never raised her eyes from her work. – "I did not think my daughter was so fond of chess as to burst into the house of a dying beggar with such a phrase in her mouth." – "It was I said it, Madonna," said the priest, reverting to his game, on which he hung with soul and eye intent on his recent victory. "Holy saints!" said Donna Clara, still more and more perplexed, "I thought the usual phrase on such occasions was *pax vobiscum*,[30] or" – Before Father Jose could reply, a shriek from Isidora pierced the ears of every one. All gathered round her in a moment, reinforced by four female attendants and two pages, whom the unusual sound had summoned from the antichamber. Isidora had not fainted; she still stood among them pale as death, speechless, her eye wandering round the groupe that encircled her, without seeming to distinguish them. But she retained that presence of mind which never deserts woman where a secret is to be guarded, and she neither pointed with finger, or glanced with eye, towards the casement, where the cause of her alarm had presented itself. Pressed with a thousand questions, she appeared incapable of answering them, and, declining assistance, leaned against the casement for support.

'Donna Clara was now advancing with measured step to proffer a bottle of curious essences, which she drew from a pocket of a depth beyond calculation, when one of the female attendants, aware of her favourite habits, proposed reviving her by the scent of the flowers that clustered round the frame of the casement; and collecting a handful of roses, offered them to Isidora. The sight and scent of these beautiful flowers, revived the former associations of Isidora; and, waving away her attendant, she exclaimed, "There are no roses like those which surrounded me when he beheld me first!" – "He! – who, daughter?" said the alarmed Donna Clara. "Speak, I charge you, sister," said the irritable Fernan, "to whom do you allude?" – "She raves," said the priest, whose habitual penetration discovered there was a secret, – and whose professional jealousy decided that no one, not mother or brother, should share it with him; "she raves – ye are to blame – forbear to hang round and to question her. Madonna, retire to rest, and the saints watch round your bed!" Isidora, bending thankfully for this permission, retired to her apartment; and Father Jose for an hour appeared to contend with the suspicious fears of Donna Clara, and the sullen irritability of Fernan, merely that he might induce them, in the heat of controversy, to betray all they knew or dreaded, that he might strengthen his own conjectures, and establish his own power by the discovery.

Scire volunt secreta domus, et inde timeri.[31]

'And this desire is not only natural but necessary, in a being from whose heart his profession has torn every tie of nature and of passion; and if it generates malignity, ambition, and the wish for mischief, it is the system, not the individual, we must blame.

'"Madonna," said the Father, "you are always urging your zeal for the Catholic church – and you, Senhor, are always reminding me of the honour of your family – I am anxious for both – and how can the interests of both be better secured than by Donna Isidora taking the veil?" – "The wish of my soul!" cried Donna Clara, clasping her hands, and closing her eyes, as if she witnessed her daughter's apotheosis. "I will never hear of it, Father," said Fernan; "my sister's beauty and wealth entitle *me* to claim alliance with the first families in Spain – their baboon shapes and copper-coloured visages might be redeemed for a century by such a graft on the stock, and the blood of which they boast would not be impoverished by a transfusion of the *aurum potabile*[32] of ours into it." – "You forget, son," said the priest, "the extraordinary circumstances attendant on the early part of your sister's life. There are many of our Catholic nobility who would rather see the black blood of the banished Moors, or the proscribed Jews, flow in the veins of their descendants, than that of one who" – Here a mysterious whisper drew from Donna Clara a shudder of distress and consternation, and from her son an impatient motion of angry incredulity. "I do not credit a word of it," said the latter; "you wish that my sister should take the veil, and therefore you credit and circulate the monstrous invention." – "Take heed, son, I conjure you," said the trembling Donna Clara. "Take you heed, Madam, that you do not sacrifice your daughter to an unfounded and incredible fiction." – "Fiction!" repeated Father Jose – "Senhor, I forgive your illiberal reflections on me, – but let me remind you, that the same immunity will not be extended to the insult you offer to the Catholic faith." – "Reverend Father," said the terrified Fernan, "the Catholic church has not a more devoted and unworthy professor on earth than myself." – "I do believe the latter," said the priest. "You admit all that the holy church teaches to be irrefragably true?" – "To be sure I do." – "Then you must admit that the islands in the Indian seas are particularly under the influence of the devil?" – "I do, if the church requires me so to believe." – "And that he possessed a peculiar sway over that island where your sister was lost in her infancy?" – "I do not see how that follows," said Fernan, making a sudden stand at this premise of the Sorites. "Not see how that follows!" repeated Father Jose, crossing himself;

Excæcavit oculos corum ne viderent.[33]

'"But why waste I my Latin and logic on thee, who art incapable of both? Mark me, I will use but one unanswerable argument, the which whoso gainsayeth is a – gainsayer – that's all. The Inquisition at Goa knows the truth of what I have asserted, and who will dare deny it now?" – "Not I! – not I!" exclaimed Donna Clara; "nor, I am sure, will this stubborn boy. Son, I adjure you, make haste to believe what the reverend Father has told you." – "I am believing as fast as I can," answered Don Fernan, in the tone of one who is reluctantly swallowing a distasteful mess; "but my faith will be choaked if you don't allow it time to swallow. As for digestion," he muttered, "let that come when it pleases God." – "Daughter," said the priest, who well knew the *mollia tempora fandi*,[34] and saw that the sullen and angry Fernan could not well bear more at present; "daughter, it is enough – we must lead with gentleness those whose steps find stumbling-blocks in the paths of grace. Pray with me, daughter, that your son's eyes may yet be opened to the glory and felicity of his sister's vocation to a state where the exhaustless copiousness of divine benignity places the happy inmates above all those mean and mundane anxieties, those petty and local wants, which – Ah! – hem – verily I feel some of those wants myself at this moment. I am hoarse with speaking; and the intense heat of this night hath so exhausted my strength, that methinks the wing of a partridge would be no unseasonable refreshment."

At a sign from Donna Clara, a salver with wine appeared, and a partridge that might have provoked the French prelate to renew his meal once more, spite of his horror of *toujours perdrix*."[35] "See, daughter, see how much I am exhausted in this distressing controversy – well may I say, the zeal of thine house hath eaten me up." – "Then you and the zeal of the house will soon be *quit*," muttered Fernan as he retired. And drawing the folds of his mantle over his shoulder, he threw a glance of wonder at the happy facility with which the priest discussed the wings and breast of his favourite bird, – whispering alternately words of admonition to Donna Clara, and muttering something about the omission of pimento and lemon.

'"Father," said Don Fernan, stalking back from the door, and fronting the priest – "Father, I have a favour to ask of you." – "Glad, were it in my power to comply with it," said Father Jose, turning over the skeleton of the fowl; "but you see here is only the thigh, and that somewhat bare." – "It is not of that I speak or think, reverend Father," said Fernan, with a smile; "I have but to request, that you will not renew the subject of my sister's vocation till the return of my father." – "Certainly not, son, certainly not. Ah! you know the time to ask a favour – you know I never could refuse you at a moment like this, when my heart is warmed, and softened, and expanded, by – by – by the evidences of your contrition and humiliation, and all that your devout mother, and your zealous spiritual friend, could hope or wish for. In truth, it overcomes me – these tears – I do not often weep but on occasions like these, and then I weep abundantly, and am compelled to recruit my lack of moisture thus." – "Fetch more wine," said Donna Clara. – The order was obeyed. – "Good night, Father," said Don Fernan. – "The saints watch round you, my son! Oh I am exhausted! – I sink in this struggle! The night is hot, and requires wine to slake my thirst – and wine is a provocative, and requires food to take away its deleterious and damnable qualities – and food, especially partridge, which is a hot and stimulative nutritive, requires drink again to absorb or neutralize its exciting qualities. Observe me, Donna Clara – I speak as to the learned. There is stimulation, and there is absorption; the causes of which are manifold, and the effects such as – I am not bound to tell you at present." – "Reverend Father," said the admiring Donna Clara, not guessing, in the least, from what source all this eloquence flowed, "I trespassed on your time merely to ask a favour also." – "Ask and 'tis granted," said Father Jose, with a protrusion of his foot as proud as that of Sixtus himself. "It is merely to know, will not all the inhabitants of those accursed Indian isles be damned everlastingly?" – "Damned everlasting, and without doubt," returned the priest. "Now my mind is easy," rejoined the lady, "and I shall sleep in peace to-night."

'Sleep, however, did not visit her so soon as she expected, for an hour after she knocked at Father Jose's door, repeating,

"Damned to all eternity, Father, did you not say?" – "Be damned to all eternity!" said the priest, tossing on his feverish bed, and dreaming, in the intervals of his troubled sleep, of Don Fernan coming to confession with a drawn sword, and Donna Clara with a bottle of Xeres in her hand, which she swallowed at a draught, while his parched lips were gaping for a drop in vain, – and of the Inquisition being established in an island off the coast of Bengal, and a huge partridge seated with a cap on at the end of a table covered with black, as chief Inquisitor, – and various and monstrous chimeras, the abortive births of repletion and indigestion.

'Donna Clara, catching only the last words, returned to her apartment with light step and gladdened heart, and, full of pious consolation, renewed her devotions before the image of the virgin in her apartment, at each side of whose niche two wax tapers were burning, till the cool morning breeze made it possible for her to retire with some hope of rest.

'Isidora, in her apartment, was equally sleepless; and she, too, had prostrated herself before the sacred image, but with different thoughts. Her feverish and dreamy existence, composed of wild and irreconcileable contrasts between the forms of the present, and the visions of the past, – the difference between all that she felt within, and all that she saw around her, – between the impassioned life of recollection, and the monotonous one of reality, – was becoming too much for a heart bursting with undirected sensibilities, and a head giddy from vicissitudes that would have deeply tried much firmer faculties.

'She remained for some time repeating the usual number of ave's, to which she added the litany of the Virgin, without any corresponding impulses of solace or illumination, till at length, feeling that her prayers were not the expressions of her heart, and dreading this heterodoxy of the heart more than the violation of the ritual, she ventured to address the image of the Virgin in language of her own.

' "Mild and beautiful Spirit!" she cried, prostrating herself before the figure – "you whose lips alone have smiled on me since I reached your Christian land, – you whose countenance I have sometimes imagined to belong to those who dwelt in the stars of my own Indian sky, – hear me, and be not angry with me! Let me lose all feeling of my present existence, or all memory of the past! Why do my former thoughts return? They once made me happy, now they are thorns in my heart! Why do they retain their power since their nature is altered? I cannot be what I was – Oh, let me then no longer remember it! Let me, if possible, see, feel, and think as those around me do! Alas! I feel it is much easier to descend to their level than to raise them to mine. Time, constraint, and dullness, may do much for me, but what time could ever operate such a change on them! It would be like looking for the pearls at the bottom of the stagnant ponds which art has dug in their gardens. No, mother of the Deity! divine and mysterious woman, no! – they never shall see another throb of my burning heart. Let it consume in its own fires before a drop of their cold compassion extinguishes them! Mother divine! are not burning hearts, then, worthiest of thee? – and does not the love of nature assimilate itself to the love of God! True, we may love without religion, but can we be religious without love? Yet, mother divine! dry up my heart, since there is no longer a channel for its streams to flow through! – or turn all those streams into the river, narrow and cold, that holds its course on to eternity! Why should I think or feel, since life requires only duties that no feeling suggests, and apathy that no reflection disturbs? Here let me rest! – it is indeed the end of enjoyment, but it is also the end of suffering; and a thousand tears are a price too dear for the single smile which is sold for them in the commerce of life. Alas! it is better to wander in perpetual sterility than to be tortured with the remembrance of flowers that have withered, and odours that have died for ever." Then a gush of uncontroulable emotion overwhelming her, she again bowed before the Virgin. "Yes, help me to banish every image from my soul but his – his alone! Let my heart be like this lonely apartment, consecrated by the presence of one sole image, and illuminated only by that light which affection kindles before the object of its adoration, and worships it by for ever!"

'In an agony of enthusiasm she continued to kneel before the image; and when she rose, the silence of her apartment, and the calm smile of the celestial figure, seemed at once a contrast and a reproach to this excess of morbid indulgence. That smile appeared to her like a frown. It is certain, that in agitation we can feel no solace from features that express only profound tranquillity. We would rather wish corresponding agitation, even hostility – any thing but a calm that neutralizes and absorbs us. It is the answer of the rock to the wave – we collect, foam, dash, and disperse ourselves against it, and retire broken, shattered, and murmuring to the echoes of our disappointment.

'From the tranquil and hopeless aspect of the divinity, smiling on the misery it neither consoles or relieves, and intimating in that smile the profound and pulseless apathy of inaccessible elevation, coldly hinting that humanity must cease to be, before it can cease to suffer – from this the sufferer rushed for consolation to nature, whose ceaseless agitation seems to correspond with the vicissitudes of human destiny and the emotions of the human heart – whose alternation of storms and calms, – of clouds and sun-light, – of terrors and delights – seems to keep a kind of mysterious measure of ineffable harmony with that instrument whose chords are doomed alternately to the thrill of agony and rapture, till the hand of death sweeps over all the strings, and silences them for ever. – With such a feeling, Isidora leaned against her casement, gasped for a breath of air, which the burning night did not grant, and thought how, on such a night in her Indian isle, she could plunge into the stream shaded by her beloved tamarind, or even venture amid the still and silvery waves of the ocean, laughing at the broken beams of the moonlight, as her light form dimpled the waters – snatching with smiling delight the brilliant, tortuous, and enamelled shells that seemed to woo her white footsteps as she turned to the shore. Now all was different. The duties of the bath had been performed, but with a parade of soaps, perfumes, and, above all, attendants, who, though of her own sex, gave Isidora an unspeakable degree of disgust at the operation. The sponges and odours sickened her unsophisticated senses, and the presence of another human being seemed to close up every pore.

'She had felt no refreshment from the bath, or from her prayers – she sought it at her casement, but there also in vain. The moon was as bright as the sun of colder climates, and the heavens were all in a blaze with her light. She seemed like a gallant vessel ploughing the bright and trackless ocean alone, while a thousand stars burned in the wake of her quiet glory, like attendant vessels pursuing their course to undiscovered worlds, and pointing them out to the mortal eye that lingered on their course, and loved their light.

'Such was the scene above, but what a contrast to the scene below! The glorious and unbounded light fell on an inclosure of stiff parterres, cropped myrtles and orange-trees in tubs, and quadrangular ponds, and bowers of trellis-work, and nature tortured a thousand ways, and indignant and repulsive under her tortures every way.

'Isidora looked and wept. Tears had now become her language when alone – it was a language she dared not utter before her family. Suddenly she saw one of the moonlight alleys darkened by an approaching figure. It advanced – it uttered her name – the name she remembered and loved – the name of Immalee! "Ah!" she exclaimed, leaning from the casement, "is there then one who recognizes me by that name?" – "It is only by that name I can address you," answered the voice of the stranger – "I have not yet the honour of being acquainted with the name your Christian friends have given you." – "They call me Isidora, but do you still call me Immalee. But how is it," she added in a trembling voice, – her fears for his safety overcoming all her sudden and innocent joy at his sight – "how is it that you are here? – here, where no human being is ever beheld but the inmates of the mansion? – how did you cross the garden wall? – how did you come from India? Oh! retire for your own safety! I am among those whom I cannot trust or love. My mother is severe – my brother is violent. Oh! how did you obtain entrance into the garden? – How is it," she added in a broken voice, "that you risk so much to see one whom you have forgotten so long?" – "Fair Neophyte, beautiful Christian," answered the stranger, with a diabolical sneer, "be it known to you that I regard bolts, and bars, and walls, as much as I did the breakers and rocks of your Indian isle – that I can go where, and retire when I please, without leave asked or taken of your brother's mastiffs, or Toledos, or spring-guns, and in utter defiance of your mother's advanced guard of duennas, armed in spectacles, and flanked with a double ammunition of rosaries, with beads as large as –" "Hush! – hush! – do not utter such impious sounds – I am taught to revere those holy things. But is it you? – and did I indeed see you last night, or was it a thought such as visits me in dreams, and wraps me again in visions of that beautiful and blessed isle where first I – Oh that I never had seen you!" – "Lovely Christian! be reconciled to your horrible destiny. You saw me last night – I crossed your path twice when you were sparkling among the brightest and most beautiful of all Madrid. It was me you saw – I rivetted your eye – I transfixed your slender frame as with a flash of lightning – you fell fainting and withered under my burning glance. It was me you saw – me, the disturber of your angelical existence in that isle of paradise – the hunter of your form and your steps, even amid the complicated and artificial tracks in which you have been concealed by the false forms of the existence you have embraced!" – "Embraced! – Oh no! they seized on me – they dragged me here – they made me a Christian. They told me all was for my salvation, for my happiness here and hereafter – and I trust it will, for I have been so miserable ever since, that I ought to be happy somewhere." – "Happy," repeated the stranger with his withering sneer – "and are you not happy now? The delicacy of your exquisite frame is no longer exposed to the rage of the elements – the fine and feminine luxury of your taste is solicited and indulged by a thousand inventions of art – your bed is of down – your chamber hung with tapestry. Whether the moon be bright or dark, six wax tapers burn in your chamber all night. Whether the skies be bright or cloudy, – whether the earth be clothed with flowers, or deformed with tempests, – the art of the limner has surrounded you with 'a new heaven and a new earth'; and you may bask in suns that never set, while the heavens are dark to other eyes, – and luxuriate amid landscapes and flowers, while half your fellow-creatures are perishing amid snows and tempests!" (Such was the over-flowing acrimony of this being, that he could not speak of the beneficence of nature, or the luxuries of art, without interweaving something that seemed like a satire on, or a scorn of both.) "You also have intellectual beings to converse with instead of the chirpings of loxias, and the chatterings of monkeys." – "I have not found the conversation I encounter much more intelligible or significant," murmured Isidora, but the stranger did not appear to hear her. "You are surrounded by every thing that can flatter the senses, intoxicate the imagination, or expand the heart. All these indulgences must make you forget the voluptuous but unrefined liberty of your former existence." – "The birds in my mother's cages," said Isidora, "are for ever pecking at their gilded bars, and trampling on the clear seeds and limpid water they are supplied with – would they not rather rest in the mossy trunk of a doddered oak, and drink of whatever stream they met, and be at liberty, at all the risk of poorer food and fouler drink – would they not rather do anything than break their bills against gilded wires?" – "Then you do not feel your new existence in this Christian land so likely to surfeit you with delight as you once thought? For shame, Immalee – shame on your ingratitude and caprice! Do you remember when from your Indian isle you caught a glimpse of the Christian worship, and were entranced at the sight?" – "I remember all that ever passed in that isle. My life formerly was all anticipation, – now it is all retrospection. *The life of the happy is all hopes, – that of the unfortunate all memory.* Yes, I remember catching a glimpse of that religion so beautiful and pure; and when they brought me to a Christian land, I thought I should have found them all Christians." – "And what did you find them, then, Immalee?" – "Only Catholics." – "Are you aware of the danger of the words you utter? Do you know that in this country to hint a doubt of Catholicism and Christianity being the same, would consign you to the flames as a heretic incorrigible? Your mother, so lately known to you as a mother, would bind your hands when the covered litter came for its victim; and your father, though he has never yet beheld you, would buy with his last ducat the faggots that were to consume you to ashes; and all your relations in their gala robes would shout their hallelujahs to your dying screams of torture. Do you know that the Christianity of these countries is diametrically opposite to the Christianity of that world of which you caught a gleam, and which you may see recorded in the pages of your Bible, if you are permitted to read it?"

'Isidora wept, and confessed she had not found Christianity what she had at first believed it; but with her wild and eccentric ingenuousness, she accused herself the next moment of her confession, – and she added, "I am so ignorant in this new world, – I have so much to learn, – my senses so often deceive me, – and my habits and perceptions so different from what they ought to be – I mean from what those around me are – that I should not speak or think but as I am taught. Perhaps, after some years of instruction and suffering, I may be able to discover that happiness cannot exist in this new world, and Christianity is not so remote from Catholicism as it appears to me now." – "And have you not found yourself happy in this new world of intelligence and luxury?" said Melmoth, in a tone of involuntary softness. "I have at times." – "What times?" – "When the weary day was over, and my dreams bore me back to that island of enchantment. Sleep is to me like some bark rowed by visionary pilots, that wafts me to shores of beauty and blessedness, – and all night long I revel in my dreams with spirits. Again I live among flowers and odours – a thousand voices sing to me from the brooks and the breezes – the air is all alive and eloquent with invisible melodists – I walk amid a breathing atmosphere, and living and loving inanimation – blossoms that shed themselves beneath my steps – and streams that tremble to kiss my feet, and then retire; and then return again, wasting themselves in fondness before me, and touching me, as my lips press the holy images they have taught me to worship here!" – "Does no other image ever visit your dreams, Immalee?" – "I need not tell you," said Isidora, with that singular mixture of natural firmness, and partial obscuration of intellect, – the combined result of her original and native character, and extraordinary circumstances of her early existence – "I need not tell you – you know you are with me every night!" – "Me?" – "Yes, you; you are for ever in that canoe that bears me to the Indian isle – you gaze on me, but your expression is so changed, that I dare not speak to you – we fly over the seas in a moment, but you are for ever at the helm, though you never land – the moment the paradise isle appears, you disappear; and as we return, the ocean is all dark, and our course is as dark and swift as the storm that sweeps them – you look at me, but never speak – Oh yes! you are with me every night!" – "But, Immalee, these are all dreams – idle dreams. *I* row you over the Indian seas from Spain! – this is all a vision of your imagination." – "Is it a dream that I see you now?" said Isidora – "is it a dream that I talk with you? – Tell me, for my senses are bewildered; and it appears to me no less strange, that you should be here in Spain, than that I should be in my native island. Alas! in the life that I now lead, dreams have become realities, and realities seem only like dreams. How is it you are here, if indeed you are here? – how is it that you have wandered so far to see me? How many oceans you must have crossed, how many isles you must have seen, and none like that where I first beheld you! But is it you indeed I behold? I thought I saw you last night, but I had rather trust even my dreams than my senses. I believed you only a visitor of that isle of visions, and a haunter of the visions that recall it – but are you in truth a living being, and one whom I may hope to behold in this land of cold realities and Christian horrors?" – "Beautiful Immalee, or Isidora, or whatever other name your Indian worshippers, or Christian god-fathers and god-mothers, have called you by, I pray you listen to me, while I expound a few mysteries to you." And Melmoth, as he spoke, flung himself on a bed of hyacinths and tulips that displayed their glowing flowers, and sent up their odorous breath right under Isidora's casement. "Oh you will destroy my flowers!" cried she, while a reminiscence of her former picturesque existence, when flowers were the companions alike of her imagination and her pure heart, awoke her exclamation. "It is my vocation – I pray you pardon me!" said Melmoth, as he basked on the crushed flowers, and darted his withering sneer and scowling glance at Isidora. "I am commissioned to trample on and bruise every flower in the natural and moral world – hyacinths, hearts, and bagatelles of that kind, just as they occur. And now, Donna Isidora, with as long an *et cetera* as you or your sponsors could wish, and with no possible offence to the herald, here I am to-night – and where I shall be to-morrow night, depends on your choice. I would as soon be on the Indian seas, where your dreams send me rowing every night, or crashing through the ice near the Poles, or ploughing with my naked corse, (if corses have feeling), through the billows of that ocean where I must one day (a day that has neither sun or moon, neither commencement or termination), plough forever, and reap despair!" – "Hush! – hush! – Oh forbear such horrid sounds! Are you indeed he whom I saw in the isle? Are you he, inwoven ever since that moment with my prayers, my hopes, my heart? Are you that being upon whom hope subsisted, when life itself was failing? On my passage to this Christian land, I suffered much. I was so ill you would have pitied me – the clothes they put on me – the language they made me speak – the religion they made me believe – the country they brought me to – Oh *you*! – you alone! – the thought – the image of you, could alone have supported me! I loved, and to love is to live. Amid the disruption of every natural tie, – amid the loss of that delicious existence which seems a dream, and which still fills my dreams, and makes sleep a second existence, – I have thought of you – have dreamt of you – have loved you!" – "Loved me? – no being yet loved me but pledged me in tears." – "And have I not wept?" said Isidora – "believe these tears – they are not the first I have shed, nor I fear will be the last, since I owe the first to you." And she wept as she spoke. "Well," said the wanderer, with a bitter and self-satirizing laugh, "I shall be persuaded at last that I am 'a marvellous proper man'. Well, if it must be so, happy man be his dole! And when shall the auspicious day, beautiful Immalee, *still* beautiful Isidora, in spite of your Christian name, (to which I have a most anti-catholic objection) – when shall that bright day dawn on your long slumbering eye-lashes, and waken them with kisses, and beams, and light, and love, and all the paraphernalia with which folly arrays misery previous to their union – that glittering and empoisoned drapery that well resembles what of old Dejanira sent to her husband – when shall the day of bliss be?" And he laughed with that horrible convulsion that mingles the expression of levity with that of despair, and leaves the listener no doubt whether there is more despair in laughter, or more laughter in despair. "I understand you not," said the pure and timid Isidora; "and if you would not terrify me to madness, laugh no more – no more, at least, in that fearful way!" – "*I cannot weep,*" said Melmoth, fixing on her his dry and burning eyes, strikingly visible in the moonlight; "the fountain of tears has been long dried up within me, like that of every other human blessing." – "I can weep for both," said Isidora, "if that be all." And her tears flowed fast, as much from memory as from grief – and when those sources are united, God and the sufferer only know how fast and bitterly they fall. "Reserve them for our nuptial hour, my lovely bride," said Melmoth to himself; "you will have occasion for them then."

'There was a custom then, however indelicate and repulsive it may sound to modern ears, for ladies who were doubtful of the intentions of their lovers to demand of them the proof of their purity and honour, by requiring an appeal to their family, and a solemn union under the sanction of the church. Perhaps there was more genuine spirit of truth and chastity in this, than in all the ambiguous flirtation that is carried on with an ill-understood and mysterious dependence on principles that have never been defined, and fidelity that has never been removed. When the lady in the Italian tragedy* asks her lover, almost at their first interview, if his intentions are honourable, and requires, as the proof of their being so, that he shall espouse her immediately, does she not utter a language more unsophisticated, more intelligible, more *heartedly* pure, than all the romantic and incredible reliance that other females are supposed to place in the volatility of impulse, – in that wild and extemporaneous feeling, – that "house on the sands", – which never has its foundation in the immoveable depths of the heart. Yielding to this feeling, Isidora, in a voice that faultered at its own accents, murmured, "If you love me, seek me no more clandestinely. My mother is good, though she is austere – my brother is kind, though he is passionate – my father – I have never seen him! I know not what to say, but if he be *my* father, he will love you. Meet me in their presence, and I will no longer feel pain and shame mingled with the delight of seeing you. Invoke the sanction of the church, and then, perhaps," – "Perhaps!" retorted Melmoth; "You have learned the European 'perhaps!' – the art of suspending the meaning of an emphatic word – of affecting to draw the curtain of the heart at

* Alluding possibly to 'Romeo and Juliet.'

the moment you drop its folds closer and closer – of bidding us despair at the moment you intend we should feel hope!" – "Oh no! – no!" answered the innocent being; "I am *truth*. I am Immalee when I speak to you, – though to all others in this country, which they call Christian, I am Isidora. When I loved you first, I had only one heart to consult, – now there are many, and some who have not hearts like mine. But if you love me, you can bend to them as I have done – you can love their God, their home, their hopes, and their country. Even with *you* I could not be happy, unless you adored the cross to which your hand first pointed my wandering sight, and the religion which you reluctantly con- fessed was the most beautiful and beneficent on earth." – "Did I confess that?" echoed Melmoth; "It must have been *reluctantly* indeed. Beautiful Immalee! I am a convert to you;" and he stifled a Satanic laugh as he spoke; "to your new religion, and your beauty, and your Spanish birth and nomenclature, and every thing that you would wish. I will incontinently wait on your pious mother, and angry brother, and all your relatives, testy, proud, and ridiculous as they may be. I will encounter the starched ruffs, and rustling manteaus, and whale-boned fardin- gales of the females, from your good mother down to the oldest duenna who sits spectacled, and armed with bobbin, on her inaccessible and untempted sopha; and the twirled whiskers, plumed hats, and shouldered capas of all your male relatives. And I will drink chocolate, and strut among them; and when they refer me to your mustachoed man of law, with his thread-bare cloke of black velvet over his shoulder, his long quill in his hand, and his soul in three sheets of wide-spread parchment, I will dower you in the most ample territory ever settled on a bride." – "Oh let it be, then, in that land of music and sunshine where we first met! One spot where I might set my foot amid its flowers, is worth all the cultivated earth of Europe!" said Isidora. – "No! – it shall be in a territory with which your bearded men of law are far better acquainted, and which even your pious mother and proud family must acknowledge my claim to, when they shall hear it asserted and explained. Perchance they may be joint-tenants with *me* there; and yet (strange to say!) they will never litigate my exclusive title to possession." – "I understand nothing of this," said Isidora; "but I feel I am transgressing the decorums of a Spanish female and a Christian, in holding this conference with you any longer. If you think as you once thought, – if you feel as *I* must feel for ever, – there needs not this discussion, which only perplexes and terrifies. What have I to do with this territory of which you speak? That *you* are its possessor, is its only value in my eyes!" – "What have you to do with it?" repeated Melmoth; "Oh, you know not how much you may have to do with it and me yet! In other cases, the possession of the territory is the security for the man, – but here the man is the security for the everlasting possession of the territory. Mine heirs must inherit it for ever and ever, if they hold by my tenure. Listen to me, beautiful Immalee, or Christian, or whatever other name you choose to be called by! Nature, your first sponsor, baptized you with the dews of Indian roses – your Christian sponsors, of course, spared not water, salt, or oil, to wash away the stain of nature from your regenerated frame – and your last sponsor, if you will submit to the rite, will anoint you with a new chrism. But of that hereafter. Listen to me while I announce to you the wealth, the population, the magnificence of that region to which I will endower you. The rulers of the earth are there – all of them. There be the heroes, and the sovereigns, and the tyrants. There are their riches, and pomp, and power – Oh what a glorious accumulation! – and they have thrones, and crowns, and pedestals, and trophies of fire, that burn for ever and ever, and the light of their glory blazes eternally. There are all you read of in story, your Alexanders and Cæsars, your Ptolemies and Pharaohs. There be the princes of the East, the Nimrods, the Belshazzars, and the Holoferneses of their day. There are the princes of the North, the Odins, the Attilas, (named by your church the scourge of God), the Alarics, and

434

all those nameless and name-undeserving barbarians, who, under various titles and claims, ravaged and ruined the earth they came to conquer. There be the sovereigns of the South, and East, and West, the Mahommedans, the Caliphs, the Saracens, the Moors, with all their gorgeous pretensions and ornaments – the crescent, the Koran, and the horse-tail – the trump, the gong, and the atabal, (or to suit it to your Christianized ear, lovely Neophyte!) 'the noise of the captains, and the shoutings.' There be also those triple-crowned chieftains of the West, who hide their shorn heads under a diadem, and for every hair they shave, demand the life of a sovereign – who, pretending to humility, trample on power – whose title is, Servant of servants – and whose claim and recognizance is, Lord of lords. Oh! you will not lack company in that bright region, for bright it will be! – and what matter whether its light be borrowed from the gleam of sulphur, or the trembling light of the moon, by which I see you look so pale?" – "I look pale?" said Isidora gasping; "I *feel* pale! I know not the meaning of your words, but I know it must be horrible. Speak no more of that region, with its pride, its wickedness, and its splendour! I am willing to follow you to deserts, to solitudes, which human step never trod but yours, and where mine shall trace, with sole fidelity, the print of yours. Amid loneliness I was born; amid loneliness I could die. Let me but, wherever I live, and whenever I die, be yours! – and for the place, it matters not, let it be even" – and she shivered involuntarily as she spoke; "Let it be even" – "Even – *where?*" asked Melmoth, while a wild feeling of triumph in the devotedness of this unfortunate female, and of horror at the destination which she was unconsciously imprecating on herself, mingled in the question. "Even where you are to be," answered the devoted Isidora, "Let me be there! and there I must be happy, as in the isle of flowers and sunlight, where I first beheld you. Oh! there are no flowers so balmy and roseate as those that once blew there! There are no waters so musical, or breezes so fragrant, as those that I listened to and inhaled, when I thought that they repeated to me the echo of your steps, or the melody of your voice – that *human music* the first I ever heard, and which, when I cease to hear" – "You will hear much better!" interrupted Melmoth; "the voices of ten thousand – ten millions of spirits – beings whose tones are immortal, without cessation, without pause, without interval!" – "Oh that will be glorious!" said Isidora, clasping her hands; "the only language I have learned in this new world worth speaking, is the language of music. I caught some imperfect sounds from birds in my first world, but in my second world they taught me music; and the misery they have taught me, hardly makes a balance against that new and delicious language." – "But think," rejoined Melmoth, "if your taste for music be indeed so exquisite, how it will be indulged, how it will be enlarged, in hearing those voices accompanied and re-echoed by the thunders of ten thousand billows of fire, lashing against rocks which eternal despair has turned into adamant! They talk of the music of the spheres! – Dream of the music of those living orbs turning on their axis of fire for ever and ever, and ever singing as they shine, like your bretheren the Christians, who had the honour to illuminate Nero's garden in Rome on a rejoicing night." – "You make me tremble!" – "Tremble! – a strange effect of fire. Fie! what a coyness is this! I have promised, on your arrival at your new territory, all that is mighty and magnificent, – all that is splendid and voluptuous – the sovereign and the sensualist – the inebriated monarch and the pampered slave – the bed of roses and the canopy of fire!" – "And is this the home to which you invite me?" – "It is – it is. Come, and be mine! – myriads of voices summon you – hear and obey them! Their voices thunder in the echoes of mine – their fires flash from my eyes, and blaze in my heart. Hear me, Isidora, my beloved, hear me! I woo you in earnest, and for ever! Oh how trivial are the ties by which mortal lovers are bound, compared to those in which you and I shall be bound to eternity! Fear not the want of a numerous and splendid society. I have enumerated sovereigns, and pontiffs, and heroes, – and if you should condescend to remember the trivial amusements of your present sejour, you will have enough to revive its associations. You love music, and doubtless you will have most of the musicians who have chromatized since the first essays of Tubal Cain to Lully, who beat himself to death at one of his own oratorios, or operas, I don't know which. They will have a singular accompaniment – the eternal roar of a sea of fire makes a profound bass to the chorus of millions of singers in torture!" – "What is the meaning of this horrible description?" said the trembling Isidora; "your words are riddles to me. Do you jest with me for the sake of tormenting, or of laughing at me?" – "Laughing!" repeated her wild visitor, "that is an exquisite hint – *vive la bagatelle!* Let us laugh for ever! – we shall have enough to keep us in countenance. There will be all that ever have dared to laugh on earth – the singers, the dancers, the gay, the voluptuous, the brilliant, the beloved – all who have ever dared to mistake their destiny, so far as to imagine that enjoyment was not a crime, or that a smile was not an infringement of their duty as sufferers. All such must expiate their error under circumstances which will probably compel the most inveterate disciple of Democritus, the most *inextinguishable laugher* among them, to allow that *there*, at least, 'laughter is madness'. "I do not understand you," said Isidora, listening to him with that sinking of the heart which is produced by a combined and painful feeling of ignorance and terror. "Not understand me?" repeated Melmoth, with that sarcastic frigidity of countenance which frightfully contrasted the burning intelligence of his eyes, that seemed like the fires of a volcano bursting out amid masses of snow heaped up to its very edge; "not understand me! – are you not, then, fond of music?" – "I am." – "Of dancing, too, my graceful, beautiful love?" – "I *was*." – "What is the meaning of the different emphasis you give to those answers?" – "I love music – I must love it for ever – it is the language of recollection. A single strain of it wafts me back to the dreamy blessedness, the enchanted existence, of my own – own isle. Of dancing I cannot say so much. I have *learnt* dancing – but I *felt* music. I shall never forget the hour when I heard it for the first time, and imagined it was the language which Christians spoke to each other. I have heard them speak a different language since." – "Doubtless their language is not always melody, particularly when they address each other on controverted points in religion. Indeed, I can conceive nothing less a-kin to harmony than the debate of a Dominican and Franciscan on the respective efficacy of the cowl of the order, to ascertain the salvation of him who happens to die in it. But have you no other reason for *being* fond of music, and for only *having been* fond of dancing? Nay, let me have 'your most exquisite reason'."

'It seemed as if this unhappy being was impelled by his ineffable destiny to deride the misery he inflicted, in proportion to its bitterness. His sarcastic levity bore a direct and fearful proportion to his despair. Perhaps this is also the case in circumstances and characters less atrocious. A mirth which is not gaiety is often the mask which hides the convulsed and distorted features of agony – and laughter, which never yet was the expression of rapture, has often been the only intelligible language of madness and misery. Extacy only smiles, – despair laughs. It seemed, too, as if no keenness of ironical insult, no menace of portentous darkness, had power to revolt the feelings, or alarm the apprehensions, of the devoted being to whom they were addressed. Her "most exquisite reasons", demanded in a tone of ruthless irony, were given in one whose exquisite and tender melody seemed still to retain the modulation on which its first sounds had been formed, – that of the song of birds, mingled with the murmur of waters.

'"I love music, because when I hear it I think of you. I have ceased to love dancing, though I was at first intoxicated with it, because, when dancing, I have sometimes forgot you. When I listen to music, your image floats on every note, – I hear you in every sound. The most inarticulate murmurs that I produce on my guitar (for I am very ignorant) are like a spell of melody that raises a form indescribable – not you, but *my idea of you*. In your presence, though that seems necessary to my existence, I have never felt that exquisite delight that I have experienced in that of your image, when music has called it up from the recesses of my heart. Music seems to me like the voice of religion summoning to remember and worship the God of my heart. Dancing appears like a momentary apostasy, almost a profanation." – "That, indeed, is a sweet and subtle reason," answered Melmoth, "and one that, of course, has but one failure, – that of not being sufficiently flattering to the hearer. And so my image floats on the rich and tremulous waves of melody one moment, like a god of the overflowing billows of music, triumphing in their swells, and graceful even in their falls, – and the next moment appears, like the dancing demon of your operas, grinning at you between the brilliant movement of your fandangoes, and flinging the withering foam of his black and convulsed lips into the cup where you pledge at your banquetting. Well – dancing – music – let them go together! It seems that my image is equally mischievous in both – in one you are tortured by reminiscence, and in the other by remorse. Suppose that image is withdrawn from you for ever, – suppose that it were possible to break the tie that unites us, and whose vision has entered into the soul of both." – "You may suppose it," said Isidora, with maiden pride and tender grief blended in her voice; "and if you do, believe that I will try to suppose it too; the effort will not cost much, – nothing but – my life!"

'As Melmoth beheld this blessed and beautiful being, once so refined amid nature, and now so natural amid refinement, still possessing all the soft luxuriance of her first angelic nature, amid the artificial atmosphere where her sweets were uninhaled, and her brilliant tints doomed to wither unappreciated, – where her pure and sublime devotedness of heart was doomed to beat like a wave against a rock, – exhaust its murmurs, – and expire; – As he felt this, and gazed on her, he cursed himself; and then, with the selfishness of hopeless misery, he felt that the curse might, by dividing it, be diminished.

'"Isidora!" he whispered in the softest tones he could assume, approaching the casement, at which his pale and beautiful victim stood; "Isidora! will you then be mine?" – "What shall I say?" said Isidora; "if love requires the answer, I have said enough; if only vanity, I have said too much." – "Vanity! beautiful trifler, you know not what you say; the accusing angel himself might blot out that article from the catalogue of my sins. It is one of my prohibited and impossible offences; it is an earthly feeling, and therefore one which I can neither participate or enjoy. Certain it is that I feel some share of human pride at this moment." – "Pride! at what? Since I have known you, I have felt no pride but that of supreme devotedness, – that self-annihilating pride which renders the victim prouder of its wreath, than the sacrificer of his office." – "But I feel another pride," answered Melmoth, and in a proud tone he spoke it, – "a pride, which, like that of the storm that visited the ancient cities, whose destruction you may have read of, while it blasts, withers, and encrusts paintings, gems, music, and festivity, grasping them in its talons of annihilation, exclaims, Perish to all the world, perhaps beyond the period of its existence, but live to me in darkness and in corruption! Preserve all the exquisite modulation of your forms! all the indestructible brilliancy of your colouring! – but preserve it for me alone! – me, the single, pulseless, eyeless, heartless embracer of an unfertile bride, – the brooder over the dark and unproductive nest of eternal sterility, – the mountain whose lava of internal fire has stifled, and indurated, and inclosed for ever, all that was the joy of earth, the felicity of life, and the hope of futurity!"

'As he spoke, his expression was at once so convulsed and so derisive, so indicative of malignity and levity, so thrilling to the heart, while it withered every fibre it touched and wrung, that Isidora, with all her innocent and helpless devotedness, could not avoid shuddering before this fearful being, while, in trembling and unappeasable solicitude, she demanded, "Will you then be mine? Or what am I to understand from your terrible words? Alas! *my* heart has never enveloped itself in mysteries – never has the light of its truth burst forth amid the thunderings and burnings in which you have issued the law of my destiny." – "Will you then be mine, Isidora?" – "Consult my parents. Wed me by the rites, and in the face of the church, of which I am an unworthy member, and I will be yours for ever." – *"For ever!"* repeated Melmoth; "well-spoken, *my* bride. You will then be mine *for ever*? – will you, Isidora?" – "Yes! – yes – I have said so. But the sun is about to rise, I feel the increasing perfume of the orange blossoms, and the coolness of the morning air. Begone – I have staid too long here – the domestics may be about, and observe you – begone, I implore you." – "I go – but one word – for to me the rising of the sun, and the appearance of your domestics, and every thing in heaven above, and earth beneath, is equally unimportant. Let the sun stay below the horizon and wait for me. *You are mine!*" – "Yes, I am yours; but you must solicit my family." – "Oh, doubtless! – solicitation is so congenial to my habits." – "And" – "Well, what? – you hesitate." – "I hesitate," said the ingenuous and timid Isidora, "because" – "Well?" – "Because," she added, bursting into tears, "those with whom you speak will not utter to God language like mine. They will speak to you of wealth and dower; they will inquire about that region where you have told me your rich and wide possessions are held; and should they ask me of them, how shall I answer?"

'At these words, Melmoth approached as close as possible to the casement, and uttered a certain word which Isidora did not at first appear to hear, or understand – trembling she repeated her request. In a still lower tone the answer was returned. Incredulous, and hoping that the answer had deceived her, she again repeated her petition. A withering monosyllable, not to be told, thundered in her ears, – and she shrieked as she closed the casement. Alas! the casement only shut out the form of the stranger – not his image.'

Chapter Twenty-One

> He saw the eternal fire that keeps,
> In the unfathomable deeps,
> Its power for ever, and made a sign
> To the morning prince divine;
> Who came across the sulphurous flood,
> Obedient to the master-call,
> And in angel-beauty stood,
> High on his star-lit pedestal.

'In this part of the manuscript, which I read in the vault of Adonijah the Jew,' said Monçada, continuing his narrative, 'there were several pages destroyed, and the contents of many following wholly obliterated – nor could Adonijah supply the deficiency. From the next pages that were legible, it appeared that Isidora imprudently continued to permit her mysterious visitor to frequent the garden at night, and to converse with him from the casement, though unable to prevail on him to declare himself to her family, and perhaps conscious that his declaration would not be too favourably received. Such, at least, appeared to be the meaning of the next lines I could decypher.

'She had renewed, in these nightly conferences, her former visionary existence. Her whole day was but a long thought of the hour at which she expected to see him. In the day-time she was silent, pensive, abstracted, feeding on thought – with the evening her spirits perceptibly though softly rose, like those of one who has a secret and incommunicable store of delight; and her mind became like that flower that unfolds its leaves, and diffuses its odours, only on the approach of night.

'The season favoured this fatal delusion. It was that rage of summer when we begin to respire only towards evening, and the balmy and brilliant night is our day. The day itself is passed in a languid and feverish doze. At night alone she existed, – at her moon-lit casement alone she breathed freely; and never did the moonlight fall on a lovelier form, or gild a more angelic brow, or gleam on eyes that returned more pure and congenial rays. The mutual and friendly light seemed like the correspondence of spirits who glided on the alternate beams, and, passing from the glow of the planet to the glory of a mortal eye, felt that to reside in either was heaven.

*

'She lingered at that casement till she imagined that the clipped and artificially straitened treillage of the garden was the luxuriant and undulating foliage of the trees of her paradise isle – that the flowers had the same odour as that of the untrained and spontaneous roses that once showered their leaves under her naked feet – that the birds sung to her as they had once done when the vesper-hymn of her pure heart ascended along with their closing notes, and formed the holiest and most acceptable anthem that perhaps ever wooed the evening-breeze to waft it to heaven.

'This delusion would soon cease. The stiff and stern monotony of the parterre, where even the productions of nature held their place as if under the constraint of duty, forced the conviction of its unnatural regularity on her eye and soul, and she turned to heaven for relief. Who does not, even in the first sweet agony of passion? Then we tell that tale to heaven which we would not trust to the ear of mortal – and in the withering hour that must come to all whose love is only mortal, we again call on that heaven which we have intrusted with our secret, to send us back one bright messenger of consolation on those thousand rays that its bright, and cold, and passionless orbs, are for ever pouring on the earth as if in mockery. We ask, but is the petition heard or answered? We weep, but do not we feel that those tears are like rain falling on the sea? *Mare infructuosum.*[36] No matter. Revelation assures us there is a period coming, when all petitions suited to our state shall be granted, and when "tears shall be wiped from all eyes". In revelation, then, let us trust – in any thing but our own hearts. But Isidora had not yet learned that theology of the skies, whose text is, "Let us go into the house of mourning". To her still the night was day, and her sun was the "moon walking in its brightness". When she beheld it, the recollections of the isle rushed on her heart like a flood; and a figure soon appeared to recall and to realize them.

'That figure appeared to her every night without disturbance or interruption; and though her knowledge of the severe restraint and regularity of the household caused her some surprise at the facility with which Melmoth apparently defied both, and visited the garden every night, yet such was the influence of her former dream-like and romantic existence, that his continued presence, under circumstances so extraordinary, never drew from her a question with regard to the means by which he was enabled to surmount difficulties insurmountable to all others.

'There were, indeed, two extraordinary circumstances attendant on these meetings. Though seeing each other again in Spain, after an interval of three years elapsing since they had parted on the shores of an isle in the Indian sea, neither had ever inquired what circumstances could have led to a meeting so unexpected and extraordinary. On Isidora's part this incurious feeling was easily accounted for. Her former existence had been one of such a fabulous and fantastic character, that the improbable had become familiar to her, – and the familiar only, improbable. Wonders were her natural element; and she felt, perhaps, less surprised at seeing Melmoth in Spain, than when she first beheld him treading the sands of her lonely island. With Melmoth the cause was different, though the effect was the same. His destiny forbid alike curiosity or surprise. The world could show him no greater marvel than his own existence; and the facility with which he himself passed from region to region, mingling with, yet distinct from all his species, like a wearied and uninterested spectator rambling through the various seats of some vast theatre, where he knows none of the audience, would have prevented his feeling astonishment, had he encountered Isidora on the summit of the Andes.

'During a month, through the course of which she had tacitly permitted these nightly visits beneath her casement – (at a distance which indeed might have defied Spanish jealousy itself to devise matter of suspicion out of, – the balcony of her window being nearly fourteen feet above the level of the garden, where Melmoth stood) – during this month, Isidora rapidly, but imperceptibly, graduated through those stages of feeling which all who love have alike experienced, whether the stream of passion be smooth or obstructed. In the first, she was full of anxiety to speak and to listen, to hear and to be heard. She had all the wonders of her new existence to relate; and perhaps that indefinite and unselfish hope of magnifying herself in the eyes of him she loved, which induces us in our first encounter to display all the eloquence, all the powers, all the attractions we possess, not with the pride of a competitor, but with the humiliation of a victim. The conquered city displays all its wealth in hopes of propitiating the conqueror. It decorates him with all its spoils, and feels prouder to behold him arrayed in them, than when she wore them in triumph herself. That is the first bright hour of excitement, of trembling, but hopeful and felicitous anxiety. Then we think we never can display enough of talent, of imagination, of all that can interest, of all that can dazzle. We pride ourselves in the homage we receive from society, from the hope of sacrificing that homage to our beloved – we feel a pure and almost spiritualized delight in our own praises, from imagining they render us more worthy of meriting *his,* from whom we have received the *grace* of love to deserve them – we glorify ourselves, that we may be enabled to render back the glory to him from whom we received it, and for whom we have kept it in trust, only to tender it back with that rich and accumulated interest of the heart, of which we would pay the uttermost farthing, if the payment exacted the last vibration of its fibres, – the last drop of its blood. No saint who ever viewed a miracle performed by himself with a holy and self-annihilating abstraction from *seity,* has perhaps felt a purer sentiment of perfect devotedness, than the female who, in her first hours of love, offers, at the feet of her worshipped one, the brilliant wreath of music, painting, and eloquence, – and only hopes, with an unuttered sigh, that the rose of love will not be unnoticed in the garland.

'Oh! how delicious it is to such a being (and such was Isidora) to touch her harp amid crowds, and watch, when the noisy and tasteless bravoes have ceased, for the heart-drawn sigh of *the one,* to whom alone her soul, not her fingers, have played, – and whose single sigh is heard, and heard alone, amid the plaudits of thousands! Yet how delicious to her to whisper to herself, "I heard his sigh, but he has heard the applause!"

'And when she glides through the dance, and in touching, with easy and accustomed grace, the hands of many, she feels there is but one hand whose touch she can recognize; and, waiting for its thrilling and life-like vibration, moves on like a statue, cold and graceful, till the Pygmalion-touch warms her into woman, and the marble melts into flesh under the hands of the resistless moulder. And her movements betray, at that moment, the unwonted and half-unconscious impulses of that fair image to which love had given life, and who luxuriated in the vivid and newly-tried enjoyment of that animation which the passion of her lover had breathed into her frame. And when the splendid portfolio is displayed, or the richly-wrought tapestry expanded by outstretched arms, and cavaliers gaze, and ladies envy, and every eye is busy in examination, and every tongue loud in praise, just in the inverted proportion of the ability of the one to scrutinize with accuracy, and the other to applaud with taste – then to throw round the secret silent glance, that searches for that eye whose light alone, to her intoxicated gaze, contains all judgment, all taste, all feeling – for that lip whose very censure would be dearer than the applause of a world! – To hear, with soft and submissive tranquillity, censure and remark, praise and comment, but to turn for ever the appealing look to one who alone can understand, and whose swiftly-answering glance can alone reward it! – This – this had been Isidora's hope. Even in the isle where he first saw her in the infancy of her intellect, she had felt the consciousness of superior powers, which were then her solace, not her pride. Her value for herself rose with her devotion to him. Her passion became her pride; and the enlarged resources of her mind, (for Christianity under its most corrupt form enlarges every mind), made her at first believe, that to behold her admired as she was for her loveliness, her talents, and her wealth, would compel this proudest and most eccentric of beings to prostrate himself before her, or at least to acknowledge the power of those acquirements which she had so painfully been arrived at the knowledge of, since her involuntary introduction into European society.

'This had been her hope during the earlier period of his visits; but innocent and flattering to its object as it was, she was disappointed. To Melmoth "nothing was new under the sun". Talent was to him a burden. He knew more than man could tell him, or woman either. Accomplishments were a bauble – the rattle teazed his ear, and he flung it away. Beauty was a flower he looked on only to scorn, and touched only to wither. Wealth and distinction he appreciated as they deserved, but not with the placid disdain of the philosopher, or the holy abstraction of the saint, but with that "fearful looking for of judgment and fiery indignation", to which he believed their possessors irreversibly devoted, and to the infliction of which he looked forward with perhaps a feeling like that of those executioners who, at the command of Mithridates, poured the melted ore of his golden chains down the throat of the Roman ambassador.

'With such feelings, and others that cannot be told, Melmoth experienced an indescribable relief from the eternal fire that was already kindled within him, in the perfect and unsullied freshness of what may be called the untrodden verdure of Immalee's heart, – for she was Immalee still to him. She was the Oasis of his desert – the fountain at which he drank, and forgot his passage over the burning sands – and the *burning* sands to which his passage must conduct him. He sat under the shade of the gourd, and forgot the worm was working at its root; – perhaps the undying worm that gnawed, and coiled, and festered in his own heart, might have made him forget the corrosions of that he himself had sown in hers.

'Isidora, before the second week of their interview, had lowered her pretensions. She had given up the hope to interest or to dazzle – that hope which is twin-born with love in the purest female heart. She now had concentrated all her hopes, and all her heart, no longer in the ambition *to be* beloved, but in the sole wish *to* love. She no longer alluded to the enlargement of her faculties, the acquisition of new powers, and the expansion and cultivation of her taste. She ceased to speak – she sought only to listen – then her wish subsided into that quiet listening for his form alone, which seemed to transfer the office of hearing into the eyes, or rather, to identify both. She saw him long before he appeared, – and heard him though he did not speak. They have been in each other's presence for the short hours of a Spanish summer's night, – Isidora's eyes alternately fixed on the sun-like moon, and on her mysterious lover, – while he, without uttering a word, leaned against the pillars of her balcony, or the trunk of the giant myrtle-tree, which cast the shade he loved, even by night, over his portentous expression, – and they never uttered a word to each other, till the waving of Isidora's hand, as the dawn appeared, was the tacit signal for their parting.

'This is the marked graduation of a profound feeling. Language is no longer necessary to those whose beating hearts converse audibly – whose eyes, even by moonlight, are more intelligible to each other's stolen and shadowed glances, than the broad converse of face to face in the brightest sunshine – to whom, in the exquisite inversion of earthly feeling and habit, darkness is light, and silence eloquence.

'At their last interviews, Isidora sometimes spoke, – but it was only to remind her lover, in a soft and chastened tone, of a promise which it seems he had at one time made of disclosing himself to her parents, and demanding her at their hands. Something she murmured also of her declining health – her exhausted spirits – her breaking heart – the long delay – the hope deferred – the mysterious meeting; and while she spoke she wept, but hid her tears from him.

'It is thus, Oh God! we are doomed (and justly doomed when we fix our hearts on any thing below thee) to feel those hearts repelled like the dove who hovered over the shoreless ocean, and found not a spot where her foot might rest, – not a green leaf to bring back in her beak. Oh that the ark of mercy may open to such souls, and receive them from that stormy world of deluge and of wrath, with which they are unable to contend, and where they can find no resting place!

'Isidora now had arrived at the last stage of that painful pilgrimage through which she had been led by a stern and reluctant guide.

'In its first, with the innocent and venial art of woman, she had tried to interest him by the display of her new acquirements, without the consciousness that they were not new to him. The harmony of civilized society, of which she was at once weary and proud, was discord to his ear. He had examined all the strings that formed this curious but ill-constructed instrument, and found them all false.

'In the second, she was satisfied with merely beholding him.

His presence formed the atmosphere of her existence – in it alone she breathed. She said to herself, as evening approached, "I shall see him!" – and the burden of life rolled from her heart as she internally uttered the words. The constraint, the gloom, the monotony of her existence, vanished like clouds at the sun, or rather like those clouds assuming such gorgeous and resplendent colours, that they seemed to have been painted by the finger of happiness itself. The brilliant hue diffused itself over every object of her eye and heart. Her mother appeared no longer a cold and gloomy bigot, and even her brother seemed kind. There was not a tree in the garden whose foliage was not illumined as by the light of a setting sun; and the breeze spoke to her in a voice whose melody was borrowed from her own heart.

'When at length she saw him, – when she said to herself, He is there, – she felt as if all the felicity of earth was comprised in that single sensation, – at least she felt that all her own was. She no longer indulged the wish to attract or to subdue him – absorbed in his existence, she forgot her own – immersed in the consciousness of her own felicity, she lost the wish, or rather the pride, of BESTOWING it. In the impassioned revelry of the heart, she flung the pearl of existence into the draught in which she pledged her lover, and saw it melt away without a sigh. But now she was beginning to feel, that for this intensity of feeling, this profound devotedness, she was entitled at least to an honourable acknowledgement on the part of her lover; and that the mysterious delay in which her existence was wasted, might make that acknowledgement come perhaps too late. She expressed this to him; but to these appeals, (not the least affecting of which had no language but that of looks), he replied only by a profound but uneasy silence, or by a levity whose wild and frightful sallies had something in them still more alarming.

'At times he appeared even to insult the heart over which he had triumphed, and to affect to doubt his conquest with the air of one who is revelling in its certainty, and who mocks the captive by asking "if it is really in chains?"

'"You do not love?" he would say; – "you cannot love *me* at least. Love, in your happy Christian country, must be the result of cultivated taste, – of harmonized habits, – of a felicitous congeniality of pursuits, – of thought, and hopes, and feelings, that, in the sublime language of the Jewish poet, (prophet I mean), 'tell and certify to each other; and though they have neither speech or language, a voice is heard among them.' You cannot love a being repulsive in his appearance, – eccentric in his habits, – wild and unsearchable in his feelings, – and inaccessible in the settled purpose of his fearful and fearless existence. No," he added in a melancholy and decided tone of voice, "you cannot love me under the circumstances of your new existence. Once – but that is past. – You are now a baptized daughter of the Catholic church, – the member of a civilized community, – the child of a family that knows not the stranger. What, then, is there between me and thee, Isidora, or, as your Fra Jose would phrase it, (if he knows so much Greek), τι εμοι και σοι."[37] – "I loved you," answered the Spanish maiden, speaking in the same pure, firm, and tender voice in which she had spoken when she first was the sole goddess of her fairy and flowery isle; "I loved you before I was a Christian. They have changed my creed – but they never can change my heart. I love you still – I will be yours for ever! On the shore of the desolate isle, – from the grated window of my Christian prison, – I utter the same sounds. What can woman, what can man, in all the boasted superiority of his character and feeling, (which I have learned only since I became a Christian, or an European), do more? You but insult me when you appear to doubt that feeling, which you may wish to have analyzed, because you do not experience or cannot comprehend it. Tell me, then, *what is it to love*? I defy all your eloquence, all your sophistry, to answer the question as truly as I can. If you would wish to know what is love, inquire not at the tongue of man, but at the heart of woman." – "What is love?" said Melmoth; "is that the question?" – "You doubt that I love," said Isidora – "tell me, then, what is love?" – "You have imposed on me a task," said Melmoth smiling, but not in mirth, "so congenial to my feelings and habits of thought, that the execution will doubtless be inimitable. To love, beautiful Isidora, is to live in a world of the heart's own creation – all whose forms and colours are as brilliant as they are deceptive and unreal. To those who love there is neither day or night, summer or winter, society or solitude. They have but two eras in their delicious but visionary existence, – and those are thus marked in the heart's calendar – *presence – absence.* These are the substitutes for all the distinctions of nature and society. The world to them contains but one individual, – and that individual is to them the world as well as its single inmate. The atmosphere of his presence is the only air they can breathe in, – and the light of his eye the only sun of their creation, in whose rays they bask and live." – "Then I love," said Isidora internally. "To love," pursued Melmoth, "is to live in an existence of perpetual contradictions – to feel that absence is insupportable, and yet be doomed to experience the presence of the object as almost equally so – to be full of ten thousand thoughts while he is absent, the confession of which we dream will render our next meeting delicious, yet when the hour of meeting arrives, to feel ourselves, by a timidity alike oppressive and unaccountable, robbed of the power of expressing one – to be eloquent in his absence, and dumb in his presence – to watch for the hour of his return as for the dawn of a new existence, yet when it arrives, to feel all those powers suspended which we imagined it would restore to energy – *to be the statue that meets the sun, but without the music his presence should draw from it* – to watch for the light of his looks, as a traveller in the deserts looks for the rising of the sun; and when it bursts on our awakened world, to sink fainting under its overwhelming and intolerable glory, and almost wish it were night again – this is love!" – "Then I believe I love," said Isidora half audibly. "To feel," added Melmoth with increasing energy, "that our existence is so absorbed in his, that we have lost all consciousness but of his presence – all sympathy but of his enjoyments – all sense of suffering but when he suffers – *to be* only because *he is* – and to have no other use of being but to devote it to him, while our humiliation increases in proportion to our devotedness; and the lower you bow before your idol, the prostrations seem less and less worthy of being the expression of your devotion, – till you are only *his*, when you are not yourself. – To feel that to the sacrifice of yourself, all other sacrifices are inferior; and in it, therefore, all other sacrifices must be included. That she who loves, must remember no longer her individual existence, her natural existence – that she must consider parents, country, nature, society, religion itself – (you tremble, Immalee – Isidora I would say) – only as grains of incense flung on the altar of the heart, to burn and exhale their sacrificed odours there." – "Then I do love," said Isidora; and she wept and trembled indeed at this terrible confession – "for I have forgot the ties they told me were natural, – the country of which they said I was a native. I will renounce, if it must be so, parents, – country, – the habits which I have acquired, – the thoughts which I have learnt, – the religion which I – Oh no! my God! my Saviour!" she exclaimed, darting from the casement, and clinging to the crucifix – "No! I will never renounce you! – I will never renounce you! – you will not forsake me in the hour of death! – you will not desert me in the moment of trial! – you will not forsake me at this moment!"

'By the wax-lights that burned in her apartment, Melmoth could see her prostrate before the sacred image. He could see that devotion of the heart which made it throb almost visibly in the white and palpitating bosom – the clasped hands that seemed imploring aid against that rebellious heart, whose beatings they vainly struggled to repress; and then, locked and upraised, asked forgiveness from heaven for their fruitless opposition. He could see the wild but profound devotion with which she clung to the crucifix, – and he shuddered to behold it. He never gazed on that symbol, – his eyes were immediately averted; – yet now he looked long and intently at her as she knelt before it. He seemed to suspend the diabolical instinct that governed his existence, and to view her for the pure pleasure of sight. Her prostrate figure, – her rich robes that floated round her like drapery round an inviolate shrine, – her locks of light streaming over her naked shoulders, – her small white hands locked in agony of prayer, – the purity of expression that seemed to identify the agent with the employment, and made one believe they saw not a suppliant, but the embodied spirit of supplication, and feel that lips like those had never held communion with aught below heaven. – All this Melmoth beheld; and feeling that in this he could never participate, he turned away his head in stern and bitter agony, – and the moon-beam that met his burning eye saw no tear there.

'Had he looked a moment longer, he might have beheld a change in the expression of Isidora too flattering to his pride, if not to his heart. He might have marked all that profound and perilous absorption of the soul, when it is determined to penetrate the mysteries of love or of religion, and chuse "whom it will serve" – that *pause* on the brink of an abyss, in which all its energies, its passions, and its powers, are to be immersed – that pause, while the balance is trembling (and we tremble with it) between God and man.

'In a few moments, Isidora arose from before the cross. There was more composure, more elevation in her air. There was also that air of decision which an unreserved appeal to the Searcher of hearts never fails to communicate even to the weakest of those he has made.

'Melmoth, returning to his station beneath the casement, looked on her for some time with a mixture of compassion and wonder – feelings that he hasted to repel, as he eagerly demanded, "What proof are you ready to give of *that* love I have described –

of that which alone deserves the name?" – "Every proof," answered Isidora firmly, "that the most devoted of the daughters of man can give – my heart and hand, – my resolution to be yours amid mystery and grief, – to follow you in exile and loneliness (if it must be) through the world!"

'As she spoke, there was a light in her eye, – a glow on her brow, – an expansive and irradiated sublimity around her figure, – that made it appear like the rare and glorious vision of the personified union of passion and purity, – as if those eternal rivals had agreed to reconcile their claims, to meet on the confines of their respective dominions, and had selected the form of Isidora as the temple in which their league might be hallowed, and their union consummated – and never were the opposite divinities so deliciously lodged. They forgot their ancient feuds, and agreed to dwell there for ever.

'There was a grandeur, too, about her slender form, that seemed to announce that pride of purity, – that confidence in external weakness, and internal energy, – that conquest without armour, – that victory over the victor, which makes the latter blush at his triumph, and compels him to bow to the standard of the besieged fortress at the moment of its surrender. She stood like a woman devoted, but not humiliated by her devotion – uniting tenderness with magnanimity – willing to sacrifice every thing to her lover, but that which must lessen the value of the sacrifice in his eyes – willing to be the victim, but feeling worthy to be the priestess.

'Melmoth gazed on her as she stood. One generous, one human feeling, throbbed in his veins, and thrilled in his heart. He saw her in her beauty, – her devotedness, – her pure and perfect innocence, – her sole feeling for one who could not, by the fearful power of his unnatural existence, feel for mortal being. He turned aside, and did not weep; or if he did, wiped away his tears, as a fiend might do, with his burning talons, when he sees a new victim arrive for torture; and, *repenting of his repentance*, rends away *the blot* of compunction, and arms himself for his task of renewed infliction.

' "Well, then, Isidora, you will give me no proof of your love? Is that what I must understand?" – "Demand," answered the innocent and high-souled Isidora, "any proof that woman ought to give – more is not in human power – less would render the proof of no value!"

'Such was the impression that these words made on Melmoth, whose heart, however, plunged in unutterable crimes, had never been polluted by sensuality, that he started from the spot where he stood, – gazed on her for a moment, – and then exclaimed, "Well! you have given me proofs of love unquestionable! It remains for me to give you a proof of that love which I have described – of that love which only *you* could inspire – of that love which, under happier circumstances, I might – But no matter – it is not my business to analyse the feeling, but to give the proof." He extended his arm toward the casement at which she stood. – "Would you then consent to unite your destiny with mine? Would you indeed be mine amid mystery and sorrow? Would you follow me from land to sea, and from sea to land, – a restless, homeless, devoted being, – with the brand on your brow, and the curse on your name? Would you indeed *be mine*? – my own – my only Immalee?" – "I would – I will!" – "Then," answered Melmoth, "on this spot receive the proof of my eternal gratitude. On this spot I renounce your sight! – I disannul your engagement! – I fly from you for ever!" And as he spoke, he disappeared.'

Chapter Twenty-Two

I'll not wed Paris, – Romeo is my husband.

Shakespeare

'Isidora was so accustomed to the wild exclamations and (to her) unintelligible allusions of her mysterious lover, that she felt no unwonted alarm at his singular language, and abrupt departure. There was nothing in either more menacing or formidable than she had often witnessed; and she recollected, that after these paroxysms, he often re-appeared in a mood comparatively tranquil. She felt sustained, therefore, by this reflection, – and perhaps by that mysterious conviction impressed on the hearts of those who love profoundly – that passion must always be united with suffering; and she seemed to hear, with a kind of melancholy submission to the fatality of love, that her lot was to suffer from lips that were sure to verify the oracle. The disappearance, therefore, of Melmoth, gave her less surprise than a summons from her mother a few hours after, which was delivered in these words: "Madonna Isidora, your lady-mother desires your presence in the tapestried chamber – having received intelligence by a certain express, which she deems fitting you should be acquainted withal."

'Isidora had been in some degree prepared for extraordinary intelligence by an extraordinary bustle in this grave and quiet household. She had heard steps passing, and voices resounding, but

'She wist not what they were,'

and thought not of what they meant. She imagined that her mother might have some communication to make about some intricate point of conscience which Fra Jose had not discussed to her satisfaction, from which she would make an instant transition to the levity visible in the mode in which one attendant damsel arranged her hair, and the suspected sound of a ghitarra under the window of another, and then fly off at a tangent to inquire how the capons were fed, and why the eggs and Muscadine had not been duly prepared for Fra Jose's supper. Then would she fret about the family clock not chiming synchronically with the bells of the neighbouring church where she performed her devotions. And finally, she fretted about every thing, from the fattening of the "pullen", and the preparation for the olio, up to the increasing feuds between the Molinists and Jansenists, which had already visited Spain, and the deadly dispute between the Dominican and Franciscan orders, relative to the habit in which it was most effective to salvation for the dying body of the sinner to be wrapped. So between her kitchen and her oratory, – her prayers to the saints, and her scoldings to her servants, – her devotion and her anger, – Donna Clara continued to keep herself and domestics in a perpetual state of interesting occupation and gentle excitement.

'Something of this Isidora expected on the summons, and she was, therefore, surprised to see Donna Clara seated at her writing desk, – a large and fairly written manuscript of a letter extended before her, – and to hear words thereafter uttered thus: "Daughter, I have sent for you, that you might with me partake of the pleasure these lines should afford both; and that you may do so, I desire you to sit and hear while they are read to you."

'Donna Clara, as she uttered these words, was seated in a monstrous high-backed chair, of which she actually seemed a part, so wooden was her figure, so moveless her features, so lacklustre her eyes.

'Isidora curtsied low, and sat on one of the cushions with which the room was heaped, – while a spectacled duenna, enthroned on another cushion at the right hand of Donna Clara, read, with sundry pauses and some difficulty, the following letter, which Donna Clara had just received from her husband, who had landed, not *at Ossuna*,* but at a real seaport town in Spain, and was now on his way to join his family.

"Donna Clara,

"It is about a year since I received your letter advising me of the recovery of our daughter, whom we believed lost with her nurse on her voyage to India when an infant, to which I would sooner have replied, were I not otherwise hindered by concerns of business.

"I would have you understand, that I rejoice not so much that I have recovered a daughter, as that heaven hath regained a soul and a subject, as it were, *e faucibus Draconis – e profundis Barathri*[38] – the which terms Fra Jose will make plain to your weaker comprehension.

"I trust that, through the ministry of that devout servant of God and the church, she is now become as complete a Catholic in all points necessary, absolute, doubtful, or incomprehensible, – formal, essential, venial and indispensible, as becomes the daughter of an old Christian such as I (though unworthy of that honour) boast myself to be. Moreover, I expect to find her, as a Spanish maiden should be, equipped and accomplished with all the virtues pertaining to that character, especially those of discretion and reserve. The which qualities, as I have always perceived to reside in you, so I hope you have laboured to transfer to her, – a transfer by which the receiver is enriched, and the giver not impoverished.

"Finally, as maidens should be rewarded for their chastity and reserve by being joined in wedlock with a worthy husband, so it

---

* Vide Don Quixote, Vol. II. Smollet's Translation.

is the duty of a careful father to provide such a one for his daughter, that she do not pass her marriageable age, and sit in discontent and squalidness at home, as one overlooked of the other sex. My fatherly care, therefore, moving me, I shall bring with me one who is to be her husband, Don Gregorio Montilla, of whose qualifications I have not now leisure to speak, but whom I expect she will receive as becomes the dutiful daughter, and you as the obedient wife, of

Francisco Aliaga."

' "You have heard your father's letter, daughter," said Donna Clara, placing herself as in act to speak, "and doubtless sit silent in expectation of hearing from me a rehearsal of the duties pertaining to the state on which you are so soon to enter, and which, I take it, are three; that is to say, obedience, silence and thriftiness. And first of the first, which, as I conceive, divides itself into thirteen heads," – "Holy saints!" said the duenna under her breath, "how pale Madonna Isidora grows!" – "First of the first," continued Donna Clara, clearing her throat, elevating her spectacles with one hand, and fixing three demonstrative fingers of the other on a huge clasped volume, containing the life of St Francis Xavier, that lay on the desk before her, – "as touching the thirteen heads into which the first divides itself, the eleven first, I take it, are the most profitable – the two last I shall leave you to be instructed in by your husband. First, then," – Here she was interrupted by a slight noise, which did not, however, draw her attention, till she was startled by a scream from the duenna, who exclaimed, "The Virgin be my protection! Madonna Isidora has fainted!"

'Donna Clara lowered her spectacles, glanced at the figure of her daughter, who had fallen from her cushion, and lay breathless on the floor, and, after a short pause, replied, "She *has* fainted. Raise her. – Call for assistance, and apply some cold water, or bear her into the open air. I fear I have lost the mark in the life of this holy saint," muttered Donna Clara when alone; "this comes of this foolish business of love and marriage. I never loved in my life, thank the saints! – and as to marriage, that is according to the will of God and of our parents."

'The unfortunate Isidora was lifted from the floor, conveyed into the open air, whose breath had the same effect on her still elementary existence, that water was said to have on that of the *ombre pez*, (man-fish) of whom the popular traditions of Barcelona were at that time, and still have been, rife.

'She recovered; and sending an apology to Donna Clara for her sudden indisposition, intreated her attendants to leave her, as she wished to be alone. Alone! – that is a word to which those who love annex but one idea, – that of being in society with one who is their all. She wished in this (to her) terrible emergency, to ask counsel of him whose image was ever present to her, and whose voice she heard with the mind's ear distinctly even in absence.

'The crisis was indeed one calculated to try a female heart; and Isidora's, with its potency of feeling, opposed to utter destitution of judgement and of experience, – its native habits of resolution and self-direction, and its acquired ones of timidity and diffidence almost to despondency, – became the victim of emotions, whose struggle seemed at first to threaten her reason.

'Her former independent and instinctive existence revived in her heart at some moments, and suggested to her resolutions wild and desperate, but such as the most timid females have been known, under the pressure of a fearful exigency, to purpose, and even to execute. Then the constraint of her new habits, – the severity of her factitious existence, – and the solemn power of her newly-learned but deeply-felt religion, – made her renounce all thoughts of resistance or opposition, as offences against heaven.

'Her former feelings, her new duties, beat in terrible conflict against her heart; and, trembling at the isthmus on which she stood, she felt it, under the influence of opposing tides, narrowing every moment under her feet.

'This was a dreadful day to her. She had sufficient time for reflection, but she had within her the conviction that reflection could be of no use, – that the circumstances in which she was placed, not her own thoughts, must decide for her, – and that, situated as she was, mental power was no match for physical.

'There is not, perhaps, a more painful exercise of the mind than that of treading, with weary and impatient pace, the entire round of thought, and arriving at the same conclusion for ever; then setting out again with increased speed and diminished strength, and again returning to the very same spot – of sending out all our faculties on a voyage of discovery, and seeing them all return empty, and watch the wrecks as they drift helplessly along, and sink before the eye that hailed their outward expedition with joy and confidence.

'All that day she thought how it was possible to liberate herself from her situation, while the feeling that liberation was impossible clung to the bottom of her heart; and this sensation of the energies of the soul in all their strength, being in vain opposed to imbecility and mediocrity, when aided by circumstances, is one productive alike of melancholy and of irritation. We feel like prisoners in romance, bound by threads to which the power of magic has given the force of adamant.

'To those whose minds incline them rather to observe, than to sympathize with the varieties of human feeling, it would have been interesting to watch the restless agony of Isidora, contrasted with the cold and serene satisfaction of her mother, who employed the whole of the day in composing, with the assistance of Fra Jose, what Juvenal calls *"verbosa et grandis epistola"*,[39] in answer to that of her husband; and to conceive how two human beings, apparently of similarly-constructed organs, and destined apparently to sympathize with each other, could draw from the same fountain waters sweet and bitter.

'On her plea of continued indisposition, Isidora was excused from appearing before her mother during the remainder of the day. The night came on, – the night, which, by concealing the artificial objects and manners which surrounded her, restored to her, in some degree, the consciousness of her former existence, and gave her a sense of independence she never felt by day. The absence of Melmoth increased her anxiety. She began to apprehend that his departure was intended to be final, and her heart sunk at the thought.

'To the mere reader of romance, it may seem incredible that a female of Isidora's energy and devotedness should feel anxiety or terror in a situation so common to a heroine. She has only to stand proof against all the importunities and authority of her family, and announce her desperate resolution to share the destiny of a mysterious and unacknowledged lover. All this sounds very plausible and interesting. Romances have been written and read, whose interest arose from the noble and impossible defiance of the heroine to all powers human and superhuman alike. But neither the writers or readers seem ever to have taken into account the thousand petty external causes that operate on human agency with a force, if not more powerful, far more effective than the grand internal motive which makes so grand a figure in romance, and so rare and trivial a one in common life.

'Isidora would have died for him she loved. At the stake or the scaffold she would have avowed her passion, and triumphed in perishing as its victim. The mind can collect itself for one great effort, but it is exhausted by the eternally-recurring necessity of domestic conflicts, – victories by which she must lose, and defeats by which she might gain the praise of perseverance, and feel such gain was loss. The last single and terrible effort of the Jewish champion, in which he and his enemies perished together, must have been a luxury compared to his blind drudgery in his mill.

'Before Isidora lay that painful and perpetual struggle of fettered strength with persecuting weakness, which, if the truth were told, would divest half the heroines of romance of the power or wish to contend against the difficulties that beset them. Her mansion was a prison – she had no power (and if she possessed the power, would never have exercised it) of obtaining an unpermitted or unobserved egress from the doors of the house for one moment. Thus her escape was completely barred; and had every door in the house been thrown open, she would have felt like a bird on its first flight from the cage, without a spray that she dared to rest on. Such was her prospect, even if she could effect her escape – at home it was worse.

'The stern and cold tone of authority in which her father's letter was written, gave her but little hope that in her father she would find a friend. Then the feeble and yet imperious mediocrity of her mother – the selfish and arrogant temper of Fernan – the powerful influence and incessant documentizing of Fra Jose, whose good-nature was no match for his love of authority – the daily domestic persecution – that vinegar that would wear out any rock – the being compelled to listen day after day to the same exhausting repetition of exhortation, chiding, reproach and menace, or seek refuge in her chamber, to waste the weary hours in loneliness and tears – this strife maintained by one strong indeed in purpose, but feeble in power, against so many all sworn to work their will, and have their way – this perpetual conflict with evils so trivial in the items, but so heavy in the amount, to those who have the debt to pay daily and hourly, – was too much for the resolution of Isidora, and she wept in hopeless despondency, as she felt that already her courage shrunk from the encounter, and knew not what concessions might be extorted from her increasing inability of resistance.

' "Oh!" she cried, clasping her hands in the extremity of her distress, "Oh that he were but here to direct, to counsel me! – that he were here even no longer as my lover, but only as my adviser!"

'It is said that a certain power is always at hand to facilitate the wishes that the individual forms for his own injury; and so it should seem in the present instance, – for she had scarce uttered these words, when the shadow of Melmoth was seen darkening the garden walk, – and the next moment he was beneath the casement. As she saw him approach, she uttered a cry of mingled joy and fear, which he hushed by making a signal of silence with his hand, and then whispered, "I know it all!"

'Isidora was silent. She had nothing but her recent distress to communicate, – and of that, it appeared, he was already apprized. She waited, therefore, in mute anxiety for some words of counsel or of comfort. "I know all!" continued Melmoth; "your father has landed in Spain – he brings with him your destined husband. The fixed purpose of your whole family, as obstinate as they are weak, it will be bootless in you to resist; and this day fortnight will see you the bride of Montilla." – "I will first be the bride of the grave," said Isidora, with perfect and fearful calmness.

'At these words, Melmoth advanced and gazed on her more closely. Any thing of intense and terrible resolution, – of feeling or action in extremity, – made harmony with the powerful but disordered chords of his soul. He required her to repeat the words – she did so, with quivering lip, but unfaultering voice. He advanced still nearer to gaze on her as she spoke. It was a beautiful and fearful sight to see her as she stood; – her marble face – her moveless features – her eyes in which burned the fixed and livid light of despair, like a lamp in a sepulchral vault – the lips that half opened, and remaining unclosed, appeared as if the speaker was unconscious of the words that had escaped them, or rather, as if they had burst forth by involuntary and incontroulable impulse; – so she stood, like a statue, at her casement, the moon-light giving her white drapery the appearance of stone, and her wrought-up and determined mind lending the same rigidity to her expression. Melmoth himself felt confounded – appalled he could not feel. He retreated, and then returning, demanded, "Is this your resolution, Isidora? – and have you indeed resolution to" – "To die!" answered Isidora, with the same unaltered accent, – the same calm expression, – and seeming, as she spake, capable of all she expressed; and this union, in the same slight and tender form, of those eternal competitors, energy and fragility, beauty and death, made every human pulse in Melmoth's frame beat with a throbbing unknown before. "Can you, then," he said, with averted head, and in a tone that seemed ashamed of its own softness – "Can you, then, die for him you will not live for?" – "I have said I will die sooner than be the bride of Montilla," answered Isidora. "Of death I know nothing, nor do I know much of life – but I would rather perish, than be the perjured wife of the man I cannot love." – "And why can you not love him?" said Melmoth, toying with the heart he held in his hand, like a mischievous boy with a bird, around whose leg he has fastened a string – "Because I can love but one. You were the first human being I ever saw who could teach me language, and who taught me feeling. Your image is for ever before me, present or absent, sleeping or waking. I have seen fairer forms, – I have listened to softer voices, – I might have met gentler hearts, – but the first, the indelible image, is written on mine, and its characters will never be effaced till that heart is a clod of the valley. I loved you not for comeliness, – I loved you not for gay deportment, or fond language, or all that is said to be lovely in the eye of woman, – I loved you because you were my *first,* – the sole connecting link between the human world and my heart, – the being who brought me acquainted with that wondrous instrument that lay unknown and untouched within me, whose chords, as long as they vibrate, will disdain to obey any touch but that of their first mover – because your image is mixed in my imagination with all the glories of nature – because your voice, when I heard it first, was something in accordance with the murmur of the ocean, and the music of the stars. And still its tones recall the unimaginable blessedness of those scenes where first I heard it, – and still I listen to it like an exile who hears the music of his native country in a land that is very far off, – because nature and passion, memory

466

and hope, alike cling round your image; and amid the light of my former existence, and the gloom of my present, there is but one form that retains its reality and its power through light and shade. I am like one who has traversed many climates, and looks but to one sun as the light of all, whether bright or obscure. I have loved once – and for ever!" Then, trembling at the words she uttered, she added, with that sweet mixture of maiden pride and purity that redeems while it pledges the hostage of the heart, "The feelings I have entrusted you with may be abused, but never alienated." – "And these are your *real* feelings?" said Melmoth, pausing long, and moving his frame like one agitated by deep and uneasy thoughts. "Real!" repeated Isidora, with some transient glow on her cheek – "real! Can I utter any thing but what is real? Can I so soon forget my existence?" Melmoth looked up once more as she spoke – "If such is your resolution, – if such be your feelings indeed," – "And they are! – they are!" exclaimed Isidora, her tears bursting through the slender fingers, which, after extending towards him, she clasped over her burning eyes. "Then look to the alternative that awaits you!" said Melmoth slowly, bringing out the words with difficulty, and, as it appeared, with some feeling for his victim; "a union with the man who cannot love, – or the perpetual hostility, the wearying, wasting, almost annihilating persecution of your family! Think of days that" – "Oh let me not think!" cried Isidora, wringing her white and slender hands; "tell me – tell me what may be done to escape them!" – "Now, in good troth," answered Melmoth, knitting his brows with a most cogitative wrinkle, while it was impossible to discover whether his predominant expression was that of irony or profound and sincere feeling – "I know not what resource you have unless you wed me." – "Wed you!" cried Isidora, retreating from the window – "Wed you!" and she clasped her hands over her pale forehead; – and at this moment, when the hope of her heart, the thread on which her existence was suspended, was within her reach, she trembled to touch it. "Wed you! – but how is that possible?" – "All things are possible to those who love," said Melmoth, with his sardonic smile, which was hid by the shades of the night. "And you will wed me, then, by the rites of the church of which I am a member?" – "Aye! or of any other!" – "Oh speak not so wildly! – say not *aye* in that horrible voice! Will you wed me as a Christian maiden should be wed? – Will you love me as a Christian wife should be loved? My former existence was like a dream, – but now I am awake. If I unite my destiny to yours, – if I abandon my family, my country, my" – "If you do, how will you be the loser? – your family harasses and confines you – your country would shout to see you at the stake, for you have some heretical feelings about you, Isidora. And for the rest" – "God!" said the poor victim, clasping her hands, and looking upwards, "God, aid me in this extremity!" – "If I am to wait here only as a witness to your devotions," said Melmoth with sullen asperity, "my stay will not be long." – "You cannot leave me, then, to struggle with fear and perplexity alone! How is it possible for me to escape, even if" – "By whatever means I possess of entering this place and retiring unobserved, – by the same you may effect your escape. If you have resolution, the effort will cost you little, – if love, – nothing. Speak, shall I be here at this hour to-morrow night, to conduct you to liberty and" – Safety he would have added, but his voice faultered. *"To-morrow night,"* said Isidora, after a long pause, and in accents almost inarticulate. She closed the casement as she spoke, and Melmoth slowly departed.'

Chapter Twenty-Three

If he to thee no answer give,
    I'll give to thee a sign;
A secret known to nought that live,
    Save but to me and mine.

*

Gone to be married –

Shakespeare

'The whole of the next day was occupied by Donna Clara, to whom letter-writing was a rare, troublesome, and momentous task, in reading over and correcting her answer to her husband's letter; in which examination she found so much to correct, inter-line, alter, modify, expunge and new-model, that finally Donna Clara's epistle very much resembled the work she was now employed in, namely that of *overcasting* a piece of tapestry wrought by her grandmother, representing the meeting of king Solomon and the queen of Sheba. The new work, instead of repairing, made fearful havock among the old; but Donna Clara went on, like her countryman at Mr Peter's puppet-show, playing away (with her needle) in a perfect shower of back-strokes, fore-strokes, side-thrusts, and counter-thrusts, till not a figure in the tapestry could know himself again. The faded face of Solomon was garnished with a florid beard of scarlet silk (which Fra Jose at first told her she must rip out, as it made Solomon very little bet-ter than Judas) that made him resemble a boiled scallop. The fardingale of the queen of Sheba was expanded to an enormous hoop, of whose shrunk and pallid wearer it might be truly said,

"Minima est pars sui".[40] The dog that, in the original tapestry, stood by the spurred and booted heel of the oriental monarch, (who was clad in Spanish costume), by dint of a few tufts of black and yellow satin, was converted into a tiger, – a transformation which his grinning fangs rendered as authentic as heart could wish. And the parrot perched on the queen's shoulder, with the help of a train of green and gold, which the ignorant mistook for her majesty's mantle, proved a very passable peacock.

'As little trace of her original epistle did Donna Clara's present one bear, as did her elaborate overcasting to the original and painful labours of her grandmother. In both, however, Donna Clara (who scorned to flinch) went over the same ground with dim eye, and patient touch, and inextinguishable and remorseless assiduity. The letter, such as it was, was still sufficiently characteristic of the writer. Some passages of it the reader shall be indulged with, – and we reckon on his gratitude for not insisting on his perusal of the whole. The authentic copy, from which we are favoured with the extracts, runs thus.

*

"Your daughter takes to her religion like mother's milk; and well may she do so, considering that the trunk of our family was planted in the genuine soil of the Catholic church, and that every branch of it must flourish there or perish. For a Neophyte, (as Fra Jose wills me to word it), she is as promising a sprout as one should wish to see flourishing within the pale of the holy church; – and for a heathen, she is so amenable, submissive, and of such maidenly suavity, that for the comportment of her person, and the discreet and virtuous ordering of her mind, I have no Christian mother to envy. Nay, I sometimes take pity on them, when I see the lightness, the exceeding vain carriage, and the unadvised eagerness to be wedded, of the best trained maidens of our country. This our daughter hath nothing of, either in her outward demeanour, or inward mind. She talks little, *therefore she cannot think much*; and she dreams not of the light devices of love, and is therefore well qualified for the marriage proposed unto her.

*

"One thing, dear spouse of my soul, I would have thee to take notice of, and guard like the apple of thine eye, – our daughter is deranged, but never, on thy discretion, mention this to Don Montilla, even though he were the descendant in the right line of the Campeador, or of Gonsalvo di Cordova. Her derangement will in no wise impede or contravene her marriage, – for be it known to thee, it breaks out but at times, and at such times, that the most jealous eye of man could not spy it, unless he had a foretaught intimation of it. She hath strange fantasies swimming in her brain, such as, that heretics and heathens shall not be everlastingly damned – (God and the saints protect us!) – which must clearly proceed from madness, – but which her Catholic husband, if ever he comes to the knowledge of them, shall know how to expel, by aid of the church, and conjugal authority. That thou may'st better know the truth of what I hereby painfully certify, the saints and Fra Jose (who will not let me tell a lie, because he in a manner holds my pen) can witness, that about four days before we left Madrid, as we went to church, and I was about, while ascending the steps, to dole alms to a mendicant woman wrapt in a mantle, who held up a naked child for the receiving of charity, your daughter twitched my sleeve, while she whispered, 'Madam, she cannot be mother to that child, for she is covered, and her child is naked. If she were its mother, she would cover her child, and not be comfortably wrapt herself.' True it was, I found afterwards the wretched woman had hired the child from its more wretched mother, and my alms had paid the price of its hire for the day; but still that not a whit disproved our daughter insane, inasmuch as it showed her ignorant of the fashion and usages of the beggars of the country, and did in

471

some degree shew a doubt of the merit of alms-deeds, which thou know'st none but heretics or madmen could deny. Other and grievous proofs of her insanity doth she give daily; but not willing to incumber you with ink, (which Fra Jose willeth me to call *atramentum*), I will add but a few particulars to arouse your dormant faculties, which may be wrapt in lethargic obliviousness by the anodyne of my somniferous epistolation."

' "Reverend Father," said Donna Clara, looking up to Fra Jose, who had dictated the last line, "Don Francisco will know the last line not to be mine – he heard it in one of your sermons. Let me add the extraordinary proof of my daughter's insanity at the ball." – "Add or diminish, compose or confound, what you will, in God's name!" said Fra Jose, vexed at the frequent erasures and lituras which disfigured the lines of his dictation; "for though in style I may somewhat boast of my superiority, in scratches no hen on the best dunghill in Spain can contend with you! On, then, in the name of all the saints! – and when it pleases heaven to send an interpreter to your husband, we may hope to hear from him by the next post-angel, for surely such a letter was never written on earth."

'With this encouragement and applause, Donna Clara proceeded to relate sundry other errors and wanderings of her daughter, which, to a mind so swathed, crippled and dwarfed, by the ligatures which the hand of custom had twined round it since its first hour of consciousness, might well have appeared like the aberrations of insanity. Among other proofs, she mentioned that Isidora's first introduction to a Christian and Catholic church, was on that night of penitence in passion-week, when, the lights being extinguished, the *miserere* is chaunted in profound darkness, the penitents macerate themselves, and groans are heard on every side instead of prayers, as if the worship of Moloch was renewed without its fires; – struck with horror at the sounds she heard, and the darkness which surrounded her, Isidora demanded what they were doing. – "Worshipping God," was the answer.

'At the expiration of Lent, she was introduced to a brilliant assembly, where the gay fandango was succeeded by the soft notes of the seguedilla, – and the crackling of the castanets, and the tinkling of the guitars, marked alternate time to the light and ecstatic step of youth, and the silvery and love-tuned voice of beauty. Touched with delight at all she saw and heard, – the smiles that dimpled and sparkled over her beautiful features reflecting every shade of pleasure they encountered, like the ripplings of a brook kissed by moon-beams, – she eagerly asked, "And are not these worshipping God?" – "Out on it, daughter!" interposed Donna Clara, who happened to overhear the question; "This is a vain and sinful pastime, – the invention of the devil to delude the children of folly – hateful in the eyes of heaven and its saints, – and abhorred and renounced by the faithful." – "Then there are two Gods," said Isidora sighing, "The God of smiles and happiness, and the God of groans and blood. Would I could serve the former!" – "I will take order you shall serve the latter, heathenish and profane that you are!" answered Donna Clara, as she hurried her from the assembly, shocked at the scandal which her words might have given. These and many similar anecdotes were painfully indited in Donna Clara's long epistle, which, after being folded and sealed by Fra Jose, (who swore by the habit he wore, he had rather study twenty pages of the Polyglot fasting, than read it over once more), was duly forwarded to Don Francisco.

'The habits and movements of Don Francisco were, like those of his nation, so deliberate and dilatory, and his aversion to writing letters, except on mercantile subjects, so well known, that Donna Clara was actually alarmed at receiving, in the evening of the day in which her epistle was dispatched, another letter from her husband.

'Its contents must be guessed to be sufficiently singular, when the result was, that Donna Clara and Fra Jose sat up over them nearly the whole of the night, in consultation, anxiety and fear. So intense was their conference, that it is recorded it was never interrupted even by the lady telling her beads, or the monk thinking of his supper. All the artificial habits, the customary indulgences, the factitious existence of both, were merged in the real genuine fear which pervaded their minds, and which asserted its power over both in painful and exacting proportion to their long and hardy rejection of its influence. Their minds succumbed together, and sought and gave in vain, feeble counsel, and fruitless consolation. They read over and over again this extraordinary letter, and at every reading their minds grew darker, – and their counsels more perplexed, – and their looks more dismal. Ever and anon they turned their eyes on it, as it lay open before them on Donna Clara's ebony writing-desk, and then starting, asked each other by looks, and sometimes in words, "Did either hear some strange noise in the house?" The letter, among other matter not important to the reader, contained the singular passage following.

*

"In my travel from the place where I landed, to that whence I now write, I fortuned to be in company with strangers, from whom I heard things touching me (not as they meant, but as my fear interpreted them) in a point the most exquisite that can prick and wound the soul of a Christian father. These I shall discuss unto thee at thy more leisure. They are full of fearful matter, and such as may perchance require the aid of some churchman rightly to understand, and fully to fathom. Nevertheless this I can commend to thy discretion, that after I had parted from this strange conference, the reports of which I cannot by letter communicate to thee, I retired to my chamber full of sad and heavy thoughts, and being seated in my chair, pored over a tome containing legends of departed spirits, in nowise contradictive to the doctrine of the holy Catholic church, otherwise I would have crushed it with the sole of my foot into the fire that burned before me on the hearth, and spit

on its cinders with the spittle of my mouth. Now, whether it
was the company I fortuned to be into, (whose conversation
must never be known but to thee only), or the book I had been
reading, which contained certain extracts from Pliny, Artemi-
dore, and others, full-filled with tales which I may not now
recount, but which did relate altogether to the revivification of
the departed, appearing in due accordance with our Catholic
conceptions of Christian ghosts in purgatory, with their suitable
accoutrements of chains and flames, – as thus Pliny writeth,
'*Apparebat eidolon senex, macie et senie confectus,*'[41] – or finally, the
weariness of my lonely journey, or other things I know not, –
but feeling my mind ill-disposed for deeper converse with books
at my own thoughts, and though oppressed by sleep, unwilling
to retire to rest, – a mood which I and others have often
experienced, – I took out thy letters from the desk in which I
duly reposit them, and read over the description which thou
didst send me of our daughter, upon the first intelligence of her
being discovered in that accursed isle of heathenism, – and I do
assure thee, the description of our daughter hath been written
in such characters on the bosom to which she hath never been
clasped, that it would defy the art of all the limners in Spain to
paint it more effectually. So, thinking on those dark-blue
eyes, – and those natural ringlets which will not obey their new
mistress, art, – and that slender undulating shape, – and thinking
it would soon be folded in my arms, and ask the blessing of a
Christian father in Christian tones, I dozed as I sat in my chair;
and my dreams taking part with my waking thoughts, I was
a-dreamt that such a creature, so fair, so fond, so cherubic, sat
beside me, and asked me blessing. As I bowed to give it, I
nodded in my chair and awoke. Awoke I say, for what followed
was as palpable to human sight as the furniture of my apartment, or any other tangible object. There was a female seated
opposite me, clad in a Spanish dress, but her veil flowed down to
her feet. She sat, and seemed to expect that I should bespeak her

first. 'Damsel,' I said, 'what seekest thou? – or why art thou
here?' The figure never raised its veil, nor motioned with hand
or lip. Mine head was full of what I had heard and read of; and
after making the sign of the cross, and uttering certain prayers, I
approached that figure, and said, 'Damsel, what wantest
thou?' – 'A father,' said the form, raising its veil, and disclosing
the identical features of my daughter Isidora, as described in thy
numerous letters. Thou mayest well guess my consternation,
which I might almost term fear, at the sight and words of this
beautiful but strange and solemn figure. Nor was my perplexity
and trouble diminished but increased, when the figure, rising
and pointing to the door, through which she forthwith passed
with a mysterious grace and incredible alacrity, uttered, *in
transitu,* words like these: – 'Save me! – save me! – lose not a
moment, or I am lost!' And I swear to thee, wife, that while that
figure sat or departed, I heard not the rustling of her garments,
or the tread of her foot, or the sound of her respiration – only as
she went out, there was a rushing sound as of a wind passing
through the chamber, – and a mist seemed to hang on every
object around me, which dispersed, – and I was conscious of
heaving a deep sigh, as if a load had been removed from my
breast. I sat thereafter for an hour pondering on what I had seen,
and not knowing whether to term it a waking dream, or a
dream-like waking. I am a mortal man, sensible of fear, and
liable to error, – but I am also a Catholic Christian, and have ever
been a hearty contemner of your tales of spectres and visions,
excepting always when sanctioned by the authority of the holy
church, and recorded in the lives of her saints and martyrs.
Finding no end or fruit of these my heavy cogitations, I
withdrew myself to bed, where I long lay tossing and sleepless,
till at the approach of morning, just as I was falling into a deep
sleep, I was awoke by a noise like that of a breeze waving my
curtains. I started up, and drawing them, looked around me.
There was a glimpse of day-light appearing through the

window-shutters, but not sufficient to enable me to distinguish the objects in the room, were it not for the lamp that burned on the hearth, and whose light, though somewhat dim, was perfectly distinct. By it I discovered, near the door, a figure which my sight, rendered more acute by my terror, verified as the identical figure I had before beheld, who, waving its arm with a melancholy gesture, and uttering in a piteous voice these words, 'It is too late,' disappeared. As, I will own to thee, overcome with horror at this second visitation, I fell back on my pillow almost bereft of the use of my faculties, I remember the clock struck three."

'As Donna Clara and the priest (on their tenth perusal of the letter) arrived at these words, the clock in the hall below struck three. "That is a singular coincidence," said Fra Jose. "Do you think it nothing more, Father?" said Donna Clara, turning very pale. "I know not," said the priest; "many have told credible stories of warnings permitted by our guardian saints, to be given even by the ministry of inanimate things. But to what purpose are we warned, when we know not the evil we are to shun?" – "Hush! – hark!" said Donna Clara, "did you hear no noise?" – "None," said Fra Jose listening, not without some appearance of perturbation – "None," he added, in a more tranquil and assured voice, after a pause; "and the noise which I *did* hear about two hours ago, was of short continuance, and has not been renewed." – "What a flickering light these tapers give!" said Donna Clara, viewing them with eyes glassy and fixed with fear. "The casements are open," answered the priest. "So they have been since we sat here," returned Donna Clara; "yet now see what a stream of air comes rushing against them! Holy God! They flare as if they would go out!"

'The priest, looking up at the tapers, observed the truth of what she said, – and at the same time perceived the tapestry near the door to be considerably agitated. "There is a door open in some other direction," said he, rising. "You are not going to leave me, Father?" said Donna Clara, who sat in her chair paralyzed with terror, and unable to follow him but with her eyes.

'The Father Jose made no answer. He was now in the passage, where a circumstance which he observed had arrested all his attention, – the door of Isidora's apartment was open, and lights were burning in it. He entered it slowly at first, and gazed around, but its inmate was not there. He glanced his eye on the bed, but no human form had pressed it that night – it lay untouched and undisturbed. The casement next caught his eye, now glancing with the quickness of fear on every object. He approached it – it was wide open, – the casement that looked towards the garden. In his horror at this discovery, the good Father could not avoid uttering a cry that pierced the ears of Donna Clara, who, trembling and scarce able to make her way to the room, attempted to follow him in vain, and fell down in the passage. The priest raised and tried to assist her back to her own apartment. The wretched mother, when at last placed in her chair, neither fainted or wept; but with white and speechless lips, and a paralytic motion of her hand, tried to point towards her daughter's apartment, as if she wished to be conveyed there. "It is too late," said the priest, unconsciously using the ominous words quoted in the letter of Don Francisco.'

Chapter Twenty-Four

Responde meum argumentum – nomen est nomen
– *ergo,* quod tibi est nomen – responde argumentum.

Beaumont *and* Fletcher's
Wit at Several Weapons[42]

'That night was the one fixed on for the union of Isidora and Melmoth. She had retired early to her chamber, and sat at the casement watching for his approach for hours before she could probably expect it. It might be supposed that at this terrible crisis of her fate, she felt agitated by a thousand emotions, – that a soul susceptible like hers felt itself almost torn in pieces by the struggle, – but it was not so. When a mind strong by nature, but weakened by fettering circumstances, is driven to make one strong spring to free itself, it has no leisure to calculate the weight of its hindrances, or the width of its leap, – it sits with its chains heaped about it, thinking only of the bound that is to be its liberation – or –

'During the many hours that Isidora awaited the approach of this mysterious bridegroom, she felt nothing but the awful sense of that approach, and of the event that was to follow. So she sat at her casement, pale but resolute, and trusting in the extraordinary promise of Melmoth, that by whatever means he was enabled to visit her, by those she would be enabled to effect her escape, in spite of her well-guarded mansion, and vigilant household.

'It was near one (the hour at which Fra Jose, who was sitting in consultation with her mother over that melancholy letter, heard the noise alluded to in the preceding chapter) when Melmoth appeared in the garden, and, without uttering a word, threw up a ladder of ropes, which, in short and sullen whispers, he instructed her to fasten, and assisted her to descend. They hurried through the garden, – and Isidora, amid all the novelty of her feelings and situation, could not avoid testifying her surprise at the facility with which they passed through the well-secured garden gate.

'They were now in the open country, – a region far wilder to Isidora than the flowery paths of that untrodden isle, where she had no enemy. Now in every breeze she heard a menacing voice, – in the echoes of her own light steps she heard the sound of steps pursuing her.

'The night was very dark, – unlike the midsummer nights in that delicious climate. A blast sometimes cold, sometimes stifling from heat, indicated some extraordinary vicissitude in the atmosphere. There is something very fearful in this kind of wintry feeling in a summer night. The cold, the darkness, followed by intense heat, and a pale, meteoric lightning, seemed to unite the mingled evils of the various seasons, and to trace their sad analogy to life, – whose stormy summer allows youth little to enjoy, and whose chilling winter leaves age nothing to hope.

'To Isidora, whose sensibilities were still so acutely physical, that she could feel the state of the elements as if they were the oracles of nature, which she could interpret at sight, – this dark and troubled appearance seemed like a fearful omen. More than once she paused, trembled, and turned on Melmoth a glance of doubt and terror, – which the darkness of the night, of course, prevented him from observing. Perhaps there was another cause, – but as they hurried on, Isidora's strength and courage began to fail together. She perceived that she was borne on with a kind of supernatural velocity, – her breath failed, – her feet faultered, – and she felt like one in a dream.

' "Stay!" she exclaimed, gasping from weakness, "stay! – whither am I going? – where do you bear me?" – "To your nuptials," answered Melmoth, in low and almost inarticulate tones; – but whether rendered so by emotion, or by the speed with which they seemed to fly along, Isidora could not discover.

'In a few moments, she was forced to declare herself unable to proceed, and leaned on his arm, gasping and exhausted. "Let me pause," said she ominously, "in the name of God!" Melmoth returned no answer. He paused, however, and supported her with an appearance of anxiety, if not of tenderness.

'During this interval, she gazed around her, and tried to distinguish the objects near; but the intense darkness of the night rendered this almost impossible, – and what she *could* discover, was not calculated to dispel her alarm. They seemed to be walking on a narrow and precipitous path close by a shallow stream, as she could guess, by the hoarse and rugged sound of its waters, as they fought with every pebble to win their way. This path was edged on the other side by a few trees, whose stunted growth, and branches tossing wild and wide to the blast that now began to whisper mournfully among them, seemed to banish every image of a summer night from the senses, and almost from the memory. Every thing around was alike dreary and strange to Isidora, who had never, since her arrival at the villa, wandered beyond the precincts of the garden, – and who, even if she had, would probably have found no clue to direct her where she now was. "This is a fearful night," said she, half internally. She then repeated the same words more audibly, perhaps in hope of some answering and consolatory sounds. Melmoth was silent – and her spirits subdued by fatigue and emotion, she wept. "Do you already repent the step you have taken?" said he, laying a strange emphasis on the word – already. "No, love, no!" replied Isidora, gently wiping away her tears; "it is impossible for me ever to repent it. But this loneliness, – this darkness, – this speed, – this silence, – have in them something almost awful. I feel as if I were traversing some unknown region. Are these indeed the winds of heaven that sigh around me? Are these trees of nature's growth, that nod at me like spectres? How hollow and dismal is the sound of the blast! – it chills me though the night is sultry! – and those trees, they cast their shadows over my soul! Oh, is this like a bridal night?" she exclaimed, as Melmoth, apparently disturbed at these words, attempted to hurry her on – "Is this like a bridal? No father, no brother, to support me! – no mother near me! – no kiss of kindred to greet me! – no congratulating friends!" – and her fears increasing, she wildly exclaimed, "Where is the priest to bless our union? – where is the church under whose roof we are to be united?"

'As she spoke, Melmoth, drawing her arm under his, attempted to lead her gently forward. "There is," said he, "a ruined monastery near – you may have observed it from your window." – "No! I never saw it. Why is it in ruins?" – "I know not – there were wild stories told. It was said the Superior, or Prior, or – I know not what – had looked into certain books, the perusal of which was not altogether sanctioned by the rules of his order – books of magic they called them. There was much noise about it, I remember, and some talk of the Inquisition, – but the end of the business was, the Prior disappeared, some said into the prisons of the Inquisition, some said into safer custody – (though how that could be, I cannot well conceive) – and the brethren were drafted into other communities, and the building became deserted. There were some offers made for it by the communities of other religious houses, but the evil, though vague and wild reports, that had gone forth about it, deterred them, on inquiry, from inhabiting it, – and gradually the building fell to ruin. It still retains all that can sanctify it in the eyes of the faithful. There are crucifixes and tombstones, and here and there a cross set up where there has been murder, – for, by a singular congeniality of taste, a banditti has fixed their seat there now, – and the traffic of gold for souls, once carried on so profitably by the former inmates, is exchanged for that of souls for gold, by the present."

'At these words, Melmoth felt the slender arm that hung on his withdrawn, – and he perceived that his victim, between shuddering and struggling, had shrunk from his hold. "But there," he added, "even amid those ruins, there dwells a holy hermit, – one who has taken up his residence near the spot, – he will unite us in his oratory, according to the rites of your church. He will speak the blessing over us, – and one of us, at least, shall be blessed." – "Hold!" said Isidora, repelling, and standing at what distance from him she could, – her slight figure expanding to that queen-like dignity with which nature had once invested her as the fair and sole sovereign of her own island-paradise. "Hold!" she repeated – "approach me not by another step, – address me not by another word, – till you tell me when and where I am to be united to you, – to become your wedded wife! I have borne much of doubt and terror, – of suspicion and persecution, – but" – "Hear me, Isidora," said Melmoth, terrified at this sudden burst of resolution. "Hear *me*," answered the timid but heroic girl, springing, with the elasticity of her early movements, upon a crag that hung over their stony path, and clinging to an ash-tree that had burst through its fissures – "Hear me! Sooner will you rend this tree from its bed of stone, than me from its trunk! Sooner will I dash this body on the stony bed of the stream that groans below my feet, than descend into your arms, till you swear to me they will bear me to honour and safety! For you I have given up all that my newly-taught duties have told me was holy! – all that my heart long ago whispered I ought to love! Judge by what I *have* sacrificed, of what I *can* sacrifice – and doubt not that I would be my own victim ten thousand times sooner than yours!" – "By all that you deem holy!" cried Melmoth, humbling himself even to kneel before her as she stood, – "my intentions are as pure as your own soul! – the hermitage is not an hundred paces off. Come, and do not, by a fantastic and causeless appre-hension, frustrate all the magnanimity and tenderness you have hitherto shewed, and which have raised you in my eyes not only above your sex, but above your whole species. Had you not been what you are, and what no other but you could be, you had never been the bride of Melmoth. With whom but you did he ever seek to unite his dark and inscrutable destiny? Isidora," he added, in tones more potent and emphatic, perceiving she still hesitated, and clung to the tree – "Isidora, how weak, how unworthy of you is this! You are in my power, – absolutely, hopelessly in my power. No human eye can see *me* – no human arm can aid *you*. You are as helpless as infancy in my grasp. This dark stream would tell no tales of deeds that stained its waters, – and the blast that howls round you would never waft your groans to mortal ear! You are in my power, yet I seek not to abuse it. I offer you my hand to conduct you to a consecrated building, where we shall be united according to the fashion of your country – and will you still persevere in this fanciful and profitless waywardness?"

'As he spoke, Isidora looked round her helplessly – every object was a confirmation of his arguments – she shuddered and submitted. But as they walked on in silence, she could not help interrupting it to give utterance to the thousand anxieties that oppressed her heart.

' "But you speak," said she, in a suppressed and pleading tone, – "you speak of religion in words that make me tremble – you speak of it as the fashion of a country, – as a thing of form, of accident, of habit. What faith do you profess? – what church do you frequent? – what holy rites do you perform?" – "I venerate all faiths – alike, I hold all religious rites – pretty much in the same respect," said Melmoth, while his former wild and scoffing levity seemed to struggle vainly with a feeling of involuntary horror. "And do you then, indeed, believe in holy things?" asked Isidora. "Do you indeed?" she repeated anxiously. *"I believe in a God,"* answered Melmoth, in a voice that froze her blood; "you have heard of those who believe and tremble, – such is he who speaks to you!"

'Isidora's acquaintance with the book from which he quoted, was too limited to permit her to understand the allusion. She knew, according to the religious education she had received, more of her breviary than her Bible; and though she pursued her inquiry in a timid and anxious tone, she felt no additional terror from words she did not understand.

"'But,' she continued, "Christianity is something more than belief in a God. Do you also believe in all that the Catholic church declares to be essential to salvation? Do you believe that" – And here she added a name too sacred, and accompanied with terms too awful, to be expressed in pages so light as these.* "I believe it all – I know it all," answered Melmoth, in a voice of stern and reluctant confession. "Infidel and scoffer as I may appear to you, there is no martyr of the Christian church, who in other times blazed for his God, that has borne or exhibited a more resplendent illustration of his faith, than I shall bear one day – and for ever. There is a slight difference only between our testimonies in point of duration. They burned for the truths they loved for a few moments – not so many perchance. Some were suffocated before the flames could reach them, – but I am doomed to bear my attestation on the truth of the gospel, amid fires that shall burn for ever and ever. See with what a glorious destiny yours, my bride, is united! You, as a Christian, would doubtless exult to see your husband at the stake, – and amid the faggots to prove his devotion. How it must ennoble the sacrifice to think that it is to last to eternity!"

'Melmoth uttered these words in ears that heard no longer. Isidora had fainted; and hanging with one cold hand on his arm still, fell a helpless, senseless weight on the earth. Melmoth, at this sight, shewed more feeling than he could have been suspected of. He disentangled her from the folds of her mantle, sprinkled water from the stream on her cold cheek, and supported her frame in every direction where a breath of air was to be caught. Isidora recovered; for her swoon was that of fatigue

* Here Monçada expressed his surprise at this passage, (as savouring more of Christianity than Judaism), considering it occurred in the manuscript of a Jew.

more than fear; and, with her recovery, her lover's short-lived tenderness seemed to cease. The moment she was able to speak he urged her to proceed, – and while she feebly attempted to obey him, he assured her, her strength was perfectly recovered, and that the place they had to reach was but a few paces distant. Isidora struggled on. Their path now lay up the ascent of a steep hill, – they left the murmur of the stream, and the sighing of trees, behind them, – the wind, too, had sunk, but the night continued intensely dark, – and the absence of all sound seemed to Isidora to increase the desolateness of the scene. She wished for something to listen to beside her impeded and painful respiration, and the audible beatings of her heart. As they descended the hill on the other side, the murmuring of the waters became once more faintly audible; and this sound she had longed to hear again, had now, amid the stillness of the night, a cadence so melancholy, that she almost wished it hushed.

'Thus always, to the unhappy, the very fulfilment of their morbid wishings becomes a source of disappointment, and the change they hoped for is desirable only as it gives them cause to long for another change. In the morning they say, Would to God it were evening! – Evening comes, – and in the evening they say, Would to God it were morning! But Isidora had no time to analyse her feelings, – a new apprehension struck her, – and, as she could well guess from the increasing speed of Melmoth, and head thrown backward impatiently, and often, it had probably reached him too. A sound they had been for some time watching, (without communicating their feelings to each other), became every moment more distinct. It was the sound of a human foot, evidently pursuing them, from the increasing quickness of its speed, and a certain sharpness of tread, that irresistibly gave the idea of hot and anxious pursuit. Melmoth suddenly paused, and Isidora hung trembling on his arm. Neither of them uttered a word; but Isidora's eyes, instinctively following the slight but fearful waving of his arm, saw it directed towards a figure so obscure, that it at first appeared like a spray moving in the misty night, – then was lost in darkness as it descended the hill, – and then appeared in a human form, as far as the darkness of the night would permit its shape to be distinguishable. It came on – its steps were more and more audible, and its shape almost distinct. – Then Melmoth suddenly quitted Isidora, who, shivering with terror, but unable to utter a word that might implore him to stay, stood alone, her whole frame trembling almost to dissolution, and her feet feeling as if she were nailed to the spot where she stood. What passed she knew not. There was a short and darkened struggle between two figures, – and, in this fearful interval, she imagined she heard the voice of an ancient domestic, much attached to her, call on her, first in accents of expostulation and appeal, then in choked and breathless cries for help – help – help! – Then she heard a sound as if a heavy body fell into the water that murmured below. – It fell heavily – the wave groaned – the dark hill groaned in answer, like murderers exchanging their stilled and midnight whispers over their work of blood – and all was silent. Isidora clasped her cold and convulsed fingers over her eyes, till a whispering voice, the voice of Melmoth, uttered, "Let us hasten on, my love." – "Where?" said Isidora, not knowing the meaning of the words she uttered. – "To the ruined monastery, my love, – to the hermitage, where the holy man, the man of your faith, shall unite us." – "Where are the steps that pursued us?" said Isidora, suddenly recovering her recollection. – "They will pursue you no more." – "But I saw a figure." – "But you will see it no more." – "I heard something fall into that stream – heavily – like a corse." – "There was a stone that fell from the precipice of the hill – the waters splashed, and curled, and whitened round it for a moment, but they have swallowed it now, and appear to have such a relish for the morsel, that they will not be apt to resign it."

'In silent horror she proceeded, till Melmoth, pointing to a dusky and indefinite mass of what, in the gloom of night, bore, according to the eye or the fancy, the shape of a rock, a tuft of trees, or a massive and unlighted building, whispered, "There is the ruin, and near it stands the hermitage, – one moment more of effort, – of renewed strength and courage, and we are there." Urged by these words, and still more by an undefinable wish to put an end to this shadowy journey, – these mysterious fears, – even at the risk of finding them worse than verified at its termination, Isidora exerted all her remaining strength, and, sup-ported by Melmoth, began to ascend the sloping ground on which the monastery had once stood. There had been a path, but it was now all obstructed by stones, and rugged with the knotted and interlaced roots of the neglected trees that had once formed its shelter and its grace.

'As they approached, in spite of the darkness of the night, the ruin began to assume a distinct and characteristic appearance, and Isidora's heart beat less fearfully, when she could ascertain, from the remains of the tower and spire, the vast Eastern win-dow, and the crosses still visible on every ruined pinnacle and pediment, like religion triumphant amid grief and decay, that this had been a building destined for sacred purposes. A narrow path, that seemed to wind round the edifice, conducted them to a front which overlooked an extensive cemetery, at the extremity of which Melmoth pointed out to her an indistinct object, which he said was the hermitage, and to which he would hasten to intreat the hermit, who was also a priest, to unite them. "May I not accompany you?" said Isidora, glancing round on the graves that were to be her companions in solitude. – "It is against his vow," said Melmoth, "to admit a female into his presence, except when obliged by the course of his duties." So saying he hasted away, and Isidora, sinking on a grave for rest, wrapt her veil around her, as if its folds could exclude even thought. In a few moments, gasping for air, she withdrew it; but as her eye encountered only tomb-stone and crosses, and that dark and sepulchral vegetation that loves to shoot its roots, and trail its unlovely verdure amid the joints of gravestones, she closed it again, and sat shuddering and alone. Suddenly a faint sound, like the murmur of a breeze, reached her, – she looked up, but the wind had sunk, and the night was perfectly calm. The same sound recurring, as of a breeze sweeping past, made her turn her eyes in the direction from which it came, and, at some distance from her, she thought she beheld a human figure moving slowly along on the verge of the inclosure of the burial-ground. Though it did not seem approaching her, (but rather moving in a low circuit on the verge of her view), conceiving it must be Melmoth, she rose in expectation of his advancing to her, and, at this moment, the figure, turning and half-pausing, seemed to extend its arm towards her, and wave it once or twice, but whether with a motion or purpose of warning or repelling her, it was impossible to discover, – it then renewed its dim and silent progress, and the next moment the ruins hid it from her view. She had no time to muse on this singular appearance, for Melmoth was now at her side urging her to proceed. There was a chapel, he told her, attached to the ruins, but not like them in decay, where sacred ceremonies were still performed, and where the priest had promised to join them in a few moments. "He is there before us," said Isidora, adverting to the figure she had seen; "I think I saw him." – "Saw whom?" said Melmoth, starting, and standing immoveable till his question was answered. – "I saw a figure," said Isidora, trembling – "I thought I saw a figure moving towards the ruin." – "You are mistaken," said Melmoth; but a moment after he added, "We ought to have been there before him." And he hurried on with Isidora. Suddenly slackening his speed, he demanded, in a choaked and indistinct voice, if she had ever heard any music precede his visits to her, – any sounds in the air. "Never," was the answer. – "You are sure?" – "Perfectly sure."

'At this moment they were ascending the fractured and rugged steps that led to the entrance of the chapel, now they passed under the dark and ivied porch, – now they entered the chapel, which, even in darkness, appeared to the eyes of Isidora ruinous and deserted. "He has not yet arrived," said Melmoth, in a disturbed voice; "Wait there a moment." And Isidora, enfeebled by terror beyond the power of resistance, or even intreaty, saw him depart without an effort to detain him. She felt as if the effort would be hopeless. Left thus alone, she glanced her eyes around, and a faint and watery moon-beam breaking at that moment through the heavy clouds, threw its light on the objects around her. There was a window, but the stained glass of its compartments, broken and discoloured, held rare and precarious place between the fluted shafts of stone. Ivy and moss darkened the fragments of glass, and clung round the clustered pillars. Beneath were the remains of an altar and crucifix, but they seemed like the rude work of the first hands that had ever been employed on such subjects. There was also a marble vessel, that seemed designed to contain holy water, but it was empty, – and there was a stone bench, on which Isidora sunk down in weariness, but without hope of rest. Once or twice she looked up to the window, through which the moon-beams fell, with that instinctive feeling of her former existence, that made companions of the elements and of the beautiful and glorious family of heaven, under whose burning light she had once imagined the moon was her parent, and the stars her kindred. She gazed on the window still, like one who loved the light of nature, and drank health and truth from its beams, till a figure passing slowly but visibly before the pillared shafts, disclosed to her view the face of that ancient servant, whose features she remembered well. He seemed to regard her with a look, first of intent contemplation, – then of compassion, – the figure then passed from before the ruined window, and a faint and wailing cry rung in the ears of Isidora as it disappeared.

'At that moment the moon, that had so faintly lit the chapel, sunk behind a cloud, and every thing was enveloped in darkness so profound, that Isidora did not recognize the figure of Melmoth till her hand was clasped in his, and his voice whispered, "He is here – ready to unite us." The long-protracted terrors of this bridal left her not a breath to utter a word withal, and she leaned on the arm that she felt, not in confidence, but for support. The place, the hour, the objects, all were hid in darkness. She heard a faint rustling as of the approach of another person, – she tried to catch certain words, but she knew not what they were, – she attempted also to speak, but she knew not what she said. All was mist and darkness with her, – she knew not what was muttered, – she felt not that the hand of Melmoth grasped hers, – but she felt that the hand that united them, and clasped their palms within his own, was as *cold as that of death.*'

Chapter Twenty-Five

Τηλε μέιργουοι ψυχαι, ειδοωλα καμονιων.

Homer[43]

'We have now to retrace a short period of our narrative to the night on which Don Francisco di Aliaga, the father of Isidora, "fortuned," as he termed it, to be among the company whose conversation had produced so extraordinary an effect on him.

'He was journeying homewards, full of the contemplation of his wealth, – the certainty of having attained complete security against the evils that harass life, – and being able to set at defiance all external causes of infelicity. He felt like a man "at ease in his possessions", and he felt also a grave and placid satisfaction at the thought of meeting a family who looked up to him with profound respect as the author of their fortunes, – of walking in his own house, amid bowing domestics and obsequious relatives, with the same slow authoritative step with which he paced that mart among wealthy merchants, and saw the wealthiest bow as he approached, – and when he had passed, point out the man of whose grave salute they were proud, and whisper, That is Aliaga the rich. – So thinking and feeling, as most prosperous men do, with an honest pride in their worldly success, – an exaggerated expectation of the homage of society, – (which they often find frustrated by its contempt), – and an ultimate reliance on the respect and devotion of their family whom they have enriched, making them ample amends for the slights they may be exposed to where their wealth is unknown, and their newly assumed consequence unappreciated, – or if appreciated, not valued: – So thinking and feeling, Don Francisco journeyed homeward.

'At a wretched inn where he was compelled to halt, he found the accommodation so bad, and the heat of the weather so intolerable in the low, narrow, and unwindowed rooms, that he preferred taking his supper in the open air, on a stone bench at the door of the inn. We cannot say that he there imagined himself to be feasted with trout and white bread, like Don Quixote, – and still less that he fancied he was ministered unto by damsels of rank; – on the contrary, Don Francisco was digesting a sorry meal with wretched wine, with a perfect internal consciousness of the mediocrity of both, when he beheld a person ride by, who paused, and looked as if he was inclined to stop at the inn. (The interval of this pause was not long enough to permit Don Francisco to observe particularly the figure or face of the horseman, or indeed to recognize him on any future occasion of meeting; nor was there any thing remarkable in his appearance to invite or arrest observation.) He made a sign to the host, who approached him with a slow and unwilling pace, – appeared to answer all his inquiries with sturdy negatives, – and finally, as the stranger rode on, returned to his station, crossing himself with every mark of terror and deprecation.

'There was something more in this than the ordinary surliness of a Spanish innkeeper. Don Francisco's curiosity was excited, and he asked the innkeeper, whether the stranger had proposed to pass the night at the inn, as the weather seemed to threaten a storm? "I know not what he proposes," answered the man, "but this I know, that I would not suffer him to pass an hour under my roof for the revenues of Toledo. If there be a storm coming on, I care not – those who can raise them are the fittest to meet them!"

'Don Francisco inquired the cause of these extraordinary expressions of aversion and terror, but the innkeeper shook his head and remained silent, with, as it were, the circumspective fear of one who is inclosed within the sorcerer's circle, and dreads to pass its verge, lest he become the prey of the spirits who are waiting beyond it to take advantage of his transgression.

'At last, at Don Francisco's repeated instances, he said, "Your worship must needs be a stranger in this part of Spain not to have heard of Melmoth the wanderer." – "I have never heard of the name before," said Don Francisco; "and I conjure you, brother, to tell me what you know of this person, whose character, if I may judge by the manner in which you speak of him, must have in it something extraordinary." – "Senhor," answered the man, "were I to relate what is told of that person, I should not be able to close an eye to-night; or if I did, it would be to dream of things so horrible, that I had rather lie awake for ever. But, if I am not mistaken, there is in the house one who can gratify your curiosity – it is a gentleman who is preparing for the press a collection of facts relative to that person, and who has been, for some time, in vain soliciting for a license to print them, they being such as the government, in its wisdom, thinks not fit to be perused by the eyes of Catholics, or circulated among a Christian community."

'As the innkeeper spoke, and spoke with an earnestness that at least made the hearer believe he felt the conviction he tried to impress, the person of whom he spoke was standing beside Don Francisco. He had apparently overheard their conversation, and seemed not indisposed to continue it. He was a man of a grave and composed aspect, and altogether so remote from any appearance of imposition, or theatrical and conjuror-like display, that Don Francisco, grave, suspicious and deliberate as a Spaniard, and moreover a Spanish merchant, may be, could not avoid giving him his confidence at sight, though he forbore any external expression of it.

"Senhor," said the stranger, "mine host has told you but the truth. The person whom you saw ride by, is one of those beings after whom human curiosity pants in vain, – whose life is doomed to be recorded in incredible legends that moulder in the libraries of the curious, and to be disbelieved and scorned even by those who exhaust sums on their collection, and ungratefully depreciate the contents of the volumes on whose aggregate its value depends. There has been, however, I believe, no other instance of a person still alive, and apparently exercising all the functions of a human agent, who has become already the subject of written memoirs, and the theme of traditional history. Several circumstances relating to this extraordinary being are even now in the hands of curious and eager collectors; and I have myself attained to the knowledge of one or two that are not among the least extraordinary. The marvellous period of life said to be assigned him, and the facility with which he has been observed to pass from region to region, (knowing all, and known to none), have been the principal causes why the adventures in which he is engaged, should be at once so numerous and so similar."

'As the stranger ceased to speak, the evening grew dark, and a few large and heavy drops of rain fell. "This night threatens a storm," said the stranger, looking abroad with some degree of anxiety – "we had better retire within doors; and if you, Senhor, are not otherwise occupied, I am willing to pass away some hours of this unpleasant night in relating to you some circumstances relating to the wanderer, which have come within my certain knowledge."

'Don Francisco assented to this proposal as much from curiosity, as from the impatience of solitude, which is never more insupportable than in an inn, and during stormy weather. Don Montilla, too, had left him on a visit to his father, who was in a declining state, and was not to join him again till his arrival in the neighbourhood of Madrid. He therefore bid his servants shew the way to his apartment, whither he courteously invited his new acquaintance.

'Imagine them now seated in the wretched upper apartment of a Spanish inn, whose appearance, though dreary and comfortless, had in it, nevertheless, something picturesque, and not inappropriate, as the scene where a wild and wondrous tale was to be related and listened to. There was no luxury of inventive art to flatter the senses, or enervate the attention, – to enable the hearer to break the spell that binds him to the world of horrors, and recover to all the soothing realities and comforts of ordinary life, like one who starts from a dream of the rack, and finds himself waking on a bed of down. The walls were bare, and the roofs were raftered, and the only furniture was a table, beside which Don Francisco and his companion sat, the one on a huge high-backed chair, the other on a stool so low, that he seemed seated at the listener's foot. A lamp stood on the table, whose light flickering in the wind, that sighed through many apertures of the jarring door, fell alternately on lips that quivered as they read, and cheeks that grew paler as the listener bent to catch the sounds to which fear gave a more broken and hollow tone, at the close of every page. The rising voice of the stormy night seemed to make wild and dreary harmony with the tones of the listener's feelings. The storm came on, not with sudden violence, but with sullen and long-suspended wrath – often receding, as it were, to the verge of the horizon, and then returning and rolling its deepening and awful peals over the very roof. And as the stranger proceeded in his narrative, every pause, which emotion or weariness might cause, was meetly filled by the deep rushing of the rain that fell in torrents, – the sighs of the wind, – and now and then a faint, distant, but long-continued peal of thunder. "It sounds," said the stranger, raising his eyes from the manuscript, "like the chidings of the spirits, that their secrets are disclosed!" '

Chapter Twenty-Six

– And the twain were playing dice.

*

The game is done, I've won, I've won,
Quoth she, and whistled thrice.

Coleridge – *Rhyme of the Ancient Mariner*

The Tale of Guzman's Family

' "Of what I am about to read to you," said the stranger, "I have witnessed part myself, and the remainder is established on a basis as strong as human evidence can make it.

' "In the city of Seville, where I lived many years, I knew a wealthy merchant, far advanced in years, who was known by the name of Guzman the rich. He was of obscure birth, – and those who honoured his wealth sufficiently to borrow from him frequently, never honoured his name so far as to prefix Don to it, or to add his surname, of which, indeed, most were ignorant, and among the number, it is said, the wealthy merchant himself. He was well respected, however; and when Guzman was seen, as regularly as the bell tolled for vespers, to issue from the narrow door of his house, – lock it carefully, – view it twice or thrice with a wistful eye, – then deposit the key in his bosom, and move slowly to church, feeling for the key in his vest the whole way, – the proudest heads in Seville were uncovered as he passed, – and the children who were playing in the streets, desisted from their sports till he had halted by them.

' "Guzman had neither wife or child, – relative or friend. An old female domestic constituted his whole household, and his personal expences were calculated on a scale of the most pinching frugality; it was therefore matter of anxious conjecture to many, how his enormous wealth would be bestowed after his death. This anxiety gave rise to inquiries about the possibility of Guzman having relatives, though in remoteness and obscurity; and the diligence of inquiry, when stimulated at once by avarice and curiosity, is indefatigable. Thus it was at length discovered that Guzman had formerly a sister, many years younger than himself, who, at a very early age, had married a German musician, a Protestant, and had shortly after quitted Spain. It was remembered, or reported, that she had made many efforts to soften the heart and open the hand of her brother, who was even then very wealthy, and to induce him to be reconciled to their union, and to enable her and her husband to remain in Spain. Guzman was inflexible. Wealthy, and proud of his wealth as he was, he might have digested the unpalatable morsel of her union with a poor man, whom he could have made rich; but he could not even swallow the intelligence that she had married a Protestant. Ines, for that was her name, and her husband, went to Germany, partly in dependence on his musical talents, which were highly appreciated in that country, – partly in the vague hope of emigrants, that change of place will be attended with change of circumstances, – and partly, also, from the feeling, that misfortune is better tolerated any where than in the presence of those who inflict it. Such was the tale told by the old, who affected to remember the facts, – and believed by the young, whose imagination supplied all the defects of memory, and pictured to them an interesting beauty, with her children hanging about her, embarking, with a heretic husband, for a distant country, and sadly bidding farewell to the land and the religion of her fathers.

'"Now, while these things were talked of at Seville, Guzman fell sick, and was given over by the physicians, whom with considerable reluctance he had suffered to be called in.

' "In the progress of his illness, whether nature revisited a heart she long appeared to have deserted, – or whether he conceived that the hand of a relative might be a more grateful support to his dying head than that of a rapacious and mercenary menial, – or whether his resentful feelings burnt faintly at the expected approach of death, as artificial fires wax dim at the appearance of morning; – so it was, that Guzman in his illness bethought himself of his sister and her family – sent off, at a considerable expense, an express to that part of Germany where she resided, to invite her to return and be reconciled to him, – and prayed devoutly that he might be permitted to survive till he could breathe his last amid the arms of her and her children. Moreover, there was a report at this time, in which the hearers probably took more interest than in any thing that related merely to the life or death of Guzman, – and this was, that he had rescinded his former will, and sent for a notary, with whom, in spite of his apparent debility, he remained locked up for some hours, dictating in a tone which, however clear to the notary, did not leave one distinct impression of sound on the ears that were strained, even to an agony of listening, at the double-locked door of his chamber.

' "All Guzman's friends had endeavoured to dissuade him from making this exertion, which, they assured him, would only hasten his dissolution. But to their surprise, and doubtless their delight, from the moment his will was made, Guzman's health began to amend, – and in less than a week he began to walk about his chamber, and calculate what time it might take an express to reach Germany, and how soon he might expect intelligence from his family.

' "Some months had passed away, and the priests took advantage of the interval to get about Guzman. But after exhausting every effort of ingenuity, – after plying him powerfully but unavailingly on the side of conscience, of duty, of fear and of religion, – they began to understand their interest, and change their battery. And finding that the settled purpose of Guzman's soul was not to be changed, and that he was determined on recalling his sister and her family to Spain, they contented themselves with requiring that he should have no communication with the heretic family, except through them, – and never see his sister or her children unless they were witnesses to the interview.

' "This condition was easily complied with, for Guzman felt no decided inclination for seeing his sister, whose presence might have reminded him of feelings alienated, and duties forgot. Besides, he was a man of fixed habits; and the presence of the most interesting being on earth, that threatened the slightest interruption or suspension of those habits, would have been to him insupportable.

' "Thus we are all indurated by age and habit, – and feel ultimately, that the dearest connections of nature or passion may be sacrificed to those petty indulgences which the presence or influence of a stranger may disturb. So Guzman compromised between his conscience and his feelings. He determined, in spite of all the priests in Seville, to invite his sister and her family to Spain, and to leave the mass of his immense fortune to them; (and to that effect he wrote, and wrote repeatedly and explicitly). But, on the other hand, he promised and swore to his spiritual counsellors, that he never would see one individual of the family; and that, though his sister might inherit his fortune, she never – never should see his face. The priests were satisfied, or appeared to be so, with this declaration; and Guzman, having propitiated them with ample offerings to the shrines of various saints, to each of whom his recovery was exclusively attributed, sat down to calculate the probable expence of his sister's return to Spain, and the necessity of providing for her family, whom he had, as it were, rooted from their native bed; and therefore felt bound, in all honesty, to make them flourish in the soil into which he had transplanted them.

' "Within the year, his sister, her husband, and four children, returned to Spain. Her name was Ines, her husband's was Walberg. He was an industrious man, and an excellent musician. His talents had obtained for him the place of *Maestro di Capella* to the Duke of Saxony; and his children were educated (according to his means) to supply his place when vacated by death or accident, or to employ themselves as musical teachers in the courts of German princes. He and his wife had lived with the utmost frugality, and looked to their children for the means of increasing, by the exercise of their talents, that subsistence which it was their daily labour to provide.

' "The eldest son, who was called Everhard, inherited his father's musical talents. The daughters, Julia and Ines, were musical also, and very skilful in embroidery. The youngest child, Maurice, was by turns the delight and the torment of the family.

' "They had struggled on for many years in difficulties too petty to be made the subject of detail, yet too severe not to be painfully felt by those whose lot is to encounter them every day, and every hour of the day, – when the sudden intelligence, brought by an express from Spain, of their wealthy relative Guzman inviting them to return thither, and proclaiming them heirs to all his vast riches, burst on them like the first dawn of his half-year's summer on the crouching and squalid inmate of a Lapland hut. All trouble was forgot, – all cares postponed, – their few debts paid off, – and their preparations made for an instant departure to Spain.

' "So to Spain they went, and journeyed on to the city of Seville, where, on their arrival, they were waited on by a grave ecclesiastic, who acquainted them with Guzman's resolution of never seeing his offending sister or her family, while at the same time he assured them of his intention of supporting and supplying them with every comfort, till his decease put them in possession of his wealth. The family were somewhat disturbed at this intelligence, and the mother wept at being denied the sight of her brother, for whom she still cherished the affection of memory; while the priest, by way of softening the discharge of his commission, dropt some words of a change of their heretical opinions being most likely to open a channel of communication between them and their relative. The silence with which this hint was received spoke more than many words, and the priest departed.

' "This was the first cloud that had intercepted their view of felicity since the express arrived in Germany, and they sat gloomily enough under its shadow for the remainder of the evening. Walberg, in the confidence of expected wealth, had not only brought over his children to Spain, but had written to his father and mother, who were very old, and wretchedly poor, to join him in Seville; and by the sale of his house and furniture, had been enabled to remit them money for the heavy expences of so long a journey. They were now hourly expected, and the children, who had a faint but grateful recollection of the blessing bestowed on their infant heads by quivering lips and withered hands, looked out with joy for the arrival of the ancient pair. Ines had often said to her husband, 'Would it not be better to let your father and mother remain in Germany, and remit them money for their support, than put them to the fatigue of so long a journey at their far advanced age?' – And he had always answered, 'Let them rather die under my roof, than live under that of strangers.'

' "This night he perhaps began to feel the prudence of his wife's advice; – she saw it, and with cautious gentleness forbore, for that very reason, to remind him of it.

' "The weather was gloomy and cold that evening, – it was unlike a night in Spain. Its chill appeared to extend to the party. Ines sat and worked in silence – the children, collected at the window, communicated in whispers their hopes and conjectures about the arrival of the aged travellers, and Walberg, who was restlessly traversing the room, sometimes sighed as he overheard them.

' "The next day was sunny and cloudless. The priest again called on them, and, after regretting that Guzman's resolution was inflexible, informed them, that he was directed to pay them an annual sum for their support, which he named, and which appeared to them enormous; and to appropriate another for the education of the children, which seemed to be calculated on a scale of princely munificence. He put deeds, properly drawn and attested for this purpose, into their hands, and then withdrew, after repeating the assurance, that they would be the undoubted heirs of Guzman's wealth at his decease, and that, as the interval would be passed in affluence, it might well be passed without repining. The priest had scarcely retired, when the aged parents of Walberg arrived, feeble from joy and fatigue, but not exhausted, and the whole family sat down to a meal that appeared to them luxurious, in that placid contemplation of future felicity, which is often more exquisite than its actual enjoyment.

' "I saw them," said the stranger, interrupting himself, – "I saw them on the evening of that day of union, and a painter, who wished to embody the image of domestic felicity in a group of living figures, need have gone no further than the mansion of Walberg. He and his wife were seated at the head of the table, smiling on their children, and seeing them smile in return, without the intervention of one anxious thought, – one present harassing of petty difficulty, or heavy presage of future mischance, – *one fear of the morrow,* or aching remembrance of the past. Their children formed indeed a groupe on which the eye of painter or of parent, the gaze of taste or of affection, might have hung with equal delight. Everhard their eldest son, now sixteen, possessed too much beauty for his sex, and his delicate and brilliant complexion, his slender and exquisitely moulded form, and the modulation of his tender and tremulous voice, inspired that mingled interest, with which we watch, in youth, over the strife of present debility with the promise of future strength, and infused into his parents' hearts that fond anxiety with which we mark the progress of a mild but cloudy morning in spring, rejoicing in the mild and balmy glories of its dawn, but fearing lest clouds may overshade them before noon. The daughters, Ines

and Julia, had all the loveliness of their colder climate – the luxuriant ringlets of golden hair, the large bright blue eyes, the
snow-like whiteness of their bosoms, and slender arms, and the
rose-leaf tint and peachiness of their delicate cheeks, made them,
as they attended their parents with graceful and fond officiousness, resemble two young Hebes ministering cups, which their
touch alone was enough to turn into nectar.

‘ "The spirits of these young persons had been early depressed
by the difficulties in which their parents were involved; and even
in childhood they had acquired the timid tread, the whispered
tone, the anxious and inquiring look, that the constant sense of
domestic distress painfully teaches even to children, and which it
is the most exquisite pain to a parent to witness. But now there
was nothing to restrain their young hearts, – that stranger, a
smile, fled back rejoicing to the lovely home of their lips, – and
the timidity of their former habits only lent a grateful shade to
the brilliant exuberance of youthful happiness. Just opposite this
picture, whose hues were so bright, and whose shades were so
tender, were seated the figures of the aged grandfather and
grandmother. The contrast was very strong; there was no connecting link, no graduated medium, – you passed at once from
the first and fairest flowers of spring, to the withered and rootless
barrenness of winter.

‘ "These very aged persons, however, had something in their
looks to soothe the eye, and Teniers or Wouverman would perhaps have valued their figures and costume far beyond those of
their young and lovely grandchildren. They were stiffly and
quaintly habited in their German garb – the old man in his dou-
blet and cap, and the old woman in her ruff, stomacher and
head-gear resembling a skull-cap, with long depending pinners,
through which a few white, but very long hairs, appeared on her
wrinkled cheeks; but on the countenances of both there was a
gleam of joy, like the cold smile of a setting sun on a wintry landscape. They did not distinctly hear the kind importunities of their

son and daughter, to partake more amply of the most plentiful meal they had ever witnessed in their frugal lives, – but they bowed and smiled with that thankfulness which is at once wounding and grateful to the hearts of affectionate children. They smiled also at the beauty of Everhard and their elder grandchildren, – at the wild pranks of Maurice, who was as wild in the hour of trouble as in the hour of prosperity; – and finally, they smiled at all that was said, though they did not hear half of it, and at all they saw, though they could enjoy very little – and that *smile of age,* that placid submission to the pleasures of the young, mingled with undoubted anticipations of a more pure and perfect felicity, gave an almost heavenly expression to features, that would otherwise have borne only the withering look of debility and decay.

' "Some circumstances occurred during this family feast, which were sufficiently characteristic of the partakers. Walberg (himself a very temperate man) pressed his father repeatedly to take more wine than he was accustomed to, – the old man gently declined it. The son still pressed it heartfully, and the old man complied with a wish to gratify his son, not himself.

' "The younger children, too, caressed their grandmother with the boisterous fondness of children. Their mother reproached them. – 'Nay, let be,' said the gentle old woman. 'They trouble you, mother,' said the wife of Walberg. – 'They cannot trouble me long,' said the grandmother, with an emphatic smile. 'Father,' said Walberg, 'is not Everhard grown very tall?' – 'The last time I saw him,' said the grandfather, 'I stooped to kiss him; now I think he must stoop to kiss me.' And, at the word, Everhard darted like an arrow into the trembling arms that were opened to receive him, and his red and hairless lips were pressed to the snowy beard of his grandfather. 'Cling there, my child,' said the exulting father. – 'God grant your kiss may never be applied to lips less pure.' – 'They never shall, my father!' said the susceptible boy, blushing at his own emotions – 'I never wish to press any lips but those that will bless me like those of my grandfather.' – 'And do you wish,' said the old man jocularly, 'that the blessing should *always* issue from lips as rough and hoary as mine?' Everhard stood blushing behind the old man's chair at this question, and Walberg, who heard the clock strike the hour at which he had been always accustomed, in prosperity or adversity, to summon his family to prayer, made a signal which his children well understood, and which was communicated in whispers to their aged relatives. – 'Thank God,' said the aged grandmother to the young whisperer, and as she spoke, she sunk on her knees. Her grandchildren assisted her. 'Thank God,' echoed the old man, bending his stiffened knees, and doffing his cap – 'Thank God for this "shadow of a great rock in a weary land!"' – and he knelt, while Walberg, after reading a chapter or two from a German Bible which he held in his hands, pronounced an extempore prayer, imploring God to fill their hearts with gratitude for the temporal blessings they enjoyed, and to enable them 'so to pass through things temporal, that they might not finally lose the things eternal.' At the close of the prayer, the family rose and saluted each other with that affection which has not its root in earth, and whose blossoms, however diminutive and colourless to the eye of man in this wretched soil, shall yet bear glorious fruit in the garden of God. It was a lovely sight to behold the young people assisting their aged relatives to arise from their knees, – and it was a lovelier hearing, to listen to the happy good-nights exchanged among the parting family. The wife of Walberg was most assiduous in preparing the comforts of her husband's parents, and Walberg yielded to her with that proud gratitude, that feels more exaltation in a benefit conferred by those we love, than if we conferred it ourselves. He loved his parents, but he was proud of his wife loving them because they were his. To the repeated offers of his children to assist or attend their ancient relatives, he answered, 'No, dear children, your mother will do better, – your mother always does best.' As he spoke, his children, according to a custom now forgot, kneeled before him to ask his blessing. His hand, tremulous with affection, rested first on the curling locks of the darling Everhard, whose head towered proudly above those of his kneeling sisters, and of Maurice, who, with the irrepressible and venial levity of joyous childhood, laughed as he knelt. 'God bless you!' said Walberg – 'God bless you all, – and may he make you as good as your mother, and as happy as – your father is this night;' and as he spoke, the happy father turned aside and wept." '

Chapter Twenty-Seven

– Quæque ipsa miserrima vidi,
Et quorum pars magna fui.

Virgil[44]

' "The wife of Walberg, who was naturally of a cool sedate temper, and to whom misfortune had taught an anxious and jealous prevoyance, was not so intoxicated with the present prosperity of the family, as its young, or even its aged members. Her mind was full of thoughts which she would not communicate to her husband, and sometimes did not wish to acknowledge to herself; but to the priest, who visited them frequently with renewed marks of Guzman's bounty, she spoke explicitly. She said, that however grateful for her brother's kindness, for the enjoyment of present competence, and the hope of future wealth, she wished that her children might be permitted to acquire the means of independent subsistence for themselves, and that the money destined by Guzman's liberality for their ornamental education, might be applied to the purpose of ensuring them the power of supporting themselves, and assisting their parents. She alluded slightly to the possible future change in her brother's favourable feelings towards her, and dwelt much on the circumstance of her children being strangers in the country, wholly unacquainted with its language, and averse from its religion; and she mildly but strongly stated the difficulties to which a heretic family of strangers might be exposed in a Catholic country, and implored the priest to employ his mediation and influence with her brother, that her children might be enabled, through his bounty, to acquire the means of independent subsistence, as if—and she paused. The good and friendly priest (for he was truly both) listened to her with attention; and after satisfying his conscience, by adjuring her to renounce her heretical opinions, as the only means of obtaining a reconciliation with God and her brother, and receiving a calm, but firm negative, proceeded to give her his best LAY advice, which was to comply with her brother's wishes in every thing, to educate her children in the manner which he prescribed, and to the full extent of the means which he so amply furnished. He added, *en confiance,* that Guzman, though, during his long life, he had never been suspected of any passion but that of accumulating money, was now possessed with a spirit much harder to expel, and was resolved that the heirs of his wealth should be, in point of all that might embellish polished society, on a level with the descendants of the first nobility of Spain. Finally, he counselled submission to her brother's wishes in all things, – and the wife of Walberg complied with tears, which she tried to conceal from the priest, and had completely effaced the traces of before she again met her husband.

' "In the mean time, the plan of Guzman was rapidly realized. A handsome house was taken for Walberg, – his sons and daughters were splendidly arrayed, and sumptuously lodged; and, though education was, and still is, on a very low level in Spain, they were taught all that was then supposed to qualify them as companions for the descendants of Hidalgoes. Any attempt, or even allusion to their being prepared for the ordinary occupations of life, was strictly forbidden by the orders of Guzman. The father triumphed in this, – the mother regretted it, but she kept her regret to herself, and consoled herself with thinking, that the ornamental education her children were receiving might ultimately be turned to account; for the wife of Walberg was a woman whom the experience of misfortune had taught to look to the future with an anxious eye, and that eye, with ominous accuracy, had seldom failed to detect a speck of evil in the brightest beam of sun-shine that had ever trembled on her chequered existence.

' "The injunctions of Guzman were obeyed, – the family lived in luxury. The young people plunged into their new life of enjoyment with an avidity proportioned to their youthful sensibility of pleasure, and to a taste for refinement and elegant pursuits, which their former obscurity had repressed, but never extinguished. The proud and happy father exulted in the personal beauty, and improving talents of his children. The anxious mother sighed sometimes, but took care the sigh should never reach her husband's ear. The aged grandfather and grandmother, whose infirmities had been much increased by their journey to Spain, and possibly still more by that strong emotion which is a habit to youth, but a convulsion to age, sat in their ample chairs comfortably idle, dozing away life in intervals of unuttered though conscious satisfaction, and calm but venerable apathy; – they slept much, but when they awoke, they smiled at their grandchildren, and at each other.

' "The wife of Walberg, during this interval, which seemed one of undisturbed felicity to all but her, sometimes suggested a gentle caution, – a doubtful and anxious hint, – a possibility of future disappointment, but this was soon smiled away by the rosy, and laughing, and kissful lips of her children, till the mother at last began to smile at her apprehensions herself. At times, however, she led them anxiously in the direction of their uncle's house. She walked up and down the street before his door with her children, and sometimes lifted up her veil, as if to try whether her eye could pierce through walls as hard as the miser's heart, or windows barred like his coffers, – then glancing on her children's costly dress, while her eye darted far into futurity, she sighed and returned slowly home. This state of suspense was soon to be terminated.

' "The priest, Guzman's confessor, visited them often; first in quality of almoner or agent of his bounty, which was amply and punctually bestowed through his hands; and secondly, in quality of a professed chess-player, at which game he had met, even in Spain, no antagonist like Walberg. He also felt an interest in the family and their fortunes, which, though his orthodoxy disowned, his heart could not forbear to acknowledge, – so the good priest compromised matters by playing chess with the father, and praying for the conversion of his family on his return to Guzman's house. It was while engaged in the former exercise, that a message arrived to summon him on the instant home, – the priest left his queen *en prise*, and hurried into the passage to speak with the messenger. The family of Walberg, with agitation unspeakable, half rose to follow him. They paused at the door, and then retreated with a mixed feeling of anxiety for the intelligence, and shame at the attitude in which they might be discovered. As they retreated, however, they could not help hearing the words of the messenger, – 'He is at his last gasp, – he has sent for you, – you must not lose a moment.' As the messenger spoke, the priest and he departed.

' "The family returned to their apartment, and for some hours sat in profound silence, interrupted only by the ticking of the clock, which was distinctly and solely heard, and which seemed too loud to their quickened ears, amid that deep stillness on which it broke incessantly, – or by the echoes of Walberg's hurried step, as he started from his chair and traversed the apartment. At this sound they turned, as if expecting a messenger, then, glancing at the silent figure of Walberg, sunk on their seats again. The family sat up all that long night of unuttered, and indeed unutterable emotion. The lights burnt low, and were at length extinguished, but no one noticed them; – the pale light of the dawn broke feebly into the room, but no one observed it was morning. 'God! – how long he lingers!' exclaimed Walberg involuntarily; and these words, though uttered under his breath, made all the listeners start, as at the first sounds of a human voice, which they had not heard for many hours.

' "At this moment a knock was heard at the door, – a step trod slowly along the passage that led to the room, – the door opened, and the priest appeared. He advanced into the room without speaking, or being spoken to. And the contrast of strong emotion and unbroken silence, – this conflict of speech that strangled thought in the utterance, and of thought that in vain asked aid of speech, – the agony and the muteness, – formed a terrible momentary association. It was but momentary, – the priest, as he stood, uttered the words – 'All is over!' Walberg clasped his hands over his forehead, and in ecstatic agony exclaimed, – 'Thank God!' and wildly catching at the object nearest him, as if imagining it one of his children, he clasped and hugged it to his breast. His wife wept for a moment at the thought of her brother's death, but roused herself for her children's sake to hear all that was to be told. The priest could tell no more but that Guzman was dead, – seals had been put on every chest, drawer and coffer in the house, – not a cabinet had escaped the diligence of the persons employed, and the will was to be read the following day.

' "For the following day the family remained in that intensity of expectation that precluded all thought. The servants prepared the usual meal, but it remained untasted. The family pressed each other to partake of it; but as the importunity was not enforced by the inviter setting any example of the lesson he tried to teach, the meal remained untasted. About noon a grave person, in the habit of a notary, was announced, and summoned Walberg to be present at the opening of Guzman's will. As Walberg prepared to obey the summons, one of his children officiously offered him his hat, another his cloke, both of which he had forgot in the trepidation of his anxiety; and these instances of reminiscence and attention in his children, contrasted with his own abstraction, completely overcame him, and he sunk down on a seat to recover himself. 'You had better not go, my love,' said his wife mildly. 'I believe I shall – I *must* take your advice,' said Walberg, relapsing on the seat from which he had half risen. The notary, with a formal bow, was retiring. 'I *will* go!' said Walberg, swearing a German oath, whose guttural sound made the notary start, – 'I *will* go!' and as he spoke he fell on the floor, exhausted by fatigue and want of refreshment, and emotion indescribable but to a father. The notary retired, and a few hours more were exhausted in torturing conjecture, expressed on the mother's part only by clasped hands and smothered sighs, – on the father's by profound silence, averted countenance, and hands that seemed to feel for those of his children, and then shrink from the touch, – and on the children's by rapidly varying auguries of hope and of disappointment. The aged pair sat motionless among their family; – they knew not what was going on, but they knew if it was good they must partake of it, – and in the perception or expectation of the approach of evil, their faculties had latterly become very obtuse.

' "The day was far advanced, – it was noon. The servants, with whom the munificence of the deceased had amply supplied their establishment, announced that dinner was prepared; and Ines, who retained more presence of mind than the rest, gently suggested to her husband the necessity of not betraying their emotions to their servants. He obeyed her hint mechanically, and walked into the dining-hall, forgetting for the first time to offer his arm to his infirm father. His family followed, but, when seated at the table, they seemed not to know for what purpose they were collected there. Walberg, consumed by that *thirst of anxiety* which nothing seems sufficient to quench, called repeatedly for wine; and his wife, who found even the attempt to eat impossible in the presence of the gazing and unmoved attendants, dismissed them by a signal, but did not feel the desire of food restored by their absence. The old couple eat as usual, and sometimes looked up with an expression of vague and vacant wonder, and a kind of sluggish reluctance to admit the fear or belief of approaching calamity. Towards the end of their cheerless meal, Walberg was called out; he returned in a few minutes, and there was no appearance of change in his countenance. He seated himself, and only his wife perceived the traces of a wild smile stealing over the trembling lines of his face, as he filled a large glass of wine, and raised it to his lips, pronouncing – 'A health to the heirs of Guzman.' But instead of drinking the wine, he dashed the glass to the floor, and burying his head in the drapery of the table on which he flung himself, he exclaimed, 'Not a ducat, – not a ducat, – all left to the church! – Not a ducat!'

*

' "In the evening the priest called, and found the family much more composed. The certainty of evil had given them a kind of courage. Suspence is the only evil against which it is impossible to set up a defence, – and, like young mariners in an untried sea, they almost felt ready to welcome the storm, as a relief from the deadly and loathsome sickness of anxiety. The honest resentment, and encouraging manner of the priest, were a cordial to their ears and hearts. He declared his belief, that nothing but the foulest means that might be resorted to by interested and bigotted monks, could have extorted such a will from the dying man, – his readiness to attest, in every court in Spain, the intentions of the testator (till within a few hours of his death) to have bequeathed his whole fortune to his family – intentions which he had repeatedly expressed to him and others, and to whose effect he had seen a former will of no long date, – and, finally, gave his strenuous advice to Walberg to bring the matter to legal arbitration, in aid of which he promised his personal exertions, his influence with the ablest advocates in Seville, and every thing – but money.

' "The family that night went to bed with spirits exalted by hope, and slept in peace. One circumstance alone marked a change in their feelings and habits. As they were retiring, the old man laid his tremulous hand on the shoulder of Walberg, and said mildly, 'My son, shall we pray before we retire?' – 'Not to-night, father,' said Walberg, who perhaps feared the mention of their heretical worship might alienate the friendly priest, or who felt the agitation of his heart too great for the solemn exercise; 'Not to-night, I am – too happy!'

' "The priest was as good as his word, – the ablest advocates in Seville undertook the cause of Walberg. Proofs of undue influence, of imposition, and of terror being exercised on the mind of the testator, were ingeniously made out by the diligence and spiritual authority of the priest, and skilfully arranged and ably pleaded by the advocates. Walberg's spirits rose with every hour. The family, at the time of Guzman's death, were in possession of a considerable sum of money, but this was soon expended, together with another sum which the frugality of Ines had enabled her to save, and which she now cheerfully produced in aid of her husband's exigencies, and in confidence of eventual success. When all was gone, other resources still remained, – the spacious house was disposed of, the servants dismissed, the furniture sold (as usual) for about a fourth of its value, and, in their new and humble abode in the suburbs of Seville, Ines and her daughters contentedly resumed those domestic duties which they had been in the habit of performing in their quiet home in Germany. Amid these changes, the grandfather and grandmother experienced none but mere change of place, of which they hardly appeared conscious. The assiduous attention of Ines to their comforts was increased, not diminished, by the necessity of being herself the sole ministrant to them; and smiling she pleaded want of appetite, or trifling indisposition, as an excuse for her own and her children's meal, while theirs was composed of every thing that could tempt the tasteless palate of age, or that she remembered was acceptable to theirs.

' "The cause had now come to a hearing, and for the two first days the advocates of Walberg carried all before them. On the third the ecclesiastical advocates made a firm and vigorous stand. Walberg returned much dispirited; – his wife saw it, and therefore assumed no airs of cheerfulness, which only increase the irritation of misfortune, but she was equable, and steadily and tranquilly occupied in domestic business the whole evening in his sight. As they were separating for the night, by a singular contingency, the old man again reminded his son of the forgotten hour of family prayer. 'Not to-night, father,' said Walberg impatiently; 'not to-night; I am – too unhappy!' – 'Thus,' said the old man, lifting up his withered hands, and speaking with an energy he had not showed for years, – 'thus, O my God! Prosperity and adversity alike furnish us with excuses for neglecting thee!' As he tottered from the room, Walberg declined his head on the bosom of his wife, who sat beside him, and shed a few bitter tears. And Ines whispered to herself, 'The sacrifice of God is a troubled spirit, – a broken heart he will not despise.'

*

' "The cause had been carried on with a spirit and expedition that had no precedent in the courts of Spain, and the fourth day was fixed on for a final hearing and termination of the cause. The day dawned, and at the dawn of day Walberg arose, and walked for some hours before the gates of the hall of justice; and when they were opened, he entered, and sat down mechanically on a seat in the vacant hall, with the same look of profound attention, and anxious interest, that he would have assumed had the court been seated, and the cause about to be decided. After a few moments' pause, he sighed, started and appearing to awake from a dream, quitted his seat, and walked up and down the empty passages till the court was prepared to sit.

' "The court met early that day, and the cause was powerfully advocated. Walberg sat on one seat, without ever changing his place, till all was over; and it was then late in the evening, and he had taken no refreshment the entire day, and he had never changed his place, and he had never changed the close and corrupted atmosphere of the crowded court for a moment. *Quid multis morer?*[45] The chance of a heretic stranger, against the interests of churchmen in Spain, may be calculated by the most shallow capacity.

' "The family had all that day sat in the innermost room of their humble dwelling. Everhard had wished to accompany his father to the court, – his mother withheld him. The sisters involuntarily dropt their work from time to time, and their mother gently reminded them of the necessity of renewing it. They did resume it, but their hands, at variance with their feelings, made such blunders, that their mother, δακρυοεν γελασασα,[46] removed their work, and suggested to them some active employment in household affairs. While they were thus engaged, evening came on, – the family from time to time suspended their ordinary occupations, and crowded to the window to watch the return of their father. Their mother no longer interfered, – she sat in silence, and this silence formed a strong contrast to the restless impatience of her children. 'That is my father,' exclaimed the voices of the four at once, as a figure crossed the street. 'That is not my father,' they repeated, as the figure slowly retired. A knock was heard at the door, – Ines herself rushed forward to open it. A figure retreated, advanced again, and again retreated. Then it seemed to rush past her, and enter the house like a shadow. In terror she followed it, and with terror unutterable saw her husband kneeling among his children, who in vain attempted to raise him, while he continued to repeat, 'No, let me kneel, – let me kneel, I have undone you all! The cause is lost, and I have made beggars of you all!' – 'Rise, – rise, dearest father,' cried the children, gathering round him, 'nothing is lost, if you are saved!' – 'Rise, my love, from that horrible and unnatural humiliation,' cried Ines, grasping the arms of her husband; 'help me, my children, – father, – mother, will you not help me?' – and as she spoke, the tottering, helpless and almost lifeless figures of the aged grandfather and grandmother arose from their chairs, and staggering forwards, added their feeble strength, – their *vis impotentiæ,*[47] to sustain or succour the weight that dragged heavily on the arms of the children and their mother. By this sight, more than by any effort, Walberg was raised from the posture that agonized his family, and placed in a chair, around which hung the wife and children, while the aged father and mother, retreating torpidly to their seats, seemed to lose in a few moments the keen consciousness of evil that had inspired them for an instant with a force almost miraculous. Ines and her children hung round Walberg, and uttered all of consolation that helpless affection could suggest; but perhaps there is not a more barbed arrow can be sent through the heart, than by the thought that the hands that clasp ours so fondly cannot earn for us or themselves the means of another meal, – that the lips that are pressed to ours so warmly, may the next ask us for bread, and – ask in vain!

' "It was perhaps fortunate for this unhappy family, that the very extremity of their grief rendered its long indulgence impossible, – the voice of necessity made itself be heard distinctly and loudly amid all the cry and clamour of that hour of agony. Something must be done for the morrow, – and it was to be done immediately. 'What money have you?' was the first articulate sentence Walberg uttered to his wife; and when she whispered the small sum that the expences of their lost cause had left them, he shivered with a brief emphatic spasm of horror, – then bursting from their arms, and rising, he crossed the room, as if he wished to be alone for a moment. As he did so, he saw his youngest child playing with the long strings of his grandfather's band, – a mode of sportive teazing in which the urchin delighted, and which was at once chid and smiled at. Walberg struck the poor child vehemently, and then catching him in his arms, bid him – 'Smile as long as he could!'

*

' "They had means of subsistence at least for the following week; and that was such a source of comfort to them, as it is to men who are quitting a wreck, and drifting on a bare raft with a slender provision towards some coast, which they hope to reach before it is exhausted. They sat up all that night together in earnest counsel, after Ines had taken care to see the father and mother of her husband comfortably placed in their apartment. Amid their long and melancholy conference, hope sprung up insensibly in the hearts of the speakers, and a plan was gradually formed for obtaining the means of subsistence. Walberg was to offer his talents as a musical teacher, – Ines and her daughters were to undertake embroidery, – and Everhard, who possessed exquisite taste both in music and drawing, was to make an effort in both departments, and the friendly priest was to be applied to for his needful interest and recommendation for all. The morning broke on their long-protracted consultation, and found them unwearied in discussing its subject. 'We shall not starve,' said the children hopefully. – 'I trust not,' said Walberg sighingly. – His wife, who knew Spain, said not a word. –"'

Chapter Twenty-Eight

– This to me
In dreadful secrecy they did impart,
And I with them the third night kept the watch.

Shakespeare

' "As they spoke, a soft knock was heard, such as kindness gives at
the door of misfortune, and Everhard started up to answer it.
'Stay,' said Walberg, absently, 'Where are the servants?' Then recollecting himself, he smiled agonizingly, and waved his hand to
his son to go. It was the good priest. He entered, and sat down in
silence, – no one spoke to him. It might be truly said, as it is sub-
limely said in the original, 'There was neither speech nor
language, but voices were heard among them – *and felt too.*' The
worthy priest piqued himself on his orthodoxy of all matters of
belief and form enjoined by the Catholic church; and, moreover,
had acquired a kind of monastic apathy, of sanctified stoicism,
which priests sometimes imagine is the conquest of grace over
the rebellion of nature, when it is merely the result of a profession that denies nature its objects and its ties. Yet so it was, that as
he sat among this afflicted family, after complaining of the keenness of the morning air, and wiping away in vain the moisture,
which he said it had brought into his eyes, he at last yielded to his
feelings, and 'lifted up his voice and wept'. But tears were not all
he had to offer. On hearing the plans of Walberg and his family,
he promised, with a faultering voice, his ready assistance in promoting them; and, as he rose to depart, observing that he had
been entrusted by the faithful with a small sum for the relief of

the unfortunate, and knew not where it could be better bestowed, he dropped from the sleeve of his habit a well filled purse on the floor, and hurried away.

' "The family retired to rest as the day approached, but rose in a few hours afterwards without having slept; and the remainder of that day, and the whole of the three following, were devoted to applications at every door where encouragement might be expected, or employment obtained, the priest in person aiding every application. But there were many circumstances unfavour- able to the ill-starred family of Walberg. They were strangers, and, with the exception of their mother, who acted as interpreter, ignorant of the language of the country. This was 'a sore evil', extending almost to the total preclusion of their exertions as teachers. They were also heretics, – and this alone was a sufficient bar to their success in Seville. In some families the beauty of the daughters, in others that of the son, was gravely debated as an important objection. In others the recollection of their former splendour, suggested a mean and rancorous motive to jealous inferiority to insult them by a rejection, for which no other cause could be assigned. Unwearied and undismayed, they renewed their applications every day, at every house where admission could be obtained, and at many where it was denied; and each day they returned to examine the diminished stock, to divide the scantier meal, calculate how far it was possible to reduce the claims of nature to the level of their ebbing means, and smile when they talked of the morrow to each other, but weep when they thought of it alone. There is a withering monotony in the diary of misery, – 'one day telleth another'. But there came at length a day, when the last coin was expended, the last meal devoured, the last resource exhausted, the last hope annihilated, and the friendly priest himself told them weeping, he had noth- ing to give them but his prayers.

' "That evening the family sat in profound and stupified silence together for some hours, till the aged mother of Walberg, who had not for some months uttered any thing but indistinct mono-syllables, or appeared conscious of any thing that was going on, suddenly, with that ominous energy that announces its effort to be the last, – that bright flash of parting life that precedes its total extinction, exclaimed aloud, apparently addressing her husband, 'There is something wrong here, – why did they bring us from Germany? They might have suffered us to die there, – they have brought us here to mock us, I think. Yesterday, – (her memory evidently confounding the dates of her son's prosperous and adverse fortune), yesterday they clothed me in silk, and I drank wine, and to-day they give me this sorry crust, – (flinging away the piece of bread which had been her share of the miserable meal), – there is something wrong here. I will go back to Ger-many, – I will!' and she rose from her seat in the sight of the astonished family, who, horror-struck, as they would have been at the sudden resuscitation of a corse, ventured not to oppose her by word or movement. 'I will go back to Germany,' she repeated; and, rising, she actually took three or four firm and equal steps on the floor, while no one attempted to approach her. Then her force, both physical and mental, seemed to fail, – she tottered, – her voice sunk into hollow mutterings, as she repeated, 'I know the way, – I know the way, – if it was not so dark. – I have not far to go, – I am very near – *home!*' As she spoke, she fell across the feet of Walberg. The family collected round her, and raised – a corse. 'Thank God!' exclaimed her son, as he gazed on his mother's corse. – And this reversion of the strongest feeling of nature, – this wish for the death of those for whom, in other cir-cumstances, we could ourselves have died, makes those who have experienced it feel as if there was no evil in life but want, and no object of rational pursuit but the means of avoiding it. Alas! if it be so, for what purpose were hearts that beat, and minds that burn, bestowed on us? Is all the energy of intellect, and all the enthusiasm of feeling, to be expended in contrivances how to meet or shift off the petty but torturing pangs of hourly necessity? Is the fire caught from heaven to be employed in lighting a faggot to keep the cold from the numbed and wasted fingers of poverty. Pardon this digression, Senhor,' said the stranger, 'but *I had a painful feeling, that forced me to make it.*' He then proceeded.

' "The family collected around the dead body, – and it might have been a subject worthy the pencil of the first of painters, to witness its interment, as it took place the following night. As the deceased was a heretic, the corse was not allowed to be laid in consecrated ground; and the family, solicitous to avoid giving offence, or attracting notice on the subject of their religion, were the only attendants on the funeral. In a small inclosure, at the rear of their wretched abode, her son dug his mother's grave, and Ines and her daughters placed the body in it. Everhard was absent in search of employment, – as they hoped, – and a light was held by the youngest child, who smiled as he watched the scene, as if it had been a pageant got up for his amusement. That light, feeble as it was, showed the strong and varying expression of the countenances on which it fell; – in Walberg's there was a stern and fearful joy, that she whom they were laying to rest had been 'taken from the evil to come', – in that of Ines there was grief, mingled with something of horror, at this mute and unhallowed ceremony. – Her daughters, pale with grief and fear, wept silently; but their tears were checked, and the whole course of their feelings changed, when the light fell on another figure who appeared suddenly standing among them on the edge of the grave, – it was that of Walberg's father. Impatient of being left alone, and wholly unconscious of the cause, he had groped and tottered his way till he reached the spot; and now, as he saw his son heap up the earth over the grave, he exclaimed, with a brief and feeble effort of reminiscence, sinking on the ground, 'Me, too, – lay me there, the same spot will serve for both!' His children raised and supported him into the house, where the sight of Everhard, with an unexpected supply of provisions, made them forget the horrors of the late scene, and postpone once more the fears of want till to-morrow. No inquiry how this supply was obtained, could extort more from Everhard than that it was the gift of charity. He looked exhausted and dreadfully pale, – and, forbearing to press him with further questions, they partook of this manna-meal, – this food that seemed to have dropped from heaven, and separated for the night.

*

' "Ines had, during this period of calamity, unremittingly enforced the application of her daughters to those accomplishments from which she still derived the hopes of their subsistence. Whatever were the privations and disappointments of the day, their musical and other exercises were strictly attended to; and hands enfeebled by want and grief, plied their task with as much assiduity as when occupation was only a variation of luxury. This attention to the ornaments of life, when its actual necessaries are wanted, – this sound of music in a house where the murmurs of domestic anxiety are heard every moment, – this subservience of talent to necessity, all its generous enthusiasm lost, and only its possible utility remembered or valued, – is perhaps the bitterest strife that ever was fought between the opposing claims of our artificial and our natural existence. But things had now occurred that shook not only the resolution of Ines, but even affected her feelings beyond the power of repression. She had been accustomed to hear, with delight, the eager application of her daughters to their musical studies; – now – when she heard them, the morning after the interment of their grandmother, renewing that application – she felt as if the sounds struck through her heart. She entered the room where they were, and they turned towards her with their usual smiling demand for her approbation.

' "The mother, with the forced smile of a sickening heart, said she believed there was no occasion for their practising any further that day. The daughters, who understood her too well, relinquished their instruments, and, accustomed to see every article of furniture converted into the means of casual subsistence, they thought no worse than that their ghitarras might be disposed of this day, and the next they hoped they would have to teach on those of their pupils. They were mistaken. Other symptoms of failing resolution, – of utter and hopeless abandonment, appeared that day. Walberg had always felt and expressed the strongest feelings of tender respect towards his parents – his father particularly, whose age far exceeded that of his mother. At the division of their meal that day, he shewed a kind of wolfish and greedy jealousy that made Ines tremble. He whispered to her – 'How much my father eats – how heartily he feeds while we have scarce a morsel!' – 'And let us want that morsel, before your father wants one!' said Ines in a whisper – 'I have scarce tasted any thing myself.' – 'Father – father,' cried Walberg, shouting in the ear of the doting old man, 'you are eating heartily, while Ines and her children are starving!' And he snatched the food from his father's hand, who gazed at him vacantly, and resigned the contested morsel without a struggle. A moment afterwards the old man rose from his seat, and with horrid unnatural force, tore the untasted meat from his grandchildren's lips, and swallowed it himself, while his rivelled and toothless mouth grinned at them in mockery at once infantine and malicious.

' "'Squabbling about your supper?' cried Everhard, bursting among them with a wild and feeble laugh, – 'Why, here's enough for to-morrow – and to-morrow.' And he flung indeed ample means for two days' subsistence on the table, but he looked *paler and paler*. The hungry family devoured the hoard, and forgot to ask the cause of his increasing paleness, and obviously diminished strength.

*

' "They had long been without any domestics, and as Everhard disappeared mysteriously every day, the daughters were sometimes employed on the humble errands of the family. The beauty of the elder daughter, Julia, was so conspicuous, that her mother had often undertaken the most menial errands herself, rather than send her daughter into the streets unprotected. The following evening, however, being intently employed in some domestic occupation, she allowed Julia to go out to purchase their food for to-morrow, and lent her veil for the purpose, directing her daughter to arrange it in the Spanish fashion, with which she was well acquainted, so as to hide her face.

' "Julia, who went with trembling steps on her brief errand, had somehow deranged her veil, and a glimpse of her beauty was caught by a cavalier who was passing. The meanness of her dress and occupation suggested hopes to him which he ventured to express. Julia burst from him with the mingled terror and indignation of insulted purity, but her eyes rested with unconscious avidity on the handful of gold which glittered in his hand. – She thought of her famishing parents, – of her own declining strength, and neglected useless talents. The gold still sparkled before her, – she felt – she knew not what, and to escape from some feelings is perhaps the best victory we can obtain over them. But when she arrived at home, she eagerly thrust the small purchase she had made into her mother's hand, and, though hitherto gentle, submissive, and tractable, announced, in a tone of decision that seemed to her startled mother (whose thoughts were always limited to the exigencies of the hour) like that of sudden insanity, that she would rather starve than ever again tread the streets of Seville alone.

' "As Ines retired to her bed, she thought she heard a feeble moan from the room where Everhard lay, and where, from their being compelled to sell the necessary furniture of the bed, he had entreated his parents to allow Maurice to sleep with him, alleging that the warmth of his body would be a substitute for artificial covering to his little brother. Twice those moans were heard, but Ines did not dare to awake Walberg, who had sunk into that profound sleep which is as often the refuge of intolerable misery, as that of saturated enjoyment. A few moments after, when the moans had ceased, and she had half persuaded herself it was only the echo of that wave that seems for ever beating in the ears of the unfortunate, – the curtains of her bed were thrown open, and the figure of a child covered with blood, stained in breast, arms, and legs, appeared before her, and cried, – 'It is Everhard's blood – he is bleeding to death, – I am covered with his blood! – Mother – mother – rise and save Everhard's life!' The object, the voice, the words, seemed to Ines like the imagery of some terrible dream, such as had lately often visited her sleep, till the tones of Maurice, her youngest, and (in her heart) her favourite child, made her spring from the bed, and hurry after the little blood-spotted figure that paddled before her on its naked feet, till she reached the adjoining room where Everhard lay. Amid all her anguish and fear, she trod as lightly as Maurice, lest she should awake Walberg.

' "The moon-light fell strongly through the unshuttered windows on the wretched closet that just contained the bed. Its furniture was sufficiently scanty, and in his spasms Everhard had thrown off the sheet. So he lay, as Ines approached his bed, in a kind of corse-like beauty, to which the light of the moon gave an effect that would have rendered the figure worthy the pencil of a Murillo, a Rosa, or any of those painters, who, inspired by the genius of suffering, delight in representing the most exquisite of human forms in the extremity of human agony. A St Bartholomew flayed, with his skin hanging about him in graceful drapery – a St Laurence, broiled on a gridiron, and exhibiting his finely-formed anatomy on its bars, while naked slaves are blowing the coals beneath it, – even these were inferior to the form half-veiled, – half-disclosed by the moon-light as it lay. The snow-white limbs of Everhard were extended as if for the inspection of a sculptor, and moveless, as if they were indeed what they resembled, in hue and symmetry, those of a marble statue. His arms were tossed above his head, and the blood was trickling fast from

the opened veins of both, – his bright and curled hair was clotted
with the red stream that flowed from his arms, – his lips were
blue, and a faint and fainter moan issued from them as his mother
hung over him. This sight banished in a moment all other fears
and feelings, and Ines shrieked aloud to her husband for assistance. Walberg, staggering from his sleep, entered the room, – the
object before him was enough. Ines had only strength left to
point to it. The wretched father rushed out in quest of medical
aid, which he was obliged to solicit gratuitously, and in bad Spanish, while his accents betrayed him at every door he knocked
at, – and closed them against him as a foreigner and a heretic. At
length a barber-surgeon (for the professions were united in Seville) consented, with many a yawn, to attend him, and came
duly armed with lint and styptics. The distance was short, and he
was soon by the bed of the young sufferer. The parents observed,
with consternation unspeakable, the languid looks of recognition, the ghastly smile of consciousness, that Everhard viewed
him with, as he approached the bed; and when he had succeeded
in stopping the hæmorrhage, and bound up the arms, a whisper
passed between him and the patient, and the latter raised his
bloodless hand to his lips, and uttered, 'Remember our bargain.'
As the man retired, Walberg followed, and demanded to know
the meaning of the words he had heard. Walberg was a German,
and choleric – the surgeon was a Spaniard, and cool. 'I shall tell
you to-morrow, Senhor,' said he, putting up his instruments, – 'in
the mean time be assured of my gratuitous attendance on your
son, and of his certain recovery. We deem you heretics in Seville,
but that youth is enough to canonize the whole family, and cover
a multitude of sins.' And with these words he departed. The next
day he attended Everhard, and so for several, till he was completely recovered, always refusing the slightest remuneration, till
the father, whom misery had made suspicious of every thing and
nothing, watched at the door, and heard the horrible secret. He
did not disclose it to his wife, – but from that hour, it was observed

that his gloom became more intense, and the communications he used to hold with his family, on the subject of their distress, and the modes of evading it by hourly expedients, utterly and finally ceased.

' "Everhard, now recovered, but still pale as the widow of Seneca, was at last able to join the family consultation, and give advice, and suggest resources, with a mental energy that his physical weakness could not overcome. The next day, when they were assembled to debate on the means of procuring subsistence for the following one, they for the first time missed their father. At every word that was uttered, they turned to ask for his sanction – but he was not there. At last he entered the room, but without taking a part in their consultation. He leaned gloomily against the wall, and while Everhard and Julia, at every sentence, turned their appealing looks towards him, he sullenly averted his head. Ines, appearing to pursue some work, while her trembling fingers could scarce direct the needle, made a sign to her children not to observe him. Their voices were instantly depressed, and their heads bent closely towards each other. Mendicity appeared the only resource of this unfortunate family, – and they agreed, that the evening was the best time for trying its effect. The unhappy father remained rocking against the shattered wainscot till the arrival of evening. Ines repaired the clothes of the children, which were now so decayed, that every attempt at repair made a fresh rent, and the very thread she worked with seemed less attenuated than the worn-out materials it wrought on.

' "The grandfather, still seated in his ample chair by the care of Ines, (for his son had grown very indifferent about him), watched her moving fingers, and exclaimed, with the petulance of dotage, 'Aye, – you are arraying them in embroidery, while I am in rags. – In rags!' he repeated, holding out the slender garments which the beggared family could with difficulty spare him. Ines tried to pacify him, and showed her work, to prove that it was the remnants of her children's former dress she was repairing; but, with horror unutterable, she perceived her husband incensed at these expressions of dotage, and venting his frantic and fearful indignation in language that she tried to bury the sound of, by pressing closer to the old man, and attempting to fix his bewildered attention on herself and her work. This was easily accomplished, and all was well, till they were about to separate on their wretched precarious errands. Then a new and untold feeling trembled at the heart of one of the young wanderers. Julia remembered the occurrence of a preceding evening, – she thought of the tempting gold, the flattering language, and the tender tone of the young cavalier. She saw her family perishing around her for want, – she felt it consuming her own vitals, – and as she cast her eye round the squalid room, the gold glittered brighter and brighter in her eye. A faint hope, aided perhaps by a still more faint suggestion of venial pride, swelled in her heart. 'Perhaps he might love me,' she whispered to herself, 'and think me not unworthy of his hand.' Then despair returned to the charge. 'I must die of famine,' she thought, 'if I return unaided, – and why may I not by my death benefit my family! I will never survive shame, but they may, – for they will not know it!' – She went out, and took a direction different from that of the family.

' "Night came on, – the wanderers returned slowly one by one, – *Julia was the last*. Her brothers and sisters had each obtained a trifling alms, for they had learned Spanish enough to beg in, – and the old man's face wore a vacant smile, as he saw the store produced, which was, after all, scarce sufficient to afford a meal for the youngest. 'And have you brought us nothing, Julia?' said her parents. She stood apart, and in silence. Her father repeated the question in a raised and angry voice. She started at the sound, and, rushing forward, buried her head in her mother's bosom. 'Nothing, – nothing,' she cried, in a broken and suffocated voice; 'I tried, – my weak and wicked heart submitted to the thought for a moment, – but no, – no, not even to save you from perishing, could I! – I came home to perish first myself!' Her shuddering parents comprehended her, – and amid their agony they blessed her and wept, – but not from grief. The meal was divided, of which Julia at first steadily refused to partake, as she had not contributed to it, till her reluctance was overcome by the affectionate importunity of the rest, and she complied.

' "It was during this division of what all believed to be their last meal, that Walberg gave one of those proofs of sudden and fearful violence of temper, bordering on insanity, which he had betrayed latterly. He seemed to notice, with sullen displeasure, that his wife had (as she always did) reserved the largest portion for his father. He eyed it askance at first, muttering angrily to himself. Then he spoke more aloud, though not so as to be heard by the deaf old man, who was sluggishly devouring his sordid meal. Then the sufferings of his children seemed to inspire him with a kind of wild resentment, and he started up, exclaiming, 'My son sells his blood to a surgeon, to save us from perishing!* My daughter trembles on the verge of prostitution, to procure us a meal!' Then fiercely addressing his father, 'And what dost thou do, old dotard? Rise up, – rise up, and beg for us thyself, or thou must starve!' – and, as he spoke, he raised his arm against the helpless old man. At this horrid sight, Ines shrieked aloud, and the children, rushing forward, interposed. The wretched father, incensed to madness, dealt blows among them, which were borne without a murmur; and then, the storm being exhausted, he sat down and wept.

' "At this moment, to the astonishment and terror of all except Walberg, the old man, who, since the night of his wife's interment, had never moved but from his chair to his bed, and that not without assistance, rose suddenly from his seat, and, apparently in obedience to his son, walked with a firm and steady pace towards the door. When he had reached it, he paused, looked back on them with a fruitless effort at recollection, and went out slowly; – and such was the terror felt by all at this last ghastly

---

* Fact, – it occurred in a French family not many years ago.

look, which seemed like that of a corse moving on to the place of its interment, that no one attempted to oppose his passage, and several moments elapsed before Everhard had the recollection to pursue him.

'"In the mean time, Ines had dismissed her children, and sitting as near as she dared to the wretched father, attempted to address some soothing expressions to him. Her voice, which was exquisitely sweet and soft, seemed to produce a mechanical effect on him. He turned towards her at first, – then leaning his head on his arm, he shed a few silent tears, – then flinging it on his wife's bosom, he wept aloud. Ines seized this moment to impress on his heart the horror she felt from the outrage he had committed, and adjured him to supplicate the mercy of God for a crime, which, in her eyes, appeared scarce short of parricide. Walberg wildly asked what she alluded to; and when, shuddering, she uttered the words, – 'Your father, – your poor old father!' – he smiled with an expression of mysterious and supernatural confidence that froze her blood, and, approaching her ear, softly whispered, 'I have no father! He is dead, – long dead! I buried him the night I dug my mother's grave! Poor old man,' he added with a sigh, 'it was the better for him, – he would have lived only to weep, and perish perhaps with hunger. But I will tell you, Ines, – and let it be a secret, I wondered what made our provisions decrease so, till what was yesterday sufficient for four, is not to-day sufficient for one. I watched, and at last I discovered – it must be a secret – an old goblin, who daily visited this house. It came in the likeness of an old man in rags, and with a long white beard, and it devoured every thing on the table, while the children stood hungry by! But I struck at – I cursed it, – I chased it in the name of the All-powerful, and it is gone. Oh it was a fell devouring goblin! – but it will haunt us no more, and we shall have enough. Enough,' said the wretched man, involuntarily returning to his habitual associations, – 'enough for to-morrow!'

'"Ines, overcome with horror at this obvious proof of insanity, neither interrupted or opposed him; she attempted only to

soothe him, internally praying against the too probable disturbance of her own intellects. Walberg saw her look of distrust, and,
with the quick jealousy of partial insanity, said, 'If you do not
credit me in that, still less, I suppose, will you in the account of
that fearful visitation with which I have latterly been familiar.' –
'Oh, my beloved!' said Ines, who recognized in these words the
source of a fear that had latterly, from some extraordinary circumstances in her husband's conduct, taken possession of her
soul, and made the fear even of famine trifling in comparison, –
'I dread lest I understand you too well. The anguish of want and
of famine I could have borne, – aye, and seen you bear, but the
horrid words you have lately uttered, the horrid thoughts that
escape you in your sleep, – when I think on these, and guess at' –
'You need not guess,' said Walberg, interrupting her, 'I will tell
you all.' And, as he spoke, his countenance changed from its
expression of wildness to one of perfect sanity and calm confidence, – his features relaxed, his eye became steady, and his tone
firm. – 'Every night since our late distresses, I have wandered out
in search of some relief, and supplicated every passing stranger; –
latterly, I have met every night the enemy of man, who' – 'Oh
cease, my love, to indulge these horrible thoughts, – they are the
results of your disturbed unhappy state of mind.' – 'Ines, listen to
me. I see that figure as plainly as I see yours, – I hear his voice as
distinctly as you hear mine this moment. Want and misery are
not naturally fertile in the production of imagination, – they
grasp at realities too closely. No man, who wants a meal, con-
ceives that a banquet is spread before him, and that the tempter
invites him to sit down and eat at his ease. No, – no, Ines, the evil
one, or some devoted agent of his in human form, besets me
every night, – and how I shall longer resist the snare, I know
not.' – 'And in what form does he appear?' said Ines, hoping to
turn the channel of his gloomy thoughts, while she appeared to
follow their direction. 'In that of a middle-aged man, of a serious
and staid demeanour, and with nothing remarkable in his aspect

except the light of two burning eyes, whose lustre is almost intolerable. He fixes them on me sometimes, and I feel as if there was fascination in their glare. Every night he besets me, and few like me could have resisted his seductions. He has offered, and proved to me, that it is in his power to bestow all that human cupidity could thirst for, on the condition that – I cannot utter! It is one so full of horror and impiety, that, even to listen to it, is scarce less a crime than to comply with it!'

' "Ines, still incredulous, yet imagining that to soothe his delirium was perhaps the best way to overcome it, demanded what that condition was. Though they were alone, Walberg would communicate it only in a whisper; and Ines, fortified as she was by reason hitherto undisturbed, and a cool and steady temper, could not but recollect some vague reports she had heard in her early youth, before she quitted Spain, of a being permitted to wander through it, with power to tempt men under the pressure of extreme calamity with similar offers, which had been invariably rejected, even in the last extremities of despair and dissolution. She was not superstitious, – but, her memory now taking part with her husband's representation of what had befallen him, she shuddered at the possibility of his being exposed to similar temptation; and she endeavoured to fortify his mind and conscience, by arguments equally appropriate whether he was the victim of a disturbed imagination, or the real object of this fearful persecution. She reminded him, that if, even in Spain, where the abominations of Antichrist prevailed, and the triumph of the mother of witchcrafts and spiritual seduction was complete, the fearful offer he alluded to had been made and rejected with such unmitigated abhorrence, the renunciation of one who had embraced the pure doctrines of the gospel should be expressed with a tenfold energy of feeling and holy defiance. 'You,' said the heroic woman, 'you first taught me that the doctrines of salvation are to be found alone in the holy scriptures, – I believed you, and wedded you in that belief. We are united less in the body than in the soul, for in the body neither of us may probably sojourn much longer. You pointed out to me, not the legends of fabulous saints, but the lives of the primitive apostles and martyrs of the true church. There I read no tales of "voluntary humility", of self-inflicted – fruitless sufferings, but I read that the people of God were "destitute, afflicted, tormented". And shall we dare to murmur at following the examples of those you have pointed out to me as ensamples of suffering? They bore the spoiling of their goods, – they wandered about in sheep skins and goat skins, – they resisted unto blood, striving against sin. – And shall we lament the lot that has fallen to us, when our hearts have so often burned within us, as we read the holy records together? Alas! what avails feeling till it is brought to the test of fact? How we deceived ourselves, in believing that we indeed participated in the feelings of those holy men, while we were so far removed from the test by which they were proved! We read of imprisonments, of tortures, and of flames! – We closed the book, and partook of a comfortable meal, and retired to a peaceful bed, triumphing in the thought, while saturated with all the world's goods, that if their trials had been ours, we could have sustained those trials as they did. Now, *our* hour has come, – it is an hour sharp and terrible!' – 'It is!' murmured the shuddering husband. 'But shall we therefore shrink?' replied his wife. 'Your ancestors, who were the first in Germany that embraced the reformed religion, have bled and blazed for it, as you have often told me, – can there be a stronger attestation to it?' – 'I believe there can,' said Walberg, whose eyes rolled fearfully, – 'that of starving for it! – Oh Ines,' he exclaimed, as he grasped her hands convulsively, 'I have felt, – I still feel, that a death at the stake would be mercy compared to the lingering tortures of protracted famine, – to the death that we die daily – and yet do not die! What is this I hold?' he exclaimed, grasping unconsciously the hand he held in his. 'It is my hand, my love,' answered the trembling wife. – 'Yours! – no – impossible! – Your fingers were soft and cool, but these are dry, – is this a human hand?' – 'It is mine,' said the weeping wife. 'Then you must have been famishing,' said Walberg, awakening as if from a dream. 'We have all been so latterly,' answered Ines, satisfied to restore her husband's sanity, even at the expense of this horrible confession, – 'We have all been so – but I have suffered the least. When a family is famishing, the children think of their meals – but the mother thinks only of her children. I have lived on as little as – I could, – I had indeed no appetite.' – 'Hush,' said Walberg, interrupting her – 'what sound was that? – was it not like a dying groan?' – 'No – it is the children who moan in their sleep.' – 'What do they moan for?' 'Hunger I believe,' said Ines, involuntarily yielding to the dreadful conviction of habitual misery. – 'And I sit and hear this,' said Walberg, starting up, – 'I sit to hear their young sleep broken by dreams of hunger, while for a word's speaking I could pile this floor with mountains of gold, and all for the risk of' – 'Of what?' – said Ines, clinging to him, – 'of what? – Oh! think of that! – what shall a man give in exchange for his soul? – Oh! let us starve, die, rot before your eyes, rather than you should seal your perdition by that horrible' – 'Hear me, woman!' said Walberg, turning on her eyes almost as fierce and lustrous as those of Melmoth, and whose light, indeed, seemed borrowed from his; 'Hear me! – My soul is lost! They who die in the agonies of famine know no God, and want none – if I remain here to famish among my children, I shall as surely blaspheme the Author of my being, as I shall renounce him under the fearful conditions proposed to me! – Listen to me, Ines, and tremble not. To see my children die of famine will be to me instant suicide and impenitent despair! But if I close with this fearful offer, I may yet repent, – I may yet escape! – There is hope on one side – on the other there is none – none – none! Your hands cling round me, but their touch is cold! – You are wasted to a shadow with want! Shew me the means of procuring another meal, and I will spit at the tempter, and spurn him! – But where is that to be found? – Let me go, then, to meet him! – You will pray for me, Ines, – will you not? – and the children? – No, let them not pray for me! – in my despair I forgot to pray myself, and their prayers would now be a reproach to me. – Ines! – Ines! – What? am I talking to a corse?' He was indeed, for the wretched wife had sunk at his feet senseless. 'Thank God!' he again emphatically exclaimed, as he beheld her lie to all appearance lifeless before him. 'Thank God a word then has killed her, – it was a gentler death than famine! It would have been kind to have strangled her with these hands! Now for the children!' he exclaimed, while horrid thoughts chased each other over his reeling and unseated mind, and he imagined he heard the roar of a sea in its full strength thundering in his ears, and saw ten thousand waves dashing at his feet, and every wave of blood. 'Now for the children!' – and he felt about as if for some implement of destruction. In doing so, his left hand crossed his right, and grasping it, he exclaimed as if he felt a sword in his hand, – 'This will do – they will struggle – they will supplicate, – but I will tell them their mother lies dead at my feet, and then what can they say? How now,' said the miserable man, sitting calmly down, 'If they cry to me, what shall I answer? Julia, and Ines her mother's namesake, – and poor little Maurice, who smiles even amid hunger, and whose smiles are worse than curses! – I will tell them their mother is dead!' he cried, staggering towards the door of his children's apartment – 'Dead without a blow! – that shall be their answer and their doom.'

' "As he spoke, he stumbled over the senseless body of his wife; and the tone of his mind once more strung up to the highest pitch of conscious agony, he cried, 'Men! – men! – what are your pursuits and your passions? – your hopes and fears? – your struggles and your triumphs? – Look on me! – learn from a human being like yourselves, who preaches his last and fearful sermon over the corse of his wife, and approaching the bodies of his sleeping children, whom he soon hopes to see corses also – corses made so by his own hand! – Let all the world listen to me! – let them resign factitious wants and wishes, and furnish those who hang on them for subsistence with the means of bare subsistence! – There is no care, no thought beyond this! Let our children call on me for instruction, for promotion, for distinction, and call in vain – I hold myself innocent. They may find those for themselves, or want them if they list – but let them never in vain call on me for bread, as they have done, – as they do now! I hear the moans of their hungry sleep! – World – world, be wise, and let your children curse you to your face for any thing but want of bread! Oh that is the bitterest of curses, – and it is felt most when it is least uttered! I have felt it often, but I shall feel it no longer!' – And the wretch tottered towards the beds of his children.

' " 'Father! – father!' cried Julia, 'are these your hands? Oh let me live, and I will do any thing – any thing but' – 'Father! – dear father!' cried Ines, 'spare us! – to-morrow may bring another meal!' Maurice, the young child, sprung from his bed, and cried, clinging round his father, 'Oh, dear father, forgive me! – but I dreamed a wolf was in the room, and was tearing out our throats; and, father, I cried so long, that I thought you never would come. And now – Oh God! oh God!' – as he felt the hands of the frantic wretch grasping his throat, – 'are you the wolf?'

' "Fortunately those hands were powerless from the very convulsion of the agony that prompted their desperate effort. The daughters had swooned from horror, – and their swoon appeared like death. The child had the cunning to counterfeit death also, and lay extended and stopping his breath under the fierce but faultering gripe that seized his young throat – then relinquished – then grasped it again – and then relaxed its hold as at the expiration of a spasm.

' "When all was over, as the wretched father thought, he retreated from the chamber. In doing so, he stumbled over the corse-like form of his wife. – A groan announced that the sufferer was not dead. 'What does this mean?' said Walberg, staggering in his delirium, – 'does the corse reproach me for murder? – or does one surviving breath curse me for the unfinished work?'

' "As he spoke, he placed his foot on his wife's body. At this moment, a loud knock was heard at the door. 'They are come!' said Walberg, whose frenzy hurried him rapidly through the scenes of an imaginary murder, and the consequence of a judicial process. 'Well! – come in – knock again, or lift the latch – or enter as ye list – here I sit amid the bodies of my wife and children – I have murdered them – I confess it – ye come to drag me to torture, I know – but never – never can your tortures inflict on me more than the agony of seeing them perish by hunger before my eyes. Come in – come in – the deed is done! – The corse of my wife is at my foot, and the blood of my children is on my hands – what have I further to fear?' But while the wretched man spoke thus, he sunk sullenly on his chair, appearing to be employed in wiping from his fingers the traces of blood with which he imagined they were stained. At length the knocking at the door became louder, – the latch was lifted, – and three figures entered the apartment in which Walberg sat. They advanced slowly, – two from age and exhaustion, – and the third from strong emotion. Walberg heeded them not, – his eyes were fixed, – his hands locked in each other; – nor did he move a limb as they approached.

' " 'Do you know us?' said the foremost, holding up a lantern which he held in his hand. Its light fell on a groupe worthy the pencil of a Rembrandt. The room lay in complete darkness, except where that strong and unbroken light fell. It glared on the rigid and moveless obduracy of Walberg's despair, who appeared stiffening into stone as he sat. It showed the figure of the friendly priest who had been Guzman's director, and whose features, pale and haggard with age and austerities, seemed to struggle with the smile that trembled over their wrinkled lines. Behind him stood the aged father of Walberg, with an aspect of perfect apathy, except when, with a momentary effort at recollection, he shook his white head, seeming to ask himself why he was there – and wherefore he could not speak. Supporting him stood the young form of Everhard, over whose cheek and eye wandered a glow and lustre too bright to last, and instantly succeeded by paleness and dejection. He trembled, advanced, – then shrinking back, clung to his infirm grandfather, as if needing the support he appeared to give. Walberg was the first to break the silence. 'I know ye who ye are,' he said hollowly – 'ye are come to seize me – ye have heard my confession – why do you delay? Drag me away – I would rise and follow you if I could, but I feel as if I had grown to this seat – you must drag me from it yourselves.'

'As he spoke, his wife, who had remained stretched at his feet, rose slowly but firmly; and, of all that she saw or heard, appearing to comprehend only the meaning of her husband's words, she clasped her arms round him, as if to oppose his being torn from her, and gazed on the groupe with a look of impotent and ghastly defiance. 'Another witness,' cried Walberg, 'risen from the dead against me? Nay, then, it is time to be gone,' – and he attempted to rise. 'Stay, father,' said Everhard, rushing forward and detaining him in his seat; 'stay, – there is good news, and this good priest has come to tell it, – listen to him, father, I cannot speak.' – 'You! oh you! Everhard,' answered the father, with a look of mournful reproach, 'you a witness against me too, – I never raised my hand against you! – Those whom I murdered are silent, and will you be my accuser?'

' "They all now gathered round him, partly in terror and partly in consolation, – all anxious to disclose to him the tidings with which their hearts were burdened, yet fearful lest the freight might be too much for the frail vessel that rocked and reeled before them, as if the next breeze would be like a tempest to it. At last it burst forth from the priest, who, by the necessities of his profession, was ignorant of domestic feelings, and of the felicities and agonies which are inseparably twined with the fibres of conjugal and parental hearts. He knew nothing of what Walberg might feel as a husband or father, – for he could never be either; but he felt that good news must be good news, into whatever ears they were poured, or by whatever lips they might be uttered. 'We have the will,' he cried abruptly, 'the true will of Guzman. The other was – asking pardon of God and the saints for saying so – no better than a forgery. The will is found, and you and your family are heirs to all his wealth. I was coming to acquaint you, late as it was, having with difficulty obtained the Superior's permission to do so, and in my way I met this old man, whom your son was conducting, – how came he out so late?' At these words Walberg was observed to shudder with a brief but strong spasm. 'The will is found!' repeated the priest, perceiving how little effect the words seemed to have on Walberg, – and he raised his voice to its utmost pitch. 'The will of my uncle is found,' repeated Everhard. 'Found, – found, – found!' echoed the aged grandfather, not knowing what he said, but vaguely repeating the last words he heard, and then looking round as if asking for an explanation of them. 'The will is found, love,' cried Ines, who appeared restored to sudden and perfect consciousness by the sound; 'Do you not hear, love? We are wealthy, – we are happy! Speak to us, love, and do not stare so vacantly, – speak to us!' A long pause followed. At length, – 'Who are those?' said Walberg in a hollow voice, pointing to the figures before him, whom he viewed with a fixed and ghastly look, as if he was gazing on a band of spectres. 'Your son, love, – and your father, – and the good friendly priest. Why do you look so doubtfully on us?' – 'And what do they come for?' said Walberg. Again and again the import of their communication was told him, in tones that, trembling with varied emotion, scarce could express their meaning. At length he seemed faintly conscious of what was said, and, looking round on them, uttered a long and heavy sigh. They ceased to speak, and watched him in silence. – 'Wealth! – wealth! – it comes too late. Look there, – look there!' and he pointed to the room where his children lay.

' "Ines, with a dreadful presentiment at her heart, rushed into it, and beheld her daughters lying apparently lifeless. The shriek she uttered, as she fell on the bodies, brought the priest and her son to her assistance, and Walberg and the old man were left together alone, viewing each other with looks of complete insensibility; and this apathy of age, and stupefaction of despair, made a singular contrast with the fierce and wild agony of those who still retained their feelings. It was long before the daughters were recovered from their death-like swoon, and still longer before their father could be persuaded that the arms that clasped him, and the tears that fell on his cold cheek, were those of his living children.

' "All that night his wife and family struggled with his despair. At last recollection seemed to burst on him at once. He shed some tears; – then, with a minuteness of reminiscence that was equally singular and affecting, he flung himself before the old man, who, speechless and exhausted, sat passively in his chair, and exclaiming, 'Father, forgive me!' buried his head between his father's knees.

*

' "Happiness is a powerful restorative, – in a few days the spirits of all appeared to have subsided into a calm. They wept sometimes, but their tears were no longer painful; – they resembled those showers in a fine spring morning, which announce the increasing warmth and beauty of the day. The infirmities of Walberg's father made the son resolve not to leave Spain till his dissolution, which took place in a few months. He died in peace, blessing and blessed. His son was his only spiritual attendant, and a brief and partial interval of recollection enabled him to understand and express his joy and confidence in the holy texts which were read to him from the scriptures. The wealth of the family had now given them importance; and, by the interest of the friendly priest, the body was permitted to be interred in consecrated ground. The family then set out for Germany, where they reside in prosperous felicity; – but to this hour Walberg shudders with horror when he recals the fearful temptations of the stranger, whom he met in his nightly wanderings in the hour of his adversity, and the horrors of this visitation appear to oppress his recollection more than even the images of his family perishing with want.

' "There are other narratives," continued the stranger, "relating to this mysterious being, which I am in possession of, and which I have collected with much difficulty; for the unhappy, who are exposed to his temptations, consider their misfortunes as a crime, and conceal, with the most anxious secresy, every circumstance of this horrible visitation. Should we again meet, Senhor, I may communicate them to you, and you will find them no less extraordinary than that I have just related. But it is now late, and you need repose after the fatigue of your journey." – So saying, the stranger departed.

'Don Francisco remained seated in his chair, musing on the singular tale he had listened to, till the lateness of the hour, combining with his fatigue, and the profound attention he had paid to the narrative of the stranger, plunged him insensibly into a deep slumber. He was awoke in a few minutes by a slight noise in the room, and looking up perceived seated opposite to him another person, whom he never recollected to have seen before, but who was indeed the same who had been refused admittance under the roof of that house the preceding day. He appeared seated perfectly at his ease, however; and to Don Francisco's look of surprise and inquiry, replied that he was a traveller, who had been by mistake shown into that apartment, – that finding its occupant asleep and undisturbed by his entrance, he had taken the liberty of remaining there, but was willing to retire if his presence was considered intrusive.

'As he spoke, Don Francisco had leisure to observe him. There was something remarkable in his expression, though the observer did not find it easy to define what it was; and his manner, though not courtly or conciliating, had an ease which appeared more the result of independence of thought, than of the acquired habitudes of society.

'Don Francisco welcomed him gravely and slowly, not without a sensation of awe for which he could scarcely account; – and the stranger returned the salutation in a manner that was not likely to diminish that impression. A long silence followed. The stranger (who did not announce his name) was the first to break it, by apologizing for having, while seated in an adjacent apartment, involuntarily overheard an extraordinary tale or narrative related to Don Francisco, in which he confessed he took a profound interest, such as (he added, bowing with an air of grim and reluctant civility) would, he trusted, palliate his impropriety in listening to a communication not addressed to him.

'To all this Don Francisco could only reply by bows equally rigid, (his body scarce forming an acute angle with his limbs as he sat), and by looks of uneasy and doubtful curiosity directed towards his strange visitor, who, however, kept his seat immoveably, and seemed, after all his apologies, resolved to sit out Don Francisco.

'Another long pause was broken by the visitor. "You were listening, I think," he said, "to a wild and terrible story of a being who was commissioned on an unutterable errand, – even to tempt spirits in woe, at their last mortal extremity, to barter their hopes of future happiness for a short remission of their temporary sufferings." – "I heard nothing of that," said Don Francisco, whose recollection, none of the clearest naturally, was not much improved by the length of the narrative he had just listened to, and by the sleep into which he had fallen since he heard it. "Nothing?" said the visitor, with something of abruptness and asperity in his tone that made the hearer start – "nothing! – I thought there was mention too of that unhappy being to whom Walberg confessed his severest trials were owing, – in comparison with whose fearful visitations those of even famine were as dust in the balance." – "Yes, yes," answered Don Francisco, startled into sudden recollection, "I remember there was a mention of the devil, – or his agent, – or something" – "Senhor," said the stranger interrupting him, with an expression of wild and fierce derision, which was lost on Aliaga – "Senhor, I beg you will not confound personages who have the honour to be so nearly allied, and yet so perfectly distinct as the devil and his agent, or agents. You yourself, Senhor, who, of course, as an orthodox and inveterate Catholic, must abhor the enemy of mankind, have often acted as his agent, and yet would be somewhat offended at being mistaken for him." Don Francisco crossed himself repeatedly, and devoutly disavowed his ever having been an agent of the enemy of man. "Will you dare to say so?" said his singular visitor, not raising his voice as the insolence of the question seemed to require, but depressing it to the lowest whisper as he drew his seat nearer his astonished companion – "Will you dare to say so? – Have you never erred? – Have you never felt one impure sensation? – Have you never indulged a transient feeling of hatred, or malice, or revenge? – Have you never forgot to do the good you ought to do, – or remembered to do the evil you ought not to have done? – Have you never in trade over-reached a dealer, or banquetted on the spoils of your starving debtor? – Have you never, as you went to your daily devotions, cursed from your heart the wanderings of your heretical brethren, – and while you dipped your fingers in the holy water, hoped that every drop that touched your pores, would be visited on them in drops of brimstone and sulphur? – Have you never, as you beheld the famished, illiterate, degraded populace of your country, exulted in the wretched and temporary superiority your wealth has given you, – and felt that the wheels of your carriage would not roll less smoothly if the way was paved with the heads of your countrymen? Orthodox Catholic – old Christian – as you boast yourself to be, – is not this true? – and dare you say you have not been an agent of Satan? I tell you, whenever you indulge one brutal passion, one sordid desire, one impure imagination – whenever you uttered one

word that wrung the heart, or embittered the spirit of your fel-
low-creature – whenever you made that hour pass in pain to
whose flight you might have lent wings of down – whenever you
have seen the tear, which your hand might have wiped away, fall
uncaught, or forced it from an eye which would have smiled on
you in light had you permitted it – whenever you have done this,
you have been ten times more an agent of the enemy of man
than all the wretches whom terror, enfeebled nerves, or visionary
credulity, has forced into the confession of an incredible compact
with the author of evil, and whose confession has consigned
them to flames much more substantial than those the imagination of their persecutors pictured them doomed to for an
eternity of suffering! Enemy of mankind!" the speaker continued, – "Alas! how absurdly is that title bestowed on the great
angelic chief, – the morning star fallen from its sphere! What
enemy has man so deadly as himself? If he would ask on whom
he should bestow that title aright, let him smite his bosom, and
his heart will answer, – Bestow it here!"

'The emotion with which the stranger spoke, roused and
affected even the sluggish and incrusted spirit of the listener. His
conscience, like a state coach-horse, had hitherto only been
brought on solemn and pompous occasions, and then paced
heavily along a smooth and well-prepared course, under the gorgeous trappings of ceremony; – now it resembled the same
animal suddenly bestrid by a fierce and vigorous rider, and urged
by lash and spur along a new and rugged road. And slow and
reluctant as he was to own it, he felt the power of the weight that
pressed, and the bit that galled him. He answered by a hasty and
trembling renunciation of all engagements, direct or indirect,
with the evil power; but he added, that he must acknowledge he
had been too often the victim of his seductions, and trusted for
the forgiveness of his wanderings to the power of the holy
church, and the intercession of the saints.

'The stranger (though he smiled somewhat grimly at this declaration) seemed to accept the concession, and apologized, in his turn, for the warmth with which he had spoken; and which he begged Don Francisco would interpret as a mark of interest in his spiritual concerns. This explanation, though it seemed to commence favourably, was not followed, however, by any attempt at renewed conversation. The parties appeared to stand aloof from each other, till the stranger again alluded to his having overheard the singular conversation and subsequent narrative in Aliaga's apartment. "Senhor," he added, in a voice whose solemnity deeply impressed the hearer, wearied as he was, – "I am acquainted with circumstances relating to the extraordinary person who was the daily watcher of Walberg's miseries, and the nightly tempter of his thoughts, – known but to him and me. Indeed I may add, without the imputation of vanity or presumption, that I am as well acquainted as himself with every event of his extraordinary existence; and that your curiosity, if excited at all about him, could be gratified by none so amply and faithfully as by myself." – "I thank you, Senhor," answered Don Francisco, whose blood seemed congealing in his veins at the voice and expression of the stranger, he knew not why – "I thank you, but my curiosity has been completely satisfied by the narrative I have already listened to. The night is far spent, and I have to pursue my journey to-morrow; I will therefore defer hearing the particulars you offer to gratify me with till our next meeting."

'As he spoke, he rose from his seat, hoping that this action would intimate to the intruder, that his presence was no longer desirable. The latter continued, in spite of the intimation, fixed in his seat. At length, starting as if from a trance, he exclaimed, "When shall our next meeting be?"

'Don Francisco, who did not feel particularly anxious to renew the intimacy, slightly mentioned, that he was on his journey to the neighbourhood of Madrid, where his family, whom he had not seen for many years, resided – that the stages of his journey were uncertain, as he would be obliged to wait for communications from a friend and future relative, – (he alluded to Montilla his intended son-in-law, and as he spoke, the stranger gave a peculiar smile), – and also from certain mercantile correspondents, whose letters were of the utmost importance. Finally, he added, in a disturbed tone, (for the awe of the stranger's presence hung round him like a chilling atmosphere, and seemed to freeze even his words as they issued from his mouth), he could not – easily – tell when he might again have the honour of meeting the stranger. "You cannot," said the stranger, rising and drawing his mantle over one shoulder, while his reverted eyes glanced fearfully on the pale auditor – "You cannot, – but I can. Don Francisco di Aliaga, we shall meet to-morrow night!"

'As he spoke, he still continued to stand near the door, fixing on Aliaga eyes whose light seemed to burn more intensely amid the dimness of the wretched apartment. Aliaga had risen also, and was gazing on his strange visitor with dim and troubled vision, – when the latter, suddenly retreating from the door, approached him and said, in a stifled and mysterious whisper, "Would you wish to witness the fate of those whose curiosity or presumption breaks on the secrets of that mysterious being, and dares to touch the folds of the veil in which his destiny has been enshrouded by eternity? If you do, look here!" And as he spoke, he pointed to a door which Don Francisco well remembered to be that which the person whom he had met at the inn the preceding evening, and who had related to him the tale of Guzman's family, (or rather relatives), had retired by. Obeying mechanically the waving of the arm, and the beckoning of the stranger's awful eye, rather than the impulse of his own will, Aliaga followed him. They entered the apartment; it was narrow, and dark, and empty. The stranger held a candle aloft, whose dim light fell on a wretched bed, where lay what had been the form of a living man within a few hours. "Look there!" said the stranger; and Aliaga with horror beheld the figure of the being who had been conversing with him the preceding part of that very evening, – extended a corse!

"Advance – look – observe!" said the stranger, tearing off the sheet which had been the only covering of the sleeper who had now sunk into the long and last slumber – "There is no mark of violence, no distortion of feature, or convulsion of limb – no hand of man was on him. He sought the possession of a desperate secret – he obtained it, but he paid for it the dreadful price that can be paid but once by mortals. So perish those whose presumption exceeds their power!"

'Aliaga, as he beheld the body, and heard the words of the stranger, felt himself disposed to summon the inmates of the house, and accuse the stranger of murder; but the natural cowardice of a mercantile spirit, mingled with other feelings which he could not analyse, and dared not own, withheld him, – and he continued to gaze alternately on the corse and the corse-like stranger. The latter, after pointing emphatically to the body, as if intimating the danger of imprudent curiosity, or unavailing disclosure, repeated the words, "We meet again to-morrow night!" and departed.

'Aliaga, overcome by fatigue and emotion, sunk down by the corse, and remained in that trance-like state till the servants of the inn entered the room. They were shocked to find a dead body in the bed, and scarce less shocked at the death-like state in which they found Aliaga. His known wealth and distinction procured for him those attentions which otherwise their terrors or their suspicions might have withheld. A sheet was cast over the body, and Aliaga was conveyed to another apartment, and attended sedulously by the domestics.

'In the mean time, the Alcaide arrived; and having learned that the person who had died suddenly in the inn was one totally unknown, as being only a writer, and a man of no importance in public or private life, and that the person found near his bed in a passive stupor was a wealthy merchant, – snatched, with some trepidation, the pen from the ink-horn which hung at his button-hole, and sketched the record of this sapient inquest: – "That a guest had died in the house, none could deny; but no one could suspect Don Francisco di Aliaga of murder."

"As Don Francisco mounted his mule the following day, on the strength of this just verdict, a person, who did not apparently belong to the house, was particularly solicitous in adjusting his stirrups, &c.; and while the obsequious Alcaide bowed oft and profoundly to the wealthy merchant, (whose liberality he had amply experienced for the favourable colour he had given to the strong circumstantial evidence against him), this person whispered, in a voice that reached only the ears of Don Francisco, "We meet to-night!"

'Don Francisco checked his mule as he heard the words. He looked round him – the speaker was gone. Don Francisco rode on with a feeling known to few, and which those who have felt are perhaps the least willing to communicate.'

Chapter Twenty-Nine

Χαλεπου δε το φιλησαι
χαλεπου το μη φιλησαι
χαλεπωτερου δε παυτου
αποτυγχανειυ φιλουυτα[48]

'Don Francisco rode on most of that day. The weather was mild, and his servants holding occasionally large umbrellas over him as he rode, rendered travelling supportable. In consequence of his long absence from Spain, he was wholly unacquainted with his route, and obliged to depend on a guide; and the fidelity of a Spanish guide being as proverbial and trust-worthy as Punic faith, towards evening Don Francisco found himself just where the Princess Micomicona, in the romance of his countryman, is said to have discovered Don Quixote, – 'amid a labyrinth of rocks.' He immediately dispatched his attendants in various directions, to discover the track they were to pursue. The guide gallopped after as fast as his wearied mule could go, and Don Francisco, looking round, after a long delay on the part of his attendants, found himself completely alone. Neither the weather nor the prospect was calculated to raise his spirits. The evening was very misty, unlike the brief and brilliant twilight that precedes the nights of the favoured climates of the south. Heavy showers fell from time to time, – not incessant, but seeming like the discharge of passing clouds, that were instantly succeeded by others. Those clouds gathered blacker and deeper every moment, and hung in fantastic wreaths over the stony mountains that formed a gloomy perspective to the eye of the traveller. As the mists wandered over them, they seemed to rise and fade, and shift their shapes and their stations like the hills of Ubeda*, as indistinct in form and as dim in hue, as the atmospheric illusions which in that dreary and deceptive light sometimes gave them the appearance of primeval mountains, and sometimes that of fleecy and baseless clouds.

'Don Francisco at first dropt the reins on his mule's neck, and uttered sundry ejaculations to the Virgin. Finding this did no good, – that the hills still seemed to wander before his bewildered eyes, and the mule, on the other hand, remained immoveable, he bethought himself of calling on a variety of saints, whose names the echoes of the hills returned with the most perfect punctuality, but not one of whom happened just then to be at leisure to attend to his petitions. Finding the case thus desperate, Don Francisco struck spurs into his mule, and gallopped up a rocky defile, where the hoofs of his beast struck fire at every step, and their echo from the rocks of granite made the rider tremble, lest he was pursued by banditti at every step he took. The mule, so provoked, gallopped fiercely on, till the rider, weary as he was, and some-what incommoded by its speed, drew up the reins more tightly, at hearing the steps of another rider close behind him. The mule paused instantly. Some say that animals have a kind of instinct in discovering and recognizing the approach of beings not of this world. However that may be, Don Francisco's mule stood as if its feet had been nailed to the road, till the approach of the traveller set it once more into a gallop, on which, as it appeared, the gallop of the pursuer, whose course seemed fleeter than that of an earthly rider, gained fast, and in a few moments a singular figure rode close beside Don Francisco.

'He was not in a riding dress, but muffled from head to foot in a long cloke, whose folds were so ample as almost to hide the flanks of his beast. As soon as he was abreast with Aliaga, he removed that part of the cloke which covered his head and shoul-

* Vide Cervantes, apud Don Quixote de Collibus Ubedæ.

ders, and, turning towards him, disclosed the unwelcome countenance of his mysterious visitor the preceding night. "We meet again, Senhor," said the stranger, with his peculiar smile, "and fortunately for you, I trust. Your guide has ridden off with the money you advanced him for his services, and your servants are ignorant of the roads, which, in this part of the country, are singularly perplexed. If you will accept of me as your guide, you will, I believe, have reason to congratulate yourself on our encounter."

'Don Francisco, who felt that no choice was left, acquiesced in silence, and rode on, not without reluctance, by the side of his strange companion. The silence was at length broken, by the stranger's pointing out the village at which Aliaga proposed to pass the night, at no very great distance, and at the same time noticing the approaching of his servants, who were returning to their master, after having made a similar discovery. These circumstances contributing to restore Aliaga's courage, he proceeded with some degree of confidence, and even began to listen with interest to the conversation of the stranger; particularly as he observed, that though the village was near, the windings of the road were likely to retard their arrival for some hours. The interest which had thus been excited, the stranger seemed resolved to improve to the uttermost. He rapidly unfolded the stores of his rich and copiously furnished mind; and, by skilfully blending his displays of general knowledge with particular references to the oriental countries where Aliaga had resided, their commerce, their customs, and their manners, and with a perfect acquaintance with the most minute topics of mercantile discourse, – he so far conciliated his fellow-traveller, that the journey, begun in terror, ended in delight, and Aliaga heard with a kind of pleasure, (not however unmixed with awful reminiscences), the stranger announce his intention of passing the night at the same inn.

'During the supper, the stranger redoubled his efforts, and confirmed his success. He was indeed a man who could please when he pleased, and whom. His powerful intellects, extensive knowledge, and accurate memory, qualified him to render the hour of companionship delightful to all whom genius could interest, or information amuse. He possessed a fund of anecdotical history, and, from the fidelity of his paintings, always appeared himself to have been an agent in the scenes he described. This night, too, that the attractions of his conversation might want no charm, and have no shade, he watchfully forbore those bursts of passion, – those fierce explosions of misanthropy and malediction, and that bitter and burning irony with which, at other times, he seemed to delight to interrupt himself and confound his hearer.

'The evening thus passed pleasurably; and it was not till supper was removed, and the lamp placed on the table beside which the stranger and he were seated alone, that the ghastly scene of the preceding night rose like a vision before the eyes of Aliaga. He thought he saw the corse lying in a corner of the room, and waving its dead hand, as if to beckon him away from the society of the stranger. The vision passed away, – he looked up, – they were alone. It was with the utmost effort of his mixed politeness and fear, that he prepared himself to listen to the tale which the stranger had frequently, amid their miscellaneous conversation, alluded to, and showed an evident anxiety to relate.

'These allusions were attended with unpleasant reminiscences to the hearer, – but he saw that it was to be, and armed himself as he might with courage to hear. "I would not intrude on you, Senhor," said the stranger, with an air of grave interest which Aliaga had never seen him assume before – "I would not intrude on you with a narrative in which you can feel but little interest, were I not conscious that its relation may operate as a warning the most awful, salutary, and efficacious to yourself." – "Me!" exclaimed Don Francisco, revolting with all the horror of an orthodox Catholic at the sound. – "Me!" he repeated, uttering a dozen ejaculations to the saints, and making the sign of the cross twice that number

of times. – "Me!" he continued, discharging a whole volley of ful-
mination against all those who, being entangled in the snares of
Satan, sought to draw others into them, whether in the shape of
heresy, witchcraft, or otherwise. It might be observed, however,
that he laid most stress on heresy, the latter evil, from the rigour
of their mythology, or other causes, which it were not unworthy
philosophical curiosity to inquire into, being almost unknown in
Spain; – and he uttered this protestation (which was doubtless
very sincere) with such a hostile and denunciatory tone, that
Satan, if he was present, (as the speaker half imagined), would
have been almost justified in making reprisals. Amid the assumed
consequence which passion, whether natural or artificial, always
gives to a man of mediocrity, he felt himself withering in the wild
laugh of the stranger. "You, – you!" he exclaimed, after a burst of
sound that seemed rather like the convulsion of a demoniac,
than the mirth, however frantic, of a human being – "you! – oh,
there's metal more attractive! Satan himself, however depraved,
has a better taste than to crunch such a withered scrap of orthodoxy as you between his iron teeth. No! – the interest I alluded to
as possible for you to feel, refers to another one, for whom you
ought to feel if possible more than for yourself. Now, worthy
Aliaga, your personal fears being removed, sit and listen to my
tale. You are sufficiently acquainted, through the medium of
commercial feelings, and the general information which your
habits have forced on you, with the history and manners of those
heretics who inhabit the country called England."

'Don Francisco, as a merchant, avouched his knowledge of
their being fair dealers, and wealthy liberal speculators in trade;
but (crossing himself frequently) he pronounced his utter detes-
tation of them as enemies to the holy church, and implored the
stranger to believe that he would rather renounce the most
advantageous contract he had ever made with them in the mercantile line, than be suspected of – "I suspect nothing," said the
stranger, interrupting him, with that smile that spoke darker and

bitterer things than the fiercest frown that ever wrinkled the features of man. – "Interrupt me no more, – listen, as you value the safety of a being of more value than all your race beside. You are acquainted tolerably with the English history, and manners, and habits; the latter events of their history are indeed in the mouths of all Europe." Aliaga was silent, and the stranger proceeded.

The Lovers' Tale

' "In a part of that heretic country lies a portion of land they call Shropshire, ('I have had dealings with Shrewsbury merchants,' said Aliaga to himself, 'they furnished goods, and paid bills with distinguished punctuality,') – there stood Mortimer Castle, the seat of a family who boasted of their descent from the age of the Norman Conqueror, and had never mortgaged an acre, or cut down a tree, or lowered a banner on their towers at the approach of a foe, for five hundred years. Mortimer Castle had held out during the wars of Stephen and Matilda, – it had even defied the powers that summoned it to capitulation alternately, (about once a week), during the struggle between the houses of York and Lancaster, – it had also disdained the summons of Richard and Richmond, as their successive blasts shook its battlements, while the armies of the respective leaders advanced to the field of Bosworth. The Mortimer family, in fact, by their power, their extensive influence, their immense wealth, and the independency of their spirit, had rendered themselves formidable to every party, and superior to all.

' "At the time of the Reformation, Sir Roger Mortimer, the descendant of this powerful family, vigorously espoused the cause of the Reformers; and when the nobility and gentry of the neighbourhood sent their usual dole, at Christmas, of beef and ale to their tenants, Sir Roger, with his chaplain attending him, went about from cottage to cottage, distributing Bibles in English, of the edition printed by Tyndal in Holland. But his loyalism prevailed so far, that he circulated along with them the uncouth print, cut out of his own copy, of the King (Henry VIII) dispensing copies of the Bible from both hands, which the people, as represented in the engraving, caught at with theirs, and seemed to devour as the word of life, almost before it could reach them.

' "In the short reign of Edward, the family was protected and cherished, and the godly Sir Edmund, son and successor to Sir Roger, had the Bible laid open in his hall window, that while his domestics passed on their errands, as he expressed himself, – 'he that runs may read'. In that of Mary, they were oppressed, confiscated and menaced. Two of their servants were burned at Shrewsbury; and it was said that nothing but a large sum, advanced to defray the expenses of the entertainments made at Court on the arrival of Philip of Spain, saved the godly Sir Edmund from the same fate.

' "Sir Edmund, to whatever cause he owed his safety, did not enjoy it long. He had seen his faithful and ancient servants brought to the stake, for the opinions he had taught them, – he had attended them in person to the awful spot, and seen the Bibles he had attempted to place in their hands flung into the flames, as they were kindled round them, – he had turned with tottering steps from the scene, but the crowd, in the triumph of their barbarity, gathered round, and kept him close, so that he not only involuntarily witnessed the whole spectacle, but felt the very heat of the flames that were consuming the bodies of the sufferers. Sir Edmund returned to Mortimer Castle, and died.

' "His successor, during the reign of Elizabeth, stoutly defended the rights of the Reformers, and sometimes grumbled at those of prerogative. These grumblings were said to have cost him dear – the court of purveyors charged him £3000, an enormous sum in those days, for an expected visit of the Queen and her court – a visit which was never paid. The money was, however, paid; and it was said that Sir Orlando de Mortimer raised part of the money by disposing of his falcons, the best in England, to the Earl of Leicester, the *then* favourite of the Queen. At all events, there was a tradition in the family, that when, on his last ride through his territorial demesne, Sir Orlando saw his favourite remaining bird fly from the falconer's hand, and break her jesses, he exclaimed, 'Let her fly; she knows the way to my lord of Leicester's.'

' "During the reign of James, the Mortimer family took a more decided part. The influence of the Puritans (whom James hated with a hatred passing that of even a controversialist, and remembered with pardonable filial resentment, as the inveterate enemies of his ill-fated mother) was now increasing every hour. Sir Arthur Mortimer was standing by King James at the first representation of 'Bartholomew Fair', written by Ben Jonson, when the prologue uttered these words:*

> 'Your Majesty is welcome to a Fair;
> Such place, such men, such language, and such ware,
> You must expect – with these the *zealous noise*
> Of your land's faction, scandalized at toys.'

'My lord,' said the King, (for Sir Arthur was one of the lords of the privy council), 'how deem you by that?' – 'Please your Majesty,' answered Sir Arthur, 'those Puritans, as I rode to London, cut off mine horse's tail, as they said the ribbons with which it was tied savoured too much of the pride of the beast on which the scarlet whore sits. Pray God their shears may never extend from the tails of horses to the heads of kings!' And as he spoke with affectionate and ominous solicitude, he happened to place his hand on the head of Prince Charles, (afterwards Charles I), who was sitting next his brother Henry, Prince of Wales, and to

---

* Vide Jonson's play, in which is introduced a Puritan preacher, a *Banbury man*, named Zeal-of-the-land Busy.

whom Sir Arthur Mortimer had had the high honour to be sponsor, as proxy for a sovereign prince.

' "The awful and troubled times which Sir Arthur had predicted soon arrived, though he did not live to witness them. His son, Sir Roger Mortimer, a man lofty alike in pride and in principle, and immoveable in both, – an Arminian in creed, and an aristocrat in politics, – the zealous friend of the misguided Laud, and the bosom-companion of the unfortunate Strafford, – was among the first to urge King Charles to those high-handed and impolitic measures, the result of which was so fatal.

' "When the war broke out between the King and the Parliament, Sir Roger espoused the royal cause with heart and hand, – raised a large sum in vain, to prevent the sale of the crown-jewels in Holland, – and led five hundred of his tenants, armed at his own expence, to the battles of Edge-hill and Marston-moor.

' "His wife was dead, but his sister, Mrs Ann Mortimer, a woman of uncommon beauty, spirit and dignity of character, and as firmly attached as her brother to the cause of the court, of which she had been once the most brilliant ornament, presided over his household, and by her talents, courage and promptitude, had been of considerable service to the cause.

' "The time came, however, when valour and rank, and loyalty and beauty, found all their efforts ineffectual; and of the five hundred brave men that Sir Roger had led into the field to his sovereign's aid, he brought back thirty maimed and mutilated veterans to Mortimer Castle, on the disastrous day that King Charles was persuaded to put himself into the hands of the disaffected and mercenary Scots, who sold him for their arrears of pay due by the Parliament.

' "The reign of rebellion soon commenced, – and Sir Roger, as a distinguished loyalist, felt the severest scourge of its power. Sequestrations and compositions, – fines for malignancy, and forced loans for the support of a cause he detested, – drained the well-filled coffers, and depressed the high spirit, of the aged loyalist. Domestic inquietude was added to his other calamities. He had three children. – His eldest son had fallen fighting in the King's cause at the battle of Newbury, leaving an infant daughter, then supposed the heiress of immense wealth. His second son had embraced the Puritanic cause, and, lapsing from error to error, married the daughter of an Independent, whose creed he had adopted; and, according to the custom of those days, fought all day at the head of his regiment, and preached and prayed to them all night, in strict conformity with that verse in the psalms, which served him alternately for his text and his battle-word – 'Let the praises of God be in their mouth, and a two-edged sword in their hands.' This double exercise of the sword and the word, however, proved too much for the strength of the saint-militant; and after having, during Cromwell's Irish campaign, vigorously headed the attack on Cloghan Castle*, the ancient seat of the O'Moores, princes of Leix, – and being scalded through his buff-coat by a discharge of hot water from the bartizan, – and then imprudently given the word of exhortation for an hour and forty minutes to his soldiers, on the bare heath that surrounded the castle, and under a drenching rain, – he died of a pleurisy in three days, and left, like his brother, an infant daughter who had remained in England, and had been educated by her mother. It

---

* I have been an inmate in this castle for many months – it is still inhabited by the venerable descendant of that ancient family. His son is now High-Sheriff of the King's county. Half the castle was battered down by Oliver Cromwell's forces, and rebuilt in the reign of Charles the Second. The remains of the *castle* are a tower of about forty feet square, and five stories high, with a single spacious apartment on each floor, and a narrow staircase communicating with each, and reaching to the bartizan. A beautiful ash-plant, which I have often admired, is now displaying its foliage between the stones of the bartizan, – and how it got or grew there, heaven only knows. There it is, however; and it is better to see it there than to feel the discharge of hot water or molten lead from the apertures.

was said in the family, that this man had written the first lines of Milton's poem 'on the new forcers of conscience under the Long Parliament.' It is certain, at least, that when the fanatics who surrounded his dying bed were lifting up their voices to sing a hymn, he thundered with his last breath,

> 'Because ye have thrown off your prelate lord,
> And with stiff vows renounce his Liturgy,
> To seize the widowed – e pluralitie,
> From them whose sin ye envied not, abhorr'd,' &c.

' "Sir Roger felt, though from different causes, pretty much the same degree of emotion on the deaths of his two sons. He was fortified against affliction at the death of the elder, from the consolation afforded him by the cause in which he had fallen; and that in which the apostate, as his father always called him, had perished, was an equal preventive against his feeling any deep or bitter grief on his dissolution.

' "When his eldest son fell in the royal cause, and his friends gathered round him in officious condolence, the old loyalist replied, with a spirit worthy of the proudest days of classic heroism, 'It is not for my dead son that I should weep, but for my living one.' His tears, however, were flowing at that time for another cause.

' "His only daughter, during his absence, in spite of the vigilance of Mrs Ann, had been seduced by some Puritan servants in a neighbouring family, to hear an Independent preacher of the name of Sandal, who was then a serjeant in Colonel Pride's regiment, and who was preaching in a barn in the neighbourhood, in the intervals of his military exercises. This man was a natural orator, and a vehement enthusiast; and, with the license of the day, that compromised between a pun and a text, and delighted in the union of both, this serjeant-preacher had baptized himself by the name of – 'Thou-art-not-worthy-to-unloose-the-latchets-of-his-shoes, – *Sandal*'.

' "This was the text on which he preached, and his eloquence had such effect on the daughter of Sir Roger Mortimer, that, forgetting the dignity of her birth, and the loyalty of her family, she united her destiny with this low-born man; and, believing herself to be suddenly inspired from this felicitous conjunction, she actually out-preached two female Quakers in a fortnight after their marriage, and wrote a letter (very ill-spelled) to her father, in which she announced her intention to 'suffer affliction with the people of God', and denounced his eternal damnation, if he declined embracing the creed of her husband; – which creed was changed the following week, on his hearing a sermon from the celebrated Hugh Peters, and a month after, on hearing an itinerant preacher of the Ranters or Antinomians, who was surrounded by a troop of licentious, half-naked, drunken disciples, whose vociferations of – 'We are the naked truth', completely silenced a fifth-monarchy man, who was preaching from a tub on the other side of the road. To this preacher Sandal was introduced, and being a man of violent passions, and unsettled principles, he instantly embraced the opinions of the last speaker, (dragging his wife along with him into every gulph of polemical or political difficulty he plunged in), till he happened to hear another preacher of the Cameronians, whose constant topic, whether of triumph or of consolation, was the unavailing efforts made in the preceding reign, to force the Episcopalian system down the throat of the Scots; and, in default of a text, always repeated the words of Archy, jester to Charles the First, who, on the first intimation of the reluctance of the Scots to admit Episcopal jurisdiction, exclaimed to Archbishop Laud, 'My Lord, who is the fool now?' – for which he had his coat stripped over his head, and was forbid the court. So Sandal vacillated between creed and creed, between preacher and preacher, till he died, leaving his widow with one son. Sir Roger announced to his widowed daughter, his determined purpose never to see her more, but he promised his protection to her son, if entrusted to his care. The widow was too poor to decline compliance with the offer of her deserted father.

' "So in Mortimer Castle were, in their infancy, assembled the three grandchildren, born under such various auspices and destinies. Margaret Mortimer the heiress, a beautiful, intelligent, spirited girl, heiress of all the pride, aristocratical principle and possible wealth of the family; Elinor Mortimer, the daughter of the Apostate, received rather than admitted into the house, and educated in all the strictness of her Independent family; and John Sandal, the son of the rejected daughter, whom Sir Roger admitted into the Castle only on the condition of his being engaged in the service of the royal family, banished and persecuted as they were; and he renewed his correspondence with some emigrant loyalists in Holland, for the establishment of his protegé, whom he described, in language borrowed from the Puritan preachers, as 'a brand snatched from the burning'.

' "While matters were thus at the Castle, intelligence arrived of Monk's unexpected exertions in favour of the banished family. The result was as rapid as it was auspicious. The Restoration took place within a few days after, and the Mortimer family were then esteemed of so much consequence, that an express, girthed from his waist to his shoulders, was dispatched from London to announce the intelligence. He arrived when Sir Roger, whose chaplain he had been compelled by the ruling party to dismiss as a malignant, was reading prayers himself to his family. The return and restoration of Charles the Second was announced. The old loyalist rose from his knees, waved his cap, (which he had reverently taken from his white head), and, suddenly changing his tone of supplication for one of triumph, exclaimed, 'Lord, now lettest thou thy servant depart in peace, according to thy word, for mine eyes have seen thy salvation!' As he spoke, the old man sunk on the cushion which Mrs Ann had placed beneath his knees. His grandchildren rose from their knees to assist him, – it was too late, – his spirit had parted in that last exclamation." '

Chapter Thirty

– She sat, and thought
Of what a sailor suffers.

Cowper

' "The intelligence that was the cause of old Sir Roger's death, who might be said to be conducted from this world to the next by a blessed *euthanasia*, (a kind of passing with a light and lofty step from a narrow entry to a spacious and glorious apartment, without ever feeling he trod the dark and rugged threshold that lies between), was the signal and pledge to this ancient family of the restitution of their faded honours, and fast-declining possessions. Grants, reversals of fine, restoration of land and chattels and offer of pensions, and provisions, and remunerations, and all that royal gratitude, in the effervescence of its enthusiasm, could bestow, came showering on the Mortimer family, as fast and faster than fines, confiscations and sequestrations, had poured on them in the reign of the usurper. In fact, the language of King Charles to the Mortimers was like that of the Eastern monarchs to their favourites, – 'Ask what thou wilt, and it shall be granted to thee, even to the half of my kingdom.' The Mortimers asked only for their own, – and being thus more reasonable, both in their expectations and demands, than most other applicants at that period, they succeeded in obtaining what they required.

' "Thus Mrs Margaret Mortimer (so unmarried females were named at the date of the narrative) was again acknowledged as the wealthy and noble heiress of the Castle. Numerous invitations were sent to her to visit the court, which, though recommended by letters from divers of the court-ladies, who had been acquainted, traditionally at least, with her family, and enforced by a letter from Catherine of Braganza, written by her own hand, in which she acknowledged the obligations of the king to the house of Mortimer, were steadily rejected by the high-minded heiress of its honours and its spirit. – 'From these towers,' said she to Mrs Ann, 'my grandfather led forth his vassals and tenants in aid of his king, – to these towers he led what was left of them back, when the royal cause seemed lost for ever. Here he lived and died for his sovereign, – and here will I live and die. And I feel that I shall do more effectual service to his Majesty, by residing on my estates, and protecting my tenants, and repairing,' – she added with a smile, – 'even with my needle, the rents made in the banners of our house by many a Puritan's bullet, than if I flaunted it in Hyde-Park in my glass coach, or masqueraded it all night in that of St James's*, even though I were sure to encounter the Duchess of Cleveland on one side, and Louise de Querouaille on the other, – fitter place for them than me.' – And so saying, Mrs Margaret Mortimer resumed her tapestry work. Mrs Ann looked at her with an eye that spoke volumes, – and the tear that trembled in it made the lines more legible.

' "After the decided refusal of Mrs Margaret Mortimer to go to London, the family resumed their former ancestorial habits of stately regularity, and decorous grandeur, such as became a magnificent and well-ordered household, of which a noble maiden was the head and president. But this regularity was without rigour, and this monotony without apathy – the minds of these highly fated females were too familiar with trains of lofty thinking, and images of noble deeds, to sink into vacancy, or feel

---

* See a comedy of Wycherly's, entitled, 'Love in a Wood, or St James's Park,' where the company are represented going there at night in masks and with torches.

depression from solitude. I behold them," said the stranger, "as I once saw them, seated in a vast irregularly shaped apartment, wainscotted with oak richly and quaintly carved, and as black as ebony – Mrs Ann Mortimer, in a recess which terminated in an ancient casement window, the upper panes of which were gorgeously emblazoned with the arms of the Mortimers, and some legendary achievements of the former heroes of the family. A book she valued much* lay on her knee, on which she fixed her eyes intently – the light that came through the casement chequering its dark lettered pages with hues of such glorious and fantastic colouring, that they resembled the leaves of some splendidly-illuminated missal, with all its pomp of gold, and azure and vermilion.

' "At a little distance sat her two grand-nieces, employed in work, and relieving their attention to it by conversation, for which they had ample materials. They spoke of the poor whom they had visited and assisted, – of the rewards they had distributed among the industrious and orderly, – and of the books which they were studying; and of which the well-filled shelves of the library furnished them with copious and noble stores.

' "Sir Roger had been a man of letters as well as of arms. He had been often heard to say, that next to a well-stocked armoury in time of war, was a well-stocked library in time of peace; and even in the midst of his latter grievances and privations, he contrived every year to make an addition to his own.

' "His grand-daughters, well instructed by him in the French and Latin languages, had read Mezeray, Thuanus and Sully. In English, they had Froissart in the black-letter translation of Pynson, imprinted 1525. Their poetry, exclusive of the classics, consisted chiefly of Waller, Donne and that constellation of writers that illuminated the drama in the latter end of the reign of Elizabeth,

* Taylor's Book of Martyrs.

and the commencement of that of James, – Marlow, and Massinger, and Shirley, and Ford – *cum multis aliis.*[49] Fairfax's translations had made them familiar with the continental poets; and Sir Roger had consented to admit, among his modern collection, the Latin poems (the only ones then published) of Milton, for the sake of that *in Quintum Novembris*, – for Sir Roger, next to the fanatics, held the Catholics in utter abomination."

' "Then he will be damned to all eternity," said Aliaga, "and that's some satisfaction."

' "Thus, their retirement was not inelegant, nor unaccompanied with those delights at once soothing and elating, which arise from a judicious mixture of useful occupation and literary tastes.

' "On all they read or conversed of, Mrs Ann Mortimer was a living comment. Her conversation, rich in anecdote, and accurate to minuteness, sometimes rising to the loftiest strains of eloquence, as she related 'deeds of the days of old', and often borrowing the sublimity of inspiration, as the reminiscences of religion softened and solemnized the spirit with which she spake, – like the influence of time on fine paintings, that consecrates the tints it mellows, and makes the colours it has half obscured more precious to the eye of feeling and of taste, than they were in the glow of their early beauty, – her conversation was to her grand-nieces at once history and poetry.

' "The events of English history then not recorded, had a kind of traditional history more vivid, if not so faithful as the records of modern historians, in the memories of those who had been agents and sufferers (the terms are probably synonimous) in those memorable periods.

' "There was an entertainment then, banished by modern dissipation now, but alluded to by the great poet of that nation, whom your orthodox and undeniable creed justly devotes to eternal damnation.

'In winter's tedious nights sit by the fire,

*

– and tell the tales
Of woful ages long ago betid;

*

And send the hearers weeping to their beds.
We cited up a thousand heavy times.'

*

' "When memory thus becomes the dispository of grief, how faithfully is the charge kept! – and how much superior are the touches of one who paints from the life, and the heart, and the senses, – to those of one who dips his pen in his ink-stand, and casts his eye on a heap of musty parchments, to glean his facts or his feelings from them! Mrs Ann Mortimer had much to tell, – and she told it well. If history was the subject, she could relate the events of the civil wars – events which resembled indeed those of all civil wars, but which derived a peculiar strength of character, and brilliancy of colouring, from the hand by which they were sketched. She told of the time when she rode behind her brother, Sir Roger, to meet the King at Shrewsbury; and she almost echoed the shout uttered in the streets of that loyal city, when the University of Oxford sent in its plate to be coined for the exigences of the royal cause. She told also, with grave humour, the anecdote of Queen Henrietta making her escape with some difficulty from a house on fire, – and, when her life was scarce secure from the flames that consumed it, rushing back among them – to save her lapdog!

' "But of all her historical anecdotes, Mrs Ann valued most what she had to relate of her own family. On the virtue and valour of her brother Sir Roger, she dwelt with an unction whose balm imparted itself to her hearers; and even Elinor, in spite of the Puritanism of her early principles, wept as she listened. But when Mrs Ann told of the King taking shelter for one night in the Castle, under the protection only of her mother and herself, to whom he intrusted his rank and his misfortunes, (arriving under a disguise), – (Sir Roger being absent fighting his battles in York-shire) – when she added that her aged mother, Lady Mortimer, then seventy-four, after spreading her richest velvet mantle, lined with fur, as a quilt for the bed of her persecuted sovereign, tot-tered into the armoury, and, presenting the few servants that followed her with what arms could be found, adjured them by brand and blade, by lady's love, and their hopes of heaven, to defend her royal guest. When she related that a band of fanatics, after robbing a church of all its silver-plate, and burning the adja-cent vicarage, drunk with their success, had invested the Castle, and cried aloud for '*the man*' to be brought unto them, that he might be hewed to pieces before the Lord in Gilgal – and Lady Mortimer had called on a young French officer in Prince Rupert's corps, who, with his men, had been billetted on the Castle for some days – and that this youth, but seventeen years of age, had met two desperate attacks of the assailants, and twice retired covered with his own blood and that of the assailants, whom he had in vain attempted to repel – and that Lady Mortimer, finding all was lost, had counselled the royal fugitive to make his escape, – and furnished him with the best horse left in Sir Roger's stables to effect his flight, while she returned to the great hall, whose win-dows were now shattered by the balls that hissed and flew round her head, and whose doors were fast yielding to the crows and other instruments which a Puritan smith, who was both chaplain and colonel of the band, had lent them, and instructed them in the use of – and how Lady Mortimer fell on her knees before the young Frenchman, and adjured him to make good the defence till King Charles was safe, and free, and far – and how the young Frenchman had done all that man could do; – and finally, when the Castle, after an hour's obstinate resistance, yielded to the assault of the fanatics, he had staggered, covered with blood, to the foot of the great chair which that ancient lady had immove-ably occupied, (paralyzed by terror and exhaustion), and dropping his sword, *then for the first time*, exclaimed, 'J'ai fait mon devoir!'[50] and expired at her feet – and how her mother sat in the same rigour of attitude, while the fanatics ravaged through the Castle, – drank half the wines in the cellar, – thrust their bayonets through the family-pictures, which they called the idols of the high-places, – fired bullets through the wainscot, and converted half the female servants after their own way, – and on finding their search after the King fruitless, in mere wantonness of mischief, were about to discharge a piece of ordnance in the hall that must have shattered it in pieces, while Lady Mortimer sat torpidly looking on, – till, perceiving that the piece was accidentally pointed towards the very door through which King Charles had passed from the hall, her recollection seemed suddenly to return, and starting up and before the mouth of the piece, exclaimed, '*Not there*! – you shall not *there*!' – and as she spoke, dropt dead in the hall. When Mrs Ann told these and other thrilling tales of the magnanimity, the loyalty, and the sufferings of her high ancestry, in a voice that alternately swelled with energy, and trembled with emotion, and as she told them, pointed to the spot where each had happened, – her young hearers felt a deep stirring of the heart, – a proud yet mellowed elation that never yet was felt by the reader of a written history, though its pages were as legitimate as any sanctioned by the royal licenser at Madrid.

'"Nor was Mrs Ann Mortimer less qualified to take an interesting share in their lighter studies. When Waller's poetry was its subject, she could tell of the charms of his Sacharissa, whom she knew well, – the Lady Dorothea Sidney, daughter of the Earl of Leicester, – and compare, with those of his Amoret, the Lady Sophia Murray. And in balancing the claims of these poetical heroines, she gave so accurate an account of their opposite styles of beauty, – entered so minutely into the details of their dress and deportment, – and so affectingly hinted, with a mysterious sigh, that there was *one* then at court whom Lucius, Lord Falkland, the gallant, the learned, and the polished, had whispered was far superior to both, – that her auditors more than suspected she had herself been one of the most brilliant stars in that galaxy whose faded glories were still reflected in her memory, – and that Mrs Ann, amid her piety and patriotism, still blended a fond reminiscence of the gallantries of that court where her youth had been spent, – and over which the beauty, the magnificent taste, and national *gaieté* of the ill-fated Henrietta, had once thrown a light as dazzling as it was transient. She was listened to by Margaret and Elinor with equal interest, but with far different feelings. Margaret, beautiful, vivacious, haughty and generous, and resembling her grandfather and his sister alike in character and person, could have listened for ever to narrations that, while they confirmed her principles, gave a kind of holiness to the governing feelings of her heart, and made her enthusiasm a kind of virtue in her eyes. An aristocrat in politics, she could not conceive that public virtue could soar to a higher pitch than a devoted attachment to the house of Stuart afforded for its flight; and her religion had never given her any disturbance. – Strictly attached to the Church of England, as her forefathers had been from its first establishment, she included in an adherence to this not only all the graces of religion, but all the virtues of morality; and she could hardly conceive how there could be majesty in the sovereign, or loyalty in the subject, or valour in man, or virtue in woman, unless they were comprised within the pale of the Church of England. These qualities, with their adjuncts, had been always represented to her as co-existent with an attachment to monarchy and Episcopacy, and vested solely in those heroic characters of her ancestry, whose lives, and even deaths, it was a proud delight to their young descendant to listen to, – while all the opposite qualities, – all that man can hate, or woman despise, – had been represented to her as instinctively resident in the partizans of republicanism and the Presbytery. Thus her feelings and her principles, – her reasoning powers and the habits of her life, all took one way; and she was not only unable to make the least allowance for a divergence from this way, but utterly unable to conceive that another existed for those who believed in a God, or acknowledged human power at all. She was as much at a loss to conceive how any good could come out of that Nazareth of her abhorrence, as an ancient geographer would have been to have pointed out America in a classical map. – Such was Margaret.

' "Elinor, on the other hand, bred up amid a clamour of perpetual contention, – for the house of her mother's family, in which her first years had been passed, was, in the language of the profane of those times, a scruple-shop, where the godly of all denominations held their conferences of contradiction, – had her mind early awakened to differences of opinion, and opposition of principle. Accustomed to hear these differences and oppositions often expressed with the most unruly vehemence, she had never, like Margaret, indulged in a splendid aristocracy of imagination, that bore every thing before it, and made prosperity and adversity alike pay tribute to the pride of its triumph. Since her admission into the house of her grandfather, the mind of Elinor had become still more humble and patient, – more subdued and self-denied. Compelled to hear the opinions she was attached to decried, and the characters she reverenced vilified, she sat in reflective silence; and, balancing the opposite extremes which she was destined to witness, she came to the right conclusion, – that there must be good on both sides, however obscured or defaced by passion and by interest, and that great and noble qualities must exist in either party, where so much intellectual power, and so much physical energy, had been displayed by both. Nor could she believe that these clear and mighty spirits would be for ever opposed to each other in their future destinations, – she loved to view them as children who had 'fallen out by the way', from mistaking the path that led to their father's house, but who would yet rejoice together in the light of his presence, and smile at the differences that divided them on their journey.

' "In spite of the influence of her early education, Elinor had learned to appreciate the advantages of her residence in her grandfather's castle. She was fond of literature and of poetry. She possessed imagination and enthusiasm, – and these qualities met with their loveliest indulgence amid the picturesque and historical scenery that surrounded the Castle, – the lofty tales told within its walls, and to which every stone in them seemed to cry out in attestation, – and the heroic and chivalrous characters of its inmates, with whom the portraits of their high descended ancestry seemed starting from their gorgeous frames to converse, as the tale of their virtues and their valour was told in their presence. This was a different scene from that in which she had passed her childhood. The gloomy and narrow apartments, divested of all ornament, and awaking no associations but those of an awful futurity – the uncouth habits, austere visages, denunciatory language and polemical fury of its inmates or guests, struck her with a feeling for which she reproached herself, but did not suppress; and though she continued a rigid Calvinist in her creed, and listened whenever she could to the preaching of the non-conformist ministers, she had adopted in her pursuits the literary tastes, and in her manners the dignified courtesy, that became the descendant of the Mortimers.

' "Elinor's beauty, though of a style quite different from that of her cousin, was yet beauty of the first and finest character. Margaret's was luxuriant, lavish and triumphant, – every movement displayed a conscious grace, – every look demanded homage, and obtained it the moment it was demanded. Elinor's was pale, contemplative, and touching; – her hair was as black as jet, and the thousand small curls into which, according to the fashion of the day, it was woven, seemed as if every one of them had been twined by the hand of nature, – they hung so softly and shadowingly, that they appeared like a veil dropping over the features of a nun, till she shook them back, and there beamed among them an eye of dark and brilliant light, like a star amid the deepening shades of twilight. She wore the rich dress prescribed by taste and habits of Mrs Ann, who had never, even in the hour of extreme adversity, relaxed in what may be called the rigour of her aristocratical costume, and would have thought it little less than a desecration of the solemnity, had she appeared at prayers, even though celebrated (as she loved to term it) in the Castle-hall, unless arrayed in satins and velvets, that, like ancient suits of armour, could have stood alone and erect without the aid of human inhabitant. There was a soft and yielding tone in the gently modulated harmony of Elinor's form and movements, – a gracious melancholy in her smile, – a tremulous sweetness in her voice, – an appeal in her look, which the heart that refused to answer could not have living pulse within its region. No head of Rembrandt's, amid its contrasted luxuries of light and shade, – no form of Guido's, hovering in exquisite and speechful undulation between earth and heaven, could vie with the tint and character of Elinor's countenance and form. There was but one touch to be added to the picture of her beauty, and that touch was given by no physical grace, – no exterior charm. It was borrowed from a feeling as pure as it was intense, – as unconscious as it was profound. The secret fire that lit her eyes with that lambent glory, while it amused the paleness of her young cheek, – that preyed on her heart, while it seemed to her imagination that she clasped a young cherub in her arms, like the unfortunate queen of Virgil, – that fire was a secret even to herself. – She knew she felt, but knew not what she felt.

' "When first admitted into the Castle, and treated with sufficient *hauteur* by her grandfather and his sister, who could not forget the mean descent and fanatic principles of her father's family, she remembered, that, amid the appalling grandeur and austere reserve of her reception, her cousin, John Sandal, was the only one who spoke to her in accents of tenderness, or turned on her an eye that beamed consolation. She remembered him as the beautiful and gentle boy who had lightened all her tasks, and partaken in all her recreations.

' "At an early age John Sandal, at his own request, had been sent to sea, and had never since visited the Castle. On the Restoration, the remembered services of the Mortimer family, and the high fame of the youth's courage and ability, had procured him a distinguished situation in the navy. John Sandal's consequence now rose in the eyes of the family, of whom he was at first an inmate on toleration only; and even Mrs Ann Mortimer began to express some anxiety to hear tidings of her valiant cousin John. When she spoke thus, the light of Elinor's eye fell on her aunt with as rich a glow as ever summer sun on an evening landscape; but she felt, at the same moment, an oppression, – an indefinable suspension of thought, of speech, almost of breath, which was only relieved by the tears which, when retired from her aunt's presence, she indulged in. Soon this feeling was exchanged for one of deeper and more agitating interest. The war with the Dutch broke out, and Captain John Sandal's name, in spite of his youth, appeared conspicuous among those of the officers appointed to that memorable service.

' "Mrs Ann, long accustomed to hear the names of her family uttered always in the same breath with the stirring report of high heroic deeds, felt the elation of spirit she had experienced in bygone days, combined with happier associations, and more prosperous auguries. Though far advanced in life, and much declined in strength, it was observed, that during the reports of the war, and while she listened to the accounts of her kinsman's valour and fast-advancing eminence, her step became firm and elastic, her lofty figure dilated to its youthful height, and a colour at times visited her cheek, with as rich and brilliant a tinge as when the first sighs of love murmured over its young roses. The high minded Margaret, partaking that enthusiasm which merged all personal feeling in the glory of her family and of her country, heard of the perils to which her cousin (whom she hardly remembered) was exposed, only with a haughty confidence that he would meet them as she felt she would have met them herself, had she been, like him, the last male descendant of the family of Mortimer. Elinor trembled and wept, – and when alone she prayed fervently.

' "It was observable, however, that the respectful interest with which she had hitherto listened to the family legends so eloquently told by Mrs Ann, was now exchanged for a restless and unappeaseable anxiety for tales of the naval heroes who had dignified the family history. Happily she found a willing narrator in Mrs Ann, who had little need to search her memory, and no occasion to consult her invention, for splendid stories of those whose home was the deep, and whose battle-field was the wild waste ocean. Amid the gallery richly hung with family portraits, she pointed out the likeness of many a bold adventurer, whom the report of the riches and felicities of the new discovered world had tempted on speculations sometimes wild and disastrous, sometimes prosperous beyond the golden dreams of cupidity. 'How precarious! – how perilous!' murmured Elinor, shuddering. But when Mrs Ann told the tale of her uncle, the literary speculator, the polished scholar, the brave and gentle of the family, who had accompanied Sir Walter Raleigh on his calamitous expedition, and years after died of grief for his calamitous death, Elinor, with a start of horror, caught her aunt's arm, emphatically extended towards the portrait, and implored her to desist. The decorum of the family was so great, that this liberty could not be taken without an apology for indisposition; – it was duly though faintly made, and Elinor retired to her apartment.

' "From February 1665, – from the first intelligence of De Ruyter's enterprises, till the animating period when the Duke of York was appointed to the command of the Royal fleet, – all was eager and anticipative excitement, and eloquent expatiations on ancient achievements, and presageful hopes of new honours, on the part of the heiress of Mortimer and Mrs Ann, and profound and speechless emotion on that of Elinor.

' "The hour arrived, and an express was dispatched from London to Mortimer Castle with intelligence, in which King Charles, with that splendid courtesy which half redeemed his vices, announced himself most deeply interested, inasmuch as it added to the honours of the loyal family, whose services he appreciated so highly. The victory was complete, – and Captain John Sandal, in the phrase which the King's attachment to French manners and language was beginning to render popular, had 'covered himself with glory'. Amid the thickest of the fight, in an open boat, he had carried a message from Lord Sandwich to the Duke of York, under a shower of balls, and when older officers had stoutly declined the perilous errand; and when, on his return, Opdam the Dutch Admiral's ship blew up, amid the crater of the explosion John Sandal plunged into the sea, to save the half-drowning, half-burning wretches who clung to the fragments that scorched them, or sunk in the boiling waves; and then, – dismissed on another fearful errand, flung himself between the Duke of York and the ball that struck at one blow the Earl of Falmouth, Lord Muskerry, and Mr Boyle, and when they all fell at the same moment, wiped, with unfaultering hand, and on bended knee, their brains and gore, with which the Duke of York was covered from head to foot. When this was read by Mrs Ann Mortimer, with many pauses, caused by sight dim with age, and diffused with tears, – and when at length, finishing the long and laborious read detail, Mrs Ann exclaimed – 'He is a hero!' Elinor tremblingly whispered to herself – 'He is a Christian.'

' "The details of such an event forming a kind of era in a family so sequestered, imaginative and heroic, as that of the Mortimers, the contents of the letter signed by the King's own hand were read over and over again. They formed the theme of converse at their meals, and the subject of their study and comment when alone. Margaret dwelt much on the gallantry of the action, and half-imagined she saw the tremendous explosion of Opdam's ship. Elinor repeated to herself, 'And he plunged amid the burning wave to save the lives of the men he had conquered!' And some months elapsed before the brilliant vision of glory, and of grateful royalty, faded from their imagination; and when it did, like that of Micyllus, it left honey on the eye-lids of the dreamer.

' "From the date of the arrival of this intelligence, a change had taken place in the habits and manners of Elinor, so striking as to become the object of notice to all but herself. Her health, her rest, and her imagination, became the prey of indefinable fantasies. The cherished images of the past, – the lovely visions of her golden childhood, – seemed fearfully and insanely contrasted in her imagination with the ideas of slaughter and blood, – of decks strewed with corses, – and of a young and terrible conqueror bestriding them amid showers of ball and clouds of fire. Her very senses reeled between these opposite impressions. Her reason could not brook the sudden transition from the smiling and Cupid-like companion of her childhood, to the hero of the embattled deep, and of nations and navies on fire, – garments rolled in blood, – the thunder of the battle and the shouting.

' "She sat and tried, as well as her wandering fancy would allow her, to reconcile the images of that remembered eye, whose beam rested on her like the dark blue of a summer heaven swimming in dewy light, – with the flash that darted from the burning eye of the conqueror, whose light was as fatal where it fell as his sword. She saw him, as he had once sat beside her, smiling like the first morning in spring, – and smiled in return. The slender form, the soft and springy movements, the kiss of childhood that felt like velvet, and scented like balm, – was suddenly exchanged in her dream (for all her thoughts were dreams) for a fearful figure of one drenched in blood, and spattered with brains and gore. And Elinor, half-screaming, exclaimed, 'Is this he whom I loved?' Thus her mind, vacillating between contrasts so strongly opposed, began to feel its moorings give way. She drifted from rock to rock, and on every rock she struck a wreck.

' "Elinor relinquished her usual meetings with the family – she sat in her own apartment all the day, and most of the evening. It was a lonely turret projecting so far from the walls of the Castle, that there were windows, or rather casements, on three sides. There Elinor sat to catch the blast, let it blow as it would, and imagined she heard in its moaning the cries of drowning seamen. No music that her lute, or that which Margaret touched with a more powerful and brilliant finger, could wean her from this melancholy indulgence.

' "'Hush!' she would say to the females who attended her – 'Hush! let me listen to the blast! – It waves many a banner spread for victory, – it sighs over many a head that has been laid low!'

' "Her amazement that a being could be at once so gentle and so ferocious – her dread that the habits of his life must have converted the *angel of her wilderness* into a brave but brutal seaman, estranged from the feelings that had rendered the beautiful boy so indulgent to her errors, – so propitiatory between her and her proud relatives, – so aidant in all her amusements, – so necessary to her very existence. – The tones of this dreamy life harmonized, awfully for Elinor, with the sound of the blast as it shook the turrets of the Castle, or swept the woods that groaned and bowed beneath its awful visitings. And this secluded life, intense feeling, and profound and heart-rooted secret of her silent passion, held perhaps fearful and indescribable alliance with that aberration of mind, that prostration at once of the heart and the intellect, that have been found to bring forth, according as the agents were impelled, 'the savour of life unto life, or of death unto death'. She had all the intensity of passion, combined with all the devotedness of religion; but she knew not which way to steer, or what gale to follow. She trembled and shrunk from her doubtful pilotage, and the rudder was left to the mercy of the winds and waves. Slender mercy do those experience who commit themselves to the tempests of the mental world – better if they had sunk at once amid the strife of the dark waters in their wild and wintry rage; there they would soon have arrived at the haven where they would be secure.

' "Such was the state of Elinor, when the arrival of one who had been long a stranger in the vicinity of the Castle caused a strong sensation in its inhabitants.

' "The widow Sandal, the mother of the young seaman, who had hitherto lived in obscurity on the interest of the small fortune bequeathed her by Sir Roger, (under the rigid injunction of never visiting the Castle), suddenly arrived in Shrewsbury, which was scarce a mile from it, and declared her intention of fixing her residence there.

' "The affection of her son had showered on her, with the profusion of a sailor, and the fondness of a child, all the rewards of his services – but their glory; – and in comparative affluence, and honoured and pointed to as the mother of the young hero who stood high in royal favour, the widow of many sorrows took up her abode once more near the seat of her ancestors.

' "At this period, every step taken by the member of a family was a subject of anxious and solemn consultation to those who considered themselves its heads, and there was a kind of chapter held in Mortimer Castle on this singular movement of the widow Sandal. Elinor's heart beat hard during the debate – it subsided, however, at the determination, that the severe sentence of Sir Roger was not to be extended beyond his death, and that a descendant of the House of Mortimer should never live neglected while almost under the shadow of its walls.

' "The visit was accordingly solemnly paid, and gratefully received, – there was much stately courtesy on the part of Mrs Ann towards her niece, (whom she called cousin after the old English fashion), and a due degree of retrospective humility and decorous dejection on that of the widow. They parted mutually softened towards, if not pleased with each other, and the intercourse thus opened was unremittingly sustained by Elinor, whose weekly visits of ceremony soon became the daily visits of interest and of habit. The object of the thoughts of both was the theme of the tongue of but one; and, as is not uncommon, she who said nothing felt the most. The details of his exploits, the description of his person, the fond enumeration of the promises of his childhood, and the graces and goodliness of his youth, were dangerous topics for the listener, to whom the bare mention of his name caused an intoxication of the heart, from which it scarce recovered for hours.

' "The frequency of these visits was not observed to be diminished by a faint rumour, which the widow seemed to believe, rather from hope than probability, that Captain Sandal was about to visit the neighbourhood of the Castle. It was one evening in autumn, that Elinor, who had been prevented during the day from visiting her aunt, set out attended only by her maid and her usher. There was a private path through the park, that opened by a small door on the verge of the suburbs where the widow lived. Elinor, on her arrival, found her aunt from home, and was informed she had gone to pass the evening with a friend in Shrewsbury. Elinor hesitated for a moment, and then recollecting that this friend was a grave staid widow of one of Oliver's knights, wealthy, however, and well respected, and a common acquaintance, she resolved to follow her thither. As she entered the room, which was spacious, but dimly lit by an old-fashioned casement window, she was surprised to see it filled with an unusual number of persons, some of whom were seated, but the greater number were collected in the ample recess of the window, and among them Elinor saw a figure, remarkable rather for its height, than its attitude or pretension, – it was that of a tall slender boy, about eighteen, with a beautiful infant in his arms, whom he was caressing with a tenderness that seemed rather associated with the retrospective fondness of brotherhood, than the anticipated hope of paternity. The mother of the infant, proud of the notice bestowed on her child, made, however, the usual incredulous apology for its troubling him.

' " 'Troubling me!' said the boy, in tones that made Elinor think it was the first time she had heard music. 'Oh, no – if you knew how fond I am of children, – how long it is since I had the delight of pressing one to my breast – how long it may be again before' – and averting his head, he bowed it over the babe. The room was very dark, from the increasing shades of evening, deepened by the effect of the heavy wainscotting of its walls; but at this moment, the last bright light of an autumnal evening, in all its rich and fading glory, burst on the casement, pouring on every object a golden and purpureal light. That end of the apartment in which Elinor sat remained in the deepest shade. She then distinctly beheld the figure which her heart seemed to recognize before her senses. His luxuriant hair, of the richest brown, (its feathery summits tinged by the light resembling the halo round some glorified head), hung, according to the fashion of the day, in clusters on his bosom, and half-concealed the face of the infant, as it lay like a nestling among them.

'"His dress was that of a naval officer, – it was splendidly adorned with lace, and the superb insignia of a foreign order, the guerdon of some daring deed; and as the infant played with these, and then looked upward, as if to repose its dazzled sight on the smile of its young protector, Elinor thought she had never beheld association and contrast so touchingly united, – it was like a finely coloured painting, where the tints are so mellowed and mingled into each other, that the eye feels no transition in passing from one brilliant hue to another, with such exquisite imperceptibility are they graduated, – it was like a fine piece of music, where the art of the modulator prevents your knowing that you pass from one key to another; so softly are the intermediate tones of harmony touched, that the ear knows not where it wanders, but wherever it wanders, feels its path is pleasant. The young loveliness of the infant, almost assimilated to the beauty of the youthful caresser, and yet contrasted with the high and heroic air of his figure, and the adornments of his dress, (splendid as they were), all emblematic of deeds of peril and of death, seemed to the imagination of Elinor like the cherub-angel of peace reposing on the breast of valour, and whispering that his toils were done. She was awoke from her vision by the voice of the widow. – 'Niece, this is your cousin John Sandal.' Elinor started, and received the salute of her kinsman, thus abruptly introduced, with an emotion, which, if it deprived her of those courtly graces which ought to have embellished her reception of the distinguished stranger, gave her, at least, the more touching ones of diffidence.

' "The forms of the day admitted of, and even sanctioned, a mode of salutation since exploded; and as Elinor felt the pressure of a lip as vermeil as her own, she trembled to think that that lip had often given the war-word to beings athirst for human blood, and that the arm that enfolded her so tenderly had pointed the weapons of death with resistless and terrible aim against bosoms that beat with all the cords of human affection. She loved her young kinsman, but she trembled in the arms of the hero.

' "John Sandal sat down by her, and in a few moments the melody of his tones, the gentle facility of his manner, the eyes that smiled when the lips were closed, and the lips whose smile was more eloquent in silence than the language of the brightest eyes, made her gradually feel at ease with herself – she attempted to converse, but paused to listen – she tried to look up, but felt like the worshippers of the sun, sickening under the blaze she gazed on, – and *averted her eyes that she might see.* There was a mild, inoppressive, but most seductive light in the dark-blue eyes that fell so softly on hers, like moon-light floating over a fine landscape. And there was a young and eloquent tenderness in the tones of that voice, which she expected to have spoken in thunder, that disarmed and dulcified speech almost to luxury. Elinor sat, and imbibed poison at every inlet of the senses, ear and eye, and touch, for her kinsman, with a venial, and to her imperceptible licence, had taken her hand as he spoke. And he spoke much, but not of war and blood, of the scenes where he had been so eminent, and of the events to which his simple allusion would have given interest and dignity, – but of his return to his family, of the delight he felt at again beholding his mother, and of the hopes that he indulged of being not an unwelcome visitor at the Castle. He inquired after Margaret with affectionate earnestness, and after Mrs Ann with reverential regard, and in mentioning the names of these relatives, he spoke like one whose heart was at home before his steps, and whose heart could make every spot where it rested a home to itself and to others. Elinor could have listened for ever. The names of the relatives she loved and revered sounded in her ears like music, but the advancing night warned her of the necessity of returning to the Castle, where the hours were scrupulously observed; and when John Sandal offered to attend her home, she had no longer a motive to delay her departure.

' "It had appeared dark in the room where they were sitting, but it was still rich and purple twilight in the sky, when they set out for the Castle.

' "Elinor took the path through the park, and, absorbed in new feelings, was for the first time insensible of its woodland beauty, at once gloomy and resplendent, mellowed by the tints of autumnal colouring, and glorious with the light of an autumnal evening, – till she was roused to attention by the exclamations of her companion, who appeared rapt into delight at what he beheld. This sensibility of nature, this fresh and unworn feeling, in one whom she had believed hardened by scenes of toil and terror against the perception of beauty, – whom her imagination had painted to her as *fitter to cross the Alps, than to luxuriate in Campania*, touched her deeply. She attempted to reply, but was unable, – she remembered how her quick susceptibility of nature had enabled her to sympathize with and improve on the admiration expressed by others, and she wondered at her silence, for she knew not its cause.

' "As they approached the Castle, the scene became glorious beyond the imagination of a painter, whose eye has dreamed of sun-set in foreign climes. The vast edifice lay buried in shade, – all

its varied and strongly charactered features of tower and pinnacle, bartizan and battlement, were melted into one dense and
sombrous mass. The distant hills, with their conical summits,
were still clearly defined in the dark-blue heaven, and their peaks
still retained a hue of purple so brilliant and lovely, that it seemed
as if the light had loved to linger there, and, parting, had left that
tint as the promise of a glorious morning. The woods that surrounded the Castle stood as dark, and apparently as solid as itself.
Sometimes a gleam like gold trembled over the tufted foliage of
their summits, and at length, through a glade which opened
among the dark and massive boles of the ancient trees, one last
rich and gorgeous flood of light burst in, turned every blade of
grass it touched into emerald for a moment, – paused on its
lovely work – and parted. The effect was so instantaneous, brilliant, and evanishing, that Elinor had scarce time for a half uttered
exclamation, as she extended her arm in the direction where the
light had fallen so brightly and so briefly. She raised her eyes to
her companion, in that full consciousness of perfect sympathy
that makes words seem like counters, compared to the sterling
gold of a heart-minted look. Her companion had turned towards
it too. He neither uttered exclamation, nor pointed with finger, –
he smiled, and his countenance was as that of an angel. It seemed
to reflect and answer the last bright farewell of day, as if friends
had parted smiling at each other. It was not alone the lips that
smiled, – the eyes, the cheeks, every feature had its share in that
effulgent light that was diffused over his aspect, and all combined
to make that harmony to the eye, which is often as deliciously
perceptible, as the combination of the most exquisite voices with
the most perfect modulation, is to the ear. To the last hour of her
mortal existence, that smile, and the scene where it was *uttered*,
were engraved on the heart of Elinor. It announced at once a
spirit, that, like the ancient statue, answered every ray of light
that fell on it with a voice of melody, and blended the triumph of
the glories of nature with the profound and tender felicities of

the heart. They spoke no more during the remainder of their walk, but there was more eloquence in their silence than in many words.

*

' "It was almost night before they arrived at the Castle. Mrs Ann received her distinguished kinsman with stately cordiality, and affection mingled with pride. Margaret welcomed him rather as the hero than the relative; and John, after the ceremonies of introduction, turned to repose himself on the smile of Elinor. They had arrived just at the time when the chaplain was about to read the evening prayers, – a form so strictly adhered to at the Castle, that not even the arrival of a stranger was permitted to interfere with its observance. Elinor watched this moment with peculiar solicitude; – her religious feelings were profound, and amid all the young hero's vivid display of the gentlest affections, and purest sensibilities by which our wretched existence can be enhanced or beautified, she still dreaded that religion, the companion of deep thought and solemn habits, might wander far for an abode before it settled in the heart of a sailor. The last doubt passed from her mind, as she beheld the intense but silent devotion with which John mingled in the family rite. There is something very ennobling in the sight of male piety. To see that lofty form, that never bowed to man, bowed to the earth to God, – to behold the knee, whose joints would be as adamant under the influence of mortal force or threat, as flexible as those of infancy in the presence of the Almighty, – to see the locked and lifted hands, to hear the fervent aspiration, to feel the sound of the mortal weapon as it drags on the floor beside the kneeling warrior, – these are things that touch the senses and the heart at once, and suggest the awful and affecting image of all physical energy prostrate before the power of the Divinity. Elinor watched him even to the forgetfulness of her own devotions; – and when his white hands, that seemed never formed to grasp a weapon of destruction, were clasped in devotion, and one of them slightly and occasionally raised to part the redundant curls that shaded his face as he knelt, she thought that she beheld at once angelic strength and angelic purity.

' "When the service concluded, Mrs Ann, after repeating her solemn welcome to her nephew, could not help expressing her satisfaction at the devotion he had showed; but she mingled with that expression a kind of incredulity, that men accustomed to toil and peril could ever have devotional feelings. John Sandal bowed to the congratulatory part of Mrs Ann's speech, and, resting one hand on his short sword, and with the other removing the thick ringlets of his luxuriant hair, he stood before them a hero in deed, and a boy in form. A blush overspread his young features, as he said, in accents at once emphatic and tremulous, 'Dear Aunt, why should you accuse those of neglecting the protection of the Almighty who need it most. They who "go down to the sea in ships, and occupy their business in the great waters", have the best right to feel, in their hour of peril, "it is but the wind and the storm fulfilling his word". A seaman without a belief and hope in God, is worse off than a seaman without chart or pilot.'

' "As he spoke with that trembling eloquence that makes conviction be felt almost before it is heard, Mrs Ann held out to him her withered but still snow-white hand to kiss. Margaret presented hers also, like a heroine to a feudal knight; and Elinor turned aside, and wept in delicious agony.

*

' "When we set ourselves resolutely to discover perfection in a character, we are always sure to find it. But Elinor needed little aid from the pencil of imagination to colour the object that had been stamped by an ineffaceable touch upon her heart. Her kinsman's character and temper developed themselves slowly, or rather were developed by external and accidental causes; for a diffidence almost feminine prevented his ever saying much, – and when he did, himself was the last theme he touched on. He unfolded himself like a blowing flower, – the soft and silken leaves expanded imperceptibly to the eye, and every day the tints were deepening, and the scent becoming richer, till Elinor was dazzled by their lustre, and inebriated with the fragrance.

' "This wish to discover excellencies in the object we love, and to identify esteem and passion by seeking the union of moral beauty and physical grace, is a proof that love is of a very ennobling character, – that, however the stream may be troubled by many things, the source at least is pure, – and that the heart capable of feeling it intensely, proves it possesses an energy that may one day be rewarded by a brighter object, and a holier flame, than earth ever afforded, or nature ever could kindle.

*

' "Since her son's arrival, the widow Sandal had betrayed a marked degree of anxiety, and a kind of restless precaution against some invisible evil. She was now frequently at the Castle. She could not be blind to the increasing attachment of John and Elinor, – and her only thought was how to prevent the possibility of their union, by which the interest of the former and her own importance would be materially affected.

' "She had obtained, by indirect means, a knowledge of the contents of Sir Roger's will; and the whole force of a mind which possessed more of art than of power, and of a temper which had more passion than energy, was strained to realize the hopes it suggested. Sir Roger's will was singular. Alienated as he was from his daughter Sandal, and his younger son the father of Elinor, by the connexions they had adopted, it seemed to be the strongest object of his wishes to unite their descendants, and invest the wealth and rank of the house of Mortimer in the last of its representatives. He had therefore bequeathed his immense estates to his grand-daughter Margaret, in the event of her marrying her kinsman John Sandal; – in the case of his marrying Elinor, he was

entitled to no more than her fortune of £5000; – and the bequest
of the greater part of the property to a distant relative who bore
the name of Mortimer, was to be the consequence of the non-
intermarriage of Sandal with either of his cousins.

' "Mrs Ann Mortimer, anticipating the effect that this opposition of interest to affection might produce in the family, had kept
the contents of the will a secret, – but Mrs Sandal had discovered
it by means of the domestics at the Castle, and her mind wrought
intensely on the discovery. She was a woman too long familiar
with want and privation to dread any evil but their continuance,
and too ambitious of the remembered distinctions of her early
life, not to risk any thing that might enable her to recover them.
She felt a personal feminine jealousy of the high-minded Mrs
Ann, and the noble-hearted beautiful Margaret, which was unappeasable; and she hovered round the walls of the Castle like a
departed spirit groaning for its re-admission to the place from
which it had been driven, and feeling and giving no peace till its
restoration was accomplished.

' "When with these feelings was united the anxiety of maternal
ambition for her son, who might be raised to a noble inheritance,
or sunk to comparative mediocrity by his choice, the result may
be easily guessed; and the widow Sandal, once determined on the
end, felt little scruple about the means. Want and envy had given
her an unslakeable appetite for the restored splendours of her
former state; and false religion had taught her every shade and
penumbra of hypocrisy, every meanness of artifice, every obliquity of insinuation. In her varied life she had known the good,
and chosen the evil. The widow Sandal was now determined to
interpose an insurmountable obstruction to their union.

*

' "Mrs Ann still flattered herself that the secret of Sir Roger's will
was suppressed. She saw the intense and disruptable feeling that
seemed to mark John and Elinor for each other; and, with a

feeling half-borrowed from magnanimity, half from romance, (for Mrs Ann had been fond of the high-toned romances of her day), she looked forward to the felicity of their union as being little disturbed by the loss of land and lordship, – of the immense revenues, – and the far descended titles of the Mortimer family.

' "Highly as she prized these distinctions, dear to every noble mind, she prized still more highly the union of devoted hearts and congenial spirits, who, trampling on the golden apples that were flung in their path, pressed forward with unremitting ardour for the prize of felicity.

' "The wedding-day of John and Elinor was fixed, – the bridal clothes were made, – the noble and numerous friends summoned, – the Castle hall decorated, the bells of the parish church ringing out a loud and merry peal, and the blue-coated serving men adorned with favours, and employed in garnishing the wassail bowl, which was doomed by many a thirsty eye to be often drained and often replenished. Mrs Ann herself took with her own hands, from an ample chest of ebony, a robe of velvet and satin, which she had worn at the court of James the First, on the marriage of the princess Elizabeth with the prince palatine, of whom the former, to borrow the language of a contemporary writer, had 'brided and bridled it so well, and indeed became herself so handsomely,' that Mrs Ann, as she arrayed herself, thought she saw the splendid vision of the royal bridal float before her faded eyes in dim but gorgeous pageantry once more. The heiress, too, attired herself splendidly, but it was observed, that her beautiful cheek was paler than even that of the bride, and the smile which held a fixed unjoyous station on her features all that morning, seemed more like the effort of resolution than the expression of felicity. The widow Sandal had betrayed considerable agitation, and quitted the Castle at an early hour. The bridegroom had not yet appeared, and the company, after having in vain for some time awaited his arrival, set out for the church, where they supposed he was impatiently expecting them.

' "The cavalcade was magnificent and numerous – the dignity and consequence of the Mortimer family had assembled all who had aspired to the distinction of their acquaintance, and such was then the feudal grandeur attendant on the nuptials of a high-descended family, that relatives, however remote in blood or in local distance, collected for sixty miles in every direction around the Castle, and presented a 'host of friends, gorgeously arrayed and attended on that eventful morning'.

' "Most of the company, even including the females, were mounted on horseback, and this, by apparently increasing the number of the procession, added to its tumultuous magnificence. There were some cumbrous vehicles, misnamed carriages of a fashion indescribably inconvenient, but gorgeously gilded and painted, – and the Cupids on the pannels had been re-touched for the occasion. The bride was lifted on her palfrey by two peers, – Margaret rode beside her gallantly attended, – and Mrs Ann, who once more saw nobles contending for her withered hand, and adjusting her silken rein, felt the long-faded glories of her family revive, and led the van of the pompous procession with as much dignity of demeanour, and as much glow of faded beauty, once eminent and resistless, as if she still followed the gorgeous nuptial progress of the princess palatine. They arrived at the church, – the bride, the relatives, the splendid company, the minister – all but the bridegroom, were there. There was a long painful silence. Several gentlemen of the bridal party rode rapidly out in every direction in which it was thought probable to meet him, – the clergyman stood at the altar, till, weary of standing, he retired. The crowd from the neighbouring villages, combined with the numerous attendants, filled the church-yard. Their acclamations were incessant, – the heat and distraction became intolerable, and Elinor begged for a few moments to be allowed to retire to the vestry.

' "There was a casement window which opened on the road, and Mrs Ann supported the bride as she tottered towards it, attempting to loose her wimple, and veil of costly lace. As Elinor approached the casement, the thundering hoofs of a horse at full speed shook the road. Elinor looked up mechanically, – the rider was John Sandal, – he cast a look of horror at the pale bride, and plunging his desperate spurs deeper, disappeared in a moment.

*

' "A year after this event, two figures were seen to walk, or rather wander, almost every evening, in the neighbourhood of a small hamlet in a remote part of Yorkshire. The vicinage was pictur-esque and attractive, but these figures seemed to move amid the scenery like beings, who, if they still retained eyes for nature, had lost all heart for it. That wan and attenuated form, so young, yet so withered, whose dark eyes emit a fearful light amid features chill and white as those of a statue, and the young graces of whose form seem to have been nipt like those of a lily that bloomed too soon in spring, and was destroyed by the frost of the treacherous season, whose whispers had first invited it to bud, – that is Elinor Mortimer, – and that figure that walks beside her, so stiff and rectangular, that it seems as its motion was regulated by mechanism, whose sharp eyes are directed so straight forward, that they see neither tree on the right hand, or glade on the left, or heaven above, or earth beneath, or any thing but a dim vision of mystic theology for ever before them, which is aptly reflected in their cold contemplative light, that is the Puritan maiden sister of her mother, with whom Elinor had fixed her residence. Her dress is arranged with as much precision as if a mathematician had calculated the angles of every fold, – every pin's point knows its place, and does its duty – the plaits of her round-eared cap do not permit one hair to appear on her narrow forehead, and her large hood, adjusted after the fashion in which it was worn by the godly sisters, who rode out to meet Prynne on his return from the pillory, lends a deeper shade to her rigid features, – a wretched-looking lacquey is carrying a huge clasped bible after her, in the mode in which she remembered to have seen Lady Lambert and Lady Desborough march to prayer, attended by their pages, while she proudly followed in their train, distinguished as the sister of that godly man and powerful preacher of the world, Sandal. From the day of her disappointed nuptials, Elinor, with that insulted feeling of maiden pride, which not even the anguish of her broken heart could suppress, had felt an unappeaseable anxiety to quit the scene of her disgrace and her misfortune. It was vainly opposed by her aunt and Margaret, who, horror-struck at the event of those disastrous nuptials, and wholly unconscious of the cause, had implored her, with all the energy of affection, to fix her residence at the Castle, within whose walls they pledged themselves he who had abandoned her should never be permitted to place his foot. Elinor answered the impassioned importunities, only by eager and clinging pressures of her cold hands, and by tears which trembled on her eyelids, without the power to fall. – 'Nay, stay with us,' said the kind and noble-hearted Margaret, 'you shall not leave us!' And she pressed the hands of her kinswoman, with that cordial touch that gives a welcome as much to the heart as to the home of the inviter. – 'Dearest cousin,' said Elinor, answering, for the first time, this affectionate appeal with a faint and ghastly smile – 'I have so many enemies within these walls, that I can no longer encounter them with safety to my life.' – 'Enemies!' repeated Margaret. – 'Yes, dearest cousin – there is not a spot where *he* trod – not a prospect on which he has gazed – not an echo which has repeated the sound of his voice, – that does not send daggers through my heart, which those who wish me to live would not willingly see infixed any longer.' To the emphatic agony with which these words were uttered, Margaret had nothing to reply but with tears; and Elinor set out on her journey to the relative of her mother, a rigid Puritan, who resided in Yorkshire.

' "As the carriage was ordered for her departure, Mrs Ann, supported by her female attendants, stood on the drawbridge to take leave of her niece, with solemn and affectionate courtesy. Margaret wept bitterly, and aloud, as she stood at a casement, and waved her hand to Elinor. Her aunt never shed a tear, till out of the presence of the domestics, – but when all was over, – 'she entered into her chamber, and wept there'.

' "When her carriage had driven some miles from the Castle, a servant on a fleet horse followed it at full speed with Elinor's lute, which had been forgotten, – it was offered to her, and after viewing it for some moments with a look in which memory struggled with grief, she ordered its strings to be broken on the spot, and proceeded on her journey.

' "The retreat to which Elinor had retired, did not afford her the tranquillity she expected. Thus, change of place always deceives us with the tantalizing hope of relief, as we toss on the feverish bed of life.

' "She went in a faint expectation of the revival of her religious feelings – she went to wed, amid the solitude and desert where she had first known him, the immortal bridegroom, who would never desert her as the mortal one had done, – but she did not find him there – the voice of God was no longer heard in the garden – either her religious sensibility had abated, or those from whom she first received the impression, had no longer power to renew it, or perhaps the heart which has exhausted itself on a mortal object, does not find its powers soon recruited to meet the image of celestial beneficence, and exchange at once the visible for the invisible, – the felt and present, for the future and the unknown.

' "Elinor returned to the residence of her mother's family in the hope of renewing former images, but she found only the words that had conveyed those ideas, and she looked around in vain for the impressions they had once suggested. When we thus come to feel that *all* has been illusion, even on the most solemn subjects, – that the future world seems to be deserting us along with the present, and that our own hearts, with all their treachery, have done us no more wrong than the false impressions which we have received from our religious instructors, we are like the deity in the painting of the great Italian artist, extending one hand to the sun, and the other to the moon, but touching neither. Elinor had imagined or hoped, that the language of her aunt would have revived her habitual associations – she was disappointed. It is true no pains were spared – when Elinor wished to read, she was furnished amply with the Westminster Confession, or Prynne's Histriomastix, or if she wished for lighter pages, for the Belles Lettres of Puritanism, there were John Bunyan's Holy War, or the life of Mr Badman. If she closed the book in despair at the insensibility of her untouched heart, she was invited to a godly conference, where the non-conformist ministers, who had been, in the language of the day, extinguished under the Bartholomew bushel*, met to give the precious word in season to the scattered fold of the Lord. Elinor knelt and wept too at these meetings; but, while her form was prostrated before the Deity, her tears fell for one whom she dared not name. When, in incontroulable agony, she sought, like Joseph, where she might weep unobserved and unrestrained, and rushed into the narrow garden that skirted the cottage of her aunt, and wept there, she was followed by the quiet, sedate figure, moving at the rate of an inch in a minute, who offered her for her consolation, the newly published and difficultly obtained work of Marshall on Sanctification.

' "Elinor, accustomed too much to that fatal excitement of the heart, which renders all other excitement as faint and feeble as the air of heaven to one who has been inhaling the potent inebriation of the strongest perfumes, wondered how this being, so abstracted, cold, and unearthly, could tolerate her motionless existence. She rose at a fixed hour, – at a fixed hour she prayed, – at a fixed hour received the godly friends who visited her, and whose existence was as monotonous and apathetic as her

* Anachronism – n'importe.

own, – at a fixed hour she dined, – and at a fixed hour she prayed again, and then retired, – yet she prayed without unction, and fed without appetite, and retired to rest without the least inclination to sleep. Her life was mere mechanism; but the machine was so well wound up, that it appeared to have some quiet consciousness and sullen satisfaction in its movements.

' "Elinor struggled in vain for the renewal of this life of cold mediocrity, – she thirsted for it as one who, in the deserts of Africa, expiring for want of water, would wish for the moment to be an inmate of Lapland, to drink of their eternal snows, – yet at that moment wonders how its inhabitants can live among SNOW. She saw a being far inferior to herself in mental power, – of feelings that hardly deserved the name – *tranquil*, and wondered that she herself was wretched. – Alas! she did not know, that the heartless and unimaginative are those alone who entitle themselves to the comforts of life, and who can alone enjoy them. A cold and sluggish mediocrity in their occupations or their amusements, is all they require – pleasure has with them no meaning but the exemption from actual suffering, nor do they annex any idea to pain but the immediate infliction of corporeal suffering, or of external calamity – the source of pain or pleasure is never found in their *hearts* – while those who have profound feelings scarce ever look elsewhere for either. So much the worse for them, – the being reduced to providing for the necessities of human life, and being satisfied when that provision is made, is perhaps the best condition of human life – beyond that, all is the dream of insanity, or the agony of disappointment. Far better the dull and dusky winter's day, whose gloom, if it never abates, never increases, – (and to which we lift up an eye of listlessness, in which there is no apprehension of future and added terrors), – to the glorious fierceness of the summer's day, whose sun sets amid purple and gold, – while, panting under its parting beams, we see the clouds collecting in the darkening East, and view the armies of heaven on their march, whose thunders are to break our rest, and whose lightnings may crumble us to ashes.

*

' "Elinor strove hard with her fate, – the strength of her intellect had been much developed since her residence at Mortimer Castle, and there also the energies of her heart had been developed fatally. How dreadful is the conflict of superior intellect and a burning heart, with the perfect mediocrity of the characters and circumstances they are generally doomed to live with! The battering-rams play against woolbags, – the lightnings glance on ice, hiss, and are extinguished. The greater strength we exhibit, we feel we are more and more paralyzed by the weakness of our enemies, – our very energy becomes our bitterest enemy, as it fights in vain against the impregnable fortress of total vacuity! It is in vain we assail a foe who neither knows our language or uses our weapons. Elinor gave it up, – yet still she struggled with her own feelings; and perhaps the conflict which she now undertook was the hardest of all. She had received her first religious impressions under the roof of her Puritanic aunt, and, true or false, they had been so vivid, that she was anxious to revive them. When the heart is robbed of its first-born, there is nothing it will not try to adopt. Elinor remembered a very affecting scene that had occurred in her childhood, beneath the roof where she now resided.

' "An old non-conformist minister, a very Saint John for sanctity of life, and simplicity of manners, had been seized by a magistrate while giving the word of consolation to a few of his flock who had met at the cottage of her aunt.

' "The old man had supplicated for a moment's delay on the part of the civil power, and its officers, by an unusual effort of toleration or of humanity, complied. Turning to his congregation, who, amid the tumult of the arrest, had never risen from their knees, and only changed the voice of supplication from praying with their pastor, to praying for him, – he quoted to them that beautiful passage from the prophet Malachi, which appears to give such delightful encouragement to the spiritual intercourse of Christians, – 'Then they that feared the Lord, spoke often to one another, and the Lord heard it', &c. As he spoke, the old man was dragged away by some rougher hands, and died soon after in confinement.

' "On the young imagination of Elinor, this scene was indelibly written. Amid the magnificence of Mortimer Castle, it had never been effaced or obscured, and now she tried to make herself in love with the sounds and the scene that had so deeply touched her infant heart.

' "Resolute in her purposes, she spared no pains to excite this reminiscence of religion, – it was her last resource. Like the wife of Phineas, she struggled to bear an heir of the soul, even while she named him *Ichabod*, – and felt the glory was departed. She went to the narrow apartment, – she seated herself in the very chair that venerable man occupied when he was torn from it, and his departure appeared to her like that of an ascending prophet. She would *then* have caught the folds of his mantle, and mounted with him, even though his flight had led to prison and to death. She tried, by repeating his last words, to produce the same effect they had once had on her heart, and wept in indescribable agony at feeling those words had no meaning now for her. When life and passion have thus rejected us, the backward steps we are compelled to tread towards the path we have wandered from, are ten thousand times more torturing and arduous than those we have exhausted in their pursuit. Hope then supported our hands every step we took. Remorse and disappointment scourge us back, and every step is tinged with tears or with blood; and well it is for the pilgrim if that blood is drained from his heart, for then – his pilgrimage will be sooner terminated.

*

598

' "At times Elinor, who had forgotten neither the language or habits of her former existence, would speak in a manner that gave her Puritanic relative hopes that, according to the language of the times, 'the root of the matter was in her', and when the old lady, in confidence of her returning orthodoxy, discussed long and learnedly on the election and perseverance of the saints, the listener would startle her by a burst of feeling, that seemed to her aunt more like the ravings of a demoniac, than the language of a human being, – especially one who had from her youth known the Scriptures, She would say, 'Dearest aunt, I am not insensible of what you say; from a child, (thanks to your care), I have known the holy scriptures. I *have* felt the power of religion. At a latter period I have experienced all the enjoyments of an intellectual existence. Surrounded by splendour, I have conversed with enlarged minds, – I have seen all that life can shew me, – I have lived with the mean and the rich, – the spiritual in their poverty, and the worldly-minded in their grandeur, – I have deeply drank of the cup which both modes of existence held to my lip, – and at this moment I swear to you, – *one moment of heart*, – one dream such as once I dreamed, (and though I should never awake from), is worth all the existence that the earthlyminded lavish on this world, and those who mystify expend on the next!' – 'Unfortunate wretch! and undone for everlasting!' cried the terrified Calvinist, lifting up her hands. – 'Cease, cease,' said Elinor with that dignity which grief alone can give, – 'If I have indeed devoted to an earthly love that which is due to God alone, is not my punishment certain in a future state? Has it not already commenced here? May not then all reproaches be spared when we are suffering more than human enmity can wish us, – when our very existence is a bitterer reproach to us than malignity can utter?' – As she spoke, she added, wiping a cold tear from her wasted cheek, 'My stroke is heavier than my groaning!'

' "At other times she appeared to listen to the language of the Puritan preachers (for all were preachers who frequented the house) with some appearance of attention, and then, rushing from them without any conviction but that of despair, exclaimed in her haste, 'All men are liars!' Thus it fares with those who wish to make an instant transition from one world to another, – it is impossible, – the cold wave interposes – for ever interposes, between the wilderness and the land of promise – and we may as soon expect to tread the threshold which parts life and death without pain, as to cross the interval which separates two modes of existence so distinct as those of passion and religion, without struggles of the soul inexpressible – without groanings which cannot be uttered.

'"To these struggles there was soon to be an addition. Letters at this period circulated very slowly, and were written only on important occasions. Within a very short period, Elinor received two letters by express from Mortimer Castle, written by her cousin Margaret. The first announced the arrival of John Sandal at the Castle, – the second, the death of Mrs Ann, – the post-scriptums of both contained certain mysterious hints relative to the interruption of the marriage, – intimations that the cause was known only to the writer, to Sandal and to his mother, – and entreaties that Elinor would return to the Castle, and partake of the *sisterly* love with which Margaret and John Sandal would be glad to receive her. The letters dropt from her hand as she received them, – of John Sandal she had never ceased to think, but she had never ceased to wish not to think, – and his name even now gave her a pang which she could neither utter or suppress, and which burst forth in an involuntary shriek, that seemed like the last string that breaks in the exquisite and too-highly strung instrument of the human heart.

'"Over the account of Mrs Ann's death, she lingered with that fearful feeling that a young adventurer experiences, who sees a noble vessel set out before him on a voyage of discovery, and wishes, while lingering in harbour himself, that he was already at the shore where *it* has arrived, and tasted of its repose, and participated in its treasures.

' "Mrs Ann's death had not been unworthy of that life of magnanimity and high heroic feeling which had marked every hour of her mortal existence – she had espoused the cause of the rejected Elinor, and sworn in the chapel of Mortimer Castle, while Margaret knelt beside, never to admit within its walls the deserter of his betrothed bride.

' "On a dim autumnal evening, when Mrs Ann, with fading sight but undiminished feeling, was poring over some of Lady Russell's letters in manuscript, and, to relieve her eyes, sometimes glanced on the manuscript of Nelson's Fasts and Festivals of the Church of England, it was announced to her that a Cavalier (the servants well knew the charm of that name to the ear of the ancient loyalist) had crossed the draw-bridge, entered the hall, and was advancing to the apartment where she sat. 'Let him be admitted,' was her answer, and rising from her chair, which was so lofty and so spacious, that as she lifted herself from it to greet the stranger with a courtly reception, her form appeared like a spectre rising from an ancient monument, – she stood facing the entrance – at that entrance appeared John Sandal. She bent forwards for a moment, but her eyes, bright and piercing, still recognized him in a moment.

' " 'Back! – back!' – exclaimed the stately ancestress, waving him off with her withered hand – 'Back! – profane not this floor with another step!' – 'Hear me, madam, for one moment – suffer me to address you, even on my knees – I pay the homage to your rank and relationship – misunderstand it not as an acknowledgement of guilt on my part!'

' "Mrs Ann's features at this action underwent a slight contraction – a short spasmodic affection. 'Rise, Sir – rise,' she said – 'and say what you have to say – but utter it, Sir, at the door whose threshold you are unworthy to tread.'

' "John Sandal rose from his knees, and pointed instinctively as he rose to the portrait of Sir Roger Mortimer, to whom he bore a striking resemblance. Mrs Ann acknowledged the appeal – she advanced a few steps on the oaken floor – she stood erect for a moment, and then, pointing with a dignity of action which no pencil could embody to the portrait, seemed to consider her attitude as a valid and eloquent answer – it said – he to whose resemblance you point, and claim protection from, never like you dishonoured these walls by an act of baseness – of heartless treachery! Betrayer! – look to his portrait! Her expression had in it something of the sublime – the next moment a strong spasm contracted her features – she attempted to speak, but her lips no longer obeyed her – she seemed to speak, but was not heard even by herself. She stood for a moment before John Sandal in that rigid immoveable attitude that says, 'Advance not another step at your peril – insult not the portraits of your ancestors – insult not their living representative, by another step of intrusion!' As she spoke thus, (for her attitude spoke), a stronger spasm contracted her features. She attempted to move – the same rigid constriction extended to her limbs; and, waving her prohibitory arm still, as if in defiance at once of the approach of death and of her rejected kinsman, she dropt at his feet.

*

' "She did not long survive the interview, nor did she ever recover the use of speech. Her powerful intellect was, however, unimpaired; and to the last she expressed herself most intelligibly by action, as determined not to hear a word explanatory of Sandal's conduct. This explanation was therefore made to Margaret, who, though much shocked and agitated at the first disclosure, seemed afterwards perfectly reconciled to it.

*

' "Shortly after the receipt of these letters, Elinor took a sudden, but perhaps not singular resolution, – she determined to set out immediately for Mortimer Castle. It was not her weariness of the withering life, the αβιωτος βιος[51] she lived at her Puritanic aunt's – it was not the wish to enjoy again the stately and splendid ceremonial of Mortimer Castle, contrasted with the frugal fare and monastic rigour of the cottage in Yorkshire – it was not even the wish for that change of place that always flatters us with change of circumstance, as if we did not carry our own hearts with us wherever we go, and might not therefore be sure that an innate and eroding ulcer must be our companion from the Pole to the Equator – it was not this, but a whisper half unheard, yet believed, (just in proportion as it was inaudible and incredible), that murmured from the bottom of her credulous heart, 'Go – and *perhaps*' –

' "Elinor set out on her journey, and after having performed it with fewer difficulties than can be imagined, considering the state of the roads, and the modes of travelling in the year 1667 or thereabouts, she arrived in the vicinity of Mortimer Castle. It was a scene of reminiscence to her, – her heart throbbed audibly as the carriage stopped at a Gothic gate, through which there was a walk between two rows of lofty elms. She alighted, and to the request of the servant who followed her, that he might be permitted to shew her the way through a path entangled by the intersecting roots of the trees, and dim with twilight, she answered only by her tears. She waved him off, and advanced on foot and alone. She remembered, from the bottom of her soul, how she had once wandered amid that very grove with John Sandal – how his smile had shed a richer light on the landscape, than even the purple smile of the dying day-light. She thought of that smile, and lingered to catch it amid the rich and burning hues flung by the fading light on the many-tinted boles of the ancient trees. The trees were there – and the light was there – but his smile, that once eclipsed the sun-light, was there no longer!

' "She advanced alone – the lofty avenue of trees still retained its magnificent depth of shade, and gorgeous colouring of trunk and leaf. She sought among them for that which she had once felt – and God and nature alone are conscious of the agony with which we demand from them the object which we are conscious was once consecrated to our hearts, and which we now require of both in vain! God withholds, – and Nature denies them!

' "As Elinor with trembling steps advanced towards the Castle, she saw the funeral scutcheon which Mrs Margaret, in honour of her grand-aunt, had caused to be affixed over the principal tower since her decease, with the same heraldic decorum as if the last male of the Mortimer family were extinct. Elinor looked up, and many thoughts rushed on her heart. – 'There is one departed,' she thought, 'whose mind was always fixed on glorious thoughts – the most exalted actions of humanity, or the sublime associations of eternity! Her noble heart had room but for two illustrious guests – the love of God, and the love of her country. They tarried with her to the last, for they found the abode worthy of them; and when they parted, the inmate found the mansion untenantable any longer – the soul fled with its glorious visitors to heaven! My treacherous heart welcomed another inmate, and how has he repaid its hospitality? – By leaving the mansion in ruins!' As she spoke thus, she approached the entrance of the Castle.

' "In the spacious hall she was received by Margaret Mortimer with the embrace of rooted affection, and by John Sandal, who advanced after the first enthusiasm of meeting was over, with that calm and brother-like good-will, from which there was – nothing to be hoped. There was the same heavenly smile, the same clasp of the hand, the same tender and almost feminine expression of anxiety for her safety – even Margaret herself, who must have felt, and who did feel the perils of the long journey, did not enter into them with that circumstantiality, or appear to sympathize with them so vividly, or, when the tale of toil and travel was told, appear to urge the necessity of speedy retirement, with such solicitude as did John Sandal. Elinor, faint and gasping, grasped the hands of both, and by an involuntary motion locked both together. The widow Sandal was present – she shewed much agitation at the appearance of Elinor; but when she saw this extraordinary and spontaneous movement, it was observed she smiled.

' "Soon after, Elinor retired to the apartment she had formerly occupied. By the affectionate and delicate prevoyance of Margaret, the furniture had all been changed – there was nothing to remind her of former days, except her heart. She sat for some time reflecting on her reception, and hope died within her heart as she thought of it. The strongest expression of aversion or disdain would not have been so withering.

' "It is certain that the fiercest passions may be exchanged for their widest extremes in a time incredibly short, and by means the most incalculable. Within the narrow circle of a day, enemies may embrace, and lovers may hate, – but, in the course of centuries, pure complacency and cordial good-will never can be exalted into passion. The wretched Elinor felt this, – and feeling it, knew that all was lost.

' "She had now, for many days, to undergo the torture of complacent and fraternal affection from the man she loved, – and perhaps a keener torture was never endured. To feel hands that we long to press to our burning hearts, touch ours with cool and pulseless tranquillity – to see eyes in whose light we live, throw on us a cold but smiling beam, that gives light, but not fertility, to the parched and thirsting soil of the heart – to hear the ordinary language of affectionate civility addressed to us in tones of the most delicious suavity – to seek in these expressions an ulterior meaning, and to find it not – This – this is an agony which only those who have felt can conceive!

' "Elinor, with an effort that cost her heart many a pang, mingled in the habits of the house, which had been greatly changed since the death of Mrs Ann. The numerous suitors of the wealthy and noble heiress, now crowded to the Castle; and, according to the custom of the times, they were sumptuously entertained, and invited to prolong their stay by numerous banquets.

' "On these occasions, John Sandal was the first to pay distinguished attention to Elinor. They danced together; and though her Puritanic education had taught her an abhorrence of those 'devil's measures', as her family was accustomed to term them, she tried to adapt herself to the gay steps of the Canaries*, and the stately movements of the Measures – (for the newer dances had not, even in report, reached Mortimer Castle) – and her slender and graceful form needed no other inspiration than the support of John Sandal's arms, (who was himself an exquisite dancer), to assume all the graces of that delightful exercise. Even the practised courtiers applauded her. But, when it was over, Elinor felt, that had John Sandal been dancing with a being the most indifferent to him on earth, his manner would have been exactly the same. No one could point with more smiling grace to her slight deviations from the figure, – no one could attend her to her seat with more tender and anxious politeness, and wave the vast fan of those days over her with more graceful and assiduous courtesy. But Elinor felt that these attentions, however flattering, were offered not by a lover.

*

' "Sandal was absent on a visit to some neighbouring nobleman, and Margaret and Elinor were one evening completely alone. Each seemed equally anxious for an explanation, which neither appeared willing to begin. Elinor had lingered till twilight at the casement, from which she had seen him ride, and lingered still

---

* In Cowley's 'Cutter of Coleman Street,' Mrs Tabitha, a rigid Puritan, tells her husband she had danced the Canaries in her youth. And in Rushworth's Collections, if I remember right, Prynne vindicates himself from the charge of a general denunciation against dancing, and even speaks of the 'Measures', a stately, solemn dance, with some approbation.

when to see him was no longer possible. Her sight was strained to catch a glimpse of him through the gathering clouds, as her imagination still toiled to catch a gleam of that light of the heart, which now struggled dimly amid clouds of gloomy and unpierceable mystery. 'Elinor,' said Margaret emphatically, 'look for him no longer, – he never can be yours!'

' "The sudden address, and the imperative tone of conviction, had upon Elinor the effect of being addressed by a supernatural monitor. She was unable even to ask how the terrible intelligence that burst on her so decisively, was obtained.

' "There is a state of mind in which we listen thus to a human voice as if it were an oracle, – and instead of asking an explanation of the destiny it announces, we wait submissively for what yet remains to be told. In this mood, Elinor slowly advanced from the casement, and asked in a voice of fearful calmness, 'Has he explained himself perfectly to you?' – 'Perfectly.' – 'And there is nothing to expect?' – 'Nothing.' – 'And you have heard this from himself – his very self?' – 'I have; and, dear Elinor, let us never again speak on the subject.' – 'Never!' answered Elinor, – 'Never!'

' "The veracity and dignity of Margaret's character, were inviolable securities for the truth of what she uttered; and perhaps that was the very reason why Elinor tried to shrink most from the conviction. In a morbid state of heart, we cannot bear truth – the falsehood that intoxicates us for a moment, is worth more than the truth that would disenchant us for life. – *I hate him because he tells me the truth*, is the language natural to the human mind, from the slave of power to the slave of passion.

*

' "Other symptoms that could not escape the notice of the most shallow, struck her every hour. That devotion of the eye and heart, – of the language and the look, that cannot be mistaken, – were all obviously directed to Margaret. Still Elinor lingered in the Castle, and said to herself, while every day she saw and felt what was passing, 'Perhaps.' That is the last word that quits the lips of those who love.

*

' "She saw with all her eyes, – she felt to the bottom of her soul, – the obviously increasing attachment of John Sandal and Margaret; yet still she dreamed of interposing obstacles, – of *an explanation*. When passion is deprived of its proper aliment, there is no telling the food on which it will prey, – the impossibilities to which, like a famished garrison, it will look for its wretched sustenance.

' "Elinor had ceased to demand the heart of the being she was devoted to. She now lived on his looks. She said to herself, Let him smile, though not on me, and I am happy still – wherever the sun-light falls, the earth must be blessed. Then she sunk to lower claims. She said, Let me but be in his presence, and that is enough – let his smiles and his soul be devoted to another, one wandering ray may reach me, and that will be enough!

' "Love is a very noble and exalting sentiment in its first germ and principle. We never love without arraying the object in all the glories of moral as well as physical perfection, and deriving a kind of dignity to ourselves from our capacity of admiring a creature so excellent and dignified; but this lavish and magnificent prodigality of the imagination often leaves the heart a bankrupt. Love in its iron age of disappointment, becomes very degraded – it submits to be satisfied with merely exterior indulgences – a look, a touch of the hand, though occurring by accident – a kind word, though uttered almost unconsciously, suffices for its humble existence. In its first state, it is like man before the fall, inhaling the odours of paradise, and enjoying the communion of the Deity; in the latter, it is like the same being toiling amid the briar and the thistle, barely to maintain a squalid existence without enjoyment, utility, or loveliness.

*

' "About this time, her Puritan aunt made a strong effort to recover

Elinor out of the snare of the enemy. She wrote a long letter (a great exertion for a woman far advanced in years, and never in the habits of epistolary composition) adjuring her apostate niece to return to the guide of her youth, and the covenant of her God, – to take shelter in the everlasting arms while they were still held out to her, – and to flee to the city of refuge while its gates were yet open to receive her. She urged on her the truth, power, and blessedness of the system of Calvin, which she termed the gospel. – She supported and defended it with all the metaphysical skill, and all the scriptural knowledge she possessed, – and the latter was not scanty. – And she affectingly reminded her, that the hand that traced these lines, would be unable ever to repeat the admonition, and would probably be mouldering into dust while she was employed in their perusal.

'"Elinor wept while she read, but that was all. She wept from physical emotion, not from mental conviction; nor is there such an induration of heart caused by any other power, as by that of the passion which seems to soften it most. She answered the letter, however, and the effort scarce cost her less than it did her decrepid and dying relative. She acknowledged her dereliction of all religious feeling, and bewailed it – the more, she added with painful sincerity, because I *feel my grief is not sincere.* 'Oh, my God!' she continued, 'you who have clothed my heart with such burning energies – you who have given to it a power of loving so intense, so devoted, so concentrated – you have not given it in vain; – no, in some happier world, or perhaps even in this, when this "tyranny is overpast", you will fill my heart with an image worthier than him whom I once believed your image on earth. The stars, though their light appears so dim and distant to us, were not lit by the Almighty hand in vain. Their glorious light burns for remote and happier worlds; and the beam of religion that glows so feebly to eyes almost blind with earthly tears, may be rekindled when a broken heart has been my passport to a place of rest.

★

' " 'Do not think me, dear aunt, deserted by all hope of religion, even though I have lost the sense of it. Was it not said by unerring lips to a sinner, that her transgressions were forgiven because she *loved much*? And does not this capacity of love prove that it will one day be more worthily filled, and more happily employed.

*

' " 'Miserable wretch that I am! At this moment, a voice from the bottom of my heart asks me *"Whom* hast thou loved so much? Was it man or God, that thou darest to compare thyself with her who knelt and wept – not before a mortal idol, but at the feet of an incarnate divinity?"

*

' " 'It may yet befall, that the ark which has floated through the waste of waters may find its resting-place, and the trembling inmate debark on the shores of an unknown but purer world.' " '

Chapter Thirty-One

There is an oak beside the froth-clad pool,
Where in old time, as I have often heard,
A woman desperate, a wretch like me,
Ended her woes! – Her woes were not like mine!

*

– Ronan will know;
When he beholds me floating on the stream,
His heart will tell him why Rivine died!

Home's Fatal Discovery

' "The increasing decline of Elinor's health was marked by all the family; the very servant who stood behind her chair looked sadder every day – even Margaret began to repent of the invitation she had given her to the Castle.

' "Elinor felt this, and would have spared her what pain she could; but it was not possible for herself to be insensible of the fast-fading remains of her withering youth and blighted beauty. The place – the place itself, was the principal cause of that mortal disease that was consuming her; yet from that place she felt she had less resolution to tear herself every day. So she lived, like those sufferers in eastern prisons, who are not allowed to taste food unless mixed with poison, and who must perish alike whether they eat or forbear.

' "Once, urged by intolerable pain of heart, (tortured by living in the placid light of John Sandal's sunny smile), she confessed this to Margaret. She said, 'It is impossible for me to support this existence – impossible! To tread the floor which those steps have trod – to listen for their approach, and when they come, feel they do not bear him we seek – to see every object around me reflect his image, but never – never to see the reality – to see the door open which once disclosed his figure, and when it opens, not to see *him*, and when he does appear, to see him not what he saw – to feel he is the same and not the same, – the same to the eye, but not to the heart – to struggle thus between the dream of imagination and the cruel awaking of reality – Oh! Margaret – that undeception plants a dagger in the heart, whose point no human hand can extract, and whose venom no human hand can heal!' Margaret wept as Elinor spoke thus, and slowly, very slowly, expressed her consent that Elinor should quit the Castle, if it was necessary for her peace.

'"It was the very evening after this conversation, that Elinor, whose habit was to wander among the woods that surrounded the Castle unattended, met with John Sandal. It was a glorious autumnal evening, just like that on which they had first met, – the associations of nature were the same, those of the heart alone had suffered change. There is that light in an autumnal sky, – that shade in autumnal woods, – that dim and hallowed glory in the evening of the year, which is indefinably combined with recollections. Sandal, as they met, had spoken to her in the same voice of melody, and with the same heart-thrilling tenderness of manner, that had never ceased to visit her ear since their first meeting, like music in dreams. She imagined there was more than usual feeling in his manner; and the spot where they were, and which memory made populous and eloquent with the imagery and speech of other days, flattered this illusion. A vague hope trembled at the bottom of her heart, – she thought of what she dared not to utter, and yet dared to believe. They walked on together, – together they watched the last light on the purple hills, the deep repose of the woods, whose summits were still like 'feathers of gold,' – together they once more tasted the confidence of nature, and, amid the most perfect silence, there was a mutual and unutterable eloquence in their hearts. The thoughts of other days rushed on Elinor, – she ventured to raise her eyes to that countenance which she once more saw 'as it had been that of an angel'. The glow and the smile, that made it appear like a reflection of heaven, were there still, – but that glow was borrowed from the bright flush of the glorious west, and that smile was for nature, – not for her. She lingered till she felt it fade with the fading light, – and a *last conviction* striking her heart, she burst into an agony of tears. To his words of affectionate surprise, and gentle consolation, she answered only by fixing her appealing eyes on him, and agonizingly invoking his name. She had trusted to nature, and to this scene of their first meeting, to act as an interpreter between them, – and still even in despair she trusted to it.

' "Perhaps there is not a more agonizing moment than that in which we feel the aspect of nature give a perfect vitality to the association of *our* hearts, while they lie buried in those in which we try *in vain to revive them*.

' "She was soon undeceived. With that benignity which, while it speaks of consolation, forbids hope – with that smile which angels may be supposed to give on the last conflict of a sufferer who is casting off the garments of mortality in pain and hope – with such an expression he whom she loved regarded her. From another world he might have cast such a glance on her, – and it sealed her doom in this for ever.

*

' "As, unable to witness the agony of the wound he had inflicted but could not heal, he turned from her, the last light of day faded from the hills – the sun of both worlds set on her eye and soul – she sunk on the earth, and notes of faint music that seemed designed to echo the words – 'No – no – no – never – never more!' trembled in her ears. They were as simple and monotonous as the words themselves, and were played accidentally by a peasant boy who was wandering in the woods. But to the unfortunate, every thing seems prophetic; and amid the shades of evening, and accompanied by the sound of his departing footsteps, the breaking heart of Elinor accepted the augury of these melancholy notes.*

' "A few days after this final meeting, Elinor wrote to her aunt in York to announce, that if she still lived, and was not unwilling to admit her, she would reside with her for life; and she could not help intimating, that *her* life would probably not outlast that of her hostess. She did not tell what the widow Sandal had a whispered to her at her first arrival at the Castle, and what she now ventured to repeat with a tone that struggled between the imperative and the persuasive, – the conciliating and the intimidative. Elinor yielded, – and the indelicacy of this representation, had only the effect to make her shrink from its repetition.

' "On her departure, Margaret wept, and Sandal shewed as much tender officiousness about her journey, as if it were to terminate in their renewed bridal. To escape from this, Elinor hastened her preparations for departure.

' "When she arrived at a certain distance from the Castle, she dismissed the family carriage, and said she would go on foot with her female servant to the farmhouse where horses were awaiting her. She went there, but remained concealed, for the report of the approaching bridal resounded in her ears.

* As this whole scene is taken from fact, I subjoin the notes whose modulation is so simple, and whose effect was so profound.

*

' "The day arrived – Elinor rose very early – the bells rung out a merry peal – (as she had once heard them do on another occasion) – the troops of friends arrived in greater numbers, and with equal gaiety as they had once assembled to escort her – she saw their equipages gleaming along – she heard the joyous shouts of half the county – she imagined to herself the timid smile of Margaret, and the irradiated countenance of him who had been *her* bridegroom.

' "Suddenly there was a pause. She felt that the ceremony was going on – was finished – that the irrevocable words were spoken – the indissoluble tie was knit! Again the shout and wild joyance burst forth as the sumptuous cavalcade returned to the Castle. The glare of the equipages, – the splendid habits of the riders, – the cheerful groupe of shouting tenantry, – she saw it all!

*

' "When all was over, Elinor glanced accidentally at her dress – it was white like her bridal habit; – shuddering she exchanged it for a mourning habit, and set out, as she hoped, on her last journey." '

Chapter Thirty-Two

Fuimus, non sumus.[52]

' "When Elinor arrived in Yorkshire, she found her aunt was dead. Elinor went to visit her grave. It was, in compliance with her last request, placed near the window of the independent meeting-house, and bore for inscription her favourite text, 'Those whom he foreknew, he also predestinated', &c. &c. Elinor stood by the grave some time, but could not shed a tear. This contrast of a life so rigid, and a death so hopeful, – this silence of humanity, and eloquence of the grave, – pierced through her heart, as it will through every heart that has indulged in the inebriation of human passion, and feels that the draught has been drawn from broken cisterns.

' "Her aunt's death made Elinor's life, if possible, more secluded, and her habits more monotonous than they would otherwise have been. She was very charitable to the cottagers in her neighbourhood; but except to visit their habitations, she never quitted her own.

*

' "Often she contemplated a small stream that flowed at the end of her garden. As she had lost all her sensibility of nature, another motive was assigned for this mute and dark contemplation; and her servant, much attached to her, watched her close.

*

' "She was roused from this fearful state of stupefaction and despair, which those who have felt shudder at the attempt to describe, by a letter from Margaret. She had received several from her which lay unanswered, (no unusual thing in those days), but this she tore open, read with interest inconceivable, and prepared instantly to answer by action.

' "Margaret's high spirits seemed to have sunk in her hour of danger. She hinted that that hour was rapidly approaching, and that she earnestly implored the presence of her affectionate kinswoman to soothe and sustain in the moment of her approaching peril. She added, that the manly and affectionate tenderness of John Sandal at this period, had touched her heart more deeply, if possible, than all the former testimonies of his affection – but that she could not bear his resignation of all his usual habits of rural amusement, and of the neighbouring society – that she in vain had chided him from her couch, where she lingered in pain and hope, and hoped that Elinor's presence might induce him to yield to her request, as he must feel, on her arrival, the dearest companion of her youth was present – and that, at such a moment, a female companion was more suitable than even the gentlest and most affectionate of the other sex.

*

' "Elinor set out directly. The purity of her feelings had formed an impenetrable barrier between her heart and its object, – and she apprehended no more danger from the presence of one who was wedded, and wedded to her relative, than from that of her own brother.

' "She arrived at the Castle – Margaret's hour of danger had begun – she had been very ill during the preceding period. The natural consequences of her situation had been aggravated by a feeling of dignified responsibility of the birth of an heir to the house of Mortimer – and this feeling had not contributed to render that situation more supportable.

' "Elinor bent over the bed of pain – pressed her cold lips to the burning lips of the sufferer – and prayed for her.

' "The first medical assistance in the country (then very rarely employed on such occasions) had been obtained at a vast expence. The widow Sandal, declining all attendance on the sufferer, paced through the adjacent apartments in agony unutterable and *unuttered*.

' "Two days and nights went on in hope and terror – the bell-ringers sat up in every church within ten miles round – the tenantry crowded round the Castle with honest heartfelt solicitude – the neighbouring nobility sent their messages of inquiry every hour. An accouchement in a noble family was then an event of importance.

' "The hour came – twins were born dead – and the young mother was fated to follow them within a few hours! While life yet remained, Margaret shewed the remains of the lofty spirit of the Mortimers. She sought with her cold hand that of her wretched husband and of the weeping Elinor. She joined them in an embrace which one of them at least understood, and prayed that their union might be eternal. She then begged to see the bodies of her infant sons – they were produced; and it was said that she uttered expressions, intimating that, had they not been the heirs of the Mortimer family – had not expectation been wound so high, and supported by all the hopes that life and youth could flatter her with, – she and they might yet have existed.

' "As she spoke, her voice grew feebler, and her eyes dim – their last light was turned on him she loved, and when sight was gone, she still felt his arms enfold her. The next moment they enfolded – nothing!

' "In the terrible spasms of masculine agony – the more intensely felt as they are more rarely indulged – the young widower dashed himself on the bed, which shook with his convulsive grief; and Elinor, losing all sense but that of a calamity so sudden and so terrible, echoed his deep and suffocating sobs, as if she whom they deplored had not been the only obstacle to her happiness.

★

' "Amid the voice of mourning that rung through the Castle from vault to tower in that day of trouble, none was loud like that of the widow Sandal – her wailings were shrieks, her grief was despair. Rushing through the rooms like one distracted, she tore her hair out by the roots, and imprecated the most fearful curses on her head. At length she approached the apartment where the corse lay. The servants, shocked at her distraction, would have withheld her from entering it, but could not. She burst into the room, cast one wild look on its inmates – the still corse and the dumb mourners – and then, flinging herself on her knees before her son, confessed the secret of her guilt, and developed to its foul base the foundation of that pile of iniquity and sorrow which had now reached its summit.

' "Her son listened to this horrible confession with fixed eye and features unmoved; and at its conclusion, when the wretched penitent implored the assistance of her son to raise her from her knees, he repelled her outstretched hands, and with a weak wild laugh, sunk back on the bed. He never could be removed from it till the corse to which he clung was borne away, and then the mourners hardly knew which to deplore – her who was deprived of the light of life, or him in whom the light of reason was extinguished for ever!

*

' "The wretched, guilty mother, (but for her fate no one can be solicitous), a few months after, on her dying bed, declared the secret of her crime to a minister of an independent congregation, who was induced, by the report of her despair, to visit her. She confessed that, being instigated by avarice, and still more by the desire of regaining her lost consequence in the family, and knowing the wealth and dignity her son would acquire, and in which she must participate, by his marriage with Margaret, she had, after using all the means of persuasion and intreaty, been driven, in despair at her disappointment, to fabricate a tale as false as it was horrible, which she related to her deluded son on the evening before his intended nuptials with Elinor. She had assured him he was not her son, but the offspring of the illicit commerce of her husband the preacher with the puritan mother of Elinor, who had formerly been one of his congregation, and whose well-known and strongly-expressed admiration of his preaching had been once supposed extended to his person, – had caused her much jealous anxiety in the early years of their marriage, and was now made the basis of this horrible fiction. She added, that Margaret's obvious attachment to her cousin had, in some degree, palliated her guilt to herself; but that, when she saw him quit her house in despair on the morning of his intended marriage and rush he knew not whither, she was half tempted to recall him, and confess the truth. Her mind again became hardened, and she reflected that her secret was safe, as she had bound him by an oath, from respect to his father's memory, and compassion to the guilty mother of Elinor, never to disclose the truth to her daughter.

' "The event had succeeded to her guilty wishes. – Sandal beheld Elinor with the eyes of a brother, and the image of Margaret easily found a place in his unoccupied affections. But, as often befals to the dealers in falsehood and obliquity, the apparent accomplishment of her hopes proved her ruin. In the event of the marriage of John and Margaret proving issueless, the estates and title went to the distant relative named in the will; and her son, deprived of reason by the calamities in which her arts had involved him, was by them also deprived of the wealth and rank to which they were meant to raise him, and reduced to the small pension obtained by his former services – the poverty of the King, then himself a pensioner of Lewis XIV, forbidding the possibility of added remuneration. When the minister heard to the last the terrible confession of the dying penitent, in the awful language ascribed to Bishop Burnet when consulted by another criminal, – he bid her 'almost despair', and departed.

*

' "Elinor has retired, with the helpless object of her unfading love and unceasing care, to her cottage in Yorkshire. There, in the language of that divine and blind old man, the fame of whose poetry has not yet reached this country, it is

'Her delight to see him sitting in the house,'

and watch, like the father of the Jewish champion, the growth of that 'God-given strength', that intellectual power, which, unlike Samson's, will never return.

' "After an interval of two years, during which she had expended a large part of the capital of her fortune in obtaining the first medical advice for the patient, and 'suffered many things of many physicians', she gave up all hope, – and, reflecting that the interest of her fortune thus diminished would be but sufficient to procure the comforts of life for herself and him whom she has resolved never to forsake, she sat down in patient misery with her melancholy companion, and added one more to the many proofs of woman's heart, 'unwearied in well-doing', without the intoxication of passion, the excitement of applause, or even the gratitude of the unconscious object.

' "Were this a life of calm privation, and pulseless apathy, her efforts would scarce have merit, and her sufferings hardly demand compassion; but it is one of pain incessant and immitigable. The first-born of her heart lies dead within it; but that heart is still alive with all its keenest sensibilities, its most vivid hopes, and its most exquisite sense of grief.

*

' "She sits beside him all day – she watches that eye whose light was life, and sees it fixed on her in glassy and unmeaning complacency – she dreams of that smile which burst on her soul like the morning sun over a landscape in spring, and sees that smile of vacancy which tries to convey satisfaction, but cannot give it the language of expression. Averting her head, she thinks of other days. A vision passes before her. – Lovely and glorious things, the hues of whose colouring are not of this world, and whose web is too fine to be woven in the loom of life, – rise to her eye like the illusions of enchantment. A strain of rich remembered music floats in her hearing – she dreams of the hero, the lover, the beloved, – him in whom were united all that could dazzle the eye, inebriate the imagination, and melt the heart. She sees him as he first appeared to her, – and the mirage of the desert presents not a vision more delicious and deceptive – she bends to drink of that false fountain, and the stream disappears – she starts from her reverie, and hears the weak laugh of the sufferer, as he moves a little water in a shell, and imagines he sees the ocean in a storm!

*

' "She has one consolation. When a short interval of recollection returns, – when his speech becomes articulate, – he utters *her* name, not that of Margaret, and a beam of early hope dances on her heart as she hears it, but fades away as fast as the rare and wandering ray of intellect from the lost mind of the sufferer!

*

' "Unceasingly attentive to his health and his comforts, she walked out with him every evening, but led him through the most sequestered paths, to avoid those whose mockful persecution, or whose vacant pity, might be equally torturing to her feelings, or harassing to her still gentle and smiling companion.

' "It was at this period," said the stranger to Aliaga, "I first became acquainted with – I mean – at this time a stranger, who had taken up his abode near the hamlet where Elinor resided, was seen to watch the two figures as they passed slowly on their retired walk. Evening after evening he watched them. He knew the history of these two unhappy beings, and prepared himself to take advantage of it. It was impossible, considering their secluded mode of existence, to obtain an introduction. He tried to recommend himself by his occasional attentions to the invalid – he sometimes picked up the flowers that an unconscious hand flung into the stream, and listened, with a gracious smile, to the indistinct sounds in which the sufferer, who still retained all the graciousness of his perished mind, attempted to thank him.

' "Elinor felt grateful for these occasional attentions; but she was somewhat alarmed at the assiduity with which the stranger attended their melancholy walk every evening, – and, whether encouraged, neglected, or even repelled, still found the means of insinuating himself into companionship. Even the mournful dignity of Elinor's demeanour, – her deep dejection, – her bows or brief replies, – were unavailing against the gentle but indefatigable importunity of the intruder.

' "By degrees he ventured to speak to her of her misfortunes, – and that topic is a sure key to the confidence of the unhappy. Elinor began to listen to him; – and, though somewhat amazed at the knowledge he displayed of every circumstance of her life, she could not but feel soothed by the tone of sympathy in which he spoke, and excited by the mysterious hints of hope which he sometimes suffered to escape him as if involuntarily. It was observed soon by the inmates of the hamlet, whom idleness and the want of any object of excitement had made curious, that Elinor and the stranger were inseparable in their evening walks.

*

' "It was about a fortnight after this observation was first made, that Elinor, unattended, drenched with rain, and her head uncovered, loudly and eagerly demanded admittance, at a late hour, at the house of a neighbouring clergyman. She was admitted, – and the surprise of her reverend host at this visit, equally unseasonable and unexpected, was exchanged for a deeper feeling of wonder and terror as she related the cause of it. He at first imagined (knowing her unhappy situation) that the constant presence of an insane person might have a contagious effect on the intellects of one so perseveringly exposed to that presence.

' "As Elinor, however, proceeded to disclose the awful proposal, and the scarcely less awful name of the unholy intruder, the clergyman betrayed considerable emotion; and, after a long pause, desired permission to accompany her on their next meeting. This was to be the following evening, for the stranger was unremitting in his attendance on her lonely walks.

' "It is necessary to mention, that this clergyman had been for some years abroad – that events had occurred to him in foreign countries, of which strange reports were spread, but on the subject of which he had been always profoundly silent – and that having but lately fixed his residence in the neighbourhood, he was equally a stranger to Elinor, and to the circumstances of her past life, and of her present situation.

*

' "It was now autumn, – the evenings were growing short, – and the brief twilight was rapidly succeeded by night. On the dubious verge of both, the clergyman quitted his house, and went in the direction where Elinor told him she was accustomed to meet the stranger.

' "They were there before him; and in the shuddering and averted form of Elinor, and the stern but calm importunity of her companion, he read the terrible secret of their conference. Suddenly he advanced and stood before the stranger. They immediately recognized each other. An expression that was never before beheld there – an expression of fear – wandered over the features of the stranger! He paused for a moment, and then departed without uttering a word – nor was Elinor ever again molested by his presence.

*

' "It was some days before the clergyman recovered from the shock of this singular encounter sufficiently to see Elinor, and explain to her the cause of his deep and painful agitation.

' "He sent to announce to her when he was able to receive her, and appointed the night for the time of meeting, for he knew that during the day she never forsook the helpless object of her un-alienated heart. The night arrived – imagine them seated in the antique study of the clergyman, whose shelves were filled with the ponderous volumes of ancient learning – the embers of a peat fire shed a dim and fitful light through the room, and the single candle that burned in a distant oaken stand, seemed to shed its light on that alone – not a ray fell on the figures of Elinor and her companion, as they sat in their massive chairs of carved-like figures in the richly-wrought nitches of some Catholic place of worship –"

' "That is a most profane and abominable comparison," said Aliaga, starting from the doze in which he had frequently indulged during this long narrative.

' "But hear the result," said the pertinacious narrator. "The clergyman confessed to Elinor that he had been acquainted with an Irishman of the name of Melmoth, whose various erudition, profound intellect, and intense appetency for information, had interested him so deeply as to lead to a perfect intimacy between them. At the breaking out of the troubles in England, the clergy-man had been compelled, with his father's family, to seek refuge in Holland. There again he met Melmoth, who proposed to him a journey to Poland – the offer was accepted, and to Poland they went. The clergyman here told many extraordinary tales of Dr Dee, and of Albert Alasco, the Polish adventurer, who were their companions both in England and Poland – and he added, that he felt his companion Melmoth was irrevocably attached to the study of that art which is held in just abomination by all 'who name the name of Christ'. The power of the intellectual vessel was too great for the narrow seas where it was coasting – it longed to set out on a voyage of discovery – in other words, Melmoth attached himself to those impostors, or worse, who promised him the knowledge and the power of the future world – on conditions that are unutterable. A strange expression crossed his face as he spoke. He recovered himself, and added, 'From that hour our intercourse ceased. I conceived of him as of one given up to diabolical delusions – to the power of the enemy.

' " 'I had not seen Melmoth for some years. I was preparing to quit Germany, when, on the eve of my departure, I received a message from a person who announced himself as my friend, and who, believing himself dying, wished for the attendance of a Protestant minister. We were then in the territories of a Catholic electoral bishop. I lost no time in attending the sick person. As I entered his room, conducted by a servant, who immediately closed the door and retired, I was astonished to see the room filled with an astrological apparatus, books and implements of a science I did not understand; in a corner there was a bed, near which there was neither priest or physician, relative or friend – on it lay extended the form of Melmoth. I approached, and attempted to address to him some words of consolation. He waved his hand to me to be silent – and I was so. The recollection of his former habits and pursuits, and the view of his present situation, had an effect that appalled more than it amazed me. "Come near," said Melmoth, speaking very faintly – "nearer. I am dying – how my life has been passed you know but too well. Mine was the great angelic sin – pride and intellectual glorying! It was the first mortal sin – a boundless aspiration after forbidden knowledge! I am now dying. I ask for no forms of religion – I wish not to hear words that have to me no meaning, or that I wish had none! Spare your look of horror. I sent for you to exact your solemn promise that you will conceal from every human being the fact of my death – let no man know that I died, or when, or where."

' " 'He spoke with a distinctness of tone, and energy of manner, that convinced me he could not be in the state he described himself to be, and I said, "But I cannot believe you are dying – your intellects are clear, your voice is strong, your language is coherent, and but for the paleness of your face, and your lying extended on that bed, I could not even imagine you were ill." He answered, "Have you patience and courage to abide by the proof that what I say is true?" I replied, that I doubtless had patience, and for the courage, I looked to that Being for whose name I had too much reverence to utter in his hearing. He acknowledged my forbearance by a ghastly smile which I understood too well, and pointed to a clock that stood at the foot of his bed. "Observe," said he, "the hour-hand is on eleven, and I am now sane, clear of speech, and apparently healthful – tarry but an hour, and you yourself will behold me dead!"

' " 'I remained by his bed-side – the eyes of both were fixed intently on the slow motion of the clock. From time to time he spoke, but his strength now appeared obviously declining. He repeatedly urged on me the necessity of profound secresy, its importance to myself, and yet he hinted at the possibility of our future meeting. I asked why he thought proper to confide to me a secret whose divulgement was so perilous, and which might have been so easily concealed? Unknowing whether he existed, or where, I must have been equally ignorant of the mode and place of his death. To this he returned no answer. As the hand of the clock approached the hour of twelve, his countenance changed – his eyes became dim – his speech inarticulate – his jaw dropped – his respiration ceased. I applied a glass to his lips – but there was not a breath to stain it. I felt his wrist – but there was no pulse. I placed my hand on his heart – there was not the slightest vibration. In a few minutes the body was perfectly cold. I did not quit the room till nearly an hour after – the body gave no signs of returning animation.

' " 'Unhappy circumstances detained me long abroad. I was in various parts of the Continent, and every where I was haunted with the report of Melmoth being still alive. To these reports

I gave no credit, and returned to England in the full conviction of his being dead. *Yet it was Melmoth who walked and spoke with you the last night of our meeting.* My eyes never more faithfully attested the presence of living being. It was Melmoth himself, such as I beheld him many years ago, when my hairs were dark and my steps were firm. I am changed, but he is the same – time seems to have forborne to touch him from terror. By what means or power he is thus enabled to continue his posthumous and preternatural existence, it is impossible to conceive, unless the fearful report that every where followed his steps on the Continent, be indeed true.'

'"Elinor, impelled by terror and wild curiosity, inquired into that report which dreadful experience had anticipated the meaning of. 'Seek no farther,' said the minister, 'you know already more than should ever have reached the human ear, or entered into the conception of the human mind. Enough that you have been enabled by Divine Power to repel the assaults of the evil one – the trial was terrible, but the result will be glorious. Should the foe persevere in his attempts, remember that he has been already repelled amid the horrors of the dungeon and of the scaffold, the screams of Bedlam and the flames of the Inquisition – he is yet to be subdued by a foe that he deemed of all others the least invincible – the withered energies of a broken heart. He has traversed the earth in search of victims, "Seeking whom he might devour", and has found no prey, even where he might seek for it with all the cupidity of infernal expectation. Let it be your glory and crown of rejoicing, that even the feeblest of his adversaries has repulsed him with a power that will always annihilate his.'

*

'"Who is that faded form that supports with difficulty an emaciated invalid, and seems at every step to need the support she gives? – It is still Elinor tending John. Their path is the same, but the season is changed – and that change seems to her to have

628

passed alike on the mental and physical world. It is a dreary evening in Autumn – the stream flows dark and turbid beside their path – the blast is groaning among the trees, and the dry discoloured leaves are sounding under their feet – their walk is uncheered by human converse, for one of them no longer thinks, and seldom speaks!

' "Suddenly he gives a sign that he wishes to be seated – it is complied with, and she sits beside him on the felled trunk of a tree. He declines his head on her bosom, and she feels with delighted amazement, a few tears streaming on it for the first time for years – a soft but conscious pressure of her hand, seems to her like the signal of reviving intelligence – with breathless hope she watches him as he slowly raises his head, and fixes his eyes – God of all consolation, there is intelligence in his glance! He thanks her with an unutterable look for all her care, her long and painful labour of love! His lips are open, but long unaccustomed to utter human sounds, the effort is made with difficulty – again that effort is repeated and fails – his strength is exhausted – his eyes close – his last gentle sigh is breathed on the bosom of faith and love – and Elinor soon after said to those who surrounded her bed, that she died happy, since he knew her once more! She gave one parting awful sign to the minister, which was understood and answered!" '

Chapter Thirty-Three

Cum mihi non tantum furesque feræque, suëtæ,
Hunc vexare locum, curæ sunt atque labori;
Quantum carminibus quæ versant atque venenis,
Humanos animos.[53]

Horace

' "It is inconceivable to me," said Don Aliaga to himself, as he pursued his journey the next day – "it is inconceivable to me how this person forces himself on my company, harasses me with tales that have no more application to me than the legend of the Cid, and may be as apocryphal as the ballad of Roncesvalles – and now he has ridden by my side all day, and, as if to make amends for his former uninvited and unwelcome communicativeness, he has never once opened his lips."

' "Senhor," said the stranger, then speaking for the first time, as if he read Aliaga's thoughts – "I acknowledge myself in error for relating to you a narrative in which you must have felt there was little to interest you. Permit me to atone for it, by recounting to you a very brief one, in which I flatter myself you will be disposed to feel a very peculiar interest." – "You assure me it will be brief," said Aliaga. "Not only so, but the last I shall obtrude on your patience," replied the stranger. "On that condition," said Aliaga, "in God's name, brother, proceed. And look you handle the matter discreetly, as you have said."

"There was," said the stranger, "a certain Spanish merchant, who set out prosperously in business; but, after a few years, finding his affairs assume an unfavourable aspect, and being tempted by an offer of partnership with a relative who was settled in the East Indies, had embarked for those countries with his wife and son, leaving behind him an infant daughter in Spain." – "That was exactly my case," said Aliaga, wholly unsuspicious of the tendency of this tale.

'"Two years of successful occupation restored him to opulence, and to the hope of vast and future accumulation. Thus encouraged, our Spanish merchant entertained ideas of settling in the East Indies, and sent over for his young daughter with her nurse, who embarked for the East Indies with the first opportunity, which was then very rare." – "This reminds me exactly of what occurred to myself," said Aliaga, whose faculties were somewhat obtuse.

'"The nurse and infant were supposed to have perished in a storm which wrecked the vessel on an isle near the mouth of a river, and in which the crew and passengers perished. It was said that the nurse and child alone escaped; that by some extraordinary chance they arrived at this isle, where the nurse died from fatigue and want of nourishment, and the child survived, and grew up a wild and beautiful daughter of nature, feeding on fruits, – and sleeping amid roses, – and drinking the pure element, – and inhaling the harmonies of heaven, – and repeating to herself the few Christian words her nurse had taught her, in answer to the melody of the birds that sung to her, and of the stream whose waves murmured in accordance to the pure and holy music of her unearthly heart." – "I never heard a word of this before," muttered Aliaga to himself. The stranger went on.

'"It was said that some vessel in distress arrived at the isle, – that the captain had rescued this lovely lonely being from the brutality of the sailors, – and, discovering from some remains of the Spanish tongue which she still spoke, and which he supposed must have been cultivated during the visits of some other wanderer to the isle, he undertook, like a man of honour, to conduct her to her parents, whose names she could tell, though not their residence, so acute and tenacious is the memory of infancy. He fulfilled his promise, and the pure and innocent being was restored to her family, who were then residing in the city of Benares." Aliaga, at these words, stared with a look of intelligence somewhat ghastly. He could not interrupt the stranger – he drew in his breath, and closed his teeth.

' "I have since heard," said the stranger, "that the family has returned to Spain, – that the beautiful inhabitant of the foreign isle is become the idol of your cavaliers of Madrid, – your loungers of the Prado, – your *sacravienses*, – your – by what other name of contempt shall I call them? But listen to me, – there is an eye fixed on her, and its fascination is more deadly than that fabled of the snake! – There is an arm extended to seize her, in whose grasp humanity withers! – That arm even now relaxes for a moment, – its fibres thrill with pity and horror, – it releases the victim for a moment, – it even beckons her father to her aid! – Don Francisco, do you understand me now? – Has this tale interest or application for you?"

'He paused, but Aliaga, chilled with horror, was unable to answer him but by a feeble exclamation. "If it has," resumed the stranger, "lose not a moment to save your daughter!" and, clapping spurs to his mule, he disappeared through a narrow passage among the rocks, apparently never intended to be trod by earthly traveller. Aliaga was not a man susceptible of strong impressions from nature; but, if he had been, the scene amid which this mysterious warning was uttered would have powerfully ministered to its effect. The time was evening, – grey and misty twilight hung over every object; – the way lay through a rocky road, that wound among mountains, or rather stony hills, bleak and bare as those which the weary traveller through the western isles* sees rising amid the moors, to which they form a contrast without giving a relief. Heavy rains had made deep gullies amid the hills,

---

* Ireland, – forsan.

and here and there a mountain-stream brawled amid its stony channel, like a proud and noisy upstart, while the vast chasms that had been the beds of torrents which once swept through them in thunder, now stood gaping and ghastly like the deserted abodes of ruined nobility. Not a sound broke on the stillness, except the monotonous echo of the hoofs of the mules answered from the hollows of the hill, and the screams of the birds, which, after a few short circles in the damp and cloudy air, fled back to their retreats amid the cliffs.

*

'It is almost incredible, that after this warning, enforced as it was by the perfect acquaintance which the stranger displayed of Aliaga's former life and family-circumstances, it should not have had the effect of making him hurry homewards immediately, particularly as it seems he thought it of sufficient importance to make it the subject of correspondence with his wife. So it was however.

'At the moment of the stranger's departure, it was his resolution not to lose a moment in hastening homewards; but at the next stage he arrived at, there were letters of business awaiting him. A mercantile correspondent gave him the information of the probable failure of a house in a distant part of Spain, where his speedy presence might be of vital consequence. There were also letters from Montilla, his intended son-in-law, informing him that the state of his father's health was so precarious, it was impossible to leave him till his fate was decided. As the decisions of fate involved equally the wealth of the son, and the life of the father, Aliaga could not help thinking there was as much prudence as affection in this resolution.

'After reading these letters, Aliaga's mind began to flow in its usual channel. There is no breaking through the inveterate habitudes of a thorough-paced mercantile mind, "though one rose from the dead". Besides, by this time the mysterious image of the stranger's presence and communications were fading fast from a mind not at all habituated to visionary impressions. He shook off the terrors of this visitation by the aid of time, and gave his courage the credit due to that aid. Thus we all deal with the illusions of the imagination, – with this difference only, that the impassioned recal them with the tear of regret, and the unimaginative with the blush of shame. Aliaga set out for the distant part of Spain where his presence was to save this tottering house in which he had an extensive concern, and wrote to Donna Clara, that it might be some months before he returned to the neighbourhood of Madrid.'

Chapter Thirty-Four

Husband, husband, I've the ring
Thou gavest to-day to me;
And thou to me art ever wed,
As I am wed to thee!

Little's Poems

'The remainder of that dreadful night when Isidora disappeared, had been passed almost in despair by Donna Clara, who, amid all her rigour and chilling mediocrity, had still the feelings of a mother – and by Fra Jose, who, with all his selfish luxury and love of domination, had a heart where distress never knocked for admittance, that she did not find pity ready to open the door.

'The distress of Donna Clara was aggravated by her fear of her husband, of whom she stood in great awe, and who, she dreaded, might reproach her with unpardonable negligence of her maternal authority.

'In this night of distress, she was often tempted to call on her son for advice and assistance; but the recollection of his violent passions deterred her, and she sat in passive despair till day. Then, with an unaccountable impulse, she rose from her seat, and hurried to her daughter's apartment, as if she imagined that the events of the preceding night were only a fearful and false illusion that would be dispersed by the approach of day.

'It seemed, indeed, as if they were, for on the bed lay Isidora in a profound sleep, with the same pure and placid smile as when she was lulled into slumber by the melodies of nature, and the sound was prolonged in her dream by the whispered songs of the spirits of the Indian Ocean. Donna Clara uttered a shriek of surprise, that had the singular effect of rousing Fra Jose from a deep sleep into which he had fallen at the approach of day. Starting at the sound, the good natured, pampered priest, tottered into the room, and saw, with incredulity that slowly yielded to frequent application to his obstinate and adhesive eye-lids, the form of Isidora extended in profound slumber.

' "Oh what an exquisite enjoyment!" said the yawning priest, as he looked on the sleeping beauty without another emotion than that of the delight of an uninterrupted repose. – "Pray, don't disturb her," he said, yawning himself out of the room – "after such a night as we all have had, sleep must be a very refreshing and laudable exercise; and so I commend you to the protection of the holy saints!" – "Oh, reverend Father! – Oh holy Father!" cried Donna Clara clinging to him, "desert me not in this extremity – this has been the work of magic – of infernal spirits. See how profoundly she sleeps, though we are speaking, and it is now daylight." – "Daughter, you are much mistaken," answered the drowsy priest; "people can sleep soundly even in the day-time; and for proof send me, as I am now retiring to rest, a bottle of Foncarral or Valdepenas – not that I value the richest vintage of Spain from the Chacoli of Biscay to the Mataro of Catalonia*, but I would never have it said that I slept in the day-time, but for sufficient reason." – "Holy Father!" answered Donna Clara, "do you not think my daughter's disappearance and intense slumber are the result of preternatural causes?" – "Daughter," answered the priest, contracting his brows, "let me have some wine to slake the intolerable thirst caused by my anxiety for the welfare of your family, and let me meditate some hours afterwards on the measures best to be adopted, and then – when I awake, I will give you my opinion." – "Holy Father, you shall judge for me in every thing." – "It were not amiss, daughter," said the priest retiring, "if

* Vide Dillon's travels through Spain.

a few slices of ham, or some poignant sausages, accompanied the wine – it might, as it were, abate the deleterious effects of that abominable liquor, which I never drink but on emergencies like these." – "Holy Father, they shall be ordered," said the anxious mother – "but do you not think my daughter's sleep is supernatural?" – "Follow me to mine apartment, daughter," answered the priest, exchanging his cowl for a night-cap, which one of the numerous household obsequiously presented him, "and you will soon see that sleep is a natural effect of a natural cause. Your daughter has doubtless passed a very fatiguing night, and so have you, and so have I, though perhaps from very different causes; but all those causes dispose us to a profound repose. – I have no doubt of mine – fetch up the wine and sausages – I am very weary – Oh I am weak and worn with fasts and watching, and the labours of exhortation. My tongue cleaves to the roof of my mouth, and my jaws cling together, – perhaps a draught or two might dissolve their parching adhesion. But I do so hate wine – why the devil don't you fetch up the bottle?"

'The attendant domestic, terrified by the tone of wrath in which the last words were uttered, hurried on with submissive expedition, and Fra Jose sat down at length in his apartment to ruminate on the calamities and perplexities of the family, till he was actually overcome by the subject, and exclaimed in a tone of despair, "Both bottles empty! Then it is useless to meditate further on this subject."

*

'He was roused at an earlier hour than he wished, by a message from Donna Clara, who, in the distress of a weak mind, accustomed always to factitious and external support, now felt as if every step she took without it, must lead to actual and instant perdition. Her fear of her husband, next to her superstitious fears, held the strongest power over her mind, and that morning she called Fra Jose to an early consultation of terror and inquietude. – Her great object was to conceal, if possible, the absence of her daughter on that eventful night; and finding that none of the domestics appeared conscious of it, and that amid the numerous household, only *one aged servant was absent*, of whose absence no one took notice amid the superfluous multitude of a Spanish establishment, her courage began to revive. It was raised still higher by a letter from Aliaga, announcing the necessity of his visiting a distant part of Spain, and of the marriage of his daughter with Montilla being deferred for some months – this sounded like reprieve in the ears of Donna Clara – she consulted with the priest, who answered in words of comfort, that if Donna Isidora's short absence were known, it was but a slight evil, and if it were not known, it was none at all, – and he recommended to her, to ensure the secresy of the servants by means that he swore by his habit were infallible, as he had known them operate effectively among the servants of a far more powerful and extensive establishment. – "Reverend Father," said Donna Clara, "I know of no establishment among the grandees of Spain more splendid than ours." – "But I do, daughter," said the priest, "and the head of that establishment is – the Pope; – but go now, and awake your daughter, who deserves to sleep till doomsday, as she seems totally to have forgotten the hour of breakfast. It is not for myself I speak, daughter, but I cannot bear to see the regularity of a magnificent household thus interrupted; for myself, a basin of chocolate, and a cluster of grapes, will be sufficient; and to allay the crudity of the grapes, a glass of Malaga. – Your glasses, by the bye, are the shallowest I ever drank out of – could you not find some means to get from Ildefonso* glasses of the right make, with short shanks and ample bodies; Yours resemble those of Quichotte, all limbs and no trunk. I like one that resembles his squire, a spacious body and a shank that may be measured by my little finger." – "I will send to St Ildefonso this day," answered

---

* The celebrated manufactory for glass in Spain.

Donna Clara. – "Go and awake your daughter first," said the priest.

'As he spoke, Isidora entered the room – the mother and the priest both stood amazed. Her countenance was as serene, her step as equal, and her mien as composed, as if she were totally unconscious of the terror and distress her disappearance the preceding night had caused. To the first short silence of amazement, succeeded a storm of interrogations from Donna Clara and Fra Jose in concert – why – where – wherefore – and what, and with whom and how – that was all they could articulate. They might as well have spared themselves the trouble, for neither that day nor many following, could the remonstrances, intreaties, or menaces of her mother, aided by the spiritual authority and more powerful anxiety of the priest, extort from her a word of explanation on the cause of her absence that awful night. When closely and sternly pressed, Isidora's mind seemed to assume something of the wild but potent spirit of independence, which her early habits and feelings might have communicated to her. She had been her own teacher and mistress for seventeen years, and though naturally gentle and tractable, when imperious mediocrity attempted to tyrannize over her, she felt a sense of disdain which she expressed only by profound silence.

'Fra Jose, incensed at her obstinacy, and trembling for the loss of his power over the family, threatened to exclude her from confession, unless she disclosed to him the secret of that night – "Then I will confess to God!" said Isidora. Her mother's importunity she found it more difficult to resist, for her feminine heart loved all that was feminine even in its most unattractive shape, and the persecution from that quarter was alike monotonous and unremitting.

'There was a weak but harassing tenacity about Donna Clara, that is the general adjunct to the female character when it combines intellectual mediocrity with rigid principle. When she laid siege to a secret, the garrison might as well capitulate at once. – What she wanted in vigour and ability, she supplied by a minute and gnawing assiduity. She never ventured to carry the fort by storm, but her obstinacy blockaded it till it was forced to surrender. But here even *her* importunity failed. – Isidora remained respectfully, but resolutely silent; finding matters thus desperate, Donna Clara, who had a fine talent for keeping as well as discovering a secret, agreed with Fra Jose not to utter a syllable of the business to her father and brother. – "We will show," said Donna Clara, with a sagacious and self-approving nod, "that we can keep a secret as well as she." – "Right, daughter," said Fra Jose, "imitate her in the only point in which you can flatter yourself with the hope of resemblance."

*

'The secret was, however, soon disclosed. Some months had elapsed, and the visits of her husband began to give an habitual calm and confidence to the mind of Isidora. He imperceptibly was exchanging his ferocious misanthropy for a kind of pensive gloom. – It was like the dark, cold, but unterrific and comparatively soothing night, that succeeds to a day of storm and earthquake. The sufferers remember the terrors of the day, and the still darkness of the night feels to them like a shelter. Isidora gazed on her espoused with delight, when she saw no longer his withering frown, or more withering smile; and she felt the hope that the calm purity of female hearts always suggests, that its influence will one day float over the formless and the void, like the spirit that moved upon the face of the waters, and that the unbelieving husband may yet be saved by the believing wife.

'These thoughts were her comfort, and it was well she had thoughts to comfort her, for facts are miserable allies when imagination fights its battle with despair. On one of those nights that she expected Melmoth, he found her employed in her usual hymn to the Virgin, which she accompanied on her lute. "Is it not rather late to sing your vesper hymn to the Virgin after midnight," said Melmoth with a ghastly smile. "Her ear is open at all times, I have been told," answered Isidora. – "If it is, then, love," said Melmoth, vaulting as usual through the casement, "add a stanza to your hymn in favour of me." – "Alas!" said Isidora, dropping her lute, "you do not believe, love, in what the Holy Church requires." – "Yes, I do believe, when I listen to you." – "And only then?" – "Sing again your hymn to the Virgin."

'Isidora complied, and watched the effect on the listener. He seemed affected – he motioned to her to repeat it. "My love," said Isidora, "is not this more like the repetition of a theatrical song called for by an audience, than a hymn which he who listens to loves his wife better for, because she loves her God." – "It is a shrewd question," said Melmoth, "but why am I in your imagination excluded from the love of God?" – "Do you ever visit the church," answered the anxious Isidora. A profound silence. – "Do you ever receive the Holy Sacrament?" – Melmoth did not utter a word. – "Have you ever, at my earnest solicitation, enabled me to announce to my anxious family the tie that united us?" – No answer. – "And now – that – perhaps – I dare not utter what I feel! Oh, how shall I appear before eyes that watch me even now so closely? – what shall I say? – a wife without a husband – a mother without a father for her child, or one whom a fearful oath has bound her never to declare! Oh! Melmoth, pity me, – deliver me from this life of constraint, falsehood, and dissimulation. Claim me as your wedded wife in the face of my family, and in the face of ruin your wedded wife will follow – will cling to – will perish with you!" Her arms clung round him, her cold but heart-wrung tears fell fast on his cheek, and the imploring arms of woman supplicating for deliverance in her hour of shame and terror, seldom are twined round us in vain. Melmoth felt the appeal – it was but for a moment. He caught the white arms extended towards him – he fixed an eager and fearful look of inquiry on his victim-consort, as he asked – "And is it so?" The pale and shuddering wife shrunk from his arms at the question – her silence answered him. The agonies of nature throbbed audibly in his heart. He said to himself – it is mine – the fruit of affection – the first-born of the heart and of nature – mine – mine, – and whatever becomes of me, there shall yet be a human being on earth who traces me in its external form, and who will be taught to pray for its father, even when its prayer falls parched and hissing on the fires that burn for ever, like a wandering drop of dew on the burning sands of the desert!"

*

'From the period of this communication, Melmoth's tenderness for his wife visibly increased.

'Heaven only knows the source of that wild fondness with which he contemplated her, and in which was still mingled something of ferocity. His warm look seemed like the glow of a sultry summer day, whose heat announces a storm, and compels us by its burning oppression, to look to the storm almost for relief.

'It is not impossible that he looked to some future object of his fearful experiment – and a being so perfectly in his power as his own child, might have appeared to him fatally fitted for his purpose – the quantum of misery, too, necessary to qualify the probationer, it was always in his own power to inflict. Whatever was his motive, he assumed as much tenderness as it was possible for him to assume, and spoke of the approaching event with the anxious interest of a human father.

'Soothed by his altered manner, Isidora bore with silent sufferance the burden of her situation, with all its painful accompaniments of indisposition and dejection, aggravated by hourly fear and mysterious secrecy. She hoped he would at length reward her by an open and honourable declaration, but this hope was expressed only in her patient smiles. The hour approached fast, and fearful and indefinite apprehensions began to overshadow her mind, relative to the fate of the infant about to be born under circumstances so mysterious.

'At his next nightly visit, Melmoth found her in tears.

' "Alas!" said she in answer to his abrupt inquiry, and brief attempt at consolation, "How many causes have I for tears – and how few have I shed? If you would have them wiped away, be assured it is only your hand can do it. I feel," she added, "that this event will be fatal to me – I know I shall not live to see my child – I demand from you the only promise that can support me even under this conviction" – Melmoth interrupted her by the assurance, that these apprehensions were the inseparable concomitants of her situation, and that many mothers, surrounded by a numerous offspring, smiled as they recollected their fears that the birth of each would be fatal to them.

'Isidora shook her head. "The presages," said she, "that visit me, are such as never visited mortality in vain. I have always believed, that as we approach the invisible world, its voice becomes more audible to us, and grief and pain are very eloquent interpreters between us and eternity – quite distinct from all corporeal suffering, even from all mental terror, is that deep and unutterable impression which is alike incommunicable and ineffaceable – it is as if heaven spoke to us alone, and told us to keep its secret, or divulge it on the condition of never being believed. Oh! Melmoth, do not give that fearful smile when I speak of heaven – soon I may be your only intercessor there." "My dear saint," said Melmoth, laughing and kneeling to her in mockery, "let me make early interest for your mediation – how many ducats will it cost me to get you canonized? – you will furnish me, I hope, with an authentic account of legitimate miracles – one is ashamed of the nonsense that is sent monthly to the Vatican." "*Let your conversion be the first miracle on the list,*" said Isidora, with an energy that made Melmoth tremble – it was dark – but she felt that he trembled – she pursued her imagined triumph – "Melmoth," she exclaimed, "I have a right to demand one promise from you – for you I have sacrificed every thing – never was woman more devoted – never did woman give proofs of devotion like mine.

I might have been the noble, honoured wife of one who would have laid his wealth and titles at my feet. In this my hour of danger and suffering, the first families in Spain would have been waiting round my door. Alone, unaided, unsustained, unconsoled, I must undergo the terrible struggle of nature – terrible to those whose beds are smoothed by the hands of affection, whose agonies are soothed by the presence of a mother – who hears the first feeble cry of her infant echoed by the joy of exulting noble relatives. Oh Melmoth! what must be mine! I must suffer in secresy and in silence! I must see my babe torn from me before I have even kissed it, – and the chrism-mantle will be one of that mysterious darkness which your fingers have woven! Yet grant me one thing – one thing!" continued the suppliant, growing earnest in her prayer even to agony: "swear to me that my child shall be baptised according to the forms of the Catholic church, – that it shall be a Christian as far as those forms can make it, – and I shall feel that, if all my fearful presages are fulfilled, I shall leave behind me one who will pray for his father, and whose prayer may be accepted. Promise me, – swear to me," she added, in intenser agony, "that my child shall be a Christian! Alas! if my voice be not worthy to be heard in heaven, that of a cherub may! Christ himself suffered children to come unto him while on earth, and will he repel them in heaven? – Oh! no, – no! he will not repel *yours*!"

'Melmoth listened to her with feelings that it is better to suppress than explain or expatiate on. Thus solemnly adjured, however, he promised that the child should be baptised; and added, with an expression which Isidora's delight at this concession did not give her time to understand, that it should be a Christian as far as the rites and ceremonies of the Catholic church could make it one. While he added many a bitter hint of the inefficacy of any external rites – and the impotentiality of any hierarchy – and of the deadly and desperate impositions of priests under every dispensation – and exposed them with a spirit at once ludicrous and Satanic, – a spirit that mingled ridicule with horror, and seemed like a Harlequin in the infernal regions, flirting with the furies, Isidora still repeated her solemn request that her child, if it survived her, should be baptised. To this he assented; and added, with a sarcastic and appalling levity, – "And a Mahometan, if you should change your mind, – or any other mythology you please to adopt; – only send me word, – priests are easily obtained, and ceremonies cheaply purchased! Only let me know your future intentions, – when you know them yourself." – "I shall not be here to tell you," said Isidora, replying with profound conviction to this withering levity, like a cold winter day to the glow of a capricious summer one, that blends the sunshine and the lightning; – "Melmoth, I shall not be here then!" And this energy of despair in a creature so young, so inexperienced, except in the vicissitudes of the heart, formed a strong contrast to the stony apathy of one who had traversed life from Dan to Beersheba, and found all barren, or – made it so.

'At this moment, while Isidora wept the cold tears of despair, without daring to ask the hand of him she loved to dry them, the bells of a neighbouring convent, where they were performing a mass for the soul of a departed brother, suddenly rung out. Isidora seized that moment, when the very air was eloquent with the voice of religion, to impress its power on that mysterious being whose presence inspired her equally with terror and with love. "Listen, – listen!" she cried. The sounds came slowly and stilly on, as if it was an involuntary expression of that profound sentiment that night always inspires, – the reverberating watchword from sentinel to sentinel, when wakeful and reflecting minds have become the "watchers of the night"*. The effect of these sounds was increased, by their catching from time to time the deep and thrilling chorus of the voices, – these voices more than harmonized, they were coincident with the toll of the bell,

* He called unto me out of Seir, Watchman, what of the night? – Watchman, what of the night? – ISAIAH.

and seemed like them set in involuntary motion, – music played by invisible hands.

'"Listen," repeated Isidora, "is there no truth in the voice that speaks to you in tones like these? Alas! if there be no truth in religion, there is none on earth! Passion itself evanishes into an illusion, unless it is hallowed by the consciousness of a God and of futurity. That sterility of the heart that forbids the growth of divine feeling, must be hostile also to every tender and generous sentiment. *He who is without a God must be without a heart!* Oh my love, will you not, as you bend over my grave, wish my last slumbers to have been soothed by sounds like these, – wish that they may whisper peace to your own? Promise me, at least, that you will lead your child to my tomb-stone, – that you will suffer it to read the inscription that tells I died in the faith of Christ, and the hope of immortality. Its tears will be powerful pleaders to you not to deny it the consolation that faith has given me in hours of suffering, and the hopes with which it will illuminate my parting hour. Oh promise me this at least, that you will suffer your child to visit my grave – that is all. Do not interrupt or distract the impression by sophistry or levity, or by that wild and withering eloquence that flashes from your lips, not to enlighten but to blast. You will not weep, but you will be silent, – leave Heaven and nature free to their work. The voice of God will speak to its heart, and my spirit, as it witnesses the conflict, will tremble though in paradise, – and, even in heaven, will feel an added joy, when it beholds the victory won. Promise me, then, – swear to me!" she added, with agonizing energy of tone and gesture. "Your child shall be a Christian!" said Melmoth.'

Chapter Thirty-Five

> – Oh, spare me, Grimbald!
> I will tempt hermits for thee in their cells.
> And virgins in their dreams.
>
> Dryden's King Arthur

'It is a singular, but well-attested fact, that women who are compelled to undergo all the inconveniences and uneasiness of clandestine pregnancy, often fare better than those whose situation is watched over by tender and anxious relatives; and that concealed or illegitimate births are actually attended with less danger and suffering than those which have all the aid that skill and affection can give. So it appeared likely to fare with Isidora. The retirement in which her family lived – the temper of Donna Clara, as slow to suspect from want of penetration, as she was eager in pursuing an object once discovered, from the natural cupidity of a vacant mind – these circumstances, combined with the dress of the day, the enormous and enveloping fardingale, gave safety to her secret, at least till the arrival of its crisis. As this crisis approached, one may easily imagine the secret and trembling preparation – the important nurse, proud of the trust reposed in her – the confidential maid – the faithful and discreet medical attendant – to obtain all these Melmoth supplied her amply with money – a circumstance that would have surprised Isidora, as his appearance was always remarkably plain and private, if, at this moment of anxiety, any thought but that of *the hour* could have found room in her mind.

*

'On the evening supposed to be that preceding the dreaded event, Melmoth had thrown an unusual degree of tenderness into his manner – he gazed on her frequently with anxious and silent fondness – he seemed to have something to communicate which he had not courage to disclose. Isidora, well versed in the language of the countenance, which is often, more than that of words, the language of the heart, intreated him to tell her what he *looked*. "Your father is returning," said Melmoth reluctantly. "He will certainly be here in a few days, perhaps in a few hours." Isidora heard him in silent horror. "My father!" she cried – "I have never seen my father. – Oh, how shall I meet him now! And is my mother ignorant of this? – would she not have apprized me?" – "She is ignorant at present; but she will not long be so." – "And from whence could *you* have obtained intelligence that she is ignorant of?" Melmoth paused some time, – his features assumed a more contracted and gloomy character than they had done laterally – he answered with slow and stern reluctance – "Never again ask me that question – the intelligence that I can give you must be of more importance to you than the means by which I obtain it – enough for you that it is true." – "Pardon me, love," said Isidora; "it is probable that I may never again offend you – will you not, then, forgive my *last* offence?"

'Melmoth seemed too intently occupied with his own thoughts to answer even her tears. He added, after a short and sullen pause, "Your betrothed bridegroom is coming with your father – Montilla's father is dead – the arrangements are all concluded for your nuptials – your bridegroom is coming to wed the wife of another – with him comes your fiery, foolish brother, who has set out to meet his father and his future relative. There will be a feast prepared in the house on the occasion of your future nuptials – you may hear of a strange guest appearing at your festival – I will be there!"

'Isidora stood stupified with horror. "Festival!" she repeated –

"a bridal festival! – and I already wedded to you, and about to become a mother!"

*

'At this moment the trampling of many horsemen was heard as they approached the villa – the tumult of the domestics hurrying to admit and receive them, resounded through the apartments – and Melmoth, with a gesture that seemed to Isidora rather like a menace than a farewell, instantly disappeared; and within an hour, Isidora knelt to the father she had never till then beheld – suffered herself to be saluted by Montilla – and accepted the embrace of her brother, who, in the petulance of his spirit, half rejected the chill and altered form that advanced to greet him.

*

'Every thing at the family meeting was conducted in true Spanish formality. Aliaga kissed the cold hand of his withered wife – the numerous domestics exhibited a grave joy at the return of their master – Fra Jose assumed increased importance, and called for dinner in a louder tone. Montilla, the lover, a cold and quiet character, took things as they occurred.

'Every thing lay hushed under a brief and treacherous calm. Isidora, who trembled at the approaching danger, felt her terrors on a sudden suspended. It was not so very near as she apprehended – and she bore with tolerable patience the daily mention of her approaching nuptials, while she was momently harassed by her confidential servants with hints of the impossibility of the event of which they were in expectation, being much longer delayed. Isidora heard, felt, endured all with courage – the grave congratulation of her father and mother – the self-complacent attentions of Montilla, sure of the bride and of her dower – the sullen compliance of the brother, who, unable to refuse his consent, was for ever hinting that *his* sister might have formed a

649

higher connection. All these passed over her mind like a dream – the reality of her existence seemed internal, and she said to herself. – "Were I at the altar, were my hand locked in that of Montilla, Melmoth would rend me from him." A wild but deeply-fixed conviction – a wandering image of preternatural power, overshadowed her mind while she thought of Melmoth; – and this image, which had caused her so much terror and inquietude in her early hours of love, now formed her only resource against the hour of inconceivable suffering; as those unfortunate females in the Eastern Tales, whose beauty has attracted the fearful passion of some evil genie, are supposed to depend, at their nuptial hour, on the presence of the seducing spirit, to tear from the arms of the agonized parent, and the distracted bridegroom, the victim whom he has reserved for himself, and whose wild devotion to him gives a dignity to the union so unhallowed and unnatural.*

*

'Aliaga's heart expanded amid the approaching completion of the felicitous plans he had formed, and with his heart, his purse, which was its depositary, opened also, and he resolved to give a splendid fete in honour of his daughter's nuptials. Isidora remembered Melmoth's prediction of a fatal festival; and his words, "I will be there," gave her for a time a kind of trembling confidence. But as the preparations were carried on under her very eye, – as she was hourly consulted about the disposal of the ornaments, and the decorations of the apartments, – her resolution failed, and while she uttered a few incoherent words, her eye was glazed with horror.

'The entertainment was to be a masked ball; and Isidora, who imagined that this might suggest to Melmoth some auspicious

---

* Vide the beautiful tale of Auheta the Princess of Egypt, and Maugraby the Sorcerer, in the Arabian Tales.

expedient for her escape, watched in vain for some hint of hope, – some allusion to the probability of this event facilitating her extrication from those snares of death that seemed compassing her about. He never uttered a word, and her dependence on him was at one moment confirmed, at another shaken to its foundation, by this terrible silence. In one of these latter moments, the anguish of which was increased beyond expression by a conviction that her hour of danger was not far distant, she exclaimed to Melmoth – "Take me – take me from this place! My existence is nothing – it is a vapour that soon must be exhaled – but my reason is threatened every moment! I cannot sustain the horrors to which I am exposed! All this day I have been dragged through rooms decorated for my impossible nuptials! – Oh, Melmoth, if you no longer love me, at least commiserate me! Save me from a situation of horror unspeakable! – have mercy on your child, if not on me! I have hung on your looks, – I have watched for a word of hope – you have not uttered a sound – you have not cast a glance of hope on me! I am wild! – I am reckless of all but the imminent and *present* horrors of to-morrow – you have talked of your power to approach, to enter these walls without suspicion or discovery – you boasted of that cloud of mystery in which you could envelope yourself. Oh! in this last moment of my extremity, wrap me in its tremendous folds, and let me escape in them, though they prove my shroud! – Think of the terrible night of our marriage! I followed you then in fear and confidence – your touch dissolved every earthly barrier – your steps trod an unknown path, yet I followed you! – Oh! If you really possess that mysterious and inscrutable power, which I dare not either question or believe, exert it for me in this terrible emergency – aid my escape – and though I feel I shall never live to thank you, the *silent suppliant* will remind you by its smiles of the tears that I now shed; and if they are shed in vain, its smile will have a bitter eloquence as it plays with the flowers on its mother's grave!"

'Melmoth, as she spoke, was profoundly silent, and deeply

attentive. He said at last, "Do you then resign yourself to me?" – "Alas! have I not?" – "A question is not an answer. Will you, renouncing all other engagements, all other hopes, depend on me solely for your extrication from this fearful emergency?" – "I will – I do!" – "Will you promise, that if I render you the service you require, if I employ the power you say I have alluded to, you will be *mine*?" – "*Yours!* – Alas! am I not yours already?" – "You embrace *my* protection, then? You voluntarily seek the shelter of that power which I can promise? You yourself will me to employ that power in effecting your escape? – Speak – do I interpret your sentiments aright? – I am unable to exercise those powers you invest me with, unless you yourself require me to do so. I have waited – I have watched for the demand – it has been made – would that it never had!" An expression of the fiercest agony corrugated his stern features as he spoke. – "But it may yet be withdrawn – reflect!" – "And you will not then save me from shame and danger? Is this the proof of your love – is this the boast of your power?" said Isidora, half frantic at this delay. "If I adjure you to pause – if I myself hesitate and tremble – it is to give time for the salutary whisper of your better angel." "Oh! save me, and you shall be my angel!" said Isidora, falling at his feet. Melmoth shook through his whole frame as he heard these words. He raised and soothed her, however, with promises of safety, though in a voice that seemed to announce despair – and then turning from her, burst into a passionate soliloquy. "Immortal Heaven! what is man? – A being with the ignorance, but not the instinct, of the feeblest animals! – They are like birds – when thy hand, O Thou whom I dare not call Father, is on them, they scream and quiver, though the gentle pressure is intended only to convey the wanderer back to his cage – while, to shun the light fear that scares their senses, they rush into the snare that is spread in their sight, and where their captivity is hopeless!" As he spoke, hastily traversing the room, his foot struck against a chair on which a gorgeous dress was spread. "What is this?" he exclaimed – "What ideot trumpery, what May-queen foolery is this?" – "It is the habit I am to wear at the feast to-night," said Isidora – "My attendants are coming – I hear them at the door – oh, with what a throbbing heart I shall put on this glittering mockery! – But you will not desert me then?" she added, with wild and breathless anxiety. "Fear not," said Melmoth, solemnly – "You have demanded my aid, and it shall be accorded. May your heart tremble no more when you throw off that habit, than now when you are about to put it on!"

'The hour approached, and the guests were arriving. Isidora, arrayed in a splendid and fanciful garb, and rejoicing in the shelter which her mask afforded to the expression of her pale features, mingled among the groupe. She walked one measure with Montilla, and then declined dancing on the pretence of assisting her mother in receiving and entertaining her guests.

'After a sumptuous banquet, dancing was renewed in the spacious hall, and Isidora followed the company thither with a beating heart. Twelve was the hour at which Melmoth had promised to meet her, and by the clock, which was placed over the door of the hall, she saw it wanted but a quarter to twelve. The hand moved on – it arrived at the hour – the clock struck! Isidora, whose eyes had been rivetted on its movements, now withdrew them in despair. At that moment she felt her arm gently touched, and one of the maskers, bending towards her, whispered, "I am here!" and he added the sign which Melmoth and she had agreed on as the signal of their meeting. Isidora, unable to reply, could only return the sign. "Make haste," he added – "All is arranged for your flight – there is not a moment to be lost – I will leave you now, but meet me in a few moments in the western portico – the lamps are extinguished there, and the servants have neglected to relight them – be silent and be swift!" He disappeared as he spoke, and Isidora, after a few moments, followed him. Though the portico was dark, a faint gleam from the splendidly illuminated rooms disclosed to her the figure of Melmoth. He drew her arm under his in silence, and proceeded to hurry her from the spot. "Stop, villain, stop!" exclaimed the voice of her brother, who, followed by Montilla, sprung from the balcony – "Where do you drag my sister? – and you, degraded wretch, where are you about to fly, and with whom?" Melmoth attempted to pass him, supporting Isidora with one arm, while the other was extended to repel his approach; but Fernan, drawing his sword, placed himself directly in their way, at the same time calling on Montilla to raise the household, and tear Isidora from his arms. "Off, fool – off!" exclaimed Melmoth – "Rush not on destruction! – I seek not your life – one victim of your house is enough – let us pass ere you perish!" – "Boaster, prove your words!" said Fernan, making a desperate thrust at him, which Melmoth coolly put by with his hand. "Draw, coward!" cried Fernan, rendered furious by this action – "My next will be more successful!" Melmoth slowly drew his sword. "Boy!" said he in an awful voice – "If I turn this point against you, your life is not worth a moment's purchase – be wise and let us pass." Fernan made no answer but by a fierce attack, which was instantly met by his antagonist.

'The shrieks of Isidora had now reached the ears of the revellers, who rushed in crowds to the garden – the servants followed them with flambeaux snatched from the walls adorned for this ill-omened festival, and the scene of the combat was in a moment as light as day, and surrounded by a hundred spectators.

' "Part them – part them – save them!" shrieked Isidora, writhing at the feet of her father and mother, who, with the rest, were gazing in stupid horror at the scene – "Save my brother – save my husband!" The whole dreadful truth rushed on Donna Clara's mind at these words, and casting a conscious look at the terrified priest, she fell to the ground. The combat was short as it was unequal, – in two moments Melmoth passed his sword twice through the body of Fernan, who sunk beside Isidora, and expired! There was a universal pause of horror for some moments – at length a cry of – "Seize the murderer!" burst from every lip, and the crowd began to close around Melmoth. He attempted no defence. He retreated a few paces, and sheathing his sword, waved them back only with his arm; and this movement, that seemed to announce an internal power above all physical force, had the effect of nailing every spectator to the spot where he stood.

'The light of the torches, which the trembling servants held up to gaze on him, fell full on his countenance, and the voices of a few shuddering speakers exclaimed, "MELMOTH THE WANDERER!" – "I am – I am!" said that unfortunate being – "and who now will oppose my passing – who will become my companion? – I seek not to injure now – but I will not be detained. Would that breathless fool had yielded to my bidding, not to my sword – there was but one human chord that vibrated in my heart – it is broken to-night, and for ever! I will never tempt woman more! Why should the whirlwind, that can shake mountains, and overwhelm cities with its breath, descend to scatter the leaves of the rosebud?" As he spoke, his eyes fell on the form of Isidora, which lay at his feet extended beside that of Fernan. He bent over it for a moment – a pulsation like returning life agitated her frame. He bent nearer – he whispered, unheard by the rest, – "Isidora, will you fly with me – this is the moment – every arm is paralysed – every mind is frozen to its centre! – Isidora, rise and fly with me – this is your hour of safety!" Isidora, who recognized the voice but not the speaker, raised herself for a moment – looked on Melmoth – cast a glance on the bleeding bosom of Fernan, and fell on it dyed in that blood. Melmoth started up – there was a slight movement of hostility among some of the guests – he turned one brief and withering glance on them – they stood every man his hand on his sword, without the power to draw them, and the very domestics held up the torches in their trembling hands, as if with involuntary awe they were lighting him out. So he passed on unmolested amid the groupe, till he reached the spot where Aliaga, stupified with horror, stood beside the bodies of his son and daughter. "Wretched old man!" he exclaimed, looking on him as the unhappy father strained his glazing and dilated eyes to see who spoke to him, and at length with difficulty recognized the form of *the stranger* – the companion of his fearful journey some months past – "Wretched old man – you were warned – but you neglected the warning – I adjured you to save your daughter – *I best* knew her danger – you saved your gold – now estimate the value of the dross you grasped, and the precious ore you dropt! *I stood between myself and her* – I warned – I menaced – it was not for me to intreat. Wretched old man – see the result!" – and he turned slowly to depart. An involuntary sound of execration and horror, half a howl and half a hiss, pursued his parting steps, and the priest, with a dignity that more became his profession than his character, exclaimed aloud, "Depart accursed, and trouble us not – go, cursing and to curse." – "I go conquering and to conquer," answered Melmoth with wild and fierce triumph – "wretches! your vices, your passions, and your weaknesses, make you my victims. Upbraid yourselves, and not me. Heroes in your guilt, but cowards in your despair, you would kneel at my feet for the terrible immunity with which I pass through you at this moment. – I go accursed of every human heart, yet untouched by one human hand!" – As he retired slowly, the murmur of suppressed but instinctive and irrepressible horror and hatred burst from the groupe. He past on scowling at them like a lion on a pack of bayed hounds, and departed unmolested – unassayed – no weapon was drawn – no arm was lifted – the mark was on his brow, – and those who could read it knew that all human power was alike forceless and needless, – and those who could not succumbed in passive horror. Every sword was in its sheath as Melmoth quitted the garden. "Leave him to God!" – was the universal exclamation. "You could not leave him in worse hands," exclaimed Fra Jose – "He will certainly be damned – and – that is some comfort to this afflicted family.'"

Chapter Thirty-Six

Nunc animum pietas, et materna nomina frangunt.[54]

'In less than half an hour, the superb apartments, the illuminated gardens of Aliaga, did not echo a footstep; all were gone, except a few who lingered, some from curiosity, some from humanity, to witness or condole with the sufferings of the wretched parents. The sumptuously decorated garden now presented a sight horrid from the contrasted figures and scenery. The domestics stood like statues, holding the torches still in their hands – Isidora lay beside the bloody corse of her brother, till an attempt was made to remove it, and then she clung to it with a strength that required strength to tear her from it – Aliaga, who had not uttered a word, and scarcely drawn a breath, sunk on his knees to curse his half-lifeless daughter – Donna Clara, who still retained a woman's heart, lost all fear of her husband in this dreadful emergency, and, kneeling beside him, held his uplifted hands, and struggled hard for the suspension of the malediction – Fra Jose, the only one of the groupe who appeared to possess any power of recollection or of mental sanity, addressed repeatedly to Isidora the question, "Are you married, – and married to that fearful being?" – "I am married!" answered the victim, rising from beside the corse of her brother. "I am married!" she added, glancing a look at her splendid habit, and displaying it with a frantic laugh. A loud knocking at the garden gate was heard at this moment. "I *am* married!" shrieked Isidora, "and here comes the witness of my nuptials!"

'As she spoke, some peasants from the neighbourhood, assisted

657

by the domestics of Don Aliaga, brought in a corse, so altered from the fearful change that passes on the mortal frame, that the nearest relative could not have known it. Isidora recognized it in a moment for the body of the old domestic who had disappeared so mysteriously on the night of her frightful nuptials. The body had been discovered but that evening by the peasants; it was lacerated as by a fall from rocks, and so disfigured and decayed as to retain no resemblance to humanity. It was recognizable only by the livery of Aliaga, which, though much defaced, was still distinguishable by some peculiarities in the dress, that announced that those defaced garments covered the mortal remains of the old domestic. "There!" cried Isidora with delirious energy – "There is the witness of my fatal marriage!"

'Fra Jose hung over the illegible fragments of that whereon nature had once written – "This is a human being," and, turning his eyes on Isidora, with involuntary horror he exclaimed, "Your witness is dumb!" As the wretched Isidora was dragged away by those who surrounded her, she felt the first throes of maternal suffering, and exclaimed, "Oh! there will be a living witness – if you permit it to live!" Her words were soon realized; she was conveyed to her apartment, and a few hours after, scarcely assisted and wholly unpitied by her attendants, gave birth to a daughter.

'This event excited a sentiment in the family at once ludicrous and horrible. Aliaga, who had remained in a state of stupefaction since his son's death, uttered but one exclamation – "Let the wife of the sorcerer, and their accursed offspring, be delivered into the hands of the merciful and holy tribunal, the Inquisition." He afterwards muttered something about his property being confiscated, but nobody paid attention. Donna Clara was almost distracted between compassion for her wretched daughter, and being grandmother to an infant demon, for such she deemed the child of "Melmoth the Wanderer" must be – and Fra Jose, while he baptized the infant with trembling hands, almost expected a fearful sponsor to appear and blast the rite with his horrible negative to the appeal made in the name of all that is holy among Christians. The baptismal ceremony was performed, however, with an omission which the goodnatured priest overlooked – there was no sponsor – the lowest domestic in the house declined with horror the proposal of being sponsor for the child of that terrible union. The wretched mother heard them from her bed of pain, and loved her infant better for its utter destitution.

*

'A few hours put an end to the consternation of the family, on the score of religion at least. The officers of the Inquisition arrived, armed with all the powers of their tribunal, and strongly excited by the report, that the Wanderer of whom they had been long in search, had lately perpetrated an act that brought him within the sphere of their jurisdiction, by involving the life of the only being his solitary existence held alliance with. "We hold him by the cords of a man," said the chief inquisitor, speaking more from what he read than what he felt – "if he burst these cords he is more than man. He has a wife and child, and if there be human elements in him, if there be any thing mortal clinging to his heart, we shall wind round the roots of it, and extract it."

*

'It was not till after some weeks, that Isidora recovered her perfect recollection. When she did, she was in a prison, a pallet of straw was her bed, a crucifix and a death's head the only furniture of her cell; the light struggled through a narrow grate, and struggled in vain, to cast one gleam on the squalid apartment that it visited and shrunk from. Isidora looked round her – she had light enough to see her child – she clasped it to her bosom, from which it had unconsciously drawn its feverish nourishment, and wept in extasy. "It is my own," she sobbed, "and only mine! It has no father – he is at the ends of the earth – he has left me alone – but I am not alone while you are left to me!"

'She was left in solitary confinement for many days, undisturbed and unvisited. The persons in whose hands she was had strong reasons for this mode of treatment. They were desirous that she should recover perfect sanity of intellect previous to her examination, and they also wished to give her time to form that profound attachment to the innocent companion of her solitude, that might be a powerful engine in their hands in discovering those circumstances relative to Melmoth that had hitherto baffled all the power and penetration of the Inquisition itself. All reports agreed that the Wanderer had never before been known to make a woman the object of his temptation, or to entrust her with the terrible secret of his destiny;* and the Inquisitors were heard to say to each other, "Now that we have got the Delilah in our hands, we shall soon have the Sampson."

'It was on the night previous to her examination, (of which she was unapprized), that Isidora saw the door of her cell opened, and a figure appear at it, whom, amid the dreary obscurity that surrounded her, she recognized in a moment, – it was Fra Jose. After a long pause of mutual horror, she knelt in silence to receive his benediction, which he gave with feeling solemnity; and then the good monk, whose propensities, though somewhat "earthly and sensual", were never "devilish", after vainly drawing his cowl over his face to stifle his sobs, lifted up his voice and "wept bitterly".

"Isidora was silent, but her silence was not that of sullen apathy, or of conscience-seared impenitence. At length Fra Jose seated himself on the foot of the pallet, at some distance from the prisoner, who was also sitting, and bending her cheek, down which a cold tear slowly flowed, over her infant. "Daughter," said the monk, collecting himself, "it is to the indulgence of the holy office I owe this permission to visit you." – "I thank them," said Isidora,

---

* From this it should seem that they were unacquainted with the story of Elinor Mortimer.

and her tears flowed fast and relievingly. "I am permitted also to tell you that your examination will take place to-morrow, – to adjure you to prepare for it, – and, if there be any thing which" – "My examination!" repeated Isidora with surprise, but evidently without terror, "on what subject am I then to be examined?" – "On that of your inconceivable union with a being devoted and ac-cursed." His voice was choked with horror, and he added, "Daughter, are you then indeed the wife of – of – that being, whose name makes the flesh creep, and the hair stand on end?" – "I am." – "Who were the witnesses of your marriage, and what hand dared to bind yours with that unholy and unnatural bond?" – "There were not witnesses – we were wedded in dark-ness. I saw no form, but I thought I heard words uttered – I know I felt a hand place mine in Melmoth's – its touch was as cold as that of the dead." – "Oh complicated and mysterious horror!" said the priest, turning pale, and crossing himself with marks of unfeigned terror: he bowed his head on his arm for some time, and remained silent from unutterable emotion. "Father," said Isi-dora at length, "you knew the hermit who lived amid the ruins of the monastery near our house, – he was a priest also, he was a holy man, it was he who united us!" Her voice trembled – "Wretched victim!" groaned the priest, without raising his head, "you know not what you utter – that holy man is known to have died the very night preceding that of your dreadful union."

"Another pause of mute horror followed, which the priest at length broke. – "Unhappy daughter," said he in a composed and solemn voice, "I am indulged with permission to give you the benefit of the sacrament of confession, previous to your exami-nation. I adjure you to unburden your soul to me, – will you?" – "I will, my father." – "Will you answer me, as you would answer at the tribunal of God?" – "Yes, – as I would answer at the tribunal of God." As she spake, she prostrated herself before the priest in the attitude of confession.

*

' "And you have now disclosed the whole burden of your spirit?" – "I have, my father." The priest sat thoughtfully for a considerable time. He then put to her several singular questions relative to Melmoth, which she was wholly unable to answer. They seemed chiefly the result of those impressions of supernatural power and terror, which were every where associated with his image. "My father," said Isidora, when he had ceased, in a faultering voice, "My father, may I inquire about my unhappy parents?" The priest shook his head, and remained silent. At length, affected by the agony with which she urged her inquiry, he reluctantly said she might guess the effect which the death of their son, and the imprisonment of their daughter in the Inquisition, must have on parents, who were no less eminent for their zeal for the Catholic faith, than for their parental affection. "Are they alive?" said Isidora. – "Spare yourself the pain of further inquiries, daughter," said the priest, "and be assured, that if the answer was such as could give you comfort, it would not be withheld."

'At this moment a bell was heard to sound in a distant part of the structure. "That bell," said the priest, "announces that the hour of your examination approaches – farewell, and may the saints be with you." – "Stay, father, – stay one moment, – but one moment!" cried Isidora, rushing franticly between him and the door. Fra Jose paused. Isidora sunk before him, and, hiding her face with her hands, exclaimed in a voice choaked with agony, "Father, do you think – that I am – lost for ever?" – "Daughter," said the priest in heavy accents, and in a troubled and doubting spirit, "Daughter, – I have given you what comfort I could – press for no more, lest what I have given (with many struggles of conscience) may be withdrawn. Perhaps you are in a state on which I can form no judgment, and pronounce no sentence. May God be merciful to you, and may the holy tribunal judge you in its mercy also." – "Yet stay, father – stay one moment – only one moment – only one question more." As she spoke, she caught her pale and innocent companion from the pallet where it slept, and held it up to the priest. "Father, tell me, *can* this be the child of a demon? – can it be, this creature that smiles on me – that smiles on you, while you are mustering curses against it? – Oh, holy drops have sprinkled it from your own hand! – Father, you have spoke holy words over it. Father, let them tear me with their pincers, let them roast me on their flames, but will not my child escape – my innocent child, that smiles on you? – Holy father, dear father, look back on your child." And she crawled after him on her knees, holding up the miserable infant in her arms, whose weak cry and wasted frame, pleaded against the dungeon-life to which its infancy had been doomed.

'Fra Jose melted at the appeal, and he was about to bestow many a kiss and many a prayer on the wretched babe, when the bell again was sounded, and hasting away, he had but time to exclaim, "My daughter, may God protect you!" – "God protect me," said Isidora, clasping her infant to her bosom. The bell sounded again, and Isidora knew that the hour of her trial approached.'

Chapter Thirty-Seven

Fear not now the fever's fire,
　Fear not now the death-bed groan;
Pangs that torture, pains that tine
　Bed-rid age with feeble moan.

Mason

'The first examination of Isidora was conducted with the circumspective formality that has always been known to mark the proceedings of that tribunal. The second and the third were alike strict, penetrating and inoperative, and the holy office began to feel its highest functionaries were no match for the extraordinary prisoner who stood before them, who, combining the extremes of simplicity and magnanimity, uttered every thing that might criminate herself, but evaded with skill that baffled all the arts of inquisitorial examination, every question that referred to Melmoth.

'In the course of the first examination, they hinted at the torture. Isidora, with something of the free and nature-taught dignity of her early existence, smiled as they spoke of it. An official whispered one of the inquisitors, as he observed the peculiar expression of her countenance, and the torture was mentioned no more.

'A second – a third examination followed at long intervals – but it was observed, that every time the mode of examination was less severe, and the treatment of the prisoner more and more indulgent – her youth, her beauty, her profound simplicity of character and language, developed strongly on this singular emergency, and the affecting circumstance of her always appearing with her child in her arms, whose feeble cries she tried to hush, while she bent forward to hear and answer the questions addressed to her – all these seemed to have wrought powerfully on the minds of men not accustomed to yield to external impressions. There was also a docility, a submission, about this beautiful and unfortunate being – a contrite and bending spirit – a sense of wretchedness for the misfortunes of her family – a consciousness of her own, that touched the hearts even of inquisitors.

'After repeated examinations, when nothing could be extorted from the prisoner, a skilful and profound artist in the school of mental anatomy, whispered to the inquisitor something about the infant whom she held in her arms. "She has defied the rack," was the answer. "Try her on *that rack*," was rejoined, and the hint was taken.

'After the usual formalities were gone through, Isidora's sentence was read to her. She was condemned, as a suspected heretic, to perpetual confinement in the prison of the Inquisition – her child was to be taken from her, and brought up in a convent, in order to –

'Here, the reading of the sentence was interrupted by the prisoner, who, uttering one dreadful shriek of maternal agony, louder than any other mode of torture had ever before extorted, fell prostrate on the floor. When she was restored to sensation, no authority or terror of the place or the judges, could prevent her pouring forth those wild and piercing supplications, which, from the energy with which they are uttered, appear to the speaker himself like commands, – that the latter part of her sentence might be remitted – the former appeared to make not the least impression on her – eternal solitude, passed in eternal darkness, seemed to give her neither fear nor pain, but she wept, and pleaded, and raved, that she might not be separated from her infant.

'The judges listened with fortified hearts, and in unbroken

silence. When she found all was over, she rose from her posture of humiliation and agony – and there was something even of dignity about her as she demanded, in a calm and altered voice, that her child might not be removed from her till the following day. She had also self-possession enough to enforce her petition by the remark, that its life might be the sacrifice if it was too suddenly deprived of the nourishment it was accustomed to receive from her. To this request the judges acceded, and she was remanded to her cell.

*

'The time elapsed. The person who brought her food departed without uttering a word; nor did she utter a word to him. It was about midnight that the door of her cell was unlocked, and two persons in official habits appeared at it. They seemed to pause, like the heralds at the tent of Achilles, and then, like them, forced themselves to enter. These men had haggard and livid faces – their attitudes were perfectly stony and automaton-like – their movements appeared the result of mere mechanism – yet these men were touched. The miserable light within hardly shewed the pallet on which the prisoner was seated; but a strong red light from the torch the attendant held, flared broadly on the arch of the door under which the figures appeared. They approached with a motion that seemed simultaneous and involuntary – and uttered together, in accents that seemed to issue from one mouth, "Deliver your child to us." In a voice as hoarse, dry, and natureless, the prisoner answered, "Take it!"

'The men looked about the cell – it seemed as if they knew not where to find the offspring of humanity amid the cells of the Inquisition. The prisoner was silent and motionless during their search. It was not long – the narrow apartment, the scanty furniture, afforded little room for the investigation. When it was concluded, however, the prisoner, bursting into a wild laugh, exclaimed, "Where would you search for a child but in its mother's bosom? Here – here it is – take it – take it!" And she put it into their hands. "Oh what fools ye were to seek my child any where but on its mother's bosom! It is yours now!" she shrieked in a voice that froze the officials. – "Take it – take it from me!"

'The agents of the holy office advanced; and the technicality of their movements was somewhat suspended when Isidora placed in their hands the corse of her infant daughter. Around the throat of the miserable infant, born amid agony, and nursed in a dungeon, there was a black mark, which the officials made their use of in representing this extraordinary circumstance to the holy office. By some it was deemed as the sign impressed by the evil one at its birth – by others as the fearful effect of maternal despair.

'It was determined that the prisoner should appear before them within four-and-twenty hours, and account for the death of her child.

*

'Within less than half that number of hours, a mightier arm than that of the Inquisition was dealing with the prisoner – an arm that seemed to menace, but was indeed stretched out to save, and before whose touch the barriers of the dreaded Inquisition itself were as frail as the fortress of the spider who hung her web on its walls. Isidora was dying of a disease not the less mortal because it makes no appearance in an obituary – she was dying of that internal and incurable wound – a broken heart.

'When the inquisitors were at last convinced that there was nothing more to be obtained by torture, bodily or mental torture, they suffered her to die unmolested, and granted her last request, that Fra Jose might be permitted to visit her.

*

'It was midnight, but its approach was unknown in that place, where day and night are the same. A dim lamp was substituted for that weak and struggling beam that counterfeited day-light. The penitent was stretched on her bed of rest – the humane priest sat beside her; and if his presence gave no dignity to the scene, it at least softened it by the touches of humanity.

*

' "My father," said the dying Isidora, "you pronounced me for-given." – "Yes, my daughter," said the priest, "you have assured me you are innocent of the death of your infant." – "You never could have believed me guilty," said Isidora, raising herself on her pallet at the appeal – "the consciousness of *its* existence alone would have kept me alive, even in my prison. Oh, my father, how was it possible it could live, buried with me in this dreadful place almost as soon as it respired? Even the morbid nourishment it received from me was dried up when my sentence was read. It moaned all night – towards morning its moans grew fainter, and I was glad – at last they ceased, and I was very happy!" But, as she talked of this fearful happiness, she wept.

' "My daughter, is your heart disengaged from that awful and disastrous tie that bound it to misfortune here, and to perdition hereafter?" It was long before she could answer; at length she said in a broken voice. "My father, I have not now strength to search or to struggle with my heart. Death must very soon break every tie that was twined with it, and it is useless to anticipate my liber-ation; the effort would be agony – fruitless agony, for, while I live, I must love my destroyer! Alas! in being the enemy of mankind, was not his hostility to me inevitable and fatal? In rejecting his last terrible temptation – in resigning him to his destiny, and pre-ferring submission to my own, I feel my triumph complete, and my salvation assured." – "Daughter, I do not comprehend you." – "Melmoth," said Isidora, with a strong effort, "Melmoth was here last night – within the walls of the Inquisition – within this very cell!" The priest crossed himself with the marks of the profound-est horror, and, as the wind swept hollowly through the long passage, almost expected the shaken door would burst open, and disclose the figure of the Wanderer.

*

' "My father, I have had many dreams," answered the penitent, shaking her head at a suggestion of the priest's, "many – many wanderings, but this was no dream. I have dreamed of the garden-land where I beheld him first – I have dreamed of the nights when he stood at my casement, and trembled in sleep at the sound of my mother's step – and I have had holy and hopeful visions, in which celestial forms appeared to me, and promised me his conversion – but this was no dream – I saw him last night. Father, he was here the whole night – he promised – he assured me – he adjured me to accept of liberation and safety, of life and of felicity. He told me, nor could I doubt him, that, by whatever means he effected his entrance, he could also effect my escape. He offered to live with me in that Indian isle – that paradise of ocean, far from human resort or human persecution. – He offered to love me alone, and for ever – and then I listened to him. Oh, my father. I am very young, and life and love sounded sweetly in my ears, when I looked at my dungeon, and thought of dying on this floor of stone! But – when he whispered the terrible condition on which the fulfilment of his promise depended – when he told me that" –

'Her voice failed with her failing strength, and she could utter no more. "Daughter," said the priest, bending over her bed, "daughter, I adjure you, by the image represented on this cross I hold to your dying lips – by your hopes of that salvation which depends on the truth you utter to me, your priest and your friend – the conditions proposed by your tempter!" "Promise me absolution for repeating the words, for I should wish that my last breath might not be exhaled in uttering – what I must." – "*Te absolvo,*" &c. said the priest, and bent his ear to catch the sounds. The moment they were uttered, he started as from the sting of a serpent, and, seating himself at the extremity of the cell, rocked in dumb horror. "My father, you promised me absolution," said the penitent. *"Jam tibi dedi, moribunda,"*[55] answered the priest, in the confusion of thoughts using the language appropriated to the service of religion. "Moribunda indeed!" said the sufferer, falling back on her pallet. "Father, let me feel a human hand in mine as I part!" – "Call upon God, daughter!" said the priest, applying the crucifix to her cold lips. "I loved his religion," said the penitent, kissing it devoutly, "I loved it before I knew it, and God must have been my teacher, for I had no other! Oh!" she exclaimed, with that deep conviction that must thrill every dying heart, and whose echo (would God) might pierce every living one – "Oh that I have loved none but God – how profound would have been my peace – how glorious my departure – *now* – *his* image pursues me even to the brink of the grave, into which I plunge to escape it!"

' "My daughter," said the priest, while the tears rolled fast down his cheeks – "my daughter, you are passing to bliss – the conflict was fierce and short, but the victory is sure – harps are tuned to a new song, even a song of welcome, and wreaths of palm are weaving for you in paradise!"

' "Paradise!" uttered Isidora, with her last breath – *"Will he be there!"* '

Chapter Thirty-Eight

Loud tolled the bell, the priests prayed well,
    The tapers they all burned bright,
The monk her son, and her daughter the nun,
    They told their beads all night!

        *

The second night –

        *

The monk and the nun they told their beads
    As fast as they could tell,
And aye the louder grew the noise,
    The faster went the bell!

        *

The third night came –

        *

The monk and the nun forgot their beads,
    They fell to the ground dismayed,
There was not a single saint in heaven
    Whom they did not call to their aid!

    Southey

Monçada here concluded the tale of the Indian, – the victim of Melmoth's passion, no less than of his destiny, both alike unhallowed and unutterable. And he announced his intention of disclosing to him the fates of the other victims, whose skeletons were preserved in the vault of the Jew Adonijah in Madrid. He added, that the circumstances relating to them, were of a character still darker and more awful than those he had recited, as they were the result of impressions made on masculine minds, without any excitement but that of looking into futurity. He mentioned, too, that the circumstances of his residence in the house of the Jew, his escape from it, and the reasons of his subsequent arrival in Ireland, were scarcely less extraordinary than any thing he had hitherto related. Young Melmoth, (whose name perhaps the reader has forgot) did 'seriously incline' to the purpose of having his dangerous curiosity further gratified, nor was he perhaps altogether without the wild hope of seeing the original of that portrait he had destroyed, burst from the walls and take up the fearful tale himself.

The narrative of the Spaniard had occupied many days; at their termination, young Melmoth signified to his guest that he was prepared to hear the sequel.

A night was fixed for the continuation of the recital. Young Melmoth and his guest met in the usual apartment – it was a dreary, stormy night – the rain that had fallen all day, seemed now to have yielded to the wind, that came in strong and sudden bursts, suddenly hushed, as if collecting strength for the tempest of the night. Monçada and Melmoth drew their chairs closer to the fire, looking at each other with the aspect of men who wish to inspire each other with courage to listen, and to tell, and are the more eager to inspire it, because neither feels it himself.

At length Monçada collected his voice and resolution to proceed, but as he went on, he perceived he could not fix his hearer's attention, and he paused.

'I thought,' said Melmoth, answering his silence, 'I thought I heard a noise – as of a person walking in the passage.' 'Hush! and listen,' said Monçada, 'I would not wish to be overheard.' They paused and held their breath – the sound was renewed – it was evidently that of steps approaching the door, and then retiring from it. 'We are watched,' said Melmoth, half-rising from his chair, but at that moment the door opened, and a figure appeared at it, which Monçada recognized for the subject of his narrative, and his mysterious visitor in the prison of the Inquisition, and Melmoth for the original of the picture, and the being whose unaccountable appearance had filled him with consternation, as he sat beside his dying uncle's bed.

The figure stood at the door for some time, and then advancing slowly till it gained the centre of the room, it remained there fixed for some time, but without looking at them. It then approached the table where they sat, in a slow but distinctly heard step, and stood before them as a living being. The profound horror that was equally felt by both, was differently expressed by each. Monçada crossed himself repeatedly, and attempted to utter many prayers. Melmoth, nailed to his chair, fixed his sightless eyes on the form that stood before him – it was indeed Melmoth the Wanderer – the same as he was in the past century – the same as he may be in centuries to come, should the fearful terms of his existence be renewed. His 'natural force was not abated', but 'his eye was dim', – that appalling and supernatural lustre of the visual organ, that beacon lit by an infernal fire, to tempt or to warn the adventurers of despair from that coast on which many struck, and some sunk – that portentous light was no longer visible – the form and figure were those of a living man, of the age indicated in the portrait which the young Melmoth had destroyed, but the eyes were as the eyes of the dead.

*

As the Wanderer advanced still nearer till his figure touched the table, Monçada and Melmoth started up in irrepressible horror, and stood in attitudes of defence, though conscious at the moment that all defence was hopeless against a being that withered and mocked at human power. The Wanderer waved his arm with an action that spoke defiance without hostility – and the strange and solemn accents of the only human voice that had respired mortal air beyond the period of mortal life, and never spoken but to the ear of guilt or suffering, and never uttered to that ear aught but despair, rolled slowly on their hearing like a peal of distant thunder.

'Mortals – you are here to talk of my destiny, and the events which it has involved. That destiny is accomplished, I believe, and with it terminate those events that have stimulated your wild and wretched curiosity. I am here to tell you of both! – I – I – of whom you speak, am here! – Who can tell so well of Melmoth the Wanderer as himself, now that he is about to resign that existence which has been the object of terror and wonder to the world? – Melmoth, you behold your ancestor – the being on whose portrait is inscribed the date of a century and a half, is before you. – Monçada, you see an acquaintance of a later date.' – (A grim smile of recognition wandered over his features as he spoke.) – 'Fear nothing,' he added, observing the agony and terror of his involuntary hearers – 'What have you to fear?' he continued, while a flash of derisive malignity once more lit up the sockets of his dead eyes – 'You, Senhor, are armed with your beads – and you, Melmoth, are fortified by that vain and desperate inquisitiveness, which might, at a former period, have made you my victim,' – (and his features underwent a short but horrible convulsion) – 'but now makes you only my mockery.

*

'Have you aught to quench my thirst?' he added, seating himself. The senses of Monçada and his companion reeled in delirious terror, and the former, in a kind of wild confidence, filled a glass of water, and offered it to the Wanderer with a hand as steady, but somewhat colder, as he would have presented it to one who sat beside him in human companionship. The Wanderer raised it to his lips, and tasted a few drops, then replacing it on the table, said with a laugh, wild indeed, but no longer ferocious – 'Have you seen,' said he to Monçada and Melmoth, who gazed with dim and troubled sight on this vision, and wist not what to think – 'Have you seen the fate of Don Juan, not as he is pantomimed on your paltry stage, but as he is represented in the real horrors of his destiny by the Spanish writer*? There the spectre returns the hospitality of his inviter, and summons him in turn to a feast. – The banquet-hall is a church – he arrives – it is illuminated with a mysterious light – invisible hands hold lamps fed by no earthly substance, to light the apostate to his doom! – He enters the church, and is greeted by a numerous company – the spirits of those whom he has wronged and murdered, uprisen from their charnel, and swathed in shrouds, stand there to welcome him! – As he passes among them, they call on him in hollow sounds to pledge them in goblets of blood which they present to him – and beneath the altar, by which stands the spirit of him whom the parricide has murdered, the gulph of perdition is yawning to receive him! – Through such a band I must soon prepare to pass! – Isidora! thy form will be the last I must encounter – and – the most terrible! Now for the last drop I must taste of earth's produce – the last that shall wet my mortal lips!' He slowly finished the draught of water. Neither of his companions had the power to speak. He sat down in a posture of heavy musing, and neither ventured to interrupt him.

They kept silence till the morning was dawning, and a faint light streamed through the closed shutters. Then the Wanderer raised his heavy eyes, and fixed them on Melmoth. 'Your ancestor has come home,' he said; 'his wanderings are over! – What has been told or believed of me is now of light avail to me. The secret of my destiny rests with myself. If all that fear has invented, and credulity believed of me be true, to what does it amount? That if my crimes have exceeded those of mortality, so will my punishment. I have been on earth a terror, but not an evil to its inhabitants. None can participate in my destiny but with his own consent – *none have consented* – none can be involved in its

* Vide the original play, of which there is a curious and very obsolete translation.

tremendous penalties, but by participation. I alone must sustain the penalty. If I have put forth my hand, and eaten of the fruit of the interdicted tree, am I not driven from the presence of God and the region of paradise, and sent to wander amid worlds of barrenness and curse for ever and ever?

'It has been reported of me, that I obtained from the enemy of souls a range of existence beyond the period allotted to mortality – a power to pass over space without disturbance or delay, and visit remote regions with the swiftness of thought – to encounter tempests without the *hope* of their blasting me, and penetrate into dungeons, whose bolts were as flax and tow at my touch. It has been said that this power was accorded to me, that I might be enabled to tempt wretches in their fearful hour of extremity, with the promise of deliverance and immunity, on condition of their exchanging situations with me. If this be true, it bears attestation to a truth uttered by the lips of one I may not name, and echoed by every human heart in the habitable world.

'No one has ever exchanged destinies with Melmoth the Wanderer. *I have traversed the world in the search, and no one to gain that world, would lose his own soul!* Not Stanton in his cell – nor you, Monçada, in the prison of the Inquisition – nor Walberg, who saw his children perishing with want – not – another' –

He paused, and though on the verge of his dark and doubtful voyage, he seemed to cast one look of bitter and retrospective anguish on the receding shore of life, and see, through the mists of memory, one form that stood there to bid him farewell. He rose – 'Let me, if possible, obtain an hour's repose. Aye, repose – sleep!' he repeated, answering the silent astonishment of his hearers' looks, 'my existence is still human!' – and a ghastly and derisive smile wandered over his features for the last time, as he spoke. How often had that smile frozen the blood of his victims! Melmoth and Monçada quitted the apartment; and the Wanderer, sinking back in his chair, slept profoundly. He slept, but what were the visions of his last earthly slumber?

Chapter Thirty-Eight

The Wanderer's Dream

He dreamed that he stood on the summit of a precipice, whose downward height no eye could have measured, but for the fearful waves of a fiery ocean that lashed, and blazed, and roared at its bottom, sending its burning spray far up, so as to drench the dreamer with its sulphurous rain. The whole glowing ocean below was alive – every billow bore an agonizing soul, that rose like a wreck or a putrid corse on the waves of earth's ocean – uttered a shriek as it burst against that adamantine precipice – sunk – and rose again to repeat the tremendous experiment! Every billow of fire was thus instinct with immortal and agonizing existence, – each was freighted with a soul, that rose on the burning wave in torturing hope, burst on the rock in despair, added its eternal shriek to the roar of that fiery ocean, and sunk to rise again – in vain, and – for ever!

Suddenly the Wanderer felt himself flung half-way down the precipice. He stood, in his dream, tottering on a crag midway down the precipice – he looked upward, but the upper air (for there was no heaven) showed only blackness unshadowed and impenetrable – but, blacker than that blackness, he could distinguish a gigantic outstretched arm, that held him as in sport on the ridge of that infernal precipice, while another, that seemed in its motions to hold fearful and invisible conjunction with the arm that grasped him, as if both belonged to some being too vast and horrible even for the imagery of a dream to shape, pointed upwards to a dial-plate fixed on the top of that precipice, and which the flashes of that ocean of fire made fearfully conspicuous. He saw the mysterious single hand revolve – he saw it reach the appointed period of 150 years – (for in this mystic plate centuries were marked, not hours) – he shrieked in his dream, and, with that strong impulse often felt in sleep, burst from the arm that held him, to arrest the motion of the hand.

In the effort he fell, and falling grasped at aught that might save him. His fall seemed perpendicular – there was nought to save him – the rock was as smooth as ice – the ocean of fire broke at its foot! Suddenly a groupe of figures appeared, ascending as he fell. He grasped at them successively; – first Stanton – then Walberg – Elinor Mortimer – Isidora – Monçada – all passed him, – to each he seemed in his slumber to cling in order to break his fall – all ascended the precipice. He caught at each in his downward flight, but all forsook him and ascended.

His last despairing reverted glance was fixed on the clock of eternity – the upraised black arm seemed to push forward the hand – it arrived at its period – he fell – he sunk – he blazed – he shrieked! The burning waves boomed over his sinking head, and the clock of eternity rung out its awful chime – 'Room for the soul of the Wanderer!' – and the waves of the burning ocean answered, as they lashed the adamantine rock – 'There is room for more!' – The Wanderer awoke.

Chapter Thirty-Nine

And in he came with eyes of flame,
The fiend to fetch the dead.

Southey's *Old Woman of Berkeley*

Melmoth and Monçada did not dare to approach the door till about noon. They then knocked gently at the door, and finding the summons unanswered, they entered slowly and irresolutely. The apartment was in the same state in which they had left it the preceding night, or rather morning; it was dusky and silent, the shutters had not been opened, and the Wanderer still seemed sleeping in his chair.

At the sound of their approach he half-started up, and demanded what was the hour. They told him. 'My hour is come,' said the Wanderer, 'it is an hour you must neither partake or witness – the clock of eternity is about to strike, but its knell must be unheard by mortal ears!' As he spoke they approached nearer, and saw with horror the change the last few hours had wrought on him. The fearful lustre of his eyes had been deadened before their late interview, but now the lines of extreme age were visible in every feature. His hairs were as white as snow, his mouth had fallen in, the muscles of his face were relaxed and withered – he was the very image of hoary decrepid debility. He started himself at the impression which his appearance visibly made on the intruders. 'You see what I feel,' he exclaimed, 'the hour then is come. I am summoned, and I must obey the summons – my master has other work for me! When a meteor blazes in your atmosphere – when a comet pursues its burning path towards the

sun – look up, and perhaps you may think of the spirit condemned to guide the blazing and erratic orb.'

The spirits, that had risen to a kind of wild elation, as suddenly
subsided, and he added, 'Leave me, I must be alone for the few
last hours of my mortal existence – if indeed they are to be the
last. He spoke this with an inward shuddering, that was felt by his
hearers. 'In this apartment,' he continued, 'I first drew breath, in
this I must perhaps resign it, – would – would I had never been
born!

★

'Men – retire – leave me alone. Whatever noises you hear in the
course of the awful night that is approaching, come not near this
apartment, at peril of your lives. Remember,' raising his voice,
which still retained all its powers, 'remember your lives will be
the forfeit of your desperate curiosity. For the same stake I risked
more than life – and lost it! – Be warned – retire!'

They retired, and passed the remainder of that day without
even thinking of food, from that intense and burning anxiety that
seemed to prey on their very vitals. At night they retired, and
though each lay down, it was without a thought of repose.
Repose indeed would have been impossible. The sounds that
soon after midnight began to issue from the apartment of the
Wanderer, were at first of a description not to alarm, but they
were soon exchanged for others of such indescribable horror,
that Melmoth, though he had taken the precaution of dismissing
the servants to sleep in the adjacent offices, began to fear that
those sounds might reach them, and, restless himself from insupportable inquietude, rose and walked up and down the passage
that led to that room of horror. As he was thus occupied, he
thought he saw a figure at the lower end of the passage. So disturbed was his vision, that he did not at first recognize Monçada.
Neither asked the other the reason of his being there – they
walked up and down together silently.

In a short time the sounds became so terrible, that scarcely had the awful warning of the Wanderer power to withhold them from attempting to burst into the room. These noises were of the most mixed and indescribable kind. They could not distinguish whether they were the shrieks of supplication, or the yell of blasphemy – they hoped inwardly they might be the former.

Towards morning the sounds suddenly ceased – they were stilled as in a moment. The silence that succeeded seemed to them for a few moments more terrible than all that preceded. After consulting each other by a glance, they hastened together to the apartment. They entered – it was empty – not a vestige of its last inhabitant was to be traced within.

After looking around in fruitless amazement, they perceived a small door opposite to that by which they had entered. It communicated with a back staircase, and was open. As they approached it, they discovered the traces of footsteps that appeared to be those of a person who had been walking in damp sand or clay. These traces were exceedingly plain – they followed them to a door that opened on the garden – that door was open also. They traced the footmarks distinctly through the narrow gravel walk, which was terminated by a broken fence, and opened on a heathy field which spread half-way up a rock whose summit overlooked the sea. The weather had been rainy, and they could trace the steps distinctly through that heathy field. They ascended the rock together.

Early as it was, the cottagers, who were poor fishermen residing on the shore, were all up, and assuring Melmoth and his companion that they had been disturbed and terrified the preceding night by sounds which they could not describe. It was singular that these men, accustomed by nature and habit alike to exaggeration and superstition, used not the language of either on this occasion.

There is an overwhelming mass of conviction that falls on the mind, that annihilates idiom and peculiarities, and crushes out truth from the heart. Melmoth waved back all who offered to accompany him to the precipice which overhung the sea. Monçada alone followed him.

Through the furze that clothed this rock, almost to its summit, there was a kind of track as if a person had dragged, or been dragged, his way through it – a down-trodden track, over which no footsteps but those of one impelled by force had ever passed. Melmoth and Monçada gained at last the summit of the rock. The ocean was beneath – the wide, waste, engulphing ocean! On a crag beneath them, something hung as floating to the blast. Melmoth clambered down and caught it. It was the handkerchief which the Wanderer had worn about his neck the preceding night – that was the last trace of the Wanderer!

Melmoth and Monçada exchanged looks of silent and unutterable horror, and returned slowly home.

FINIS

End Notes

1. *Apparebat eidolon senex*: A phantom appeared in the shape of an old man (Pliny, *Letters*, VII, xxvii, 5).
2. *a l'outrance*: To the point of exaggeration.
3. *Væ victis*: Woe to the conquered (Livy, *History*, v. xlviii, 9).
4. *faedi oculi*: Mistake for foedi: with bloodshot eyes (Sallust, *Catiline*, xv.5, Loeb trans.).
5. *vi et armis*: By force of arms.
6. *in pontificalibus*: In his robes of office.
7. *Fiat voluntas tua*: Have it your own way.
8. *auto da fe*: Act of faith.
9. *Satana . . . Satana*: Get thee behind me, Satan. Matt. xvi, 23.
10. *in ordine ad spiritualia*: In the ranks of the spiritual.
11. *Τηλε μὲιργοναι ψυχαι, ειδοωλα καδουιων*: 'Afar do the spirits keep me aloof, the phantoms of men that have done with toils', Homer (*Iliad*, xxiii, 72).
12. *Ex uno disce omnes*: From one, judge of all. (Virgil, *Aeneid*, ii, 65–6.)
13. *Apage Satana*: Get thee behind me, Satan. Matt. xvi, 23.
14. *diabole te adjuro*: Devil, I bind you under a curse.
15. *Pandere . . . mersas*: To unfold secrets buried in the depths and darkness of the earth (Virgil, *Aeneid*, vi, 267).
16. *rictus Sardonicus*: Facial symptoms resembling those of laughter, after which death occurred.
17. *me ipso teste*: Lit. 'with myself as witness'.
18. *Heu . . . venis?*: 'How greatly changed, alas, from what he seemed – From what shores, Hector, long-awaited, have you come?' (Virgil, *Aeneid*, ii, 274, 282–3 – Grant).

    Heu fuge: 'Ah, flee.'

    Venit . . . tempus: 'the final day has come and the inevitable hour'

19. *vox stridula*: 'Creaking voice' (Seneca, *Epistles*, lvi, 2).

20. *Misericordia por amor di Dios*: Pity, for the love of God.

21. *Orate pro anima*: Pray for the soul of . . .

22. *Juravi . . . gero*: 'My tongue has sworn; the mind I have has sworn no oath' (Cicero, *De Officiis*, III, xxix, 108).

23. *Quilibet postea paterfamilias . . . etc.*: 'Then some head of the household comes forward first into the centre bearing a cock before him in his hands. He then approaches the expiation and strikes the cock three times on his own head accompanying each blow with these words, "Let this cock be a substitute for me, etc." Then placing his hands on the cock he slays it at once.'

24. *Statim . . . gallum*': At once he slays the cock.

25. *ευ-τουτω-υικα*: By this, Conquer.

26. *Unde . . . merentur*: 'Why should they fear the anger of the Gods, who deserve their favour?'

27. *Aer . . . longevitatem*: 'The shutting out of draughts contributes to longevity.'

28. *Miseram . . . Apollinis*: 'All things terrify wretched me, the noise of the sea, and the rocks, and solitude, and the sanctity of Apollo' (Sextus Turpilius, *Leucadia*, frag. XI).

29. *Ευθα υησου μακαρωυ Αυραι περιπυεουσιυ*. Here the breezes blow around the isle of the blessed; adapted from Pindar, *Olympian Odes*, ii, 72.

30. *pax vobiscum*: Peace be with you. Having mistaken his first exclamation for an item of reported speech, the puritanical Madonna now mistakes his address to her as an indecorous exclamation, and supplies him with a periphrasis more suitable to his priestly condition.

31. *Scire . . . timeri*: They wish to know the family secrets, and so to be feared (Juvenal, *Satires*, iii, 113).

32. *aurum potabile*: 'Potable gold': the analogy is between the hierarchy of alchemical metals and the hierarchy of races. Reflects the Spanish obsession with the purity of blood.

33. *Excaecavit . . . viderent*: 'He blinded their eyes so that they did not see.'

34. *mollia tempora fandi*: Happy moments for speech. (Adapted from Virgil, *Aeneid*, iv, 293).

35. *toujours perdrix*: Partridge yet again!

36. *Mare infructuosum*: The unfruitful sea.

37. *τι εμοι και σοι*: What [is there between] thee and me? John ii, 4.

38. *e faucibus Draconis – e profundis Barathri*: From the jaws of the dragon, from the depths of the abyss.

39. *verbosa et grandis epistola*: 'A great, long-winded letter' (Juvenal, *Satires*, x, 71).

40. *Minima . . . sui*: She is the smallest part of herself.

41. *Apparebat . . . confectus*: See above, note 1.

42. *Responde . . . argumentum*: (Lit.) 'Reply to my argument – a name is a name – therefore what is your name – reply to my argument . . .'

43. *Τηλε μὲιργουσι ψυχαι, ειδοωλα καμουιων* (Homer, *Iliad*, xxiii, 72). See above, note 12.

44. *Quaeque . . . fui*: The sights most piteous that I myself saw, and whereof I was no small part (Virgil, *Aeneid*, ii, 5–6: Grant).

45. *Quid multis morer*: Why do I delay so much? (Terence, *Andria*, 114: Grant).

46. *δακρυοεν γελασασα*: Smiling through her tears (Homer, *Iliad*, vi, 484: Grant).

47. *vis impotentiae*: 'Force of impotence'.

48.   Woe 'tis to love not, and to love is woe

                  But worst it is of woes

                  To love and lose.

                (*Anacreontea*, xxix, 1 – 4. Loeb trans.)

49. *cum multis aliis*: Along with many others.

50. *j'ai fait mon devoir*: I have done my duty.

51. *αβιωτος βιος*: An intolerable (lit: 'unliveable') life (Aristophanes, *Plutus*, 1.969).

52. *We were, but are no more* (unidentified).

53. 'Tis not so much the thieves and beasts wont to infest the place that

685

cause me care and trouble, as the witches who with spells and drugs vex human souls' (Horace, *Satires*, I, viii, 17–20).

54. 'Now love and the name of mother break me down' (Ovid, *Metamorphoses*, viii, 508).

55. *Te absolvo*: I absolve you.

   Jam tibi dedi, moribunda: I have just now given it to you, you who are about to die.

Melmoth the Wanderer

by Alethea Hayter

A writer's description of the moment at which an idea for a new book surfaced in his imagination is often puzzling as a clue to his completed book. 'One sees a fin passing far out', wrote Virginia Woolf in 1926, and five years later 'I have netted that fin in the waste of water which appeared to me over the marshes out of my window at Rodmell when I was coming to an end of *To the Lighthouse*'. But the fish that is finally caught may seem, when it is shown to the world, a very different creature from the one suggested by that momentary glimpse of a passing fin.

Charles Robert Maturin gave his own account of how the idea of his greatest novel, *Melmoth the Wanderer*, dawned on him. It came from one of his own sermons. He was preaching about sin and salvation, and a rhetorical question which he threw out at his congregation hit back at himself like a boomerang. The question which he asked from the pulpit was 'At this moment is there one of us present, however we may have departed from the Lord, disobeyed His will, and disregarded His word – is there one of us who would, at this moment, accept all that man could bestow, or earth afford, to resign the hope of his salvation? – No, there is not one – not such a fool on earth, were the enemy of mankind to traverse it with the offer.'

But was there one present, one who desperately wanted and needed what man could bestow and the earth afford, who felt he had been shut out from his just rewards, who was fascinated by the techniques which the enemy of mankind might bring to bear, and by the black and secret corners of his empire, one who might be tempted – the preacher himself? Maturin would not have admitted to feeling any such temptation, but the novel which took its starting-point from this sermon was much more an exploration of the power of evil than a vindication of the supreme inducement of salvation.

Maturin's feeling that life had not been fair to him was due more to a disappointed imagination than to any excessive privations or distresses. Speaking of himself in the third person, he told Walter Scott that he was one who 'borrowed the gloomy colouring of his own pages from the shade of obscurity and misfortune under which his existence had been wasted' and who had 'hitherto known little of life but labour, distress and difficulty'. He had a slight persecution mania, originating perhaps in his father's unjust treatment by his employers, the Post Office, and his own failure to secure promotion in the Church. He compensated for this by Timon-like fantasies that his family had formerly been courted by the great, but abandoned when their fortunes declined, and by a flattering legend of his descent from an aristocratic foundling who was abandoned in the rue des Mathurins in Paris (which he believed to be the origin of his his surname), picked up by a lady of rank – actually his real mother – educated in a seminary, and imprisoned in the Bastille whence he escaped to Ireland. The story is probably apocryphal, but Maturin undoubtedly was descended from a Huguenot pastor who fled to Ireland from France, and many of his forebears in Ireland were Protestant clergymen.

Maturin was born in Dublin in 1782, one of a family of six children. At the age of 15 he went to Trinity College Dublin, where he took his degree after some years. His strongest bent was for the stage; he had a real talent for acting, production and décor, and at one time thought of becoming an actor, but decided to follow family tradition and enter the Church. For two years after his ordination at the age of 21, he was a curate in a remote country parish; then in 1806 he became curate at Saint Peter's Dublin, where he remained for the rest of his life.

Shortly after his ordination he married Henrietta Kingsbury, a

beauty and an accomplished singer. The marriage was a happy
one. Maturin adored and was proud of his wife all his life; he
liked her to dress in the height of fashion, and insisted on her
wearing rouge. His family responsibilities made it essential for
him to earn more money than his £90-a-year curacy provided.
He took pupils, but that was not enough to keep the wolf from
the door. From sheer need, and not from natural impulse, he
turned to the writing of novels. As he said in his Preface to *Melmoth the Wanderer*, 'I cannot again appear before the public in so
unseemly a character as that of a writer of romances, without
regretting the necessity that compels me to it. Did my profession
furnish me with the means of subsistence, I should hold myself
culpable indeed in having recourse to any other.'

Under this compelling necessity he published *The Fatal Revenge,
or the Family of the Montorio* in 1807, *The Wild Irish Boy* in 1808, *The
Milesian Chief* in 1812 and *Woman, or Pour et Contre* in 1818. His
novels brought him very little money, and in 1816 he turned to the
drama, and had his first real success with a tragedy, *Bertram*,
which was produced in London by Edmund Kean, who played
the title role. This was the peak of Maturin's prosperity and happiness. The financial proceeds of the Drury Lane production
were handsome; he visited London, met some of the literary
lions, and enjoyed something of the intellectual stimulus which
he felt was lacking in the Dublin of his day; and he transformed
his Dublin home with painted ceilings, chandeliers, marble tables,
scarlet divans and sumptuous carpets, in the likeness of his splendid dreams.

His prosperity did not last long. Two more tragedies, *Manuel*
and *Fredolfo*, proved failures. In 1820 he returned to novel-writing
and published *Melmoth the Wanderer*, which was widely read but
had many hostile reviews; and his last novel, *The Albigenses*, published in 1824 in the year he died, attracted little attention. His
harassing money difficulties returned; the resplendent house
became shabby, dark and gloomy, with the stone floors now once

more bare of carpets; it began to be uncertain where the next meal was coming from. Maturin again knew that torturing hour, 'the Hour in which the Heart of Man is tried above any other, the Hour in which your children ask you for Food, and you have no answer', as he said to Walter Scott. It was an experience of which he made use in *Melmoth the Wanderer*, in the 'Tale of Guzman's Family', working out to its extreme possibilities the situation which he had actually endured in a milder form.

'There was in him a strange vacillation of temperament between gaiety and gloom', wrote a Dublin friend about Maturin after his death. When alone he was often deeply melancholy, but in social life, which he loved, he was gay to flippancy, volatile, easily deceived, gentle and kind in manner though tenacious of his own opinions. His conversation could sometimes be fascinating, but was not often really brilliant, and could be merely superficial. He preferred the company of women to that of men. As a clergyman he was conscientious in his duties and an eloquent preacher, much liked by his parishioners, but the world in general thought him rather more frivolous and sociable than was suitable for a man in Holy Orders. His penchant for dancing was particularly reprobated, although he was discriminating about it; his great passion was for elegant dances of French origin such as the quadrille, and he detested English country dances which he considered only fit for the kitchen and the scullery. Quirks of this kind, a sort of buoyant freakishness, made him an endless source of gossip in Dublin. The power and eccentricity of his imagination puzzled the narrower minds all around him. What could he mean, for instance, by his strange habit of knocking at the doors of any old and dilapidated houses in Dublin which seemed to have an air of mystery about them, or some historical association, and making some excuse to be allowed to see over them? He became a legend in his own lifetime, not without some deliberate contributions from himself. His appearance helped; he was tall, handsome and graceful, with a romantically haggard face

and large dreamy eyes, and in the days of his prosperity almost
foppishly well dressed, but in his poverty-stricken last years he
looked like Don Quixote, pale and hollow-eyed, wandering about
the streets of Dublin in well-worn shoes and a long shabby cape.
He was exhausted by his struggle with poverty, his long nights of
writing, and he dreamed of a suicide's death – he held that suicide was nowhere positively condemned in the Bible. 'To pass
away from the sorrows of earth to the peace of eternity, by reposing on a bed of eastern poppy flowers, where sleep is death,
would be the most enviable mode of earthly exit,' he said. There
is no firm evidence that his death on 30 October 1824 was anything but natural, but it was rumoured that his end was hastened
by taking the wrong medicine; perhaps it was a deliberate over-
dose.

The Maturin who sat up half the night writing tales of terror
was a different Maturin from the gay and elegant dancer of qua-
drilles that the outside world knew. That this darker self was a
puzzle and a mystery to his friends is shown by the odd conflict-
ing legends that grew up round his writing methods. To protect
his solitude he used to write with a wafer pasted to his forehead,
to indicate that if any of his family entered his study they must
not speak to him. So runs one of these legends; but another,
probably an equally garbled version of the same originating incident, told that he liked to have other people in the room talking,
or his wife singing, while he was writing, but used to gag his
mouth with a paste of bread and water to prevent himself from
joining in the conversation. In the long night sessions he was
committing to paper what he had already arranged in his mind;
he explained to a friend that 'I compose on a long walk; but then
the day must be neither too hot, nor cold: it must be reduced
to that medium from which you feel no inconvenience one way
or the other; and then when I am perfectly free from the city, and
experience no annoyance from the weather, my mind becomes
lighted by sunshine, and I arrange my plan perfectly to my own

satisfaction'. The sunlit mood which irradiated his mind on these afternoon walks was not reflected in the literary labours of the night, which lasted – with the help of brandy – till 3 or 4 a.m.; during these hours of direful imaginings his glassy-eyed pallor gave him the look of a cataleptic.

In these night hours his subterranean fears and hatreds emerged to transform the fictions he had planned in his afternoon walks into something more urgent, less logical, less controlled. His conscious religious stance (he described himself as a 'high Calvinist') made him anti-Papist, but there was something more emotive and personal than a logical conviction of error in his virulent hatred of anything that seemed to him to be ecclesiastical cruelty in any form. His attacks and satires on Popery were thought excessive and intemperate even by contemporary reviewers, and have made a modern critic oddly describe him as writing with 'an avowed atheism'. Such criticisms as that forced him to point out, in a footnote to *Melmoth the Wanderer*, how unfair it was to suggest that the worst sentiments of his worst characters were necessarily his own sentiments; but this was not accepted as an excuse by the hostile *Edinburgh Review* critique of his novel, which maintained that there was no need to introduce such characters at all; it was a cheap device to dazzle and terrify the reader, an effect like the pictures of Fuseli. The accusation of affectation is unjust; it was an unacknowledged inner compulsion, not a calculated dramatic verisimilitude, still less an eye-catching trick, that informed the bitter and effective onslaughts on religion, patriotism, law, monarchy, capitalism, which he put into Melmoth's mouth. The daytime logical Calvinist Maturin was an upholder of law and order, but a nihilist second self couched in his sub-conscious, and was let out to speak through Melmoth with an abrasive voice which many readers today may find congenial. Maturin himself, though he made literary use of the night side of his personality, was frightened of it and clung to his daylight self. 'There are some *criminals of the imagination*, whom if we could plunge into the *oubliettes* of its magnificent but lightly-based fabric, its lord would reign more happy,' he confessed.

The criticisms of established institutions expressed in Maturin's novels are mainly destructive; he had no positive programme or active political interests, beyond an Irish nationalism rooted in history and folklore. History – the texture and local colour of particular periods – appealed strongly to him. He was an omnivorous reader, and his memory was a huge but disorderly storehouse from which he could always pluck out a more-or-less appropriate, more-or-less accurate quotation for any possible event or emotion in his narratives. His pages are peppered with tags and historical and mythological references – from the Bible, from Homer, Virgil, Dante, Shakespeare, Cervantes, but also from obscure travel books, memoirs, studies of witchcraft, of botany, of Indian antiquities. The writers whom he most admired were not the ones by whom he was most influenced. He revered the elegance of Pope, and among his own contemporaries his preferences went to the austerity of Crabbe, the lyric lightness of Moore and the sunny humour of Scott; he had little admiration for Byron, and none for Coleridge or Wordsworth. He had a great taste for the Restoration dramatists, their witty indecorum and frivolity, their affectations and absurdities, and he made himself into a real authority on the theatre and the social framework of the late seventeenth century.

These were his avowed and daylight tastes, the pleasures of reason and good company, of wit and concinnity. The man who sat up late writing *Melmoth the Wanderer* might never have heard of Pope or Crabbe or Moore, for all the influence they had on the world which he created in his novel, a world of violence and black despair where logic and elegance had no place. The denizens of this world came partly from the hidden self of his dreams (he seems to have been a habitual dreamer; he writes of a special kind of creaking voice which we hear only in dreams, and of 'a dull twilight, such as one always sees in his sleep (no man ever dreamed of sunlight)' – an erroneous but revealing statement), and partly from the legendary repertoire of European literature and folklore. His Melmoth, human but exempt from death, a lost soul and a tempter, is descended from both Faust and Mephistopheles, from the Flying Dutchman and the Wandering Jew of European legends; Marlowe, Milton, Goethe, Godwin, Beckford, Schiller, Hoffmann, all contributed to the idea of this sardonic invulnerable rover with mesmeric eyes and a grating laugh.

Maturin is apt to be placed in the English school of Gothick romance-writers originating with Horace Walpole, and grouped with Mrs Radcliffe and 'Monk' Lewis, or with the more general European tradition of the *Schauer-romantik*, the tale of romantic terror. But this is not much more than a historical accident. He really had little in common with Walpole and Mrs Radcliffe, and not much with Lewis. They all used certain effects popular at the time – the terrors of the Inquisition, the oppressions and miseries of monastic life, unjust imprisonments and improbable escapes, mysterious wanderers with hypnotic eyes, ambiguous portraits in dark corners, stained manuscripts found in mouldering chests; just as today many fiction-writers with very different aims and tastes and levels of accomplishment use espionage as a framework for what they want to say. It is easy, and has been a favourite game with commentators on Maturin, to trace the sources of various incidents in *Melmoth the Wanderer* to previous writers who influenced Maturin. Thus the love of the child of nature, Immalee, for the first man that she has ever seen has been identified as based on Miranda's reaction to Ferdinand in *The Tempest*, or on Bernardin de St Pierre's Virginie or Mrs Radcliffe's Emily, or even on *Gulliver's Travels* or Coleridge's woman wailing for her demon lover in *Kubla Khan*. Such identifications do not prove much more than that Maturin, a well-read man, had not blocked off his imagination from the images and situations floating in European literary tradition.

In a wide sense the novels clustered together as Gothick or terror romances were of course all in the current of the whole Romantic inundation that swept away the Age of Reason – the whirlpools of revolutionary struggle, the overflow of guilt no longer safely canalized by religion, the upsurge into consciousness of childhood anxieties and of impulses long ignored or suppressed. But they have this in common, not only with each other but with nearly all the artistic manifestations of the time, making a category too large to tell us much about them. It has been suggested that what distinguishes the Gothick or terror novels is their concentration on arousing the sense of fear in the reader. The public for which Maturin wrote – like readers today, but unlike those of the earlier eighteenth century and of the later nineteenth century – liked being frightened, and valued strong emotions of any kind far above self-control. The Gothick novels have sometimes been grouped according to the type of fear which they inspire in the reader; those like Mrs Radcliffe's which aim, by suggestion and suspense, to make the reader feel terror, and those like Lewis's which aim, by explicit descriptions of cruel and disgusting scenes, to make him feel horror.

Maturin cannot be completely fitted into any of these categories, or convincingly grouped with any of his Gothick predecessors. He does not share Lewis's gloating fascination with charnel-house horrors, with pollution and decay. He does indeed have an unpleasant obsession with two forms of horror – death by burning, and death by mob violence connected with religious intolerance – which he describes in ghastly and explicit detail, but these seem like permanent nightmares of his own which he cannot forget or dispel, rather than deliberate indulgences in sadism as in Lewis; apart from them, he goes in for terror, not horror. Nor does he share Beckford's fantastic visual and sensory effects, the huge perspectives and fuming vapours of *Vathek* which produce terror in the reader by combining the sensations of agoraphobia and of suffocation. The fear produced by Maturin's narrative does not depend on any strongly visualized effect of place, of shape or colour or light. His difference from Mrs Radcliffe, often identified as the strongest influence on him, is a radical one. Mrs Radcliffe was preoccupied with the raptures and fears of the solitary imagination in relation to nature, architecture and history. Her characters barely exist in relation to each other; all their strongest emotions are aroused by mountain landscapes, ruined castles, storms, sunsets, crypts, tapestries, secret doors, by solitary indulgence in music and poetry, by solitary musings and memories, by isolated fears and imagined dangers. To find an equivalent in painting for her novels one would have to look to the landscape painters – to Turner's mountain gorges, to Richard Wilson's castle-crowned crags, to Caspar David Friedrich's ruined abbeys buried in the forest.

Maturin's effects of terror in *Melmoth the Wanderer* are not achieved by any such means as that. To him, fear was a man-made sensation, which would be unknown to a human being in real solitude. Nature has no terrors for his Immalee on her desert isle.

> 'The elements might be supposed to have impressed her imagination with some terrible ideas; but the periodical regularity of these phenomena, in the climate she inhabited, divested them of their terrors to one who had been accustomed to them, as to the alternation of night and day – who could not remember the fearful impression of the first, and, above all, who had never heard any terror of them expressed by *another*, perhaps the primitive cause of fear in most minds'.

Not so, not with this tranquil insensibility, would one of Mrs Radcliffe's heroines have reacted to the thrilling horror of a thunderstorm. The descriptions of nature in Maturin's novels are all anthropomorphic; some of his pictures of clouded and lowering skies are fine, but they are always inserted to illustrate and reinforce a human mood, the depression or apprehension of one of his characters. *Melmoth the Wanderer* contains no solitary ruined castles or abbeys; nearly all its scenes take place in populated habitations – even in a monastery or the prisons of the Inquisition, the victim is seldom left alone, the footstep of his persecutor or his rescuer is always at the door. The fear which Maturin portrayed arose out of extreme relationships between man and man, all seen as tyrants or victims, none ever really alone. Irish village gossips, strolling Spanish crowds, Indian fishermen, people his scenes. The equivalent in painting for Maturin's novel would have to be Goya. Maturin's heroine, Immalee, among the crowds in the Madrid street is just like one of Goya's round-cheeked girls under a parasol, with a raddled hag glimpsed behind her shoulder; deeper in, one comes to a Goya of the Inquisition, of faces blankly idiotic with fear under high dunce caps; deeper in still, the staring eyes and shrouded forms of hidden sufferings as in Goya's *Disparates*. It was man's inhumanity to man that inspired Maturin's worst terrors, terrors which he communicates to his readers. He dissociated himself from the Gothick formula; 'You must expect no romance-horrors, Sir, from my narrative' he makes the chief narrator in *Melmoth* say. He belongs, not with the exponents of ruin-sensibility, but in a category or school for which a new name perhaps needs to be invented – a school which would include Godwin, some of Edgar Allan Poe, the Sheridan Le Fanu of *Uncle Silas*, the Marryat of *The Phantom Ship*, a school whose technique is the turn of the screw, the extreme pressure of one human personality on another.

What Maturin said in *Melmoth* of the Inquisition, that it was a 'tremendous monument of the power, and crime, and gloom of the human mind', might be a description of his own basic theme, one which ran through all his novels and plays, from the beginning of his writing career. Of his first work, *The Fatal Revenge, or the Family of the Montorio*, he said that its interest was based entirely on the emotion of supernatural terror, because terror was a universal emotion to which every reader could respond, while the passion of love, the usual theme of novels, was one which in real life is only felt in any depth by the few. Five years later, in the Preface to his *Milesian Chief*, he made what is often quoted as his clearest summary of his own literary character and aims: 'If I possess any talent, it is that of darkening the gloomy and of deepening the sad; of painting life in extremes, and representing those struggles of passion when the soul trembles on the verge of the unlawful and unhallowed.'

'Painting life in extremes'; that was Maturin's speciality, his real interest – describing, not the normal, average, everyday man and woman, but the exceptions, the freaks, the monsters, the despairing, the utterly crushed, the insane. He perceived a kind of grandeur, which he even calls magnanimity, in the excesses of evil, as when he makes Alonzo de Monçada speak of 'the last struggles of the impenitent malefactor, – that agony without remorse, that suffering without requital or consolation, that, if I may say so, arrays crime in the dazzling robe of magnanimity, and makes us admire the fallen spirit, with whom we dare not sympathize'.

The deprecating 'if I may say so' was not enough to avert suspicion as to where his secret sympathies really lay. Contemporary reviewers condemned him as a sadist, though the actual term was not then in use and it is not known whether Maturin ever read Sade's works. The *Edinburgh Review* accused him of having a positive taste for horrible and revolting scenes, such as cannibalism and burning alive; and the *New Monthly Review*, more percipiently, noted that 'He will ransack the forgotten records of crime, or the dusty museums of natural history, to discover a new horror. He is a passionate connoisseur in agony. His taste for strong emotion evidently hurries him on almost without the concurrence of the will.'

Was Maturin a 'connoisseur in agony', who actually enjoyed the spectacle of human suffering? He was certainly aware that some men do have such tastes; in the character of the parricide monk who helps Alonzo to escape from the monastery, Maturin depicted a self-confessed 'amateur in suffering', who analysed his own enjoyment in watching the tortures and miseries of others, seeing it as a gratification of power and superiority, a taste which, he claimed, every human being feels in some degree. 'You will call this cruelty, I call it curiosity – that curiosity that brings thousands to witness a tragedy, and makes the most delicate female feast on groans and agonies.' Two motives – the desire for power, for domination, for reinforcement of superiority, and the desire for knowledge – are here confounded, and Maturin himself probably felt only the latter, a taste for what he called 'moral botany', for observation of the wildest anomalies of its variation of species. His curiosity was extreme; he had an absorbed interest in the possible contortions of human nature, but it was the interest of a man watching a skilled gymnast or a Houdini whose every muscle is in play, not the pleasure of a man watching torture, a pleasure very evident in Lewis's *The Monk*. Maturin might perhaps be called a voyeur, but I doubt if he could justly be described as a sadist, though sadists may derive pleasure from his novel.

It is a fair comment that he 'will ransack the forgotten records of crime'. He was a great collector of anecdotes and case-histories of obsession and morbid psychology, and when he introduced such themes into his novels he often testified in a footnote that they were based on real-life cases. His pictures of the inmates of a madhouse – the religious fanatic with his infernal and erotic visions, the alcoholic, the woman driven insane by the deaths of her children in the Fire of London – are Hogarthian in their intensity. But the most interesting parts of *Melmoth the Wanderer*, and the ones most relevant to our own times, are his studies of the psychology of prisoners, and how this can be manipulated by brain-washers. He portrays every stage in the mental state of a man long imprisoned: the first period, while the prisoner still remains resolute to resist, to remain the captain of his soul; his education in cunning, in feigned submission, in the avoidance of traps; his gradual loss of self-respect, of cleanliness, of effort, of presence of mind, of the power of logical thought; the growth of automatism, of indifference and stupor, the abdication of moral responsibility, the willing submission to any authority, good or bad; the horrible dislocation of human relationships, that 'confidence of hostility ... in which we cling to each other's hate, instead of to each other's love'; and the last extremity, that loss of identity in which any attention, even that of a torturer, is better than none – 'While people think it worth their while to torment us, we are never without some dignity, though painful and imaginary. Even in the Inquisition I belonged to somebody, – I was watched and guarded.'

In flashes of insight like that, Maturin is at his height. Equally extraordinary is his penetration into the psychology of the gaoler and the interrogator. Melmoth himself is an expert brainwasher, whether he is taunting, bullying and tempting Stanton in the madhouse with a crushingly convincing forecast of the madness bound to overwhelm Stanton in the end, or destroying Immalee's illusions and poisoning her imagination. But Maturin's fullest study of brainwashing techniques is his description of the methods employed, by the Monçada family confessor and by the Superior and all the monks of the monastery where Alonzo de Monçada is shut up, to force him into a monastic vocation. This section of the novel is, by Maturin's own account, one to which he gave very careful thought; as he said in his Preface, he 'made the misery of conventual life depend less on the startling adventures one meets with in romances, than on that irritating series of petty torments which constitutes the misery of life in general, and which, amid the tideless stagnation of monastic existence, solitude gives its inmates leisure to invent, and power combined with malignity, the full disposition to practise'.

The 'series of petty torments' which Maturin describes reads like an instruction-manual for brainwashers. It is all there: the alternations of threats and pleading, of flattery and blandishments with sarcasm and derision; the deployment of specious arguments, plausible pretexts, and illogical and irrelevant statements which break down all reasonable sequence; the use of moral blackmail through the prisoner's family affections; unceasing watching and spying; tantalizing by half-audible mysteries and hints; continual attempts to secure recantation; the use of *agents provocateurs*. Then, when these preliminary weapons do not succeed, the more drastic ones; incarceration in total darkness, alternating with relaxation and indulgence; deprivation of all personal belongings which could reinforce the prisoner's sense of identity; continual repetition in his hearing of false dogmas and blasphemies; humiliation by filth and disgusting objects; deprivation of sleep; isolation by the planned recoil of all other human beings whom the prisoner encounters. In his descriptions of what seem inexplicable caprices of tyranny, but are really carefully devised techniques, forcing on the prisoner the conviction that he is guilty of a crime never explained to him, Maturin seems the forerunner of Kafka.

His own forerunner, as Professor Mario Praz has shown in *The Romantic Agony*, was Diderot, from whose *La Réligieuse* Maturin took without acknowledgement many of the details of methods used to force an unwilling victim into a monastic vocation. But the atmosphere in Maturin's novel is utterly different, though so many of the incidents are the same. Diderot's nun is a tough and argumentative woman who gives as good as she gets, except in physical ill-treatment, and the motives and behaviour of all concerned, though unpleasant, are explicable and not excessive; there is none of the almost motiveless malignity of Maturin's persecutors. The difference is perhaps because Diderot, though he disapproved of much in the monastic life, could see that for some people it had some point; to Maturin the whole institution was a ghastly error. He had no belief in the efficacy or even the reality of the contemplative life; to him all ecstasy was suspect, a purely physical condition as easily induced by drugs as by prayer and abstinence. His interest in abnormal states of mind did not extend in that direction.

In depicting normal states of mind and feeling, Maturin was apt to be perfunctory and unconvincing. He was not good at portraying *l'homme moyen sensuel*, the personality with some good impulses and a fair amount of selfishness and vanity. When, as with Father José or Don Francisco or Juan de Monçada, he attempted such characters, they came out very flat; and flatter still were his attempts at moral paragons – the Walberg family, Elinor Mortimer and John Sandal; while Alonzo de Monçada, the nearest approach to a hero that the book affords, is a passive, almost detached, reporter of his own dangers and sufferings, not much more than a narrative tool. Maturin did, however, make some interesting observations of the oddities of virtue, as well as of vice. The Bishop to whom Alonzo appeals against his persecutors is a clever study of an upright, chilly, cerebral type jolted by an exceptional situation. 'Rigid minds, when they yield themselves to emotion, do it with a vehemence inconceivable, for to them everything is a duty, and passion (when it occurs) among the rest. Perhaps the novelty of emotion, too, may be a delightful surprise to them.' Equally well observed is the stiff severe old Puritan with her monotonous routine; 'her life was mere mechanism, but the machine was so well wound up, that it appeared to have some quiet consciousness and sullen satisfaction in its movements'. As Oliver Elton said of Maturin's observation of this kind, 'he was the first to find a notation and rhythm for obscure, damped and half-paralysed feeling'.

The greatest feat which Maturin's imagination achieved when it turned to the observation of oddities of goodness was its creation of the character of Immalee. Immalee is a freak, an abnormal creature, because she has lived alone on a desert island since earliest childhood and therefore has none of the knowledge and feelings of human society. But she is an enchanting freak, the only delightful creature in this sombre book; the description of her and her island comes as a much needed breath of fresh air after the stenches and suffocations of monastic dungeons. Naked except for garlands of flowers, her long hair hung with lustrous green seashells, she moves about her fragrant island, attended by peacocks and living on figs and tamarinds; watching stormy seas and glassy calms, dawn and moonrise, monkeys and fishes and parrots, with an absorbed and serene innocence. Maturin has penetrated with imaginative sympathy into such an untouched mind, scarcely aware of separate identities, so that she can feel totally at one with the movement of a huge wave, but thinks her own reflection in the water is another woman, whose cold lips she stoops to kiss; the distant fishermen seem to her to be plants, the moon-reflections on the sea to be branches and flowers of light which break as she tries to gather them. The impact on such a mind of Melmoth's searingly cynical experience is genuinely pathetic, as we see her mind groping in what she at first rejoicingly calls 'the world of answers', but soon comes sadly to recognize as 'the world that suffers'.

Maturin occasionally derided the myth, so fashionable in his day, of the Noble Savage. His Immalee is admirable because she is totally unaffected and spontaneous, all her impulses are fresh, her values unconventional; but she has no armour of innate ethical standards to preserve her from the worst miseries. She falls in love with Melmoth, the first man to whom she has ever spoken, and becomes his helpless prey; though she too, like all the other chief characters in the novel, finds the strength to choose death rather than rescue on his terms, at the price of her soul. To this ostensible theme of the whole book – the final inefficacy of fear to imperil the soul – Maturin returns rather hastily in his last pages, when Melmoth admits that none of his victims finally consented to pay the price he asked; 'I have been on earth a terror, but not an evil to its inhabitants ... I have traversed the world in the search, and no one, to gain that world, would lose his own soul.' But the moments of choice, which ought to have been the great crises of the book, pass almost perfunctorily in the main part of the narrative. Maturin was more interested in the chase than in the kill.

Melmoth the Wanderer was originally planned as a series of tales, rather than as a single narrative, and it is a pity that Maturin did not adhere to this plan, and present a set of short stories of various periods and countries, all of them depicting encounters with the tempter Melmoth, but each separately communicated to the reader either by an omniscient impersonal narrator or by the protagonist of each encounter. Instead, Maturin chose a narrative method which, from the first in the *Quarterly*'s abrasive review and by many critics ever since, has been condemned as Chinese-box perversity – story within story within story, a perpetual shift and distancing of narrator from reader which chills the latter's interest and belief. Conrad's most elaborate effects of distancing by reported narrative are as nothing to Maturin's. At one point we have Melmoth himself relating the 'Lovers' Tale', a fifty-page affair complete with dialogues, internal meditations, descriptions of dress, a catalogue of the contents of a library, and a few bars of music, *viva voce* to Don Francisco, who is described as a bored and uncomprehending listener but who nevertheless somehow, by means not described, repeats the whole story verbatim to an aged Jew, who writes it down; the written narrative is later copied by Alonzo de Monçada who apparently commits it, and a much longer narrative within which it is embedded, so perfectly to memory that many years later he too is able to repeat the whole thing verbatim in a month-long conversation with young John Melmoth; and it is only via that conversation that it reaches the reader. To read many eighteenth-century and early nineteenth-century novels with pleasure it is necessary to accept and ignore the convention that immense dialogues can be remembered and reported verbatim – Richardson and Fanny Burney are two obvious examples – but Maturin demands a much greater suspension of disbelief from his readers, more than most of them can consistently accord. Maturin himself could not keep it up throughout; at times he finds that one of his sets of brackets has slipped off, and he is a stage or two stages nearer direct contact with the reader than he meant, and has to make a hastily-contrived retreat; or he deliberately bursts out through half a dozen layers of Chinese box to address and exhort the reader in his own authorial voice. His complicated machinery has found some defenders, who feel that its breaks and shifts and mystifications enhance the morbid dream-like effect of the story, but the majority of readers are more likely to be fretted by so much gratuitous implausibility.

Maturin's style is very individual, a mixture of headlong violence and pithy aphorism in which some critics have heard a characteristically Irish tone of voice. He was a great coiner of words – 'sateless', 'mockful', 'ancestorial', 'obdured', 'anecdotical', 'exhaustless' – some of which seem merely the result of hasty careless writing under pressure, but he certainly wanted to extend the expressive possibilities of the language, and had his own idiosyncratic raptures and excruciations of the ear; he detested puns, for instance, and had an aversion to rhyme.

When *Melmoth the Wanderer* was published in 1820, it received a lot of publicity in the main literary reviews of the day; much of the criticism was hostile – the *Quarterly* and *Edinburgh* condemned and abused it out of hand – but the comments were at least attentive and interest-provoking, and the book was widely read, and became part of the furniture of many young imaginations. Its influence was even greater abroad than in England. Five years after it appeared, it had already reached Italy and inspired a section on a victim forced into a monastic vocation in Manzoni's *I Promessi Sposi*; five years after that, Pushkin, in *Eugene Onegin*, was classing Melmoth with Byron's and Rousseau's heroes as a denizen of the love-dreams of young Russian girls; and a few years later Poe in America was showing in many of his tales how much he had learned from Maturin. But Maturin's power was greatest in France (*Melmoth* was translated into French a year after its publication); his influence can be seen on Victor Hugo, on Soulié and Sue and Dumas *père*, and specially on Balzac, who actually wrote a story called *Melmoth Reconcilié*. Among English writers his influence is less obvious, but the character of Melmoth had passed into literary mythology. Thackeray, casting round for a description of Goethe's brilliant piercing gaze, compared it with 'the eyes of the hero of a certain romance called "Melmoth the Wanderer", which used to alarm us boys thirty years ago'; William Rossetti remembered how he and his brother Dante Gabriel used to sit up far into the night reading Maturin's novel over each other's shoulders with breathless absorption; and Oscar Wilde (who was actually a connection of Maturin's, and may have taken certain features of *The Picture of Dorian Gray* from Maturin's novel) used the pseudonym Sebastian Melmoth after he came out of prison. Some critics have seen Maturin's influence not only on nineteenth-century suspense novels like those of Wilkie Collins, Sheridan Le Fanu and Stevenson, but even on the modern detective story and science fiction. One might, for instance, see, in the description of Melmoth's sudden ageing to his full 200-year-old decrepitude in the last hours of his life, the source of a similar incident in James Hilton's *Lost Horizon*.

There have always been some readers to whom Maturin's book was disgusting. The *Edinburgh Review* critique said that it made 'women, and people of weak nerves' feel sick, while those with stouter nerves were moved to laughter, but no one to tears of sympathy. The French critic and translator, Amédée Pichot, said that when he read Maturin he felt the same unpleasant sensation as he did when confronted with a beggar who deliberately brought on an epileptic attack in order to extort alms. To such critics, Maturin's work seemed shrill, pretentious, absurd, a farrago of ill-constructed exaggeration. At the other extreme, he has been credited with producing the masterpiece of the school of terror romance, of having created a character worthy to be set between Goethe's Faust and Byron's Manfred. His power, originality, brilliant imagination and psychological insight have been lavishly praised; the grim realism of the opening chapters depicting the death of the miser in his decaying house has been greatly admired, the refreshing beauty of Immalee and her desert island has been enthusiastically welcomed, and even the 'Tale of Guzman's Family' and the 'Lovers' Tale' – turgid as these may seem to readers today – were warmly loved in their time.

The comment which Walter Scott made on an earlier novel of Maturin's is perhaps the best summary of the reader's reaction to *Melmoth the Wanderer*. 'We rose from his strange chaotic novel unrefreshed and unamused, yet strongly impressed by many of the ideas which had been so vaguely and wildly presented to our imagination.' As a sustained design, the novel fails; its ostensible theme, the power of the human mind to triumph over suffering and to resist temptation, is often forgotten and, when remembered, per functorily treated, and the whole story ends with a weary effect, as though Maturin had lost interest, and with many loose ends left dangling. Melmoth's last appearance is fiasco – he hangs about the house, asks for a glass of water has a short sleep, and then vanishes into the night, thoughtfully dropping a handkerchief as he plunges over a cliff, so that his fate should be clear to the searchers. This low-keyed ending is a dismal contrast with the terrifying last night of Marlowe's Dr Faustus, from which Maturin cribbed some of his incidents without producing any of the same effect of horror.

Yet this shabby and unsuccessful tempter has previously been depicted with real power, as a personality racked by brilliant contradictions, an imaginative creation not easy to forget. He is capable of tenderness and of admiration for virtue, yet envying, hating and destroying what he can never emulate; knowing himself doomed, yet still tortured by hope; an outcast who has chosen to be so, and yet resents his isolation. Maturin uncovered an element in the human subconscious, and gave it a personified life which many will recognize as a shadow in their own identities. Baudelaire, himself a voluntary outcast, saluted the figure of the *'célèbre voyageur Melmoth, la grande création satanique du révérend Maturin'* in a famous passage in his essay *De L'Essence Du Rire*:

> 'What could be greater, what could have more power over poor human beings, than this pale bored Melmoth? And yet, there is an aspect of him that is feeble, abject, unspiritual, lustreless. How he laughs, how he laughs, endlessly comparing himself with the poor human worms – he so strong, so intelligent, he for whom some of the physical and intellectual laws, which condition the existence of other men, no longer exist! And this laughter is the perpetual paroxysm of his wrath and his suffering. It is, you understand, the necessary result of his contradictory double nature, which is infinitely great in relation to mankind, infinitely vile and base in relation to absolute Truth and Justice'.

PENGUIN ENGLISH
LIBRARY

OTHER TITLES IN THIS SERIES

The War of the Worlds
H. G. WELLS

"'Death!" I shouted. "Death is coming! Death!"'

In this pioneering, shocking and nightmarish tale, naïve suburban Londoners investigate a strange cylinder from space, but are instantly incinerated by an all-destroying heat-ray. Soon, gigantic killing machines that chase and feed on human prey are threatening the whole of humanity.

A pioneering work of alien invasion fiction, *The War of the Worlds*'s journalistic style contrasts disturbingly with its horrifying visions of the human race under siege.